Praise for
The Circle of the Swan:
Book One of the DragonFire Series

*"...well told, with good, rounded characters
and enjoyable prose."* Science Fiction Chronicle

*"THE CIRCLE OF THE SWAN pleased and delighted
me much as did the early works of Anne McCaffrey.
The delineation of good and evil, the strength of female
characters and the likeability of the good guys contribute
to a story that you don't read so much as you actually
seem to participate in."* Baryon Magazine

*"... reading this book is a much better thing to do
than sit in a movie theater for three hours if you
are wanting a taste of wizardry."* Blue Iris Journal

MAGESPELL PRESS

Titles by
Jana G. Oliver

The Lover's Knot

The DragonFire Fantasy Series
The Circle of the Swan (Book One)
The Summoning Stone (Book Two)

THE
SUMMONING STONE

BOOK TWO OF THE
DRAGONFIRE FANTASY SERIES

JANA G. OLIVER

Vikki & Sam,

May Peace Reign!

Jana G. Oliver

MAGESPELL PRESS

Published by
MageSpell Press
P.O. Box 1126
Atlanta, GA 30091

This novel is a work of fiction. Names, characters, places, and
incidents are the product of the author's imagination and are not to
be construed as real. Any resemblance to actual persons, living or
dead, events, or locales is entirely coincidental.

THE SUMMONING STONE
Copyright © 2002 by Jana G. Oliver

Cover Design by LS&W Productions, LC

Cover Painting by L.W. Perkins © 2002

Library of Congress Control Number: 2002101798

ISBN: 0-9704490-2-X

Printed in the United States of America
by QUESTprint

September 2002

10 9 8 7 6 5 4 3 2 1

I DEDICATE THIS BOOK TO
TO ALL WHO SUFFER
AT THE HANDS OF OPPRESSORS,
THOSE WHO CRY OUT FOR
PEACE AND ARE GIVEN
THE POINT OF A SWORD.

MAY YOU BE GRANTED SANCTUARY
IN THIS WORLD OR THE NEXT ...

Acknowledgements

To claim a novel is merely the work of one person is a falsehood. I owe this book to many people and here are a few who warrant very special attention:

L.W. "Lynn" Perkins, the incredibly talented artist who takes my humble descriptions and crafts the most fantastic cover paintings I've ever seen. She continues to amaze and delight me as she does my readers. Bless you, Lynn, for your talent and your great sense of humor!

LS&W Productions for creating another awesome book cover. Elvis would be proud!

To Harold, the long-suffering husband. Being wed to an author truly requires endless patience and diplomacy. Fortunately, Harold possesses both those qualities and so much more. Thanks, luv.

To Melody, dear friend and the proofreader of this tome. Every manuscript harbors little typos and her sharp eyes found them. Thanks, Mel, you're a gem!

To Aiodhan Bryghtblade, wiccan, warrior and good friend. Because of your tutelage I did not have to rewrite the battle scenes countless times like before. Thanks for your valued input on weaponry, wicca and what-not. Bright Blessings!

To Midnight, who continues to sit in my office window and remind this writer that humility is reserved for humans, not felines. Cats and dragons have a lot in common, me thinks.

To my intrepid 'beta' readers.

Harold Buehl ~~ Tina Lampe
NJ Olds-Magnotta ~~ Laurie Yochim

A 'beta' reader's task is not a simple one, for they alone are allowed to see the work before it is ready for publication. The 'betas' for *Summoning Stone* waded through almost five-hundred pages of rough manuscript, offering their candid opinions on characterization, plotting, flow, etc. They rooted out the inconsistencies, the little plot twists that didn't twist and told me what was strong and what was weak. Their insights were incredible and their excellent suggestions readily taken to heart. The book ascended to a higher level after their hands touched it.

Bless You One & All!

Author's Notes

Names and Places

The names and places spoken of in this tale come from many sources. Some are pure imagination while many of the names have Anglo-Saxon, Irish, Scottish or Welsh origins. For example; the word for horse in Welsh is *ceffyl* and that is the name of Belwyn's steed. *Adwyth* is Welsh for evil and *Aithne* means fire. *Phelan* is a wolf and *Corryn* means spider. This writer could not resist the temptation of using names that so readily described the characters.

The geography of this mythical realm is loosely based on Wales, a magnificent country full of wonderful people. My love of Wales began in 1987 when I first visited Caerphilly Castle and stood gazing out across the moat, allowing my fertile imagination to imagine what the fortress was like in the day of Gilbert de Clare. Little did I know that one day I'd have the opportunity to write an entire fantasy series with Wales as the backdrop.

For a comprehensive list of names and a pronunciation guide, please see the Glossary at the back of the book.

On this Book

Inner strength is often only made manifest in times of horrific struggle. Caewlin, the young iarel, is given the impossible task of preventing the wholesale extermination of his people. Knowing there is no one else left to take up the reins, he steps into the role of iarel with all the fortitude he can muster, despite the fear of failure that rages within him. He puts those fears aside and works for the survival of his people. His struggle mirrors our struggle in a world no less dangerous than his. The quest for peace is neverending.

Y Ddraig Goch Ddyry Cychwyn!

ONE

The impact of horses' hooves on the dry ground caught his attention first, for though travelers would occasionally stop at the mirrored lake to water their animals, they usually did not gallop to the destination. Peter dropped the empty water bucket in the verdant grass at his feet and strained his eyes through the morning's dim light to determine who was in such a hurry. Some basic instinct warned him of danger and so he left the bucket by the lake and scurried back toward the small hut that served as his home. As he ran, a quartet of riders passed him and reined to a halt in front of the structure.

Their apparent leader, a burly and unkempt man, bellowed,

"Morwyn! Come out, now!"

Peter shivered as he skirted around the horses and skidded to a stop near the door. To his relief the door opened and his mother, Riona, appeared. He immediately darted up to stand next to her. She unconsciously smoothed back his brown hair and took stock of the four riders in front of her. They were a curious lot, mismatched in their appearance. Two of them, a man and a woman, stopped a short distance away from the others. They appeared disconcerted. The young man had the bearing of a warrior with intense dark eyes. The woman was nondescript, though Riona could sense from her behavior she was not a camp follower. The couple gave her no clue as to why they were here. The smell of horse sweat caught her nose as the mounts stomped and shook their heads in the morning air. Turning her scrutiny to the others, she sensed these two men were of a different mold. A feeling of foreboding tracked through her, for she saw volatility and growing lust on both their faces. She decided to brave it out.

"Who are you, sir, to come shouting at my door so early?" Riona's voice was even, but loaded with fear. She pulled the hut's worn door closed behind her.

"I seek Morwyn! Have her show herself!" the gruff man replied. He was clearly eyeing the woman, sizing her up, as was one of his companions.

"I do not know of whom you speak of, sir. Now go, leave us in peace!" Riona replied.

"Do not lie to me, woman! Morwyn lives here as well as her two bastards by the Eldest of the House of Aderyn." He paused and then shouted louder as his eyes moved toward the hut's door, "Come out, Morwyn, or I will cut this woman's throat instead of yours!"

Before Riona had a chance to respond the door creaked opened and a young woman in her early twenties appeared. She was tall and thin, clothed in peasant garb, her long black hair in a single braid that fell well below her waist. She buckled on her sword and then placed a hand on its hilt.

"Braen." She uttered the word as if it was a vile curse, her eyes cold and unfeeling. *You have found me, you bastard.*

He had not changed much, she noted, he was still heavyset with unruly blonde hair and a scraggly beard. His eyes were no less cruel.

"Morwyn, there you are," he smirked. "You have been out of sight for a very long time." It had taken him over three years to learn what had befallen her and now he was here to settle matters between them.

"What is it you want, Braen?" *I must bluff him, if he believes I still wield the magic he will leave us be.*

"What do I want, Morwyn?" he retorted, as if that was an absurd question. "I would think that was obvious. I have waited all these years to *have* you and now you have neither the warrior nor your magic to save you." His grizzled face broadened into a wide and gloating smile.

He knows. Morwyn kept the stark jolt of fear off her face and answered in a steely voice, "Leave, Braen, we have nothing in common."

"Oh, we have very much in common, Morwyn, for we are both castoffs. The smithy did not like how I handled his daughter so I am no longer welcome in our village. You've been bedded by the Eldest of Aderyn and have had bastards by him. You are spurned as well."

He gestured widely to encompass the humble hut she called home as if to illustrate his point. She thought a moment and then surmised the man's plan. Braen was greedy, besides being cruel.

"Belwyn does not acknowledge his children. He does not care," she lied. The eldest son of Aderyn did not even know the children existed, she had never told him. She prayed Braen did not know this. As it was, her falsehood was not enough to sway the brutish man from his purpose.

Braen's eyes grew dark and angry. "It does not matter. His father will pay ransom for his grandchildren even if his son does not claim they are his. I am here to settle the score with Aderyn and with you."

Morwyn's heart pounded in her chest. She traded looks with Riona and saw rampant fear in her friend's eyes. Two women against three men were uneven odds, at best. Morwyn knew what she must do.

"I will go with you, Braen, I will do whatever you demand of me, but leave my children and my friends out of it."

"No, that is not enough, not this time. My men deserve a good time and you women will provide it." Braen heaved himself out of his saddle, as did one of the other men, both moving forward in a threatening manner.

"Braen, what is this?" the third man asked, the one that rode with the woman. He was clearly upset.

"It is what we came for, Ifor," Braen snarled, displeased to have his actions challenged.

"You said there was gold to be had, not stealing someone's children and harassing women," the man came back instantly. His tone was more demanding.

"If you don't want your turn, that's more for Malvern and me," Braen replied dismissively and set his sights back on Morwyn. Sensing his intent, Riona pulled her knife from the small sheath at her waist as Morwyn unsheathed her sword.

"Run, Peter!" Riona commanded, but the boy did not comply. He shook his head and snatched up a staff where it leaned near the door, brandishing it as a weapon.

"No, mother, I stay!"

Malvern, a bear of a man, began to snicker at the sight.

"Well, this shouldn't be too difficult. Two women and a boy." He had a leer on his face that chilled Riona to the core.

Braen pulled his sword and moved toward Morwyn with deliberate steps, clearly relishing the moment.

"I will have you either way, cut or not, it is your choice."

Morwyn did not reply and waited for him to come within range of her sword, her heart racing. Somehow, Braen had learned who had fathered her children and that she no longer possessed the power of magic to destroy him. He had attempted to assault her once before, in their village, before she had become an adept and wielded the magic. That time, Belwyn had come to her rescue. Today there was no warrior to protect her or her friends – it would come down to the might of the sword. She pushed down her fear and waited for the man to make the first move.

Braen found her a dangerous foe. She knew how to wield the weapon, for she was the daughter of a warrior, and fear for her children gave her needed courage. He sustained a deep cut the moment they engaged in combat and blood coursed down his arm in crimson rivers.

"Powers!" he shouted and drove at her again, swinging wildly. She ducked and slashed at him, nearly impaling him as her anger pushed her. Out of the corner of her eye she was aware of a desperate struggle between Riona and the other man. She realized that the third bandit remained on his horse, choosing to stay out of the brawl. That gave her some measure of hope, for if she could slay Braen they may have a chance to survive this confrontation.

Malvern howled in pain as little Peter struck him hard with the staff. He backhanded him and the lad went to the ground immediately. With his attention diverted, Riona managed to inflict a knife wound on her attacker, but a blow dropped her to the ground near her son. She quickly regained her feet and helped Peter rise.

"Come on, woman, make it easy on yourself. I'll be good fun," Malvern taunted her.

"Dead is what you'll be, you bastard," Peter snarled back and despite being only twelve-years-old, managed to sweep the staff under the man's feet and drop him in a heap. The bandit pulled himself back up and ignored the lad, setting his sights on the woman. He threw himself on Riona and they fell together, her knife knocked from her grasp. She screamed as Peter desperately began to strike at her assailant with the staff.

It would have been very entertaining if the situation had not been so desperate – a little boy, less than three years of age, charged out of the hut brandishing a small stick. He made straight for Braen, shouting in a little child's voice. Morwyn's concentration was broken by the small figure running past her and she cried in horror,

"Pyrs, no!" Fearing for her son's life, Morwyn attempted to divert Braen's attention. She cut at him with her sword, but was off balance. He seized that moment of distraction and plunged his blade into Morwyn's right shoulder. She reeled back from the pain but managed to knock his weapon from his grasp and it fell between them. She moved forward, standing over the blade as Braen shouted his indignation. She could feel blood pouring out of the wound as she fought to keep her feet. Braen reached out and gave Pyrs a vicious kick, sending the little boy tumbling across the ground like one would a pinecone. Shouting her wrath, Morwyn moved forward to kill the monster but met with his knife as it sunk into her flesh near her collarbone. She stumbled back and then sank to her knees instantly, dizziness encompassing her. Braen sheathed his knife and strode to the boy, scooping him up in his arms. Pyrs shouted and howled, fighting the brute.

"Silence, brat! Hold still or I'll cut you, too!" he threatened but the little boy did not stop battling him. Pyrs bit him hard on the hand eliciting a vehement oath.

"Ifor, come here and take this bastard!" he commanded. Ifor reluctantly dismounted and took the screaming boy from Braen. As he retreated with the struggling child his eyes caught those of his companion who sat ashen faced on her horse.

Her voice quavered, "This is not right, Ifor."

He nodded, he had no taste for this.

Braen shifted his attention back to the wounded woman. He reclaimed his sword and sheathed it, not bothering to cleanse it of the blood that coated the tip. He put his hands on his hips, reveling in the moment. Morwyn tightened her grip on her sword and struggled to rise. She felt a strange wave of warmth fly through her body. She half-turned to find her small daughter, Gwyn, Pyrs's twin sister, with her hand on her mother's elbow.

"Safe, mother," the little girl said and then toddled over to where Riona and Malvern fought on the ground. She stopped, as if waiting for something. Peter slammed the staff down on the man's head and he reeled from the blow, rolling off the woman beneath him. The sight of Riona's torn clothes and blood-streaked face incensed her son. The young lad swore an oath and then charged the stunned man again, striking him solidly on the chest and the shoulder. Malvern cursed and backed away, slowly rising to his feet. He turned his knife toward the boy, slicing at him. Peter had no choice but to retreat. As Riona struggled to rise she gasped, feeling the same odd warmth as Morwyn had. She turned to find Gwyn near her, touching her with her outstretched hand.

"Gwyn?" she asked, as the sensation poured through her, making her feel faint.

The little girl only murmured, "Riona, safe." She made her way to Peter and repeated the gesture to him as well. Then, despite the danger and the brutality around her, she walked toward the horses and the woman who had come with the attackers. The woman stared at the small girl in disbelief as Gwyn stretched out her arms as if wanting to be held. After only a moment's hesitation, the woman climbed off her horse and scooped her up. The little girl did not fight her, if anything she welcomed her embrace. There was a strange look of contentment on the child's face. Gwyn turned her calm blue-grey eyes on Ifor, who stood next to her, still clutching her distraught twin.

As Morwyn's head cleared she found her nemesis towering over her. He laughed, knowing that there was little fight left in her. Intent on violation, he grappled her down. As soon he touched her, began to rip at her clothes, he screamed in mortal agony and hurtled off her. He lurched to his feet, holding his hands out in front of him as they shook in intense pain. The skin on his hands began to turn deep red.

"Curse you! What devilry is this?" Morwyn's dazed mind could not comprehend what was happening. She heard a similar shriek from the other outlaw after he resumed his attack on Riona.

"It is evil magic!" Malvern exclaimed. Like his companion's, his hands were red and swollen, scalded as if he had plunged them in a boiling kettle of water. In obvious discomfort he pulled his sword, determined to slay Riona, but he could not come close to her or Peter. Searing pain scorched through his body. It lessened when he retreated from them, flared two-fold when he moved closer. He lurched back and stayed in place as curses tumbled out of his mouth.

Braen bellowed in anger and surged forward, determined to slaughter Morwyn as she endeavored to rise to a fighting position. He met the same fate as Malvern, unable to come near for the pain that seared through him. He began to swear, cursing her for her vile sorcery. Something made Morwyn turn her eyes toward her small daughter nestled peacefully within the arms of the bandits' female companion. Her daughter's tranquil expression told the story.

Gwyn has done this. My daughter has saved us. She allowed no hint of this revelation to show and spun the truth in another direction to keep her daughter safe. She knew Braen would try to kill the girl if he suspected her of such powerful magic.

Summoning a strong voice she retorted, "You deserve to burn, Braen." He spat at her and cursed even more. When his eyes fell on Pyrs he moved toward the small boy with deadly determination, intent on unholy revenge. Ifor shook his head and sheltered the struggling boy.

"No, none of that, Braen!" Pyrs continued to fight and only ceased his struggles when Ifor wrapped him tightly in a blanket so he could not flail. He began to howl, piteously, and the sound of her son's frightened voice wounded Morwyn more than any blade Braen could turn on her.

"Braen, please, leave the children!" He turned his cold eyes on her and shook his head, pulling a piece of rolled parchment out from under his shirt. The blood on his hands stained it immediately as he cast it towards her in disdain.

His voice was deep and icy. "Tell Aderyn if they do not want these children butchered they must pay what I demand. You know me, Morwyn, I will kill them and enjoy every moment of it." He pulled himself back on his horse, his crippled hands complicating the task as his companions did the same. The young woman made sure that Gwyn was safely seated right in front of her before Ifor hoisted the blanket-entombed little boy onto the horse. Pyrs continued to wail in fear and anger. His cries only lessened to quiet sobs when Gwyn reached out and touched her twin brother's cheek.

Braen took one last look at Morwyn and a strange look of triumph crossed his face.

He muttered, "You are worm's meat, woman. My knife was poisoned." Morwyn shivered involuntarily, knowing he did not lie.

Through a haze of pain she replied, "I will live to see you hang, Braen." Her voice was defiant as tears coursed down her cheeks. Her eyes moved to her children and she saw Gwyn's placid face as she kept her hand on her brother for comfort. Braen wheeled his horse with an oath and the four riders left the hut behind at a full gallop.

Peter helped his mother up from the ground and they hugged, lingering over the embrace. She kissed him on the forehead, smoothed his hair back and spoke her love for him.

"I am so proud of you, Peter, so proud." The young boy only hugged her harder, his heart still pounding, his gut knotted in fright. Riona shifted her gaze toward Morwyn. She was on her knees again, her shoulder bleeding heavily. She dropped her sword and pressed her free hand to the shoulder wound. Blood began to trickle around her fingers, coating them.

"Riona," she began and paused to try to work through a spasm of pain that overtook her. She felt arms around her and heard her friend's voice in her ear.

"Hold fast, you are badly injured."

"Go to Aderyn, tell them what has happened and beg them to rescue Gwyn and Pyrs. Please, you must…" Morwyn's strength faded before she could complete the request and she slipped to the ground.

The riders swept through the forest to the main road and then galloped north. Braen did not allow them to stop until the horses were wheezing and near to collapse. When they could go no further, he reluctantly halted. He threw himself off his mount and stomped some distance away in a black mood, his shoulder throbbing viciously from the wound Morwyn had given him. He had planned to send the note to Aderyn in the hands of the other woman at the hut, after he and his men had finished with her. He did not intend to leave Morwyn behind, he wanted her with him so he could extract the full measure of brutality she deserved. Now, it was very likely the wench would die from the poisoned wound. He swore oaths again, loud and long. His burning gaze shifted over to Ifor and his woman, Cara, as they lifted the children down from her horse.

"At least we have his bastards," Braen muttered and strode to his mount, yanking off his wineskin from the saddle horn. Ignoring the needs of his horse, he began to drink and brood.

TWO

They lay Morwyn upon her cot and Riona began to tend her wounds. The sword cut was deep and it bled profusely, though in time the flow was stanched by firm pressure. The knife wound bled very little and that puzzled her, for it was a wicked gash. She said nothing to Morwyn and the wounded woman remained quiet the entire time, tears in her eyes. Once the wounds were bound, Riona called to her son. Peter instantly appeared in the doorway at the sound of her voice.

"Hitch the horse to the cart. We must go to Aderyn to deliver the ransom note and seek treatment for Morwyn and ourselves."

"Yes, mother." The boy vanished to do his mother's bidding. Still in a daze, Riona changed her dress, mechanically washing the blood off her face and hands. Nausea bubbled through her and it took all her effort to keep from collapsing in tears. She steadied herself and then knelt down to cleanse the blood off her friend's hands and arms.

"He will kill them, Riona," Morwyn said in a shaky voice.

Riona shook her head, "No, he won't. They are his pouch of gold. He'll keep them alive just to claim the money."

"Maybe, but once he has the money he will kill them, for he hates me that much. I should have gone with him, allowed him his way…"

"It would not have mattered." Morwyn searched her friend's face and knew she spoke the truth. *It would not have mattered, either way. My pride has caused this. The children would have been safe with their father. I am to blame.*

Riona rose and began to pack herbs, linens and food for the journey to Aderyn. As his mother completed her preparations, Peter announced the cart and horse were ready. His face was a mass of dirty scrapes and his clothes stained and torn from the violence of the assault. After making him wash and change into different clothes, she handed him a cup of herb-laced wine to drink. He sniffed the cup suspiciously and asked,

"What is this? It smells awful."

"It is needed, son. We must remain strong to help Morwyn and the children." He nodded and slowly drank the concoction, his face settling into a noticeable grimace at the taste. He handed the cup back to his mother and pulled out the ransom note Braen had left behind in the grass at Morwyn's feet.

"I cannot read it, mother, it is not very clear." Riona took the document in her hands, which were shaking again, and read the demands.

"You cannot read it, son, because of the language. That villain is not even literate."

"And not worthy of life, either, mother," the young boy came back, steel in his voice. She gazed down at him and realized the boy had taken a step closer to manhood.

"No, Aderyn will kill him and I pray they do it slowly." She gave the note back to the boy for safekeeping and they helped Morwyn into the small cart, tucking blankets around her for warmth. Peter guided the horse through the forest toward the main road. Once they reached that point, they would turn south toward Aderyn's holdings. The road was dry this time of year so the journey would go smoothly providing they didn't encounter any further perils.

"Was that your spell that kept the men off us?" Riona asked. A slight shake of the woman's head was her answer. "Then it was Gwyn's magic?" A nod in the affirmative this time. "Powers," Riona replied in amazement.

Braen was drunk within a short time making further travel impossible. They moved the horses to a sheltered area and made camp for the night. Pyrs was now silent and his sister remained next to him for comfort. Cara pulled out some bread and cheese and tore the food into small pieces for the children to eat. Gwyn ate what she was given, Pyrs refused to touch the food.

"He is too upset to eat," Cara said to her lover. Ifor nodded. He looked over at Braen some distance from him and shook his head.

"I had no idea this is what he planned. I would not have done this, Cara."

"I know," she replied and continued to feed bits of bread and cheese to Gwyn.

"Aderyn will hunt us and kill us," he said quietly.

She only nodded and continued her attentions to the little girl.

Riona provided what healing she could over the two full days it took to journey to the House of Aderyn, but it was apparent there was more at work than just the wounds. Morwyn began to shiver and chill late the first night and then a roaring fever took hold. Riona changed the bandages but found no sign of infection at either site. The sword wound's bandage had blood on it, as one would expect. The knife wound, the one at Morwyn's collarbone, did not. The wound was pale and felt unnaturally cold to the touch. It made no sense to Riona and she asked Morwyn of it.

"Braen said the knife was poisoned," Morwyn replied as another shiver overtook her.

"How do I counter it?" Riona asked. Morwyn mumbled something, but it made no sense. Riona was an apprentice healer and did not know the means to treat a wound tainted by poison.

"Mother?" Peter asked, noticing her worried face.

"We must press on, Peter. Make sure the horse is sufficiently rested and let us be on our way." He nodded and rose to tend the beast.

The further they traveled the more incoherent Morwyn became. Initially she alternated between fits of chills and burning fever. In time, it was all fever. Peter kept the horse moving forward steadily, speeding up the cart when the road allowed. Sensing time was waning for their friend, they did not stop except to allow the beast to rest and take water.

The guard at Aderyn's main gate was perplexed to see a small cart moving toward him at a fairly fast pace along the well-worn path. It was late in the day, the light was fading, and he squinted to assure himself of what he was seeing. He called to a fellow guard and they watched as the cart approached. They were wary.

"It is not a peddler's cart, it moves too fast."

"I will tell the Master of Guard, lest there be trouble."

The first man nodded his agreement and kept his eyes on the approaching conveyance. Dillan, the Master of the Guard, appeared moments later. His keen eyes sought out the cart and he frowned.

Placing his hand on his sword hilt he muttered, "It is a boy." He began to walk forward, one of the guards at his side, and they intercepted the two-wheeled wagon as it approached the outer wall of the holdings. Behind them stood ten men, armed, standing guard in front of the main gate. Dillan was known for his caution.

"Sir! Good sir, please, we need help!" Peter called, in a breathless voice. To Dillan, the boy appeared to be no more than eleven or twelve years old of age. His face bruised and he moved stiffly as if there were other wounds they could not see. In the back of the cart was a woman, actually two women. One sat upright beside the body of the other and appeared to be tending her. Gazing into the back of the cart, even in the dim light, Dillan recognized the inert figure lying there. He took a sharp intact of breath.

"By the Powers, it is her!" he exclaimed and Riona raised her eyes toward him at the sound of his voice.

Thank the Powers, he remembers her!

"She is wounded, sir. We seek shelter and aid from the House of Aderyn. Please help us," she asked, her voice quavering.

"You shall have it." Dillan took hold of the horse's bridle and led the beast and the cart into the courtyard as one of the guard hurried to report the situation to their master.

Owain the Elder, master of the house, and his eldest son, Belwyn, were at the evening repast with their guests. Seated at Belwyn's right was Lord Morgan, only son of Lord Bardyn. A friend of Belwyn's and the future Lord of the Eastern March, Morgan was a handsome and well-mannered man with long blonde hair and a strong face. His looks contrasted with Belwyn's, for though handsome, the eldest son of Aderyn had shoulder length dark hair and intense eyes. The other guest, also a close friend, was Ulwyn the Bard, a young lad with a cheery smile and a ready wit. Well featured with long brown hair flowing down his back, his presence had insured the evening passed in song and jest. The merriment ended the moment the guard appeared and reported that Morwyn the Healer had arrived at the holdings, badly wounded.

Morwyn was fiery to the touch and did not stir when Dillan removed her from the back of the cart. He knew that boded ill. He strode toward Aderyn's main hall with Morwyn lying in his arms, keenly aware of the reaction her arrival would cause. Once inside he found himself surrounded by concerned faces.

"By the Powers," was all Owain the Elder could mutter. He had not seen Morwyn since the great battle over three years before. Her face was older, more worn.

"What has happened to her?" Belwyn demanded.

"She is wounded, sir, by both sword and knife," Riona replied wearily. The journey to Aderyn, at such a furious pace, had taken its toll on her and her son.

"Surely that would not account for her being so ill. Are the wounds infected?" the bard asked, puzzled. His wife was a healer and he knew something was amiss.

"No, the wounds are clean. One of wounds is poisoned."

"Powers Prevent!" Ulwyn replied, shaking his head, worry in his eyes.

"But how has this happened?" Morgan asked, haunted by the sight of the seriously ill woman.

"We were attacked, sirs, attacked at our home," Riona answered and then began to waver on her feet from fatigue. Her son caught her around the waist to steady her.

Noting the woman's exhausted condition, Owain the Elder said,

"You are not well, either, madam, and it appears both of you have taken hurt in this matter. Come, let us find you a place by the fire and we will sort this out."

"Peter, give them the note," Riona ordered. Her son complied, pulling the rolled parchment out from under his rough linen shirt and handing it to the master of the house.

Dillan set off for one of the rooms on the lower floor of the great hall as Riona and her son followed behind him. Belwyn's eyes were only on the injured young woman as he followed the procession, his face pale and drawn. Owain the Elder was transfixed by the scrawled words on the parchment in his hand. His face grew grey.

Morgan noticed the change in his host and paused near him.

"Owain? What is it?" he pressed.

The older man's eyes raised from the paper. "Ill news."

He strode on, Morgan behind him, and entered the room as Dillan placed the injured woman on the bed. Owain paused and read the note again. It was misspelled and spattered with blood, but its demands were clear. The revelations it contained was earthshaking – he had grandchildren, someone had taken them by force from their mother and threatened to kill them if ransom was not paid. His anger kindled.

They have my grandchildren!

Belwyn helped Aderyn's healer, Iola, remove Morwyn's boots and then stepped away. Iola spread a clean linen sheet over the woman's body and began to remove her sweat-soaked clothes under the cover. Riona, despite her weariness, assisted the healer. They placed a clean chemise on Morwyn and cut out the right shoulder so the sword wound could be easily accessed.

"Tell me what treatment you have given her," Iola asked as she began to examine both wounds. The shoulder wound, though deep, was clean and beginning to heal. The cut near Morwyn's collarbone was uncharacteristically pale, bloodless.

"I have kept the wounds clean and they are not infected, but she burns with fever. Morwyn said the knife wound was poisoned," Riona explained. "I am only an apprentice healer, I do not know how to combat this and she could not tell me." The older healer nodded and placed her hand on Riona's arm for comfort.

"How long ago did this happen?"

"Two days. We traveled without rest to come here." The older healer nodded her understanding.

"Tell me her symptoms and I will see what can be done." Riona began to relate what traits Morwyn had exhibited and eventually the healer nodded once again.

"I know of the poison. It is a crude and slow-acting one or she would have died the day of the injury. I will apply a poultice with a drawing out herb. It may turn her course."

"Thank you, I felt so powerless," Riona replied, her voice thick with emotion. She felt someone's strong arm around her waist and turned to find it was the young man with the long brown hair. His face was kind and gentle.

"Come, sit by the fire. Iola will care for her."

"Thank you," she murmured.

"I am Ulwyn the Bard. This is Lord Morgan," he gestured toward the tall blonde man hovering near the bed, "Belwyn, the Eldest of Aderyn," pointing to the dark-haired man, "and Owain the Elder, master of the house."

She gave a very slight bow. "I am Riona and this is my son, Peter."

"Then come, Riona, sit and rest. You as well, Peter, for both of you are obviously very weary," Ulwyn said as he guided the woman over to a chair by the fire.

Belwyn pulled a chair over by the bed and sank down on it, taking Morwyn's feverish hand in his. His face was as blanched as the wounded woman's was scarlet.

"Owain?" Morgan asked again, sensing something dreadful was playing out given the man's grave countenance.

Owain the Elder looked over at Riona.

"If you are well enough, madam, please explain the sequence of events that led you to our door before I reveal the contents of this message." The hand holding the parchment was unsteady and the dried blood on the document seemed to glow in the firelight.

A cup of wine appeared in front of Riona, courtesy of Ulwyn, and she took a big sip to steady her nerves. She glanced over and found Peter was in a chair near her, covered with blankets and a cup of wine in his hands as well. He gave her a faint smile, one of encouragement. She turned her attention back to the master of the house.

"My son and I live with Morwyn near the mirrored lake north of here. Yesterday, three men and a woman came to our hut just after dawn. One of them was named Braen and he …"

The man's name triggered an instant oath from Belwyn.

"That bastard, what did he want?"

"He was there for two things, sir. He wanted Morwyn and he sought – her children."

"Children?" Morgan asked, bewilderment on his face. He glanced down at the unconscious woman on the bed. The healer was cleaning the deep shoulder wound and the sight of it made him grimace.

"Morwyn has twins, Gwyn and Pyrs. They are just two and half years old," Riona replied, her eyes moving to Belwyn. The man blinked and she knew he was beginning to work out the ramifications of that revelation.

"Who is the father?" Morgan asked, instantly apprehensive.

"They were sired by …" Riona paused. She kept her eyes on Belwyn and waited. *He must acknowledge the truth himself.*

He fixed his gaze on Riona and replied, "By me." he murmured. "If they are that age they are my children."

"Yes, they were sired by you, sir, the night Morwyn broke your enchantment."

Belwyn had realized the truth almost instantly. He had always wondered if new life was created that night, for their loving was an act of strong magic that had freed him of his enchantment and cost Morwyn most of her powers. His mind had consoled himself that she would tell him if he were a father. His heart had told him otherwise, but he had allowed his mind to rule him.

"I did not know," he said.

"I do not understand," Morgan muttered, growing angry. He had once been Morwyn's lover, years before she took the vow of celibacy as a practitioner of the *Way*. His love still burned bright. "She cannot be with a man without losing her powers and yet you say…" It suddenly made sense to him and his mind screamed at the injustice. "You took her to your bed to break the enchantment, knowing what would happen to her?" His voice was raw and unyielding in its intensity.

"Now is not the time, Morgan, there are greater matters at hand." Owain's voice rose in timbre as he waved the parchment in his hand. "This is a ransom note."

Morgan opened his mouth to retort and then reined back his anger. He nodded reluctantly.

"I will hold my tongue for now. As you say, there are greater matters at hand." He gave Belwyn a thinly disguised glare and then moved his eyes down to the woman on the bed. The healer was applying a poultice to the knife wound as Morwyn continued deep within the fever.

"This states that they demand money for my grandchildren. If we do not pay the ransom they will slit their throats and leave their bodies to be torn apart by scavengers."

"No!" Belwyn's voice rose in anger. "Braen seeks revenge upon me. By the Powers, father, we must save them!"

"We shall, my son and make the villains pay for their greed." He paused and then bellowed, "Dillan!" The man appeared instantly at his master's side, his face grim, for he had heard what the note contained.

"Sir?"

"We are to ride to Ilspath. The note speaks of an inn where we must leave the ransom money. We will leave in the morning, before dawn so that we can arrive during daylight. I wish to have every opportunity to locate the children once the ransom is paid."

"I will prepare men for the journey, sir."

Ulwyn cleared his throat. "Where I agree force is usually a good thing, Owain," the bard said cautiously, "too many of us will unsettle them. I believe it would be best if only Belwyn, Morgan and I go to Ilspath, along with Riona if she feels able. The children know her and they will be very frightened. Her presence may give them comfort." The older man studied the bard for a moment and reluctantly nodded his agreement.

"You are quite right, a show of force may cause them to act irrationally and harm the children. I will regret not bringing all the might of Aderyn against those monsters."

"I wish to go as well, father," a different voice added, having listened intently to the demands contained in the parchment.

"Owain?" his father asked, surprised to see his youngest son and namesake standing in doorway of the room. His presence at the holdings was a surprise for he had sent no word of his impending visit. Owain the Younger crossed to his father and embraced him.

He turned and asked, "Riona, how are you?"

"I am only sore and bruised, Owain. Peter kept me safe," she answered honestly. Owain gave the young man a smile.

"You are a brave lad, your father would be proud of you," he said as he tousled the boy's hair. The lad blushed slightly.

"I was very frightened," he admitted.

"As was I, son," Riona replied. "You fought like a man and I am so proud of you." The boy looked down, overwhelmed by the feelings raging inside him. Owain the Younger gave a quick nod to acknowledge Ulwyn and then went to stand by his brother and Morgan as they kept vigil over the desperately ill woman.

"How is she?" he asked Iola, his face registering his worry.

"Very weak. A fever burns because one of the wounds is poisoned," the woman replied.

"May the Powers aid you, healer." He put his arm on his brother's shoulder in a comforting gesture.

"I am confused ..." Morgan began, sensing something amiss. He pressed ahead without thinking, his mind in turmoil over Morwyn's injury and the revelation she had children. "You appear to know Riona and her son. Did you know of Morwyn's twins?" He immediately realized that was not a question he should have asked at this time. Chagrined, he apologized, "I'm sorry, perhaps I overstep myself."

There was a very awkward silence and finally young Owain nodded in resignation.

"I have visited Morwyn at the mirrored lake a number of times since she broke Belwyn's enchantment. I learned of her pregnancy only a month or so before she delivered. I have seen the twins every few months since then."

"Why, in the Powers' name, did you not tell me?" Belwyn demanded as rose from his chair, clearly agitated. His brother did not move away, readily accepting his sibling's anger.

"She made me vow not to. Only her brother and I knew, she refused to allow us to tell anyone else, even our father. She and I argued about that more than once, but you know Morwyn, she can be very stubborn."

"Why did she not want me to know I had children?" Belwyn challenged. He was clearly distraught that his own brother knew of his offspring and yet had not told him. "It would have made all the difference, Owain, can't you see that?"

"I know, she would not let me."

"Still, you have not said why …" Belwyn pressed.

"They were all she had, Belwyn. She feared you would take them from her."

"I would not have!" His life had been empty since that night. The spell had been broken, against his wishes, for he suspected the heavy price she would pay. "The years would have been bearable if I had known." His voice cracked betraying the emotional anguish raging inside of him.

"I know. She was not willing to risk it."

"They are my children as well …" Belwyn began and it was Owain the Elder who finished the statement,

"And they are the heirs to the House of Aderyn and must be protected. These villains will pay with their lives."

"They shall trice over," was all Belwyn could utter and he sunk back down onto the chair, his strength gone.

The mood was somber that night. Morwyn remained desperately ill, though Iola reported that the fever's fury was lessening. That was badly needed news for all those who sat vigil either at her bedside or in the main gathering room of the hall. Iola sent Riona to bed with a sleeping draught, concerned for the woman's welfare after the injuries she had taken in the attack. Peter could not sleep, his mind was too full of the events of the past two days, so he sat with the men and recounted the attack, in detail.

"Not all of them were party to the raid?" Ulwyn asked in surprise.

"No, one of them refused. He was the one with the woman. They appeared to be disconcerted by what Braen intended, as if they had not known ahead of time."

"Well, that speaks well of his honor, to some extent," Ulwyn replied. He took another sip of ale as Peter continued with the tale, telling them of Pyrs' futile attempt to save his mother.

"He attacked Braen?" Owain the Younger asked incredulously. "Pyrs has always been fearless, but that is remarkable!" He shook his head at the thought of it.

"He could not harm the monster. His actions only distracted his mother and it was then she was wounded. Nevertheless, I was very proud of him," Peter remarked.

Ulwyn chuckled, "He sounds as fearless as his father." Belwyn caught his friend's eyes and a faint smile appeared on his worn face.

"What can you tell me of the little ones, Peter?" he asked, his mind still trying to accept that he was a father twice over.

Peter cleared his throat and explained, "Morwyn said she came to the lake after the enchantment was broken. She built the hut and bore the children that first winter. My mother and I came to live with her the following autumn. My father is dead, sir, and my mother wished to learn the healing arts. Morwyn offered to teach her. Pyrs and Gwyn are like brother and sister to me. Pyrs loves to play with small river stones, building little skirmish lines in the dirt and moving them around like they were battle formations. He has a wicked temper and is so brave, more than is good at his age, to be honest. He is inseparable from his sister. Gwyn is, well, a child of magic, as my mother says. She talks with animals in forest and they come to be with her for hours on end. Morwyn says she wields the Old Magic."

"Powers," Ulwyn murmured. *The Old Magic!*

"I saw a wolf come up her once, one of the large grey ones. I thought it meant to carry her off, but it was not there to harm her, for she had called it to her. I still remember her standing by it, clutching its fur to keep her balance. She said her first two words – *wolf friend.* She only speaks two words at a time, you see." Peter's voice was growing faint and it was evident the boy was winding down, the adrenaline no longer fueling his mind. He yawned without warning and was instantly chagrined. Belwyn put his arm on the lad's shoulder in a heartfelt gesture.

"Thank you, Peter, you have been such a comfort. Your courage has been unfailing."

"I wish I could have prevented Morwyn from being hurt," the boy said sadly.

"You kept them alive, young man," Owain the Elder observed, "and that is no mean feat."

"Gwyn did that sir, not me." At that he explained the strange spell the girl had used to keep them from further harm.

"By the Powers," Ulwyn muttered, "she wields as much magic as her mother once did, but at such a young age."

"In that case, Braen may not be able to harm them," Owain the Younger offered.

"Let us pray that is the case, brother. I should have killed him that day in Argel," Belwyn replied darkly.

"Your turn will come soon enough, my son," his father replied and then gestured for one of the servants to walk Peter to the room where his mother slept so the lad could rest.

"I have children," Belwyn said quietly, more to himself than the others seated around him. It was his way of allowing the truth to sink in. It still stunned and amazed him.

"They were not to be," his brother replied. Belwyn gave him a startled look. "Morwyn told me that she took herbs to prevent conception before she came to your room that night. She did not want children of such a union, Belwyn, she knew it would not be right. Clearly, the Powers wanted the twins to exist."

There was silence for a time, each man deep in his own thoughts. Morgan's voice finally broke the silence, for he had spoken little during the evening. His eyes betrayed his inner turmoil, they were dark and unsettled.

"I have waited patiently, Belwyn, but I have not heard you explain how you could so casually bed her, knowing the harm it would bring her." His words were at odds with his emotions, in deference to his host he held his anger in check.

Belwyn sighed. "You are right, I have not said a word about that. I think you and I should speak privately."

"As you wish." Morgan's tone did not waver.

Belwyn's brother shot his father a look of concern, but Owain the Elder only shook his head slightly. After Belwyn and Morgan left the room the older man explained,

"It is between them, son, for they both love the woman equally."

"I fear Morgan's passion may take this too far," Owain the Younger replied, a slight frown on his face.

"It may, but there is nothing we can do. They must make peace now or be enemies in the future," the older man replied. He rose and left the room, heading to his bed. As he trudged up the long staircase to the second floor he uttered a prayer that Morgan's good reason would prevail.

THREE

◆

It was a beautiful summer evening and the sound of crickets echoed around them as the two warriors strode away from the hall into the waxing moonlight. They did not speak a word until they reached the stable. Belwyn found a place to sit on one of the crude wooden benches outside the building while Morgan remained standing, his mind in tumult. His anger had only grown during their silent walk.

"Now that we are away from the others and I no longer need to hold my tongue in deference to your father ..." his voice seethed. "How could you *do* that to her? You can have any woman you want, yet you bed her as if she was but a camp wench and of no value, knowing you would destroy her!" Morgan's face was cold and raw anger flickered in his eyes.

Belwyn studied his friend, Morwyn's first love, the man who would, in time, be his liege lord. He felt the raging anger and his own guilt for having caused it.

"I love her, Morgan, I know that is difficult for you to hear, for I know you love her as well."

"Do not taint your actions in love, Belwyn! You slaked your lust on her to free yourself and now she pays the price!" The young lord grew stormier. "I should strike you dead for what you have done to her!" The threat was genuine, for his hand was on the hilt of his sword, his knuckles white.

"It is best I tell you all of it, from the very beginning, and then you can judge if you wish to remain my friend or slay me. For if you feel I have wronged Morwyn, then I deserve just that."

In a quiet voice, full of aching memories, he started his tale. He told his fellow warrior of his confrontation with the village brute, Braen, in Argel, and how he had saved Morwyn from violation. He spoke of his enchantment and why Adwyth the Adept chose him to exact her revenge against the House of Aderyn.

"She pulled my memory of Braen's attack upon Morwyn from my mind and wove it into a vicious enchantment. I saw myself forcing and then killing her repeatedly in my nightmares. They were as consuming as if I had done the deed each time. Only by the intervention of the Powers did I not take my own life."

Morgan held his silence. He had heard only bits and pieces of this strange story over the years, but never from Belwyn himself. The real tale had remained out of the light of day.

Belwyn continued, "I learned that Adwyth was my father's lover and that my grandfather, Trahern, sought her death because she carried an heir to Aderyn. My uncle forcibly took the child from her to prevent my grandsire from killing her and the infant. I have a half-sister somewhere in this world, Morgan, and neither my brother nor I can find her." His voice rung with sadness at that admission.

"We believe she still lives, for she was fostered with a family further to the south of my uncle's holdings. They have passed over and no further word has been heard of her. We don't even know what she is called, for apparently the name Adwyth gave her was changed to further shield her identity and to prevent my grandfather's wrath from falling upon them."

He paused and stared at the moon for a moment and then recounted the journey he and Morwyn undertook to see the Ancient One, the dragon, where she learned how to break his enchantment.

"She did not tell me what the dragon demanded of her, Morgan, but I knew it was grave by the way she reacted. I did not know she had to break the enchantment by being with me or I would not have permitted it."

Morgan held his tongue, his mind beginning to absorb this amazing tale. Sensing he did not intend to speak, Belwyn continued, "She came to my bed that night, performed a healing spell, and then told me she was there to break the enchantment. I started to protest but she spellbound me, Morgan, it was the only way I would lie with her. I knew that to make love to her was to destroy her."

A sheen of tears appeared in his eyes. "The next morning I found a broken swan's feather in my bed, she used to wear them in her hair, and that helped me piece together what had happened between us. I remember we made love, twice …" At that he tugged a silver locket from under his jerkin and held it reverently, caressing its reflective surface with his thumb. "I have that feather here, in this locket, and I have worn it since."

He paused for a moment and then explained, "I love her, Morgan, but we can never be together, not if she wishes to keep what little magic she has left. I know, now, why she kept the children a secret, why she was given them in the first place, despite her wishes. I believe it was the Powers' way of granting her peace-of-mind after what she lost. Though I regret not having the children in my arms all these years, I understand why she kept them hidden. They were her only solace."

As the story progressed, Morgan's veil of righteous anger shredded and he glimpsed the depth of pain and immeasurable sadness Belwyn carried within. He clearly saw Morwyn making her sacrifice for a man she loved more than her life. He turned and watched the moon for a time, no word coming from him as his heart weighed all he had heard.

Finally, he addressed his friend in a melancholy voice, "No, I shall not slay you, Belwyn, for I see that no mortal sword could wound you as deep as the Powers have. Morwyn had no choice and neither did you. It was destined that you fall in love and be separated as you are, though I do not understand why They could be so harsh. I was angry when I thought you had destroyed her magic solely to break the spell you endured. I thought you callous, taking her to your bed only so that you could be whole once more. I see now that neither of you are whole, not until you are together." He paused and then added with a voice that sounded like his heart was bleeding, "I know now that Morwyn will forever love you more than she does me."

Belwyn rose and they embraced for a long time. Both had tears in their eyes and it took considerable time for the Eldest of Aderyn to speak.

"You are an honorable and decent man and I so wish Morwyn had taken your offers of marriage when they were made. Even if the crone had slain me, and she had the right to do so, Morwyn would have had a full life."

Morgan's voice was intense, "It was not to be, Belwyn, I see that now. I ask the Powers, no I *beseech* the Powers, that They find some mercy in Their hearts and heal both of you, if not for your sakes, then for your children." Belwyn inclined his head at the supplication.

"At least for the children," he stated and then they turned and walked back to the house in heavy silence.

Belwyn rose before the sun, preparing for the journey that lay ahead. He spent some time near Morwyn's bed, holding her hand as she lay muttering to herself in a language he could not comprehend. Iola was dozing in a chair near the fire, weary from her care of her fellow healer.

"We go for the children, Morwyn," Belwyn said quietly near her ear. He was not sure she could understand him, but it was important that he said it. He gently kissed her sweaty cheek and left the room.

Their faces were grim and the men were heavily armed as they rode out of Aderyn's front gate right after sunrise. In his saddlebag Belwyn carried a pouch of gold coins as specified in the ransom demand. Owain the Elder had added even more to the sum for he wanted nothing to stand in the way of the children's safe return. By unspoken agreement they rode steadily for the whole day making only brief halts along the way to allow the horses to rest. Conversation was minimal, there was not much to say. Riona knew that if they did find the children, the men who had taken them would no doubt be slaughtered without mercy. She steeled herself for that. Her best hope was that the woman who had accompanied the kidnappers was tending to Gwyn and Pyrs, keeping them healthy and safe from Braen.

It was near the end of the day when Belwyn finally spoke with Riona. They had drifted to the back of the group for a private conversation for he had a number of things he needed to resolve in his own mind. He had tried to conjure a picture of Gwyn and Pyrs, based on Riona and her son's descriptions. That had proved difficult.

"You say the children do not resemble each other, but more resemble Morwyn and I?" he asked, puzzled.

Riona nodded. "Morwyn told me that Gwyn was conceived during the act of loving that broke the enchantment. That is why magic is so much a part of her. Pyrs was conceived during your second joining, the one Morwyn said was borne of your passion for each other. So they are indeed twins, but not identical."

"I see. That makes sense and would explain why Pyrs is so fiery and passionate. What little I remember of that night bears that out."

"Gwyn looks almost exactly like her mother and Pyrs like you. There are some subtle differences and I suspect as they age they will change."

"I have missed so much of their lives. I would have loved to watch them as they learned to walk," he said in a melancholy tone.

"You wouldn't have wanted to be around Pyrs. He would stumble, fall, pick himself up and if you tried to comfort him he'd grow angry with you and throw a tantrum. We learned it was best to leave him be. He has a very strong personality. He refuses to allow anything to best him. He may be bruised and battered, but he will continue until he masters whatever skill he wants to learn."

"He will be formidable as he grows older," Belwyn observed with a proud smile.

Riona chuckled, "He is formidable now. Only the calming influence of his sister and his mother's strong hand have kept him in line."

"I hope to be able to help her with that." Riona felt the anguish behind the statement, the deep concern that Morwyn would not allow him to be part of the twins' future.

"Morwyn was the one who sent us to Aderyn to plead for your help. She knows the twins' lives will be different from on. I believe she always intended to tell you about them once they were older."

He nodded and fell silent, his mind continuing to work on the faces of children. For some reason that was very important to him at this moment.

Braen was drunk and in a vile mood. He had expected to spend the last two days with Morwyn, reveling in his mastery over her. He knew she would have had no choice but to submit to whatever he demanded, for he held her children in bondage. Somehow, she had escaped him again and if the poison acted as it should, she would be dying at this moment. He swore under his breath, irate that she might now have found a way to evade him forever. His eyes kept tracking over to the little girl as she sat quietly in Cara's lap, her irritable brother near her. Pyrs was not eating and refused to have anyone touch him but his sister. He was clearly traumatized by the kidnapping, though Gwyn appeared just the opposite. The little boy regularly glared at Braen, unaware of the volatile reaction that might ignite.

"Why do we not just go to Ilspath, Braen?" Malvern asked. He was drunk as well and sported a blood-soaked bandage on his arm where Riona had wounded him.

"Aderyn will arrive there soon enough and I do not wish to have them find us too soon. If we stay out of Ilspath until it is time to collect the ransom, we have a better chance of survival. I cannot doubt that Owain the Elder has sent most of his men to hunt me."

"If his son claims the bastards, you mean," Malvern shot back. He'd not enjoyed the past few days in the forest, preferring the taverns and the brothels of Ilspath.

"Even if the warrior denies they are his seed, his father will not. We will go to Ilspath tomorrow morning and no doubt they will be waiting for us." Malvern appeared mollified by the answer and turned his attention back to the dried beef in his hand.

Braen drank more wine and then turned his eyes to Cara. She was not his woman, but tonight it did not matter. He gestured to her to come to him. She set Gwyn down and rose warily.

"What do you want, Braen?" she asked.

"You. I have need of a woman and where you are not Morwyn, you will do."

"I am not yours, Braen," she answered instantly. She sensed her lover shift his weight behind her, on the alert.

"I don't care tonight who you belong to, I need a woman and you will do."

"No, that is not possible." She sat back down as Braen lurched unsteadily on his feet.

"You require payment? So be it," he growled and pulled a copper coin out of his pouch. It landed near her feet. "Now come here." She shook her head and her lover rose at this overt insult.

"Braen, leave her be, she is no camp follower. Cara is my woman. You can have a wench in Ilspath once you've collected the ransom."

Braen snorted and shook his head. His eyes fell on young Gwyn again and Cara drew her into his arms, fearing for the child.

"She so looks like her mother," he said as his bile rose. He could not harm Morwyn, but he could her daughter. He pulled his knife and gestured for Cara to let lose of the girl. "Send her over to me. I cannot carve her mother as I wish, but she is another matter."

"By the Powers, leave the child alone!" Cara retorted and hugged Gwyn tighter. She felt a slight tingle course through her, unaware that Gwyn had placed a tiny spell of protection upon her.

"Send her to me, Cara. I will leave the boy alive, for he is worth the ransom. They will not miss a girl child." Gwyn's face did not change, did not reflect any fear or anxiety, though it appeared she understood some of what he said. "She is not normal, look at her!"

"No, Braen, leave her be. Go away and sleep off the wine," Cara replied.

"Bring her to me!" Braen bellowed. Ifor put his hand on the hilt of his sword.

"Braen, you're drunk. Let the matter be. If you are so eager to revenge yourself, then go back to the hut and finish what you started."

Braen shook his head and snorted, "I cut her with my knife. It is poisoned, so she is worm's fodder."

"What?" Cara asked, stunned.

"You heard me." He strode toward where Cara sat with the little girl and found Ifor baring his way.

"Leave it be, Braen. The child is innocent."

"I will kill you and then I will have your woman and cut the girl as I wish." Ifor pulled his sword at this and then hefted Gwyn in his arms to protect her.

"You've made your choice, Ifor," Braen replied. He reached down and grabbed onto Cara, roughly pulling her up off the ground by her arm. He drew her close him, his knife at her throat. "A good trade. I'll have your woman back to you soon enough." He began to drag Cara away at knife point as Ifor swore loudly.

"You bastard! Let her go!" He felt the little girl's hand on his face but did not turn toward her.

"It is your choice," Braen retorted. "Your woman for the girl."

Ifor thought it through and then prayed. If Braen told the truth the knife was poisoned. He had few choices. He saw the fear in Cara's eyes and he cursed himself for putting her in such danger.

Braen shot a quick glance at Malvern who understood what his leader wanted. He rose silently behind Ifor, his knife drawn out of sight, waiting for the right moment to strike. Pyrs sat motionless on the ground, his face full of dread as if he understood what was playing out in front of him. Ifor kept his eyes on Cara and saw her shake her head very slightly. He looked over at Gwyn's innocent face and knew he could not allow Braen to harm the child no matter the cost.

"Powers, help us," he begged. He had made a decision that no man should be forced to make.

"They will," little Gwyn replied and smiled gently.

Behind them, Malvern made his move.

Screams of terror echoed in the clearing, then there was total silence. The children were gone, one of the three men lay dead and Cara was huddled up against a broad tree trunk, her eyes wide and her mind filled with dread. Left behind was a sputtering campfire and an arc of glimmering fog that dissipated as the sun slowly rose in the east.

FOUR

Ulwyn's *gift* had been troubling him since dawn. With each step his unease grew. He vividly remembered this sensation from years past and that made him all the more apprehensive. He finally glanced over at Belwyn, who rode next to him. He was not surprised to see that the warrior had a strange frown on his face.

"Belwyn, do you sense …?" the bard began.

"Yes, I do, Ulwyn." He did not have an opportunity to say anything further as a figure appeared on the road in front of them, staggering out of the forest in a flight of panic. The woman's dark hair was disheveled, her clothes askew and her eyes wild. She flagged them down as they rode toward her, oblivious as to whether they were friend or foe.

Riona recognized her immediately.

"This woman was with the kidnappers!" she exclaimed. Belwyn reined his horse and jumped off the mare, striding toward the terrified figure.

"You there!" he called. She ran toward him and fell into his arms, crying and shaking.

"Save us, Powers, please, save us!"

"Hold fast, woman, tell us what has happened!" he commanded, easing her to the ground for she could not stand without aid. Riona appeared with a wineskin and Cara eagerly took a long drink, gulping the liquid down. Some of the wine trickled out of the side of her mouth and she unconsciously wiped it away with the palm of her hand.

"Where are the children?" Belwyn demanded.

Cara looked up at him with sudden insight. "You are their father! You look like the little boy!"

"Where are they?" he asked again, fear rising with each passing moment.

"It took them! By the Powers, it took them! It killed Malvern and then it was gone!"

"*What* took them?" Belwyn demanded, shaking her.

"Please, help us. Ifor is wounded, he could not go any further and …" she struggled to get the words out.

"Tell us what happened!" Belwyn shot back.

"Easy, Belwyn, she is very frightened," Ulwyn said from over his shoulder and then stooped down to put his hand on the woman in a comforting gesture. "Tell us what happened." His soft voice seemed to reassure her. Cara's haunted eyes scanned the faces ringed around her and she began her tale after another long drink of the wine.

"Braen was going to kill the little girl. Ifor protected her and then Braen put a knife to my throat, demanding he give him the child. Ifor would not, so Malvern stabbed him. I thought all was lost and then … *it* came." Cara's shivering continued and a blanket appeared, courtesy of Morgan. Riona wrapped the woman inside it and made her drink more wine to steady her nerves. Once she had finished drinking Cara's words came out in a torrent, all the while shaking intensely.

"It was huge and dark grey in color. It billowed fire at us and then grabbed Malvern and tore him apart as you or I would a dry leaf." She stopped and shuddered at the memory and then continued, "It turned toward me and I saw its eyes. I thought it meant to burn me, but it went for Braen instead."

"Then he is dead as well?" Morgan asked, his hand on his sword hilt. He shot a quick look around to see if anyone else was near. He saw no sign of a beast, whatever it may be, nor anyone else but those of his party and the frightened woman.

"I don't know. He threw me towards the monster and I fell to the ground. I felt a blast of flame pass over me and I heard him scream. I never saw him after that."

"And the children?" Belwyn asked, his voice trembling in apprehension.

"She did not fear it! She walked right up to the beast. Her brother ran to be with her and then they were … gone."

"What sort of beast took them?" Owain the Younger pressed. He could not comprehend what the woman was describing.

Belwyn knew what had taken his children, knew it in his soul. Her description had conjured up lucid memories from years before. He remembered the strange sensation he'd felt when he stood in front of the Ancient One. It was one of their kind.

"It was a dragon," he said quietly and the woman bobbed her head in agreement.

"It was, just like they speak of in the legends. By the Powers, it was so frightening!"

"It killed one man, perhaps two and yet it did not harm the children?" Morgan asked, frowning.

"No," Cara replied, shaking her head.

The dragons wield the Old Magic, as does Gwyn, Ulwyn thought to himself with sudden insight. *It came to help them.*

"Please, Ifor is wounded! I told him I would find him help!" Cara's voice grew desperate as she pointed back into the forest.

Belwyn rose as one in a dream. He began to stride in the direction the woman had indicated though he didn't need her to show him the path, he could feel the residual power the beast had left behind. Ulwyn appeared at his side and they hiked into the forest together, no words passing between them. They found Ifor lying up against a broad oak tree. He had a knife wound to his side and it was bleeding steadily. The bard dropped to his knees and began to minister to the man. Ifor opened his eyes at the movement, his hand tightening on the sword next to him. When he realized it wasn't Braen he released the weapon and spoke in a rushed voice,

"The thing took them! Powers, I could not stop it!"

"We know, the woman told us," Belwyn said, his voice strangely cold and unfeeling.

"Cara? Is she safe?" the man asked instantly.

"She is safe." Belwyn watched for only a moment, sensing the wound was not mortal, and he set off into the forest alone, pulled forward by a force he could comprehend.

In time the others appeared, once Cara was capable of moving. Her face was less pale, but she had a haunted look in her eyes. Once she spied Ifor she hurried over to him, dropping into the deep grass on her knees by his side.

"You are still alive!" Her eyes filled with tears. She kissed him and he touched her face in a loving gesture, heedless of the dried blood on his hand.

"I am," he replied quietly. Ulwyn stood and let Riona take his place. He turned his eyes toward where Belwyn had vanished into the forest and set off after him.

Morgan's eyes searched the nearby woods and asked, "Did Braen survive?"

Ifor nodded. "Yes, he fled, though he was badly burnt. It killed Malvern, but then that is no loss."

"I understand you undertook to protect the children," Owain the Younger said evenly. He was kneeling next to Riona as she examined the wound.

Ifor gritted his teeth for a moment as her fingers probed the wound and then answered, "I tried, for Braen is a vile beast. I did not know he intended to steal them when we rode to the hut. I should have guessed that he and Malvern had their eyes on the women, for there is little else they thought of. Neither of those acts were something I wished to be part of."

"Riona told us of how you and Cara stood back from the fray, how you protected Pyrs from Braen's anger," Owain said, judging the man's words.

"I did not do enough, for I should have stopped them from harming the women. That was wrong on my part," Ifor replied grimly. "I expect Aderyn will wish us tried and hung. We are as guilty as Braen in this." His voice was full of resignation.

Owain the Younger shook his head. He had no notion what his father or his brother might think, but these people had sheltered and kept the children from harm.

"No, I think not, sir. You and your lady's honor stood fast in the midst of evil. That is not something to be punished for." He rose and set off in search of his brother, Morgan at his side.

"Who is he?" Cara asked, puzzled.

"Owain the Younger, youngest of the House of Aderyn, uncle to the children," Riona replied.

"And the other man?"

"Lord Morgan, Lord Bardyn's heir."

Ifor shot Cara a look. "By the Powers."

"How does that feel?" Riona asked as she finished tying the bandage.

"Much better, thank you," he said, shifting his attention back to the healer.

"The blade skidded along the ribs and only penetrated a short distance. Though it bled a fair amount, you are very fortunate."

"I may not be, for Malvern's blade may have been poisoned," Ifor replied calmly.

"No, it was not. I now know how a poisoned wound behaves. This one was not, for it bled."

"Then I owe the Powers much this day," the wounded man replied. With Cara's help he slowly rose, the effort taking its toll.

"Once we camp I'll give you something for the pain so you can rest."

"Bless you," Cara replied and kept tight hold of her lover.

The devastation was telling. One man's body lay in two torn sections on the ground near the campfire, his dark blood staining the earth. His mouth was open in a final death scream, unreasoned fear imprinted on his face. Nearby, trees displayed scorch marks some twenty feet in the air and there was a heavy sulfur scent that clung to the morning mist. Belwyn walked past the body and stopped in the middle of the clearing, bending down to touch the earth. The power of the dragon was still in the soil. His strength fled and he fell to his knees, weeping openly.

"Why do they not just slay me or take me to their accursed land and torture me for eternity? Why must everyone that I love suffer? Why?" the man's anguished voice demanded in a heart crushing tone. Ulwyn knelt at the side of the grieving man, desperate to offer comfort to his dear friend.

"The dragon saved them, Belwyn. It will not harm them, for that is not their nature. They only kill mortals that threaten them. Your children are safe."

"But I have lost them! How do I tell Morwyn that her children are gone?" the man's voice came back, raw with pain.

"You tell her they are safe, Belwyn. They would not have been if the dragon had not come." Ulwyn put every bit of his bard gift into these words. He prayed it would be enough for his devastated friend.

As Belwyn continued to kneel with Ulwyn at his side, deep within his personal agony, Owain and Morgan collected Malvern's remains. It was a grim task. They mounded a small cairn of stones over his shredded body, but did nothing more.

"May the Powers judge his soul and find him wanting," Morgan intoned and Owain nodded his agreement.

"May They make it so."

Braen ran half-crazed through the forest, flailing his way through the thick underbrush. He fell numerous times, but rose and fled as if the beast was still behind him. His entire left side was burnt, scorched deep and he could only see out of his right eye. His right hand was whole, his left twisted into a claw. He finally ceased his headlong flight and fell into a small stream. The water stung his burns and made him scream in agony. The pain proved too much for him to bear and he swooned where he lie.

They bedded down a good distance away from the original camp where the death had occurred. Ifor went to sleep after Riona administered a draught to cut the pain in his side. Cara stayed near him and Morgan spoke quietly with her, comforting her as best he could. She told him more of her life and he came to learn she had family in Ilspath.

"We can arrange to have you return to them, Cara," he offered. She shuddered immediately and shook her head.

"No, I cannot go back there."

Morgan frowned at that." Surely your mother and father would want to know you are safe."

"My mother would. My stepfather … he would want me home for his own reasons." The woman's eyes were not meeting Morgan's at this point.

"I see, you do not trust him," Morgan replied carefully, sensing her unease.

"No, I am too much to his liking. When I refused his attentions, he became abusive. I left my home because of that and have made my own way."

"I have heard such stories from some of the sporting wenches. It is a sad thing when one is not safe within one's own home."

"My mother does not know. I could not tell her. I lived in Ilspath for a time and then I met Ifor a few months back." Her eyes dropped down to the sleeping form near her and she gently touched his hair.

"He appears to be an honorable man, Cara."

"He is. We just needed money to begin a new life."

"Perhaps the Powers will find another way for that to happen," Morgan replied in a consoling voice.

Riona offered a sleeping draught to Belwyn, knowing the man was in shock and needed rest.

"No." His voice was firm, though his face was grey and his eyes unseeing. He sat all night without moving. His companions rested, though by unspoken agreement each of the men took turns standing guard throughout the evening. Braen was still in the woods and every time the guard rotated they voiced a personal prayer that he would return so they would be the one to plunge their sword into his heart.

The dawn was dark and cloudy; there was no light in the sky just as there was no hope in Belwyn's heart. He refused to eat, staring out into nothingness as his companions consumed their bread and dried beef in silence. Riona knew she needed to pull the distraught father back from the darkness that beckoned him. She hunted through her belongings and found Pyrs' collection of small stones.

"Belwyn?" she asked as she sat down near him. His eyes moved slowly up to hers, eyes that made her wince. "These are Pyrs' stones. He plays with them all the time, as if they are little armies. It is right that you should have them."

She held them for a moment, almost reverently, and then handed the small parcel to the children's sire. Belwyn untied the rawhide cord and opened the rough cloth. A considerable number of small flat stones resided within. They were almost too big to fit in a small child's hand. He could almost imagine a little boy laying these stones out on the ground, playing with them just as if they were armies. In time he closed the cloth, tied the cord and tucked the sack full of stones into the saddlebag at his side. The stones did what Riona had prayed they would – they tugged the bereft man out of his gloom and gave him a moment of hope. Perhaps if the Powers were merciful Belwyn would have the opportunity to hand them back to his only son.

"We will find them, Belwyn. We will go to the Ancient One and demand he return them," Morgan said defiantly. Belwyn looked up at his friend, the man who loved Morwyn as much as he did. The man, who but for fate, could have well been Gwyn and Pyrs's father.

"You have no idea of what you suggest, Morgan, though I sincerely appreciate your offer." His eyes radiated gratitude.

"I will go." The young lord's voice was resolute and the expression on his face matched it.

"It may cost you your life, the dragon is very unforgiving when it comes to mortals."

"Then it costs me my life, for I do not fear death," Morgan replied honestly. His face was set and Belwyn knew he would not be dissuaded.

"I do not fear death either, my friend. What I fear is telling Morwyn I failed to protect her children from the dragon."

"There was no way for you to protect them, Belwyn," Morgan replied in all honesty. Belwyn only shook his head, he would not allow reality to intrude upon his grief.

Owain the Younger offered, "We will return to Aderyn and let father know what has happened here."

Belwyn nodded. His eyes moved to Cara, who sat quietly next to Ifor, her hand in his. They saw no anger on his face, only sadness and loss.

Morgan saw the look and suggested, "Owain, if you would, take Cara and Ifor with you so that his treatment may continue."

"Yes, take them to father, he will see they are kept safe," Belwyn agreed.

Cara bowed her head, never expecting such decency from the father of the children.

"We do not deserve …" she began but Belwyn cut her off.

"You kept my children well and unharmed as long as you could. We will help you because of that."

"We did not expect such forgiveness," Ifor said solemnly. Belwyn only nodded woodenly. His heart was not here, but wherever the twins were.

Morgan rose from his bedding and asked, "Where to, my friend?" Belwyn rose as well, methodically shaking his blanket and folding it before he replied.

"North, I think." He slung his pack on the back of Ceffyl, secured it, and then pulled himself up in the saddle. He did everything by rote, the need to find his children overriding every other thought. With Bardyn's son at his side, he turned his horse north. For the second time in his life, the Eldest of the House of Aderyn went to seek the ddraig.

As the two men rode back toward the main road the others broke camp rather quickly, eager to report the news of the children to their grandsire, though it was not exactly what they'd hoped for. Cara rode with Ulwyn and remained silent most of the journey, her eyes constantly on her lover, Ifor, as he rode with Riona. Ulwyn finally persuaded her to talk and learned she was a seamstress by trade.

"Can you sew fine gowns, Cara?" Owain the Younger asked, intrigued.

"Yes, I have sewn for the merchant's wives in Ilspath." Owain thought for a moment and smile appeared on his face.

"I have someone in search of a good seamstress, Cara. She needs someone near her she can trust," he replied. In his mind, both Cara and Ifor had proven themselves.

Ulwyn gave him a strange look and asked, "Are things that unsure at Aldyn's holdings?"

"Yes, they are. Lord Corryn and his ilk continue to plague the woman. He has carefully placed spies that report to him. We've rooted out a couple, but I know there are more."

"They still press her to remarry?"

"Yes, they do."

"They are vultures, every one," Ulwyn came back in disdain.

"Sir, are you suggesting I would sew for a noblewoman?" Cara asked in surprise, finally getting the drift of the conversation.

"Yes, I am. You will be out of Braen's sight and safe within Lady Aldyn's holdings. I have no doubt I can find a worthy task to set your hands to as well, Ifor." The wounded man's eyes expressed his gratitude at this offer.

"I … I …" Cara began.

"It will be for the best," Owain replied. "Aldyn needs a seamstress, all she wears is black and it is not her best color."

"Sir?"

"She has worn black since her husband died over three years ago."

"She mourns him that long?" Cara asked, astounded.

"On the contrary, the man wasn't worth one day's mourning. He was a cruel brute and beat her unmercifully," Owain's voice came back with a tinge of frost to it. "No, she wears black for a number of reasons, but not for her dead husband."

"What color is her hair, sir?" Cara asked, captivated by this most unusual woman.

"Auburn, the most lovely shade of auburn you'll ever see," Owain replied, his voice shifting tone. Ulwyn sensed the shift and smiled to himself. It was clear the man was smitten with his mistress.

"She would look very fair in light green, sir, or a rust brown if she must wear darker colors."

Owain beamed. "See, that is what she should hear! She is far too beautiful to remain in black the rest of her years."

Cara smiled and turned her eyes toward her lover. He returned a warm smile, astonished at the turn of events.

The journey back to Owain the Elder's was uneventful. They elected to continue through the night rather than stop for rest. A league out from the holdings, they were met by two of Aderyn's men. The man bowed to Owain as his companion rode up next to him in the moonlight.

"Sir, Dillan sent us to watch for you."

"Send word to my father that we return unharmed and that Lord Morgan and Belwyn have ridden north to claim the children. The last we knew, my niece and nephew were well."

"Yes, sir."

"We will arrive soon, for we will not stop this night. We all are in need of hot food and a soft bed."

"I will relay that, sir. Do you wish one of us to remain as escort?" the man asked. Owain smiled to himself. Dillan's men were diligent in their service to the House of Aderyn.

"No, thank you. No threat presses us at present, only weariness."

"As you wish, sir." The two men turned their horses and galloped back down the road out of sight.

"Good, that means there will be ample food and wine when we reach your holdings, Owain," Ulwyn remarked. His friend chuckled, knowing Ulwyn's love of both.

"Something that a bard always delights in," he jested back.

"This bard, at least."

As soon as the riders entered the courtyard late that night, the drowsy stableboy ran to help them. Dillan appeared in their midst as they pulled their packs off the weary horses.

"A repast awaits you and your father is awake to hear your news."

Owain the Younger nodded and headed for the hall without delay. As Ifor and Cara dismounted, Dillan studied the strangers.

"Are you the pair that were with Braen when he took the children?" Dillan asked solemnly, his hands on his hips.

"Yes, sir," Ifor replied honestly.

"Bard?" Dillan asked, switching his eyes over to Ulwyn.

"They are here at Belwyn's request," Ulwyn explained. Dillan arched an eyebrow at this.

"Sir, if you are more comfortable, I will readily offer up my weapons before entering your lord's house," Ifor said. Dillan gave the man a measured look.

"I will accept that offer." Ifor removed his knife and sword as Dillan gestured for a nearby guard to take possession of them.

"We stand ready to accept the judgment of the House of Aderyn, sir. We did not know what evil Braen had planned, but we were part of it, nonetheless," Ifor said in a solemn voice.

"Your fate will be determined by the master of the house," Dillan replied in a noncommittal tone and gestured for the couple to follow him. Ulwyn trailed behind them, his face set. He knew Owain the Elder to be a just man, but this matter was closer to his heart than most. He prayed good sense would prevail when it came to the matter of Ifor and Cara.

Owain the Elder was waiting for them in the dining hall, seated at the long oak table. There was no plate in front of him, for he had no appetite. Places had been set for all the rest of them, with amply chilled wine and mead, roasted lamb, vegetables and fresh bread scattered down the table. Tantalizing smells enveloped them the moment they entered the room. The master of the house rose and embraced his youngest son.

"What has befallen the children?" he asked. Owain the Younger looked downward at this but did not answer immediately. "I see, it is something grave."

"I can say that they were alive, father, when we last knew of them. But it becomes more difficult after that."

"Then that is at least some good news." He did not press his son at this point, sensing the weariness that weighed upon the party. He gestured for the travelers to avail themselves of fresh water and clean towels set nearby so that they might wash before they ate. Dillan hovered, his eyes on the newcomers. Once he had cleansed his face and hands, Owain the Younger took his place at the table across from his father. He savored a long drink of cool mead, letting it settle into him and refresh him from within. He put the cup down and then addressed his sire as he gestured down the table.

"Father, this is Cara and Ifor. They were with Braen and the other man when the children were kidnapped. We found Cara on the road yesterday morning in obvious distress and Ifor wounded nearby. Cara told of us of what had happened to Gwyn and Pyrs and it is a tale unlike any other." Owain the Elder gazed down the table at the woman and she dropped her eyes immediately. No matter how hard she tried, she could not keep her composure and began to cry. Ifor's comforting hand went to her shoulder.

"Go ahead, son, for she is in no shape to tell the tale." Owain the Elder's voice was noticeably cooler now.

"Braen intended to kill Gwyn, no doubt in retribution against her mother. Cara and Ifor stopped him, at risk to their own lives."

"I see." His father's tone softened somewhat.

"I have no better way to say this, father, but it appears a dragon came for the children. It killed one of the kidnappers and would have killed Braen if the coward had not taken to his heels. It took Gwyn and Pyrs with it, father, and disappeared."

"By the Powers!" The older man's voice was heavy with shock. He caught Dillan's eyes where he stood nearby and the man's expression mirrored his.

"Belwyn goes to ask the dragon to return his children. Morgan offered to go with him and could not be dissuaded."

"He does not understand the danger in that," Ulwyn replied honestly as he slathered honey on a thick slice of bread. He had spoken at length with

Belwyn about his time before the Ancient One and knew that any contact with a ddraig was fraught with danger.

"How long does it take to make this journey?" Dillan asked.

"Belwyn said it took at least three days, as best he can remember, depending on whether the beast wishes to be found or not," Ulwyn replied.

"You mean it may hide itself?" Owain the Younger asked in obvious consternation.

"Yes, though I suspect the Old One has a reason for all this. He seems to have a reason for everything," Ulwyn replied. *What value do they have to a ddraig?* That was the puzzle he'd turned over in his mind since the moment he'd learned the children had been spirited away. His thoughts drifted to his own children. Little Hugh was the same age as Belwyn's twins, his new daughter was only six months old. Ulwyn shivered slightly, sensing what torment must be in Belwyn's heart at this moment. *Powers, guide them.* He was pulled back to the present discussion by Owain the Elder's voice.

"So it will be at least a week or more before we hear anything about their fate," Gloom settled on the older man like a thick coat of snow.

"Yes, father."

"This will harder on Morwyn than any of us."

Cara blurted out, "She lives? Braen said his knife was poisoned. We thought the woman dead!"

"She is alive and the wounds are mending, according to our healer. However, we are not sure what damage the poison or the fever may have done to her mind."

"No!" Riona said. "That would be cruel if Belwyn and Morgan find the children and return them unharmed, only to learn that their mother is ..."

"Yes, that would be cruel and I do not think the Powers are that heartless," Owain the Elder replied and then sank into silence. He rose from his chair and left the room, numb. His grandchildren, his eldest son and his best friend's heir were in the grip of a power he could not comprehend. His son's lover, the mother of his grandchildren, was still desperately ill. He was a man of action and this situation made him feel utterly helpless. He went to his bed, but sleep would not come.

Dillan arranged for a room for Cara and Ifor, one not close to his master's chambers. He'd watched the two the entire evening and found nothing in their manner that warranted worry. Still, he was a cautious man and until Owain the Elder indicated they were free to wander at will, they would remain under scrutiny.

"My master will speak with you in the morning about your part in all this. By necessity, I will be posting a guard at your door, " Dillan replied.

"I would expect no less, sir," Ifor replied and then entered the designated chamber with Cara, closing the door behind them. They were surprised to find a fire in the hearth and hot water for bathing. A change of clothes for each of them lay on the end of the large bed.

Cara gave a gasp of surprise. "Look at this! We are being treated like guests, Ifor, not villains!"

"It is very strange. I expected to be put to the sword immediately or at least clapped in chains in some dismal cell until a trial was convened. Yet, here we have a cozy fire, mead at our elbow, fresh clothes and a soft bed. It makes no sense!" His strong face sported a frown for he was thoroughly perplexed.

Cara picked up the dress that lay on the end of the bed. It was plain, but well made and of good quality. It looked to be very close to her size. A chemise lay next to it along with a pair of breeches, a shirt and a jerkin for her lover. "These clothes are not castoffs, Ifor, they are of good quality. This is all so strange, I can hardly fathom it."

He sighed and sank into a chair near the fire, his side aching.

"The Hands of the Powers are at work in a way I've never seen before. That little girl touched me right before the dragon came, I swear that is why I was not slain."

Cara's eyes widened. "She touched me as well!"

"Do you remember how Braen and Malvern could not come near to the women after the little girl appeared in their midst?"

"I did not think of that! She must wield magic in some way. I knew she was different, she was so calm and unaffected, as if she was not afraid that she or her brother would be harmed."

"We are amongst those of legend, my love."

She knelt by his side and lay her head on his knee. He gently placed his hand on her head, caressing her hair, his face pensive.

"I pray you are right, my love," she said.

The next morning the bard and Owain the Younger purposely made the effort to talk to the master of the house regarding the couple. Dillan was present by his master's side, listening intently, for the matter was his concern as well.

"You feel I should forgive them for being part of this travesty?" Owain the Elder's voice sounded more unfeeling then he wished. He'd not slept well for days and the lack of rest was taking its toll upon him.

"I do," Ulwyn replied in a strong voice. He was near the fire, sitting in a chair next to Owain the Younger. Dillan and his master were seated nearby.

"We have only the woman's word that things fell out as they did," Dillan observed.

"Yes, that is true. Nevertheless, my gift did not sense falsehood as she told the tale. It appears they found themselves in the middle of something unholy and acted as decently as they could, given the circumstances."

The master of the house sighed heavily. "And you, my son, do you agree with Ulwyn on this?"

The young man nodded. "I do, father. There is no evil in them. Ifor protected Gwyn from the brute. He faced the choice to hand over Gwyn to be slaughtered like a spring lamb or watch his lover be violated by Braen, perhaps die at the brute's hand. It is not a decision I would want to make."

The older man's dark eyes studied his master of the guard.

"Dillan?"

"I have to agree, sir. I see no evil in them. I sense that life has not been easy for either of them and they made a poor choice in joining with Braen."

"Have they been with that fiend for very long?" Owain the Elder pressed.

His son answered his question, "No, father. They met Braen on the road and joined with him. They were out of money and he never told them the whole plan, only that there was gold to be had for little work."

"What of her family?"

"She cannot return home for her step-father has attempted to take liberties with her." He had overheard Cara's conversation with Morgan and found it disquieting.

"I see," the older man replied. He sat quiet for a time and then queried, "Who am I to seek vengeance against them if the Powers acted to spare them from the beast?"

Owain the Younger's face broke out into a smile.

"Good, then Aldyn will have her seamstress." The confused look on his father's face made him explain the comment and the conversation changed direction. While they talked, Dillan set off to escort the couple to his master.

The journey to stand before the master of the House of Aderyn proved difficult, for Dillan gave no indication of his master's decision. Ifor had his arm around Cara and his face was set. He was resolved to meet his fate without fear or complaint. Cara's face was pale, for though they were treated well since they arrived, that could easily change.

"Come, sit," Owain the Elder's voice commanded and he beckoned them into the room. The pair settled into chairs near him and he observed them for a moment. "I have taken evidence from Riona and Peter and heard the sage advice of the bard, my youngest son and my Master of the Guard. They all feel you are not to blame in this matter."

Ifor blinked, caught off guard. "Sir, I ..." Owain waved his hand to cut him off.

"We all find ourselves in situations that are not of our liking. It is the test of a man, or for that matter, of a woman, in how they handle themselves. You both proved to be worthy of my regard for you protected my grandchildren from harm."

"It is us that owe you, sir, for your granddaughter saved us from the beast. In some way she spun magic that kept it from killing us, for she touched both of us before the thing came. She did not touch Malvern or Braen and they were harmed."

Owain Elder frowned and shot a quizzical look at Ulwyn.

"It is possible, Owain. Gwyn may have put a spell of protection on them or in some fashion marked them so that the dragon would not harm them."

"Powers," the older man murmured.

"We will do whatever you ask, sir, for you have been more than fair with us," Ifor replied.

"I will send you with my son to Lady Aldyn's holdings. She appears to have need of a seamstress and you have the look of a warrior, Ifor."

"I am, sir. I am an archer by training, though I do not carry a bow at present." He had sold it to buy food some weeks previous.

"Excellent," the youngest of Aderyn exclaimed, "we need archers as well."

"Then that is settled. Now if we can have my grandchildren back, all will be well."

"May the Powers make it so," Ifor replied, sealing the supplication.

FIVE

t was a slow and anxious journey into the North hills. They did not talk much the first day, but on the second Belwyn related in depth how he and Morwyn had been interrogated the last time he stood before a ddraig.

"It was made clear that if I did not answer its questions honestly, I would die."

"I see," was all Morgan responded.

"Take care, Morgan, tell the truth no matter how hard it is to say. The beast is unforgiving," Belwyn cautioned.

"I see," Morgan repeated and said no more.

It was on the fourth day that the path finally disappeared and Belwyn began moving forward solely on instinct. He was keenly aware they could wander for eternity if the dragon did not want to be found. When he voiced this concern to Morgan his friend did not completely understand.

"The last time Morwyn found our way long after the path disappeared," Belwyn explained, worry endemic in his voice. "At present I am guessing the direction by what I feel, Morgan."

"And if the dragon does not wish us to find it?" Morgan asked.

"Then I will have lost my children forever."

"I pray to the Powers that They are merciful and help us in this quest.

"As do I."

They rode on for another three hours or so, oblivious to the slow change in scenery around them. Where there was once green and lush grass, blooming meadows laced with bright flowers and the lyrical songs of birds perched in the trees around them, now there was nearly barren ground and eerie silence. The birds seemed to have lost their will to sing. The delicate scent of blooming flowers that once floated through the air had vanished, replaced by the choking smell of dust kicked up by their horses' hooves.

When Belwyn's mind began to chastise him, hound him with negative thoughts, he knew they were nearing the end of their journey. This had happened the last time that he came near the beast.

"Morgan, is your mind playing games with you?"

His fellow warrior gave him a startled look and then nodded grimly.

"Yes, it is."

"Then we are close, that is why your mind is plaguing you."

"I do not like it."

"No, it is not pleasant," was the reply, "but it will end soon."

As if in answer to Belwyn's remark Ceffyl reared suddenly, as did Morgan's mount. It took considerable skill to remain in their saddles.

"What in the name of the Powers?" Morgan shouted as his horse wheeled around and began to skitter sideways, snorting wildly.

"Get off your horse!" Belwyn commanded. Morgan jumped down from his steed just as the beast shied again, twisting his ankle as he landed. His companion leapt off Ceffyl, keeping tight hold of the reins and then began to pull the mare back the way they had just came. When she became less skittish, he secured her to a tree. Morgan joined him shortly, limping on the injured foot. Belwyn took the reins from him and tied the horse near Ceffyl. Both of the beasts remained nervous, snorting and pawing the ground. Morgan settled down on a nearby rock and began to tug off his boot to examine the foot, all the while glancing around nervously.

"What caused that?" he asked. A wince of pain tracked across his face when the boot finally slid off.

"We are near the dragon, the horses cannot stand to be so close." Belwyn paused and watched the man examine his ankle. "Is it broken?" he asked, in deep concern.

"No, I twisted it, nothing more. It will slow us down, I fear."

"Then you must stay here, walking on such an injury may do it further harm. " Morgan shook his head immediately and carefully pulled back on his boot. He tried to stand and despite his attempts to mask it, a slight groan of pain came out of his mouth.

"No, I go with you." He gritted his teeth to further conceal his discomfort, sinking back down on the rock. His brave words were at odds with his behavior.

"Morgan, you cannot. The way to the ddraig is uphill, you'll not stand this," his friend explained.

"I go, Belwyn. Believe me, you're not the only stubborn one in this, my friend." Belwyn frowned and sighed. He pulled his sword and strode back toward where the horses were tethered. After a few moments he returned with a stout branch.

"Well, then, my stubborn friend, here is a staff to aid you."

Morgan nodded, took the oak branch out of Belwyn's hand and rose slowly to standing position. His friend could see the effort was excruciating by the sweat beading on the man's forehead, but Morgan made no further comment and begin to hobble deliberately up the hill with Belwyn at his side.

It was slow going, what with the crippled man, but they made steady progress. Belwyn's worry for Morgan grew, it was evident he was in a great deal of pain though he did not voice it. He finally sank on a nearby stone in exhaustion, his face sweaty and pale. With some dark amusement he noted that the stone was graced with scorch marks. As waves of discomfort radiated upward through his leg he studied the bleached bones of the travelers who had made this journey before him.

Well, if I am to die here at least my ankle will stop hurting, he thought ruefully.

Belwyn stood stock-still, staring at the terrain he had once covered with the adept. There were fresh bone piles now, evidence of those who had displeased the Ancient One. He felt fear rising in him and he knew no way to dampen it down.

The voice caught them unaware, booming in their minds.

Spawn of Anarawd, you return. Did you not learn to fear me the last time? The beast materialized in front of them in a swirl of smoke. Although Belwyn had witnessed the dragon's grandeur before, its size still stunned him. He knew Morgan had to be dumfounded. He glanced toward him and saw his face was pure white in terror. He suspected it mirrored his own.

Morgan's eyes tracked up the entire length of the beast. It stood almost twenty-five feet in the air and seemed to fill the space in front of them. He saw one of its claws, huge and sharp-edged and he remembered the dismembered body of one of Braen's companions. The beast's massive tail twitched at the very end, apparent evidence of its displeasure at being disturbed. Its multi-hued wings were close to its body, but not completely tucked down. It made the dragon appear almost like a massive bird, ready to spring on some unwary prey.

Belwyn bowed low. "I have come to claim my children, Ancient One."

The beast ignored Belwyn and turned its sights on Morgan, who had risen and now clung to the makeshift staff like a small bird in a gale.

Morgan's heart thudded in his chest and he shook. He bowed, instinctively, and began to introduce himself, "Ancient One, I am …"

You are Morgan, newly minted heir and bastard son of Bardyn. We know your tale. The voice was sarcastic and unimpressed.

Morgan did not know what to say so he held his silence. The ddraig changed tactics and its voice changed tone as well.

Tell me, Morgan the Bastard, tell me what you wish for most in life.

Belwyn shot a nervous glance at his friend, knowing the dragon's cunning. He prayed the warrior understood that his life hung in the balance.

Morgan's eyes narrowed and he replied firmly, "I wish that Belwyn be reunited with his children." The smoke swirled again and the dragon casually shifted a claw to remind the mortals of its size.

No, you do not answer honestly. The dragon gestured toward Belwyn with the sharpened claw, **As this insignificant mortal can tell you, the lack of honestly will cost you your life.** It paused and retracted the claw. **Tell me**

what you wish for *most* in life.

Morgan paused and then said it loud and clear, "To be accepted as Bardyn's son and heir."

The ground rumbled. **You still do not tell the truth! You have one more chance, warrior.** Sweat ran down Morgan's back and he felt death regarding him. He gave Belwyn a quick glance and saw dread on the man's face.

Morgan swallowed and replied, "To accept *myself* as Lord Bardyn's son and heir."

He heard the dragon hiss in agreement, **Ah, that would be it, wouldn't it? Years of living without a father, knowing you are a man's moment of idle pleasure, one of countless seeds thrown to the wind. Then fate decrees that you learn that your father is a mighty lord, one who did not know you existed, but loves you nonetheless. While others accept you, you do not accept yourself.**

The dragon had cut to the heart of the matter – while others considered him Bardyn's only heir, he felt unworthy.

"That is it, ddraig. I fear letting the man down."

Hummpppfff. Well, you've already done more than you were supposed to, Morgan the Bastard, for you are alive.

"I … do not understand," Morgan stammered.

No, you would not. You were to die at the hands of Merioneth that day on the battlefield.

Morgan was totally confused. "But … I … how?"

Morwyn the Adept stayed the hand of the rogue lord long enough for his bride to kill him. Your death was foretold to her, but she altered your future against the wishes of the Powers. She paid for that act of defiance, for the Powers do not allow one to circumvent Their will without penalty. *Even I do not enjoy that freedom.*

Morgan was overwhelmed. "I was to die that day?"

Yes, isn't that ironic? Now you must prove your worth to yourself and to your father for the remainder of your days, where before all you had to do to become legend … was to die.

"By the Powers," Morgan muttered as his eyes fell from the beast in front him He stared into nothingness as the truth to changed him.

Inwardly pleased at the life-changing revelation he'd just delivered, the dragon turned its deep emerald eyes toward the other warrior.

You come for your children, do you?

"Yes, I do."

Why?

"They are my children!" Belwyn retorted, frowning.

I had to send a fledgling to protect *your* children. Where were you?

"Hunting them, dragon." Belwyn's voice held no deference, only steel.

Really? Such fatherly concern for two baseborn children you did not even know you had sired. Did it not occur to you that to break your enchantment in that way might cause a life to be created, that your seed might take root?

Belwyn nodded in agreement. "I feared such a thing, dragon."

And yet you lie with her anyway. Like most mortals you appear incapable of controlling your lust, even if it harms another.

"I have control, dragon. You were the one who told Morwyn she had to lie with me to break my enchantment."

I did and the enchantment is broken. Is that not enough for you? the beast chuffed back, probing.

"No, it is not. I want my children."

Why do you want these children so badly, Eldest of Aderyn? Only a few days previous you did not even know they existed.

"I wish some good to come of this."

You have your life back, mortal, the spell is gone, the beast observed, keeping the warrior under its intense scrutiny.

"It is, but what life is it that I have, dragon? I cannot be with the woman I love."

That was *your* price, warrior. We spoke of that the last time you stood before me.

"Yes, and I have paid it for over three years. I want my children."

And if I will not return them? the dragon pushed.

"Then I will meet my death at your claws with defiance on my face and my curse against all dragons on my breath!" the father stormed back, his hand on the hilt of his sword. Morgan's eyes widened and he swallowed hard.

An unholy laugh bellowed out of the beast's mouth. Belwyn steeled himself for the killing blow, hoping at least to be able to draw his sword before he met his end. The dragon's claws did not move.

You are willing to die for them, then?

"Yes."

Even if their mother does not survive to chastise you for not saving them?

"Morwyn is …" Belwyn asked, not realizing the beast was baiting him. He paused, closed his eyes and intoned a prayer for her departed soul. He knew Morgan was doing the same. He opened his eyes again and looked solemnly at the monstrosity in front of him. "Even if she is dead, dragon. They are my children, the seed of Aderyn. We protect our own."

Inwardly the dragon was satisfied but allowed nothing to show on its inscrutable face.

What *price* will you play to have your two fledglings returned?

Belwyn glared and immediately shot back, "What price do you demand?

But I must know, do you dragons pay a fee for your infinite arrogance as well?" The beast reacted immediately as the ground shook, sweeping both of the men off their feet. A blast of red-hot flame shot over the top of them, missing them by mere inches.

"Powers!" Morgan exclaimed.

A ddraig pays a price beyond your ken, mortal! the voice thundered around them. **We are *all* bound by the Laws, though some more than others.**

Belwyn rose to his feet and then helped Morgan up. As they dusted themselves off Belwyn demanded again, "What price do you ask?"

The beast glared at him for a moment and then settled down, though its voice was irate and its tail flicking with extreme irritation.

Their youth. It made no sense to either man.

"I do not understand," Belwyn replied.

The ddraig remarked mockingly, **That seems to be a common statement amongst you mortals.**

"Why would you want their youth?"

Do you agree? the dragon prodded.

"I cannot agree to something I do not understand!" Belwyn shouted back, angry at this entire confrontation. The beast studied him as if he was a small tasty insect on a branch.

Their youth is the price. It is your choice, mortal.

"I want my children, but I will not allow them to pay for their return," he stated, his voice quavering.

The dragon gave him one long penetrating gaze and a half nod.

Then you accept some of the price yourself?

"Yes, just give me my children!" Belwyn shouted back, incapable of keeping his emotions in check any longer. Though the warrior did not know it, he had passed yet another of the Ancient One's cunning tests.

It will cost you much, warrior, more than just their childhood.

"I just want them alive and well." Belwyn's anger overflowed and his desperation rose. *I owe Morwyn that.*

Then take them, Eldest of Aderyn, and depart, for I am finished with them at the moment. The smoke increased, as did the smell of raw sulfur. Both men's eyes began to water and Morgan wiped his face with his sleeve as tears rained down. Through the thick mist the warriors could see the dragon gently raise both its wings and standing under each immense iridescent canopy was a child. It was Gwyn and her brother. They appeared to be almost eight years now, covered only in cloaks cast off from those unfortunates that had not survived the dragon's fiery inquisition.

"By the Powers! They are …" Morgan murmured.

"My children," Belwyn said and extended his arms to them. His hands were shaking and tears were in his eyes. Gwyn and Pyrs walked out from under the wings and then stopped and turned to face the massive beast. They both bowed and the warriors heard Gwyn say,

"Farewell, Dragon Father."

Farewell, my kin. Your mother awaits your return. Morgan shot a stunned look at Belwyn and the Eldest of Aderyn only sighed. *She is alive.* The dragon had sparred with him and won yet another round.

The two children solemnly walked to where Morgan and Belwyn waited. There was no doubt whose children they were. Gwyn stood tall and thin, her coal black hair and eyes identical to her mother's. Pyrs was Belwyn even to his stature and the way his hair lie. Gwyn readily entered her father's embrace. Pyrs did not, but stood aloof. Morgan gave him a warm smile and the young lad moved to him and accepted an embrace, clearly avoiding his father. Belwyn saw the gesture and it hurt his heart.

That is part of the price you will be forced to pay, mortal, the dragon's voice explained.

"As long as they are safe, I will accept it."

A low chuckle erupted from the beast. **Perhaps.**

The two children extricated themselves from the warriors and continued down the hill towards where the horses were tethered, clutching the long cloaks around them. The two men, after one last look at the Ancient One, followed the twins in silence.

The dragon watched them depart, a slight frown on his furrowed brow and murmured to itself, **Though you do not know it, mortal, we will pay a debt as heavy as you.**

He paused for a moment, his eagle-sharp eyes watching the two children retreat down the hill. **Perhaps they will prove to be strong enough. If not then ...** The ddraig let the thought pass as he vanished in a cloud of sulfur-tinged smoke.

They found the two children standing by the horses, still clutching the ragged cloaks around them. Belwyn could not restrain himself and he hugged Gwyn again, hard. She accepted his embrace, knowing he needed the physical contact more than she did.

"By the Powers, you are safe, I feared you were lost forever," his voice was flush with emotion. His eyes ranged over her, marveling at how much she resembled her mother, even to the color of her eyes. She was even prettier than his mind had imagined.

"The Ancient One would not hurt us, father," Gwyn answered calmly. Belwyn turned to Pyrs and would have embraced him but the boy rebuffed him again.

"No, I'll have nothing to do with you!" His eyes were dark and angry.

Belwyn felt the boy's disdain keenly.

"I shall keep my distance, son, but are you well? You have not been harmed, have you?" Pyrs frowned and shook his head.

"I am well."

"I do not understand, you appear to be … almost …" Belwyn stopped, unable to put a number to the children's age.

"We are almost eight years, father," his daughter answered solemnly. Belwyn thought he could see a tinge of sadness in her eyes at the admission.

"The dragon said he would take your youth," he said, running a hand through his long hair. He was attempting to adjust to this unexpected change. All the provisions Riona had sent with him were appropriate to small children, not ones of this size.

"And so he has," Gwyn replied quietly. Belwyn saw her gather the cloak around her once again attempting to retain some semblance of modesty for apparently she had no other clothes on under the garment.

"You appear to need a sash, daughter," he remarked in some desperation to regain a sense of normalcy.

"That would be best, father." The girl spoke as if she was a decade older than her physical age.

Belwyn fished around in his saddlebag, found a hunk of rope and cut two lengths, handing one to each of the children. Gwyn gave him a shy smile, wound the rope around her waist, tucked in the cloak and then tied the rope tightly. Belwyn pulled out his knife and walked to where Pyrs was tying his own rope belt, intending to cut off the cloak's excess length where it flowed around him on the ground. The boy shook his head immediately, not willing to allow any contact with his sire.

"You are more obstinate than your mother, Pyrs," Belwyn muttered and handed the boy the knife. He watched as the lad deftly trimmed off the cloak, leaving it much longer than he should have. "I believe you will want it shorter than that."

"I believe not," the boy's voice came back in a diffident tone and then he walked over to his sister and performed the same operation, leaving her cloak long as well. He pointedly handed the knife to Gwyn and she returned to her father. Everything in the boy's actions spoke of contempt for his sire.

Morgan finally perched on a nearby rock and as the crisis appeared over, the pain in his ankle took precedence. A low moan escaped his lips as he began to tug off his boot. His face was pale and sweaty again, for the effort to stand during the dragon's inquisition had taken its toll. Gwyn knelt in front of him and helped him remove the boot, though it proved no easy task as the ankle was viciously swollen. The young girl examined the foot and then put both hands around the ankle as she recited a healing spell. The pain lessened and the swelling decreased so that Morgan was able to put his boot back on easily.

"Gwyn, that is marvelous, it is so much better! The pain is quite tolerable now," he explained in an amazed voice.

She only nodded. "When we stop for rest tonight I will repeat the spell. It should be completely healed in a day or so."

"You have your mother's magic in you." Gwyn gave him a curious look and then a shy smile.

Morwyn's fever broke at dawn on the day that Belwyn and Morgan stood in front of the Ancient One. Riona sat with the patient and when she saw the physical evidence that the fever had fled, the soaked bed linens and chemise, Riona thanked the Powers and sent Peter to tell the master of the house the good news. A female servant helped her bathe Morwyn, change the bed linens and bandages. Once their care was complete, Owain the Elder took up vigil near Morwyn's bed.

"Sir, it may be some time before she awakes," Riona warned.

"I know, but I owe her this. She once gave me a reason to live so I might see my eldest son returned to me, though I thought him dead. I wish to be the first to tell her what has befallen her children."

"I understand, sir."

Owain the Elder's vigil was not lengthy. Morwyn awoke only a couple of hours after her fever broke. As her eyes fluttered opened she attempted to focus on unfamiliar surroundings.

"Morwyn?" The voice sounded familiar and brought back memories. Those memories triggered ones that were more recent. Braen's brutal attack flooded her mind and then she remembered the loss of her children.

"Gwyn? Pyrs?" she called as she struggled to sit upright in the bed.

"Easy, lie back. You have been ill for some time," the voice replied full of compassion. She turned to find Owain the Elder at her bedside. She persisted in her attempts to sit upright so he helped her, propping thick pillows behind her and arranging the covers around her just as she had once done for him.

"Where am I?" Her voice was thin and weak.

"Aderyn.

Her eyes widened "Are Gwyn and Pyrs here?"

"No, they are not, but they are out of harm's reach," he answered. It was not a completely honest answer for he did not know the children's final fate, but their mother needed reassurance.

"Where are they? Does Braen still have them?" her voice edged into panic as her eyes pleaded with him for any news he was willing to impart.

"Braen does not have them," he paused, searching for the best way to explain all of this. Morwyn's voice cracked and her eyes were now full of fear.

"Owain, are they dead?"

"No!" He realized his insubstantial answers had only frightened her more. "They were rescued from Braen by a ... dragon."

"What?" she shot back instantly, her voice stronger. She shook her head to clear the cobwebs and his face became clearer. He did not appear any older, only very tired.

"A grey dragon came for them," he explained.

"Powers," her voice whispered. "A fledgling ..." Her eyes moved back to his. "Tell me all of it, Owain, leave nothing out."

He related the tale as best he could. She listened quietly and her fears slowly evaporated. Owain was concerned the tale would terrify the woman. It appeared to have the opposite effect.

"It will not harm them, Owain," she reassured, "it is not their way." A look of resigned calm descended on her face.

He took her hand and held it. "That is what the bard said. I pray you are both right."

"Now Belwyn knows of his children," she murmured.

"Yes, he does. So does Morgan, who did not take the news kindly."

She frowned. "Why would that trouble him?"

"He was angry because he felt my son used you to end his enchantment."

She shook her head immediately. "No, I gave Belwyn no choice. It was what the Ancient One decreed."

"They have made peace now, but for a time Morgan was very wroth."

She sighed. "Your son is certainly a descendant of Anarawd the Dragon-Slayer if he would venture in front of the Ancient One again." She remembered their first encounter with the old dragon – it had nearly paralyzed her with fear.

"He will return with them," Owain observed in a solemn voice. *Or die in the attempt.*

"Why would the Ancient One want my children?" her puzzled voice asked.

"Perhaps he feels they are his in some way, for he did command you to break the enchantment by lying with my son."

"I do not know. There is more here, Owain, more than I can see. Gwyn did not fear going with Braen and his men. Could she have known the dragon would come for them?"

Owain shook his head, he did not know. "I cannot say. So much is odd about this, Morwyn. At least you live and your mind is sound."

"The fever lasted that long?"

"Yes. You have been ill for over a week."

"I remember little other than hideous dreams of Braen. Is he still alive?"

"It would appear so. Often the most evil in our midst are the hardest to kill."

"Pyrs will settle that score," she said without thinking and then blinked in surprise. She had no idea where that had come from. Owain chuckled, not realizing she'd been granted a vision.

"Well, if he does, he'll have to grow a bit first."

She let the unnerving sensation past and replied, "His temper will make up for his size, I suspect."

"Peter said he has a wicked temperament."

"He does. He was born with it. I have no idea where he got it, for his father and I are fairly even tempered."

"No doubt from his great-grandfather. Trahern had a monstrous temper."

"That's possible," she mused. "He can throw one very royal tantrum when he wishes." A smile appeared on her face and Owain could tell she missed her children profoundly.

"The presence of his father and his grandsire may help in that matter. We can channel some of that temper into arms training when he gets old enough." He waited to gauge her reaction.

Is she willing to allow us to raise her children?

"You are right, my time with them is nearly at an end."

Owain vigorously shook his head. "No, it is not. They need *both* their parents, Morwyn."

"It will prove difficult, Owain."

"You still love Belwyn, don't you?"

"Yes." The admission fell from her lips like a stone.

"He will ask you to marry him, to make the children legitimate."

"I know."

He saw the apprehension in her eyes.

"He loves you as well. If you cannot live together as man and wife, we can find a way that you are near your children as they grow, Morwyn. You are their mother and they need you."

"I know. I fear …" she paused, unsure of how to explain this to the grandsire of her twins.

"You fear being near my son. You fear your love will overcome your desire to sustain the magic."

She nodded slowly. "Yes."

"That I cannot help you with. Know that you are welcome at Aderyn and I will thrash any man who speaks ill of you for your past decisions."

She smiled gently. "You have not changed, Owain the Elder."

"Neither have you, Morwyn the Adept, you are still as stubborn."

She shook her head. "I am an adept no longer, Owain."

"In my eyes you still are." He reached over and placed a light kiss on her forehead. "I have missed you," he said and squeezed her hand.

"As I have missed you."

He paused and then switched the subject rather abruptly, "Are you hungry or thirsty?"

"I am both, it appears."

"Good! I will have food brought to you and let our healer know you are awake."

"Are Riona and Peter still here?"

"Yes. Ulwyn as well. Do you wish to see them?"

"After I eat and rest some more. I have missed Ulwyn's beautiful voice and his lute playing."

"I will see what we can do for you."

She gave him a long look. "When they fetch a tray for me have one brought for you as well. You do not look like you have eaten or rested for a number of days."

"I have not. It has been hard to just wait and do nothing."

"I understand. Be patient, the waiting is almost at an end." He nodded his assent and left the room.

It took over four days to reach Aderyn's holdings. At dawn on all four of those days they awoke to find the children two years older. The first morning Morgan and Belwyn were astonished to discover the twins physically altered.

"Gwyn, what is this?" Belwyn asked, disquieted as he studied them.

"The Ancient One told you, father, he claims our youth."

"But he has already claimed six years! How much more does he require?"

"All of it," Gwyn replied somewhat wistfully and then would say no more, no matter how much her worried father pressed her.

On the second morning Belwyn asked his son, "You knew this would happen, didn't you? That is why you cut the cloaks longer than was necessary."

Pyrs only nodded and did not reply. He was rapidly growing into a smaller version of his father, complete with his sire's dark eyes and build. Nevertheless, his attitude towards Belwyn did not shift. He despised his progenitor, blaming him for leaving his mother alone to raise them. No amount of pleading by Morgan on Belwyn's behalf made any difference. In contrast, Gwyn was quite pleasant with her father and apparently held no grudge against him. She grew like a tall tree as she blossomed into womanhood. She spoke more now, but she was still a daughter of the magic.

The changes continued each morning, two years at a time.

"When will this stop, Gwyn?" Belwyn asked, fearful that this ill sorcery would not cease and he would be burying his children in a matter of a month.

Gwyn sensed his concern and shook her head, "It will stop soon, father. He does not take our lives, only our youth."

"Why?" he pressed, desperate to understand.

"It is the price for the knowledge."

"What knowledge?" Belwyn came back presently. *I have finished with them,* the dragon had said. "The knowledge the dragon taught you?"

Gwyn only nodded and would said no more.

Its wings were not tired, but it was so excited it was hard to fly straight. It was something he had never dared dream. He, the smallest of the litter, the one who had never grown as fast as his fellow hatchlings was chosen to watch over a mortal dragon daughter, the girl Gwyn. He had been summoned by the oldest of dragons and tested until he thought his little wings would fall off, interrogated until the Ancient One was sure he was the best choice to guard over the girl. In the end he was chosen over all the others. Now he flew to find her and begin his task of protection. It was a responsibility that weighed heavily on his small heart. He knew that he must perform it well, even at the cost of his own life, for the mortal girl Gwyn was of the Old Magic and must be guarded no matter the cost.

As they journeyed, Pyrs stayed at Morgan's side or at Gwyn's, but refused to come near his father. His behavior only became more insolent and he took every chance to challenge or insult his sire. Belwyn knew they would have to settle this, but he honestly did not know how to handle the boy's deep-seated ire.

By the third night, as they made camp, Belwyn's patience had ended. Pyrs had been particularly abusive during the preceding hours and he knew the time had come to confront the boy. He waited until after they ate their evening repast and then spoke privately to Morgan and Gwyn. Both understood the need for the father to settle matters with his son. The couple walked out into the forest, talking quietly, leaving Belwyn and the boy by the campfire. Immediately uncomfortable, Pyrs began to rise and join them, but Belwyn did not allow him the opportunity to leave.

"We must talk, son."

"I am Morwyn's son, not yours!" the lad instantly shot back, his eyes glaring. He began to pace around the fire, physical evidence of his displeasure at the subject of this conversation. He had dreaded this moment as much as the man who claimed to be his father. He looked out in the direction his sister had gone and wished she were here. She was out of sight and that made him feel vulnerable. He had no choice but to stay.

"You are mine as well, Pyrs, whether you claim me or not," Belwyn replied in a surprisingly mellow tone.

"I have no wish to be your son."

"In that you have no choice, I'm afraid. How much did your mother tell you of how you came to be?"

He frowned. "If you mean all that about the enchantment and the dragon and how she had to share your bed to keep you from fading – yes, I know that. How she birthed us alone, without any help. I know that as well. I know *why* my mother did what she did, she loves you and that will never change, though I do question her judgment. Now that I come to know you, my opinion has not changed."

Belwyn's mind caught at a small bit of information. "She bore you alone?" That hurt deep within him, for he had lost the simple joy of attending his children's birth, holding them in his hands during their first moments of life.

"There was no one there for her."

"By the Powers, I so wish she had come to me. She could have been safe in our house, attended by a healer, her every need met. I would have done anything to help her." Though his voice was full of sincerity the boy chose to ignore it.

"I doubt that. You did not come to her, not once. If you had, you would have known you had sired bastards on her. You did not come. Now you dare to claim that you would have done anything to help her, to help us!" Pyrs's hands were on his hips, his eyes blazing. He did not allow his father to answer and continued, his wrath growing. Unknowingly he charged Belwyn with the same crime Morgan once had. "You took her, used her and left her, you heartless bastard!"

Belwyn stood, his own anger rising with him.

"You will do well not to call me a bastard, my son, for I am a legitimate son of the House of Aderyn."

"Unlike my sister and I who were sired in some foggy enchantment and left to starve with our mother in some miserable hovel in the forest." He was bending the truth somewhat, but it felt good to hurt the man in any way he could.

"By the Powers, boy, I did not know you even existed! I could not come and aid your mother if she did not tell me of you. I would have gladly given whatever she needed to keep you fed and clothed, even if she insisted we live apart. It is my fault in how you were sired, but it is your mother's for not telling me she was with child!"

"You dare to criticize my mother, you bastard!" Pyrs flamed back.

"You push me too far, Pyrs, for I love your mother beyond all things. There has been no one all these years, *no one*. My heart is hers, though we cannot be together."

"If you had cared you would have come to her and learned of us!" Pyrs shouted. "You had your way with her and then moved on to your next conquest!"

"I refuse to take the blame for not caring for you when I did not know of you!"

As the couple stood gazing at the moon, the sound of angry voices reached them through the forest. Morgan shot Gwyn a concerned look.

"This bodes ill," he said and turned back toward the camp, fearing the argument would only widen the rift between father and son.

"My brother's anger has overwhelmed him, yet again," Gwyn sighed and followed the warrior back to her family.

six

Pyrs pressed ahead, hunting for the jugular. "Your callous indifference brought Braen to our door. If it had not been for Gwyn he would have …" the boy stopped for a moment, overwhelmed by the emotions boiling inside him. "He learned of us! Why didn't you?"

"I do not know!" Belwyn shouted back for his son had struck his guilt straight on. "I can not reverse what has happened, but I can make it right. I will marry your mother and make you legitimate. "

"No, you shall not, for I will never allow it!" Pyrs proclaimed, clearly irrational at this point, his insecurity and anger bubbling over in torrents. He snatched up Belwyn's sword where it lay on his bedding, drew it out of the scabbard and turned it on his own father. "You will only hurt her more, I see it plain. I will not allow it, no, by the Powers, I will not!" He lunged at his father, fury overwhelming him. Shocked at the boy's behavior, Belwyn stood motionless and did not attempt to evade the sword thrust.

"Pyrs!" Morgan's voice cut through the air as he seized the lad's hand and wrenched the sword away from him. He tossed it on a nearby blanket and placed himself as a shield between the man and boy.

"Pyrs, stop! What are you doing?" Gwyn's voice called out. Her brother stepped back immediately with his fists clenched at his sides, his chest heaving.

"He would marry mother just to ease his vile conscience!" he explained.

"Do you not see that your love of our mother has clouded your mind to his intentions? You must realize that you *both* share that love and that is your bond, even if you never reconcile as father and son," she said. She was stunned at how far her brother's temper had taken him. Gwyn's strong words cut into Pyrs. He hung his head, ashamed at his actions. Belwyn was in a daze, realizing his son would have struck him, perhaps even killed him if Morgan had not interfered. He caught Morgan's eyes and nodded his gratitude at his friend's timely intervention.

Sensing her twin was gaining control Gwyn took him in her arms and embraced him. He hugged her intensely, for she was the one sure thing in his life.

"I am sorry, Gwyn," he murmured and barely kept the tears from flowing. He refused to cry in front of the man that she considered their father. She continued the embrace, adding a calming spell to settle her brother's emotions. She felt him relax in her arms and she drew back.

"It is not easy, Pyrs. One day we are small children and now we are nearly grown. It is so hard to know what to feel. I am confused myself and it must be equally hard for you." *Harder, I think, for the magic gives me comfort.*

He nodded. "I don't know who I am, Gwyn, and he ..." he paused and turned his dark eyes on his sire, "and now *he* wants to be our father. He wasn't there when we needed him! Now, I am so unsure." He was talking as if Belwyn was not present. A sudden look of comprehension appeared on Morgan's face.

"Powers, Belwyn, we did not think! Remember what it was like when we were his age and we didn't know what to think or how to act? Can you imagine what it is like for Gwyn and Pyrs to suddenly be fourteen or fifteen years of age in a matter of days?"

Belwyn sighed and his voice quavered as he spoke.

"Pyrs, son, I am so sorry. I cannot undo what has happened in the past. I can only promise to be a loving father. Please give us a chance at a future together." Pyrs tried to glower at him, but failed. His anger was melting.

"I can never forgive you for not coming for us," he said honestly.

"I should have found your mother and made sure that I did not get her with child. I will never forgive myself for that, for I have lost your first years of life, time I cannot recapture." Belwyn held out his hands, not knowing if the boy would accept the overture. Pyrs stood and stared at him and then his remaining fury withered, replaced by uncertainly. He shook his head.

"I cannot."

Belwyn dropped his hands in resignation. "I accept that, Pyrs."

"Do you really love our mother?" the lad asked suddenly.

Belwyn nodded, "For me there is no one else. If we cannot find a means to be together, then there will be no one for the rest of my days."

"I see." The boy took a step back and closed his eyes for a moment, sending a prayer to the Powers that his mother would be well by the time they reached Aderyn. He opened his eyes and then bent to pick up his father's sword where it lay nearby. He cleaned it on his cloak and began to place it back in its scabbard.

"Wait, Pyrs, it is considered unlucky to not have blooded a drawn sword," Morgan explained. He took the blade from the boy, nicked his thumb on it, wiped the blood from the steel and then allowed Pyrs to sheath the weapon. The scabbard's intricate carvings caught the lad's attention and he studied it intently. Belwyn saw his interest and sensed a chance to tell the boy of his lineage.

"That sword was given to your great-great grandsire, Rhyd, after the battle that placed Awstin on the High Throne. Awstin's brother, the High King, was assassinated by the Lord of the Eastern March, Lord Wann, and it led to war. Rhyd fought at Awstin's side and was presented this sword and scabbard in acknowledgement of his skill at arms and his loyalty. Rhyd was an honorable man and when he was offered the lordship of the Eastern March and all of Wann's lands, he refused, feeling that there was another man more worthy of it."

Pyrs glanced up and asked, "Who was more worthy?"

Belwyn smiled and gestured toward Bardyn's son.

"Morgan's great-grandsire became Lord of the Eastern March, which is why Lord Bardyn now holds the title rather than your grandsire. In time, Morgan will be Lord of the Eastern March instead of me. To be honest, that does not trouble me in the least." He gave his fellow warrior a light smile and Morgan shook his head at the comment.

"I often wish the title had gone to your family, not ours, Belwyn. The weight on my shoulders would be much less," he replied honestly.

"It would, but it deserves to be where it was bestowed." Morgan shrugged at that.

"The sword and scabbard are that old?" Pyrs asked in amazement, still fixed on the tale his father had told him.

"You are the fifty-eighth in line of the House of Aderyn, my son. You have a noble heritage behind you."

"I am not a legitimate heir to that claim," Pyrs came back immediately.

"You are my son and there are no other heirs."

"In time Uncle Owain will no doubt marry and have sons by his bride, there is no doubt of that." Belwyn gave the boy a curious look; it was like talking to a young lad of fourteen going on forty.

"If so, then the line will follow his heirs. As of now, you are the eldest son of the eldest son."

Pyrs muttered quietly, "And a bastard."

He heard Morgan chuckle, "As am I, young Pyrs, and though it is not a desirable station in life, it is what we have been given. As with Belwyn, my father was not able to marry my mother, she refused him twice. So I am baseborn, for good or ill."

"You?" Pyrs looked shocked at the revelation.

"Yes, so we have much in common, though I pray to the Powers your situation is changeable where mine is not." Pyrs' estimation of Morgan rose. He studied the scabbard for a moment longer and then handed the ancient weapon back to his sire.

"Your sword …" He paused for a very long time but did not say *father.*

"Thank you, my son."

Gwyn smiled to herself and settled near the fire. The crisis had passed and some small bonding had occurred between her headstrong brother and their guilt-ridden sire. She knew only time could heal the breach. When she found Morgan's intense eyes lingering on her she turned her thoughts inward, trying to contain the strange feelings within her.

Ulwyn entertained Morwyn and the other guests of the household that night and his music and jests put all at ease. Later, he and Morwyn had a chance to catch up on their lives.

"Two children?" she asked with a grin on her face. She knew his wife had been with child at the time of the battle with Lord Merioneth, but now there appeared to be yet another little one in his family.

"A girl, just six months old. Her name is Eres, it means *wonderful* in the old language."

"I am so happy to hear of it, Ulwyn. I have often thought of you over the years and wondered how you and Rhosyn were faring."

"We fare very well, Morwyn." His smile was warm and full of contentment.

"I also fared well. Gwyn and Pyrs are good children and the years passed quickly."

"Belwyn will make an excellent father," Ulwyn said. He knew it might be difficult for her to think of the future, but she needed to accept that everything had changed the moment Braen appeared at the door of her hut.

Morwyn readily agreed. "He will. He will adore Gwyn. As for Pyrs, well, one ever knows." She chuckled at that.

Ulwyn nodded. "He will adjust in time."

"I hope so. Gwyn has always had the magic to give her security. Pyrs keenly missed having a father and knowing the lad's temper, I suspect he will find it difficult to suddenly be presented with one." She frowned for a moment, sensing something and then it flitted by her.

"Morwyn?" the bard asked, seeing her curious look.

"It is nothing, For some reason I am sensing more than I usually do."

"It may be the effects of the fever," he replied. "I have heard that it can cause one to see visions for some time after it passes."

"I don't know," she answered. At that Ulwyn began to play a lilting melody on his lute and she allowed the music to soothe her unease.

The following morning Peter and his mother set off for Ilspath. Morwyn had recommended that Riona seek out a healer named Brenna, who could complete her training. They reluctantly took leave of their friend and made Morwyn promise to send word of the children. Owain the Elder detailed two of his men to insure their journey would be safe. Shortly after their departure the bard set off for Lord Bardyn's holdings some two days' journey to the southeast of Aderyn. He carried a letter to Bardyn in which Owain related the extraordinary tale of his newfound grandchildren. Their lord would naturally be worried about his son and so Owain the Elder promised to send word as soon as Morgan and Belwyn returned from their quest.

Dillan restored Ifor's weapons to him and once the man's wound was less troublesome, he began to help around the holdings as he best he could. Cara mended clothes for both the master of the house and the servants. Her nimble figures made easy work of the repairs and Owain the Younger knew the woman was perfect for the tasks ahead at Aldyn's holdings.

As the days passed, Morwyn rose from her sickbed and sat vigil in one of the smaller gathering rooms downstairs. She was clearly on the mend, but her mind was not at peace, not until her children and their father returned.

The fluttering of wings brought the two men out of their reverie. The warriors were eating their morning repast and Pyrs was still asleep, curled up in his blankets. Gwyn sat quietly mediating, her face radiating a peace that Belwyn remembered on her mother's face years before.

It must be the magic that gives her such serenity.

The swoosh of the wings continued and at first Morgan thought it was a raven or a crow hovering just a few feet from Gwyn. She extended her arm and the creature landed, its wings shaking from the exertion of the lengthy flight. It was not a bird. Morgan blinked, twice. A small dragon the size of a man's fist was perched on Gwyn's arm. It was pure black in color with deep multi-hued eyes.

Morgan exclaimed in awe, "Powers!" Pyrs rose at this point, drowsy, for the warrior's exclamation pulled him out of his sleep.

"Powers!" he muttered as well, a grin on his face at the sight.

"Gwyn?" Belwyn asked, instantly nervous.

"All is well, father." She turned her eyes back to the small beast. "You are a guardian dragon, are you not?" she asked.

It nodded its small head and answered in her mind, **I am to protect you.**

What is your name, little one? she asked. The little dragon revealed its name to her, giving her power over it. *I am Gwyn, daughter of Morwyn the Adept, Dragon Daughter and Wielder of the Old Magic,* she replied making the proper formal introduction through the mental link.

The little one nodded and then yawned involuntarily.

"You are very weary from your flight." She returned to verbal speech for the benefit of the others. They were captivated by the small creature.

I am.

"Then rest, my dragon friend, for there is no peril here in this camp."

The dragon slowly inched its way up to her shoulder and settled here, careful not to harm her with its sharp claws. It surveyed the men, judged them in its mind and decided they presented no harm to his charge. It moved its eyes over to Pyrs.

Dragon brother.

"Welcome, brother," Pyrs replied. His father shot him a strange look but the boy ignored it. Certain that all seemed in order, the little dragon curled its tail around a section of Gwyn's long hair and fell fast asleep.

"By the Powers, I never thought I'd see something like that," Morgan said in wonder. "I can only imagine what it could can do if it felt threatened."

"Like a small watchdog," Belwyn said with a chuckle in his voice. *A dragon guards my daughter!*

"With claws and teeth that can rip a man apart," Pyrs replied, sarcastically.

Belwyn caught the boy's tone and chided back, "So, son, why don't you have one of those on your shoulder? Is it perhaps because your temper is sufficient to keep your enemies at bay?"

Pyrs glared at him and refused to answer.

"That would be the reason, father," Gwyn replied, jesting with her brother. He awarded her a sour look. Belwyn chuckled and then dug through his saddlebag, hunting for Pyrs' small bag of stones. What with the events of the past few days he'd nearly forgotten them.

"Here, something to soothe that attitude of yours, son." He handed him the bag and Pyrs' face erupted in a grin as he recognized the bundle immediately. He opened the tie, spread the cloth on the ground and started pushing the stones around.

"I had thought they were lost," he said and smiled up at his father, not realizing he had.

"Riona brought them from the hut. She knew you were fond of them."

"Bless her! Mother picked them up for me. I kept asking for more stones and each trip she went for water at the lake she would take time to find some that were just perfect."

"Why are you so fascinated with these, Pyrs?" Morgan asked, intrigued.

Pyrs pushed a few more of them around and explained,

"They're armies, you see. I can do battles all day long with these stones, trying different means of attack." His eyes shown bright as he talked.

"You need to speak to your Uncle Elrehan, he is a tactician as well," Morgan replied.

"I remember him visiting us. He would sit and watch me work the stones as if he understood what I was doing."

"No doubt he did," Belwyn replied. "Your uncle planned the diversion that kept Morgan's father alive when Lord Merioneth attempted to take him hostage. Elrehan's plan was brilliant and it worked perfectly."

"I shall ask him about that," Pyrs said and then turned his attention to the stones, moving them around in an orderly fashion. Belwyn gave Morgan a look and his friend nodded back. Young Pyrs, despite his legendary temper, had the makings of an excellent warrior.

There was pleasant conversation on the ride that day and that made the journey seem easier. Pyrs was less tense, though it was still evident he was unsure of his father. The boy was confused for he had demonized his sire and now he found him an honest and decent man. Gwyn had chastised him for his animosity, reminding him that their mother would hardly consort with a scoundrel and a liar. Pyrs had not liked that remark and had buried it deep after his sister had uttered it. Now, he knew her to be right. Nevertheless, he still did not entirely trust the man. He eventually began to talk, but he turned his inquisitive mind toward Morgan. He quizzed Bardyn's heir about his life and the warrior readily told him of it.

"So your father never knew of you?" Pyrs asked curiously. He was still riding with Morgan, not with his sire.

"No, he did not."

"And it made no difference in how you feel about him?" Morgan knew what the boy was trying to work out in his own mind. He answered honestly, for the parallels between his life and the lad's were not that different.

"No, it does not. He could in no way be my father if my mother did not tell him of me. He sorely wished to marry her, he tried to win her hand twice and she refused him both times. It was not meant to be." His voice was melancholy.

"I see. Like you and my mother?" Morgan half turned in the saddle and looked back at the boy behind him with a startled expression.

"She told you of us?"

"Yes, she told us stories each night before we went to sleep and when we sat in watching the fireflies on the lake. I do not believe that she thought children as young as us would remember them, but we both do. She spoke of a gallant blonde-haired warrior who asked for her hand three times and she said that she denied him each time. She told us he was Lord Bardyn's son and a honorable man."

Morgan smiled at the memory of his time with this boy's mother and for a moment was lost in the past. Pyrs sensed the man's reverie and remained silent. It was evident that the warrior still loved his mother.

"When we met she was near your sister's age, fair and lovely. I would have placed a kingdom at her feet if it had gained her hand. Alas, I had nothing to offer but myself. The call of the magic was too strong for her even then."

"You could have been our father," Pyrs said quietly. Morgan had no answer for this, ensnared in memories.

Belwyn heard the boy's observation and replied, "I wish that had happened, Pyrs, for he would have been there for you." Pyrs's eyebrow raised at that.

Morgan shook his head and said, "No, you forget, Belwyn, I was to die that day on the battlefield. I may have been there for the first three or so years, but Pyrs and Gwyn would have grown up without a father during the time they needed one most. It is was not to be."

"We would not have been allowed to survive if Merioneth had triumphed," Gwyn observed. "He would have put all of Lord Bardyn's family to the sword, even mother and ourselves."

Pyrs gave her a startled look. "I suppose you are right. I never thought of that."

"We are pawns in the Powers' game, are we not?" Belwyn asked, knowing his son was working all of this over in his mind.

"We are, and as you once observed, this pawn grows weary," Morgan replied.

Owain the Elder rejoiced at his eldest son's homecoming. He greeted Belwyn with a tight embrace, welcomed Morgan warmly and then he spied the children.

"By the Powers!" he sputtered in shock. Pyrs was the image of Belwyn and Gwyn was her mother, down to those unique blue-grey eyes.

Belwyn performed the introductions, enjoying every word.

"Father, this is Gwyn and Pyrs, my children by Morwyn."

"By the Powers," was all the man could say. "But how, they are, what, fourteen, fifteen years? This is not possible!" The older man was completely confounded.

"They seem to have settled on somewhere near fifteen, as best as we can tell," Belwyn replied with a twinkle in his eyes. "They have been to see the Ancient One and the dragon caused them to age faster than their years. Both should be less than three years old, but now they are nearly grown."

The older man just stood there shaking his head as they crowded around him in the courtyard. He greeted Pyrs first, for he was nearest to him.

"My grandson, you are a fine young man." He engulfed Pyrs's hand in his and shook it heartily. His eyes caught Gwyn's and a gentle smile appeared on his face. He strode over to her and took her hands in his. "You are so lovely, Gwyn, you look so much like your mother." He missed the girl's slight tension at that comment.

"How is she, sir?" Pyrs asked, a tinge of worry in his voice.

"Her fever has broke and she waits inside."

"Then it will be a joyous reunion!" Morgan remarked, his face awash in a smile.

"Come on in, let these children see their mother and then we will eat and they can tell us their tale for it will be most astounding I hear for many a year."

Pyrs found no reason to dislike the older man, he was warm and hospitable. He walked next to his grandsire as they strode toward the main hall, talking the entire way, Owain the Elder's hand on the boy's shoulder as if they'd known each other for years.

"I would say your son has bonded with your father," Morgan observed as he pulled his pack down from his horse.

"He has and that is a good thing. Even if he never accepts me, my father will help him grow into manhood," Belwyn replied. The dragon had warned him he would pay his own personal price for the children's return. He steeled himself for the possibility that his son would be closer to his grandsire than him.

"Give him time, father," Gwyn said knowingly. "Pyrs inherited our mother's stubbornness."

"Yes, he did, twice over."

The main hall of Aderyn had stood for over four centuries. Its high-beamed ceiling was of fine dark oak, the side walls constructed of grey stone with tall mullioned windows. Pyrs was dumbstruck the moment he crossed the threshold into the great hall. It was not the size of the room that halted his progress, but what the room contained. His eyes were enthralled by count-less pieces of weaponry displayed on the walls. Unlike most holdings where the weapons and armor were stored in an armory, Aderyn displayed theirs in the open for all to see. It made for a formidable impression. The room seemed to shimmer in a thousand little pinpoints as the wall-ensconced can-dles reflected off the polished armor. A meticulously arranged sword display caught Pyrs's attention and without meaning to be rude, he struck off from his grandsire's side and went to study them. They were like the lineage sword, but less ornate. One was shorter and he suspected the younger sons of the family carried it as they grew into manhood. There was an open space where another sword would normally rest. He surmised that one was currently in possession of his sire.

Next to the swords was a massive tapestry, one of three in the room. It was no less than ten-feet tall and twenty-feet wide. Its once vibrant colors, now muted in age, added an unexpected depth to the scene depicted upon it. Pyrs's eyes were drawn to the center of the tapestry where a dark-haired war-rior was kneeling in homage, his hands outstretched to receive a sword from his king. The sword looked familiar, even when worked in thread.

"The lineage sword," Pyrs said. He didn't see his grandfather smile at that comment as he took his place behind the lad.

"That is our lineage sword being presented to your great-great grandsire, Rhyd." He was pleased the boy had homed in on that particular piece of family history. "Your father carries it at present."

"I have held it." *And nearly killed him with it,* Pyrs thought ruefully.

"Good, for it will be yours in time. But come now, we best have your mother know you are well and then we can talk at length about your ancestors." Pyrs nodded and trailed behind his grandfather through the massive room. It took all his concentration not to pause to examine a certain piece of armor or one of the countless bows positioned along the walls.

"Sir?" It was an older man's voice and both Pyrs and his grandsire turned towards it. A greying man with strong arms and a wide chest came striding toward them across the hall.

"Dillan!" Owain's exuberant voice boomed. Pyrs could tell the moment the newcomer's eyes focused on him for his mouth fell open in astonishment.

"Sir?"

Owain the Elder made the introduction, savoring the moment.

"Dillan, this is my grandson, Pyrs, son of Morwyn. I wish him made welcome as an heir to the House of Aderyn should be." To his credit Dillan did not stay astonished for long. He gave a slight bow and replied in a reasonably steady voice, "Welcome, young master."

"Pyrs, this is Dillan, Aderyn's Master of the Guard and a dear friend of mine for over two decades."

"Master of the Guard, I am very pleased to meet you," Pyrs replied in deference, for clearly he was a man not to be trifled with.

Dillan continued to stare.

"My lord, the lad is ..." he began. Owain waved his hand in the air, dismissing this very salient observation.

"Enchantment, just leave it at that, Dillan. We both know he and his sister should be toddlers, but now they are nearly grown. We shall have to adapt." At this Owain laughed heartily at the improbability of the situation. Dillan gave the boy yet another long look and shook his head in surrender. There was no mistake, the boy was the image of a young Belwyn.

"Come, grandson, your mother is in here." Pyrs followed him and the moment his grandsire opened the door into an adjoining room, he saw her. She was in a chair, her face full of tears for she had heard Owain's resounding voice in the distance speaking of her children.

"Pyrs," she said and then blinked. She had not caught all of what Owain had said, only that her children had returned. "Powers, you are ..." Her face was full of bewilderment. Pyrs flew across the room and embraced her, hard. He felt her wince and only then did he remember her wounds.

"Oh, mother, I am sorry!" He backed off and she shook her head.

"No, I can handle a little pain, son. Come hug me again, for I have so missed you."

They were still embracing when Gwyn and her father appeared in the doorway. Morwyn's mouth dropped open in wonder.

"Gwyn?" she asked and Pyrs immediately extricated himself from her arms to allow his sister to take his place.

"Mother," she said and crossed to her to accept an embrace. The little dragon flitted up from Gwyn's shoulder, hovering above the girl. He sensed no danger here, only love, and allowed the mother the needed closeness with her daughter. As Morwyn hugged her daughter, the child that looked so much like her, her eyes met those of the twins' father. The emotions that hovered between them at that moment nearly brought him to his knees. Morwyn broke the contact first and with Pyrs's help, rose to judge her daughter's height. She was as tall as Morwyn.

"Gwyn, you are grown!"

"I am, mother." The dragon settled back down on the girl's shoulder and Morwyn just stared.

"Powers, that is a …" she started and then stopped.

"Yes, it is a guardian dragon."

Morwyn sank into the chair. "And I was worried about you." She shook her head at her unneeded anxiety.

"I don't have a dragon," Pyrs remarked. "I was in peril, you should have worried about me."

"You? Hardly. I know *your* temper, son."

"He does have one, I've noticed," Belwyn added as he joined his family, sensing the moment was right.

"It's been there since the moment of his birth," Morwyn said with a shrug. Pyrs squirmed a bit, uncomfortable with all the jesting at his expense. "I've been to see a dragon, mother, like you," he boasted.

"So I am told. Is there any particular reason why you and your sister are now no longer small and cuddly, my son?"

Gwyn answered. "The dragon took our youth in return for knowledge." Morwyn's eyes lost their jovial quality, as if she seemed to comprehend what this meant.

"I see. Well, it was what the Powers wished and I am not about to argue." She put one arm around Pyrs, kissed his forehead, and allowed the other arm, the injured one, to hang at her side near Gwyn. "Your grandsire has been keen to spend time with you, so we best not disappoint him."

"No, mother, we should not," Pyrs replied. The wide smile on his face made Belwyn's heart rejoice.

Owain the Younger appeared only a short time later and he was equally astonished at the children's size.

"You are such a tall lad!" he said to Pyrs and that elicited a big smile from the boy. "Gwyn," he said as his eyes fell on her. He took her in his arms and collected a hug from her.

"Uncle Owain," she replied and returned the embrace with enthusiasm.

"I am so pleased to see you both safe. We were very worried."

"No reason to worry, uncle, the dragon would not harm us."

"We were not so sure, Gwyn," the young man replied. He hugged her again for good measure.

Morgan joined them and he placed a gentle kiss on Morwyn's cheek. She gave him a look of gratitude.

"I thank you for going with Belwyn to the ddraig. That is not a journey to be taken lightly."

"No, I did not care for it. I hope that is the last dragon I ever meet."

"Hopefully that will be case," Morwyn replied sensing there was something more behind his words. Morgan's eyes moved over to Gwyn where she stood by her grandsire, quiet and composed. *You are exactly like your mother when I first met her,* he thought. Her eyes caught his and he broke contact first.

Cara and Ifor were summoned from their tasks and their reaction to the children's return was full of happiness and surprise.

"Powers, this is amazing!" Ifor said, giving Cara a quick glance. Pyrs was eyeing him and Ifor knew why. "I am sorry for what I did to you," he said in apology, knowing the boy no doubt remembered his unpleasant binding with the blanket.

"No harm was done," Pyrs said evenly and then smiled. "I do, however, regret not being this size when Braen came to visit us at the hut. The end would have been different."

"He lurks somewhere. The Powers may still give you your chance at his head," Belwyn remarked.

"I hope so, I owe that bastard much grief."

They gathered in the small dining hall and all ate with a hearty appetite, Morwyn included. Owain the Elder managed to keep his questions to a minimum until everyone had dined, but then he could contain himself no longer.

"So tell us your tale, my grandchildren, for it sounds to be one unlike any other." Pyrs glanced at Gwyn and she nodded for him to do the telling. She knew he needed this moment more than she did. With everyone's eyes on him, Pyrs told the amazing tale of their rescue by a fledgling and the thrilling flight to the North.

"I remember telling the Ancient One to release us, that our mother would be very angry," the boy remarked.

"And what did it say?" Belwyn asked.

"It said that she would be, but our father more so."

"It did not search your soul or threaten you?" his father quizzed.

"No, it did not. It was kind to us. It taught us many things, most of which I cannot speak of." He gave Gwyn a sideways look at that.

"That is remarkable! Every time I am in front of the beast it delights in frightening me to death," Belwyn replied. Pyrs looked over at him and saw the truth on his face. *The Ancient One said you were an honorable man, but I did not want to believe it.*

Morgan spoke up, "It makes sense, Belwyn. We adults know how to bury our feelings. Small children have not learned that cunning so they would be totally honest with the beast and not fear its wrath."

"I believe you are right, for all the dragon ever sought from any of us was the truth," Belwyn replied.

"The truth is preeminent, it said," Pyrs replied. Gwyn nodded solemnly, her little guardian asleep on her shoulder.

Owain the Elder chortled enthusiastically. "This is most amazing. Less than a fortnight ago I had no grandchildren and now I have two of the finest in the realm." He was obviously proud of them and that had won Pyrs's affection from the start.

"Thank you, grandsire," Pyrs replied. Gwyn gave her grandfather a sweet smile, one that melted his heart.

"I do have one question," Morwyn started, "it was your spell at the hut, wasn't it, Gwyn?"

"Yes, mother."

A look of sudden confirmation came upon Ifor's face.

"Then it is as Cara and I thought – you placed a spell on both of us in the clearing. That is why the dragon did not threaten either of us."

"Yes, I put a sign on you so it knew you should not be harmed."

"You knew the dragon was coming for you?" Belwyn asked, stunned.

"Yes, that is why I did not harm Braen and the others at the hut. He was our means to reach the Ancient One." Morwyn's face became pensive at this, her mind asking further questions she dare not voice at present.

Morgan snorted, "You see, Belwyn, even Braen is a pawn in the hands of the Powers."

"A very burnt one," Cara remarked. "I would be surprised if he survives those injuries."

"He will," Morwyn said, sensing the man was not dead. "The Powers are still playing him. His time has not come yet." Gwyn nodded solemnly and the conversation set off in a different direction as Owain the Younger spoke of Lady Aldyn and her numerous suitors. Despite her dubious history and the fact she had slain her husband, swains were still keenly pursuing her.

"She can't hold out forever," his father advised.

"I know," the young man replied in resignation. He feared the day she finally succumbed and agreed to marry just to end it all.

Belwyn gave his father a quick glance and a subtle nod returned. They'd both caught the unspoken feelings behind the young man's words.

"Then perhaps you should marry her," Belwyn said and that occasioned a number of startled looks at the table given his unpleasant history with the lady.

"I do not think she cares for me, brother," was the honest reply.

"She would be a good wife for you," Belwyn remarked. "She is not as I knew her for her lessons at the hands of Merioneth were bitterly learned."

"I have no objections to the match," Morgan said as he smiled broadly. "Besides, Aldyn knows how to deal with you if you get out of hand. She was quite capable of dispatching Merioneth when the time came." He shifted his eyes over to Morwyn at that moment, remembering the dragon's words about her part in that drama.

A low chuckle erupted from Owain the Elder. "Perhaps it would be best to hide any stray blades, should you wed."

"Especially on your wedding night," Morwyn mused. Owain the Younger frowned for only a moment and then dipped his head in acceptance.

"How true. I suspect she does not find me of interest, either. Her late husband caused her much grief and I don't think she'll allow anyone that close again."

Morwyn's eyebrow raised and when she turned her eyes over to her daughter she saw a faint nod in reply.

"Time is a great healer, my son. Be patient," Owain the Elder advised.

"I hope so," the younger man replied and would say no more on the matter.

Only Owain the Elder, Morgan, Pyrs and his father remained awake, talking into the night. The conversation was light and aimed at how best to begin Pyrs's training as the eldest son of the house. He was uncomfortable with this, for despite his youth he knew he was not worthy of the title given his particulars of birth. Seeing the magnificence of Aderyn's ancient hall had only reinforced his feelings in this regard. He took a deep breath and addressed his grandsire in a serious tone,

"Grandsire, I am not worthy of ..." he paused, trying to find the best way to explain his feelings. Morgan was the first to divine what the boy was trying to say.

"Pyrs ..." He gave the lad a slight frown. He thought they'd already covered that issue quite thoroughly.

Pyrs was not dissuaded. "No, I must say it. I am a baseborn, not a legitimate heir." Again, he sounded far older than his years. He turned his dark eyes on his father and continued, "I am beginning to understand more of the circumstances regarding my birth, grandsire, and I do not hold my sire as accountable for my station in life as I once did. Nonetheless, this is an old and honorable house and I am not fit to ..."

"Nonsense, boy! You are the eldest son of the House of Aderyn and until your uncle provides us with a son in wedlock, that is as it will remain. Even if Owain sires a son, you are my first grandson and will hold that position in my heart forever, lad." Pyrs studied the man's face and saw unstinting devotion.

"I wanted to tell my thoughts on this, sir."

"You are much like your father, Pyrs, though I suspect at this age you would prefer not to be. You have his sense of honor, that is clear. I value that more than any long lineage. Men without honor, even those with a title and a trail of ancestors back to the beginning of time, are worthless. Men who *have* honor, no matter how they are sired, are worthy of consideration. Young Morgan, here, though he is indeed illegitimate, is as honorable a man as I have seen. I will serve him more readily than a dozen of those long-sired knaves in the Council of Nobles."

"I understand, grandsire."

"Pyrs, it is possible that your mother may consent to marry me, though we could not live together as a man and wife should," Belwyn began cautiously. He still wasn't sure where his son's heart lay on this matter given his previous violent outburst.

"It is possible." the boy allowed, "I am not sure if it is the right thing to do."

"I will leave it to her, Pyrs," Belwyn acquiesced.

"I think that is wise," he responded and then rose and headed for bed, his mind troubled.

As Belwyn made his way to his room he paused near Morwyn's bedchamber. There was light under the door. He knocked and was granted entrance.

"Morwyn?" She knew why he was there and it hurt her heart in ways she never imagined. "May we speak together for a moment?"

She nodded and he entered the room, closing the door behind him. There was silence as he brought a chair over by hers near the fire. He looked as strong and handsome as the first time she'd met him in the village – the day he stood up to Braen. She pushed those memories aside.

"We have two fine children," he said, stalling.

"We do. Pyrs will be a warrior like his father. As for Gwyn, well, I do not know where her future lies. She wields the magic differently than I did."

A smile appeared on his face. "I never thought I'd have such wonderful children. I have you to thank." He paused, unsure of what to say next.

"You have the Powers to thank, Belwyn. I tried to prevent becoming pregnant and They did not allow it. It goes to prove They know more than us mortals."

"There is a matter we must discuss," he started, apprehensive. "We both know that the future of our children is paramount. I would ask that you consider marriage so that both Gwyn and Pyrs will be legitimate heirs to the House of Aderyn." His heart wrenched at this. He should be on one knee, asking for her hand, yet he was not. It felt more like barter between two merchants rather than a proposal of marriage.

She said nothing but looked down at her thin hands in her lap.

"Morwyn?"

"I will marry you, for them." Her voice was strained.

"I want you to know I love you. I ask this not only for our children, but for myself as well. I wish to be your husband, Morwyn." His dark eyes were pleading for her to believe him.

"I know." Another awkward pause ensued. "I request that we employ a proxy for the consummation, so the marriage will be legal."

He had anticipated this and shook his head immediately.

"No, I will not have another woman stand in your place for our wedding night. I will not take my pleasure with anyone else but my wife." His voice was adamant.

A slight frown appeared on her face at this. "Belwyn, you know I cannot ..."

"I know you cannot or will not be with me. I shall not press the matter. What happens between us in our marital bed is for us, alone. No one need know that the marriage was not consummated."

"There may be a cloud on Pyrs's title in the years to come."

"Whoever raises the issue will find my sword at their throat," Belwyn came back instantly.

His answer was as she anticipated. "Then make the plans, but keep them very simple."

His face looked hurt. "Morwyn, though we cannot be together as the Powers intended, there is no reason to not make this a celebration. We both love each other ..."

"No, I do not want a celebration, for after the wedding I will be asking for a Writ of Divorcement."

"Why?" he asked, stunned. "I promise not to touch you unless you are willing. I can restrain myself, Morwyn." He thought that her concern. Her eyes were surprisingly gentle and she took his hands in hers and kissed them.

"It is not *your* lack of restraint I fear, Belwyn."

Her words hit him. "I see." Another pause and then, "You do love me, don't you?"

"Yes, more than anything in my life," she answered and he saw a faint glistening of tears in her eyes.

"Except the magic." She did not reply. "I must say that I find it confusing, this need you have for the spells and illusions. You may not see it,

Morwyn, but the Powers have blessed you. Other women are forced to marry men they do not love, share their lives and their bodies with mates they fear or dislike in circumstances far more humble than this. I would have thought you would be overjoyed at the prospect of marriage to a man you care for, the father of your children, the heir to one of the oldest and most noble houses in the realm. Yet it does not suffice."

Tears were now slowly tracking down her cheeks.

"I wish that it would suffice, Belwyn." Her thick voice cracked at this admission.

"Why doesn't it?" he asked, pulling his hands out of her grasp, the hurt growing.

"I need to be …" she paused. *How do I explain this?*

"Yes?" He gave her no quarter.

"I need to be different, special," she replied. The words sounded hollow in her ears.

He sighed. "You are like the tale of the woman who refused to marry a poor man because she believed only riches would make her happy. Though his purse was not full of coins, it would not have mattered, for he would have treated her like a queen. Try as she might, she was not worthy enough for any rich man and so she never married. When she returned to beg the poor man's forgiveness, to accept his offer of marriage, she found him wed to another. She realized that the poor man's wife possessed a treasure she would never have – happiness. His love had provided what all the gold coins in the realm could not. In the end, the woman had nothing, neither riches nor love. "

"I will have my magic," Morwyn replied, defiantly.

He sighed and it almost sounded like his heart was breaking.

"And in the end, that will be nothing." He paused and then muttered, "I will make the preparations for two days hence." He left Morwyn to her tears.

SEVEN

When Morgan learned that Morwyn would be seeking a Writ of Divorcement after the wedding, he left before the ceremony, disconcerted. The news brought him no joy. Owain the Younger felt a similar foreboding and took the opportunity to journey back to his mistress' side. Ifor and Cara went with him. In the end, it was Owain the Elder, Pyrs, Gwyn and Dillan who stood as witnesses to a union none thought they would ever see.

The occasion was solemn and formal. The prelate conducting the ceremony could not help but feel the undercurrent of tension. He sensed love between the couple, but something stood in the way, something he could not fathom. He finished the service, declined the offer of food and left the holdings with sincere misgivings.

The evening repast after the ceremony was subdued and there was no celebration. Morwyn smiled, intermittently, as did Belwyn, but it was evident that not all was right with the couple. As Morwyn took her leave from the table to prepare for her wedding night, Gwyn walked beside her through the halls of the old building.

"This is most difficult, Gwyn," Morwyn murmured.

"I know, mother." *You have made it that way.*

"I will ask your father for a Writ of Divorcement and I take my leave in the morning." That did not seem to surprise her daughter.

Gwyn answered cryptically, "Mother, one must *rule* the magic, not allow the magic to rule you."

Morwyn gave her a confused look. "I do not understand."

"No, you do not and that is the problem." The girl's tone reminded her mother of the Ancient's One chiding voice and that irritated her. On the defensive, she took that opportunity to ask a question that had plagued her since the day she was injured.

"Why did you not put the protection spell on us at the hut *before* Braen wounded me? Why did you wait?"

Gwyn gave her mother a knowing look and replied, "Because you would have found a way to not tell Aderyn about us. Only if you were wounded would they learn of us. Am I not right?"

"It was my choice!"

Gwyn shook her head. "No, it was not. You waited too long to tell father of us."

Morwyn frowned but did not reply. Satisfied she had made her point, the girl left her mother standing alone, deep in thought.

Still you have not learned the lesson the Powers wish, Gwyn thought as she made her way to her own room. *How long will it take, mother? How long?*

Belwyn found Morwyn sitting by the fire combing her long hair, clad in a light shift. Her simple beauty struck him.

"Wife," he said, "you look very lovely tonight." Her eyes turned toward him and he could see she appreciated the compliment.

Morwyn did not hesitate. "And you never more handsome."

"Then come, let us lie in each other's arms, for it is our wedding night." Her eyes widened and he added, "I do not ask more than you can give, Morwyn."

She nodded and took her time coming to the bed. He joined her presently, pulled her to him and the memories of their only night together flooded through his brain. She fingered the locket around his neck.

"It is the swan's feather I found in my bed after the first time we lie together," he said, his voice thick. "I still can recollect bits and pieces of that night. I remember the loving, the pleasure and the passion, Morwyn." His eyes burned brightly.

"As do I." She was watching him intently. He pulled off the locket and set it aside, for in his mind he no longer needed to wear it. She was his and if he was fortunate she would not press her request for the divorcement.

"The memories of that night have kept me warm for many a year." He felt her slight nod and then a gentle kiss on his cheek. He so wished to love her, be with her as he had that night, to share his life with her. He sensed it was not to be.

"I love you, Belwyn, never doubt that." Her voice was laden with emotion.

"I know." He kissed her again, a more sensuous kiss, one full of promise and then he felt her body stiffen in his arms. He broke the kiss, tugged her into his arms and willed himself to stop wanting her. It was a difficult struggle, but eventually his mind overruled his passion and he fell asleep. Morwyn studied his face and felt nothing but emptiness.

I am different, her mind intoned while her heart begged her to wake her new husband and share his love fully. What was the magic to the loving they would share? Her mind reined back her heart and told her it must not happen. She rolled over on her side, out of Belwyn's arms, tears burning in her eyes. *I cannot, I cannot.*

As they sat in his room, Gwyn told Pyrs what he did not want to hear.

"Mother has not learned the lesson and will flee from the pain, just as she did the morning after we were conceived."

"She is as obstinate as I am," Pyrs remarked glumly as he sat on the edge of his bed swinging his feet back and forth.

"Yes, she is. Father has learned what the Powers wished, but not mother."

"Will it ever be otherwise?" her brother asked, his face begging for some semblance of hope.

Gwyn searched forward and shook her head. "I cannot see, Pyrs, it is too changeable." Her voice echoed her despair. Only with her twin could she be this open and honest.

"I pray that when I fall in love it will not be so, sister, for the pain our parents carry is more than I know I could bear."

Gwyn nodded solemnly and retreated to her own room.

Pyrs waited for his mother near the stable at dawn. He watched as the servants spread ashes from the hearths and collected wood to kindle the cooking fires. As time passed he slumped down on a wooden bench, digging his boot heel into the dry soil, waiting. His mother appeared just as his sister had foretold. Morwyn did not appear surprised, somehow she knew he would be here.

"Pyrs."

"Mother," he replied. His face was immensely sad and that tugged at Morwyn's heart. Her hand shaking, she handed him a rolled parchment secured by her silver wedding band.

"Give this to your father when he rises. It explains what I am doing and why." The document reiterated her love for him and formally asked for the Writ of Divorcement so that Belwyn would be free to remarry.

Pyrs nodded and then embraced his mother. "I will miss you, mother. Please keep yourself safe."

"I will, son." She broke the embrace and examined the boy's face. A pang shot through her heart – it was the face of the man asleep in their marital bed. "I am not sure where I will go. I dare not go back to the hut, Braen knows of that, and Ilspath is too close to his haunts."

"Gwyn told me to say you should *'ride as far south as you can and there you will be sorely needed.'* Those were her exact words."

Morwyn nodded with a sigh. "Gwyn sees more of the future than all of us. I pray she can find a way to heal your father."

"No, mother, only you can do that," Pyrs replied honestly. They embraced again and he helped his mother saddle a horse. By the time the sun was filtering through the trees Morwyn was on the path to the main road, leaving her children and her new husband behind.

After an uneventful journey, Owain the Younger arrived at Lady Aldyn's fortress at midday. Cadmon, Lady Aldyn's Master of the Guard, met him in the castle's courtyard and a smile of relief spread all over his face.

"Master Owain, it is indeed good to see you!" He shifted his gaze to the couple trailing behind Owain and appraised them with a knowing eye.

"Is all well, Cadmon?" Owain asked, anxious.

"Tolerable, sir. Lord Fercos is with our mistress at present, allegedly negotiating grain prices. To be honest, he's here for the food and for another attempt to angle himself into her bed."

"You would think he would tire of the pursuit, Cadmon," Owain replied darkly as he dismounted and pulled off his pack from the horse. Cara and Ifor followed suit and then stood waiting for orders.

"Not likely, sir." Owain began to stride toward the main entrance and then halted rather abruptly. In his overwhelming concern for his mistress he had forgotten the couple behind them. He made amends.

"Cadmon, this is Ifor and Cara. I am going to recommend that Cara become Lady Aldyn's seamstress. Ifor has battle training, he is an archer, and is an honorable man. I would appreciate if you could find work for his hands."

Cadmon nodded, he'd already deduced the man was a warrior by the way he carried himself.

"We have need of armed men. I will judge your skill and then make my decision." Ifor nodded his approval.

"So you are aware, Cadmon, I vouch for this couple's integrity. They have recently served my father's house in a matter of great import and acquitted themselves well." Ifor's eyebrow raised at this, surprised at the man's comment. He had felt sure Owain would tell others of what had fallen out with Braen and the children. It appeared that was past, at least in Owain's mind, and they had a start at a new life. He caught Cara's eyes and gave her a slight smile. She returned it.

"Follow me, Ifor, I'll show you to the warrior's barracks." Ifor gave his lover a slight squeeze on the shoulder and a warm smile and then set off with the Master of the Guard.

"Come on, Cara, I'll show you where Lady Aldyn spends her days," Owain offered and they continued their trek through the courtyard.

Lady Aldyn's voice sounded strained. "If we could return to the more important matter at hand, Lord Fercos. I am more concerned about the amount of grain we will have for this winter than whether or not I am wed by the first snowfall." She was sitting in a chair, ramrod straight, clearly uncomfortable with the man seated at her table. Her auburn hair was up in a bun and she wore one of her signature black gowns, though it was delicately edged in elegant silver lace. Barely twenty-six years of age, the years hung on her.

"But, Lady, surely you see they are connected," Fercos came back with a sly smile on his face. He was a middle-aged man with slightly greying hair, a widower with ambition and sporting an impressive paunch. He was clearly a master of the serving knife rather than of the sword.

"Do you suggest, sir, that grain is only available if I wed to your satisfaction?" she asked, her voice cloaked in frost.

"No, good lady, I do not suggest that at all," the man lied, though the falsehood was patently apparent for he had no skill to hide his thoughts. "However, you would not need to worry about such issues if you had a husband to handle such things."

Aldyn's patience was at an end. "I am quite capable of handling the affairs of my subjects, Lord Fercos."

"As you are, Lady, but it is still a strain that women are not meant to bear," he replied in a condescending tone.

She gave him a narrow look. "The Powers have decried that women must bear children, sir, and from what I see, my task is much easier than a woman lying in her birthing bed."

"That I would not know, Lady," Fercos came back smoothly.

"Let us return to the matter of the grain. What is the price you ask for twenty wagon loads to be delivered to my holdings?" The man quoted a figure and Aldyn frowned.

"That is too high, sir. Far too high."

"We may be willing to negotiate that figure, Lady, providing certain conditions are met in regard to …"

"Lady Aldyn, I apologize, I was delayed on the road!" Owain the Younger skillfully sliced through the other man's mandate, sweeping forward into the room with a decided flourish. He knelt on one knee beside his mistress' chair and delivered a deep bow.

"Councilor, it is good to see you have returned. I trust nothing of an ill nature befell you," Aldyn replied politely, only her strong self-control keeping the look of consummate relief off her face.

"Some issues that were difficult at the time, milady, but all is well resolved."

"That is excellent news. Would you sit and dine with us?" she asked. She sensed Lord Fercos displeasure at Owain's presence and was keen to press the advantage.

"I am fresh from the road, Lady, and not fit for company until I bathe," Owain demurred, knowing what his mistress would do.

"No, sit and eat. There is plenty of food and I would like your opinion on these outrageous grain prices Lord Fercos is quoting."

"As you wish, my lady." A servant appeared with a chair and he set himself next to his mistress as a plate, cup and utensils appeared over one shoulder. Owain the Younger turned his attention to the disgruntled lord across the table from him.

"And now, Lord Fercos, what was that price? No doubt you meant for *two* wagon loads, not one." He felt a sharp kick impact his leg under the table, courtesy of his mistress. He barely kept the smirk off his face. Lord Fercos departed shortly thereafter, obviously displeased with the precipitous return of the lady's councilor.

"Ill timing," he muttered as he hefted himself up on his horse and left the castle proper.

Once Fercos left, Owain bowed to his mistress and swept out of the room, obviously pleased with himself. The nobles had yet to learn that Aldyn had a backbone of steel. They thought if they harried her long enough she would acquiesce and marry one of them. It was not to be.

Mair, Lady Aldyn's personal maid, was waiting for him in the corridor outside the dining room. She was an older woman with thick silver hair and a merry look on her face.

"Welcome home, Master Owain."

"Thank you, Mair." He spied Cara standing quietly by herself, waiting as he had instructed.

"Mair, this is Cara. She is a seamstress and I would like to recommend she sew for Lady Aldyn." Mair had already spoken with the young woman and learned her purpose at the holdings, but she allowed Owain the right of introduction.

"Certainly, sir. Come, Cara, I will show you where you will sleep and the room in which you will work."

"Thank you." Cara turned for a half a second to Owain and smiled. "Bless, you, sir." Owain just winked. At that Jestin, his page, appeared at his elbow.

"Sir, I have water heating for you." The boy was all of fifteen, full of energy and possessed a keen sense of humor.

"Excellent, Jestin. I am in sore need of a hot bath and some rest. I am more than weary." The young boy scooted off ahead of Owain as he strode through the halls. As he passed various servants along the way to his chambers, cautious smiles began to appear on their faces. They knew that as long as Owain the Younger stood at their mistress' side, all would be well.

The swirling darkness did not leave him until he found his hands awash in blood. He did not remember what had happened, but now he stood over the body of a woman, her throat cut. Her husband lay dead only a few steps away, in his bed. He had been asleep when the wounded viper in their midst struck them down.

Braen examined his hands in an attempt to piece together a memory of the deed. The woman's voice echoed in his ears and then another one, that of her daughter. He glanced around but did not see a third body. They had cared for him, he thought, attempted to heal him of his vicious burns. Now they were dead and the blood on his hands felt like a soothing balm. Kneeling painfully by the woman, Braen cut off a switch of her long dark hair and tied it to his belt with a cord. His left hand was badly burnt, almost claw-like, yet he still accomplished the task. His injuries did not allow him to do more to her, for his days of having any women he wanted were gone, destroyed by the dragon's fire. Somehow the violence he had bestowed on her was compensation for that loss. *Almost enough*, he thought.

He heard the door to the small hut creak open as the daughter of the house returned from collecting firewood. His eyes turned on her and the darkness returned. Only her quickness saved her. She dropped the wood in a heap and fled into the forest in screaming panic at the sight of her parents' bodies. He could not run fast enough to catch her, to cut her as he had her mother and add yet another long hank of hair to his belt. As the darkness faded he limped out of the hut into the forest with no clear direction in mind, only the need to ease the unquenchable pain within him.

€iGhT

Caewlin, Iarel of the Red Hawk Clan, found himself in the unholy position of executing a raid on one of the Northern villages along the seacoast. This was not to his liking. The Southern Isle Clans had remained apart from the Northerners for centuries and only fate and the whimsy of the Gods had forced them together. Separated by the sea, he and his people occupied one of the numerous islands in an archipelago that served as home for over three-thousand clan members. Divided into five distinct groups, they had dwelt on their respective islands time out of memory and had always flourished. Then for some inexplicable reason, the Gods removed their favor and the clans no longer prospered, perishing in great numbers in the wake of unrelenting famine.

In the end, Caewlin had no choice. He had been instrumental in pushing for trade with the Northerners when it was learned their lands did not suffer the same drought as did the isles. Two of the five iarels did not wish to trade, preferring war. Caewlin had successfully argued for peace and so bartering became the lifeline for his people. The clans' rich store of animal pelts traded for food kept his people alive as the drought drug on for yet another year.

Erc, the impetuous and quarrelsome iarel of the Badger Clan started the war with the Northerners by plundering some of the smaller villages near the seacoast. The lure of food, women and goods fired his lust for battle. He bragged that someday he would sack the fortified city of Kell, though all knew it was just a boast. In retaliation for his raids trade was suspended and Lord Phelan, Kell's master, set his warriors loose on the southern clans. The result was the progressive decimation of their people. Now, over two years later, only a third of the clansmen survived, some twelve-hundred starving men, women and children.

Caewlin's men did not know that he wept in his furs at night over the deaths of his kin. They did not know how he offered prayers for the starving children. Nor did they know he had asked the Gods to take him as sacrifice to save his people. The Gods did not heed his pleas and now he was forced to make this raid or his people would perish.

I am no better than Erc, he thought, *I have failed my people.*

As he stood on the prow of his longship, his tawny blonde hair flowing free in the light breeze, he was summoned out of his dark reverie by a red-tailed hawk. It caught his attention immediately and that of most of the clansmen in the other longboats as well. It swooped low over them and settled on the carved hawk prow of his ship, glaring at him with its intense eyes. It paused as if surveying its kingdom, preened a feather, and then took wing again, floating low over the boats. It sailed across the rock-strewn beach and into the verdant forest beyond, a blur of crimson on the silken mist.

"By the Gods, did you see that?" his second-in-command asked. Nerian was an older man, stocky and dark skinned, one of the fiercest fighters in the clan. He had served Caewlin's father and now stood at the young iarel's side to offer guidance and his might with the sword.

"Yes, I did. A very good omen, I should think," Caewlin answered softly, keeping his voice low.

"A very good omen. Today will bring us the provisions we need to keep the children fed this winter," a tall young man standing near them commented. Galen served as Saga, or bard, for the clan. He had requested permission to travel with his iarel on this raid to see the land of the Northern pagans. He wished to write ballads about the land and its people. The trip proved difficult for him, he was no seaman, but his presence had made the voyage seem shorter through his songs and storytelling.

"Let us pray you are right, Galen. I would gladly have this be our only voyage to this place. There is something unsettling about this land." *As unsettling as the death we are about to unleash upon them,* he thought grimly.

"As it should be, Iarel, for they do not worship the Gods as we do." The voice belonged to Devona, the priestess, seated only a short distance away on a low chair, her multihued robes tucked around her. Though young for a priestess, she was held in awe by her people, even by their leader. It was her choice where they landed their ships, when they could return and what sacrifices they would have to make to appease the Gods that ruled the waters. If the deities were not pleased their longships would wander and never reach their hearth and home. Devona was possessed with sharp eyes and a sharper intellect. She understood her power and wielded it judiciously, for a Wise. She knew that their leader was a believer, though his father, Brecc, had not been. Brecc was with his ancestors now some fifteen moons and young Caewlin was iarel, though he was barely twenty-years-old. The Gods had chosen their leader and it was her task to aid him so that he might understand Their will. She knew his fears and the dread he held in his heart, that he would be the last iarel as his people vanished from this world.

"Is it time yet, Wise?" Caewlin asked. She stood near him now, a power staff in her thin hands. It was adorned with hawk feathers and the small shells from their isle.

"It is time, the Red Hawk has given us Her blessing."

Caewlin raised his hand to signal the other ships. He shifted his eyes back toward Devona for a moment and said quietly, "Let us pray this is our last raid." The woman nodded, she had no taste for the bloodshed, whether their foes were barbarians or not. It was not their clan's way, but now they had no choice.

The morning mist proved to be their ally as they struck at the village located a short distance from the shore. It was a hamlet of some size and until today had remained untouched by the vicious Southern warriors' raids. The alarm was raised when the village's pack of hounds began to bark incessantly, but by that time the raiders were already in their midst. Men fell as they rose from their beds even before they could reach their weapons. Women snatched up their children and fled to the relative safety of the forest. The cries of the dying intermingled with the wails of children as the clansmen moved like a wave through the village.

Caewlin did not participate in the plundering and though he understood the necessity, it sickened him nonetheless. His morals resented stealing, even to keep his people alive. Nevertheless, the food was desperately needed and in some way the raid would allow his men to feel they were doing something for their families. He had warned them to avoid random butchery, for it only sullied their souls. He also urged them to treat the Northern women with decency and for the most part almost all complied. He knew some of the healthier and prettier woman would be taken captive and returned to their isle. If they survived the trip and adjusted to the life within the Red Hawk Clan, marriages would no doubt occur. Many of the clansmen had lost their mates and sought women to share their furs and care for their orphaned children.

He strode around the center of the village, staying clear of the fighting, keeping his eye on the flow of the battle. The smell of fresh blood assailed him and he felt nauseous. As he continued his trek he heard an impassioned shout and turned his eyes toward the sound. Fyren, one of his men, had just stabbed a villager and he had fallen to the ground in the arms of a woman, no doubt his mate. As Fyren reached down to grab her, he jerked his hand back yelping in pain. Blood ran from a deep wound on his arm for the woman had taken her mate's sword and risen to stand over him, striking their attacker a strong blow.

Before Caewlin could react, Fyren howled in rage and swung his blade at the woman, intent on beheading her. She deftly ducked his vicious swipe, holding her ground while cursing in her language. The heavy cloak she wore fell to the ground revealing torrents of long red hair and a belly swollen with child. Her next blow barely missed the clansman and he lurched back, surprised at the intensity of her attack. He eyed her, noted her condition, and instead of leaving her to tend her fallen mate, he moved forward, intent on possessing the red-haired pagan. Caewlin knew this warrior's habits all too well; he was not a man of honor and had an unchecked desire for women.

As the iarel strode toward them, he shouted across the din of the battle, "Fyren!"

The sound of his name broke the warrior's concentration and he stepped back, turning toward his leader.

"Iarel," the clansman replied, eyeing him, though he did execute a very slight bow.

Caewlin judged the situation and it proved difficult. He could not tolerate any harm to befall the woman and yet the moment he opened his mouth to order Fyren to leave, he changed his mind. Fyren had little respect for the iarel and no doubt would wait until Caewlin's attention was elsewhere and then return to claim the pagan as his own. Given this particular clansman's dislike of Northerners he would no doubt kill her after he had finished with her. Caewlin's mind raced to determine a means to protect the defiant fire-haired female who stood over her wounded man and defended him even as his lifeblood poured into the ground at her bare feet.

"I claim her as clan-gild, Fyren." The warrior's face erupted into an angry frown but he had to back off. It was clan law – one of higher rank could claim any plunder he chose, including the female in front of them.

"As you command, Iarel," Fyren replied with a slight snarl to his voice. He stepped further back, gave another half bow and then strode further into the village, seeking a new victim.

The woman looked puzzled, but he noted that her guard did not drop. Caewlin moved within a few paces of where she stood and observed the scene more closely. It was clear that the wound to her mate's chest was mortal. The man feebly moved his hands, trying to rise in a futile attempt to protect his wife and unborn child. The gesture struck Caewlin in the heart.

They are so like us, they care for the same things in life.

He moved his eyes back up to the woman and found a seething expression of anger and fear. She still gripped the sword firmly as the other hand, red with her husband's blood, lay on her bulging belly as if in protection.

Caewlin shook his head and sheathed his sword to indicate he meant no harm. He had a dilemma, for though he had stopped Fyren's advances he could not stand next to her for much longer. His fellow clansmen would prize her fiery red hair, for women such as her were rarely seen. To return to the isles with such a woman as a potential mate would significantly raise a man's stature within the clan. He knew that it would not happen without her being injured, for it was plain she would fight any man who came near. She feared them all and given the situation, he could not blame her.

The sound of the battle shifted and he cast a wary eye around him. The clansmen were clearly victorious and goods were now moving in a steady line toward the ships. He had taken too much time with this female, for she was not clan, and his attention was not where it should be. Cursing himself for his fixation, he half turned to leave her to whatever fate her gods would decree. At that moment a slight breeze stirred through the village fanning the fires, causing the woman's long waist-length hair to float around her in a cloud of scarlet. In Caewlin's mind it called up the image of the Red Hawk gliding on the wind. It suddenly became clear to him why their clan deity had appeared to them in such a way. He reached under his heavy leather tunic to pull out the amulet that lay on his chest, one with a flying hawk upon it, the symbol of his people. He slowly removed the amulet, kissed it in reverence and held it toward the sky in acknowledgement of the power that lived within it. He paused for only a moment and then cast it at the bare woman's feet. She lurched back, involuntarily, and stared at him, confused. The sword sunk a bit in her hand, for no doubt her arm ached from the weight of the weapon and the battle with Fyren.

Forgetting she did not speak his language, Caewlin tried to explain, "It is the seal of our clan. If you wear it, no one will harm you." The woman only looked puzzled as the sounds of the battle died down around them. Caewlin's conscience pricked at him. He needed to be with his men so he pointed to the amulet on the ground, indicating she should pick it up.

"You must wear it. It will keep you safe!" he tried again, realizing she understood none of his speech. He cursed himself for never having learned the pagan language. She frowned and then gingerly fished the amulet off the ground with the tip of her sword, only shifting her eyes to the item at the last moment. She pulled the object off the end of the blade and studied it intensely. Caewlin repeated the donning movement, his face more anxious now. Her frown deepened but she did not do his bidding.

"Iarel!" Nerian's voice called across the compound as he strode to stand by his leader's side. He spied the sacred amulet in the Northern woman's hand and his eyes widened.

"What is it?" Caewlin snapped back, his mind in turmoil.

Nerian shot his leader a look and then announced, "The ships are being loaded and it is time to leave."

"How has it gone?" Caewlin asked, his mind pricking at him that he had not been much of a leader this day.

"It has gone well." Nerian studied the pagan woman for a moment and asked, "What is this, Iarel?" It suddenly dawned on him what iarel's intention might be. "Is it your wish she come with you to share your furs?"

Caewlin's mind raced through that possibility and he knew the answer. He shook his head.

"No. The Red Hawk has shown me this woman must wear the amulet so none will harm her. She does not understand me and I cannot speak their language."

Nerian's eyebrow raised at that and then he thought for a moment, struggling to pull forward what few words of the Northern speech he could remember. He uttered a couple quick phrases and the woman's eyes darted to him. She quickly asked a question and Nerian answered in fragments of sentences. The frown began to evaporate and she nodded.

"I have told her what she must do to keep from being taken to our isle, if that be the Red Hawk's wish."

Keeping the sword in one hand, the woman pulled the amulet on and let it fall on her chest. Caewlin contemplated her dark eyes for a few more moments, smiled, nodded his head in approval and then strode away, Nerian at his side. None of his men would dare touch her now that she wore the amulet of the clan, to do so would cause their immediate execution. Even Fyren would fear that, so in his own way Caewlin had saved a pagan woman from possible defilement and death. It seemed right.

It is Her will, he thought as he glanced upward hoping to catch sight of his clan's deity. She was not in the air above them and so he worked his way back toward the shore. His men were in the process of loading the goods and livestock onto the boats, along with the wailing women who chosen to return to the clansite. There were perhaps ten in all, his men had indeed restrained themselves. Fyren trudged to a nearby ship laden with a sack of grain on his shoulder. He had a gloating look in his eye and his face badly scratched. As he hefted the sack aboard he boasted to one of the men of what sport he'd found ashore. Nerian snapped at him, ordering him into the longboat, suspecting what evil the man had performed while in the village.

As Fyren climbed aboard he caught sight of the iarel standing on the shore, alone. The red-haired woman was nowhere in sight, either on the shore or in any of the ships. The clansman furrowed his face into a frown and glanced back toward the village, hesitating. Another sack of plunder was thrust into his hands and he became part of chain of men moving the goods from the shore to the boat. He grudgingly complied, his eyes fuming, loathe to leave such a valuable woman behind.

Caewlin kept his eyes on his men and watched as the steady stream of goods were loaded and packed down for the voyage. Nerian gave him a satisfied nod and Caewlin returned it. The ships were filling rapidly and he knew the men had not taken everything they had found. He had ordered that food be left behind so those in the village would not know the gnawing hunger his people had endured for the past two years.

We must survive this and return to ways of peace or this life will taint us forever. Fyren's kind will become our way of life. We must survive this.

He shifted his gaze back toward the village. Many of the huts were burning and the flames shot high into the air, causing swirls in the mist that now hovered near the tops of the trees. He squinted and in the distance he saw that the red-haired woman still stood over her mate, one hand on the sword, the other on the amulet around her neck. Any clansman who came near her retreated immediately. Though puzzled, none questioned how the amulet came to be in her possession and they returned to the ships. None would dare ask the iarel, so they held their silence.

As the longships left the shore and headed along the coastline to where they would turn south, into the sea, Caewlin stood alone on the prow of the lead ship and pondered what madness had overtaken him this day. He had resolved to have Orva teach him the Northerner's language, but that was not the cause of his uneasiness. It was deeper and more personal. He felt a presence near him and knew it was Galen.

"The Red Hawk spoke to you today, Iarel," the man said quietly. "To save one of Her own may turn our fortune," the Saga observed.

"It is my prayer," Caewlin replied. He found it odd that Galen considered the pagan woman one of the Hawk's *own*. Apparently, the man had witnessed his actions within the village.

As if Galen knew his thoughts, he explained, "As the Red Hawk protects her mate and her young, so did the fire-haired pagan."

Caewlin nodded solemnly.

The Saga observed, "The tale does not end here, Iarel." He turned at that and wove his way back through the men and the goods in the boat, his mind intrigued by the twist of fate the Gods had sent his leader this day.

As swiftly as they had come, the clansmen were gone, their ships weighted down with the chattel of the village. Slowly the inhabitants returned to their burning huts and began to tend to their wounded, determine who was missing and begin the sad task of burying their dead. Women were sobbing at the sight of their slain or wounded mates, children were crying in shock and in the middle of it all, Aithne still stood watch over her husband. When she realized that the invaders had departed she knelt down, took her man's head into her arms and held him as he slowly passed beyond. As he died he reached out to touch his child in her belly. Her weeping soon joined the others.

She prepared him for burial and built a cairn of stones over his body, offering prayers and laying flowers to call the Powers to his grave so that his soul would not be allowed to wander. Her hut was intact so she made ready for the birthing that was due within the next moon. She salvaged what food she could, hunted in the forest to bring down hares and then dried the meat against the time when she would not be well enough to hunt. All the while she worked alone, no words of comfort or assistance coming from her fellow villagers. They had noted the tall blonde leader of the Southern horde gave her some talisman that had protected her. Though her husband had died, she had not been spirited away as had some of the other women. Distrust grew and they began to speak against her.

The child did not wait the full month and labor began one week, to the day, after the raid. She bore the infant in the middle of the night, alone, and cared for him as best she could for he was weak from the moment of his birth. As she drifted off into deep sleep, her newborn lying in her arms, she felt the warm weight of the amulet that lie on her chest, nestled between her milk-laden breasts.

The parchment in his hands announced something joyous, at least in his mind, but he knew nothing but sadness had come from it.

"Owain, is there something wrong at Aderyn?" Lady Aldyn asked, sensing the young man's change in attitude and knowing the letter was from his brother. They sat in her chambers late one evening, Mair nearby mending linens.

"Belwyn and Morwyn have married," he announced.

"But surely that is good news!" Aldyn replied, puzzled at his melancholy tone. He had given her a full report of the events that had kept him from her side, but had not mentioned that his brother and Morwyn were intending to wed.

"It is, but she departed Aderyn the morning after the ceremony leaving behind a note asking for a Writ of Divorcement."

"Why?" Aldyn asked, puzzled. "I thought she loved him! She could do no better than your brother, for he is a good and honorable man."

"Belwyn says that she feared being near him, that she would not be able to keep her vow of celibacy as required by the magic."

"That is sad. How is he handling this?" Aldyn asked, concern in her voice.

"As well as can be expected. He loves her, there is no one else for him, so he has refused the divorce."

"Did she return to her hut near the lake?"

"No, Pyrs reported that she was headed south."

"Will the Powers never allow those two any peace?" she mused.

"I don't know, milady. At least Belwyn has the children." He studied the parchment a moment longer and said, "It appears Gwyn will go the Circle of the Swan to be with the adepts. I would suppose they will be training her as they once trained her mother."

"And Pyrs?"

"Aderyn has taken over his education. My brother writes that Pyrs has much to learn, but he possesses a keen mind so he masters things quite quickly. It appears he still has not addressed Belwyn as *father*."

"They are not close?" Aldyn asked.

"No, but apparently the rift is being healed each day."

"Good." Her eyes moved over toward two stacks of fabric near her. One was light green and the other rust brown, carefully chosen by her councilor, with Cara's assistance.

"I trust you find the fabric to your liking, milady," Owain hedged. She had been stunned by the gift and that had pleased him immensely.

"It is very rich, Owain."

"The brown will look particularly good, milady," Mair offered, aware of the councilor's gambit to encourage the young woman to cease wearing mourning gowns.

"I don't know." Aldyn's voice was unsure.

"Lady, please, something other than black," Owain pleaded and his mistress conceded at a warm smile at that. She reached out and stroked the fabric again and this time her fingers lingered.

"It was very kind of you to think of me, Owain," she said softly. He gave her a broad smile, rose to take his leave and executed a deep bow.

"I always think of you, milady." Once the door closed behind him, Mair walked over to examine the fabrics.

"They *are* very fine, my lady."

"Yes, they are. I cannot understand what drove him to buy them for me."

"You cannot?" Mair asked, a hint of amusement in her old eyes.

Aldyn gave her a startled look and shook her head. "No, Mair, it is not that. He is a like a brother to me."

"If that is what you want to believe, milady." The servant hoisted up the two piles of fabric and carried them from the room without further comment.

Aldyn shook her head again. "No, that is not the reason. It cannot be …"

Gwyn's prophecy came true in a way that unnerved her mother. '*Ride as far south as you can and there you will be sorely needed,*' was what the girl had said. Morwyn did exactly as instructed, riding for almost two weeks on the main road from Ilspath south to the old seaport of Kell. She rode through Kell's massive wooden gates and stopped, for beyond the city lie the sea.

Her first day in Kell found her at an inn, one called The Old Port. She had sufficient coin with her so she purchased a hot meal and a small room to allow her time to become acquainted with the city. There was an undercurrent here, one she could not quite fathom. Though bustling with trade and activity, there was a sickness beneath the surface of Kell, an illness of the spirit that claimed the lives of the poor, the ill and the unwary. She saw no beggars, a common sight in Ilspath, and found that odd. For a time she thought Kell was so prosperous that all found work upon which to set their hands. The innkeeper dissuaded her of that notion as she took her meal in the corner of his common room.

"There are few beggars in Kell, madam, because they are not encouraged." The innkeeper appeared anxious to be speaking about such things in the common room within earshot of the other guests.

"I see," Morwyn replied. "Is there a House of Healing in this city?"

The man nodded and refilled her cup. "Yes, there is." He was not like any innkeeper she'd ever met. Most were brimming with information and far too eager to share it with any soul they could pin down. This one was reticent and nervous.

"Thank you, innkeeper." She ate her food and tried to observe the others in the room without being obvious. A wide range of merchants were present, most from the North, though some wore the more characteristic shades of brown the citizens of Kell seemed to favor. There was a table full of men near the front door who were progressively becoming louder as they fell further into their cups. By their clothes they appeared to be city guards. A nobleman and his wife rose and left the room as soon as they finished eating, apparently uncomfortable with the guards' presence.

As the guards grew more raucous, singing and jesting with each other as they called for more ale, Morwyn kept her eyes down, sensing the need to return to her room as quickly as possible after her repast. A jarring voice broke her reverie.

"Woman, are you available for sport?" the voice asked. She looked up into the bloodshot eyes of a guard, one of those from the far table. He was an older man and deep in his cups.

"No, sir, I am not available. I am not a sporting wench."

The man laughed and noisily dropped a single copper coin on the table near her plate of dark bread. A street wench would have been insulted by the pittance the man offered. He adopted a wide stance with his hands on his hips as if to accentuate his manliness.

"All women are available if the coins are sufficient."

"Sir, I am not …" Morwyn began as the innkeeper materialized from nowhere and reclaimed the coin off the table. He genially put his arm around the guard and walked him out of the inn, talking the entire time, not allowing him the option of growing angry. The innkeeper returned a few minutes later, alone, and gestured for Morwyn to follow him.

"Come, it will be safer for you in kitchen." He scooped up her dishes as she took her cup of ale and her belongings and they walked back to the kitchen area. A small wooden table sat in the corner and he placed her food there. Serving girls hurried by them, delivering full plates of food into the common room and then returning with the dirty dishes. Once Morwyn sat down the man's attitude abruptly changed.

"I am Benen, innkeeper of this house. I am sorry you were troubled like that." His voice sounded sincere and he stuck out his thick hand in greeting.

She smiled, gave his hand a shake and replied, "I am Morwyn and I thank you for your assistance. Apparently, your customs are different in Kell. A man would not proposition a woman in such a manner in Ilspath, at least not in a common room."

"Things are very different here, Morwyn." He pulled up a chair and asked one of the serving girls to bring him ale. She scooted off and the drink appeared at his elbow almost immediately.

Sensing a more open attitude she asked, "Perhaps you can explain why this city feels so … odd."

"Kell was once like Ilspath …" he paused and glanced around the kitchen. The only people near them were his servants. "It was once a good place to live. It is now a place of illness and death. It is as if the Powers have cursed it."

"How did this come to be?" she asked and then began to eat some of the dark bread.

"It changed when Lord Phelan came to power. He is a greedy man and a dangerous one. He has taken to cleansing the city of any that he deems are unfit. Beggars are killed by the city guards and if anyone should attempt to aid them, they are burnt to death in the city square."

"Powers!" Morwyn's mouth fell open. "That is unholy!"

Benen nodded in agreement. "That is the best way to explain Kell. It is unholy."

"Benen, we need you!" a tall blonde serving girl called. "One of the guards has decided he wishes to be with Meara and she does not find him to her liking," Benen sighed.

"I should just escort the whole lot of them down the street to the brothel. They are not fit for my girls." He rose and left Morwyn to her food amidst the noise and pungent smells of the busy kitchen.

The child perished as little ones often do. No matter the healing skills Aithne possessed, the infant sickened and died. At no time did her fellow villagers offer to help her. They continued to shun her and spat at her as she walked amongst them. She carried her month-old baby to the place where her husband lie in his grave and buried the child, placing a small cairn of stones upon him. She intoned prayers and offered flowers, unable to comprehend why the Powers had been so cruel to rob her of both her mate and her newborn son. She tried not to believe the villager's malicious voices, though they did not speak to her directly. *It was the will of the Powers that her child died,* they said, *her punishment for the favor shown by the Southern heathen,* they murmured. She ignored them for she knew nothing would bring her son or her husband back to life. Once the burial rites were complete, she dusted the dirt off her hands and returned to her hut to grieve in private. She saw no further reason to remain here, this was her husband's village, not hers. She knew she must set aside her grief and leave this place behind.

The report of Erc's death reached Caewlin only four weeks after his raid, the one during which he saved the pagan woman. One of Erc's men had escaped in a small boat and made the perilous journey across the open sea to report the massacre. Caewlin set sail with five of his ten longships in hope of finding more survivors. His men rowed when the wind did not move them fast enough and they covered the distance between his clansite and Erc's in half the usual time. Fear and anger drove them.

Phelan's men had decimated the clan's holdings. Huts and tents were ablaze, shrines defiled and livestock slaughtered. All of Badger Clan's ships lay burning where they sat moored in the wide harbor. Caewlin strode through the site, his eyes stinging from the smoke of the still smoldering fires. His men were wary, swords drawn, unsure if any of the attackers remained.

"Iarel, where are the dead?" Nerian asked, unnerved by the absence of bodies.

Caewlin stopped and ran his eyes over the scene. Despite the devastation there were no corpses. He strode to where Erc's hall stood in the center of the clansite. It was untouched though there was a thick trail of blood on the threshold. He frowned at that and halted abruptly, the hair rising on the back of his neck. Nerian dispatched ten of his men to reconnoiter the building, lest it be a trap. The clansmen entered but no sounds of battle came forth for there was no enemy within. As they exited the hall, their faces told of something far worse.

"My iarel," one of the men said and fell on his knees in shock, his face ashen grey. He was one of the more seasoned fighters, older than the rest. His companions shared the haunted look on his face. Caewlin gave Nerian a quick glance and marched into the hall that had once served as center of the Badger Clan's life.

The sound of buzzing flies and the rank stench of death filled the iarel's nose and he swallowed to keep his gorge from rising. Erc's body was secured to the center pole, hideously mutilated. He had not died as a clansman should, with a sword in his hand, but at the torturous hands of Phelan's men. Caewlin's eyes tracked down, for though Erc's body was disturbing to view, it was those below that caught his attention. Those adults not bound in chains on Phelan's ships were lying in a great heap at the base of Erc's pole. Caewlin's mind could not calculate how many dead lay there, but he knew Erc's clan was once over five-hundred strong. He estimated that at least two-hundred corpses lie at their iarel's feet, as if in sacrifice. The sight was chilling, but that was not what caused his men to stumble out of the hall in profound shock.

"Iarel ..." it was Nerian's voice and he pointed into the gloom of the hall. Caewlin's eyes followed the man's outstretched arm. The sun was pouring through one of the open windows, the heavy leather covering tied back. The shaft of light struck a far corner, as if guiding them there.

"By the Gods!" He moved nearer and then stopped, unable to conceive of the horror his eyes beheld.

"The children," Nerian murmured and he fell to his knees on the blood-soaked earth. An immense pile of corpses lay in the far corner, all children ranging in age from one day to eight years. All of them had their throats cut. One little girl clutched her baby brother to her in death. Another little boy was holding a mongrel puppy, no doubt trying to flee with it when the butchers killed them both. The bodies lay entangled as if thrown onto the heap in careless abandon.

Caewlin's strength fled him and he fell to his knees in the bloody dirt of the hall. It was unthinkable for an iarel to weep in front of his men, for it was an unforgivable sign of weakness. He wept without reserve. Sobs racked him and though he did not know it, his men arrayed themselves on their knees behind him, grieving as one. They remained there, grieving, as the sunlight tracked away from the dead children. Where war encompassed adults, it was unthinkable to slaughter a child. That was not the clan way. Yet, Phelan had indiscriminately ordered his men to kill any child too young to work as a slave. He had struck at the very heart of the clans by killing their future.

Caewlin rose slowly, his tears vented, his cold fury swelling. He pulled his knife and walked toward the pile of corpses. Turning so his men could see him clearly, he cut the fleshy part of his left palm with the blade causing blood to flow instantly.

"They are now of our blood," he said and began to drop his life essence on the nearest corpses, claiming them as their own.

Nerian strode forward, pulled his knife and did the same, repeating, "They are now of our blood."

Men followed, some sixty of them, and each made the vow, casting their blood on the dead children, uniting the bodies into the Red Hawk Clan. Caewlin moved to where the other bodies lie below Erc and claimed them as well. As he strode out of the building his men repeated the gesture and then assembled at his side some distance from the hall. He looked at their shattered faces wet with tears, each man's left palm stained with their lifeblood.

He stood silent for the time, sensing that their lives had changed. He sought the strength of his ancestors, praying that wisdom and courage would infuse him.

"Their enemies are ours, their blood now mingled with our clan. We will avenge their deaths, even to the smallest child. I make this vow to the Gods and to the Red Hawk," Caewlin's voice sung through the air. He nodded to Nerian and commanded, "Fire the hall, let the dead ascend to the Gods so They can see who has done this deed. In that way may They come to our aid as we hunt and kill without mercy." Nerian nodded and with the aid of two of his men they set fire to the structure, intoning prayers for the dead as the brilliant flames marched up the outer walls.

The flames were still visible some distance out to sea as the great hall burned into the dark night. They found only a handful of survivors, enough for barely one longship. The rest were dead or enslaved. Caewlin kept his eyes on the burning hall as long as he could see it in the distance across the sea and then finally turned toward the bow of the ship.

"How many did we bring home with us, Nerian?"

"Four hands and three, my iarel." Nerian answered. Twenty-three.

"By the Gods," Caewlin intoned and fell silent.

He sent messengers to the other three clans informing them of the destruction of the Badger Clan and how it had come to pass. He warned them to be wary as their clansites lay closer to Phelan's holdings than did his. The iarels responded and set guards further afield, cognizant that the fate of the Badger Clan could well encompass them. He did not tell the other iarels everything he knew. He had learned that Badger Clan's holiest relic was gone, stolen by Phelan and his men. Ironically, it was not one of the Badger Clan that told him, but Devona, the Wise.

"I do not understand," he said, for he did not. She spoke of some mythical Stone and its power.

"I saw it in my vision. I saw the butchery at Erc's clansite. I saw it all. The Stone was claimed by our enemy even as you sailed to Badger Clan's harbor."

"But what is this relic? Surely you are not speaking of what the legends call a Stone of Summoning?"

Devona nodded solemnly. "That is what I speak of."

"No, that can't be." His voice was full of awe and dread. She nodded again. "Gods!" Caewlin's brown eyes widened. "But that means ..." His mouth could not say the words.

Devona pronounced their doom for him. "If our enemy learns what the Stone is capable of, he will summon an Old One and bind it to his will."

"Gods!" Caewlin repeated, quieter now. "But surely there are none of their kind left now. They are of the old legends."

"Legends all have some basis in truth."

Caewlin fixed her strange eyes with his and asked the burning question.

"Are there any of their kind alive, Wise?"

Her slight nod confirmed his worst fears.

nine

Impassive at the bloodied and battered prisoner secured to the wooden table in front of him, the young lord's resonate voice remarked calmly, "I had thought this one beyond your talents."

"There are few that can hold out the length of my patience, milord," his subordinate replied as he washed his bloody hands in a bucket of cold water. Once his hands were toweled dry by a servant he took the bucket of water and delivered his master a distinct look of warning.

Lord Phelan moved himself some distance back and watched as the cold water flew over the prisoner, jarring him from his stupor. The water ran in torrents over the man's broken body, washing some of the blood and burnt flesh off him in one motion. Phelan returned to stand near the prisoner, an older man. The only part of him that was whole was his tongue, for that was the most important part.

"Tell me what that stone is."

The man began to babble in the Southern dialect and that occasioned a blow on the face from his torturer. The man stopped and began again in the Northern tongue.

"It is an egg," the man said, staggered at his weakness. Once they discovered he spoke the Northern tongue the torture had lasted days beyond his reckoning. Now he had no choice, he could no longer tolerate the agony, the burning and the mutilation. He begged his Gods to forgive him, accept his weakness of mind and body.

"It is solid, you fool!" Phelan growled back and scowled menacingly. His torturer did not strike the man again, there was no need. Pain must be administered in precise doses. He knew the prisoner would speak if given the time.

A silence ensued and then, "It is an egg ... that did not hatch." That did not make much sense to the impatient lord. He stared down at the small cold object clutched in his hand. He could easily close it within his fist and yet it never grew warm from his touch.

"So why do your people venerate it, die for it?" Just days before he had watched in amazement as fifty Southern clansmen fought and died to protect the cold grey orb. When they had fallen, women had moved in the way of his troops' swords, dying in great bloody heaps to keep the cold orb from him. The thing had value, fifty warriors' lives worth of value. He just needed to know why.

"It is from Them," the man muttered through cracked and bleeding lips. "It is the way you summon Them."

"Summon *who?*" Phelan pressed. The stench of the tortured man rose up to meet him and he unconsciously swallowed to keep from being physically ill.

"Them ... ddraig."

Phelan thought for a moment and then asked, "You mean if you possess this stone you can summon a dragon?"

"Yes." The man began his prayers again, asking for forgiveness. He did not expect it, for he knew his weakness would lead to the destruction of his people, of countless others. The Gods would torment him forever and the torture he had endured the last few days would be inconsequential compared to Their wrath. *I beg for sanctuary, even if it be eternal torment,* he prayed, his lips moving silently.

"How do I call one?" Phelan asked, his eyes widening in comprehension. His voice rose, "Answer me, how do I call a dragon?"

This time the prisoner did not answer for his Gods had heard his prayers and had taken him home, carried him to where Phelan and his torturer could no longer hurt him. In Their mercy they did not condemn the man for his weakness, but granted him sanctuary as he asked, for he had performed Their will without knowing it.

The dreams would not leave him be. He saw the bodies of the children, the mound growing larger each time he dreamt. He had awoken bathed in sweat more than once over the past month since Erc's clan ceased to exist. His dreams spoke of death and destruction, no hope for life. He no longer asked for one of the girls to share his furs and his people noted that. They knew he was troubled and they feared for his health, for there was no son to take his place should he sicken and pass beyond. Rumors began to weave their way through the clan and Galen took his concerns to his leader.

"No matter the issue, Iarel, the people know you are not well. They do not need more worry for they have fears enough of their own."

"It is the nightmares, Galen. I do not understand them," Caewlin replied, his eyes sunken and his voice exhausted.

"Take them to the Wise, Iarel. She will help you. And, please, invite a girl to your furs. That will settle some of the worry your people have for you."

"I will go to the Wise, but no girl shall share my furs, Galen. I cannot take pleasure when all I see are dead children in my mind." Galen reluctantly acquiesced, satisfied that the iarel would at least speak with Devona about his nightmares.

The Wise did not look surprised to see him. She knew he was not well and that he had forsaken the company of women. She gestured for him to sit in front of her on a thick brown fur.

"Tell me what troubles you, Iarel."

He told her all of it. She sat impassive as he related the horrific nightmares in full detail, the dead children and the hollowed-eyed starving people who encompassed him. When he finished he gazed into her strangely hued eyes and waited for some words of comfort to come forth. There were none.

Gathering her multicolored robes around her, she rose and fetched a cup of spring water from a bucket in the back of her hut. She sat back down, composed herself and then cast some black power incense into the fire near them. The intense smell of it swirled around the inside of the small hut, temporarily blinding the iarel to her actions. Caewlin grew dizzy and his eyes stung. He felt a cup pressed into his hands. The liquid had a strong smell, though he did detect some of the ritual herbs their clan used to obtain visions, if the Gods were willing.

"Drink and we will see what the Red Hawk will tell us." He drank of the cup's contents without hesitation. The potion had a queer taste, as if it had been contained in a cask of burnt wood. He nearly gagged, but downed it all and handed the cup back to her. He felt her hands on him and as he swooned she eased him onto the furs beneath him.

"Fly with Red Hawk, Iarel, see what She sees!" she said in a breathless voice as he fell headlong into the vision as the herbs possessed his mind and body.

Though the fog around him was thick, he saw *Her* on the wind above him, *Her* cries echoing in the morning air. He stood alone in the bow of his ship, none of his men around him. As if by its own will the craft beached on a familiar shore.

Not home, he thought. *North. She* sailed over him, leading him forward with shrieks in the air. He followed the flash of crimson into the forest as the Red Hawk winged her way. He saw the dead walking by him, long troops of men, women and children, their wounds clearly visible. The little boy with the puppy hiked by him. The small animal wiggled in his chubby hands, licking his face in enthusiasm. When Caewlin reached out to touch the boy his hand went through him, yet the small lad did not appear to notice.

Fades, he thought, *the shadows of those passed.* The troop was neverending, the number killed by Phelan, starvation, and disease. All were clan. All were no more. He heard the cries of the Red Hawk again and followed them striding further into the forest, eager to avoid the walking dead.

Caewlin struggled to see more clearly, pushing himself deeper into the vision. The woman stood alone. The dead at her feet were not clansmen, but Northern men, corpses by the multitudes. In the midst of them she stood like a shield-maiden – the pagan woman, the fire-hair. In her right hand was a sword stained with the gore of those at her feet and in her left was an infant, newly birthed, blood still upon it. It was a boy, red of hair. Though just born he did not cry but gazed at the iarel with penetrating eyes and then turned to suckle from his mother's heavily laden breast. Her skirts were deep green and flowed down to the earth and then into the soil, as if she was rooted there. On one of the woman's shoulders perched a falcon, one keen of eye and talon. On the other shoulder was the Red Hawk, the Goddess of their clan. The amulet hung between the pagan's two full breasts. He fell on his knees in front of the vision, bowing. As he touched his forehead to the blood-anointed earth in homage, he knew no more.

Morwyn was standing in the entryway of Kell's House of Healing and she could feel the illness and pain within as easily as if it were a sword in her chest.

"The need here is great," the young man said, a deep sadness in his eyes at the admission.

"I am willing to serve," she replied, shouldering her heavy pack again. The herbs and medicines within weighed it down. She had sold her horse and converted the money into whatever supplies she could buy in the market.

"We can only pay with a bed and meager food, nothing more," the young man replied. He was tall, gaunt, with short dark brown hair.

"I accept," she replied and he gestured her inside, closing the heavy door behind her.

The House of Healing was an old institution, started by a healer when the city was no more than a small village. As Kell quickly grew to a major city, a bustling seaport, the House thrived with it. All manner of patients came to be healed here; seamen injured in their work or in the taverns, sporting wenches, local citizens and traders. The House could hold twenty patients and at present it held thirty-three. The most ill had their own bed, the others a pallet on the floor. It was the best the healers could do. Many more patients came to the House during the day for treatment, returning to their own lodgings at night.

The contents of Morwyn's pack were sorely needed. She washed her hands and set immediately to work. Her first case was a man who had sustained a burn on his leg when a blazing log had rolled out of the hearth catching his breeches on fire. She cleaned the wound, set a poultice upon it and then gave the man a small amount of a painkilling herb. All the while the young healer, Siarl, watched from a discreet distance. Once he knew Morwyn was as she claimed, he departed and left her to her work. She worked for eighteen hours that first day and fell asleep exhausted onto a small cot in a room she shared with two other healers. As she drifted off to sleep, she thought of Gwyn and her prophecy.

I am needed.

She quickly became friends with Benen, the innkeeper, and would often go to his inn to treat one of his girls or a guest. She was paid in food and with something extra to take back to the other healers. Benen was full of gossip once he knew her and often they would spend time in the kitchen talking as Morwyn ate whatever they put in front of her.

"Phelan has vanquished one of the five earls, one named Erc."

Morwyn raised an eyebrow at that. "How? I thought the Southerners were accomplished warriors."

"They are reputed to be so, but they're ill because a prolonged drought has claimed their game for the past two years. From what I hear they are starving to death." Benen's eyes were grim at this admission.

"Why is Phelan persecuting them?" she asked, curious.

"The Southerners initially traded with us, traded furs for food. Erc and one of the other iarels decided that wasn't enough and attacked some of the smaller villages on the coast. Phelan had no choice but to retaliate, though to be honest I believe it was the perfect excuse for him to make war," Benen explained. He paused a moment and gave the scullery maid a slight frown. She stopped talking to the stableboy and returned to her pot scrubbing. "Off with you, lad, you can court her later." The boy disappeared through the side door and Benen shook his head at such youthful antics.

"So he makes war on those that have attacked the villages," Morwyn said in an attempt to bring the innkeeper back to the conversation. He had a habit of veering off in a new direction without warning.

"No, he makes war on all of the Southern clans. He means to kill them or enslave those who are healthy enough to work."

"He enslaves them?" Morwyn asked, her voice cooler.

"Yes. The men go to quarry stone or to the forests to cut timber. The women are …" Benen paused and ran a hand over the stubble on his broad chin. "The women, if they're pretty, are sold to the brothels here in Kell or up north."

"Powers," Morwyn exclaimed in disgust.

"That is why you must be careful, Morwyn. You are young and pretty and in this city being a healer will not save you from Phelan's men."

"I see. Kell's citizens are as much victims as are the Southern clansmen."

"Yes, we are." Benen rose at that and abruptly changed the subject. "Thank you for your care of that silly drunk noble. You would think the Powers would have given him more sense than to imbibe all that wine and then expect to be able to walk upstairs without hurting himself."

"Nobles usually are rather light on good sense, I've found," Morwyn replied.

Benen rewarded her with a smile, happy to move to lighter subjects.

"Powers, you are right," he replied and then packed food for her to take back to the House of Healing.

The iarel remained insensible for over one full day as the physical effects of the vision faded. During that time Nerian assured the people their leader was well and told them he had flown with the Red Hawk. The clan was comforted to learn their iarel sought guidance. When Caewlin exited the Wise's hut he found small knots of his kin sitting vigil.

"The Red Hawk has shown me Her will. I will do as She asks." He did not need to tell them more, for all they wanted to know was if he had been granted a vision. They rose and went back to their tasks, sure in the knowledge that their Goddess was guiding their leader.

The Wise had helped him understand what he must do, though it made little sense to him. As soon as he felt able, Caewlin set off for the Northern shore. He found it hard not to relive his vision as he stepped into the surf and waded onto the foreign shore. He'd brought only a small boat, though he made sure to tie a red hawk feather to the mast so they would be guided and protected in their journey. The three clansmen who had accompanied him had no notion why he'd come to this shore, only that he was following the Red Hawk's bidding. The Wise had blessed the journey and that was all they needed to know. Ordering the men to remain behind, he set off into the Northern forest alone.

He found her near the twin stone cairns. She was praying at the graves as she did each dawn and on the ground near her was her pack. She had risen this morning knowing it was time to leave the village. One of the men had come to her hut a short time before knowing her to be unguarded and had attempted to lie with her. It had cost him a vicious knife wound to his thigh. She knew the villagers' wrath would fall on her once they rose from their beds and they learned of the encounter, so she packed her meager belongings and prepared to leave.

"Fire-hair," the voice came behind her, full of awe. She whirled, pulling her knife in the process and found the pagan, the blonde-haired chief of the Southerners standing only a short distance from her. His hands were at his side in a non-threatening manner. She eyed him dubiously and then realized he had spoken in her language this time.

"Why are you here?" she asked glancing around nervously. For a moment, she thought they had returned to raid the village once more, but the hounds were quiet.

"I wish that you come with me, fire-hair."

She blinked at that, surprised.

"Why?"

"The Red Hawk has said it must be so and as iarel I must obey." He pointed to the sky and then back to her chest. The amulet lay hidden under her clothes, but he knew it was there. He sensed it.

"I cannot," she objected.

"You must. You are the Red Hawk's chosen. You must come."

She frowned, glanced back toward the heart of the village for a moment and when she turned her eyes back toward the clansman, she found him on his knees, almost in supplication.

"She asks that you come with me," he pleaded and pointed up in the sky once more.

"I cannot …" she began and then saw the shape in the air, the wingspan of a bird. It was a red hawk. Her mouth fell open in astonishment. She had never seen such a bird even when she ventured far into the forest to collect herbs.

The raptor called in a high voice and swooped low across them. Aithne stepped back instinctively though she was not the bird's intended target. It headed directly at a villager now some forty feet away, a sword in his hand as he advanced upon them. It was the man who had attacked her earlier, his thigh now bandaged. He was clearly bent on revenge.

The bird dove at him and he belatedly raised his free hand to shield his face. It was not enough and the raptor's fierce talons tore at him. He crouched over, cursing in pain.

"Come now, fire-hair, please!" the iarel's voice pleaded. Aithne watched as the bird began to make another pass at the villager. This time the man raised his sword in defense and Aithne took a sharp intake of breath.

"No!" she called out, taking a step forward.

The blade stuck the hawk straight on as it dove talons first into its prey. There was a loud splintering crack and the steel blade shattered in the man's hands. He stumbled back in fright as the bird gained altitude for another attack. The man shouted for aid and turned on his heels, limping back into the center of the village.

"Powers," she whispered and looked back at the Southerner. He was on his feet again.

"She protects us," he explained. He extended his hand, his face a mixture of concern and reverence. "Come with me, please. We must leave now!"

Aithne sheathed her knife and nodded. She turned for one last downward glance at the graves near her feet and then fled with the blonde-haired man toward the seashore.

By the time villagers raised the alarm, Caewlin and the Red Hawk's Chosen were on the water. To the villagers' ire they found their boats sabotaged, a hole in the bottom of each craft to prevent them pursuing the iarel and the healer. Thwarted, they howled their indignation from the shore. Once out on the open sea the winds favored the iarel's boat and the journey was effortless. Caewlin knew it would be, for he was doing the Red Hawk's will. *I am bringing her to my people, as You have commanded.*

He stood on a tower overlooking the city of Kell. The moon was full and though Lord Phelan had no interest in magic, he knew that you ignored it at one's own peril. He had painfully pulled himself up the forty-three steps to the terrace on the top of the High Tower that sat within the fortress. His withered right leg made the journey tiring and lengthy, but he made it to the top. On the terrace he found a heavy wooden chair placed near a small table, as he had ordered. There was a pitcher of ale for refreshment and a burning brazier nearby for warmth. He poured himself a cup of ale and sank wearily into the chair as he gazed downward into the city.

Nothing in his dismal and grubby beginnings could have prepared him for this moment. Born the third son of a rich wine merchant, Phelan had the mark of fate on him at the moment of his conception. His mother was barely fourteen, a servant girl seduced by her master with the offer of a coin or two. When her belly swelled with child his interest in her waned and she was discarded in favor of a new wench. The wine merchant's wife treated the girl with contempt, for her husband found more comfort with other women than with her. No one cared when the birth pangs began. As labor progressed it was obvious not all was well and an herb seller was reluctantly summoned, one without proper training, for the girl was not worth the price of a healer.

Phelan's mother died only a few minutes after his arrival into the world. The herb seller, an old woman, acted precipitously, eager to return to her drinking. Without waiting for the child to crown fully she pulled him from his mother, an act that caused his dam's death and lent permanent damage to his right leg. Twisted like a broken doll and proclaimed a whoreson by his father's wife, he was spurned and cast off to be raised by one of the servant girls who nursed a baseborn child of her own.

He was a quiet lad, brooding and limping around the edges of the household to avoid being kicked or beaten. His silence led his father to believe he was simple and so he was treated that way. He saw no reason to act otherwise for any attention usually resulted in chastisement or blows. The middle son of the family, Taran, frequently beat him and ordered him to sleep with the dogs instead of in the kitchen. His eldest half-brother, Carr, was far more humane and smuggled food to Phelan when he could. Phelan came to adore Carr, for he was the only one who showed him any love and attention.

His father's wife died when he was ten and he did not weep. His sire continued to wench as he wished and a series of girls paraded through their household for the next decade or so. All the while Phelan watched and learned. His father was a savvy merchant and he continued to acquire his rivals' wine stocks. As the family fortune grew, Phelan learned that ruthless-ness was the means to show strength, that pity was a weakness. The only positive influence in his life was his older brother, but Carr was like a small light in the middle of a deep and dark forest. Phelan only knew abuse, deri-sion and want, despite the wealth of his family.

His eldest brother met and fell in love with a young girl, Zinna, an orphan whose father was once in the Wool Guild. Phelan's keen intuition told him she was not to be trusted, but his brother would not listen, for he was smitten. They married and appeared happy. Phelan knew otherwise, for he had seen her with Taran, her brother-in-law, sporting in the fields outside Kell. He held his silence and continued to spy, fearful of how this drama would play out. His fears were valid, for his favorite brother died six months into the marriage. Carr succumbed to a painful death over two days as his young bride dutifully sat at his bedside. Phelan mourned as he curled up with the hounds, the fleas nibbling on him as he shed his tears in private. He could not feel their bites, for the only light in his world was dying.

On the very night that she buried her husband, Zinna made sure to take her pleasure with her lover, the grieving brother. Where cries of lamentation should have come from her chambers, Phelan heard cries of delight as they coupled repeatedly. Darkness flooded his mind. He fled the house and grieved at his brother's grave until dawn. Vowing revenge, he turned his cold wrath inward. Nothing about his demeanor changed, for he remained the subservi-ent lackey his family had come to expect. In his fertile mind he set about masterminding the death of his brother, his father and the grieving widow. To his delight, his load was lightened, for his sire died a few months later, felled by the same poison that killed his eldest son. Now the middle son and his lover were heir to all the family holdings. Taran increased his reign of terror, for his half-brother was a tempting target. In derision he proclaimed Phelan *The Master of the Hounds*, mockingly calling him by that title when-ever anyone dined at their home. All through the mental and physical torment Phelan said nothing and bided his time.

For one-full year he patiently waited and planned, honing his scheme until it was a sharp as a new sword. On the anniversary of his beloved broth-er's death, he struck. Taran fell ill after the evening repast, felled by a cau-tiously administered poison that made him decay from the inside out. His hideous screams echoed throughout the household as it took him seven days and nights to occupy his grave. He died alone for Zinna cowered in her room and would not venture near him, even when he begged. The night before he was to be buried, Zinna took her usual sleeping draught and huddled in her own bed, grateful for the silence that had descended on the household. She was now sole heir and that would be her solace. Phelan was of no concern, for he was a bastard and easily discarded, just as her husband and his father had been. Taran's death had been a stroke of luck, though it unnerved her.

Phelan buried what was left of his brother's corpse that same night, under the cover of darkness. He had ordered that the casket remained unsealed and as he stood by the grave, accompanied by two gravediggers, he watched as they laid the body of the grieving widow inside with the corrupted corpse.

"You have drilled the holes in the casket as I ordered? It will not do if it is too airtight."

One of the men nodded and shuddered involuntarily.

"Dump the bucket in as well." One of the gravediggers gave the other a look and then hefted a small bucket over the top of the woman's body. The contents spilled in and immediately began to move on their own accord.

"Seal the casket and bury it!" Phelan ordered. They did not argue with him, though he was wearing grubby clothes and looked more like a beggar than a young man accustomed to giving orders. They had received considerable coin to do this onerous task and that had closed their mouths. They knew if anyone learned of what evil they performed here, they would hang.

Phelan watched as the casket was nailed shut and lowered into the uncommonly deep grave. The site was not near his family plot but a considerable distance away in the pauper's field. Taran's funeral would be tomorrow morning, just as planned, his casket filled with sacks of grain, not his moldering corpse. It had been an easy task to arrange for the diggers to do this job. Carr had generously given him a small pouch of coins in honor of his wedding to Zinna and Phelan had squirreled the unexpected largess away in his filthy bedding. That money now bought his revenge.

The men began to shovel dirt into the pit and continued until the grave was one third full. Phelan took over from there, for his two minions now lay face down on top of the casket, dead. He cleaned their blood off his knife, picked up one of the shovels and continued to fill the grave. He was nearly done when he swore he could hear faint screams deep within the earth. Perhaps it was only his imagination. Then again, the sleeping draught would not hold forever. He tried to imagine what it would be like to wake in the darkness lying face down on top of a decomposing body, entombed with a bucket-full of carrion worms who were unable to discern between the living and the dead. The holes in the coffin would insure Zinna would not suffocate too quickly, for he wanted her wanted to experience the full range of terror before she died.

He laughed coldly and advised, "Enjoy his embrace, wench, for you will sport with him for eternity." He listened for a bit longer and laughed again. "Are those screams of pleasure I hear? It sounds as if Taran is as vigorous as he was in your bed the night dear Carr lay in *his* grave. Pardon if I do not listen longer, but the morning comes and I must be away." He continued his efforts until the grave was filled and the earth leveled.

He studied his work and dusted off his hands.

"Very satisfying." Collecting the shovels, he worked his way over to Carr's grave and stood there for time. "I have avenged your death. Rest in peace, dear brother." With a smug smile on his dirty face, he hobbled off to claim his birthright.

A sound from the street below called Phelan back to the present. The city center was fairly quiet at this late hour, though just this afternoon he had ordered four Southern clansmen burnt to death at the iron stakes set in the middle of the city square. To their credit the men had not begged, but met death with their eyes open, intoning prayers to their heathen gods. As always, they were defiant to the end.

That is what makes them so dangerous, he thought to himself. *They do not fear death.*

Unlike the timid citizens of Kell who fretted over their riches and their families, the Southern clansmen feared virtually nothing. To the man, they fought and died without flinching. Even Erc, the Badger Clan's iarel, had refused to utter one scream as Phelan had him painstakingly mutilated. He had died cursing them to his gods, never once begging for mercy.

Phelan's father had taught his sons that riches and soft living made for weak enemies. Sadly, his father did not live long enough to see his youngest son's triumph, nor would he have expected it.

I proved you wrong, father, the man mused, *for I am not as simple as you thought.* Acting as the grieving half-brother, Phelan buried the grain-laden coffin that supposedly held Taran's remains. When Zinna went missing, he sued for his inheritance and was rewarded the holdings as there was no one else to claim it. When a couple more of his father's bastards appeared a few years later attempting to claim their share, they went missing as well. He used his cunning, his ruthlessness and the family fortune to build his prestige and his power. When the time was right he engaged a mercenary force and overthrew Kell's Chamberlain, a weak and pathetic man who had groveled at Phelan's feet right before he had him drawn and quartered. At the age of thirty Phelan became Lord and master of Kell. It was not enough.

"In that you were right, father. Riches and soft living make for weak enemies." The subjugation of Kell had been easy; the destruction of the clansmen was not. The clans had neither riches nor a decadent lifestyle and so they had proved to be Phelan's greatest threat. If they allied with one of his foes they would destroy him. He quickly realized that the only way to control them was to kill or enslave them all.

He put those thoughts aside and tugged a long gold chain from underneath his richly embroidered vest. The cold orb swayed in the air in front of him, captured at several points by the gold like an oversized jewel. He studied it in wonderment as he held it in his hands, judging its weight and feel. The gold glowed in contrast to its dark grey surface.

"Cold and dead," he said, "and yet …" If it had not been so vigorously protected he would have thought it a hoax, a ruse by the clansmen to make him believe it held more power than it did.

He had no clear idea how to summon a dragon. None of the other prisoners would reveal that knowledge, no matter how efficient the torturer was at his craft. He came to believe that they did not know and so he must forge his own way. Sensing it was time, he raised the orb in the air and took a deep breath.

"I hold in my hand the Stone of Summoning, revered of the Southern Isles, orb said to be of the dragons. I call forth one of their kind to come to me, to be bound to me. Come forth and serve!"

Nothing happened and that did not surprise him. A light wind kicked up and skidded the thin clouds across the moon, but nothing else of import occurred. Phelan frowned and heard the sound of intoxicated guardsmen in the streets below, singing some drinking song at full voice.

"I summon you! Come forth and serve!" he shouted and then began to feel the fool.

The singing in the streets continued, loud and off-key. As Phelan began to lower his hands, pondering whether he should toss the orb over the side of the High Tower, a shadow passed over the moon above him. He shivered, involuntarily, and then glanced up, sure it had been his imagination. The guards below broke off their song for just a moment and started up again. The shadow passed again, this time closer and Phelan saw the outline of wings and an immense tail. The singing below faltered and died.

"Powers," he said as the beast wheeled in the moonlight, massive as it floating through the clouds.

Who dares summon me? the voice asked in his mind.

Phelan nearly lost his nerve and fled. He swallowed, hard, and then muttered an oath under his breath.

Cowards do not rule, he thought and replied, "I have summoned you, dragon."

Who are you, mortal?

"I am Phelan, Lord of Kell and all that I behold. You are mine to summon and I bind you in thrall!"

A booming cry rent the air and the shape wheeled again as if in distress.

He heard in his mind, **I hear and must obey.**

He paused, unsure of how to proceed. The dragon continued its slow arc in the air above him, apparently held until he released it. A thought occurred to him and he put it into a query.

"Are there more of your kind here?"

A long pause and then, **Yes.** The beast did not offer more.

"Where are they? Why did not they not come when I summoned?" he pressed.

They are not born.

Phelan closed his eyes and smiled. He opened them again and watched the beast continue its slow circle, the moon back lighting its elongated shape.

"Tell me all," he commanded and after another long pause, the dragon complied. Phelan nodded, understanding what he'd been told.

"Then go and I will summon you when I need you."

The creature flew past the moon one last time and then vanished into the high clouds. Phelan no longer heard jests or song rising from the streets below. He knew the guards would believe the drink they had taken had created the nightmare vision they'd just witnessed.

All the better. It is not time for others to know of what power I wield. Not yet, he thought. *Not yet.*

TEN

ithne slept undisturbed for most of the voyage. Though fear should have ruled her and kept her awake, it was not to be. For some inexplicable reason she felt safe with the leader of the southern clansmen. When she awoke stiff and sore from lying in the bottom of the boat, she found the man's cloak spread over her own to keep her warm. The iarel was awake, sitting next to her, as his men eyed her cautiously. They seemed to be in as much awe of her as their leader.

She said nothing but stretched and gazed out at the scene around her. It was a pleasant sight as brown sea birds winged above them and the sun rose in the east spreading a shimmering glow on the surface of the sea. A golden sand beach edged by forest awaited them. Even from this distance Aithne could see that the woodland was not as verdant as the one she'd just left.

"We are nearing our clansite, fire-hair," the iarel explained and she nodded to indicate she understood. His command of the Northern language was good, though some words she had to fathom out by context.

"It is very beautiful, " she replied gazing out toward the island in front of them. One of the men in the boat arched an eyebrow at that.

"She said our isle is very beautiful," Caewlin translated, not knowing why he felt the need.

"Our home," the man replied, a glow in his eyes.

Caewlin repeated the words to Aithne in the Southern dialect and then in her language. She nodded. She would need to learn their tongue as quickly as possible.

"Is there someone who can teach me your language?" she asked.

"Yes, her name is Orva, she is a shield-woman. She taught me your tongue. I will have her start as soon as you are no longer weary from the journey."

"Thank you." She paused and then asked, "What is a shield-woman?" The iarel's eyebrow moved up a fraction.

"A shield-woman is permitted to fight in battle. Some might consider you a shield woman given your actions during our raid."

"I see." She fell into silence for the remainder of the voyage. It was so easy to marvel at the beauty of the sea and the island in front of them, though her mind kept asking her why she had so readily run away with this man.

All eyes fell on her the moment she stepped out of the boat. Conversations faltered, for though the clan knew their iarel had sailed they did not know to where. Though Aithne did not know it the story of the red-haired pagan woman had preceded her. It was told and retold, for there were few raiders who had not seen her or heard of the iarel's actions that day. Now she was in their midst. Most of them stared in amazement as she followed their leader through the camp.

The clansite was not as she expected. She'd heard tales about these people and most of the stories were not complimentary. Northerners believed the Southern Isle clansmen to be barbarians, unwashed and godless, too free-spirited to be decent people. They were reputed to be drunken heathens, beating their wives, lying with any woman they found of interest while ignoring their numerous bastard children. In short, they were allegedly capable of the most vile of behavior. Their seemingly unwarranted attacks on the coastal villages had only reinforced those prejudices.

Aithne found just the opposite despite the devastating effects of prolonged drought. Their clothes were clean regardless of the scarcity of fresh water. The children, though quite thin, were friendly and curious. The women were talking amongst themselves or with their mates. Sounds of laughter echoed throughout the camp. As Aithne followed the iarel through the eclectic collection of rough wood huts and hide tents she spied a mother crooning to a very small baby. Her eyes grew misty at the sight for it brought forth memories of her infant. Without thinking she paused and knelt by the mother. The woman gave her a startled look, though she did not seek to protect the infant from the stranger. Caewlin halted when he realized the fire-hair was no longer at his side.

"The baby is so small!" Aithne remarked without thinking. She was immediately chagrined at her thoughtless comment.

Hearing her, the iarel explained, "All of the babies are small now. It is lucky they survive at all." Aithne's eyes grew tears. The clanswoman saw the tears and asked Caewlin a question in their language. He nodded and they traded a few more sentences in the Southern tongue.

"Would you like to hold her child?" he asked.

Aithne's eyes grew wide at the kind offer and she nodded.

"I would so much like to hold the little one." The woman did not need this translated and handed her small child to the stranger in a gesture of trust that transcended words. Aithne cradled the infant and began to sing to it, unaware of the curious crowd gathering around her. Her actions had caught the attention of the clan and the sight of a Northern woman singing to one of their infants fascinated them. Caewlin did not intervene, allowing his people the rare opportunity to see that not all Northerners were like Phelan. He heard murmurs of approval and kept the smile off his face.

Galen watched from a distance with a pleased expression on his face. He felt a presence at his elbow and turned to see the Wise next to him.

"She has come to us," Devona observed.

"Already she makes her presence felt," he remarked.

"She will do more than that, Saga, if the oracles be right."

In time, Aithne returned the baby to the mother and offered her thanks which Caewlin related to his kinswoman. The woman responded with a question and he nodded in the affirmative. A look of understanding flooded her face for she now knew the elemental force that had pulled the Northern woman to her infant.

"Tell her I am sorry she has lost her child," the clanswoman said sadly.

Caewlin relayed the message and Aithne barely held back further tears as she rose to her feet. She was disconcerted to find herself encompassed by a ring of people until she saw gentle expressions on many of their faces. They, too, had lost children. They understood the ache she carried in her heart.

"Come, fire-hair," the iarel offered, sensing her discomfort and guided her through the crowd to his hut near the center of the camp. It was a bit larger than other structures nearby, but not sizeable. She found it odd that there was no indication on the hut's exterior that it belonged to the leader of the clan. He pulled back the leather flap that covered the entrance and gestured for her to enter. As soon as her eyes adjusted to the semi-darkness she saw one set of furs on the ground near the fire pit. Her mind caught at that and she could not help but stare.

Of course, he will want to lie with me.

She took a sharp intake of breath and tried to get a grip on her apprehension. She had thought he would be married, have children, yet there was no evidence of a family in this dwelling. Suddenly her purpose here began to make sense.

I am to be his wench. I am no different from the other women they have taken from their homes except that I came willingly.

She closed her eyes for a moment and then reopened them as the iarel watched her intently. He seemed to know her thoughts before she spoke them.

"I do not demand that you share my furs, woman, that is not my way." He walked around her and began to rearrange the bedding into two separate sections, clearly his bed and hers.

"Aithne," she replied, her concern lessening for the moment. "My name is Aithne. It means fire in my language."

His intense brown eyes sought hers as he completed his task.

"Ath-nay," he repeated. "I am Caewlin, Iarel of the Red Hawk Clan."

"Iarel," she replied solemnly. This was very awkward for her.

"I am Caewlin to you, fire-hair." He stood and then regarded her without pretense.

"Caewlin," she repeated as an unsure smile appeared on her face.

He dropped his eyes back down to the twin fur beds now in place on the dirt floor of the hut.

"If in time you wish to be with me all you need do is return the furs to how they once were. That will tell me you are willing."

"And if I am never willing?" she asked, her eyes narrowing at this.

"Then I am not favored by the Gods," he replied in an honest tone and departed without another word. She settled on the furthest set of furs and began to rummage through her pack, as if that activity would calm her raging thoughts.

Why in the Powers am I here? What possessed me to come with him? Her mind had no answers and so she buried her anxiety and began the difficult adjustment to her new home.

Eventually, she forced herself to wander around the camp in an attempt to get a sense of it all. Though the clan did not want to be rude, they could not help but stare. They murmured to themselves and she caught the word *iarel* more than once. It was obvious they thought her to be their leader's woman. She hadn't wandered for very long before she was intercepted by two clans-women, one older, one younger. The older woman's hair was blonde salted with grey and her eyes were bright and intelligent. The young woman had the same tawny hair as the iarel and her face was similar to his.

She spoke first in the Northern language.

"I am Fea, daughter of Brecc, shield-maiden and sister to the iarel." As she spoke she took Aithne's hand in a warm embrace. She stood half a head shorter than Caewlin but had the same fine features as her brother.

"I am Aithne."

"I am Orva, shield-woman of the clan," the older woman said cordially. There was no reserve in their speech, it was as if they were greeting long lost kin.

"I am pleased to meet both of you," Aithne replied sincerely, glad of the company and for someone she could understand. "Caewlin … the iarel said that you will be teaching me your language."

Orva nodded. "We will start tomorrow morning, once you are rested."

"Good." As they talked Aithne's eyes caught sight of a familiar face. The woman was shaking out bedding near the entrance to a small tent.

Orva followed her line of sight. "That is one of the women taken from your village."

"Has it gone well for her?" Aithne asked. She remembered her as a sharp-tongued and unpleasant sort though fair of features.

"No, she does not thrive here. Though, to be honest, none of us are thriving at the moment," Fea replied with a touch of irony in her voice.

"She was not one to thrive in my village, either," Aithne came back. The woman glanced their direction and rewarded her with a thinly veiled glare, though she was too distant to hear their conversation.

"Some women make the best of their new lives, others do not. It is not an easy life, but for the most part the men are kind to them and treat them with respect," Fea replied. "She has made things difficult for herself, refusing to marry two men who have offered to share their furs with her."

"So what does she do?" Aithne asked.

"Her behavior has been unworthy. She is now a ..." Fea hunted for the proper word in the northern language that corresponded to the woman's lower status, "she is now a servant."

"Is she required to share the furs of any man who asks her?"

"Only if she is willing, for our men do not force women to their furs, even those lower in rank within our clan. She has not been willing and because of that has not found her master as caring as he might be."

"I see." It was plain, if the woman had adjusted to clan life and taken either of the offers of marriage, life would be better for her. "And your brother, how does he treat his women?" Aithne asked before she could stop herself. She was wearier than she realized and that made her more candid than was prudent. Fea's eyebrow went up and Aithne knew she had offended the girl.

"Caewlin treats his women with respect. He does not strike them, nor does he demand they lie with him unless they wish." The voice was cooler now.

Aithne sighed, knowing she had stepped over the line. "I am sorry. I am tired and I am ... nervous." A look of understanding appeared in Fea's eyes.

"As any woman would be given your situation. I have heard some of the tales the Northerners tell of us, how our men are without honor and will take any woman they choose. You had cause to worry what Caewlin or any of our men intended," Fea answered.

Aithne struggled for words, seriously wishing to make amends, "I meant no offense, for he did save my life during the raid. For some reason, I made the decision to come with your brother rather quickly and ..."

"And now you regret it?" Fea asked straightforwardly. Aithne did not answer immediately, but ranged her eyes around the clansite as if assessing her decision. Orva and Fea traded looks and waited for the newcomer's verdict.

"No, I do not regret it, I just wonder what possessed me to do it." The Northern woman's candor bred a knowing smile on the young girl's face.

"The Red Hawk compelled you to accept Caewlin's offer, for She has chosen you."

"But, I do not worship her. Why would she choose me?"

"We do not question Her judgement, we only look for guidance," Fea explained. She pointed toward a large wooden structure in the middle of the camp. "Come, we will show you the center of our clan's life and you can judge us from there."

There was a small group of children playing in the corner of the great hall. They had sticks and shells and appeared to be engaged in some informal competition. Aithne enjoyed watching them, although she couldn't fathom how the sport was played. It seemed to involve a lot of running and peels of laughter, as did most children's pastimes.

"We have lost too many of our children, Aithne. They perish before birth or soon thereafter." Orva explained, her voice tinged with sadness.

"The drought has gone on for that long?" She had heard rumors of their plight in her village, though most discounted the severity as a lie put forward by the clansmen to justify their barbarous raids. The forest around them was mute testimony that the drought was real for the leaves were sickly brown and the vegetation withered.

"Two years and now half another."

"Is there no food left?"

"We fish, though the catch is poor. We gather what berries we can find and sometimes we are lucky to bring down a lean stag for meat. The small game has almost completely disappeared. That is why our iarel raided your village, our children are starving."

Fea muttered, "If Badger Clan had not been so inclined toward war, we could have continued trading, at least for a time."

"Badger Clan?" Aithne asked, puzzled.

Orva explained, "The clans are divided into five distinct groups, each named for the deity that guides them. As we serve the Red Hawk, we are Her clan. The iarel of the Badger Clan began the raids, for Erc preferred war to peace."

"I see," Aithne replied, unsure of what else to say. It was evident there were rifts between the clans.

"Caewlin told me of the death of your husband and your child," Fea said, cautiously gauging the woman's reaction.

Aithne swallowed. "To lose both was almost too much," she said.

Without hesitation, Fea embraced her and offered, "We will be your family, now." Aithne took a deep breath to hold back the tears.

Seeking to ease the woman's discomfort, Orva gestured around the hall and explained, "This hall, by tradition, is the iarel's dwelling. In his wisdom, our iarel felt it was best used for the widows and the orphaned children so they can live together and care for each other. He now lives in the dwelling that you share with him."

"He sounds like a compassionate leader."

"He is, Aithne. He is a good man," Orva explained and though the healer attempted to discern some hint of dishonesty or flattery in her words, there was none.

A woman appeared at Orva's side and they spoke together earnestly. An anxious look appeared on the older woman's face as the other hurried back toward the far corner of the hall. A loud moan and then a shrill shriek emanated from that direction.

"A birthing goes ill," Orva explained grimly.

"Surely your healer can help," Aithne said.

Orva shook her head. "Our healer perished over two moons ago. We are on our own now."

"Then *that* is why your iarel brought me here," Aithne murmured. *It was not to be his wench, but to treat his people!*

"You are skilled in the healing arts?" Orva's voice held surprise.

"Yes, I am. Surely the iarel must have surmised that or he wouldn't have brought me here."

"No, he did not, for he never mentioned it."

"Then why *did* he bring me here, if not to be his wench or the clan's healer?" Aithne pressed.

Orva paused and then answered cryptically, "*She* told him to bring you here."

"I do not understand …" Aithne began but another howl from the corner caught her attention and she knew the question must stand unanswered. She frowned and then shook her head in resignation. "I will need my pack from the iarel's tent. It contains my herbs and medicines."

"I will send someone for it," Orva answered.

It was the girl's first child and she was very young. *Young and frightened,* Aithne thought. She had vivid memories of bringing her own child into the world without any assistance. Though this girl had members of her family around her, loving and supporting her, she was still petrified, her eyes wide and her breath coming in quick gasps. Her mate, a young man, sat directly behind her, her head and shoulders lying in his lap as he devotedly sponged her face with cool water. It was a scene full of love and compassion. Aithne pushed down her momentary flash of anger at those who claimed these people to less than human, only capable of the worst atrocities.

She took a big breath and plunged in.

"Orva, will you translate for me?" The clanswoman nodded and explained the situation to the laboring girl and her mother who hovered near her. They spoke for a time as Aithne put her hands on the girl's bulging stomach and determined the quality of the contractions. The pains were strong and the child's head was firmly in the birthing canal, as it should be at this stage of labor. This was not an untoward delivery, it was the girl's fright that was slowing the birth, not some physical reason.

"Her mother says she has been in labor since late last night. She is tired and growing weak," Orva translated.

"And very afraid," Aithne observed.

Orva nodded. "Her sister died in childbirth and she fears the same will happen to her."

"I understand. I will make her a potent that will ease the birth and give her strength. Do you have some wine or mead?" Orva nodded and gestured for one of the women to pour her a cup of wine. She passed it to the healer and Aithne prepared the drink. Once it was mixed properly she passed the cup to the girl's mother. There was a long pause.

"Tell her to have her daughter drink it," Aithne instructed, suspecting the problem. Orva made the request and the answer was short and blunt. Although Aithne did not understand the words, she sensed the undercurrent.

"She does not trust you," Orva reported.

"There is nothing in that potent that will harm her!" Aithne came back sharply. She was far too tired for this sort of nonsense.

"It does not matter, you are a Northern woman."

Aithne frowned. "I am a healer and a healer does harm to no one, Northern or Southern born."

Orva translated again and the mother shook her head. Orva spoke again, reminding her that the healer was the Red Hawk's Chosen. The mother hesitated and then shook her head again. During the exchange Aithne saw increasing panic on the young father's face. The girl began to cry in shaking sobs as her husband tried to comfort her.

From somewhere behind them Fea's strong voice demanded Aithne be allowed to care for the laboring girl, but it made no difference. The mother remained resolute and though defying the sister of the iarel, she refused. Fea gave a sharp sigh and left the building in search of her brother. If needed, he could command the woman to stand aside and allow her daughter to drink the potent.

The standoff continued and it only frustrated Aithne. The girl went headlong into another strong contraction, crying out in piteous wails, and she took that moment to push the stubborn mother off-center. The healer pulled her knife out of its scabbard and handed it to an astonished Orva.

"Tell her that if her daughter dies I grant the father of the child the right to slay me." Her voice was even and strong.

Orva blinked and demanded incredulously, "Are you sure, Aithne? Many things can go wrong …"

"Tell her!" There was a tense silence as Orva carefully composed the words into her own language.

An audible gasp flew around them. The young man stared into Aithne's eyes, judged her and then nodded. He stretched out his hand and Orva handed him Aithne's blade. He uttered some short command and the mother of the girl closed her eyes, intoned a prayer, and then made the girl drink the herbed potent. She sputtered, moaned, and then complained how awful it tasted. Once it was gone she lay back to rest and her husband resumed bathing her face with cool water.

The tension was thick. Aithne was not aware of the crowd slowly forming around them as she kept her eyes riveted on her patient, constantly checking the quality of the birthing pains. Through it all the young man stalwartly comforted his wife as she continued to moan.

"How long does this take?" Orva asked, nervously.

"It will happen very soon," Aithne replied and remained fixed on the preparations for the birth. She noted a dagger resting nearby in an oily herbal mixture with only the handle protruding. When she reached to touch it Orva immediately forbade her to do so.

"It is the father's dagger, it is his task to cut the lifecord after he offers proper homage to the Gods. He is ritually cleansing the blade before the cutting. It is not for you to touch."

Aithne nodded her acquiescence. Her nose picked up a distinctive bouquet of the herbs.

"What are the herbs you use for the cleansing?"

Orva listed three or four names in the Southern tongue and Aithne did not know them.

"Describe what they look like," she said and Orva did exactly as asked.

"Of course," Aithne answered and smiled knowingly. "We use similar herbs to bind wounds. Your healers are very skilled. The herbs will prevent your babes from dying from cord-ill."

"We have done it time out of memory. We do not know why, it is just what is done."

"Then keep doing it," Aithne remarked as she kept an eye on the girl's progress. She was moaning less, beginning to relax and work with each contraction now.

"We may need to learn what herbs to use from your land as ours are vanishing with the drought."

"I will teach you what you need to know," the healer offered.

A low moan floated in the air and Aithne kept the knowing smile off her face. Subtly the quality of the girl's contractions had changed. She was now actively working with the labor pains instead of against them.

"Good," Aithne muttered and from the look on her face Orva did not need to translate for her kinsmen.

Only a few minutes later the baby, a blonde-haired boy, slid into Aithne's newly cleansed and waiting hands. He was small but appeared healthy. He howled in fury at his rude introduction into life as the healer quietly whispered a prayer of thanks to the Powers for Their assistance.

"We are favored by the Gods," Orva intoned right before unrestrained sounds of joy erupted around them. Aithne handed the babe to its mother so it could suckle and waited for the afterbirth to appear. It did in short order and was intact. The birth was now complete and it appeared there would be no complications. Aithne offered another silent prayer of thanks. She prepared a different potent and this time there was no issue of trust. The girl took it right down, still grimacing at the taste.

"It will slow her bleeding and help bring her milk on," Aithne explained and Orva translated. The new grandmother had tears in her eyes as she lovingly stroked the infant's bloody forehead. The new father was murmuring quietly, no doubt a prayer of gratitude. Once he had completed his invocation he removed the dagger out of the oily mixture and ritually severed the child's cord. Each family member placed a small stripe of cord blood on their left cheek as evidence that they had a new clansman in their midst. Some of the blood was offered to Aithne and she applied it in the manner of the others. That elicited a general murmur of approval. She caught a slight movement to her left and found the earnest brown eyes of the iarel upon her. He had some of the blood on him as well. He smiled gently, obviously pleased with the turn of events, and then disappeared out of the building.

Aithne sat with the new mother and her infant for over an hour to assure all was well. The father returned her knife and heartily embraced her, to the healer's surprise. She finally rose and headed back toward the iarel's hut, exhausted. Momentarily, she lost her way, for neither Orva or Fea were with her. When she wandered down a long row of tents she found herself face-to-face with Fyren, the man who had killed her husband.

Aithne muttered an oath, one she was sure he did not understand. He murmured something in his language and though she did not comprehend the words, she sensed the meaning. His manner was menacing and there was a leer on his face. As she drew away a small hand caught hers and it startled her. She glanced down to find a little blonde-haired boy, barely five-years old, standing near her. He ignored Fyren and tugged her along through the clansite, chattering all the while in his own tongue as if she could understand him. He finally deposited her at the iarel's hut. She had no idea who he was but gave him a big smile and then reached down and hugged him.

"Gunn?" Orva's voice called and the little boy wiggled out Aithne's arms and scooted over to accept a hug from the older clanswoman. Once that was complete he shot off into the camp in search of his friends, a merry smile on his face. Orva joined Aithne as she stood outside the hut.

"I see you've met Gunn. I sent him to find you. He is a wonderful boy."

"Whose child is he?" the healer asked.

"He is an orphan, one of the many we have now. He is one of my favorites," Orva replied.

A curious question popped into Aithne's mind. "Orva, why is the iarel not married? I would have thought he would have a wife and children, given his age and his position within the clan."

"In many ways, he is married – the clan is his bride. He has been iarel for over sixteen moons now and all that time famine has stalked us. It is important he marry so that there be sons and daughters to carry on his line, but he will not hear of it until he knows our people will survive this sad time."

"I see." Orva examined Aithne's face and sensed the exhaustion behind it. She placed a comforting hand on the healer's shoulder.

"Come, you are very weary. I will find some food for you and you must rest."

Aithne glanced up at that and advised, "Orva, I wish no more food than what all the others eat." Instinctively she suspected she would receive more since she was in the iarel's care.

A faint smile tracked over Orva's broad face. "It is custom that the family of the iarel and the healers receive more sustenance so that they may stay healthy to serve the people. The iarel has not followed custom in this way, for he has apportioned part of his food ration so that the children may eat."

"Then this healer shall do the same," Aithne replied and disappeared into the hut.

The tale of how the fire-haired pagan had delivered a baby while offering her life as a pledge of trust in the mother's stead swept through the clansite. Aithne was not allowed much rest. She ate the morsels of food Orva brought her – a small piece of fresh cooked fish and nearly tasteless bread – and then she was called to visit an ill child. Once they learned she was a healer of skill she was summoned throughout the camp. Aithne actively stepped into the void left by their deceased healer and did not return to the iarel's hut until far after the moon rose. The iarel appeared asleep in his furs. She carefully stepped around him, removed her cloak and nestled into her own set of furs.

His voice startled her when he murmured, "Thank you for your help, fire-hair. My people have much need of you."

Aithne did not answer but snuggled down into the warm furs and was asleep almost instantly.

ELEVEN

◆

I f Aithne thought Fyren was not a menace, she was naïve. She made sure to have her knife on her at all times, but everything she'd heard about clan law told her the man dare not touch her without risking not only his life, but that of his family. When she learned he was married and had two small children she could not fathom that he would jeopardize their lives solely for an opportunity to lie with her. His actions said otherwise. She would exit a hut or a tent and find him lurking in the distance, always watching, a leer on his face. She wrestled with the problem and decided not to mention this to Orva or the iarel feeling that Caewlin had too much on his mind as it was.

Fyren was inflamed with the need to possess the pagan woman, for in his mind she should have been his. The iarel's actions puzzled him for he could not understand why his leader had left such a prize behind, untouched. He consoled himself that there would be further forays and he would find other pagan women to enjoy. When there were no further raids he grew bitter and angry. Aithne's presence in the camp only ignited his desire.

When word came that Phelan had destroyed another clan, Caewlin set sail to retrieve the survivors as he had Erc's people. After the iarel departed Fyren rose from his furs late that night and headed into the forest, as if to relieve himself. Waiting a short time, he circled back and made his way to the iarel's hut. There was no fire within and so he lingered, waiting for the woman to return. He had it worked out in his mind – he would lie with her until near dawn, slay her and then row her body out into the sea. By weighting her corpse with stones it would drop into the depths where it would never rise again. Scavenger fish would make a meal of her, hiding his crime. He heard the sound of approaching footsteps in the dry dirt and saw a form coming toward him. It was the fire-hair. He smiled at his fortune and drew his dagger.

Aithne had attended a birthing and she was just returning to her bed for the night. It had been a long day and her worry for Caewlin only added to it. She had not realized how much she appreciated his quiet strength, his gentle voice and his care of her. She had tarried after the birthing as she was not looking forward to a night alone.

As she neared the hut she saw the figure of a man walking toward her. It did not concern her, there were usually clansmen up and around at all hours of the night. However, something about this one caught her attention and she instinctively put her hand on her knife. As she passed by him she belatedly realized it was Fyren.

Her knife did her no good. He whipped around, grabbed her and slapped a thick hand over her mouth as he wrestled her toward the hut. She struggled, managing a half-turn that slammed an elbow into his chest. He doubled over, cursing and his knife flashed in the moonlight. Aithne felt pain shoot through her arm but still managed to kick him in the thigh, barely missing his groin. He cried out, furious at himself for making noise. He slashed at her again and she stepped back, tripping. As she fell to the ground Fyren flung himself on top of her, his blade at her throat and curses on his lips.

Aithne never knew how it was she fought him off nor why it was she could not scream. She finally bested him and fled into the darkness, her clothes rent and her body battered. She hid herself in the forest, huddled inside an old hollow tree as she heard Fyren hunting for her in the darkness. All the while he muttered vile oaths under his breath as he slashed at the undergrowth in increasing panic. Aithne clutched her bleeding arm and felt waves of nausea flood through her. She began to shake in shock and tugged her cloak around her for warmth. Eventually she pulled her knees up and dozed inside the tree, the thick smell of earth and decaying wood around her.

When dawn came Fyren had no choice but to abandon his hunt. He washed the blood off him in the surf and returned to his furs. When his wife asked where he had been he snarled at her, struck her and began to drink. As he drank himself into a stupor, his mind conjured up the thought that the pagan was dead, that he had struck her a mortal blow and that she'd died somewhere in the forest. He prayed that was the case. To think otherwise meant his doom.

When Aithne was not in her hut and nor found to be tending a patient, a search was mounted. Gunn found her for the hollow tree was a favorite hiding place for him when it was time to bathe. He looked in at her, smiled and offered his small hand. She pulled herself out and his eyes widened at the sight of her.

"Are you hurt?" he asked, seeing the blood on her.

"Gunn," she said and gave him the most reassuring smile she could muster. She knew her disheveled appearance must be frightening to the lad.

"Come!" he urged and tugged her forward. She could not walk and sank to her feet at the base of the tree.

"Go find Orva for me. I am too tired to walk," she said, keeping her language simple for the little boy. He nodded and vanished through forest. She leaned back against the old tree trunk and let the tears fall.

The iarel returned to the clansite the next night with the remnants of the White Owl clan in his longships. His mood was grim, for he brought home pitifully few survivors. Galen was the one chosen to tell him of Aithne's fate, knowing it had best come from someone the iarel would not dare harm in his rage. As it was, Caewlin was livid. It was rare for his people to see his anger, but he did not attempt to hide it. It took all his control not to order Fyren and his family put to death the instant he learned of the attack. He regained his composure and ordered the man brought before him as he sat on the carved wooden bench from which his father and his ancestors had dispensed judgment. The bench sat in the center of the clan's hall and the building was full. All knew what crime Fyren stood accused of and that the penalty for his actions was death.

Caewlin gazed down at the bound man, his fury held in check. He had realized the crime was not against him, as iarel, but against their deity. That was far more heinous in his mind.

"The Northerners say we are heathen barbarians, Fyren, that we violate and beat our women and are godless. In that they are right if they judge us by your vile behavior. You have touched the Red Hawk's Chosen and must pay the penalty."

"It is your fault for you took her away from me!" the man shot back.

Caewlin refused to be baited. "Do you have any request before I send you to your grave?" Fyren shook his head. Caewlin eyed him cautiously. "Do you not wish to ask for the lives of your family?" It was customary for a condemned man to make that plea and so would allow an iarel leniency if he so desired.

"No! If I am to die then they shall as well." The man's cold-bloodedness rippled through the crowd. Dark murmurs flew from all sides.

Caewlin's voice was sheathed in steel. "Strip him and stake him on the beach. Make small slits on his body, just enough to draw blood so the sea crabs may find him. He will be allowed to die at his own pace. I do not want his body burnt, buried or moved in any way. His bones will bleach in the sunlight as a reminder to all who would lie with a woman without her permission. In that way we will atone to the Red Hawk for his sin against Her." His punishment was more harsh than usual, for the law decreed that the man be beheaded.

"As you wish, Iarel," Nerian replied as he hoisted the condemned clansman to his feet. Fyren said nothing, only glowered and spat at leader's his feet.

"Your contempt for me is not important, Fyren. Best you should think on your eternal torment in the talons of the Red Hawk for having harmed Her Chosen." Fyren actually paled at that. Nerian pulled him away before he could speak, marching him to the beach where they staked him out to die.

Aithne awoke to find Caewlin and Orva sitting near her in the hut.

"Fire-hair?" the iarel asked gently. He had seen the bruises on her body, the cut on her shoulder from Fyren's blade. His heart was full of guilt, he should have protected her.

"Caewlin." She thought for a moment and then offered a prayer of gratitude for he was alive.

"Aithne, I am so sorry …" he began and then his voice caught at the end. Orva gave him a measured look, sensing the depth of this man's devotion to the pagan woman.

"It is not your fault, Caewlin. He has lusted after me since the village. I should have told Orva that he was watching me, following me."

"Aithne …" he stopped, unable to say anything further. He felt impotent, ashamed.

"His assault failed and I fled into the forest. I am only bruised and sore."

"I should have acted as your family, Aithne. I apologize for not keeping you safe," Caewlin said raggedly.

"I hold no anger toward you, Caewlin."

"He is condemned to death," he replied, his voice growing stronger.

"How?"

"He is to die slowly, lying on the beach as the sea crabs consume him."

Aithne barely contained the shiver that rose within her. It was clan justice in all its unyielding severity.

"May the Powers judge him wanting and never allow his soul to rest," she intoned. Orva's eyebrow raised. It was a curse of some weight in her mind.

"There is the matter of his family …" Caewlin began. "By law I have the right to put his wife and his children to death."

Aithne's tired eyes raised immediately, "You must spare them."

"It is the law, Aithne, for he did not ask me for their lives," he replied solemnly.

"You are the iarel, you can change the law," she retorted, though she was not completely certain of this.

He shook his head as he rose to leave the hut. "An iarel is as much held in thrall by the laws as anyone." Fyren had not asked for their lives and so he had bound the iarel more than was necessary.

Aithne put her head in her hands in despair. It was only then she realized that one of them was bandaged. She had taken more injury than she thought. Caewlin left her to Orva's care and set off into the forest to calm his nerves. He needed to clear his head and allow his mind to work. In the distance he heard a raw voice calling out, begging. It was Fyren. The sea crabs had begun their task of returning his body to the earth.

Caewlin's eyes grew cold. "Die slowly, Fyren, for an eternity of pain is too swift for you."

Two small children huddled on the ground near their mother in the great hall. They sensed her fear and the sight of their wide eyes cut deep into Aithne's heart. It was two days since Fyren had attacked her and the clan had been summoned to learn the fate of his family.

"Tell us of what you know," Caewlin commanded, shifting his weight on the bench, the only physical indication of his unease.

Fyren's young wife, Mada, spoke in a halting voice,

"I knew of his lust for the pagan woman. He watched her. He would curse me at night for I was not her and strike me for he only wished to lie with her." There were tears in her eyes. One of the small children curled up tighter in her mother's embrace, needy and afraid. The other one, the older child, began to play quietly on the ground near his mother. Aithne turned her eyes toward the iarel, her heart aching.

"Did you know he would attack her that night?" Caewlin asked, his voice devoid of emotion.

"No, I did not," the woman answered honestly. The oldest child rose and tugged on his mother's hand wanting to leave, not understanding the gravity of the situation. She pulled him close, hugging him fiercely and he settled in her arms next to his sister.

Caewlin's voice rose, "Fyren attempted to lie with the woman known as Aithne without her consent and she sustained grievous injuries during his attack. As she is the Iarel's Chosen and more importantly, the Red Hawk's Chosen, the laws are even more strict."

The Iarel's Chosen. The words echoed in Aithne's mind. He had never claimed her as that before, at least in her presence.

"The laws are clear, the attacker and his family must be put to death unless the condemned asks for mercy. Fyren did not ask that his wife and children be spared. This is contrary to our way, for children are not so casually discarded."

There was absolute silence in the hall. Fyren's wife closed her eyes and hugged her children closer, fearing the moment they would be taken and slain before her eyes.

"I ask Aithne the Healer to make her feelings." His strong brown eyes reached hers and she swore she could see a plea for assistance.

He does not want to kill these people. Powers, show me a way to help him make a just decision.

She rose and cleared her throat. Her face still bore dark bruises and her body ached to the bones. She made sure her voice was clear so that all in the hall could hear her.

"Fyren had lust for me the moment he saw me in my village. He killed my husband and where that is evil, it is what happens during times of conflict. His attempt to force me the other night was something different. The Powers protected me and I have offered Them my prayers of gratitude." She paused and looked down at Fyren's wife. "Here I see another woman who has been harmed by this man, scorned and abused by a mate who favored drink and women who were not his own. I see two young children who wish nothing more than to go outside to play in the sunshine."

Her eyes were intense and her voice strong. She turned her eyes to the iarel, the man who held this trio of lives in his hand. "I know your laws, Iarel, and I can see the justice in them. I ask that you not apply justice in this case, but humanity. I wish that this woman be given the chance to find a man who would love her, care for her and raise her children to be decent and honorable. I have witnessed the death of far too many of your kin in the very short time I have been here. I ask for their lives, Iarel, so that your clan may survive." She sat down and closed her eyes, praying.

Silence reined. Caewlin closed his eyes for a time and when he finally spoke it was a low tone, though everyone in the hall could hear him.

"Our ways have not changed in all the generations. Now events are changing us. To execute a woman and her two babes because of her husband's misguided lust and lack of honor would indeed be inhuman. Therefore, I suspend the law in this case and allow that this woman and her children may live."

There was a ripple of strong approval throughout the assemblage, for they could see the decency in his decision. Tears sprang to Mada's eyes and she kissed both of her children in turn, though they had no idea what sparked their mother's sudden show of emotion.

"May the Red Hawk bless you, Iarel," she murmured through the tears.

Caewlin continued, "The healer has made a good point. If there is a man here who would take this woman as wife, if she approves, then I would bless this union, for it would heal the deep wound within our clan."

A few men shifted on their feet but no one came forward. Caewlin held his tongue and waited. A tall clansman determinedly made his way from the side of the hall, as the iarel had hoped.

"Iarel," the man said and bowed. He had a pleasant face and a courtly manner, unlike Fyren.

"Dubhan," the iarel replied.

"I am willing to offer this woman my dagger."

A slight smile appeared on Caewlin's face. "Make your offer then, for though I believe you are worthy, it is Mada's decision."

The young man nodded and shifted his position until he was on his knees in front of Fyren's wife. He pulled his dagger, lay it across his palms, and offered to her.

"I, Dubhan of the Red Hawk Clan, acknowledge you are married to another. I ask that when you are free of that bond, that you guard this dagger, protect yourself with it and keep it as long as you love me. If you accept this blade you accept my proposal and so doing you agree that you will share my furs, bear my children and tend to me all my years, no matter what the Gods set before us. In return I vow to honor you, keep you and your children safe and love you as the Gods have always loved us."

Mada smiled gently and it was only then that Aithne saw the fine hand of the iarel at work. The woman's eyes did not register surprise or distrust of the man in front of her. They radiated deep affection.

Powers! She knows him, cares for him!

"I, Mada, accept your blade and your proposal. I know you to be an honorable man and I know my life and of my children will be better for such a union."

"I am favored by the Gods!" the man said, a broad smile on his face. She took the dagger from him, held it for a time and then returned it, the ritual completed.

"Then I bless this marriage," Caewlin said with a pleased look on his face. His eyes were twinkling in delight. *You knew he would ask for her hand! You had this planned all along.* She began to feel a bit used but it did not bother her in the least. Fyren was dying on the beach and once his wife was free to wed, she would marry a man who obviously cared for her. The iarel's decision was a wise one.

All things happen as the Powers will, she thought.

The sounds from the beach were echoing in Aithne's mind and she could not sleep. If she tried to doze, Fyren's wails would wake her. She cringed at the noise and sat upright in the furs, rocking back and forth in obvious distress.

Caewlin sensed the movement and sat up, concerned. "Fire-hair, are you unwell?" He knew she had not slept soundly for the past four nights. She had refused herbs to help her sleep and he suspected her distress had nothing to do with the wounds she bore.

"I cannot sleep, not with …"

"He will die soon, Aithne." As the days progressed Fyren descended into madness from the interminable agony of hundreds of tiny nibbling crabs. Caewlin recognized that as Fyren suffered, so did the clan, for they endured his cries day and night. The iarel's righteous anger began to fade and he realized the punishment was too severe.

"It is not right, Iarel."

He caught the use of his title. "An example must be set," he replied evenly, speaking as the leader of a clan should.

"It has been."

His voice softened. "The sounds disturb you?"

"Yes," she replied honestly and sought his eyes in the dim light. "It is not me that I think of, Iarel, it is his wife and children, for they hear him as plainly as I do."

There was silence and then without a word he donned his clothes, picked up his sword and left the hut. A coarse shriek rent the air a few minutes later and then blissful silence. In time he returned, undressed and crawled into his furs.

"You are decent man, Caewlin," she said. Fyren was now with his Gods, facing Their judgement. The iarel did not reply and drifted off to sleep, knowing in his heart he'd done the right thing.

Dubhan and Mada were married that next evening and though the food was meager, the celebration was merry. Aithne remained at Caewlin's side until she felt her strength fade. When she rose and walked back to the hut she found one of the iarel's men accompanying her. She would no longer know a moment's peace, but she need not fear another Fyren in their midst.

When the fourth clan fell to Phelan's sword, Aithne traveled with Caewlin and his men to the remnants of the Black Stag clansite. He had not wanted her to come with him, but she demanded the right to go as a healer. He acquiesced, but only after warning her that she must be extremely careful, Phelan's men could still be at the site when they landed using the few survivors as bait to trap the Red Hawk Clan.

"I'll take my sword, besides my herbs," she answered defiantly.

He frowned and shook his head, recognizing a shield-woman when he saw one. Caewlin's grandmother had been one and her courage often exceeded that of his grandsire. Women had a capacity for fearlessness that he could not comprehend.

You are indeed Her chosen, fire-hair.

The pall of smoke from the fires was clearly visible from a great distance out to sea. Aithne steeled herself for what they would find for though Caewlin had never told her of what they had found at that other clansites, she had heard reports from some of the other clansmen. She feared Black Stag Clan's demise would be no less horrific.

This time there were fewer corpses.

"Phelan needs more slaves," was Nerian's grim observation. Caewlin nodded. He watched Aithne tend what wounded they could find and kept a wary eye on her. As was Phelan's way, the main hall remained intact and Caewlin knew the Black Stag's iarel and his people were within, displayed in death like Erc and his clan. When Aithne began to walk toward the entrance he immediately attempted to stop her.

"Aithne, no," he said as he put his hand on her arm in a gesture of concern.

"There may be wounded," she replied.

"There will be none left alive in there. He kills them all ... the children as well."

"I will go in," she said, fixing his eyes with hers.

"I ask you not to. The sight will haunt you forever." His voice cracked.

"I know, but I must." He took a deep breath and nodded reluctantly, sensing she would not yield to his request.

"Then I will go with you." Together they made their way into the Black Stag's hall.

The revulsion never lessened every time he stood inside one of the clan's great halls after Phelan had completed his barbarous work. As he gazed upward at the body of the Black Stag's leader on the center pole, with a jolt Caewlin realized he was now the last iarel, only the Red Hawk Clan remained. He shifted his eyes over to Aithne who stood deathly pale near the pile of corpses. He saw her lips moving in silent prayer.

Nerian came striding from across the great hall, his face puzzled.

"Iarel?"

"Yes?" Caewlin replied in a quiet voice. In his mind this was holy ground, made sacred by the blood of the dead.

"There are only a handful of children here, not as many as at the other clans."

Caewlin thought and then asked, "Could they have hidden them away when they saw Phelan's ships?" It was unlikely the clan was caught unawares for they all knew of Phelan's raids after the Badger Clan's fall. The Black Stag's leader was a cautious man, one who had campaigned for peace as earnestly as he had. *Perhaps* ...

"We will look. May the Gods make it so," Nerian replied and marched out of the structure, slim hope in his heart.

Caewlin claimed the dead as he had with Erc's kin and each clan since. He noted with some surprise that Aithne cut her palm as well, casting her blood on the corpses as she followed in line with the other clansmen. In that simple gesture, she became one of them.

The Red Hawk's Chosen has chosen us, he thought.

As the great hall burned like a roaring torch in the night sky, Caewlin and his men carefully parceled out the treasure they'd found hiding in the nearby forests. One hundred and eight children ranging in age from only a few weeks to ten years were divided amongst the longships. Aithne had a baby in her hands, a little boy of almost a week old. His eight-year-old sister sat next to her, pale and in shock. Aithne crooned to the child and tried to comfort the little girl. Around were other children and some of the clansmen had infants in their arms as well.

"How many do we bring home?" Caewlin asked, as was his grim habit.

A melancholy smile came to his second-in-command's worn face. "Twelve hands and three." One hundred twenty-three.

"The Gods have been merciful," Caewlin intoned and ordered the ships to sail. All of the Southern Isle clans were now his people, either in life or death. The weight on his shoulders grew almost too heavy to bear.

Aithne readily healed of Fyren's wounds, but the long days she put in as healer were taking their toll. She now knew why their previous healer had perished – lack of rest and nourishing food. She drug herself through the days, as did Caewlin, and they found themselves too exhausted at night to even speak to each other as they collapsed in their own furs.

The addition of over one-hundred children to feed and care for put an immense strain on the clan, immediately felt by both the iarel and the healer. Almost every household took in a child or two and stretched their meager rations to include the newcomers. The children slowly responded to the love they received, but every one of them bore the mark of their clan's death in their hearts. Caewlin was keenly aware that the clan's food supply was nearing an end and the winter would soon be upon them.

As he set his mind on new ways to obtain sustenance, Fea suggested an obvious solution to relieve Aithne's burden. It was so simple the healer cursed herself for not thinking of it sooner. If selected women were trained to handle the less serious cases, taught how to compound and apply herbal poultices, treat minor illnesses and injuries, the senior healer's duties would decline to a manageable level. Overall the clan's health would improve as much as the conditions allowed and the women would learn valuable healing skills. Aithne gave her approval at once, not even consulting the iarel. She knew he would agree and at the moment he had his own difficulties to overcome.

Fea proved to be invaluable in establishing the small healer's school. Ten women were selected and Aithne spent each morning teaching her art and the remainder of the time working amongst the clan, apprentice healers in tow. She skipped the majority of the lengthy lectures about herbal properties and moved right into practical healing. Within two weeks, she had her acolytes applying poultices, assisting at births and easing the dying into their new life. They became capable of handling the simpler cases and Aithne knew their scheme was working the night she slept straight through until dawn.

During the entirety of that time Caewlin had been warm, sociable and caring, despite the immense burden of leadership that now bore down on him. Not once had he made any move that threatened her and she was comfortable with him sleeping near her at night. He was particularly sensitive to her after Fyren's attack and as time passed, she found herself drawn to the handsome young iarel.

One night she took herself to the beach, watching the moon rise while reflecting on how her life had changed the day she stepped inside the iarel's boat. Her protector stood a discrete distance away and when she heard him speak to someone, she knew the iarel had found her. She turned and saw the guard bow and return to camp. Caewlin walked to her side. He gave her a gentle smile and she returned it. To her surprise, he put his arm around her waist, pulling her close to his side. They stood watching the waves and moon in silence. He had learned that another child had died today, despite her care. He knew the losses were pounding at her soul as they did his.

As if she knew his thoughts she murmured, "So many dead, Caewlin. How do you cope?" Her voice was barely audible above the sounds of the surf. A night bird flew above them, calling into the darkness as it hunted a moth. Their eyes tracked its progress until it disappeared into the forest.

He tightened his grip around her waist and answered, "By celebrating every day I am given, fire-hair. I thank the Gods every morning I rise. I thank Them every time I hear a new baby cry, every time I lie with a woman and experience the pleasure we share. And when I die, I will offer my thanks for They are my light in this dark world."

His faith is so simple, she thought, *and yet so strong.*

"I do not know how you push yourself forward each day. I have been here only a short time and it wears on my soul. You have struggled for almost three years."

He gazed at her for a time without answering. *You have helped me beyond measure, though you do not realize it.*

Not knowing where her heart lie, he pushed down his feelings and replied, "The Gods will see that we have persevered and They will return Their favor once again."

"I pray that it is soon," she said and fell silent. His arm remained around her waist as they walked back to the camp.

TWELVE

Morwyn gradually learned her way around the sprawling port city of Kell. It had not been easy. After the incident at the inn she quickly learned to avoid the city guards and their ill intent. Women routinely vanished off the streets only to be found in one of the brothels or dead in a gutter some days later. Families hid their young daughters and only servants went to the market to buy food. Children did not play outdoors in the sunshine as they should.

The Powers have cursed these people, she thought as she ducked down a side street for the fifth time that day. She'd mapped every back alley and side street and used them religiously. She'd already been confronted by a quartet of Phelan's guards and was only left alone as one of them, their leader, recognized her as a healer.

"What of it, Gorsedd? They make good sport as any other woman. Better, for they are healthier!" another of the guards remarked, eyeing Morwyn's lithe figure. Under her cloak she had her hand on her knife.

"No, for someday you may go to find a healer to cure whatever ill the Powers have sent you and there will be none. You will die in agony because of your lechery."

The man paused and uttered a brief prayer. Gorsedd's words sounded a bit too close to a curse for his liking.

"So be it, girl, go away!" the guard grunted. Morwyn scooted around the quartet and remained off the streets for the next two days.

Her hours were long and tiring, but the work was fulfilling. She used what little magic she had when the situation warranted it, but it made small difference. Siarl and the other four healers worked long hours and he made most of the journeys outside the House of Healing. He was too thin for work as a slave and as he often joked, he had no future as a sporting wench at one of Kell's brothels. Morwyn accompanied him when she could and they bonded their working relationship into one of friendship.

Despite her camaraderie with Siarl or the other healers, she never once told them of her past. They guessed bits and pieces given her rudimentary magic and that she did not seek respite with any man, but none dared asked her of it. She did her work, held her silence and attempted to keep her mind off her family. It was at night, right before she fell asleep, that was the hardest. She would think about her children, how they had lost their youth, and then her mind would turn to *him*. She found herself wishing she had not been so rash in leaving Aderyn, nor asking for the Writ of Divorcement. It was too late now, all that was past. Each night ended with light tears trickling down as she buried her face in her pillow. Her life was full … her life was empty. She began to see what Belwyn meant when he said that in the end she would have nothing.

I have my magic and my work. She prayed it would be enough.

Pyrs' skills grew unchecked though there were still moments when his temper got the best of him. He spent considerable time with Dillan who readily took the lad under his wing as he had Pyrs's father and uncle. The days were full of lessons, archery and sword practice. Pyrs enjoyed the time outdoors and felt sorry for Gwyn who spent her time studying old manuscripts in the library. Often he and Dillan would just sit and talk and today they were resting under a tree after a vigorous archery lesson.

A thought popped into Pyrs's mind and he asked, "What is this thing grandsire wants to talk to me about this evening? He seemed a bit mysterious about it. He said it involved women." Dillan's one eyebrow raised and he smiled. He'd heard this same question from both Belwyn and his brother when they were Pyrs's age.

"Your grandsire wants to talk to you about sporting."

"Oh, I see," Pyrs mumbled. He'd suspected as much. "I'm not very interested in that, at present." He had noted the young dairymaid, she'd been flirting with him since the moment he'd arrived. She'd stolen a kiss from him and he'd found that rather fun, but in general, his mind was elsewhere.

"You will be. It'll come and it's best to know how to take your pleasure without leaving children behind."

"Like my sister and I," the boy remarked ruefully.

"Exactly. Though your father wasn't given a choice in the matter."

"I suppose my time will come." The lad seemed resigned to it rather than eager. Watching his parents' trials had made him wary.

"I can say that it is a marvelous thing, handled in moderation."

"Morgan seems to enjoy it. He's always got a wench on his arm."

"Morgan seeks company for many reasons, not just for sport," Dillan discerned. Pyrs eyed him and knew instinctively what he meant.

"You're a wise old bird, Dillan."

"I am. Now if you've rested, you need to return to the house. It's almost time for your lessons." A groan was his answer, but Pyrs rose to his feet and dusted himself off. "After your grandsire talks to you, feel free to ask me any questions. I have no trouble talking about what a man must know."

"I will," Pyrs replied and set off for the hall and Dillan leaned back against the tree savoring the fine summer sunshine.

"Some things never change," he said.

Caewlin paused the moment he entered the hut, for was something different. The two separate sleeping furs were now together. Aithne lay in the middle of them. He knelt by the furs, examined her fire-lit face and asked in as casual tone as he could muster, "You know what this joining of the furs means?" She nodded. "You wish this, fire-hair?"

"I do."

"Why now?" he asked, intrigued. She had been with the clan over two and half moons and had never once indicated she desired to be with him.

"I wish to experience as much of life as I can before it is taken from me," she replied, her eyes shining. At this, she pulled back the furs near his knees. What part of her he could see was unclothed, her hair flowing over her chest in waves, the amulet beneath it.

"Then we shall experience it together, fire-hair." He rose, somewhat nervous if he was honest, and pulled down the hide flap over the hut's doorway to indicate the need for privacy. No doubt others in the camp would notice and tongues would wag. He did not care. He had been without a woman too long. He stripped out of his clothes and crawled into the furs next to her, his heart and mind raging at him. For the longest time he just lay there, gazing at her, his face full of wonder at his good fortune.

"Is there something wrong, Caewlin?" she asked, puzzled. She had thought he would have been more forward with his attentions.

"No, there is nothing wrong. Our people believe that the first time between a man and a woman, if they care for each other, should not be a hurried thing, but worship to the Gods."

"I see," she replied, a bit quieter. His ways were different from hers. He reached over and brushed his callused thumb across her cheek in a delicate gesture.

"You are so beautiful, fire-hair." He caressed her hair, pulling her closer. She gently kissed his cheek and he returned it.

"You are sure of this?" he asked again. "It is not required of you, Aithne." He wanted no doubt left in either of their minds.

"I am. I wish to be with you," she replied, gazing into his deep brown eyes. Her hands were gently roaming over his chest, touching him, learning each curve and muscle.

"Then I *am* favored by the gods," he replied and kissed her deeper, more intensely. He began the timeless loving ritual of his people, the gentle and determined caresses, the kisses, the embraces and finally, the joining.

As he united with her he intoned, "I am one with you and you one with me. May our loving be worship to the Gods." Then he began to make love to her in earnest.

She lay curled up in his arms after the loving, her mind at peace. She felt his soft breath in her hair, the scent of the herbal charm he wore on his neck, the gentle pressure of his hand on one of her breasts.

"Did I bring you pleasure, fire-hair?" he murmured. His eyes sought out hers, for he wished the truth.

"Yes." She did not lie.

"I have not been with a Northern woman before, I did not know if your ways were different. I feared I might not have satisfied you." She had sounded pleased, crying out as he moved with her, but one could not be sure.

"Some of your ways are different, some are not. There was not the frenzy of the loving as there often is between a man and a woman the first time they are together," she said, wrapping one of his long strands of hair around her finger. It seemed to glow like gold in the firelight.

"Then I did not bring you as much pleasure as I should have." His voice was tinged with a note of remorse.

"No, you brought me more, for this was far more than a heated rutting, Caewlin. You have been with me as if you truly love me."

There was a silence and then the answer came. "I do love you, fire-hair. I have loved you since the day I saw you standing over your mate, protecting him and your unborn child. Your bravery and your beauty captured my heart." He paused and she did not reply. He wondered if he had been too forward. "I thought I should tell you what is in my heart," the iarel said.

"Now I know why our first time was so passionate, so full. I have not known loving like this before," she said quietly.

"But surely your mate ..." Caewlin started and then caught himself, instantly chagrined at his insensitive comment.

"My husband was a good man, Caewlin, for he kept me warm and safe. He cared for me in his own way as I did him, but there was no real passion between us. The joining was for pleasure, for children, but not love."

"By the Gods," he said. *The man was a fool.*

She laid her head on his chest for a few minutes longer and then began to kiss him again, building his passion.

"I wish you again," she said.

As he pulled her closer, he said, "This time will not be like the first, we have made our offering to the Gods. This time there *will* be heat between us." He heard her chuckle and that amusement immediately changed to cries of pleasure as he strove to show the Northern woman how impassioned a Southern man could be.

When she rose in the morning, he was already gone. She found Orva waiting for her outside the hut, an unreadable look on her face. It was common knowledge that the iarel and his woman were now lovers for there were few secrets within the clan.

"You rise late, Aithne." The words were loaded with meaning.

"I do." Aithne gave her a subtle smile and Orva returned it. The look they shared spoke reams.

"I saw that the door flap on your hut was down last night."

"So all of the camp knows we were together?"

"Most of them."

"Will they accept that, given that I am a Northerner?"

"If the iarel of our clan prospers, so do we. He has not been with a woman for a very long time and that is not right. Few would raise an objection with him sharing his furs with the Red Hawk's Chosen."

"Good, for I intend to share them as long as he wants me there." Aithne shouldered her pack and set off to check on her patients from the day before. Whether it was her imagination or not, the clan acted even more differential.

She found Caewlin in the furs waiting for her that night. Though he tried to mask it, there was an eager look about him. This time she put down the outer flap. She saw him smile at that.

"The evening bodes well for me, fire-hair." His voice was soft and full of promise.

"It does," she replied, slipping off her clothes and sliding into the furs next to him. They lay together for a time as he caressed her. His hand strayed over her body, building her desire and then stopped on her flat stomach.

"Someday, Aithne, I will ask you to bear me a child," he said quietly in her ear. He knew she took herbs to prevent pregnancy, he tasted them when he kissed her.

She gave him a curious look. "I would have thought you would want a child by one of your own women."

He frowned and shook his head. "No, I want a child by you. I want my seed to find sanctuary within you and in return, you bear me a son."

"Perhaps, someday," she replied, unwilling to think that far in the future. Sensing her unease he kissed her and they turned their minds to the loving.

The conversation between the Wise, the Saga and the Iarel lasted the good portion of day. By late afternoon they were weary in both body and spirit. They had painstakingly examined every possible means to save their clan and found there were pitifully few choices. The Gods had not completely withdrawn Their favor, but They were making Their servants work for the right to remain alive. They were all in agreement that no further raids would take place. When the iarel made the suggestion they move their people to the Northern forests, Galen was stunned. Devona held her tongue while the Saga and Caewlin debated the issue vigorously.

Finally, Galen began to yield.

"I fear moving the clan so close to our enemy. It is aiding Phelan as if we were in his pay," he remarked.

"It is. However, if we stay here he will come for us as he has Erc and the others. He will butcher our children, savage our women and carry the remainder of us off to serve as his slaves. If we move the clan to the Northern forests we can hide and find abundant food. Our ability to fight is dependent on a steady food supply. There will be none here once the winter snows come."

"I know, I know," the man admitted grimly. There were few options left.

"I will ask the Red Hawk to show us the path. I suggest this should be with the clan present, for it is their future as well," Devona instructed.

Caewlin nodded solemnly. "I will abide by Her decision, Wise."

"The Gathering Night comes, that would be the best time."

Caewlin nodded and then addressed another issue that had weighed on him. His voice became softer. "I will be with the fire-hair for the Gathering Night, Wise."

Her strange eyes did not really react but her tone became strained.

"As I expected." Knowing he had disturbed her, he rose and left the woman's hut feeling decades older than his years.

Galen waited for a moment and then offered, "Devona, I would be pleased if you would be with me during the Gathering Night." She moved her uniquely colored eyes over to the Saga and nodded.

"It is as the Red Hawk wishes." Sensing she would say no more, he rose and left her to a myriad of thoughts.

The Gathering Night was one of the holiest nights of the clan's solar year. Each year, as fall arrived, they celebrated what was usually a bountiful harvest and entreated the Gods to grant them a good winter, praying for the promise of spring and her fecundity. The ceremony was a rite of food, drink and ritual joining on the shores of the sea just as their ancestors celebrated throughout the generations. This year there was no harvest to celebrate and the winter ahead of them looked bleak, filled with want and privation. This time they celebrated the fact that they were alive. This Gathering Night the clan would seek the will of the Red Hawk.

We have little future, Caewlin thought glumly as he presided over what should have been a feast. There was too little food to waste and so each person brought their own morsels to the gathering and celebrated as if the harvest was abundant as it had been in times past. He could remember this celebration as a child where the food flowed as well did the wine. He remembered his parents going to the beach, lying on the sand and joining in ritual homage to the Gods that kept them safe and healthy. Too young to participate, he stayed behind, knowing the adults would seek their pleasure on the beach until dawn. When he was old enough he did the same, choosing one of the young clanswoman to be with him for the night. Once he became iarel and did not have a wife, he made the journey to the beach with the Wise.

Their joining was more for symbolism, the combining of the powers between the iarel and the wisdom.

There is no future for us here, he thought again, saddened by the passing of a way of life. *We must flee while we still are able.*

There was silence amongst those gathered in the center of the camp, near the main hall. Nearly all the clansmen and women were present. They had spent the day bathing themselves and their clothes in preparation for this evening for this was a holy night. The moon was full, the night air clear and in the forest nearby hunting owls were on the wing. The Wise waited as the people gathered around her, the Saga and the Iarel on each side of her. Positioned in front of them were twin braziers, the light of the fires within casting shadows on the nearest faces. Inside one of the braziers was a bowl of sacred heated oil and in the other, an immense pot of warmed wine, seasoned with special herbs.

Once the Wise sensed the people had gathered, she raised her arms toward the sky in supplication, intoning prayers that had been part of their clan's religious rites for centuries. As she prayed she heard the people murmuring their own prayers, for all knew their fate would be decided this night.

The Wise slowly dropped her hands and then walked to the brazier where the oil bubbled within. The Saga handed her the ritual shell dipper and she immersed it in the mixture, careful to hold back the folds of her gown away from the oil and the flames. When she pulled forth the oil she moved to a portion of sand mounded into a heap on the ground, enclosed by a circle of stones. She closed her eyes and poured the oil, murmuring prayers the entire time. The oil cascaded down, splashing onto the sand and forming rivulets before it vanished within. She handed the dipper back to the Saga and then pulled a pouch of fine powder from her belt. Kneeling in front of the oil anointed sand, she scattered the powder on top of it. Where the oil and the powder met, a purple tint emerged, the omens she would read. Once assured all of the oil was impregnated with the powder, she dusted off her hands and began to study the omens, concentrating on each form and rivulet.

The clan was riveted on the Wise as they searched for meaning in her every movement. Knowing his peoples' anxiety, Caewlin made sure to keep his face blank, though his heart thudded in his chest and his throat was dry. He sensed Aithne behind him and without hesitation he reached back, took her hand, and brought her forward to stand by his side. Her hands were uncharacteristically cold to the touch and her eyes were as worried as his, for the strange patterns in the sand foretold their future.

As she studied the purple impressions in the sand, the Wise's mind whirled in amazement. *I have never seen such patterns!* The runes were complex, interwoven, more revelatory than the usual omens for fertility and an early spring. *Goddess, help me know Your Will.* The Wise steadied herself and began to decipher the reading in sections, keeping her mind focused and not allowing dismay to overcome her.

The crackle of the braziers, the hoarse coughs of some of the clansmen and the unending sounds of the surf in the distance surged around them as the Wise interpreted the runes. When she finally rose there was a slight sigh of relief from those nearest to her. She moved to stand on a raised platform from which all her people might be able to see and hear her. She gave no indication to the iarel of what she had learned, for it was the clan's right to know their fate at the same time their leader learned of it.

"The runes are more complex than I have ever seen. The rune for war is present in the center of the reading," she said as she pointed with a slim power-coated finger to the sand that lay five feet to her left. The iarel stared down at the center of the sand, his mind working through the runes. The Saga kept his eyes on Devona the entire time. The clan moved closer as a group, though they left a respectful distance between themselves and the reading. "To the east, south and west comes the darkness that encompasses us. It will not cease. I see that as the drought that now afflicts us."

"And to the north?" Caewlin asked, licking his lips, his throat suddenly tight.

"We have the rune for an enemy and ..." she paused and then made sure her voice carried, "a series of smaller runes that run off the main one. They are the runes for honor and rebirth." Murmurs began to flow through the crowd.

Devona continued, "In the north we have a sworn enemy, one who will destroy us if we continue as we are. Yet, his heinous actions will spawn justice, honor and rebirth amongst our people. The smaller runes are born of his sword." She paused and gathered her strength; "The runes speak of a sixth clan who will come to our aid." The murmurs became more heated now.

"All the remnants of the five clans are here, Wise, there are no others," Caewlin said, obviously confused.

"This clan resides in the north, Iarel. They will stand against our enemy as if they were to our clan born, as if they are our brothers. They will help us give rise to our rebirth."

"By the Gods," Caewlin intoned. "Then I ask, Wise, what does the Red Hawk require of us?" It was the question he had to ask.

"We must go north to meet our fellow clansmen and we will fight our enemy together. In that way the Gods will favor us and we will not perish." Her voice was resolute for she knew this was the Red Hawk's Will.

"And if we stay here?" Galen persisted.

The Wise shook her head. "There will be no help here, Saga. We must be willing to seek the aid of the others or we are doomed."

The murmuring died down. When Caewlin turned his eyes toward his people he found immense sadness residing on each face. The Wise intoned another lengthy prayer for guidance. When it was completed she raised her eyes and for those closest to her, they saw what no clansmen had ever seen – the tears of a Wise.

Seeking to regain her composure, she commanded, "Go, celebrate life as we are meant to, for we are guided to leave our home and make our way in a new place." Though stunned by her pronouncement, one-by-one the men came forward, dipped their goblets into the heated wine, and then paired off with their chosen mate.

Aithne found herself walking alongside Caewlin as they trailed down the sandy beach. He had explained the purpose of this night of physical worship and she somewhat understood. It had roots in the old spring rituals in the north, she realized, but the thought of being on the beach with her lover within clear sight of others made her very uncomfortable. He stopped at what he deemed a suitable location, lay out a heavy cloak and knelt on it, gesturing for her to do the same. She did not realize it was the exact location his parents and his grandparents had chosen for their Gathering Nights.

She remained standing, keenly aware of various couples not more than twenty feet from them. Some were talking, kissing, others were actively joining. She kept her eyes adverted but was still unnerved by the intimacy. Caewlin made sure to keep his voice light and not put undue pressure upon her. He knew this would prove difficult, as it was not her custom. He so wanted to be with her this night, to worship with her as one on the sand. He knew Galen and the Wise were already together further down the beach venerating the Gods.

"Fire-hair ..." he began and then stopped.

"We must be together ... here?" she asked glancing around again. She dropped her eyes immediately for the couple nearest them were now intimate.

"It is our way. No one will care, Aithne, they are involved in their own pleasure. The iarel must be here on this night with a woman or ..."

She almost asked if someone else could take her place and then stopped. She had already learned from Orva that in the past the Wise was his partner. Only a short time earlier she had seen Devona and Galen walking down the beach, together. There was no one else for the iarel.

She slowly knelt on the cloak and tried not to shiver.

"Come into my arms, Aithne. We need not rush, for we have all night. It is considered good fortune to be together at dawn, entwined within each other as the sun rises."

She worked her way into his arms and pushed her discomfort down. He kissed her gently and she returned the kiss. He handed her the cup of wine he had pulled from the brazier and she took a full drink. He drank from the cup as well and then set it firmly in the sand near them.

"It is only us here tonight, my fire-hair. Only us," he murmured and his kisses became more passionate. In time, her reserve fell away and they united on the beach under the moonlight, oblivious to the others loving near them.

"Wise, surely you will stay?" Galen asked, surprised when Devona began to pull on her garments. Her face remained impassive and though Galen had tried to bring her pleasure, she had remained reserved during their joining.

"We have fulfilled the rite and ..."

"We have, but we have not shared our pleasure."

She stopped dressing as if weighing his statement in her mind.

Galen tried again, "I would love you as you deserve, not some hasty coupling to satisfy the Gods. I wish to worship with you until the dawn comes."

"I ..." She no longer sounded like the confident priestess he knew, but a disconcerted young girl, for she was no more than seventeen years of age.

"I know you wished to be with him, but the Gods have sent the fire-hair as his woman."

Devona's eyes snapped up and she barely held her sharp tongue. Galen was only speaking the truth and it was not right for her to punish him for that.

"I have come to favor the iarel more than was prudent." It was an admission of some weight.

He gently touched her cheek. "As I have come to favor you, Devona." A slight expression of consternation crossed her face.

"You would be my lover for more than just this night?"

He slowly nodded and caressed her cheek again in loving tenderness.

"For all the nights that you would grant me." Not waiting for her reply he kissed her cheek and then lightly kissed her mouth. "Stay with me tonight, Devona, let us find joy with each other, for there is so little of it in our lives."

She closed her eyes and conceded, "Tonight only, Galen, for I cannot promise more than that."

He kept the disappointment off his face and replied, "Then I am favored by the Gods, at least this night." He pulled her into his arms and they slowly sank back down onto the sand.

Caewlin and Aithne remained on the beach until dawn, sharing their love. Her unease had melted, burned away by the passion they shared and she knew she would remember this night for the remainder of her days. The ritual seemed to have rich meaning now that she had partaken of it.

Despite the loving, Caewlin's sadness returned at dawn and she knew it was because they would leave this place in the coming days. She had always wandered in life, never once really having a home of her own. This *was* his home, the home of his people for generations, and now he had to leave it or watch his kin perish by starvation or the sword. She knew the ache that was in his heart and tried to bring him comfort in words and her gentle touch.

"There will be food in the forests for your people, my love. I will show them how to gather herbs and roots. I am a fair shot with a bow as well."

He gave her a gentle smile, knowing she was trying to ease his sadness. He so wanted to ask her to bear his child, but he knew he dare not. Every night for the past week he'd had the same dream, one that broke his heart. He'd hidden his tears from her in the night, for when they relocated to the Northern forests he would need to send her away. The Red Hawk had brought her to his people and now the time drew near for her to leave them.

He pulled her close to him and though weary, began to love her once more. He knew there were only a few times left he would be with her like this and he wished to cherish every moment. When they had shared their joined passion, she saw tears in his eyes.

He is sad because we must leave this place, she thought and hugged him closer. She did not realize his tears were a harbinger of their separation.

"I disagree, we do not have that much time, we must act now!" Lord Fercos's fist pounded on the heavy oak dining table to underscore the urgency. "Her councilor will sire a bastard on her and Bardyn will feel compelled to make them marry. We will lose our leverage," the man spouted. They'd finished their meal and were discussing Fercos's favorite topic – Lady Aldyn and her holdings. His fellow noble, Lord Corryn, observed his host's agitation with dispassion.

"There is no evidence they are lovers," Corryn replied evenly. He was an angular man with deep eyes and a sharp mind. He was the physical and mental opposite of his host.

"Oh, so you have your lackeys sleep under her bed every night just to see if he ruts with her or not?" Fercos growled back.

"No, I do not, but it is clear that they are not lovers for the man can barely walk." Corryn was not about to reveal his sources to someone as loose-tongued as Fercos. Every indication was that the lady had not taken a lover and was not actively searching for one.

"That will change, mark me," Fercos came back hotly. "I have seen how he looks at her. He will bed her and we will lose our advantage."

"It may happen," Corryn allowed.

"We must deal with him now, before that happens."

Corryn saw the chance to slip Fercos's head into the noose.

"And what do you recommend?" he asked casually. He knew there were at least four servants in the room, not counting his own. All of them would overhear whatever Fercos had in mind and become witnesses against him, if needed.

"A well-aimed arrow, a slip of poison in his food, a knife in the heart. There are many ways someone like Owain the Younger can die."

"If you act rashly you will bring Aderyn's wrath upon us. He is their youngest, after all." Corryn paused and took a long sip of the wine. It was of excellent vintage, but then Fercos always set a good table. "It appears your lust for the lady blinds your caution."

Fercos nodded. "Yes, I have lust for her. She'd be good sport and I'd be sure to enjoy her regularly. It is her lands I lust after more."

"No, you lust after Bardyn's holdings, not hers. She is merely the bait to catch a bigger fish."

Fercos nodded again and belched. "So who is it you have in her holdings?" His small dark eyes were dilated from all the wine he'd consumed. It has loosened his tongue more than normal.

"Someone who will not fail me. Someone they trust without realizing how dangerous she really is."

"It's a woman?" Fercos asked, gratified to learn that much. He acted more like a servant begging for crumbs rather than an equal to his fellow lord.

"Yes, it is and you'll hear no more of it, Fercos. You talk too much."

"Not as much as I drink or wench," the man chuckled as he poured himself yet another full cup of wine.

"There is that," Corryn muttered.

"Perhaps I will be in her bed by winter," Fercos mused and then took a long swig of the wine before leaning back in his chair to ponder on that possibility.

"Perhaps," Corryn replied. *More likely in your grave.*

The Red Hawk Clan began to dismantle their lives the morning after the Wise interpreted the runes. Only a handful of the clan refused to follow their iarel north, so superfluous furs, personal items and such were left to their care. Aithne packed up the iarel's meager belongings and sat in the hut for a time, alone. Caewlin was on his feet constantly now, organizing the voyages to haul all the goods and his people to the North shore. He wanted Aithne in the last ship so she would be protected at all times. She had protested, but he had refused to hear her out, uncharacteristically cutting her off mid-sentence, his nerves taunt. She held her peace and allowed him to do as he wished.

Caewlin and Nerian divided the households into three separate groups. The first group would be mostly warriors and shield women, their strongest and fiercest fighters. It was their task to secure a temporary clansite and await those who would come on the subsequent voyages. The word was passed to pack light, for they would not remain in any one location for very long. A permanent home was impossible until Phelan no longer hunted them.

Aithne packed all the herbs and potions, ready for use at their new home. She knew an abundance of herbs were available in the Northern forests, but time was needed to collect and prepare them, so she packed their stock with care. Each healer had their own individual supply and were assigned to a specific group of clan to care for them during the move. It took two days to load the ships and once all was ready, the Wise offered prayers and took omens regarding the journey. A faint smile appeared on her face.

"Our journey will be effortless, Iarel, for we do as the Gods and the Red Hawk wish."

"May it be so," Caewlin replied and ordered the ships to sail.

Thirteen

h e stood at the bow of his ship, purposely not looking back but facing forward toward their new life. He so wanted to keep his eyes on their isle, their home, on the woman he knew stood watching him from the shore, but his people needed his strength at this moment. He kept his eyes to the north as if he had no qualms about what they were doing.

"It will be better for our people, Caewlin," the Wise said quietly. He glanced over and nodded reluctantly.

"I pray it is so. We will be in the same land as Phelan. Perhaps the Gods make it easy for him to complete his slaughter of us."

She shook her head. "No, that is not what the Gods want." He did not reply but kept his eyes on the sea ahead of them. He knew that every wave he crossed took him further from his fire-hair.

Over the period of ten days the Red Hawk Clan methodically moved their kin north. The first arrivals were amazed to find green vegetation, ample game and abundant fish in the sea off the coast. It appeared a paradise to the starving survivors, but they knew a wolf prowled these woods, for Phelan's men were never far away. With the resiliency they had displayed over the past two years, they set about making themselves a new home, even if it was temporary in nature.

By the time Aithne arrived on the last ship a series of three rudimentary clansites were established and the people were drying meat, gathering nuts and laying back other portable foodstuffs against the coming winter. The longships were toted off the beach and into the forest, carefully disguised by brush, leaves and other natural materials. No matter their subterfuge, it was only a matter of time before their enemy learned that his foes were within his borders.

Once his people were settled, Caewlin had no reason to postpone his most difficult task. He spoke privately with the Wise and she confirmed his dream, the Chosen of the Red Hawk must leave the clan.

"Will we be together again?" he asked, his voice cracking. He was completely unaware of how much his love for Aithne cut into the Wise's heart.

"The oracles are unclear, Iarel." She felt a pang in her chest and knew she had not answered correctly. Her Goddess would not allow her to withhold the truth, even if it was personally painful. She acknowledged her error and added, "Your vision of the fire-hair with her child has not yet come to pass, there may be hope." The pang eased.

"Then perhaps there is a chance."

He waited until late that night to tell her of his decision, after he and Aithne had joined repeatedly in the furs. She sensed an urgency to his lovemaking, but believed it had much to do with the uncertainty of their move. She was drifting off to sleep when he rather abruptly sat up and pulled her into a sitting position.

"Caewlin?" she asked, puzzled by his strange behavior.

He reached for his dagger, pulled it out of its sheath and offered it to her, the naked blade lying across his palms. Aithne dropped her eyes down to the weapon in his slightly quaking hands. She knew what he was about to offer.

"I, Caewlin, Iarel of the Red Hawk Clan, ask that you accept my dagger as a token of my love. If you accept this my blade, you accept my proposal, and so doing you agree that you will share my furs, bear my children and tend to me all my years, no matter what the Gods set before us. In return, I vow to honor you, keep you safe and love you as the Gods have always loved us."

She did not hesitate.

"I, Aithne the Healer, accept your blade and your proposal. I will share your furs, bear your children, bind your wounds and follow you into eternity."

Caewlin's eyes grew wide and his voice broke with emotion, "You honor me, Aithne, more than you know." She took the dagger from him and carefully nicked the palm of her hand. As a small stream of blood trickled down, she handed the knife to him. He thought for a moment and realized what she was doing. He nicked his palm as well and they clasped their hands together, bonded not only in love, but also by blood. He cleaned the knife on the furs near him and put it back in the sheath, never once letting go of the handclasp they had formed.

"I love you fire-hair," he said and then paused. She saw a deep sadness descend into his eyes and it unnerved her.

She shivered involuntarily. "Caewlin?"

"I must ask a favor of you, my beloved."

"What do wish?" Her mind filled with dread.

"I wish that you leave me for the present time."

"What?" Her dread deepened.

"It is not safe here for you. You must leave us."

"I wasn't any safer at the clansite, Caewlin." She had a frown forming on her face. It served to keep the tears at bay.

"No, you were safer there, Aithne. If Phelan learns you are the iarel's chosen, he will hunt you, capture you and …" He shivered without realizing it.

"I am willing to take that risk," she said. "I wouldn't be sharing your furs if I didn't know that. Nor, for that matter, would I have accepted your offer of marriage." Her voice grew stronger.

"I know that. Phelan will only care that I love you. We both know he seeks to destroy anything I hold dear."

In that he did not lie. His foe's wrath had turned personal over the past few months, for Caewlin refused to die as he commanded and so Phelan's fury turned full bore on the iarel.

"I will not go." Her voice was firm. She pulled back from him, breaking the handclasp. Her blood continued to trickle down her palm.

"You have no choice in this. I will send two men with you and have them take you toward Kell. You must find the main road and go north. Go as far as you as need to stay out of Phelan's reach. When this is over, I will send my men to find you."

"No." Her eyes were beginning to brim with tears. They echoed what was happening inside his heart.

"If you love me, you will do this." She glared at him, furious he would play her like this.

"I cannot believe you would ask me to marry you and then send me away!"

"I asked for you in marriage because I love you. I ask for you to leave for the same reason."

She said nothing, the tears streaming down her cheeks now. His tone wavered and though he did not wish it, tears appeared in his eyes as well.

"By the Gods, Aithne, please! When he captured Erc's younger sisters he had them thrown to his guards. When they were through with them he had them burnt to death. I could not live knowing you might suffer the same fate." She swallowed, hard. She had heard the same story and it had chilled her.

"I love you, Caewlin, I cannot live without you."

Her words reached him and he pulled her back into his arms.

"If you truly love me, please, Aithne, leave me. The Red Hawk has told me you must go and I trust Her. When we have overcome Phelan I will bring you back and we will marry. I must know you are safe. I cannot worry about you and my people at the same time."

His final plea reached her. He had finally admitted it, the weight on his shoulders was too much for him to bear. If she left he could concentrate on keeping his people alive. The tears came without mercy now, pouring out of her eyes and down her face onto his shoulder. The sobs followed and finally, in a thick voice, she murmured,

"I will go."

"Bless you." he said and then mingled his tears with hers.

Aithne made the journey toward Kell with two clansmen as guard. Nerian was one of them and he said little to her during the journey, knowing her sorrow ran deeper than words. When it came time to part, the iarel's second-in-command gave her a tight embrace.

"The Gods will bring you back to us again, fire-hair. You are the Hawk's Chosen and the Chosen of the Iarel. You belong with us, for you are clan."

"I will return."

"I will miss you, Aithne," he said, quieter now.

She smiled affectionately as she was fond of the older clansman.

"Please, keep Caewlin safe and yourself as well."

"I will try. May the Gods bless your steps, Aithne Fire-Hair."

"And yours, Nerian."

She turned and set off in the forest, her heart as empty as when she'd buried her only child. It took her another two days to reach the city of Kell as she traveled west through the dense forest. She paused and gazed toward the north where the old road stretched into the distance. She shook her head, for there was nothing there that held her heart. Contrary to Caewlin's wishes, Aithne entered the city gates and set about finding herself somewhere to live.

I will be near to you, my love, no matter what befalls either of us.

The arrow flew out of nowhere and would have killed him if he had not taken that moment to step on a pinecone and lose his balance. As its target was off center, the arrow glanced off his shoulder and buried itself in the old rowan tree behind him with a thudding sound. He felt a quick stab of pain and then the telltale trickle of warm blood.

"Down!" Owain shouted and dove for cover. His two guards did the same and searched the forest around them for their assailant. Their decision to stop to allow their horses to rest had allowed an assassin to make his move.

"Any sign of him?" Owain asked as he judged the injury he'd taken. It proved minor, providing the arrow was not poisoned.

"No, sir," one of the guards replied, his sharp eyes searching the underbrush.

"This is not good." Owain muttered an oath for good measure. He was due back at the holdings this evening. It was near dusk and the thought of traveling the remaining hours with a murderer on the prowl was not appealing. The sound of another arrow's impact coincided almost exactly with a high-pitched howl. A body pitched out from a thicket some forty feet to the right, still clutching a bow in one hand and an arrow in the other. From the base of his neck protruded a missile, one that came from the man behind him.

Owain blinked and stood up cautiously for he recognized the figure behind their assailant's body.

"Ifor?" he called.

"Sir," the man replied. He warily moved forward and then rolled the body over on its side with his boot. His aim had been true and the man had died instantly. He knelt and picked up the fallen arrow and studied it with expertise. There was no gummy resin on the tip as he'd feared. He examined the other arrows in the quiver and found none carefully wrapped in soft leather, another hallmark of a poisoned missile.

"Thank the Powers," he murmured and rose to meet Owain as he closed the distance between them.

"Ifor, what are you doing here?"

"Cadmon asked me to trail behind you, sir, as he felt there was some danger. I am sorry I did not cut him down before he wounded you. I only saw him right before he loosed his arrow, for he was lying in wait."

Owain sighed. "As usual, Cadmon was right." He knelt to examine the dead man. He did not know him and there was no mark on him to indicate whom he served.

"The arrows in his possession are not poisoned, sir."

Owain shot the man a look and then nodded in understanding.

"Thank the Powers for that." He rose and pulled back the rent in his shirt and offered another prayer of gratitude.

"Sir?"

"I see no evidence the one that clipped me was poisoned, either." A telltale trail of resin would no doubt have been left as it sheered across his arm. Ifor bent down, collected the remaining arrows and bound them with a thin piece of rawhide. Owain gave him a curious look.

The archer explained. "Arrows are somewhat individual. I may be able to determine where they were made by the style and the fletching."

"Indeed." He turned his eyes to survey the terrain around them. His two men were some distance away, spaced apart, vigilant. "Shall we seek the safety of milady's fortress before someone else decides I need to die this day?" Ifor gave him a slight smile. He always appreciated Owain's dry sense of humor.

"A sound idea, sir."

The remainder of the journey was without incident. Owain's shoulder ached, but the wound was minor. But for judicious placement of a pinecone, he would have been dead.

They grow bolder, he thought.

His mistress was furious. Owain was well acquainted with her temper and it took all of his control not to chuckle in amusement as she stormed around the room, muttering oaths to all and sundry.

"It is a minor wound, Aldyn," he reassured her for what seemed the hundredth time. Their healer had bound it and pronounced it of no concern.

"It is not the wound, Owain, it is the audacity! They dare to believe that if they remove you from my side I will marry one of their worthless hides! What insolence!" As she continued to march around the room Owain shot a quick look at Mair who was sitting near the hearth. He winked at her and she winked back. Unfortunately, Aldyn caught that exchange.

Her voice challenged him. "You find this humorous, Councilor?"

He took a deep breath and shook his head. "Not really. If not for Ifor's intervention I may well have died tonight. Nevertheless, shouting about it does not help us find our enemy."

She stopped mid-stride and glared at him. He was right. Righteous anger was one thing, securing their safety was another. She slumped into the nearest chair and asked in a considerably less hostile voice, "What should we do?"

"Cadmon is already making discreet inquiries. For my money, I'd say it's either Lord Fercos or Lord Corryn. Either one have the daring to try this."

Aldyn nodded. "I should marry one of them and stab him in the back as I did my first husband. Then they'll all leave me alone."

Owain crooked a smile. "A worthy plan, milady."

She began to smirk. "So which one should I dispatch first? Corryn or Fercos?"

"I'd kill Corryn, he's more dangerous. He's more devious than Fercos and a lot quicker on his feet."

"No doubt. Fercos obviously spends most of his time at the table. I swear any wife of his would be crushed to death in their marital bed." That slightly ribald remark got Mair chortling as well.

"I fear you are right, Aldyn," her councilor replied.

The lady's face grew serious again. "I worry about you, Owain."

"As I worry about you, milady. Have no fear, we will survive." He rose at that and left the room, weary beyond the day's ride.

"Mair, I must speak with Cadmon and Ifor." Her maid raised an eyebrow.

"Yes, milady." Aldyn continued to stare into the fire as Mair set off in search of her Master of the Guard and the archer.

"I have remained passive for too long. It is time that they learn the true cost of their ambition."

Cadmon and Ifor stood in front of their mistress and waited for her to speak. She was strangely composed, though her Master of the Guard knew that Aldyn had been furious only a short time earlier. Her fit of temper had passed and now only cold resolve remained. In Cadmon's mind that was more unsettling. He knew Aldyn's strength of will, a force of nature not fathomed by those who did not know her. He had long ago judged her to be a very dangerous foe. The attempt on her councilor's life had ignited her ire and she was searching for the person upon whom she should vent it. Unfortunately, there was no immutable proof as to who had commanded the archer to his task.

They'd toted the body back to the holdings and learned what they could of the man. Careful questioning amongst the warriors in Aldyn's service gained them the knowledge that the dead archer was a paid mercenary, a bow eager for hire. It would be nearly impossible to track who had paid him for the arrow slated for Owain's heart.

Aldyn frowned. "A murderer for hire. That does not surprise me, for in that way he is of no consequence. The coins are paid and the deed done. If he does not succeed, then it is of no matter. Just hire another and another …" she let the thought trail off.

"I would guess, milady, that there are three men who could have ordered this – Fercos, Vaddon or Corryn."

Aldyn nodded. "Lord Vaddon? Possibly, I had forgotten about him for he does not plague me like the others. I do not think it is Fercos, for in his pompous arrogance he believes he can beguile me into his bed. Of the three, I would wager it is Corryn."

Cadmon nodded his agreement and out of the corner of his eye he saw Ifor doing the same.

"What rumors I have heard say it is Fercos' intention to move before the others, but I do not believe he has the manhood for it," he said bluntly. She chuckled at that keen observation.

"No, he does not. However, if Corryn planned this he is too wily to allow himself to be named the culprit. He prefers manipulating others to his own ends." A slight smile appeared on her worried face and she explained, "He is well named, for Corryn in the old language means *spider*."

Ifor smirked at that. "Milady," he began and she gestured for him to continue, "A spider is only dangerous when it has its web intact. I suggest we remove those he can manipulate, and in the end it will only be him to deal with."

"I agree, but we must move very cautiously. Owain will not necessarily approve of this, for he does not realize how grave it would be if he were no longer with us."

Cadmon shifted the weight on his feet. "I believe he is aware of what his loss would cause, my lady, but he does not warrant such a thing for fear of worrying you."

The slight incline of her head indicated she understood.

"In that you are right, Cadmon. He often tries to shelter me more than is good. I have allowed that, but now I must be totally aware of all threats against my holdings." She paused for a moment and turned her eyes back to Ifor.

"Archer, I wish to hone my skills with a bow. Will you help me?"

He blinked and then agreed instantly. "Certainly, milady. I would be honored."

"Good. Let us begin tomorrow. I would prefer that my councilor believe it to be purely a diversion. It is not and I believe you both understand why I ask to improve this skill."

"I do, milady," Ifor said.

"Would milady wish some private practice with the short sword as well?" Cadmon offered. He knew Aldyn could handle the weapon, but he also knew she had not touched one since the day she had slain her husband. She did not answer immediately and for an instant he wondered if he had gone too far.

He heard her sigh and then, "An excellent idea, Cadmon. I will look forward to tomorrow, then." Her polite dismissal granted them leave.

As the two men made their way back to the barracks Ifor observed,

"My sire was a warrior of some merit and he taught me that when a woman turns her mind to killing, the mercy of the Powers is withheld."

Cadmon gave him a long look. "Your father was a very wise man."

It was a time of unease at the Circle of the Swan. The two older adepts, now joined by a younger one named Nona, found the newcomer a handful. Gwyn was not like her mother for she came to the adept's camp in full possession of the Old Magic and with a dragon on her shoulder. Alarch, the Eldest, and Ta'wel, the second oldest of the adepts, were frankly puzzled how to deal with the girl. She sat near them clothed in a finely woven royal blue gown and a heavy purple cloak, edged in thick fur, stark contrast to her mother who had arrived years before clothed in the garments of a poor village girl.

"You refuse to accept the vow of celibacy that our path demands?" Alarch asked, her kind face wrinkled in confusion.

"I rule my own magic, it does not govern me," the girl replied, her calm eyes watching as the three adepts struggled to understand her meaning.

"That is not our way," Ta'wel replied gently.

"I know. It is my way."

Alarch sighed and allowed herself to accept the anomaly that sat in front of them on a log near the blazing campfire. She sensed the Old Magic and the imprint of the Ancient One. She sensed more, something that unnerved her.

"Why have you come to us, child?" she asked. There was no real purpose for the girl to be here. Her power and her knowledge eclipsed theirs, that was evident.

"I have come to take the Ritual of the Third Path."

Alarch blinked in surprise. The ritual was the final step before an acolyte became a full practitioner of the *Way*. It allowed a fledgling adept to plumb the depths of her own darkness. It was the most perilous portion of an adept's training.

"I see." Alarch gave Ta'wel a sideways glance.

"Gwyn, it is very dangerous to take that path if you are not properly prepared," Ta'wel explained with a note of concern.

"I know," was the answer. The dragon on her shoulder was awake and alert. It sensed no evil here, but it sensed magic and that kept it wary.

"Why do you seek this?" Alarch asked, suspecting there was more behind the girl's request. Gwyn shifted her weight and felt the dragon's claws delicately dig into her shoulder to keep it from losing its perch.

"I have aged twelve years or more in a very short period of time. I do not have the weight on my soul that many do given their years amongst other mortals. I do, however, have the need to understand who I am. I wish to take the Ritual of the Third Path to learn what I can of myself."

"You must leave your guardian behind, Gwyn. The path is not for it."

"He knows." The dragon shifted uneasily this time. It had strongly counseled Gwyn against this ritualistic journey, but to no avail.

"It is best done when the moon is full. Allow us time to prepare the proper herbs," Alarch replied solemnly.

"So be it," the young girl murmured, rose, and left the three adepts behind.

"There is more here than she is saying, Eldest," Ta'wel began.

"I know."

"Can you not refuse her, Eldest?" Nona asked. She felt extremely uncomfortable in the girl's presence.

"No, it is not right to refuse any acolyte the Ritual of the Third Path."

"She is not an acolyte, Eldest. She is … I do not know how to describe what she is," Nona replied, bewildered.

"She is a child sired in an act of Old Magic, one that has communed with the Ancient One. She is unlike us, sisters. We must trust that the Powers know what is best for her."

"I am not sure," Ta'wel replied and the adepts fell silent.

This is not for you to do, Gwyn, daughter of Morwyn. It is *their* path, not yours.

"I do not intend to tread *their* path, dragon brother. I intend to tread my own." A curious note of alarm echoed in her mind from the small beast on her shoulder. She explained further, "I will use their herbal magic to take another journey, one into the future. I must know what lies ahead."

The future changes.

"Yes, I know, but I must see it either way."

I cannot follow you there. The voice was edged in apprehension.

"I know," she said gently and reached up to scratch the beast's chin. A small humming sound echoed around her. "I must do this."

I will wait for your return, dragon sister.

Aithne settled into Kell rather quickly. She had lived in the city before moving to the village and so she knew the seaport's politics better than most. Even she was surprised to find how much had changed in the past few years since the execution of Kell's Chamberlain. Lord Phelan now ruled with an iron fist. She cautiously quizzed some of her old contacts and was warned that any association with the House of Healing could prove dangerous. True to their calling, the House of Healing routinely defied city law and treated those Phelan considered expendable. There was a pervasive feeling of foreboding, for it was felt that Kell's lord would settle that score in time. Aithne took the advice to heart and sought out Gorsedd, one of Phelan's senior guards.

The senior guard was genuinely pleased to see her and his reaction stilled her fears. If Phelan knew she was the iarel's woman, Gorsedd would not have been so warm and welcoming. She had once treated him for a vicious leg wound only a short time before she'd left Kell. If not for her skill he would have died. He still held her in high regard.

He hadn't changed much over the years, a self-effacing man with a strong face and a broad chest. His dark hair was shoulder-length and now slightly salted with grey. He sat at her table, drinking her wine, as she slowly bound and hung what fresh herbs she had gathered as she made her way to Kell. Her lodgings were a single room with a wide bed, a table, a hearth and a couple of chairs. The furs Caewlin had given her had earned her enough in the market to pay for the room and for food. Her healing skills would provide for her in the future.

"I thought I'd never see you again, Aithne. What of that village man you were to marry?"

"He was killed during a raid," she said as she continued to bind the herbs.

"One of the Southern raids?" Gorsedd asked.

"Yes."

"They didn't hurt you, did they?" he asked, suddenly concerned.

"No, they did not harm me. They were searching for food, for the most part."

"Thank the Powers. Not all of them are that decent, from what I've heard. But then if it was my family that was starving, I'd steal as well." He paused for a moment, thought, and then apologized. "I'm sorry, that was not right of me to say given they killed your husband." Aithne shook her head and sat at the table, brushing her hands on her skirt.

"I cannot forgive them for what they did," she replied solemnly. She did not forgive Fyren, so she had not lied. It was important that Gorsedd believe she had no sympathy for the clansmen. He nodded his understanding.

"You were right to come to me, Aithne. Kell is not like the city you once knew. Not since ..." he let his words trail off. "We have need of a healer for one of the garrisons. It will not be an all day task, but you will make good coin doing the work."

Aithne smiled to herself. That is what she needed – a source of money for food and supplies, and, more important, a credible source of information.

"I would be willing to do that, Gorsedd."

"It will not be difficult to convince them to accept you, given you've lost your husband to Phelan's enemies. That will tell them where your loyalties lie." He waited a moment longer and then added, "I will give you a warrant that you are a healer in service of our lord and that will keep you from the brothels." Her eyebrow raised at that.

"I have heard of Phelan's trade in flesh, but I did not realize it extended to just any woman on the street."

"It does. You are far too handsome for your own good," he said and winked in amusement. "The warrant will help and I will pass the word that if you are touched I will filet the man who dares do so."

"After I do the same," she joked back and he laughed. Gorsedd departed shortly thereafter and she allowed a smile of victory to cross her face. Guards were full of news and loved to boast in front of any woman, especially ones that were too handsome for their own good. It was simply a matter of gleaning the bragging from the truth and she'd be able to learn how Caewlin and his people fared.

"Has this been verified?" Phelan growled, tired of the unsubstantiated rumors that flew around his city like hordes of bats at midnight. One rumor had it that the Southern clansmen had poisoned the water in the city wells. That had caused a run on wine, which he did not regret as he held most of the wine stocks in the city. Still, the hearsay was annoying.

"Yes, milord, it has. We spied a large encampment of the Southern men some four days ride to the east."

"How many in the camp?"

"I would guess one hundred and fifty or so."

"Men only?"

"No, milord, men, women and children."

Phelan paced for a minute or so, his eyes pensive. It made no tactical sense for his enemy to come so close unless they had some clever plan in mind.

"What are they doing?" he demanded of the guard.

"Nothing unusual, milord. They appear to be drying game for the winter and gathering firewood."

"Did it look like they intended to stay or are they just gathering food to return to their isle?" Phelan pressed.

"They appear to be making a camp, milord. They were building those odd little shrines of theirs. I wouldn't think they'd do that if they were just going to harvest some game and then leave."

Phelan nodded in agreement, the guard's observation was a salient one.

"Put the men farther afield, by my reckoning there should be more of them. Perhaps there are other camps. I want regular reports on their activities and as close of a head count as you can get. I want to know how many of them are warriors."

The man bowed, "Yes, milord." As he left, his superior Phelan sank into the massive chair near the hearth.

"What *are* you up to, Iarel? Why make it easy for me to hunt and kill you?" There was no clear answer and he found that troubling.

The darkness that swirled around her had little to do with the moonlit night. At first Gwyn found it somewhat amusing, recalling that her mother had trod the same path. After all, she intended to bend the ritual to meet *her* needs. What she did not realize was the Ritual would not allow itself to be guided in such a manner – it took the acolyte where she must go, willing or not.

Though she did not know it, she found the sensations as unnerving as her mother once had. Every memory had a sharp edge to it, all of her senses heightened to near intolerance, making sounds, taste and colors vivid beyond imagining. She steeled herself and pressed on in the journey under the moonlight in the meadow. Her guardian dragon was not with her and she felt alone for the first time in her life.

Initially she allowed the vision to carry her wherever it took her. Since she was not that physically old, she had less to resolve than most. Once she had viewed her life and the consequences of her actions, the vision took her elsewhere, into the future where she wanted to go. She thought the worst part of ordeal to be over. It was just beginning.

What she saw there stunned her.

The roaring sound of burning wood and a high-pitched scream flew through her body. Death manifested itself in front of her in its most horrific form.

"No, it cannot be!" she cried out as the vision faded and another presented itself, hurtling into her mind with a power that shook her to the core. That vision was no more comforting, for death again reined supreme. The visions continued, relentlessly, one on top of the other, each one revealing a possible future for those she loved and those she had yet to meet.

"No, Pyrs, no!" she shouted in the dark night, the roar of an inferno coursing through her mind. As each revelation paraded itself through her very being, she felt she would go insane. Unknowingly, she did as her mother once had, rocking back and forth, crying, her arms around herself in a fierce embrace. The visions were relentless, the truth unforgiving and the future chilled.

The guardian dragon heard her cries of despair as he sat on one of the warm stones near the fire. He was resting there until he knew that his charge had ended her journey. Hearing her voice cry out again, in terror, he sighed. He had warned her and she had stubbornly chosen her path.

You are as strong as the Ancient One said you were, dragon sister, he thought to himself. He pulled his wings tight in against his body and waited, offering prayers for her safe return from the land where he could not journey.

She came out of her nightmare at dawn, hearing the small animals stirring in the forest around her. She sensed more than saw the dragon hovering in front of her, its face full of concern.

Dragon sister?

She gazed up at him, eyes red, hair disheveled, dried tears on her pale cheeks.

Dragon brother, she thought back, unable to speak aloud. She held out her arm and he settled gently upon it. He gingerly made his way up to her shoulder, curled his tail around her hair and eyed her closely.

I am pleased you have survived.

Gwyn only nodded and closed her eyes again as the small beast continued to observe her, concerned. The visions would not leave her.

The future can be changed, she thought, desperate to find some hope in what she had witnessed.

Only at great peril. He settled onto her shoulder, sighing once more.

I am a pawn in this as much as the rest of my family. We are all pawns, worthy only for the moment we serve Their needs.

Even a pawn can change their path, sister.

Her bloodshot eyes opened and she gave him a long look. She leaned over and gently kissed the top of dragon's small head and then turned toward the sunrise and began her morning prayers.

As he had anticipated, Phelan's sentries reported that the clan had two more camps deep within the forest. All were approximately the same size and all were doing the same thing, collecting and drying food at a frenetic pace. He unleashed his men against the closest camp with the orders to kill everyone who was not suitable to be a slave.

The attack went poorly from the start, for the bulk of the clan vanished into the forest taking their belongings with them. Their intricate web of sentries had given them enough time to know Phelan's intent and they packed what they could and set off for an alternate campsite. The iarel's trap had worked, but the cost was high for some ten clansmen were slain during the ensuing battle while over half of Phelan's fifty men were killed or wounded. Phelan's warriors retreated with only a handful of their foes as prisoners and began the dismal march home, knowing their lord would not be pleased.

Kell's master dutifully burnt some of the prisoners in the city square, as was his usual pleasure. He ordered the man who had commanded the raid to be burnt as well, for he had not delivered what Phelan had ordered. To insure that none misunderstood his message, he required the warriors to watch as their leader perished in the flames.

Gwyn departed the Circle of the Swan almost a fortnight after the ritual. She said little to the adepts and they had not pressed her, for it was not for them to know what she had beheld in the visions. As the girl prepared to leave them, Alarch gave her a tight embrace and whispered in her ear,

"Caution, child. A gift as strong as yours can consume the bearer as easily as it can consume others." Gwyn pulled herself out of the embrace but did not reply.

She journeyed for a considerable distance through the forest, enjoying the crisp weather as winter slowly settled in place. She woke one morning to find a light veil of snow on the ground and on herself. Her guardian had snuggled within the wide hood of her cloak overnight, huddled up in her hair to stay warm. As she rose she tugged her cloak closer to her, thankful for her grandfather's insistence on the weight and quality of her garments. She had thought them too overstated and had said so, but he had insisted, reminding her that she was a daughter of Aderyn. She had allowed him the moment just as she had allowed him the two guards who had accompanied her to the adepts. She had promised to stay there and taking her promise to heart, the men returned to Aderyn. She knew she had no need of them, but had acquiesced to their presence to mollify her sire and her grandsire. She never intended to remain at the Circle indefinitely.

"They worry too much about me," she grumbled.

As do I, the dragon's voice retorted in her mind. He had not helped her on her present quest, for he was against it. This time, however, he did press the issue, for he was not pleased with what she intended. **You do not need to speak with *them*.** His voice was unusually frank.

"I must. They have knowledge I need to obtain. They live in more than one world and I need to learn how they move from one to the other. I must know how close I can come to the Veil without crossing over and perhaps they can tell me." A tiny quake shivered through the dragon at this.

They are dangerous.

Gwyn chuckled. "So are you, my dragon friend, yet I find your knowledge worthwhile."

You do not listen very well. She reached over and scratched his chin, but this time it did not settle the beast.

"I must go," she said and discontinued the scratching, realizing it had no effect.

I must be with you. It was a statement, not a request.

"You shall be," she promised.

Later that day, near dusk, she crossed the boundary into a Ring of the Fey, a fairy circle, and she felt a slight thrill of power surge through her.

Greetings, Gwyn, daughter of Morwyn, Wielder of the Old Magic.

"Greetings, Elders. I come for what knowledge you have to offer," Gwyn answered immediately, her voice strained. Her guardian dug his claws into her shoulder in a wary stance.

What of your guardian? the voice asked, disquieted.

"He remains with me."

You will vouch for his behavior? The dragon responded with a noticeable hiss at this insult.

"I do not need to vouch for his behavior, for he is of the Ancient One."

We do not trust his kind.

Gwyn looked down at the small dragon and smiled in amusement. "And he does not trust your kind, so all is equal."

There was a lengthy pause and then, *You are welcome to our knowledge.* She said nothing further and vanished within the mists that lie inside the circle. As she crossed the boundary between the mortal world and that of the Elders, she realized it was her sixteenth birthday.

FOURTEEN

a s Aithne returned from a visit to the house of an ailing guard, she saw him taking a drink from one of the city's wells, the one nearest to her small room. She had not seen him for over two months and though the chestnut brown dye in his hair would have fooled most people, she knew who he was the moment she saw his figure. Caewlin was alert, watching for guards, and when he saw two coming toward the well he turned and inadvertently walked in her direction. The two guards found the young man of interest for they were always looking for new workers to enslave. They called to him and he acted as if he had not heard them. She made sure to put herself in his way, as if by accident. His eyes flared when he recognized her.

"Go left at the first passage," she whispered under her breath, knowingly setting him on a path that would round back to where she lived. Aithne continued on her way in the opposite direction and heard the guards call out to the stranger again. Once out of their sight she moved like a cat down the side streets, for she knew these streets intimately. She ducked into her room and waited with her heart pounding, the door not completely closed. When she saw him fly around the corner just some twenty feet up the street, she beckoned to him. Slipping on the snowy cobblestones, he scurried to safety. She closed the door behind him and bolted it, leaning against it, her eyes full of fear and her heart thudding. Their eyes met and for a moment time held its place. She saw his lips moving silently, no doubt intoning a prayer for their safety. The guards tramped down the street only a moment or so later and then the sound of curses echoed in the air. Their quarry had vanished. More curses ensued and then they set off in search of less cunning prey.

"Fire-hair," he said and without a moment's hesitation he pulled her into his arms, his passion overwhelming him. Even as he pressed her up against the heavy wooden door they began to undress, kissing and touching each other's bodies, falling into the loving without hesitation.

Sometime later they lay in her bed, her head on his bare chest as he gently stroked her hair. The room had a heady scent, he thought, the smell of drying herbs was almost overpowering. He associated that herbal bouquet with her and easily conjured up that fragrance each night as he lay alone in his furs. She looked as beautiful as ever, perhaps more so. He chastised himself for forgetting how truly magnificent she really was.

"I have so missed you and sharing your furs." The weeks apart seemed like years to him.

"Well, don't tell that wild-eyed Southern iarel or he will be quite angry at you."

"Pardon?" He didn't quite catch what she meant.

"You are not the iarel, I see that plain," she jested, tugging on a strand of his dyed hair. She far preferred his usual golden mane. "He is a very jealous man and would cut out your heart of if he knew you lie with me and brought me such pleasure."

"So I have heard, but I have already lost my heart so he will not find it that easily," he replied and kissed her full on the lips, lingering over the sensations that flooded him. The kissing led to more passion and they joined without reservation.

Eventually she rose, donned her dress and stoked the fire. As she glided around the small room he watched her every movement, unwilling to remove his eyes for a moment.

She asked the obvious question now that their desire was quenched for the time being. "Why are you here in Kell? Phelan has a hefty reward on your head." She began to pour a cup of wine for him as she spoke.

He nodded, he'd seen the posters on the walls of the city. A king's ransom was what they'd offered for him ... alive. He suspected what fate Phelan had in store for him for he vividly remembered Erc's mutilated body. If he was a corpse when thrown at his foe's feet, Phelan's joy would be diminished, for it would remove the pleasure he'd receive as he had Caewlin summarily dissected.

"We are planning a raid into Kell to kill or capture Phelan."

She stopped stunned in mid-task. "You are mad. You do not have the strength of arms for such a mission."

"We have no choice, Aithne. There are few of us left now. Even fewer than when I sent you away." His eyes were despondent. Their allies had not materialized as the Red Hawk had prophesied and though the clan had ample food, Phelan hunted them incessantly.

"I know, I have been forced to watch the executions in the city square. Young, old, men, women, it does not matter. They burn them like they are choice wood for a merry winter's fire."

"We have no other choice."

"Surely there is something else you can do, Caewlin," she replied, her face full of worry knowing this plan would fail. She walked the wine over to him and handed it to him as she settled on the bed.

He took a long sip and then sighed. "I have no other choice."

"Ask for the help of the Northern lords, Caewlin."

He shook his head immediately. "Why would they care for us? We are not kin."

"They will come. Lord Bardyn, the Lord of the Eastern March, is a fair and decent man."

He shook his head again and rose out of the bed, passing the cup back to her. As he pulled on his clothes he muttered, "They will not come. We are vermin in their eyes."

"You judge all Northerners by Phelan, my love. They are not all the same."

"And what else have I been shown?" His voice was bitter and full of repressed anger. "They wish us dead and I have aided them by moving our people north. By the Gods, I did as the Red Hawk asked, and yet we still perish!" His anguish bled through his words.

"You are not like Erc nor Fyren, to judge you by their actions is not proper. The same holds true for the Northern lords. I know that they are honorable men who would come to our aid."

"How can you say such a thing?" he demanded. His anger was growing and irrationally being displaced against her.

"I lived in the north for a time and I can attest they are honorable men."

"That is simple for you to say," he came back, his eyes dark.

"They are fine men and they will help you."

"If they were so fine, why are you not still there enjoying their respect and decency?" he pushed.

"I had my reasons for leaving," she said, her voice suddenly guarded.

"As I thought. Perhaps one of them asked more from you than you were willing to provide? Perhaps they felt you fit for only a sporting wench, a girl to keep them warm at night and provide relief for their lust?" He was pushing very hard now.

She shook her head vehemently and her voice rose to match his.

"No, I was never approached in such a manner."

"Your argument does not convince me."

"Surely you would not believe a clansman would serve a man without honor?"

Caewlin opened his mouth to retort and then stopped, realizing what she'd said. "What clansman do you speak of? What is his name?" His mind began to whirl, recalling the omens on the beach.

"Dillan. He is Master of the Guard for the House of Aderyn. I stayed in Ilspath for a time as a healer and saw him with his master. An innkeeper in Kell told me about him, for they do not often see clansmen up north."

"By the Gods!" he retorted. He sank into the nearest chair as a strange look descended on his face. "How long ago was this?"

She thought for a moment, "Nearly two years ago. Why?" She sensed his shift of emotions and went to kneel near his chair, puzzled.

"How old was this man from the Southern Isles?" he asked. His eyes were not on her but staring at the fire as if he was pulling forth some deeply buried memory.

"Old enough to be my father," she said, "if not a bit older."

"By the Gods," he murmured again and then gave her pensive look. She lay her head on his knee and felt his gentle hand caressing her hair. She did not press him, knowing he would speak of whatever was on his mind when he was ready. He did not say a word for a minute or so and then explained,

"Dillan is my grandfather's brother, my grand uncle. He is kin, Aithne. When he last us visited many years ago he said he served as Master of the Guard to a noble house."

She raised her head and smiled. "He serves one of eldest houses of the realm, Caewlin. They stand in good favor with the Lord of the Eastern March. They will come to your aid if he asks."

"You are that sure?"

"I vow it, my love."

His eyes caught hers and he sighed. "It is as the omens predicted, the sixth clan will come stand by us. The Red Hawk favors us because of you."

"No, not because of me. She favors us because the iarel of her clan refuses to surrender."

"We will ask aid from these noblemen of the North, providing I can persuade my people to allow that."

"But surely they will…" He was shaking his head before she could finish.

"Not necessarily, fire-hair. They fear the Northerners more than they fear death."

"Then you shall have to be very persuasive, my iarel." She lay her head back on his knee and let him drift off into his own thoughts.

That night he was unusually solemn. The weight of the future lay heavy on his heart. No amount of jesting on Aithne's part could pull him out of his depression. The revelation regarding his grand uncle had actually pushed him further down.

He finally put his despair into words. "I fear we will not survive. We are too stubborn, too proud of a people to ask others to come to our aid, despite the Red Hawk's omens. It is our ultimate test, Aithne, and I see us failing it."

"Your people will see the wisdom of it." She knew he needed something to live for, something that would give him heart to continue the fight against Phelan. He was too quiet for her, brooding, and it frightened her. He removed his clothes and climbed into the bed, not asking her to join him, his mood was that bleak. As he stared blankly at the herbs suspended from the ceiling rafters above him, she knew what she must do. She rose and prepared a drink for both of them.

As she sat on the bed, she offered him a tender smile and said,

"I ask that your seed find sanctuary with me. I am willing to bear you a child, Caewlin, so that your people will have a future."

His eyes widened, filled with awe and surprise. "You wish this, fire-hair?" he asked, his voice cracking. He knew that her life would be forfeit if Phelan learned she carried his child and that was why he had hesitated to ask this of her. The threat to her was grave enough. His child within her womb would seal her doom.

"Yes, I do. I love you, Caewlin." Her voice was loaded with emotion. It took all her control not to cry at the strength of the love between them.

"You will bear me a son," he said, reliving the end of his vision once more, his hope soaring. He saw her towering over their enemies, his newborn son in her arms, suckling at her breast.

"I cannot guarantee it will be a boy, Caewlin," she replied with an amused smile.

"It will be a boy, one with red hair. I have seen it," he said in a tone that brooked no argument.

"Then drink, for this wine will give us the chance to create that son. Perhaps, if the Powers are merciful, he will live to see his father and his mother living together in peace." He solemnly took the cup from her and drained half of it. She drank the remainder, blew out the candles and they settled together in the bed.

"I am yours, fire-hair, in this life and the next," he said as he ran his hand through her long hair.

She kissed him and pulled him to her, offering prayers that the Powers would grant them the new life they so desperately desired.

Four days later, in the morning, the iarel took leave of Kell, his plans to attack Phelan discarded in the wake of the revelation about Dillan. Aithne escorted him to the main gate and bid him farewell without any outward manifestation of the intimacy they had shared.

"Be safe, my love," she whispered. He had in his possession a pouch full of food and medicinal herbs, sorely needed supplies for the clan.

"I will, fire-hair. Know that I love you." She inclined her head and watched him exit the city and head up the main road where he would cut off into the forest once eyes were not upon him.

"May the Powers watch over you, beloved," she prayed and returned to her duties within the city.

Caewlin's instinct was correct, his people feared the Northerners more than the endless death that stalked them in the forest. His senior clansmen were solidly divided on the issue. Caewlin, though iarel, could not make this decision without the support of his men, it was too fraught with peril. There was no assurance that those they summoned from the North may side with

Phelan and finish the brutal work he had started, despite Aithne's belief in their honor. His grand uncle may be long dead for years had passed since she'd last seen him.

Caewlin clearly argued for a sense of reality; Phelan's raids were increasing in intensity, limiting the clan's options. They were constantly on the move now, for their foe had retaliated by sending roving bands of mercenaries to hunt them. Murmurs against Caewlin's leadership began to circulate, something that never occurred when they lived in the isles. They began to blame him for their journey to this foreign place and that death still claimed them, one by one.

When news of this dissension reached the Wise she made her presence known. She did not usually meddle with the inner workings of the clan. Her position required a more remote approach, the interaction with the Gods, the viewing of oracles. Devona knew that to ignore the Red Hawk's will would lead to their destruction. She summoned the most senior men of the clan, invoked the Gods and then unleashed her anger on them.

"As Wise I have seen many things, for I have taken the knowledge of the Wise before me and the Wise before her, through eternity. Now I have witnessed something I thought I would never see – the cowardice of the Red Hawk Clan." She paused to allow her words to have their proper effect. Men shifted uneasily where they sat, for the Wise never spoke in such straightforward terms. Some muttered under the breath, but not loudly, for they feared her power. She saw Caewlin's eyebrow inch upward, the only outward manifestation of his stunned astonishment.

"Our iarel has worked within the knowledge of the omens, followed the will of the Red Hawk, yet you bicker and complain now that you have full bellies. You even speak of the forbidden, the death of our leader, so that you may continue to skulk in the woods like little boys fearing their father's strap. If you believe this will save you, it will not!" Nerian winced at her words, though he had actively campaigned in favor of Caewlin's plan. The iarel kept his face impassive – he had known there were those who spoke against him, though he had not known the talk went as far as assassination. He quickly shifted his eyes toward one figure, Isen, and saw the man's nervous stare. *As I thought.* Isen had been the most critical of the iarel's plan.

"It is obvious that some in our midst must be shown our future, for only then will they know what we face. It is not common for a Wise to reveal what she has been shown, but I shall now, for our fate hangs in the balance. Prepare to see what I have carried in my heart and then understand why you must be men, not little boys." Devona strode to the fire pit, cast a bright powder into flames and began to chant in some ancient and archaic tongue. The smoke swirled around them and to the man, they saw a vision of what would befall the clan if they did not summon their brethren from the North.

Each man experienced it in his own way, for only then would it become personal and unforgettable. The images were unforgiving, driving to the heart of the one who experienced them. They saw the sun rising through the trees to the east as another morning dawned. Even as the sun rose the darkness began to encompass them from forest. The jubilant cries of their enemies deafened them, for they knew the clan was surrounded. The darkness overran them and began to enfold them within its cold grasp. Some saw their wives or children slain as they made a futile attempt to save them. Others witnessed their own deaths, feeling the shearing pain of the blades as they entered their bodies, the ocean of blood pouring out of their wounds.

The snow beneath them boiled crimson red, anointed with the blood of the Red Hawk's people. Above them She circled in the air, shrieking in agony as if watching a pack of ravening wolves devour her fledglings. As the individual images pummeled their minds, some of the clansmen began to weep, their strong will broken. To the man they witnessed the final death throes of their people, consumed by the darkness that Phelan had unleashed upon them. Even Isen wept.

The Wise allowed the vision to clear and granted the men time to regain their senses. She knew how hard this would strike them, for she had lived this nightmare for months. None of them lacked tears in their eyes, others were embracing each other for solace. She had not held back – the time had come for the clan to make their choice and it would not serve to withhold the truth. The men were near panic, though they held themselves and remained seated on the ground around the fire. They were all warriors, strong men who did not quail at the sight of a sword or the smell of death, but what the Wise brought to them was different.

Her eyes caught those of the iarel and his face was wet with tears. He had witnessed the annihilation of his people. He felt impotent, unworthy of the title and the mantel of leadership his father and his grandfather had carried before him. His vision revealed the secret horror he had always feared – he would be the last of the clan to die, for Phelan would not allow him the holy peace of death before he witnessed his kin's final agonies. He knew he would die alone.

The Wise cast another mixture of powder into the fire as her strong voice commanded, "Now see what our future may hold…" The smoke billowed around them again, cloaking them to the real world and taking the clansmen on yet another journey behind their ken.

Out of the mist rode a figure clad in silvery chain mail, his long blond hair flowing behind in waves. A legion surged behind him, grim men with dark eyes and fell faces. Their shields displayed the ancient symbols of the white dragon and the falcon, airborne kin to the Red Hawk. Above them She flew, shouting on the wind, as if guiding them forward. Sounds of death reeled around them as they rode on through their foes without mercy. The darkness perished under their swords and under the hooves of their steeds, spraying blood in a torrent around them. The silver-clad figure did not halt until he and his legion reached the sea where he dismounted from his horse and strode into the blue water. He knelt on one knee, lifted two handfuls of seawater into the air and invoked thanks to his Gods for their victory. As he turned the Red Hawk sailed to him, hovered and then landed on his broad shoulder.

His voice rang out, "I bring you peace, brothers." A cry of triumph rose from the legion behind him as mist overtook the vision.

This time the men did not weep, for they had witnessed the full promise of the Red Hawk. Caewlin rose to his feet, unsteady, for the visions still crowded his head.

He made sure his voice was distinct. "I leave it to you to decide our future. The Wise has shown us two paths. I pray that you choose the one that gives us life." He left the men to their consciences.

In the end, it took over thirty of Phelan's best to capture the last iarel of the Southern Isle clans. Caewlin and a dozen of his men found themselves in a pitched battle after engaging their enemy during one of their nearly continuous raids. They were grossly outnumbered and as clansmen fell, Caewlin knew his capture was eminent. When he and only six of his men remained alive, he began a prayer to his Gods that he die in battle, not at the hands of his enemy. It was not to be. A warning shouted by Dubhan came too late and the hilt of a sword crashed down on the back of his head. The blow drove him to his knees and though he struggled to rise, a second blow rendered him unconscious. When he finally woke he was in the back of a wagon, in chains, on the way to Kell. Only five of his men were with him, Dubhan included. Caewlin thanked the Gods for that, for the man's wife had already been a widow once in her life.

"Iarel?" one of the clansmen asked, seeing his leader was conscious

"The Gods did not favor me, I prayed to die as a clansman should," he muttered in remorse as the wagon jolted through the forest. Each bump made his head throb in response.

"Perhaps, Iarel, They do not want you to die at all," Dubhan replied, his calm eyes radiating benign acceptance of their current situation. "It is hard to slay your enemy if you are a *fade*."

A faint smile tracked across Caewlin's face. His smile was returned by each of his men. For the time being they lived and that was not necessarily a bad thing.

The two adversaries studied each other intently. Caewlin was in chains kneeling on the frigid stone floor of Phelan's great hall, his clansmen arrayed behind him. Phelan sat in an ornate chair, an elaborate robe on his lap and an immense hound sitting on each side of him. The dogs were well mannered, eager for their master's command. Caewlin observed them for a time and then returned his gaze to the man who now held him captive. It was chilling, for he found more humanity in the eyes of the hounds than he did their master.

The iarel judged Lord Phelan to be only a few years old than him, about thirty years or so of age. He had light-colored hair and dark eyes that missed nothing. His withered right leg was the only imperfect thing about the man, other than the lack of a soul.

From Phelan's perspective he had expected an older, more seasoned foe than the young man in chains in front of him. He knew not to underestimate the iarel, for this man had survived far longer than any of the others. Still, in some way, he was disappointed.

"Welcome, Iarel, I have been waiting for you," he said.

Caewlin did not answer, for it was not expected that he could speak the Northern tongue. Phelan gestured and one of his guards translated.

Caewlin answered back in the Southern dialect, "I ask that you release my men."

The guard translated and Phelan shook his head immediately. "No, for they will just make war on me."

"You have me, that should be enough." Phelan shook his head again.

"No, there are two more things I wish – the destruction of your people and your sister kneeling at my feet."

A bolt of terror shot through Caewlin but he banished from his face and did not answer.

"I promise you, iarel, if I catch her she will be sold to the highest bidder. There are more than a few interested in an iarel's virgin sister."

Caewlin bit the inside of his lip and still said nothing though the guard had translated his master's words precisely.

"Nothing further? So be it." He gestured toward Gorsedd, who stood nearby, and ordered, "Take them to the square and display them there until dusk."

"Yes, milord."

"Pick one of them to be burnt, it does not matter which as long as it is not the iarel."

"Yes, milord." Phelan glanced back to his bound enemy and then rose without a further word, tossing the robe aside. The harsh clanking of the prisoners' chains masked the sound of the lord's dragging foot and the impact of his wooden cane on the stone floor as he made his way out of the hall.

Gorsedd feared this onerous task would fall to him and it had – he was forced to choose which of the five clansmen would die. They were a mixed lot, one older, four younger. They were standing in the heart of city, still in chains as a crowd gathered around them in morbid fascination. Not all of the Kell's citizens found the executions repugnant. Gorsedd motioned to one of the guards who spoke the Southern dialect and took his place in front of the iarel and other prisoners.

"Translate for me, exactly." The guard nodded. "My lord has ordered that one of you must die. The iarel is not to be chosen ..." He let the rest trail off. He could tell the moment the translation was made as the faces of five men grew unreadable. They did not consult with their leader, but spoke privately amongst themselves. Finally, the older man answered in a strong voice,

"I will die, for my Gods will take me in Their arms and bear me home."

Gorsedd inwardly winced. "So be it." He shot a look at the iarel and saw his face was set. His kinsman had made his choice and he would not interfere. As the others were chained to their own individual stakes, the older man was moved to an iron stake further away from his kin and secured to it. Dry wood and kindling was placed at his feet and all the while the man was murmuring prayers, a look of serenity on his heavily-lined face.

Their faith is unshakable, Gorsedd thought. He selected a flaming torch out of a nearby brazier and marched up to the condemned man, his mind reeling at the cruelty of the act he was about to perform. To his surprise the clansman muttered something in the Northern tongue.

"The Gods do not hold you responsible." Gorsedd gazed into the man's dark brown eyes and saw the depth within.

I cannot do this to a man with such courage. No one should die like this! He thought for a moment and then pulled his knife, leaned across the brush as if to ignite the pile and then drove his blade in the man's chest at the level of his heart. The clansman shuddered for only a moment as blood rushed into his chest cavity.

He murmured, "May the Gods give you favor," and his brown eyes closed. Gorsedd removed the knife and ignited the kindling and the hem of the dead man's ragged cloak. He knew Phelan may learn of his compassion and it could cost him his life, but he did not care. Such courage demanded he act. The brush burst into flames and engulfed the body of the clansman in an upward rush. The senior guardsman stepped back for the heat was intense. Wiping his knife on his breeches, he slipped it back into the sheath. As he did he caught the eyes of the young iarel and swore he could see gratitude.

Aithne learned of Caewlin's capture from the fishmonger in the market. As he showed her a fish, supposedly fresh caught, he gleefully related that the

leader of the Southern barbarians was on display in the city's square for all
to see.

"You are sure?" she asked, barely keeping her voice even.

"Heard it from one of the guards. Said they're a brutish lot." The man
was missing more than one tooth and obviously had not bathed recently.

"I see." Aithne left the man and his fish behind and headed for the center
of Kell. Though she prayed it was only a rumor she found Caewlin with four
of his men, all chained to stakes. Nearby the burnt body of a fifth clansman
hung from another stake, smoke still spiraling in small eddies around him.
Her heart tightened at that, for no doubt she knew the man in life.

Powers, not Nerian! she thought, for the second-in-command usually
was with the iarel. She dropped her eyes and composed herself. Nearby two
of the local merchants were talking about the leader of the clan.

"So what will they do with him?" one of the locals asked another.

"Don't know, probably burn him like they did the other one," another
replied, only half interested.

"Scruffy bunch, aren't they?" the first man remarked.

"You'd be that way too if you had Phelan hunting you," the other
replied.

The first grunted. "May the Powers help them." His voice was considerably quieter now and he glanced around nervously lest anyone hear his traitorous sentiments.

"They'll have to," the other said and then went his own way.

Aithne raised her eyes and studied the bodies at the stakes in front of
her. She knew most of them. Dubhan's presence brought her nothing but sadness for she knew how much Mada had grown to love the man. She finally
willed herself to look at Caewlin. His hair was nearly blonde again, most of
the dye had faded. His face was bruised and his hair matted with blood, but he
appeared to have no other serious wounds. When their eyes finally connected
she saw his surprise and the effort needed to keep it off his face. Love flared
the ten or so feet between them. They gazed at each other just as they had in
her room, as if no one else was present. She knew he faced torture and death,
either by execution or by enslavement. She wanted him to have a reason to
live, a reason to return to her. The Powers, in Their mercy, had heard her
prayers and delivered tangible proof that they had a future together.

She placed her hand on her belly in a protective motion and smiled,
faintly. He frowned as if he did not understand what she meant by that odd
gesture. When she gave him a slight nod, the revelation overtook him. She
carried his child. She saw his lips move in a silent prayer, no doubt in thanks
to his Gods, and then fearful that one of the guards might notice them, he
dropped his head and did not raise it again. Wary of attracting any undue
attention, she left the square, not daring to turn around for one last look. Once

inside her room with the door bolted she allowed herself the release of tears. The weeping did not last long, for Aithne was not a woman of weak will. She put her grief and fears aside. It was time to determine a means of securing the release of her betrothed, the father of her unborn child.

The messenger arrived at the House of Aderyn a little over three weeks after Caewlin dispatched him, the day after his iarel knelt in thrall at his enemy's feet. Aindreas was painfully thin, exhausted and ill. His stock of food was gone and rather than take time to trap and or gather other nourishment, he had pressed on, fearful of any delay. He had no energy left, all of it spent driving himself to come to this place and find his kin.

He fell on his knees in front of the bewildered guard at the outer wall to Owain's holdings and prayed to his personal Gods to help him. He did not speak the Northern tongue fluently, few of the clan did, so he uttered what he could, trusting the guard understood him.

"I seek Dillan of the Red Hawk Clan." Once the words left his lips he fell into a heap at the guard's feet, unconscious.

Iola applied her healing arts and by nightfall the southern stranger became coherent. Aindreas found himself bathed, clothed in fresh garments and lying in a soft bed in a room with a blazing fire. He had not expected such kindness, not from pagans, despite his iarel's assurances. As he turned his head, his eyes caught those of an older man. His tawny hair was streaked with grey, but fire still reined in his eyes. There was considerable resemblance to the young iarel.

"Are you Dillan, uncle to Brecc, once a renowned warrior of the Red Hawk Clan?" Aindreas asked in a thin voice, praying his quest was over.

Dillan answered the man in the Southern tongue, "I am."

"I am Aindreas, I was sent by Caewlin, Iarel of the Red Hawk Clan."

"Brecc is no more?"

"He has passed beyond and his son is now leader." Dillan nodded, it had been over a decade since he had last seen his people and changes had no doubt occurred.

"Why have you come?"

"We are need of help."

Dillan tensed, noticeably. To have a Southerner request the aid of a Northern man, even one that was kin, meant that something catastrophic had befallen the clan.

"What has happened?"

"We are being exterminated."

"Tell me all of it," Dillan commanded. By the time the messenger had finished his tale, Dillan's head was in his broad hands. "This is grave, most grave," he mumbled in shock.

"The iarel had no choice but to send this plea."

Dillan raised his eyes and inhaled deeply. "I will speak with my master."

"Will they help us, these barbarians who believe we are savages?"

"Owain the Elder and Lord Bardyn are good men, honest and true. They will help us."

The man on the bed relaxed, not only because of his fellow clansman's assurance that the Northern lords would take interest in their plight – he had caught Dillan's use of the word *us*.

He is still clan, no matter how long he has lived among them.

Dillan left the room and went to find his master. Owain the Elder knew of the messenger's arrival and waited as patiently as he could while the man was treated. He knew a clansman would be more comfortable talking with his Master of the Guard than with himself so he sat in his chambers, Belwyn and Pyrs near him, puzzling as to what would drive one of Dillan's kin north.

"By the Powers, it must be bad," Belwyn remarked when he saw Dillan's pale countenance at the door to the room. Owain immediately waved his friend over to a chair and poured him wine, concerned as well.

"Thank you, sir." Dillan gulped down the wine and then took another deep breath.

"In all the years that you have served me, Dillan, I have seen that look on your face only once, when you came to tell me that my wife was dying." Dillan nodded, he remembered that day well. Moina had been the light of his master's life and her death had brought deep grief to the household.

"I pray you'll not see this look again."

"What has the man told you, Dillan?" Owain asked gently.

"My people, the Red Hawk Clan, are being annihilated. Their fortunes changed in the Year of the Wolf, almost three years ago by our reckoning. The spring omens were ill; the rains did not come, crops grew poorly and the fishing was scarce. The last two years were no better and the clans began to starve. They traded with the city of Kell, bartering hides for food. The trading went well, for a time, and then two of the clans broke ranks and began to raid the villages along the Southern coast. They carried off goods and women, murdering some of the villagers in the process. Caewlin, Iarel of the Red Hawk Clan, protested, knowing it would stir up the men of Kell. As he feared, trading was suspended. Caewlin finally had no choice but to take to raiding the villages as well, for his people were starving. To his credit, he only made one foray, for it sickened him to do so." Dillan's face betrayed his distaste at the news that his clan had fallen to raiding innocent villages.

"Certainly those in Kell knew of their plight, why did they not supply food, at least for the children?" Belwyn asked, astounded. Kell was not only a prosperous seaport, but also served as a market city where crops were sold from the surrounding countryside. "Do they suffer from the same drought as the Isles?"

"No, they do not. Food is available, but not in abundant quantity, for it seems held in abeyance in some way. The people of Kell are not permitted to aid the clans. Lord Phelan made it a crime to supply food to any Southerner, punishable by death."

"He's a heartless bastard," Pyrs remarked without thinking and Owain the Elder gave the boy an approving look. The lad had proven to have a mind of his own and was not ashamed of speaking it.

"So why has this man come to you?" Owain asked, his face in a slight frown now.

"The iarel seeks our aid. Lord Phelan has conquered all but one of the clans, only those of the Red Hawk remain free, if indeed they still are. It took Aindreas three weeks to come to us on foot. Phelan has made war on them, capturing them and enslaving them to work in his fields and in his quarries. The women have been sent to some of Kell's brothels and are being sold to Northern traders for the brothels in Ilspath."

"What of the children?" Owain the Elder asked, for he noted Dillan did not mention them.

"If they are not old enough to work ..." Dillan stopped at that, his iron resolve melting like snow in strong sunshine. He swallowed and then continued with a wretched ache in his voice, "they are put to the sword."

"By the Powers," Owain the Elder said as he rose from his chair. He strode to the fireplace and said nothing, overwhelmed by what he had just heard.

"Grandsire?" It was Pyrs. "Grandsire, is there nothing that Aderyn can do for these people?" His voice was more level than he thought it would sound. His anger was boiling, but he had bottled it up. He was slowly learning there were times to be furious and times to hold his wrath in check.

"Yes, my grandson, there is something the House of Aderyn can do for these people. No one deserves such treatment, not in the face of such adversity." Dillan did not react immediately, his mind too numb from the horror he felt within.

Owain the Elder advanced to his friend's side, put his hand on the man's shoulder and proclaimed in an emotional voice, "We leave for Bardyn's in the morning. If he will not aid us, we will go to Kell on our own. By the Powers, this must cease and that butcher called to account!" Dillan's eyes moved up to those of his master and he broke down into sobs.

The malady struck suddenly – Owain the Younger fell ill late in the afternoon after dining with a group of merchants in Ilspath. He had made the journey to the trading town to negotiate grain prices at a more reasonable rate than Fercos was offering. Once the negotiations were concluded he was invited to dine with the merchants. Although he preferred not to do so, he did, for it would have been discourteous to refuse. He was careful to partake of only what the others ate and felt reasonably secure as he jested and dined.

He had no more than finished the repast and rode out of Ilspath's gates when he was desperately ill, retching so hard he slid off his horse. Once the wave of body wracking illness had subsided, one of his guards helped him back on his mount. He refused to return to the city, sensing this was no common ailment. Pushing himself and his horse he made it to the courtyard of Aldyn's holdings and then fell unconscious to the ground in a sweaty heap.

"It is poison," the healer announced after she examined him. She recognized the symptoms quite clearly. "It is made from monksbane." The treatments she would administer would be purely palliative.

"What will happen?" Aldyn asked, her eyes rimmed red from tears, sensing she already knew. On the bed in front of them Owain was stripped to his breeches, semi-conscious, his face coated in sweat. He murmured incoherently as tremors surged his body.

The healer softened her voice, "Milady, it is usually fatal. Though it is said that he lost his meal very shortly after he ate, but I fear that will not be enough." Her face betrayed what she did not say. There was little hope. To her surprise, her mistress held her composure.

Aldyn turned to her Master of the Guard who stood nearby, "Determine who did this." Her tone was not weepy, but cold as the grave that beckoned her councilor.

"Yes, mistress." Cadmon bowed and left immediately, his eyes dark with anger.

"I will sit with him," Aldyn said, dragging a chair over in jerky movements, not focused enough to pick it up and carry it to the side of the bed.

"That is best, milady," the healer replied. *For it will not be long.*

FIFTEEN

The news of Owain the Younger's illness caught up with his father when he arrived at his liege lord's castle to speak to him about the clansmen. His old friend had a dark expression and Owain immediately knew something was gravely amiss.

Before he could ask Bardyn said, "Come, my friend, bring Belwyn and your grandson with you. We have news from Aldyn and it is dire." He only gave Pyrs a passing glance though he had never met the boy before. His preoccupation spoke reams.

Lord Bardyn felt a shiver of cold pass through him when he handed his friend the message that had arrived only one hour earlier, sent to him by winged messenger. *His son was dying.* He thought how devastating the news would be if it was Morgan slipping into his grave.

"Father?" Belwyn asked, his face tense.

"Your brother is on his deathbed, he has been poisoned," Owain the Elder announced, his voice uneven and raw. "The healer says it is monksbane." The color drained out of Belwyn's face and Pyrs uttered an oath under his breath.

"Who has done this?" Owain asked, his eyes moving to his lifelong friend.

Bardyn sighed. "There are many possibilities, Owain. Your son stands between Aldyn and that pack of nobles. If he were no longer at her side ..." he let the thought end there.

"Is there no hope?" Belwyn asked, his voice low and thick.

"The healer gives none, it is the Hands of the Powers," Bardyn replied. He paused and then continued, "There may be an attempt to take Aldyn's holdings if Owain does not survive. Morgan is preparing to leave with a contingent of men to bolster those in Aldyn's service." Owain the Elder nodded. It was a prudent move.

"I am so sorry to deliver such news, my old friend. I have asked that we be kept informed as to your son's condition."

"I thank you for that."

"Father, I must go to him," Belwyn began and his sire immediately shook his head.

"I understand your need, son, but there is nothing we can do for him. If he is to die, he will be gone from us before you reach his bedside. It is up to the Powers. They will aid him as They see fit." Belwyn let hope drain out of his heart. He could picture his young brother, the poison consuming him. Rage and grief struggled for supremacy within his mind.

His voice quavered. "I understand, father."

When Pyrs found Lord Bardyn studying him, he moved to kneel at his liege lord's feet.

Bardyn acknowledged him. "Young man?"

"My lord, I am Pyrs, son of Belwyn, grandson of Owain the Elder."

A slight smile played on Bardyn's face. "Indeed you are. You may not know it, but you are the fourth young man who has come to kneel in my presence from the House of Aderyn. Your uncle Owain came to offer his sword to me only a few years previous. I still remember that day." His voice was despondent. Pyrs did not reply, his mind in tumult. "Rise, young Pyrs. I am pleased to meet you at last." The lad rose and returned to stand by his father.

Bardyn turned his attention to Owain. "What has brought you to me in such haste, for you obviously did not know of your son's illness?"

Owain painstakingly related what Aindreas had told them. He watched Bardyn's face go from shock to horror to righteous anger.

"I agree, Owain, we must help these people But I wonder …"

"My lord?" Owain asked.

"Is it possible that the attack on your son and the threat to Aldyn's holdings was perpetrated to prevent us from marching south?"

Belwyn frowned and then nodded. "Perhaps it is all woven together."

"Either way, the matter at Aldyn's holdings will keep me from riding south as I soon as I should." He paused for a time and then sighed. "If you are willing to risk Belwyn, my friend, I would send him to speak with this Lord Phelan."

"Do you feel that will be of use, my lord?" Pyrs asked, clearly forgetting his junior status within the room. His father shot him a warning glance, but he did not see it.

"No, I do not. Men such as this Phelan will not respond to reason." Bardyn did not appear to be the least bit perturbed at the lad's forthright behavior. He saw a great deal of the boy's grandsire in him and he liked that.

"I am troubled, my lord. I do not wish to lose both my sons in the span of a few weeks." Owain's eyes were misty, deep and dark.

Bardyn put his hand on his comrade's shoulder. "I know. I will send Morgan as well, for Kell's lord will find it hard to ignore both of our sons."

"It will do us no good to lose both our futures," Owain observed. Bardyn examined his old friend's face and saw it furrowed in worry. The man stood to lose one son to poison and if all went ill with Kell's master, he may lose the other one as well. It was the first time Bardyn had seen fear in the man's eyes.

"Phelan will not kill my father or Lord Morgan, grandsire, they are too valuable to him. He will use them as leverage, either to keep our liege lord out of the conflict or as a means to raise coin," Pyrs observed. Bardyn's eyebrow raised, amazed at the lad's keen analysis of the situation, despite his youth.

"Elrehan tells me you have a head for strategy, young Pyrs. It appears that your mind is far more keen than most lads your age."

"Thank you, my lord," Pyrs readily acknowledged the compliment.

"I believe your grandson is correct, Owain. I am willing to take that gamble to buy us time. Once assured that Aldyn's holdings are secure I will march south, though with a smaller contingent of men than I might have. We have enemies enough in our own lands and I do not wish to put my subjects at undue risk."

"I thank you, my friend," Owain replied solemnly. "If you do not mind, I wish to rest now." He felt very old at this moment. Bardyn nodded his approval and watched as Owain left the room.

As soon as the door closed, the lord addressed Belwyn, "I will bring any news of your brother to you, before your father learns of it. That way we both can be with him if ..." Bardyn let the sentence fade. Belwyn's eyes were damp and he struggled for control.

"Thank you, my lord."

Lord Corryn chuckled at the news.

"How sad to hear that Lady Aldyn's devoted lapdog is ill, perhaps dying. How sad indeed," he said and took a long sip of ale. A faint smile appeared on his lips as he set the drink down at his elbow.

"If the man dies there will be bloodshed, Aderyn will not allow it to stand," his companion observed. He cut a hunk of cheese off a large golden wheel and began to munch on the slice in earnest.

"Ah, but it will not be our blood, will it, Vaddon?" he asked. Vaddon was a short and vain sort of man, a noble with barely enough holdings to qualify for the title.

"No, it will not, for the deed points clearly toward our most corpulent Fercos," he replied with a smirk. It had been easy to bribe one of Fercos' servants to do the poisoning, taking the place of one of the pages at the Guildhall. A quick slip of poison as he refilled Owain's cup had done the trick. That servant was now dead, carrion fodder, and could tell no one who had bought his loyalty.

"When Fercos falls to Aderyn's sword that will be one less noble in the way of the circlet," Corryn replied. Lord Vaddon nodded and cut off another hunk of succulent cheese.

The girl appeared at the castle's postern gate as if from nowhere. At least it seemed that way to the older guard on duty. He was deep in conversation when then the girl appeared in front of them.

"I am here to see Owain the Younger," she announced. She looked to be all of perhaps fifteen or sixteen years, tall, thin, with long black hair and unique eyes.

"No one is allowed inside, girl." The guard's voice was harsh and unforgiving. The news that the youngest of Aderyn was dying had put all of them on edge.

"Tell Lady Aldyn that Morwyn the Adept's daughter is here."

Morwyn's name meant nothing to him.

"I shall do no such thing, girl. Be off! We have more important things to concern ourselves than some self-important child."

Gwyn murmured a spell and the dragon on her shoulder became fully visible to the two men in front of her. She usually kept it hidden as not to frighten those she met on the road.

"Powers!" the guard sputtered, stumbling back, his eyes wide in shock. The other man allowed himself a faint smile. His garments were not those of a guard, but of higher rank. He was only a few years older than Gwyn but held himself with a pose that belied his age.

"I am no child, sir. I am Gwyn, daughter of Morwyn, wielder of the Old Magic. Summon your mistress … now!" She put a touch of power behind her words and to her irritation, the guard still did not move.

"Go, I will mind the gate while you speak to our mistress," the young man offered with a hint of amusement. The guard regained his wits and set off on his mission, hurrying across the courtyard. The remaining fellow studied Gwyn curiously. He did not appear concerned about the creature perched on her shoulder.

"Is that a real dragon or an illusion?" he asked, scrutinizing the beast intently.

"It is real," Gwyn replied, somewhat taken aback by the fellow's question. He had shoulder length blonde hair pulled back in a ponytail, tied by a rawhide cord adorned with small feathers.

"You must be important to be guarded in such a way." His voice almost sounded like it was chiding her.

A pensive expression appeared on Gwyn's face. "Perhaps."

"Are you here to heal Owain the Younger?"

"Yes."

"Thank the Powers." He paused and then began anew, his voice wroth. "He is all that stands between those whoresons who style themselves nobles and …" He stopped dead, realizing the strong language he'd used in her presence. "Pardon, please." He looked a bit chagrined.

Gwyn studied him. "You are not a guard."

He smiled, broadly, and shrugged, offering no verbal clue as to his profession. She eyed him further and then felt the ripple of the *gift*.

A bard.

He nodded, as if he had heard her thoughts.

Before she could reply a beckoning shout flew across the courtyard. Standing near an archway was Lady Aldyn with the guard at her side. She gestured and Gwyn entered through the gate, the young man trailing behind her.

"Powers, it is you!" Aldyn wavered on her feet and leaned against the stone archway for support. She was physically and mentally exhausted. "Come quickly ..." Fueled by a rush of hope that pushed down her weariness, Aldyn raised her skirts and disappeared through the archway. Gwyn and the young man took to their heels as well. Those that witnessed their passage might have found it amusing if the circumstances had been different.

Owain's color was ashen grey, his breathing labored and his murmuring indistinct. His hands were bitter cold and as Gwyn stood by his bed she sensed where he was on his personal journey. He was very near death.

She looked over at Aldyn and explained, "He is far away from us, very close to the Veil. I will do what I can." She tugged a chair over, sank into it and took a deep breath. Murmuring a prayer to the Powers, she asked for Their aid.

If it is your Will, aid me to bring him back to this life. If it is his time, let him pass in peace.

Reaching over she took both of the man's cold hands into hers. She allowed herself to sink down, drifting into the place that did not exist, the land between this world and the next. She made sure to sense the solid feel of the chair beneath her and the pressure of her feet on the stone floor, her physical connection to this world. It was too easy to drift with the dying man and be lost forever.

Owain? Uncle, can you hear me? she called into the void without speaking.

His thin voice replied in her mind. *Aldyn?*

No, it is Gwyn. You are poisoned, uncle.

I know, I am dying. There was no fear in his voice at this admission, only extreme sadness as if he knew his passing would be of great import.

If you wish to continue this journey, I will ease your passage into the other world.

There was a pause and then his voice was instantly sharp, more urgent, and it echoed in her mind.

I cannot die! They will marry her to one of them. She will kill herself rather than be hurt again. I must protect her! I must not die until she is safe!

Then you wish to live? she asked cautiously. It had to be his choice, for he alone stood at the brink.

Yes! I must ... if the Powers allow.

Then take my hand, Owain, and I will guide you back.

Can you ... are you permitted this? he asked, unsure.

I am permitted to do this if you wish, for you stand on our side of the Veil. She did not tell him that by placing his fate in the hands of the Powers he had given himself a chance at life. *We must hurry, for you are nearly beyond where even I can reach you.* She attempted to keep her voice calm and level though her heart was thundering in her chest and fear raged through her. She sensed her guardian was no longer on her shoulder though somewhere near. Though he kept silent she sensed his near panic. He could not save her if she went too far.

Then help me, for her sake! Owain's voice returned.

Take my hand, Uncle, and I will lead you back. Her voice was less strong now. The need to stand so close to the Veil drained her without respite.

Panic edged into his voice. *I cannot see it!*

Take my hand, Owain, follow my voice and reach out to my hand. Her stamina was fading, withering away. She felt herself weakening, wavering in the chair. If she did not keep her focus then she too would enter the next life as Owain crossed over. She felt a pair of hands on her shoulders and for a moment the touch of another human startled her. She thought it was perhaps Aldyn, but it was not. Warmth flooded into her, radiating throughout her being from her shoulders to the soles of her feet. Her mind told her that it was bardic power she felt and she allowed herself a moment of hope. The young man stood behind her, the one she had met at the gate. His hands were on her shoulders, his eyes closed as he poured pure energy into her.

Go ahead, I will steady you as best I can, his calm voice said in her mind. There was a long pause and then she felt it, the spectral hand of the man who stood between two worlds.

Uncle?

Yes, I feel you.

Follow me and while we walk, concentrate on the love you have for Aldyn, for that will be what will save you.

I will, the voice answered. *I will.*

In the end, Owain's faith and his unending devotion to his mistress were stronger than the poison and the lure of the world beyond. He made the long journey back to the living. It was a near thing. The healer supported his return by applying warmth and stimulants, for the poison was of short duration. Once his color and breathing had improved and Gwyn was assured he was firmly routed in this world, she rose and gave Aldyn a reassuring nod. Then she swooned from extreme exhaustion. Her guardian issued a note of alarm as the bard caught her in his arms. Once it saw she was safe, it flew beside the young man as he carried Gwyn to a bed where she could rest.

Cadmon was a very patient man and had long ago learned that not all was as it seemed when it came to the plots around the Lady Aldyn. A page that served at the Merchant Guildhall was found murdered, his throat cut, the victim of an apparent robbery. Cadmon dug deeper and discovered that the page began his work at the Guildhall only a few days before Owain met with the merchants. The meeting date and time were widely known. According to Cadmon's sources, the page was in the hire of Lord Fercos and had gone missing a few days before the meeting at Ilspath. It had been too easy to discern. Cadmon divined that the trail back to Fercos was false, but he decided to push the issue anyway.

Accompanied by five men, Ifor included, Cadmon confronted the weighty lord. Fercos balked, refusing to list his accomplices, not having the cunning to betray his own kind though they'd readily done the same to him.

Cadmon's voice was as cold as the deep of night. "Guard your health, Lord Fercos, for if we learn that you are to blame for this act of war, you will forfeit your life."

Fercos snorted, though his mind was squirming. "I do not fear you or that camp wench you serve." Menacingly, Cadmon took a step forward and Fercos's guards responded in kind.

The peace teetered precariously as Cadmon hissed, "Mind your tongue or I will remove it. You have heard the warning. If you have any sense in that fat body of yours, you will heed it." He spun on his heels and marched out of Fercos's chambers, his men behind him. The nobleman frowned and would have shouted an oath after the departing figures, but thought better of it. He gestured to one of his guards.

"Summon my Master of Guard! If I am to be blamed for this then I will reap the reward I so richly deserve."

"Yes, my lord," the man answered and set off to do his master's bidding.

Gwyn awoke to find the young man at her bedside. He was dozing, obviously tired, and it was now night. A bright blazing fire was in the hearth and she lay in a soft, comfortable bed. Her cloak and boots were removed, her long hair plaited to keep it from tangling. She frowned, sensing she had slept for a considerable length of time. For a moment she was disconcerted, for she did not see her guardian.

I am here, dragon sister.

She moved her eyes up to the carved oak headboard above her and found the beast curled around one of the bedposts. He seemed content and not the least concerned with the presence of the young man so near her.

How long have I slept? she asked.

"One full day, madam," the bard replied, again as if he could read her thoughts. Her eyes narrowed and she frowned. She opened her mouth to ask a question and he answered before she could voice it.

"Yes, I understand some of what you think and that of your guardian as well, now that I know it is not an illusion." Gwyn shot a quick glance back up at the dragon and saw the beast give a slight nod in affirmation.

"How can you sense dragon speech when it is not directed at you?" she asked, puzzled.

"I do not know. I hear and sense things others do not," he replied honestly and then yawned and stretched. Gwyn pulled herself up in bed and changed the subject.

"How is my uncle?"

"Resting quietly. He woke for a time this afternoon and spoke with Lady Aldyn. Now that she knows he is healing she has taken to her bed to rest."

"Is he aware of the residual effects of the poison?"

"Yes. He attempted to rise and he found his legs unable to support him." Gwyn sighed. "He will have to learn how to walk again."

"Can you not heal him of that weakness?" the young man asked, intrigued.

"I can, but that is not what the Powers wish."

"I see." He sounded as if he understood.

"It was your power …" she started and then stopped.

"Yes."

"I thank you …" She realized she did not know his name. Again, he answered before she could ask the question.

"I am Dru."

"I am Gwyn."

"Gwyn, daughter of Morwyn the Adept and Belwyn, the Eldest of the House of Aderyn, she who wields the Old Magic and who has communed with the Ancient One."

"You know much about my family," she replied, unnerved.

"I am bard, we study lineage," he said and shrugged, as if that was an adequate explanation. He rose at this. "I will tell the healer you are awake so that food may be sent. You are still too pale for my liking."

"I will leave in the morning," she said, having no clear idea why she felt she needed to tell him.

He halted near the door and studied her curiously. "Why so soon?"

"I am needed elsewhere," she answered frankly. He nodded and left the room. She turned her eyes to the beast above her.

"A bard who can hear our thoughts." The beast said nothing, only observed her with its glittering eyes and then resumed his tight curl around the bedpost. She pondered on the matter for a few more minutes and then fell back to sleep.

The winged messenger arrived towards dawn, for it was a long journey from Aldyn's holdings to her uncle's. A page posted near the dovecote snagged onto the bird, petted it and then removed the small parchment attached to the bird's spindly leg. He toted the message to his liege lord's chamber and handed it to his master. He was not surprised to find Bardyn awake, for everyone knew what drama played out at Aldyn's holdings. The page bowed and left his lord alone with the latest report. Bardyn swiftly skimmed Aldyn's delicately handwritten note and the news brought nothing but joy to his troubled heart.

"Powers be Praised!" he said. A smile crossed his face and then he repeated even louder, "Powers be Praised!" He stalked off toward Belwyn's room to deliver the news in person – Owain the Younger lived and would recover because of his niece, Gwyn. The House of Aderyn still had both its sons.

Gwyn left Aldyn's holdings the moment she rose from her bed. She took food from the kitchen and departed the castle without a word to either Aldyn or Owain, who slept soundly, worn out from his ordeal. Dru found her as she neared the outer gate. His presence troubled her.

"You leave us too soon," he stated as if the comment was not open to debate.

"I am needed elsewhere."

"So you have said," he replied, a strange look in his eyes.

"May the Powers bless you, Dru," Gwyn replied politely and then turned to continue her journey.

"They already have, for I have met you." Gwyn kept walking, her unease growing. She wanted to whirl around and demand why he would say such a thing, but she did not.

Because it is true, the bard's voice floated through her mind. She did turn this time, angry at his psychic intrusion, but he was not standing near the gate or anywhere she could see him. She frowned and continued the trek out the gates and into the forest beyond Aldyn's holdings, bewildered by the encounter with the enigmatic bard.

Once the rejoicing over Owain's apparent survival died down, the subject of the Southern clansmen returned full force. Morgan was appraised of what they faced and he was uncomfortable with the journey given the potential for trouble at Aldyn's holdings.

"I understand the need for us to show our displeasure at Lord Phelan's actions, but is it wise to undertake this when matters here are so unsettled?"

"I understand your concern, but I feel it is important to send a message that Phelan can not easily ignore. We do not have much time, for Phelan is pressing ahead with his war, determined to destroy the clans." Morgan sighed, knowing his sire's mind was set. He gave Belwyn a look and then a wan smile. Pyrs sat near them, a faraway look on his face.

"I've never been to Kell, this journey should prove interesting," Morgan remarked.

"I have, but it was a number of years ago. So much has changed if Aindreas' report is accurate."

"Mother is in Kell," Pyrs said, more to himself than to the others.

"What?" his father asked, for he had never learned Morwyn's final destination.

"Gwyn says she's in Kell."

Belwyn's face grew pensive. "This adds even more urgency to our journey."

Morgan nodded. "She is in danger if they are pressing women into service at the brothels."

Belwyn sighed. "Powers help her if that has happened." He saw Pyrs's eyes on him and he placed a reassuring hand on his shoulder. "I am sure she is well, son. Your mother is too resourceful to be handled in such a fashion." The boy nodded, more to reassure his sire than anything.

"We can depart in morning, Belwyn, if you are willing."

"I will be ready."

Lord Bardyn nodded his approval.

"Explain our position, son, tell him we will not condone the slaughter of the Southern clansmen. If he is the least bit tractable, ask that the clans be allowed to come to my lands. We will shelter them until the drought passes and assure they are not harmed."

"I will, father. Do you honestly believe he will heed what we say?"

"No, I agree with Pyrs on that. No doubt he will hold both of you for coin."

"Which is adequate reason for war." Morgan saw his father's plan clearly.

"More than adequate reason. I must be assured that all is secure with Aldyn's holdings before I march south, though. That may take time."

Morgan nodded. "I understand."

Bardyn sighed deeply. "Let us pray there are some of the clansmen left to assist."

When Pyrs awoke the next morning he found snowing falling at a steady pace. For a time he thought that might postpone his father's departure, but that was not the case. The warriors saddled their horses, packed extra blankets in their saddlebags and made their farewells. Though Belwyn had continually assured Pyrs that all would be well, his son knew better. His father was not riding Ceffyl, his favorite horse, nor was he carrying the lineage sword. Belwyn had divested himself of two of his most treasured possessions, as if he knew this quest was ill fated. As Pyrs watched Morgan and his father disappear out of sight into the falling snow beyond the main gate, he turned to his grandsire and commented,

"They expect an ill reception, grandsire. Father does not bear Aderyn's sword."

Owain the Elder gave the lad a measured glance and nodded. Belwyn had insisted the sword remain in his father's keeping so that it would not be lost if he fell to Phelan's men.

"Little escapes you, grandson."

"It is as if he does not expect to return," Pyrs murmured in a solemn tone.

"Only the Powers know that, Pyrs." The lad turned and walked back into the castle to begin packing for the journey home. He was keenly aware of what tasks lay ahead of him and his heart was heavy with that knowledge.

Bardyn and Owain the Elder sat in the lord's chambers and listened as Elrehan laid out his strategy to safeguard the lives of the two men riding toward Kell. It was a sound plan.

"How soon will you leave?" Bardyn asked, warming his hands near the fire.

"As soon as the storm passes," was the reply. The snowfall had only grown heavier with each passing hour since the two warriors had left. Now, at dusk, there were drifts on the road and that had delayed Owain the Elder and Pyrs from returning to Aderyn. Neither Bardyn nor Owain spoke their concern about their sons, for they were out in the weather as well.

"You have my blessing," Bardyn replied.

"Thank you, my lord," Elrehan rose and bowed.

"I am sending Duncan north with a contingent of men to aid Aldyn. I am hoping this ends soon to aid their journey."

"I spoke with a peddler newly arrived from Ilspath this afternoon, it appears the snowfall is less in that direction," Elrehan offered.

"That is promising news. I wish the matter at Aldyn's to be settled swiftly so we can turn our attention south."

Elrehan bowed again and left the room, his mind full of the preparations he would need to make before he set his horse toward Kell and his sister.

Owain the Younger quickly realized that being alive had its price. He had walked only four paces and it had been one of the hardest things he had ever done in his life. His face was drenched in sweat and his body shaking from the exertion. Though no one knew, he wept into his pillow at night, ashamed at what he had become.

"That is better than this morning!" Aldyn's overly cheery voice remarked.

He gave her a scowl and grumbled, "I do not think I can make it back to the bed."

"Sure you can." She rose and took Mair's place at his side. Peter was on his other side, his hand around his master's waist. "Come on now, that's it, turn around and back you go."

"Milady, I'm not sure ..." Owain began, her presence so near him, touching him, making it difficult to focus on the walking. He felt her hand slid down his back and to his bottom. He literally shuffled forward the remaining few steps when she deftly pinched him.

"Aldyn!" he sputtered, shocked at her behavior.

"What?" she asked, her face a mask of innocence as the hand swiftly retreated to his waist.

"You ..." he stopped and gave her another glower.

"You want to turn around and walk some more?" she asked.

A wicked grin appeared on his sweaty face. "Only if you motivate me like that again." She began to laugh and they resumed his exercises. This time he went six paces from the bed and back.

Pyrs and his grandsire returned to Aderyn once the weather abated. Both of them realized it was a waiting game. They were pleased to hear that Owain the Younger was on the mend, though so weak he was unable to walk more than a few steps. He had dictated a letter to his father and Owain the Elder found comfort in it, for his son's sense of humor remained intact. He had joked that he'd discovered the secret to being pampered by Lady Aldyn – all he had to do was come back from the dead. Underneath the light prose his father knew the young man was frightened, for he could not walk nor resume his full activities. His dedication to his mistress drove him to heal faster than was possible.

As his father rode south, Pyrs remained tense and nothing his grandsire said lightened his mood. Once at home the boy threw himself into sword practice and requested that Dillan drill him harder than ever. The Master of the Guard complied and found the lad more focused than he had been in months. Late one evening after Pyrs had retired, Dillan reported the change to his master.

"He knows his father may perish at Phelan's hands," Owain the Elder explained. His mood was constrained as well, his mind filled with worry for both his sons.

"Aye."

"Let him practice all he wishes, Dillan, for it will keep his mind off his father and his uncle."

"As you wish, sir." Dillan returned to his room and began to clean his weapons as was his evening ritual. He wanted to march south immediately but he was a man who knew that all things had their time. If his personal Gods were willing, once Lady Aldyn's holdings were secure Lord Phelan would find Dillan's sword at his throat.

Unfortunately, Lord Fercos' skills lie in various vices, not tactics. He dithered too long and lost his advantage. His Master of the Guard pushed him as hard as he dare, telling him that the heavy snow would delay Bardyn's forces and give them an advantage, but Fercos waited and fretted. He did not arrive at Aldyn's holdings until four days after Owain the Younger fell ill. If he had actually hired the assassin he would have been there the day Owain was supposed to die, eager to capitalize on the chaotic situation.

While Fercos waited, Bardyn's Master of the Guard fortified Aldyn's contingent with thirty of his liege lord's men. Though warned of the reinforcements, Fercos attacked despite the odds and half of his force fell dead or wounded. The ineffectual lord died from an arrow that cleaved his heart as he turned to flee the battlefield. He never had the pleasure of learning who sent him to his grave.

Aldyn had another arrow notched, but it was unneeded. Despite warnings to the contrary she had taken to the battlefield with her men. She was wearing a ringed mail jerkin, armed with a bow and a short sword. She did not wear a chain mail coif for she wanted her foes to know who rode against them. It was not a common sight to see a woman in battle and her men held her in awe for it. Cadmon was not awed, he was mortally afraid for her, but his worry was displaced. When he saw her arrow cut down Fercos as one would a ravening dog, he allowed himself a grim smile.

She accepted the surrender of Fercos' surviving warriors and then turned back to her holdings. All the while the face of Owain the Younger remained uppermost in her mind. He would still be sleeping when she returned to his bedside, for she had ordered the healer to give him a strong draught to keep him from learning her intent. He would be furious to learn of her participation in the battle, but that did not matter. She had sent a very clear message to her enemies in a form they could not ignore. To harm one of her own meant death.

Her councilor had not been angry, he was strangely quiet, and that, as Aldyn would come to learn, meant he was beyond anger. His eyes snapped and his voice was cool to cover his stark fear for her safety.

"In the future, madam, when you go forth to seek death at the end of some enemy's blade, please do not have me drugged. That way I will be able to insure your funeral is right and proper providing there is enough left of your ravished body to bury."

Her voice was equally cold. "I will make note of that, Councilor." She turned on her heels and departed the room, knowing he had a right to be angry. She would allow him a couple of hours to settle down and then she would return and read to him, as she did every night since his ailment began. In many ways, his poisoning had brought them closer.

As she settled in a hot tub full of steaming water to bathe the stench of battle from her body, she allowed herself a self-satisfied smile. She knew it was improper to rejoice over the death of an enemy, but it felt good.

"May the Powers judge you and find your soul wanting, Fercos," she murmured and slid further down into the warm oblivion that the bath offered.

"Powers!" Vaddon exclaimed. "She killed him herself?" he demanded of the servant who had brought the report. Corryn, his dining companion, was listening, engrossed by this improbable tale.

The servant nodded earnestly. "He was slain by an arrow, my lord, one loosed by the lady." Corryn began to laugh, heartily, pounded his thigh in amusement.

"By the Powers, that wench has spirit!"

Vaddon waved the servant off and scowled. "This changes things." Corryn continued to laugh and then finally gained control.

"Yes, it does. Fercos is no longer a problem, but the lady has proved to be more of threat than either of us thought possible."

"So how do we handle her?" Corryn thought for a time, silent. Then he nodded, more to himself than his companion.

"I will think on that. We have a couple of options." He knew his plan already, but he was not willing to share it with Vaddon.

"It cannot involve her councilor, for he will be well guarded from this time forward."

"No, he is no longer a viable target. We must be more subtle."

"Are you willing to allow me a small hint?"

Corryn shook his head. "The timing is not right, Vaddon, I must wait. But when it falls out Lady Aldyn's holdings will be secured, Aderyn will not seek revenge and Lord Bardyn will have no recourse but to acknowledge his niece's fate."

Vaddon raised a cup of wine in salute. "Then I will be in awe of you, Corryn."

The scheming lord drained his cup in acknowledgement of the toast. *As you should be.*

Their reunion was sweet, for Pyrs had sorely missed his sister. They flew into each other's arms and hugged for the longest time. She'd found him in Aderyn's library, studying books and moving his little stones around on the table to mimic whatever battle he was currently analyzing.

"Gwyn, I have so missed you!" When he finally stepped back and examined his twin he saw the small dragon clinging deftly to the girl's shoulder.

"Greetings, dragon brother," he said. The dragon gave him a slight incline of the head.

Greetings, brother. Pyrs turned his attention back to his sister and gave her another hug.

"It has been too long!"

"For me as well, Pyrs. You have grown, you look so much like father." He was now sixteen as well, a young man slowly replacing the awkward boy.

"I do, apparently." Gwyn noted that he did not bristle at the comparison, as he once would have.

"It is time, Pyrs," she said and he sighed. He knew this moment would come and it was too soon for him. "We must tell grandsire and then leave." He nodded and together they headed for Owain the Elder's study.

Gwyn patiently laid out the situation and after considerable discussion their grandsire allowed them the right to leave Aderyn.

"I agree reluctantly and with great trepidation," Owain the Elder retorted, a serious parental frown on his face. "I do demand that Dillan and Aindreas go with you. Both are keen to be with their people and Dillan can relay our plans to the iarel." Gwyn rewarded him with one of her generous smiles and his heart melted. "You are your mother, Gwyn," he had said, shaking his head. "I could never refuse her anything."

"We will be quite safe," Gwyn said, lying with a great deal of skill. She saw her grandsire's eyes narrow.

"No, you won't be, but as you've explained it, you must be there to help and so I allow it. I pray that I've not made the wrong decision."

"We will be careful, grandsire."

The twins departed at dawn with Dillan and Aindreas at their side. The weather held and though it was cold they rode toward Kell at a strong pace. As the two Southern men spoke back and forth, Pyrs listened, attempting to learn as much of their language as possible. He found it not that difficult, actually, and would throw in a word or a comment every now and then. Dillan had been patiently teaching him bits and pieces. Pyrs kept stealing looks at his sister. She seemed to have grown as much as he had over the time they were apart.

"Did you learn much from the adepts?" he asked, hoping to start a conversation.

"Yes." She offered no more and he sensed it was best not to push the issue. Still keen to wile away the time, Pyrs turned his attention back to Dillan.

"Tell me of the clans, Dillan, for I know almost nothing about them."

Pleased the boy wanted to learn of his people, Dillan captured Pyrs' attention for the next two hours as he related the history and the complex social structure of the Southern Isle Clans. Pyrs found it fascinating. When they discussed battle techniques the clan's use of shield-women riveted him.

"Women go to war, as well?" he asked, incredulous. He knew his mother could handle a sword, but the idea of women specifically trained to fight in battle was something new.

"They do and they are very ferocious. The iarel's sister, Fea, is a shield-maiden."

"Why did you leave the clan?" Pyrs asked, hoping he'd not trod on a sensitive subject. He noticed the Aindreas was listening intently, though he wondered how much the clansman actually understood of their Northern speech.

"There was a disagreement between my brother, Geraint, and myself. Geraint became iarel and chose to marry the woman I loved. Her father insisted she marry him instead of me and so I left the clan as Geraint became increasingly uncomfortable with my presence."

Pyrs frowned and thought. "You were the better choice for iarel, weren't you?" His intuition was keen, for often the eldest son was not the best choice as heir.

Dillan nodded solemnly. "There were many who thought so, for my brother was not adept at leadership. I could not allow the clan to be fragmented, so I left and made my way north."

"And in so doing you proved yourself to be the better choice for iarel," Gwyn remarked quietly. He caught her eyes and exhaled deeply.

"It is of no matter, now. Geraint is dead, his son Brecc has passed and now Caewlin is iarel. Everything Aindreas has told me says he is an excellent leader. The Powers have sent him at his people's darkest time."

"As the Powers have seen fit to you return to your people," Gwyn replied. Dillan gave her a curious look and fell silent.

The city felt odd. There were guards on every corner and where some might say they were there to protect against random attacks by the Southern clansmen, both Belwyn and Morgan knew that was not the cause. The clans were too weak to cause much harm.

"An armed camp, my friend," Morgan remarked very quietly as they rode through the main gates. The nearest guards appraised them with wary eyes and one hurried off to report the arrival of two noblemen in their midst.

"Indeed."

"Most likely to keep the citizens in line, I think," Morgan replied, still quiet.

"In that I agree."

They made their way to Phelan's large stone fortress, introduced themselves to the guard at the gate and soon they were meeting with one of his numerous ministers. This one was a disagreeably short man with a bad haircut and an over-rated sense of importance.

Belwyn made the introduction. "This is Lord Morgan, son of Lord Bardyn, Lord of the Eastern March. I am Belwyn, Eldest son of Aderyn. My lord has business with Lord Phelan."

"We wish to meet with him as soon as possible, for I bring a message of importance from my father," Morgan added. The minister sniffed at that.

"Our lord does not meet with just anyone who comes to our city."

Sensing a self-appointed gatekeeper, Belwyn leaned over and in a stern voice urged, "Pass the message to Lord Phelan or he will be searching for another pompous lackey to replace you."

"Sir! Do you threaten me?" the little toady asked in stunned surprise. He was used to reasonably deferential treatment from the citizens of Kell.

"Yes," Belwyn answered politely and placed his hand on the hilt of his sword for emphasis. The look on his face did not encourage further conversation. The lackey became extremely helpful, recommending an inn where the men could stay and promising to tell his lord of their arrival the moment Phelan returned to the city.

"Excellent," Belwyn replied. They left the little man to his muttering and set off in search of an inn. By unspoken consensus, they searched for another lodging house rather than the one recommended by Phelan's minister. They found themselves at an inn for the night and settled there in time for the evening repast and hopefully, a good night's rest. They were cautious in their speech and their movements, knowing that they were watched even as they ate their meal.

Lowri, one of The Old Port's serving girls, had been ill for the better part of a week. Benen, her employer, was fussing and worrying about her, as it should be. The three girls who worked at the inn acted as servers, or if they wished, they could spend the night with the men that came to stay there. Benen never pressured them, nor did he take a cut of what the girls made from their nightly work, knowing that each one of them had a family to support. In his mind it was not honorable work, but times were difficult and the extra coins the girls earned made all the difference. He insisted they always take herbs to prevent pregnancy and forestall illness from the men they sported with and until recently, none of them been afflicted until Lowri fell ill.

Morwyn always enjoyed visiting and tending to the Benen's girls and his other employees. The man was witty and possessed a wonderful sense of humor. She often sat and shared a meal with him while exchanging tales. She counted Benen as one of the few friends she had in the city. He was the only one in Kell who knew that Morwyn was once an adept and that she had children. Though she felt close to him she still did not reveal all of her past, for she never told him the name of her children's father nor his lineage. She preferred it that way, to speak of Belwyn only brought sharp pain to her heart. The nights were lonely enough without thinking of him during the day.

After she assured herself that Lowri's fever was in check and that she was indeed on the mend, Morwyn took Benen's offer of food in the kitchen at the inn. The meals she ate at the House of Healing tended to be filling, but not tasty. Benen's cook was quite good and Morwyn relished dining there. She sat quietly in a corner, eating the hot beef and sipping on the ale in front of her, not thinking of anything in particular. As she ate the serving girls scooted in and out on their errands. One of them, Keely, saw her sitting by herself and came over to talk.

"Morwyn, how are you?"

"I am well, Keely."

"Good! Benen tells us that Lowri is on the mend."

"She is and we must thank the Powers for that."

"Yes, we shall." Keely heard her name spoken as Benen walked over to them.

"I have an offer for you, if you're willing." He always looked a bit chagrined when passing on this sort of request. It felt sordid, but it was the nature of things now.

"Would it have something to do with those two men dining near the hearth?" Keely asked, her eyes twinkling.

"Ah, caught your attention, did they? They caught Meara's as well, especially the blonde one. As luck would have it, that one would like to arrange company for he and his friend tonight, if you are willing. Meara has already claimed him for her own, so it looks to be the dark-haired one for you. He appears to be well-mannered and honorable and no doubt he will pay well."

"Well, that is good news, for they both are quite handsome and, as you say, will no doubt pay well for warmth in their beds."

"They're of noble stock, apparently. One is the son of a powerful lord and the other, I gather, is the eldest son of a noble house."

"It appears the Powers have sent you a purse full of coins, Keely,"

Morwyn said, winking as she rose to leave.

"Good, I have need of those coins for my sister's dowry," Keely replied with a broad smile on her face. Morwyn nodded and left the kitchen, slipping out the back door and into the adjoining alley. As she made her way past the adjacent stable she saw a groom leading two fine horses, shorn of their saddles and their blankets, and she smiled to herself. Horses such as these were not common in Kell.

Most definitely nobility. May the Powers see that they are generous with their sporting and their coins.

She continued to wend her way down the streets, keeping a wary eye out for the roaming guards. For some reason her mind turned toward Belwyn at that moment and the sadness returned. She tugged her cloak hood up to keep her face covered and to hide the mist in her eyes.

The innkeeper glided to the table where the two nobles sat and paused until acknowledged. Morgan looked up and gave the man a nod.

"I trust you find the food to your liking, milord?"

"It is most excellent, especially after two weeks on the road with nothing but dried beef and stale bread," Morgan replied honestly. He gave the innkeeper a quizzical look and Benen nodded.

"As you asked, I have arranged company for both of you, milord. To be honest, my girls are looking forward to keeping such noble men as yourselves warm on this cold night."

Morgan smiled broadly, catching Belwyn's slightly startled look.

"Excellent, innkeeper. We are about finished and will wish to retire soon."

"I will be sure that all is ready, sirs." Benen moved to a nearby table to talk with some of the other patrons, asking them the standard questions about the food and the wine.

"Morgan, what have you done?" Belwyn asked, a note of upset in his voice.

"My friend, I know you have not been with a woman since well before the night of your marriage. Pyrs wrote me of what passed between you and Morwyn." He paused and then continued, "It is not right for a man to live this way, separate from women."

"Morgan, I appreciate what you are trying to do, but …"

"Belwyn, I will take it as a serious insult if you do not go to your room tonight and enjoy the company of whatever girl the innkeeper has sent to your bed. I am sure she will be willing enough, given your looks and lineage, and it will be best for both your attitude and your health, my friend."

"Attitude?" Belwyn came back a bit more sharply than he intended and then was chagrined, knowing what the man meant.

"As you see, you are more unsettled than normal, my friend. A night in a woman's arms will restore you to your usual solemn personality."

"Morgan …" Belwyn began again, a frown on his face.

"Belwyn, let me say this honestly, though it might anger you. Staying celibate just because *she* is does not make sense. She asked for the Writ of Divorcement so you could have a life of your own, so you could partake of such pleasures as a sporting wench, perhaps even remarry."

The noise of the room seemed to surround the warriors for a time. Belwyn let the hurt encompass him, for it made him feel whole. His dark eyes rose from the table and settled on his friend's concerned face.

"There is no way to dissuade you of this?" he asked.

"No, there isn't. If you do not bed the wench then pay her and don't tell me about it. If you wish to sit here and brood, that is fine, but I have willing and warm company waiting in my bed and I do not intend to miss out on what few pleasures the Powers send my way." He rose, put his hand on his friend's shoulder and added, "I hope to see you with a smile on your face tomorrow, my friend, and hear that the innkeeper has *two* very tired wenches to cope with." Morgan left the table, sought out Benen, and was directed upstairs to his room.

Belwyn sat for the longest time doing just what Morgan had said he would do … brooding. He watched the comings and goings of the inn's patrons and finally, realizing that he could not really put this off, rose and was escorted to his room. Part of him, the male part, wanted to bed a woman and feel the release he so badly needed. The other part, his heart, knew it was not to be.

Morgan found Meara more than willing and he readily took his pleasure. In time they rested, sipped on wine and talked of small matters.

"I hope my friend finds as much pleasure with the woman in his bed as I have with the one in mine." *Providing the besotted fool partakes of her.*

"Oh, he will, for she is keen to be with him," Meara said. She took another drink of wine and kept her eyes on the handsome stranger. He entranced her, for he was a generous lover and a decent man.

"Good, for he has need of that. Is she pretty like you?" he asked, gently touching her face with his fingers.

"Oh yes, very pretty."

"That is good, very good. He is a sad and lonely man, for no fault of his own. I hope he finds much joy this night." He grew quiet, pulled the girl to him and they fell back into the sporting with abandon.

Belwyn found the girl waiting in his room. She was indeed young, pretty, and no doubt would be good sport. His conscience wrestled with the issue one final time. The girl was surprised, a bit annoyed, and then mollified by the amount of coin he gave her after he announced he could not be with her.

"I do not understand, my lord. Do you not find me attractive?" she asked as she held the coins her hand, sitting on the side of the bed clad in a light chemise. The coins were double what she expected for the evening.

"I do, that is not the issue. I am married, you see." He hoped that would explain it. Unconsciously he was fingering Morwyn's ring where it lay suspended on a rawhide cord around his neck.

"But many men are married and yet they ..." she began, confused.

"I know, but I have made a commitment and I shall not break it." His voice was wavering in intensity. "I am very much in love with my wife and it would not be right to share myself you, girl, no matter how much I may need your company."

The wench grew a kind-hearted smile on her face. "You are an honorable man, sir. I pray your wife knows your value." She caught sight of the ring, silver and glinting in the firelight.

He seemed melancholy. "I do not know if she does. Perhaps in time ..."

The girl had a sudden insight and asked, "She is not with you now, is she?" His hand twisted tighter on the ring.

"No, we live apart. Though every night I pray that will soon end."

Keely rose and gave him a light kiss on the cheek and then left the room, quietly closing the door behind her. Belwyn undressed and settled into the cold bed, alone, as he had countless times since his wedding night. He knew Morgan would not be pleased, but that was of no matter. He was at peace with his decision.

"Morwyn, I miss you," he whispered and then forced himself to fall asleep.

SIXTEEN

organ was in high spirits as they lingered over the morning repast in the common room of The Old Port. It was obvious his time with the golden-haired wench was pleasurable. He chatted amiably and when Belwyn wasn't forthcoming about his evening, Morgan took the initiative.

"You are too quiet, my friend, was not the little wench I sent to your bed worth your time? Or did you decide to play the celibate and brood all night instead of enjoying what little pleasure the Powers send us?"

Belwyn gave him a sour look and retorted, "I played the celibate, just as you predicted. She was very pretty, but …" Morgan's heavy sigh cut right over the top of his fellow warrior's answer as he shook his head in resignation.

"You are truly a wonder. You and Morwyn richly deserve each other for both of you are determined to make yourselves miserable." Belwyn's sour look continued, unsure as to be angry at this observation or acknowledge the inherent truth of it. He opted for the latter.

"So it appears."

"Well, I was not celibate and I had a very fine time. Meara was good sport and full of some rather ribald jokes I will have to share with you."

Belwyn smiled and put his hand his friend's arm. "Thank you, Morgan, I sincerely appreciate what you tried to do."

Morgan gave him an irritated look and shook his head again.

"I think that after we settle matters with …" he paused and did not mention Phelan's name in such a public venue, "we shall have to hunt up your wife. I shall have a good talk with her and tell her know she's being far too intractable for her own good."

Belwyn snorted, "Don't attempt that quest, my friend, you know what she's like."

"I do. As the Powers would have it, we both have loved a woman that puts all others to shame."

Belwyn studied him for a moment. "You are as trapped by her memory as I am. It is past time you married and filled your father's holdings with heirs rather than wasting your seed on sporting wenches."

Morgan's face clouded and he exhaled heavily. "In that you are right, Belwyn, we are both in need of the same dose of medicine. Perhaps the Powers will send me someone who will remove her from my heart."

"May They make it so," Belwyn closed the supplication.

Benin appeared at that moment, his face beaming. He was in such a good mood he did not even wait acknowledgement before speaking.

"My lords, I wish to thank you for your kindness towards my girls. Times are difficult for them and I pay them what I can, so your added coins will make all the difference to their families." He'd already spoke with Keely and knew she had not spent the night with the dark-haired lord. Both her and Meara reported they'd been handsomely paid and Benin was pleased to learn that the men had acted decently toward the girls.

"Meara told me you do not take a portion of their earnings, sir, and that speaks well of you," Morgan replied.

"It would not be right. I do not wish that they trade themselves in such a way, but it is the difference between their families starving or having food on their tables."

"But surely there is adequate enough food, for the drought has not struck here," Belwyn said. Benin did a quick glance around the room and his eyes stopped on two figures loitering near the door. They were not there only a few minutes before.

"I would be pleased to help you pack for your journey, my lord," he offered as he effortlessly changed topics, his voice noticeably louder now. Morgan hesitated for only a second as he ascertained the cause for the rapid shift in conversation. The innkeeper's eyes plainly held a warning.

"We will be grateful of the assistance, innkeeper." As he spoke he caught Belwyn's eye and passed an imperceptible signal.

"A thoughtful offer, we shall be to our rooms shortly," Belwyn remarked, subtly acknowledging he was now aware of the situation. He suspected the innkeeper would be far more forthcoming in the privacy of their rooms. Benen headed for the kitchen and took a strong drink of ale before he went upstairs. Phelan's men were lurking. That never boded well.

Morwyn appeared at the inn later that afternoon to check on Lowri. The girl was eating, heartily, for she enjoyed food in all forms, and her fever was down. Morwyn advised her to have one more night's full rest and then resume her activities.

"Stay away from those eager young men for a time, Lowri, you are still not well enough to entertain," she cautioned. Lowri pouted, her crimson-apple cheeks belying her attitude.

"I will do whatever you say. As it was, I missed the opportunity to be with two of the finest men that ever came through our doors. I had to be sick, what luck!"

Morwyn grinned. "The two Northern lords?" she asked as she packed up her herbs.

"Yes, those two. Meara said the blonde one was very good sport and generous with his coins. A true lord, that one. And the other, well, he was a surprise."

"In what way?" Morwyn asked, amused. The girls maintained an earthly outlook on their other line of work.

"Apparently Meara's lord set it all up with Benen and the other one didn't know about it until after the fact. He wasn't pleased to hear a girl was going to be in his bed last night and he turned Keely down."

"Why would he do that?" Morwyn asked.

"He said he was married and would not break that vow."

Morwyn's eyebrows shot up. "Surely you jest!"

"No, Keely said he was very serious about it all. He said he would not be with her because he loved his wife, though apparently they are not together."

"Now that is a sad tale."

"He paid her nonetheless! Paid her double what she would have earned and she got a good night's sleep to boot!"

Morwyn laughed at that. "Well, I'm sure another lord will ride in here and find you of interest, Lowri. The Powers tend to even things out in due time." She shouldered her pack for the girl loved to gossip and Morwyn had other patients to see.

"I doubt it, I never get the good looking ones."

"Perhaps they'll return in a night or two."

"Odds aren't good for that – Benen says they've gone off to see Lord Phelan. Apparently, Meara's lord is to deliver some message from his father." She waved her hand in a dismissive fashion. "He's some Lord of a March or something."

"They went willingly to see Phelan? That's a foolish plan." Morwyn stopped abruptly. Something Lowri had said burned into her mind like a brand.

"What was the name of the blonde-haired lord?" she demanded.

The girl shrugged. "I don't know, you'll have to ask Benen or Keely. Is it important?" Morwyn did not answer as she was already scooting through the door, her mind whirling. She flew down the stairs and found Benen, Meara and Keely taking a brief rest in the kitchen. The moment the innkeeper saw her face he knew something was amiss.

"Morwyn, what is it? Is there a problem with Lowri?"

She shook her head immediately, her thoughts totally fixated on what she'd heard from Lowri.

"No, she is healing and should be able to work in another day or so."

"Then what is the matter? Your face is very pale. Are you unwell?"

"What as the name of the blonde-haired lord that stayed at the inn last night?"

He gave her a slight frown at this sudden demand and then glanced around the kitchen to insure they had some privacy.

"Morgan. His father is Lord Bardyn, Lord of the Eastern March."

Morwyn's face paled considerably. "And the other one, was he tall, dark-haired, dark-eyed and quite handsome?" Her pack slid off her shoulder and fell to the floor but she did not notice. Keely pushed a chair behind the healer and made her sit down, concerned she might faint.

"Yes, he was. He said his name was Belwyn and that he is the eldest son of the ..."

To Benen's surprise the healer completed the sentence,

"House of Aderyn."

"Morwyn, what is this?" he demanded.

"Have they already left the inn?"

"Yes, early this morning. They were to meet with Phelan today."

"Powers," she murmured, dread replacing the shock in her eyes.

"Please, explain!" Benen tried again.

A cup of ale appeared before her and she took a long sip, her hands clearly unsteady. When she raised her eyes they went directly to Keely.

"Lowri said that Belwyn refused to bed you. Is that true?"

Keely nodded. "Yes. I know he wished to be with me, but he would not. He said he and his wife were no longer together, but he still honored his vow. I could see how much he loves her, it was written in his eyes. They were such sad eyes."

Morwyn closed her own eyes and let the pain radiate through her, a dull aching throb from the soles of her feet to the very ends of her long hair. He had been in the other room the evening before and the Powers had not allowed them time together and now he was in Phelan's hands. She shuddered and then realized that she owed her friends an explanation.

"Belwyn is my husband. I asked him for a Writ of Divorcement, but apparently he did not issue it." *You would not let me go, would you?*

"Your husband?" Keely blurted out, stunned. "But how could you leave him?" Benen thought back on the private conversations that he and Morwyn had shared, for he, of anyone in Kell, knew the most about the mysterious healer.

"He is the father of your children, isn't he?"

"Yes, he is."

"Is he the reason you are no longer an adept?" he asked. The two serving girls listened in astonishment.

"Yes. A fellow adept from my Circle enchanted him. The only way to break the enchantment was to be with him physically. My children ... *our* children were created when the spell was severed and my powers were ..." she paused and then continued, "diminished. I still retain some elementary spells, but nothing like I once possessed."

Benen's voice had an edge to it. "You left him and your children behind because of your magic?"

Her eyes grew haunted and she nodded. "The children are older than you think, for magic played a part in that as well. I left Belwyn because ..."

"Because you loved your magic more than him." The thrill that went down his back at that moment told him he that the Powers were behind his words. He knew not to fight Them.

Morwyn shuddered again. Benen spoke the truth. The magic ruled her life, created her children and caused her to run away from the one man she would ever love.

"Yes, I loved my magic more than him." It was an admission torn from her heart and the old wound began to bleed.

"Or so you thought," Benen observed. The girls were quiet, anxious, sensing something of great import was playing out in front of them.

"Or so I thought." The strange sensation within Benen faded, leaving behind a sense of loss. As he was no longer needed as a messenger he could now offer comfort and advice.

"They are both in grave danger while they remain in Kell. So are you if Phelan learns whose wife you are."

Morwyn nodded solemnly. "I know. Why have they come south to see him?"

Benen looked around again. The kitchen was quiet for it was between meals and the cook was in the market buying food for the evening repast.

"Lord Bardyn has taken an interest in Phelan's suppression of the Southern Isle Clans. The clans have asked for his help." He glanced at the girls and ordered, "This dare not go any further than this kitchen, or we'll all be up for execution." Keely shivered as Meara nodded her understanding.

Morwyn thought for a moment and then asked, "If you were Phelan, what would you do with them?" She had witnessed the countless executions, heard the victims' torturous screams as they perished in the roaring flames. She involuntarily shuddered at the thought that Kell's lord would dare kill them in such a manner.

Benen decided honesty was the best course. "If I were Phelan, I would have two choices; I could kill the least valuable of the two and send his corpse back to Lord Bardyn as a warning or I would hold both men for ransom as assurance against any further interference."

The least valuable of the two. Morwyn's eyes squeezed shut. *Belwyn ...*

"I understand."

"You must go into hiding, Morwyn, you cannot continue to wander around the streets of Kell with this hanging over your head. Lord Morgan promised to contact me if they leave Phelan's fortress, though he honestly does not believe that will happen. I will send a message to you if they are free." Benin had promised his support to both the Northern lords, offering to relay messages north to Morgan's father. It was a dangerous gamble on the innkeeper's part, but he was impressed by their honor and decided on the spot to assist in any way he could. At present he held his silence, for none must know of the traitorous pact he'd forged.

"I will return to the House of Healing to tell them what has happened and then vanish."

"That is wise."

"He loves you," Keely said, without thinking. Her thoughts were on the young man who had so gently refused her the night before. His sad eyes still haunted her.

"I know." Morwyn accepted an embrace from her friends and slipped out into the alley. Her mind kept repeating Keely's words. *'He loves you.'*

As I love you, Belwyn. If the Powers have gone so far as to put you in the same city as I, then I will not disappoint Them. I will find you, no matter where Phelan tries to hides you.

The day continued in chaos. As Morwyn drew near the House of Healing she found it to be a smoking ruin. The smell of burnt flesh intermingled with that of the scorched wood. Bodies were being carried out of the charred building, toted on worn blankets. It was impossible to tell how many perished in the inferno, but she counted fifteen covered corpses lying on the snowy street. Instinctively, she did not made her way to the front of the crowd as she knew this was not some accidental blaze. She caught sight of one of the servants who worked in the house and made her way to stand next to the girl.

"What has happened?" she asked quietly, mindful of the need to be invisible. Guards were everywhere and the crowd of onlookers was uneasy, murmuring amongst themselves, shocked by such a catastrophe. The girl continued to tremble and subtly gestured toward some of the Phelan's guards a short distance away where they stood with their hands on their swords.

"They did this?" Morwyn asked, keeping her voice low. She turned her eyes back at the burned shell that had once housed her friends and her patients.

"It is said they came and set fire to the house. They burned them all, Morwyn, *all* of them."

"All of them?" Morwyn's voice cracked as she thought of all those that were in their care at this time. The new mother and her baby, too ill to return to her home in the North after her husband died on the road, the trader with his broken leg, the jovial wine merchant, the elderly lady who was awaiting her time to cross over … the faces paraded before her eyes as tears welled.

"All dead. I was not here, for my mother is ill. I feared you were in there as well."

"No, I was not here." Morwyn's tears fell as her caution rose. "I must go, for I endanger you." She turned and left the scene, shaken. The loss was incomprehensible.

Belwyn's father had counseled him that the more fair and flowery the greeting one received at someone's holdings, the more wary one should be. The greeting bestowed upon them by Lord Phelan was a fine example – it was as if the High King had come to Kell. It set off every nerve in the warrior's body and he knew Morgan felt exactly the same way. After only a few words with their host, they were escorted to a sumptuous bedchamber to refresh themselves and rest. A banquet was on the offing that very evening and would feature all manners of amusements in honor of their arrival in Kell. The bedchamber was well stocked with food, libations and two very lovely servant girls. They were most attentive, readily offering warmed and scented water to wash with, chilled mead and fresh beef to dine upon. They made it known that their lithe bodies were available as well, if the men wanted them.

"No, thank you, we are here for business, not for pleasure. Perhaps later," Morgan replied politely to the dark-haired one that stood very close to him, watching his every move. She was a beauty, in that there was no doubt, one of the finest sporting wenches he'd ever encountered. He was sorely tempted, but caution was more important than passion at this moment.

"But surely my lord finds me interesting," she came back, coyly. "I would be pleased to sport with you and your companion, for I will give you great pleasure."

"I'm sure you would, girl, but business must take precedence. You may leave us." She gave him a strange look, glanced over at the other girl who was attending Belwyn, and since they dare not disobey, they left the room.

"As fair a snare as can be laid," Belwyn muttered quietly to his friend as he glanced around the room.

"Very fair it is, and lesser men may have fallen for it."

"Very tempting, though," Belwyn said with a slight wolfish grin on his face as he glanced toward the door. Morgan's face erupted in a smile and he clapped his friend on the back.

"Now that's the Belwyn I remember. Obviously you are beginning to consider women once again."

"Only if it involves a certain black-haired healer, my friend."

"Either way, it is a welcome change, Belwyn."

The banquet would have rivaled those held at most of the larger houses in the North. There was an abundance of food, drink and merry entertainment. Belwyn and Morgan were the only two guests and while others would be flattered by this gesture, it only made the warriors more vigilant. They did not dare to refuse the food or the wine and they ate as sparingly as they could without insulting their host. The memory of Owain the Younger's poisoning lingered as an unpleasant reminder of how vulnerable they both were. They did not drink to excess, knowing they needed to keep their minds clear. Their host noted that and knew they had not bedded the wenches he'd sent to their room, either. These men were not ruled by their appetites.

The dancing girl at Morgan's feet was watching him intently, her golden hair tied with silken cords and her diaphanous top openly revealing her full breasts beneath. The skirt she wore swirled around her ankles every time she moved, accentuating the movement of her wide hips. She was gorgeous, but Morgan knew that in her own way she was as dangerous as her master. Belwyn's girl was no less beautiful, clothed differently, but still the fabric of her gown allowed him to see her fully underneath. Though the woman attempted to work her charms on him, Belwyn felt the weight of Morwyn's ring underneath his tunic as it lay against his chest. Though she did not know it, the girl at his feet did not have a chance against such a bond.

Phelan, in his usual manner, was blunt about their purpose,

"If they do not please you, I will have them thrown to my guards. They know the penalty for lack of good service."

With a start, Morgan realized Phelan's comment was not a jest.

"I'm sure that will not be the case, Lord Phelan. To be honest, we are here to discuss other matters than sporting wenches," the warrior replied smoothly.

"As I suspected. So, now that we've dined, tell me what brings Lord Bardyn's son and the Eldest of Aderyn to my fair city," Phelan said expansively. He leaned against the back of a heavy chair covered in thick cushions, his own girl at his feet. Her dark eyes were riveted on him, watching for any subtle command that he may give her. It was obvious she feared him. Lying on the floor some distance away were two large hounds, thin and lithe ones, built for speed. They too kept their attention on their master.

Belwyn was sitting on an overstuffed cushion and he cautiously shifted his weight. Apparently, Kell's banqueting decorum required sitting on the floor around a blazing fire pit, not at a long table. He found it unnerving because it made it hard to reach one's sword if needed. Phelan, apparently due to his crippled leg, chose to sit in a chair. Belwyn suspected it was also a subtle statement of power as their host gazed down upon those on the floor near him. Morgan appeared to be at ease, but then the man seemed to have the ability to be at ease in the most uncomfortable of situations. Belwyn sincerely envied his friend in that regard.

Morgan casually handed his empty wine goblet to the girl at his feet so that she could refill it and then answered his host, "My father is concerned about this conflict you have with the Southern isle clans."

"Really?" Phelan asked. "Why would it matter to him? It does not affect trade nor disrupt his holdings in any way."

"My father takes an interest when there are conflicts that may extend into our lands."

"I doubt your father would find such interest in these Southern bastards if he had to live with them. They have been raiding our crops, carrying away our gold, our women and our cattle since last summer."

"Why do they raid?" Belwyn asked, testing the man. He shifted on the cushion one last time. He did not want to appear to be fidgeting, but his current position was not the least bit comfortable and generated a gnawing cramp in his back.

"They claim to have some drought in their land and though they attempted to barter goods from us, we found them devious."

"So then their raiding may be out of necessity?" Morgan asked carefully.

The lord snorted at Morgan's comment, "If there be justification in looting, pillaging and rapine. You do not know the Southern men as I do. They are like the rats that inhabit this city, full of disease, skulking around and breeding with any woman they can coerce or force. They deserve to be put to the sword."

From what we've heard, a very apt description of you, Belwyn thought.

"No matter of your personal dislike for them, perhaps it would be better to offer them food until their situation passes rather than have your villages burned and your women violated," Morgan came back solemnly.

"That is not possible. Let me be blunt, sir, I make war on them. I will not be satisfied until they are either dead or enslaved."

"Your honesty is noted, sir," Morgan replied, his voice much colder.

"But what of Aderyn, what is your father's opinion in this matter?" Phelan asked, switching his attention to Belwyn. He wanted to know if both of these men were his enemy or only Bardyn's bastard.

"Aderyn stands with their liege lord on this matter, Lord Phelan. Living peacefully with one's neighbors is far more preferable than war."

"Perhaps. But, as I remember you Northerners have your own wars and I certainly did not interfere on Lord Merioneth's behalf."

Morgan's eyes narrowed. "No, you did not, but then Merioneth made war on us, not the other way around."

"Well, as we say here in the South, '*whoever is the victor decides who was the aggressor.*'" He paused, thought for a moment and then added, "I think the best way for you to know what I face is to see one of these Southern savages yourself." He gestured to one of the numerous guards in the hall and uttered a quick command. "Bring the iarel to me. No doubt he will appreciate the change of scenery from his dismal cell." The man disappeared immediately, bent on fulfilling his master's wish.

Belwyn took a slow sip of wine and waited, keeping his face devoid of any indication of his inner thoughts. *We will not be permitted to leave.*

A young man was drug across the hall and thrown on the stone floor before Phelan, his chains rattling in sharp contrast to the delicate tinkling of the wenches' ankle and arm bracelets. The two canines growled menacingly.

"See, even my hounds know a rat when they see one," Phelan jested.

The prisoner had long yellow hair, tawny in color, and his arms were tanned and thickly muscled. His clothes were tattered, his face bruised and a wide swatch of dried blood stained one of his calves. When he attempted to rise to his feet he was brutally beaten back to his knees. Though bruised and bloodied, his eyes housed a deep burning fire that Belwyn recognized.

Dillan's grand nephew, he surmised. He gave Morgan a quick glance and he saw that his friend was thinking along similar lines. The family resemblance was strong.

Phelan introduced his captive with all the charm of a generous host.

"This is Caewlin, Iarel of one of their clans. He is the *last* iarel that lives out of the five that opposed me. He has proven to be a dangerous and wily opponent, but he is now mine. He is alive solely because I will it." This last sentence he spoke with some pride.

Belwyn caught the prisoner's eyes and studied them. This was indeed no underling, but a leader, a man who had battled Phelan with all the force he could muster in growing desperation as his people succumbed to hunger, illness and the sword. Now he was in his enemy's fortress, in ponderous chains, and yet that fire was still in his eyes.

He will not surrender even at the moment of his death, Belwyn realized in awe.

From his kneeling position, Caewlin's mind reeled as he observed Phelan's noble guests. *Could they be ...?* He murmured a short prayer and kept his attention fixed upon them, hoping to receive some sign that his prayers were answered.

Seizing the moment, Belwyn uttered a short phrase in the Southern dialect Dillan had taught him as a child. If anyone else in the room spoke the language they would not understand what he had said, for it was an ancient vow between the iarels, not common speech.

Iarel to Iarel, the oath will not be broken ...

The prisoner's eyes shot back to him immediately and Caewlin instinctively completed the oath with a rough voice, *Though the bones of our enemies shall be.* He barely kept his raging emotions in check for he had heard the ancient oath of kinship coming from the lips of a pagan, a Northern lord, and he knew his kin had sent them. *The omens have come to pass!*

The conversation ended before Phelan could react. Their host was displeased, he had never considered that either of these two Northern men could speak the barbaric Southern language and he had no idea the subject of the conversation.

"What did you say?" he demanded, hotly.

Belwyn sipped his wine and then answered nonchalantly, "I said it was pity he could not share the food and the women and he replied that he would have none of it, for it was of your hand."

Phelan frowned, but he had no means to verify what the men had said to each other. He gave one of his guards an inquiring glance, for the man spoke the language and a shrug was the answer. The guard could not begin to understand the old speech.

It was time for the pleasantries to end. "So now that you have defeated these people, what do you intend to do with them?" Morgan asked.

"I will work them to death and then they will be no more," Phelan replied darkly.

"Would you consider allowing the Southern clans to come north and live in our lands? We will give them food and shelter until they can re-establish their way of life," Morgan offered. The prisoner listened intently for he sensed this offer was genuine.

"No! They are mine to do with as I choose. They have lost this war and I will put them to the sword as I wish. Their women bring good money in Kell's brothels and bring greater coin in the sporting houses of Ilspath. The men are fit for slaves and they serve that purpose well."

"And the children?" Belwyn asked in loaded voice, already knowing the answer.

"The children either work or are of no use, that is how life is in my world. I will not tolerate weakness in any form." Unconsciously, he shifted his withered leg at that moment.

"It is said that the Southern clans call us barbarians, Lord Phelan. It appears that some of us fit that name more aptly than others," Morgan observed, his voice like cold steel.

Phelan's voice turned icy in response. "Tell me, Lord Morgan, what is your father's *actual* message to me?"

"He wishes that you cease your war of extermination upon the clans and if you are unable or unwilling to care for them, then send them to the North and we will accept them as brothers."

"And if I refuse?" Phelan menaced.

"Then Lord Bardyn will take a closer interest in the war between the Southern clans and yourself."

Caewlin closed his eyes and murmured a heartfelt prayer of thanks to his Gods. *They accept us as brothers. There is still hope.*

Phelan shifted on his chair and glowered. "You have some nerve to deliver such an ultimatum when you sit as a guest in my *fortress*." He put special emphasis on the last word.

"You asked for my father's message and I have delivered it."

"I see. Frankly, Lord Morgan, I do not care what you, your father or your highborn sycophants think," his sweeping gesture included the Eldest of Aderyn. Belwyn's eyes narrowed at the grave insult. "If you are so fond of these Southern rats, then as your host I would be remiss to not allow you to share their lives as fully as you can. Perhaps in that way you'll learn what vermin they truly are." Phelan snapped his fingers and the girls at the warriors' feet fled the room in a jangle of bracelets.

"It would appear the merriment is over, my friend," Belwyn remarked as they watched the guards unsheathe their blades and the hounds rise to their feet.

"It does indeed," Morgan replied. He made no attempt to reach for his sword, that would be suicide. As his father had predicted, they were now Phelan's captives.

Still on his knees, Caewlin continued to offer prayers of gratitude to his personal deities. He had powerful allies now, men of honor, and if the Gods were willing, Phelan's evil would wither like the morning mist under a strong sun.

They were transported out of Kell that very night, in chains, sitting in a wagon full of straw, covered by thin blankets. They were allowed their clothes, boots and their heavy cloaks but everything else was taken from them. Belwyn made sure to palm Morwyn's ring and it to his relief, it was not confiscated. He hid it back under his clothes once they were secured in the wagon.

Morwyn was hurrying to Benen's inn and refuge in his attic when she saw a wagon heading toward the main gates, prisoners huddled inside, their cloak hoods down against the cold wind. It was a common occurrence to see such sights late in the evening, for Phelan often had his prisoners carried out of the city when the streets were nearly empty. After the wagon passed she crossed behind it and paused for a moment in the street, unnerved. Something troubled her, but she dare not stay in the open long enough to determine what it was. She continued on, never knowing that inside the wagon was the man who still wore her wedding ring near his heart.

The snow began falling about an hour into the journey and soon there was a thick layer of it on their cloaks. The three men huddled close for warmth as the wagon continued to bump its way to the east into the forest. All of them dozed, for it was easier than trying to stay awake and feel the numbing cold. Hours later they stopped for rest at a clearing in the forest. After being allowed to climb out and relieve themselves, the prisoners returned to the wagon, the sound of their chains jarring in the still air. A flask of water appeared but no food was forthcoming. The guards took their own repast and then bedded down next to a blazing campfire, leaving one on sentry duty. He was dozing as well, for the prisoners were chained and would make considerable noise if they tried to escape.

Once assured their captors were asleep, the men talked quietly amongst themselves.

"Well, my friend, it appears that our plan worked all too well," Belwyn joked to Morgan. "Perhaps I should have taken one of those delicious wenches to my bed, for I suspect there will be no warm comfort where we are headed."

"*This* was your plan?" Caewlin asked, a bit disconcerted. He had expected something a bit more grand. Morgan's eyebrow raised when he realized the iarel spoke their language.

"Yes, it is, and though it appears ill advised, it is one born of necessity. The best means to determine the situation was to confront it head on. If Phelan took our offer and allowed your people to move north, then all would be well. If he took us hostage, that would allow us the opportunity to make contact with your people and perhaps pass a message to you. My father would have come south without hesitation, but other matters have kept him close to home." Morgan paused for a moment and then spoke so softly Cacwlin had to strain to hear him, "My father has pledged his sword to the clans and will stand as their ally."

"Thank the Gods, perhaps some of my people will live through this horror," Caewlin murmured. His voice sounded relieved, though exhausted.

"May the Powers make it so," Morgan replied.

"Just so we know, where *are* we headed? When I asked one of the guards his answer involved a well-placed kick and a rather vile chortle," Belwyn remarked.

"We are headed to a place by the sea they call the Field of Stones."

"Is it a quarry?" Belwyn asked.

"No, not as such. Phelan needs building material so we excavate stones from dawn 'til dusk. Apparently there are not enough prisons and brothels to suit him," the iarel remarked in disgust.

Morgan gave his friend a smirk. "You're right, we should have enjoyed those wenches." At that he yawned, tugged his cloak around him and closed his eyes. Belwyn regarded the young man chained next to him with a fond smile.

"Your grand uncle sends his regards and asks you to hold on, Iarel." He spoke in the Southern tongue now.

A smile of fond memory crossed Caewlin's face. "How is he? It's been a long time since I saw him." Caewlin was only ten when Dillan had last visited the clan. By then Geraint, his grandsire, was dead and his father, Brecc, was iarel.

"He is well, but very grieved at the news of his people."

Caewlin nodded slightly, a gesture barely visible in the thin moonlight. Belwyn explained, "Dillan is like an uncle to me. He helped raise my brother and I after our mother died. He taught me how to fight, how to wench, and how to act with the dignity of my position. He is as much family to me as he is to you." Caewlin studied the warrior with renewed interest.

"Then you are truly a brother, for you could have no better teacher than Dillan of the Red Hawk Clan. He is a good man. I look forward to seeing him again." One of the guards coughed at that point as he rolled over in his bedroll near the fire. The prisoners fell silent. Belwyn eased himself down into the straw and fell into a dreamless slumber. Caewlin did not fall asleep immediately but sent his thoughts toward his beloved fire-hair and the child she carried. He uttered a prayer for their safety and then drifted off.

Morwyn the Healer was being hunted, that was the word on the streets of Kell, though no one was that keen to help Phelan's men find her. More than one household was indebted to the kindness of the House of Healing and had found their end to be unimaginably brutal. Knowing she put her friends in danger, Morwyn slipped out of Benen's side door and into the back streets of the darkened city two nights after the House of Healing burnt to the ground. She had no clear idea of what she was going to do, but remaining in The Old Port's attic was no longer possible despite Benen's pleas to the contrary. She had thought of hiding in one of the huge warehouses down by the docks, at least until she determined some reasonable course of action.

As she feared, Benen did not hear from either Morgan or her husband. Rumors began to circulate that Phelan had taken the two men prisoner and that they were now at the Field of Stones, toting rocks in service to their new lord. She found the news strangely comforting. They had a chance at survival, unlike so many of those summarily executed.

They are too valuable, she thought, *even Belwyn. They are a means to keep Bardyn and Aderyn at bay. Phelan knows he needs all the pawns he can find, for the stakes are higher now.*

She tugged her hood close to her face and scurried into the darkness, feeling like one of the wharf rats that skulked down the same streets as she trod. It was nearing midnight when she heard the echoing boot steps behind her. She cursed her bad luck, for she'd been spotted despite her cautious movements. Ducking around a corner she paused long enough to determine that there were two guards behind her, no doubt tracking her to learn what she was doing out at this late hour. She scooted down a narrow street and then paused again to listen for the sound of the guards to see if they still hunted her. Their heavy footfalls continued and panic began to take hold. As she cut down another street she found herself in a maze of small passages that eventually led to the wharf.

She hurried along the cobblestones trying not to make any noise that would echo and alert the guards to her exact location. The freshly fallen snow made the stones slippery and she nearly fell more than once. Her heart was pounding in her temples and she felt queasy from the adrenaline rushing through her. When she glanced backward she was startled to see that she was leaving a clear trail in the snowy street. Once she reached another series of passageways she purposely moved to the far side of the road where there was scant snow cover, hoping to confuse her hunters. Her boot prints would seem to disappear at the crossroads and they might not be able to determine which of the passages she had taken.

She didn't see the wharf rat until she stepped on its long spindly tail. It responded in kind by shrieking and then biting at her, sinking its long yellowed fangs into her soft boot. The sharp incisors reached her skin and she flinched in pain, but forced herself not to cry out. The beast extricated itself and scampered away as she bent down and held her ankle. She was the worse for wear from the encounter for she felt blood inside her boot, trickling warm and sticky. Morwyn swore a dark oath under her breath. The rats of Kell were as malignant as their master and the creature most likely carried any number of diseases. She shouldered her pack and entered the warehouse district, the burning pain in her ankle causing her hobble.

After a short distance she paused one last time and listened. There was no sound of her pursuers. Her ruse had apparently worked. With a little effort she discovered a quiet corner in a remote section of a massive warehouse. She had intentionally shied away from any of the buildings that stored food knowing they would be full of vermin and she had no fondness for rats at this particular moment.

When she found one that stored wool, furs, and other inedible goods, she knew this was the best she could hope for. It had been easy to work her way through a small window and into the building unseen. Luckily, the street outside was sheltered from the snow and so no tell-tale tracks would reveal her presence. She collected some discarded furs and fashioned herself a small nest. The wool was unprocessed and the cloying smell of lanolin floated around her. She shunted aside any concerns of what sort of creatures lived within these bundles and made sure to keep her cloak close to her body as she settled into the makeshift bed.

At least I shall be warm, she thought ruefully.

She pulled what ointments she possessed out of her pack and treated her ankle as best she could in total darkness. She could sense the wound was deep and that it still bled. Once Morwyn finished with the task she settled down into the furs and fell fast asleep in the darkness.

SEVENTEEN

Belwyn gazed around them, puzzled. There was nothing but wintry forest as far as he could see, though he was sure he could hear the sounds of seabirds. There were a few boulders sticking out of the snowy ground, but nothing like he had imagined.

"Where are the stones we are to haul?"

"We work on an island some distance from here," Caewlin explained, pointing toward the south. "The island has little on it except a mountain with a cavern near the top of it. We hike up there every morning, remove the stones from the mouth of the cave, and then winch them back down to sea level. They are ferried here and then taken by wagon to wherever Phelan needs them."

Morgan looked perplexed and asked, "Why don't they have you remove the stones from the base of the mountain? Is the stone of different quality near the top?" It made little sense to him. Caewlin shook his head. He glanced around again to assure the guards were not near as the prisoners were not permitted to talk amongst themselves. If caught, the punishment was usually a beating.

"The stones are the same as those near the beach where we land. It appears Phelan wishes the cavern open for some reason. We do not know why, though there are rumors, of course. Some believe there is a legendary sword inside that will make him invincible. Others believe that the High King of the North hid gold and jewels there."

"I doubt it is treasure from the north. According to our family archives the last High King never went any further south than Mersey, which is one full week's ride north of Kell," Belwyn replied. He'd learned that tidbit of history while helping Pyrs with his studies.

Caewlin shrugged. "Phelan has some reason, for he is not one for frivolous things. Everything has a purpose, either to enhance his power or to drive terror into the heart of his foes. It's only been recently that he's shifted the workers to this site and there seems to be some urgency to our tasks."

They were escorted to the largest building at the campsite, the workers' quarters, which were nothing more than two huge huts joined together. No matter how Belwyn prepared himself for what he might see inside, his mind could not comprehend the utterly dismal conditions these people faced on a daily basis. Approximately three- to four-hundred souls lived in the two interconnected structures, which should have housed only two-hundred or so bodies. There were no beds and both sexes mixed together without any attempt at privacy. The dirt floor sported a thin layer of straw and there were no windows for ventilation. Each building had a centrally located fire pit and the smoke tried to vent itself through a crude hole in the roof, usually without much success. There seemed to be a continual haze in the air that only cleared when the wind was blowing heavily. Even within this squalid existence the Southerners attempted to preserve some decency. The infirm were cared for as best they could, placed closer to the fire pits and given extra blankets donated by others who had yet to fall ill. A corner had been set aside, obscured by hanging blankets, to allow couples privacy if they wished to be together. Another corner allowed those who wished to bathe to do so in seclusion, if clean water was available. In all ways the clan strove to continue their way of life even as it disintegrated around them.

The prisoners' chains removed, they walked inside. As soon as Caewlin appeared a murmur arose and men began to come forward in obvious relief. His sudden departure from the Field of Stones had unnerved his people for they feared he was slated for execution. He had thought the same. Once he found himself displayed in front of the Northern lords at the banquet, he understood why his enemy had him brought to Kell – Phelan wanted to gloat over his enemy one more time.

Though weary, Caewlin patiently spoke with anyone who greeted him, for it was important for the clan to see that their iarel was still in command. Once the tide of men diminished he walked to the nearest fire pit and gestured toward Morgan and Belwyn.

"The Gods have sent us aid, as the omens predicted." He waved the two Northern men forward and Morgan and Belwyn found a path cleared in front of them between the ragged bodies.

"Omens?" Morgan muttered to Belwyn and his friend only shrugged. Once they reached Caewlin's side they stood silently and studied the faces around them. The clansmen and women were dressed in bits of rags with dirt-smudged faces and unkempt hair. It was their eyes that caught one's attention, for they were like their leader's – bright and full of fire.

Starved and half-dead, but not broken, Belwyn thought. *They will fight with an intensity that Phelan will never comprehend.*

Caewlin raised his voice and announced, "This is Lord Morgan, son of Lord Bardyn, Lord of the Eastern March. His companion is Belwyn, eldest son of the House of Aderyn. Our messenger reached them and related what fate has befallen our people. In response, they undertook a journey to Kell to deliver a missive from Lord Bardyn to our enemy. Bardyn demands fair treatment for our people and has asked Phelan to allow the clans to move to his lands where we could start our lives anew. Phelan denied Lord Bardyn's request and placed these men in captivity just as he has us."

"He has signed his own death warrant by such dishonorable deeds," Morgan replied in broken Southern speech. A few nodding heads meant the message was understood in some fashion.

Caewlin agreed. "He has brought the wrath of the Northern lords upon his head, not only by his actions toward our people, but toward both these men, who came in peace."

A thin clansman, one with a guarded look, demanded,

"How do we know if they are no better than Phelan, Iarel? How do we know that once he is defeated they will not enslave us as well?"

Before Caewlin could reply, Morgan spoke up. "Excellent question. You have no guarantee that my father and I are any less barbarous than your present foe."

Belwyn cleared his throat and gave Morgan a bemused look.

"May I translate for you? Your speech is a bit ... disjointed." Barely coherent was closer to the truth. Morgan nodded. He could only imagine what he'd really said for he understood the Southern tongue better than he spoke it. Belwyn translated and the thin man glared and retorted,

"That is no comfort!"

"To be honest, sir, given our present situation, none of us are in a position to bargain," Belwyn replied and then swiftly translated what he'd said for Morgan.

"Why would this high lord want us in his midst? Northerners consider us no better than the vermin that inhabit Kell. In fact, the rats eat better than we do!" the man snarled back. Caewlin remained silent, for this had to play out between the northern men and his people. He knew their fears, for they were once his own.

"One of your clansmen has fought at my father's side and that of Lord Bardyn's for many a year. He is a man known in our land for his honor and his sword arm. His integrity and loyalty have made their mark on our lord and he knows your people to be cut from the same cloth," Belwyn replied.

"And who is this clansman who is held in such high regard as to warrant your journey here?" another man demanded dubiously.

"The man is Dillan of the Red Hawk Clan," Belwyn answered, making sure his voice was clearly heard, "brother of Geraint, your iarel's grandsire." A buzz of voices flew through building at Geraint's name and small conversations began to erupt at the back of the crowd.

Belwyn continued, "Dillan has served as my father's Master of the Guard for over two decades and acted as an uncle to my brother and I. I owe him my life and so I make an oath upon his name that our purpose here is one of honor, for we are all truly brothers." He did not translate for Morgan, sensing the man was following his speech.

Caewlin knew it was time to speak. "These are the men that the Red

Hawk prophesied would come to our aid. *They* are the sixth clan."

Murmurs continued for a time and Belwyn saw a mixture of approval and dubious uncertainty on the faces nearest them. Finally one of the clansmen strode forward and extended his hand to Belwyn in a gesture of camaraderie.

"Dillan is clan and so you are clan."

Belwyn clasped the man's callused hand and replied with a well-known Southern oath, "One should judge a man by the keenness of his sword and the honesty of his word." More murmuring skirted through the crowd and then others came forward and greeted the two Northern lords. Though it appeared they'd been accepted both Belwyn and Morgan saw there were those who held back. They eventually made their way to a far corner, away from the fire.

Morgan said what both he and Belwyn were thinking, "Not all are pleased to see us here, Iarel."

"No, the hatred of Northerners runs deep, despite the Red Hawk's omens."

"Well, we shall have to prove them wrong." Caewlin nodded, yawned and then curled up on the straw floor and fell asleep almost immediately. It took Belwyn and Morgan a considerably longer time to adjust to the sounds in the building. There was endless coughing and the chilling cold seemed to penetrate through their garments. Their blankets were pitifully thin to do much good and so they both came to the same conclusion. Morgan rose, walked to where an older man and his wife were trying to rest and handed the woman his blanket. She had a racking cough and she was clearly unwell. The couple stared at him in amazement.

"Rest, for the time comes to break free of your shackles," Morgan said in a serious tone, hoping they understood his broken speech. Belwyn handed his blanket to a young boy, one close to Pyrs's age. The lad had no blanket having given his to his father who lay ill nearby. The older man saw the gesture and gave the Northern man a quizzical look.

Belwyn returned a kind smile and explained, "I have a son as well, sir. He is about your boy's age and I miss him dearly." He returned to the corner near his friend and took his place on the bitterly cold floor.

Morwyn woke to the sounds of warehousemen jesting amongst themselves as they began their labors. Her sleep had been fitful, for nightmares stalked her when she slept. The loss of her friends at the House of Healing was a heavy blow and the knowledge that Belwyn lay within Phelan's hands only made her more despondent. She shook herself awake, stretched and studied her circumstances. Now that it was light, she realized she had instinctively picked a safe place to hide. She was in a far corner, away from the main activity of the counting, sorting and stacking of wood and fur bundles. She could rest here undisturbed until darkness came.

Her throbbing right ankle reminded her of the encounter with the rat the evening before. She examined the wound with expertise and as she antici- pated, it was fiery red, burning hot to the touch and grossly swollen. She applied more ointment and tried to perform a rudimentary healing spell. It failed, a chilling reminder of how much power she had lost in the course of one night's passion. Belwyn's face flashed into her mind. She remembered him sitting by the fire at his father's holdings, Pyrs and Gwyn near him, all in high spirits. The memory caused her eyes to tear and a surge of overwhelm- ing loneliness claimed her. She missed jesting with her opinionated son, talk- ing about the mysteries of life with her daughter, and the warm embrace of her husband.

"All because of the magic," she muttered. Her mind duly reminded her those warm and loving memories only existed because of the magic. If she had not been an adept Belwyn would be dead and her children would not exist. Nevertheless, the magic did not equal the memories. She forced those feelings down and turned her attention back to her ankle. She created a ban- dage, dressed the wound and tucked it back under the furs. She fished around her pack and found some bread and cheese, courtesy of Benen, and then washed them down with water from her small flask. As she ate she pondered her options – they were limited. Belwyn and Morgan were most likely gone from Kell now, out of her reach. She had no idea where the Field of Stones lay in relation to the city.

Phelan needs pawns to keep Bardyn at bay, her practical mind taunted her. *The only way to get to Belwyn was to be a captive, one of Phelan's slaves.* She shivered at the thought and discarded it immediately. Knowing she could do nothing further at present, she snuggled back under the furs.

The sea was choppy as the flotilla of boats made their way to the island. The vessels were a motley collection of anything that would float. Inside each boat were varying numbers of workers and one or two guards. It was just past dawn and as the sea birds winged overhead in the chill morning air, Belwyn's eyes remained on the edifice looming in front of them. Contrary to Caewlin's description, it was more of a tall hill than a mountain. Centered on a small shrub-covered island it appeared to be out of place, as if the Powers had just arbitrarily deposited it there on a whim. He judged it rose some thousand feet in the air with broad craggy shoulders that sloped down to the rocky beach. His keen eyes spied a rudimentary path that snaked its way up the side ending near the top of the mountain.

"Where is the cavern?" he asked in a whisper, mindful of the guard at the back of the boat.

"Near the top, where the path ends," Caewlin replied and cautiously pointed upward to a spot on the north side of the mountain. "Only one side of the mountain is accessible, for the other three are sheer cliffs."

Morgan examined the hill looming in front of them. Again, he found that very odd, for it would be grueling work even if they loaded the stones at the shore, let alone so high on the side of a jagged hill.

"You haul the rocks all the way *down* to the sea?"

"Yes," came the answer.

"Powers," Morgan muttered back and sighed. He was already weary as the night had been short and his sleep frequently interrupted by the ambient noise in the hut. Near dawn a woman had given birth and the child had perished, followed shortly by its mother. Sounds of profound grief had awakened him and Morgan knew it to be an anthem of this place.

"Let us hope your father settles things up North as quickly as possible," Belwyn observed in as lighthearted a tone as he could muster. The cold air beat at them in the open boat and he could no longer feel his toes through his heavy boots.

"That would be best," Morgan replied.

As they drew near to the shore Belwyn shivered violently and though others may have thought it was due to the cold, it was not. He felt the surge of power in his very bones. He caught Morgan's startled eyes and asked, "Do you feel it?" His companion thought for a moment and then nodded.

"I hoped it was my imagination." He vividly remembered this same sensation from another hill, one located in the North country.

"No, it is not," Belwyn replied in a serious tone.

"Why here?"

"I have no idea."

The boats off-loaded their cargo on the rocky beach and most of the men began the hike up the side of the mountain while only a few remained at the shore. Belwyn, Morgan and the iarel were sent upward. It was tough going, for the path was not well constructed. It took them considerable time to scramble over the rocks and they only reached their destination as the sun rose above a leaden bank of clouds to the east.

"It looks like more snow," one of the clansmen remarked and another snorted in response. Belwyn turned his eyes to the east and he agreed with their observation. A thick line of clouds slowly advanced toward them, cutting the light and eliminating what beauty the sunrise might have held.

The two newcomers found themselves with ropes in hand, tugging massive boulders to a flat spot some distance from the mouth of the cavern. Belwyn found it telling that none of the other men mentioned the strange sensations that pounded him from within.

Perhaps they grow accustomed to it in some way, he thought. He watched closely as they began the task of lowering a boulder to a level beneath them and so on down the side of the mountain employing a series of flat ledges to control the boulder's descent. Once the stone reached the beach it was drug onto a flatboat to be ferried to the shore for the trip to Kell. The process was full of peril for if one of the stones escaped its mooring ropes it would cascade down dislodging other stones or sweeping the workers below it to their death. Within an hour, both Belwyn and Morgan were exhausted and blisters were swelling on their hands. As time passed the wind grew and soon their fingers were completely numb. Morgan struggled to tie a coarse rope around one of the boulders, but his fingers would not work. Belwyn knelt to help him and the men traded a look of mutual exhaustion.

The noon repast consisted of dried bread and water while trying to huddle out of the wind. They toiled the remainder of the day and as dusk neared the snow began to fall in earnest. It made the path down the mountain slippery and more than one man fell because of weariness. Belwyn did not remember much of the journey down the mountain, only the stinging cold of the snow in his face and the fact he could not feel his fingers or his toes. The wind made tears roll down his cheeks and they froze there, nestled in his growing beard.

"Powers, how have your people stood this?" Morgan murmured, his hands burning from the open sores. He tucked them under his cloak to keep them out of the biting wind and that seemed to help.

Caewlin gave him a despondent look. "They haven't, they've died in great numbers."

"Powers help us," Morgan replied.

"And soon," Belwyn added, as he hunched over in the boat, pain flooding his body.

When Morwyn woke it was late afternoon. The warehousemen were finishing their work for the day, making plans for their evening's activities. One-by-one they filed out and then she heard the huge doors bolted in place. The silence was welcome and all she could hear was the occasional squeak of a mouse and the chirping of birds high up in the rafters as they settled in for the evening. She'd spent the time between late afternoon and darkness pondering a means to reunite herself with her husband. No matter how she turned the issue over in her mind, there was only one solution – she would have to turn herself in. It was the least appealing option. There were only a few ways it could play out and none of them were appealing. At the worst, Phelan may order her immediate execution and she'd join her fellow healers in the next life. If he thought her worthwhile, she could easily find herself occupying a bed in one of Kell's numerous brothels, servicing any man with enough coins to buy her time. Even more unnerving was the possibility Phelan may keep her for his own amusement. She swallowed, hard, and then shifted her gaze upward in supplication.

"You have brought Belwyn and I this close, for the love of all that is right, help me be with him." She closed the petition with yet another prayer and then left the safety of the warehouse. She had no other choice, she had to speak with the innkeeper.

Morwyn made sure to enter the inn's kitchen very late that night after the cook had retired. She waited quietly in the corner for Benen to appear, near to the door lest she needed to flee in haste. In time, he entered bearing a tray of dirty dishes. He set it down, saw a faint movement out of the corner of his eye and then realized who it was. He seemed genuinely pleased to see her, despite the danger she brought him.

"Morwyn! Thank the Powers, you are still free!" His face beamed and he strode over and embraced her.

"Benen, it is so good to see you." She returned the hug with vigor.

"Do you need food? Sure you do, you can't purchase supplies in the market." He broke the embrace, noting how warm she felt to him. As she doffed her cloak he saw her face was flushed and her breathing heavy.

"Benen, I need your help. I wish to be arrested and sent to the Field of Stones."

His mouth gaped. "What? You know very well you are slated for execution by virtue of the fact you were at the House of Healing."

"I know that. Nevertheless, I must be with Belwyn and the only way I can do that is by being captured."

Benen sighed. "It is plain you are not well, Morwyn. Perhaps the illness is making you think irrationally."

She shook her head. "I was bitten by one of Kell's rats. I know the symptoms, Benen, it is *Gravedigger's Fever*. It will not kill me, it will only make me wish I could die. That is why it is so important I reach Belwyn as soon as possible. If I appear too ill ..."

"Phelan will have you killed, either way. Even if he decides you're worth saving for the brothels, he fears sickness, even an illness that is not usually fatal." Phelan's unreasoned fear of disease was widely known.

Her voice edged into desperation. "Please help me, Benen. Surely you know someone." He pointed to the small table and as Morwyn settled into a chair he began placing food in front of her, knowing she would be hungry. She allowed him his silence, sensing how difficult this would be for him. He would have to betray her and neither of them knew if she would survive Phelan's wrath.

"There is a man named Gorsedd, he is a senior guard in charge of one of Phelan's garrison. I have known him for many years and he is sickened by

Phelan's injustice. He is a decent man caught up in his master's madness. I will speak with him and see what he can do. There is no guarantee that even if he requests you be sent to the Field of Stones, you will go there. You are far too pretty and your compassion at the House of Healing has earned you Phelan's mark." He poured glasses of ale for both of them and sank into the chair opposite her. His face was tired, lined and full of worry.

"Then we must prove to Phelan that the wife of the Eldest of Aderyn is worthy of life and not as a sporting wench in some brothel." She began to consume a large hunk of cheese with relish. The provisions Benen had given her had run out and she was very hungry. She knew in less than a day she would be too ill to eat for the disease would progress rapidly.

"It would be better that you hide yourself, this plan is too dangerous," Benen pleaded. She noted he was not touching his ale, he was that upset.

"There is no other way. I have turned it over in my mind and this is for the best. You will receive the reward for my capture and that will insure that there is no question regarding your loyalty to Phelan. The money can be used for the girls and to help others on the run."

"I will not take blood money," he said flatly.

"I know, but there will be little choice in the matter. My heart tells me I am to be with Belwyn, my friend, so I must be there."

Benen remained silent for the length of time it took her to consume the hunk of cheese and two thick slices of brown bread slathered with thick chunks of fresh butter.

He finally acquiesced, "I will go to Gorsedd tomorrow and tell him that I know where you are hiding. I will speak with him privately so he understands why I do this ... and why *you* do this."

"He will find me near the Wool and Furrier's Guild warehouse. I will be sure to be there once the sun passes midday." Morwyn rose and embraced her friend again, both sensing this may be the last time. "I owe you so much, Benen, and I have no way to repay you. You have been a good and true friend and I will always carry you in my heart." His embrace tightened and then he released her. He dropped a small kiss on her damp forehead and then to keep his mind free of what they faced, he packed food for her in a small cloth. Once he'd handed it to her, he embraced her once more and she left the inn.

"May the Powers keep you safe, Morwyn," he whispered, "for all our sakes."

Reluctantly and with his heart full of dread, Benen did exactly as Morwyn asked. Shortly after midday, acting on information supplied by a local innkeeper, Gorsedd and two of his guards arrested Morwyn the Healer near the wharf. She did not put up any resistance and given her progressing illness, she made no attempt to escape.

"Phelan will reward the innkeeper generously for his loyalty," Gorsedd remarked loudly enough to insure all within earshot heard him. His eyes held Morwyn's and she sensed the depth behind them.

"No doubt," she said and spat in the ground in disgust at her evident betrayal.

She spent the night in a cell with a number of captives. Once they sensed she was ill they gave her considerable space and so she hunkered down, alone, in the corner of the cold stone cell and tried to sleep between the bouts of bone-shaking tremors. She was acutely ill by the time she reached Phelan's presence the next morning. *Gravedigger's Fever* was not usually fatal unless the victim was very young or infirm. Caused by the scratch or bite of an infected rat, it received its exotic name because the gravediggers often encountered vermin as they performed their grim work. Morwyn knew the disease well – she would be ill for three days and then recover. The problem would be convincing Phelan she was worth saving despite her desperate appearance.

Kell's master was pleased, for it had been a very fruitful day and it was not yet noon. He had executed three more of the Southern clansmen in the city square; Caewlin, the last iarel, was toiling in the Field of Stones along with Bardyn's bastard and the Eldest of Aderyn. Now, in front of him, was the remaining healer from the House of Healing. The woman was on her knees, head down, shaking.

No doubt from fear, he thought and he allowed himself a smug smile.

He studied the older guard standing over her and remarked, "You have done very well, Gorsedd, I am impressed. The reward is yours. But what of this one, is she handsome enough to fetch a good price at one the brothels or should I burn her like I did the others?" He'd not seen the prisoner's face yet.

"She is pretty, my lord, but ill."

"Ill?" Phelan asked, instinctively stepping back. "Lift up her head so that I may look at her."

Gorsedd did as ordered and Phelan was rewarded with the face of what was probably a handsome young woman. Her countenance was pale grey, her breathing raspy as she shivered constantly.

"By the Powers, it is a fever!" He stepped back even further. "Take her away, kill her, for we do not want that disease here in our house!"

"It is the *Gravedigger's Fever*, milord, it is not fatal. It will not pass to anyone else, though it will be some time before she is well enough for a brothel."

Phelan shuddered, "No, kill her. Take her to the city square and burn her."

"Milord, though it may not seem obvious, this woman has value."

"What possible value could she have other than an object lesson?" the lord asked, extremely irritated. He retreated a discreet distance and poured himself a cup of ale with slightly shaking hands.

Morwyn's eyes widened on cue. "No …" she began but Gorsedd's voice overrode hers.

"This woman is related to the House of Aderyn. She is the wife of Belwyn, the eldest of the house, my lord." Gorsedd allowed himself a self-important smile. It would be what Phelan would expect to see. Kell's lord stopped drinking his ale in mid-swallow and set the goblet down with a thud on a nearby table, sloshing the contents within. His penetrating eyes scrutinized the captive more carefully.

"How do you know this, Gorsedd?" he asked skeptically.

"The innkeeper of The Old Port, where the two lords lodged, said he heard the man talking about his wife. He spoke her name, Morwyn, and said she lived in Kell. Apparently he intended to contact her once he had met with you, milord," Gorsedd lied. Phelan moved closer to the captive, momentarily forgetting his concern about her illness. He took the tip of his cane and angled her face up so he could judge her reactions more clearly.

"Why are you in Kell, woman? Why are you not at Aderyn?"

She shook her head as if unwilling to answer. Phelan gave Gorsedd a gesture and Morwyn felt the razor edge of a dagger push against her throat, angling her head backward. The fear in her eyes was genuine now.

"We are estranged," she replied and dropped her eyes as if ashamed.

"Did you bear him children?"

She nodded carefully, mindful of the dagger. "Yes, twins." Gorsedd removed the blade and placed it back in its sheath, the threat no longer needed.

"By the Powers, it only gets better! You are right, Gorsedd, this woman has value!" The man thought for a moment. Morwyn slowly raised her eyes and the expression on her captor's face terrified her. "Are your children here with you, woman?" She shook her head violently.

"No, they are at Aderyn."

Phelan's voice was cold and unforgiving, "Pity, that would have been perfect!"

Gorsedd offered in a cautious tone, "My lord, may I suggest you send her to the Field of Stones. They are always in need of healers and in that way her husband will truly know you hold her life in your hands."

Phelan thought it through. "Perhaps you are right, Gorsedd. What better way to hold him on a short tether than to have his wife by his side in that place? No matter his feelings for her, he will not wish to see her shared amongst the guards."

Gorsedd remained silent, for now was not the time to speak. His lord had to make the decision himself. Phelan thought for a moment more while studying the captive at his feet. Morwyn continued to shiver from the disease and all the while prayers flew through her head in a continuous parade.

Phelan grunted his approval. "Send her to be with her husband, Gorsedd. If she dies from this disease then I will claim that I executed her. If she lives, so much the better, for she will toil at her husband's side until the work kills him." Morwyn shuddered at this and Phelan saw it. "And then I will return her here. She might prove to be an interesting amusement." He turned at that and Morwyn listened as his cane worked its way out of the room. She fell forward over her knees and silently wept in relief.

Gorsedd's face was impassive. The plan had worked; Morwyn the Healer was spared a fiery death and her wish granted, she would join her husband at the Field of Stones. *Better you should have died now, woman,* he thought to himself, *it would have been more merciful.*

Morwyn found herself chained in the back of a wagon along with a number of other unfortunates. She was, again, given a wide berth due to her illness. As the wagon bumped down the cobblestones and out of Kell's impressive wooden gates, Morwyn's fevered brain took her down into a deep sleep. When she awoke hours into the journey, drenched in sweat, she knew the disease was abating for her fever had broken. She offered a small prayer of thanks to the Powers and then drifted back to sleep, Belwyn's face on her mind.

Lord Bardyn's hands were rock solid as he read the missive, the one that demanded a king's ransom for his only son and the Eldest of Aderyn. Owain the Elder was at his side, awaiting his liege lord's explanation of the letter's contents. In his heart, he knew what it contained.

"Phelan did as we thought, Owain. The vile bastard demands ransom for our sons."

"Then let us pay the ransom he demands, with our swords," Owain replied, fire igniting in his eyes.

"Duncan!" Bardyn bellowed. His Master of the Guard appeared almost out of thin air.

"My lord?"

"We leave on the morrow. I will draft a reply and I want it back to that villain in as few days as possible."

"Yes, sire." Duncan vanished out of the room to fulfill his master's order.

"It is time to seek the release of our sons and the others within this madman's grasp." Owain the Elder nodded and left his liege lord to his preparations. He had his own to make and he was in a hurry to complete them as quickly as possible.

eighteen

a s she feared, Owain the Younger's patience vanished and Aldyn began to see a side of him she did not like. He grew surly, sullen and insolent, annoyed at his long recovery, despite the fact he could now walk from his bed to the dining hall with only Aldyn at his side. Even this did not mollify him and so he turned his insecurity and inner turmoil on those nearest him, his mistress included.

She tolerated his vile attitude for three full days, remaining cheerful and friendly while biting her tongue when he snapped at her. Jestin was becoming increasingly reticent to attend his master for he always seemed to have some harsh word for the lad. The final straw came as she was guiding her councilor into his room after a particularly tiring trip to the evening repast. He stumbled, as he often did, still unsure on his feet.

"Powers, woman are you so oblivious that you cannot help me? Must I do all this myself? Better I should summon one of the camp wenches, for at least they'd be eager to help me to my own bed!" His voice was caustic and snide. Aldyn glowered but said nothing, closing the door behind him and then escorting him to his bed. He sat down and waited for her to take off his boots.

When she did not immediately see to this task he growled, "Well? Pull off my boots!"

She eyed him and retorted, "Pull off your own accursed boots, your *lordship*! I have tolerated your belligerence for the past few days, hoping it would pass, but it has not. You are being a complete ass, Owain, scolding Jestin for nothing, snarling at me. Either you change your tone or you will be on your own from now on!" Her hands were on her hips, her eyes furious.

"Then go away! I don't need you mothering me as you do. I am tired of it all, sick of dragging myself around like some old man and hearing the servants snicker behind my back. By the Powers, I should have crossed the Veil! You would do just fine enough without me, I see that now. No doubt in one day you would have another councilor groveling at your heels, another man worshipping you. That one might have proved to your liking and at least been rewarded by being allowed to service you in bed on rare occasions."

Her face turned crimson with anger and she responded to that final insult in the most demonstrative way possible – she stormed out of his room, slamming the heavy door behind her. Aldyn commanded that no one should attend Owain the Younger, that he should stew in his own anger for at least a half an hour. Jestin nodded his agreement and readily accepted her suggestion that he retire for the night. She knew the young lad was exhausted. Caring for his master took all his time now and Owain's bitterness only made the task that much harder.

Aldyn offered, "I will watch over him, once he's cooled down."

"He's terrified that he'll never recover completely, milady," the young lad explained.

"I know. He will, though, the healer has told him that. It will just take time and effort on his part."

"It is so hard to watch him like this, for he has never had an unkind word for me. And now ..." The boy was plainly disturbed by his master's condition.

"I will speak with him and see what can be done to bolster his spirits."

"I wish you good luck with the task, milady. Good night." He bowed and headed for his own bed, praying tomorrow would be a better day for all of them.

When she returned to the patient's room she found Owain sitting in a chair near the fire, his attitude completely altered. He had obviously risen on his own and made his way to the chair unaided, an amazing feat given his disability. She expected anger, but that was not the emotion she found on his face – it was one of sheer devastation.

"Aldyn, I'm so sorry ..." he murmured and then, to her astonishment, he began to weep. Closing the door behind her for privacy, she moved to him, pulled him against her chest and held him as he wept harder. His arms went around her waist and gripped her tightly, yet the sobs did not cease.

"It is of no matter, Owain," she said, trying to calm him. She had not expected him to break apart in such a fashion and it alarmed her.

She felt him shake his head and heard, "I am so afraid." His voice shook at the admission and tears continued to pour down his face.

"I know you are. Nevertheless, you *are* making progress for your strength is returning and you walk further each day. You will be well soon enough, Owain, you must have patience."

His head shook again. "I feared I would die and ..." his voice was muffed against her gown which was growing damp with his tears.

"I understand," she said trying to comfort him. He pulled his head back away from her gown. She smoothed his long hair and gazed into his red-rimmed eyes.

"No, you do not understand. I feared I would die and leave you alone and they would hurt you. I could not stand that, Aldyn. I do not fear death, for I would gladly die a thousand times if that would keep you safe."

"I *am* safe because of you. You need not fear, we will be more vigilant."

He continued on, as if he'd not heard what she'd said.

"I feared I would die and never have a chance to ..." he stopped, abruptly, as if he had nearly revealed a profound secret, something close to his heart.

"Owain?" she asked, sensing she had to know this. There was a long pause as he released her and composed himself. She sank on her knees next to the chair and wiped the tears off his cheeks. He caught her hand, held it in both of his, his eyes full anxiety.

"I feared I would die and never have the chance to make love to you."

She took a sharp intake of breath as her heart nearly burst at this revelation. When she did not speak, he closed his eyes in resignation, his mind roiling at the thought he may have driven her away by his stark honesty.

His voice was sad, quavering. "Powers, I am sorry. I have been too forthright and I have frightened you. Please, forgive me."

She gazed up at him in wonder. "You love me?"

His eyes opened again. "Yes, I do." He saw no reason to hide it now, there was no means to retract what he'd said.

The truth finally broke through her innermost defenses and engulfed her. This time she did not try to hide from it. He was in love with her, loved her enough to die for her countless times if it meant keeping her safe. Loved her so much that his dying thoughts were of *her* safety. The truth hung between them like a newborn butterfly, beautiful in it is intensity, yet vulnerable in its fragility.

She set her fears aside.

"No, you were not too forthright, Owain, you spoke what was in your heart. It is I who have not been forthright."

"Lady?" he asked, sensing some subtle shift in her mood, but unable to comprehend the force behind it.

She tried to explain. "I have spent almost two years reassuring myself you could not possibly care for a woman like me though your every deed and word proclaimed just the opposite. How *could* you love me? I wantonly took another man to my bed while betrothed to your brother. I nearly seduced Elrehan so that he would sire a child on me so I would not have to marry Merioneth, though I did not intend to bear the child nor marry its father. I slew my own husband of two days, stabbed him full in the back. Some might say that was a noble thing, but I still feel his blood on my hands. Yet, you say you love me." Her voice was incredulous. He reached out a shaking hand and caressed her cheek in a most tender fashion.

"I love you for all that, Aldyn, for I have always seen beneath the cold exterior, the lies and the wantonness. I beheld a woman desperately afraid to give herself over to love. After Merioneth, your fear of intimacy only grew, well taught at his brutal hands. I prayed that if I stayed by you, protected you, you might come to love again. I vowed to the Powers to give my life to keep you from harm so that you might find happiness, even if it be with another man."

A single tear tracked down her cheek. He caught in with his finger, lifted to his lips and then kissed it reverently. The gesture spoke of infinite devotion.

"You are wrong, Owain, I never did know how to love. This is all new to me. As I watched you die I knew I was losing something of great value, something more important than anything I possess. I knew then I loved you, but I feared to say it."

"Do not fear, Aldyn, for I will never hurt you." His eyes were intense now, dry and full of adoration.

"I know." She paused and declared in an even voice, "I love you, Owain the Younger."

"See how easy it is to conquer one's fears?" he asked, a gentle smile on his face.

Her nodded and then her eyes turned thoughtful. "You have fears, as well and at least one I can resolve this night." At that she rose and went to the door, pausing for only a moment and then slipped the bolt, locking it soundly.

"Aldyn?" His voice was puzzled, for he did not understand her actions.

She turned back to him and the sensuous look on her face made his mind reel.

"I sent Jestin to his bed so we could talk privately, so it appears that I must be the one to help you undress and settle for the night." She walked to him, pulled him up from the chair and enveloped in her arms. They lingered over a passionate kiss and when she pulled back, his eyes were full of desire.

Owain murmured, "As much as I've dreamed of this, dear lady, I am not sure if I can be with you as you wish. I have the ardor, Aldyn, I do not know if I possess the strength to love you as you so deserve."

A knowing smile appeared on her face and her eyes flashed.

"Not to worry, Councilor, I have strength and ardor for both of us."

The kiss she gave him at that moment removed any remaining doubts he might possess.

Owain woke the next morning and instead of dreading the day that lie ahead of him, he slowly pulled himself up in bed and his face curved into a very pleasant smile. True to her predictions, Aldyn had ardor and strength enough for both of them, and though it wasn't precisely how he imagined their first time together, he was not one to complain. Her experience with other men had proved a boon and ultimately there was fire, passion and the union of two souls. They had loved twice, though he had been very weary after their first tryst. He had not cared, though, and allowed her what she wished and reveled in the love they had made. She had proved as fiery and as passionate as he had always imagined. He stood, gingerly, using the headboard as a lever and then worked his way over to a nearby chair where his clothes sat waiting for him. It seemed to take forever, but he managed to dress himself. Another smile erupted, partially of sensuous memory and part self-satisfaction. As soon as he could fall on his knees and be assured of rising again without aid, he would propose to Aldyn in the proper manner. He had no doubt she would accept his offer of marriage. The physical and emotional bond they had forged between them was unbreakable.

Jestin appeared at that moment, bearing a tray and a definite look of apprehension. His expression turned to amazement when he found his master sitting in a chair, dressed, with a warm smile on his face. He had already spoken with Lady Aldyn this morning and the last he'd heard his master was still asleep. She had assured him that Owain's mood was much improved, though she had not specifically explained *why* the change had occurred. For his part, Jestin was pleased to find his mistress was not exaggerating.

"Sir?" he asked and set down the tray on the small dining table near the hearth.

"Good morning, Jestin! I trust you slept well."

"Sir … yes, sir, I did. And you?" The master he remembered was back in full force, if not even more pleasant than before.

"I slept wonderfully." He began to rise and Jestin hurried to his side. "No, only take my arm, do not provide too much support. I need to push myself, Jestin, for I must be well as soon as possible." *So that I can wed and bed my beautiful lady as she requires,* his mind told him in a burst of enthusiasm.

"Yes, sir." They worked their way over to the table and after Owain sank onto a chair with a satisfied sigh, he gave Jestin a contrite look.

"I owe you an apology for my outrageous behavior."

"Sir, it is not expected that a …" Owain waved his hand in a dismissive manner, unknowingly using a gesture his father favored.

"I know, a master is never to apologize to a servant no matter what kind of ass he is. I disagree. You are a fine young man and did not deserve my surly behavior. I apologize and promise to behave myself in the future."

"Yes, sir." Jestin blinked. This was unexpected. He arranged the food for his master and then stoked the fire, desperately trying to figure out what had caused this sudden reversal in behavior.

"I wish to walk outside today, the fresh air will feel good in my lungs."

"Yes, sir. It snowed last night so it very beautiful."

"Good. How is Lady Aldyn this morning?" Owain asked the question all would expect him to ask. He knew very well how Aldyn fared this morning, but he kept the knowing smile off his face. It would not serve for their enemies to learn they were lovers. Though he trusted Jestin, an idle word in the wrong ear could do considerable damage.

"Very good, sir. She said that you were in better spirits."

"That I am, for she has set me right," his master replied and tucked into his morning repast like a man who had not eaten in weeks.

It took Aithne over a fortnight to work out her plan once she'd learned of the iarel's capture. One particular event spurred her on – Phelan's incarceration of the Northern lords. She had listened carefully to the guards' conversations as she made her rounds within the garrison and gleaned the identity of the two nobles now toiling at the Field of Stones with her lover. Despite the guards' boasts about their master's invincibility, Aithne knew the full weight of Lord Bardyn's wrath would come calling at Phelan's doorstep. She determined the best place for her to be was near her lover rather than trapped in a besieged city. She spoke privately with Gorsedd to arrange for her transfer to the Field of Stones. It was not difficult as the work camps were constantly seeking healers. The poor food and the brutal environment decimated even those skilled in the healing arts. Gorsedd attempted to dissuade her, but she was resolute. He did not ask why she wished to leave the city and she did not offer to explain. Both of them knew it was safer that way.

When she arrived at the camp she learned that the previous healer had perished only the week before. To her credit, she left a tolerably stocked hut. The onset of winter precluded Aithne from gathering and drying more herbs, but if the rumors swirling around Kell's streets about Lord Bardyn were true, this camp would fall to the sword soon enough. She set about treating guards and workers alike, maintaining a low profile. There was danger in her being here, for if any of the clan held a grudge against either her or the iarel, her identity might be revealed. She had weighed that danger and put it aside. Kell was equally dangerous for her.

Late in the evening on the second day she was summoned from her bed to treat a clansman. A huge rock had broken loose and crushed the man as they lowered it down the mountain. She examined him and knew his chest injuries were mortal. Where she did not know the injured worker, she did know the clansman who carried him to her hut.

Dubhan kept his composure when he recognized her and she did not attempt to communicate with him as a guard was present. Aithne turned her mind to easing the pain of the dying clansman. She chose the herbs carefully and helped the man to drink the potent that would allow him to drift into the next life without pain.

Once his raspy breathing ceased, she spoke, "He is no more." The guard nodded, a young man with an unreadable face. Dubhan took the dead man's hand, offered a brief prayer for his soul and then left with the guard. Aithne knew that within minutes Caewlin would learn she was in the camp.

The iarel shuffled into her small hut after dark on the third day, in leg irons. His eyes did not betray any surprise at her presence, as she anticipated.

If anything, she saw extreme disapproval. It unnerved her to find the Master of the Guard as the prisoner's escort. Usually he would detail this onerous chore to one of his own men. A short gnome of a man, the Master of the Guard possessed just enough shrewdness to stay in a leadership position. He was certainly not intelligent nor did he harbor any scruples.

"This one is their leader. I'll stay as he is a wicked bastard," his deep and gruff voice explained. His eyes ranged all over Aithne and he made no effort to conceal his salacious interest in the healer.

"And just what do you expect him to do?" she asked, trying to mask her annoyance. As they spoke, Caewlin was carefully rolling up one the legs of his tattered breeches to expose a vicious gash on his calf. It was red, swollen, and the leg was nearly half again the size of its mate.

"Never know with these vermin. Cut your throat or have you before you can even shout." He was still eyeing her, unaware that Caewlin could understand him.

"How did he receive this?" she asked as she bent to examine the wound. She sensed it prudent to keep her knowledge of the Southern language hidden.

"Apparently a stone shifted as they were moving it."

"When did this happen?"

"Some time back. With the other healer dead we didn't bother with it." He had only decided today to have the man treated, concerned that Phelan's pet prisoner may sicken and die.

The wound was grossly infected but bore no sign of blood fever. She offered a quick prayer of gratitude for that as she cleaned the gash. She created a poultice and then held it tight against the wound to draw out some of the corruption. She knew that hurt from Caewlin's intake of breath, but her patient said nothing, only watched her with his intense brown eyes. His hair was tawny again and hung in dirty tangles. She knew that must trouble him – the clansmen prided themselves on cleanliness.

"The previous healers and I had an arrangement, for they are usually healthier than the other girls. In return for warming my bed I keep the other men away and make sure they get regular food." He paused and then added, "You'll find me good sport."

"I do not wish a man, sir."

"Your wishes may not have much to do with it, healer. I can assure you that I have the *mettle* needed to bring you pleasure," he replied, never taking his eyes off her. Caewlin tensed at this. She gave him a reassuring look as she removed the poultice and began to bandage the leg as if nothing was untoward. Once she had finished her task, she moved to wash her hands in a nearby basin. As she dried them, she turned to the Master of Guard.

"Let me explain to you the nature of a healer, sir, for you would not make such a threat if you knew what we are capable of. We can heal and we can injure with equal talent. If a man should threaten me, I can stop him either with a very sharp knife in just the right place as to make him bleed to death or by herbs that will cause his … *mettle* … to wither and die. I suggest you turn your lust toward another woman who knows less ways to maim."

His eyebrows raised and he frowned. "Most women welcome my sporting."

"I am sure they do, however I do not."

"The other healer did not threaten me in this way," he muttered.

"She was not that gifted of a healer or she'd still be alive," Aithne lied.

"I only need to make sure you do not touch my food, wench. You cannot harm me in any other fashion," he hedged.

"Are you so sure?" she pressed. "The herbs just need to be breathed or touched and the damage is done. I know countless ways to harm a man, sir, for you are not the first to make such a demand."

His voice was considerably more unsure now. "It is not an unpleasant task I ask of you. You should consider it an honor to sport with the Master of the Guard."

She picked up the unspoken message, his sporting with her would raise his stature more than it would hers. Status and power meant more to this man than lust, though barely. She decided on a different tack.

"You come to my bed at your own risk, sir. But I must ask you, do you believe your men would follow someone who lacked … *mettle?*" She hit him where he was most vulnerable, his tenuous position as Master of the Guard. No doubt others actively sought his position and the healer's threat carried weight, for his men would not respect a man who could not sport.

Obviously disturbed at the thought he waved Caewlin up from the chair. The prisoner rose, hampered by the leg chains, and followed him, not the least bit eager to return to the cold hut with the other workers. Caewlin stopped at the door and turned for a moment, his eyes studying her midsection. It was not obviously apparent that she was pregnant under her heavy gown.

"I will need to see him again tomorrow to dress the leg once more," she said.

"So be it," was the gruff reply as the door slammed shut.

Morwyn found herself in Aithne's care the moment she crawled out of the back of the wagon. She managed to stand upright and that saved her life, for often the guards would not bother with anyone who was ill, putting them to the sword the moment they could not stand on their own.

"I am a healer," she said and then added for good measure, "and wife to one of the Northern lords." She hoped that would keep her alive and apparently it was what needed to be said as her chains were removed and she was drug to the healer's hut.

"Yes?" the healer asked, surprised at the woman's sudden appearance.

"I seek treatment," Morwyn muttered as her strength fled. Hands went around her waist and she felt a cot beneath her. There was a pause and then the voice commanded, "Drink this." Morwyn drank the mixture and her brain methodically catalogued the herbs within. The healer was skilled, for she had diagnosed Morwyn's illness and chosen the proper herbs for treatment without pause.

"My right foot is injured," Morwyn began and she felt the healer pulling her cloak back and tugging off her boot.

"A rat bite?" was the question and Morwyn nodded in the affirmative. A few more minutes elapsed as she felt the old bandage removed and new one applied. The wound stung and the smell of ointment filled her nose. The voice returned near her ear as a cold cloth resumed bathing her forehead.

"What is your name?"

"Morwyn, I am a healer."

There was a long pause and then, "You were at the House of Healing, weren't you?"

"Yes."

"Why didn't Phelan have you burnt like the rest?" Aithne asked, wary.

"I was spared as I am wife to one of the Northern lords."

"Which lord?" Aithne asked.

"Belwyn, the Eldest of Aderyn."

"Powers," Aithne muttered and then she rose to set matters right.

Lord Morgan was summoned to the healer's hut where he found a red-haired woman, the healer he supposed, and someone he recognized instantly.

"Morwyn?" he asked as he knelt by the cot. She was sound asleep, wrapped in her cloak.

"She claims to be the wife of one of the Northern lords," Aithne observed. As always, a guard hovered nearby.

"She is the wife of my companion."

Aithne nodded, a troubled look on her face. "She will sleep part of tonight. Wake her later and give her water and bread. By morning she will be much improved."

"We shall care for her." Morgan reached down, scooped up the inert body of the woman who had once been his lover and devotedly carried her to the worker's hut.

It felt like years later when Morwyn heard more voices, one in particular that cut through the low curtain of sounds around her. She worked to remember the voice, to put a name to the person to whom the voice belonged. As she swam out of her sleepy fog she felt herself being cradled in someone's arms. They were strong arms. Finally, the voice registered.

"Belwyn?" she asked in a very weak tone. She felt a subtle shift in the arms and that voice closer to her ear.

"Morwyn, you must wake and eat. You have slept too long." She slowly willed her eyes to open and though she expected it to be daylight, it was not. It was night and the room she was in was smoky and dim.

"Belwyn?" she asked again, this time her voice was a bit louder.

"Yes?" she heard back and focused her eyes on the face above her. Her husband held her, though he appeared older and dirtier than she remembered from her wedding night. He looked exhausted, dark circles arrayed under his eyes. He had a ragged beard now and it didn't suit him, making him look years older. She tried to sit upright until he deftly resettled her in his arms and leaned her against his broad chest. He seemed to know she was too weak to do anything but lie there.

"Here," he said and pushed a cup of tepid water to her lips. She drank deeply. The cup disappeared and then she found a piece of dry bread in front of her face. She took it and began the arduous task of chewing it into small manageable pieces. It took a great amount of water to wash it down, but she was grateful for any food, as her stomach was empty.

"Is she finally awake?" another voice asked and she recognized it immediately. Morgan's face appeared within her field of vision and she gave him a wan smile.

"Yes."

"Good. You were sleeping so soundly we feared for you."

"I am just tired." She shifted a bit, trying to get a clearer look at her husband's face. "Are you well?" she asked, concerned.

"As well as can be expected given what we face here. But what of you, why are you so ill?"

"One of Kell's venomous rats bit me when I stepped on the accursed thing. I am better, for the fever has passed."

"How did you come to be here?" he pressed. He had been astounded when Morgan placed his wife into his arms. Once he was reassured that she was not deathly ill, he had thanked the Powers for bringing them together, even here.

"I made sure to have myself arrested."

"Why did you seek that?" he asked incredulously.

"It was the only way I could be with my *former* husband."

He frowned at that, not quite understanding what she meant.

"I do believe I asked you for a Writ of Divorcement, Belwyn." Her eyes were completely open and he saw a strange look in them.

"I appear to have forgotten to file for it." His answer brooked no argument. He pointed down to her chest and upon it lay her ring, secured by the rawhide cord. He had placed it there as she slept. Though he preferred it to be on her hand, he knew the guards would confiscate anything of value, even a ring. There was an awkward silence and even Morgan shifted uncomfortably.

"Why does that not surprise me," she murmured and then closed her eyes. Morgan shot his friend a wink as Belwyn allowed a slow smile to cross his face.

As ordered, Caewlin returned to have his leg treated the next morning. This time it was an older guard in attendance and when Aithne took off the infection-soaked bandage and began to clean the wound, the man swallowed hard and asked if she'd mind if he stood outside.

"No, there is no difficulty with this one," she said and continued to cleanse the wound of the corruption. She considered it fortuitous that the guard who was with her today was not comfortable with wounds, blood, or infection. He frequently had to go outside the healer's hut to gain some air and to allow his queasy stomach to settle. She heard the door to the hut bang shut as he retreated, pale and swallowing frequently to keep his morning repast in its proper place.

"How is the leg?" Caewlin asked in a quiet voice.

"It is much improved since yesterday. The infection is lessening and it is beginning to heal," she answered.

"That is good news." He waited a moment and then added, "Why *are* you here?"

"To heal and to be near you," she replied.

"It is too dangerous for you." She kept her attention on the wound, knowing his eyes would reveal his displeasure in way that she would not want to see.

"No less dangerous than Kell when the battle begins." She felt him nod reluctantly.

"There will be much death and destruction." They fell into silence as she completed his treatment. Once the wound was bandaged, he rose, glanced at the door to assure they were truly alone and then placed his hand reverently on her abdomen. He whispered very softly, almost too quiet for even her to hear, "Our son grows strong within his mother." His face was a mixture of pride and wonder.

She nodded, smiled, and then asked, "A son?"

"I have seen it in a dream. It is a boy."

"Perhaps." He reached over and kissed her, delicately.

"Be careful, my love, for I cannot live without you." He left at that moment, fearing to stay any longer.

ᘉᎥᘉᎬᎢᎬᘉ

The banquet was pleasant, though not as sumptuous as the one Kell's master spread before the two Northern lords. These were flesh traders, after all, and did not deserve a lavish meal. Phelan had four of them in his fortress at present, three from Kell and one from Ilspath. His demand for slave labor was growing daily, for the workers were dying too quickly to complete the various projects he set before them. His main source of new workers, the clans, was vanishing. In retrospect, he now regretted some the executions for they were, in part, the cause of his labor shortage. To offset his expenses, he'd promptly levied a new tax on wine consumption, but that proved of marginal value. In the end, to his extreme displeasure, he found himself forced to buy workers with the profits he earned from the sale of young women to the brothels, which is why the traders where here.

His eyes lingered on the figure huddled on the cold stone floor in front of them. The traders' attention was there as well, for the girl was a beauty. Phelan had finally obtained the last prize he sought from the Southern clans and she had proved to be worth the wait, though it had cost him the lives of twenty-three of his men to effect her capture.

He announced with an edge of glee to his voice, "She is the virgin sister of Caewlin, the last iarel. She is as wild as any woman can be and if you're not careful she'll cut your heart out just for fun. We have learned to keep her bound for our safety." It was the lesson a young guard had learned the hard way when he'd gotten too close to the Southern wench. Though small in build, she'd nearly strangled him to death with her bare hands in an attempt to escape.

"Really?" the youngest trader replied as he studied her. Her face was petite, her figure slim and her long tawny hair was unbound and fell well below her waist. She was clean and her hair brushed until it glowed. She was clad only in a simple white shift that clung to her lithe body. A cloak was set over her shoulders to forestall the chill of the large room. "She is indeed a beauty. I'd not thought the clans capable of breeding such a pretty girl."

He took another sip of wine and then cut off a hunk of fresh cheese from a platter on a low table near him. Like his fellow traders he was perched on a large floor cushion near the central fire pit. As he partook of the cheese, his mind urged caution. He had no doubt that his host would have taken this wild one for his own if he had wanted. *So why are you still pure, if indeed you are?* He thought for a while and his mind answered, *Profit from selling her to the highest bidder, perhaps?* Phelan's greed was legendary, but his hatred for the Southern clans took precedence at every turn. He puzzled on that for a moment and then cast a glance at the other traders seated near him. He was the youngest, and he had to admit, the best looking of the crew. One of his competitors had a long jagged scar down the entire right side of his face. He was clearly lusting after the girl. The other two traders were nondescript. One was feigning disinterest and the third appeared to be oblivious to the merchandise. He found that odd.

"So, how much for her?" the scarred man asked as he unintentionally licked his lips. The young trader caught the girl's slight head movement at this, as if she understood what the man had said though he spoke in the Northern tongue. It was a subtle clue the others missed, his host included.

"I hadn't thought that much about it," Lord Phelan came back casually. That confirmed the young man's hunch, his host intended to sell the girl to the highest bidder this evening. The invitation had stated a Southern Isle girl would be present for their inspection. Phelan had failed to mention that she was for sale and that she was the sister of an iarel.

"Ha!" the third trader remarked, a bit into his cups and not as cautious as he should be with the notorious master of Kell. He was clad in dusty brown robes and sported a scraggly grey beard. The fourth trader remained quiet, just watching. The younger trader began to surmise that he was one of Phelan's own men, a shill to raise the price when the bidding began.

Lord Phelan tracked his dark eyes over to the young Northern trader and assessed him, yet again. He knew almost nothing about the man and he did not trust him. He had learned that he bought for brothels in Ilspath, that his coin pouch bulged with money, and that he had attended the last two slave auctions and bought three girls, all very pretty. That had earned him a place at Phelan's table this evening.

"I understand you bought a few girls this week. Apparently you've found Kell a worthy place to find new stock," Phelan remarked genially. The young trader nodded.

"I have been quite surprised at the quality available. It was sometimes hard to decide which one to purchase, for many are quite handsome and will bring good coin in Ilspath, especially those with blonde hair." He glanced back down at the girl on the floor at this point.

"I would have thought you would bring them this evening, so that we could enjoy your purchases," Phelan commented, watching the man's reaction intently.

"I usually would have, for it is common to do such a thing in Ilspath in return for your host's hospitality. However, once I heard you had a Southern Isle beauty in your stable, I though it best to send my stock north for they would not be able to compete with the girl." He was carefully praising his host and yet letting him know that he held his merchandise in high regard, not available for just anyone. The trader's reply tallied with what the lord had learned from his spies. The man had sent his three girls north with his servant just this morning, right after he had received the invitation to this evening's banquet.

"Then I ask you, what do you think of her, especially since you traffic entirely in female flesh." The Northern trader set down his wine, rose, and walked over to the girl to inspect her. He gestured her to rise, which she did, and he noticed a volatile mix of fear and hate in her eyes. He wasn't surprised. He'd heard tales about the Southern Isle folk, how they were absolutely fearless. This one was no exception, maid though she apparently was.

"You may have her remove her shift, if you wish," Phelan offered.

"No need, I can see the width of her hips and her long legs without chancing her catching a chill. She would be fine sport, though a bit skinny." He gestured for her to return to her place on the floor. "I can see what you mean, you'd just as well wake up in the morning with a knife in your throat as anything." He sat back down on the cushion, picked up his wine, and took another sip. Everything in his behavior spoke of measured indifference.

"So, is she worth money, that's the question?" Phelan asked.

The leering trader answered. "By the Powers, Lord Phelan, you jest! How often would a man get to take a virgin from the Southern Isles? I've heard they are rare and this one's an iarel's sister to boot! What better sport is there?"

"An iarel that has clan members who will hunt you to the ends of the earth for violating their clan-sister," the Northern trader replied quietly and then sipped on his wine again. He caught the girl's eyes and this time he knew she understood their language well enough.

"I never worry of such things," the man replied and rose to inspect the maiden himself.

"Is that how you received that scar on your face?" the Northern trader asked silkily.

"You're a smart one, aren't you?" the man replied in a sour voice. He pulled the girl up roughly and put his hands on her, but she did not struggle. She just glared at him with those two deep brown eyes as he manhandled her. "Well formed, yes, she would be good sport. That fire in her can be beat out in time." The young trader noted the girl tolerated the man's gross touch but did nothing to aggravate or stimulate him. *She knows now is not the time. She is more cunning than any of them believe.*

"What is the point of breaking a fiery mare to have a plough horse?" he asked in feigned amusement.

"So that you don't end up scarred like I am," the man replied and took his seat again, his hunger for the young girl raised by the touching of her.

"Do you wish to have a look at her?" Phelan asked the remaining two traders.

The greybeard shook his head. "I can see her virtues easily enough from here. Though I'd love to be her first and teach her some manners, she is not what I seek. I am here to sell workers, not buy wenches."

"And you?" Phelan asked the final man.

"No need. I offer you two gold coins for her."

"Two? You are joking, certainly. This girl is worth ten at least," Phelan replied, shaking his head.

"No, two."

"And you?" Phelan turned his eyes toward the scarred trader.

"Three."

"And what of you?" Phelan inquired of the young northern trader.

"She is not worth ten, but she is worth four."

"Five," the scarred man shot back instantly.

As they so callously bid for her, Fea listened while trying to keep her face void of emotion. She feared all of them, especially the one that put his hands on her. As her price rose she determined that whichever man bought her would die.

"This could go on all night," the Northern trader said and sighed. "Seven gold pieces."

"Eight," the scarred man retorted.

"Too much," the third bidder replied and signaled his withdrawal from the auction.

"I will pay nine if you can guarantee she is pure," the young man offered, clearly uneasy at paying such a price for one woman, no matter her provenance.

"That I vow, she is untouched," his host answered and poured himself more wine.

"Ten!" the other man crowed. His purse bulged heavily and it obvious he would not allow himself to be the loser. The Northern trader thought a while and a plan formed in his mind. He reached down, picked up the serving knife and cut himself another hunk of cheese.

Acquiescing gracefully, he remarked, "As I said before, ten is far too high. It appears that you will be the one to feel the heat of her caress or have her cut your throat. I wish you well."

"The knife will be at her throat, not mine," the scarred man replied, his eyes falling on the girl. She dropped her chin, her worst fears realized.

"Well, Lord Phelan, since my fellow trader has not yet given you the coins for the girl and I was so generous as to bid up the price, I beg a favor."

"As long as it does not harm the wench's value, I will grant it," Phelan replied in curiosity.

"I ask only of a kiss from those pure lips and that one of your seasoned wenches to be sent to my bed. For it appears that I will not be sleeping *in* the Southern Isles this evening." That ribald comment drew boisterous and raunchy laughter from the other men and his request was readily granted.

"I will send you my personal favorite, a wench who will no doubt prove as pleasurable as this young one," Phelan replied, immensely pleased with the amount of gold he'd received for his foe's sister. The money would buy countless strong backs and leave a bit left over for his coffers.

The Northern trader dipped his head in thanks, rose and walked to the girl once more. He pulled her up, grabbed her hair and crushed her to him. The kiss was not brutal, but it was demanding and she struggled against his embrace. He casually brushed her cloak off her shoulders so he could caress her body more fully. In time, he removed his lips, chuckled, stepped back and swept up her cloak off the ground. He carefully folded it over and then handed it to her in a mock gesture of gallantry.

"Your cloak, milady." The move startled her for it made no sense until he pulled her hand onto the cold steel under the garment. Her startled eyes darted up to his as he gave her a knowing nod and left the room. She dropped to her knees again, carefully tucking the sharp serving knife into the thick layers of the cloth so no one would know it was there. For a reason known only to him, the Northern flesh trader had given her the means to save herself this night, if her personal Gods so willed it.

Phelan's favorite wench appeared as promised and she had indeed been good sport. The Northern trader would have preferred not to have a woman in his bed this night, for he trusted nothing of what his host offered him. Nonetheless, not to ask for this simple hospitality and not to enjoy it would have raised his host's suspicions even further. As he spent his time with the woman, his mind kept returning to the Southern girl. Realizing his preoccupation would telegraph itself to the wench in his bed, he turned his mind to the matter at hand and partook of what his host had so generously provided him.

The young trader found himself alone at the morning repast with Lord Phelan. He knew the other traders were from Kell and had most likely returned to their homes. No doubt in his own good time Phelan would reveal the fate of the Southern girl and in more detail that he would care to hear. His host did not appear upset and that meant the girl most likely was the victim of last night's encounter, not the victor. If she had escaped, Phelan wouldn't be sitting so calmly at the morning repast as if all was right in the world.

The lord waited him out and then asked as a genial host would, "I trust the woman in your bed last night was worth the time."

"Very much worth the time. And experienced, which counts for much," the trader replied politely, cautiously baiting his host.

"As compared to a virgin from the South."

"Indeed. I'm sorry the bidding went as high as it did. If she had been properly trained, and I know her new owner will not bother with that detail, she would have brought a high price in Ilspath."

"The price was ten gold pieces, was it not?" Phelan inquired. The Northern trader nodded his head in agreement and then picked up a cup of ale to wash down the piece of freshly cooked lamb he'd just consumed.

"If you up that to eleven, she is yours." The trader put his cup down and gave the man a strange look.

"Why would I pay eleven pieces of gold for a girl who is, no doubt, so badly damaged that she will be a second-rate sporting wench?'

"Because she is pure as she was last night before she was bought." Phelan watched the man's reaction with relish.

"Has the scarred one lost his nerve?" the trader asked, puzzled.

"No, his life. She put a serving knife in his throat."

The young trader shook his head in feigned sympathy and laughed.

"That is bad news, though I did warn him. How can I be assured she is still pure, for it matters at that price?"

"I swear it, though now she is even more unruly after last night."

"That I would not doubt." He thought for a while, letting the tension build. "Seven pieces of gold."

"Seven! Why would the value drop?" Phelan demanded, a scowl on his face.

"For two reasons; first, as you say, she is even more likely to try to kill any man who touches her, and second, you already have ten gold pieces from her first purchase. Besides, you have whatever else was in the dead trader's pouch." He gambled that the man had stayed the night in Phelan's fortress or the lord would not be so knowledgeable about his demise. The lord laughed heartily, he rather liked this young trader, though he still did not trust him.

"Seven pieces of gold it is, for if she kills you I shall have your money and your coin pouch, as well."

"If that happens, you will have endless wealth simply by selling the same Southern she-devil over and over."

"Perhaps I will!" the man roared and clapped the trader on the back. "So do you still plan to train this she-devil, as you call her, or turn her over to a brothel as a maid so they can bid out her virtue?"

The trader felt the slight tug of a noose on his neck. Phelan still didn't trust him.

"Why is it of importance?" he hedged.

"I wish her brother to learn of her ruin and if you haul her to Ilspath and sell her virtue there, I lose that opportunity."

"I see." The noose grew tighter. "And if I insist on bidding out her virtue rather than claiming it myself?"

"Then the trade is off," Phelan gambled.

"I did not note you put such a stipulation on the other trader."

"I did not need to. His lust was evident. Apparently your vices do not rule you. You lust after the coins more than her body."

The trader inwardly sighed, his host had tightened the noose down firmly. It was his choice whether he leapt off the scaffold or not. It was not his intention to begin the girl's training in Kell, but he sensed Phelan might not allow him that option. If Phelan only needed to know that the girl was no longer a maiden to satisfy his grudge against the iarel, that would not hinder his plans. Where the training began was of no real import – the trade was too valuable to lose over particulars.

"Another women I would peddle as a maid and the brothel could sell them to their first man at a high price. This one I will not, not now, she is too dangerous to allow some overfed noble in Ilspath to have for the first time. If she can kill a trader, one that knows all the tricks, she will kill an aristocrat without any effort. A dead noble is not good for business."

Phelan snorted and smiled. "That is what I wish to hear, for it will allow me to drive yet another stake into the iarel's heart." He paused and then asked, "So how do you accomplish this training?

"I will teach her who is her master and instruct her how to serve a man in anyway he wishes. I do not care to break her spirit, for that is what makes a girl worth the money. However, she must learn that her life is in my hands. This one will be more difficult, for she will probably never become compliant like most of them do."

"Then why attempt it?" Phelan pushed.

A raw and virile male smile erupted on the trader's face. "The challenge, why else?"

Phelan snorted again, "Then I will have her brought to you tonight at the evening repast so you can start her education as soon as possible."

"I look forward to it." He pushed down his misgivings and the conversation turned elsewhere.

Later in the morning the trader took his leave and set off to purchase a few items in the city market. He selected some sturdy rope, smooth woven so it would not harm the girl's wrists and then he bought two chemises, an overdress, a sturdy set of boots, socks and a thin slave chain. On a whim, he acquired some ribbons. The ribbons would look good in the girl's hair and in their own way remind her that even the simplest things in life now came from him.

Their journey to Kell was uneventful, though Dillan had expected otherwise. He had continued to drill Pyrs every time they stopped to allow the horses to rest as if he knew time grew short. Even now, after their evening repast, Dillan was drilling the boy.

"May I rest now?" Pyrs asked, immensely weary from the day's long ride and the intensive sword practice.

"Only a little longer," Dillan answered, "you are still weak with your upward stroke."

"Dillan, I am exhausted and if I haven't learned how to keep myself from being butchered, then I am done for. We are a short distance from Kell and it is too late for me to improve much more."

Dillan sighed and sheathed his weapon with reluctance.

"Then you must stay close to me for I cannot abide the thought of informing your grandsire and your father that you are dead at the hands of one of Phelan's men." Pyrs shot Gwyn a look and she nodded from her position near the campfire. It was time for Dillan to know why they had made this journey.

Pyrs started, "I will not be with you, Dillan, at least not at first. I have come on this journey so that I can make my way into Kell and then to wherever father and Morgan are being held. You cannot be with me, for you must go with Aindreas and meet with the clan." He waited for the inevitable explosion, for his grandfather had not explained to Dillan precisely why both Gwyn and Pyrs needed to go south.

The Master of the Guard was instantly wroth. "By the Powers, no! I was dead set against your grandsire allowing either of you this nonsense, for you should be safe at Aderyn, not off on some childish lark. Now you say you have business in Kell, young master. I forbid it! You will stay near me or I will tie you to a tree and leave you there until this is over." Dillan's hands were on his hips and his eyes were fiery. Pyrs, remarkably, did not lose his temper. If anything, his manner softened.

"Dillan, we are here for a reason. It is essential that you go your way and Gwyn and I go ours."

"Absolutely not!" he protested vehemently and glowered at his young charge. It was evident the man would not allow them to wander off on their own.

"Come, sit, and I will explain why it is we must tread our own path," Gwyn said and gestured for Dillan to join her near the campfire. The Master of the Guard continued to frown but took his place near the fire. Aindreas studied his companions' faces, his understanding of the Northern speech was so limited he could not completely understand what was happening. Sensing his bewilderment Gwyn murmured something under her breath and the man froze, in place, where he sat on his blanket.

"Powers!" Dillan remarked as he waved a hand in front of the Southern man's face. No reaction was forthcoming.

"I have spellbound him, for what we must speak of I do not wish him to hear." Pyrs settled in next to her, his eyes bright and alert. He took a long pull on the wineskin to cool down after the vigorous training session.

Dillan turned his eyes back on her and nodded. "Go ahead, you have my attention."

"You are aware of my parents' quest to the dragon to learn how to break my father's enchantment?" Gwyn began.

"Yes, I know of it. Your father spoke of it, though not in great detail."

"They were called to the drraig for a reason, Dillan. The Ancient One foresaw a time when his kind would be threatened. He saw Phelan's rise to power and he set a plan in motion to stop him."

"Why would the dragon care about Phelan?" Dillan pressed.

"What do you know of a Stone of Summoning?" Gwyn asked. She felt her small guardian shift on her shoulder, his claws inadvertently digging into her flesh more than was usual.

Dillan huffed, "That is an old woman's tale."

"Tell me what you know of that *old woman's tale*," she ordered.

He frowned again and muttered, "It is said that with a Stone of Summoning one can bind a dragon to one's will." His eyes flitted up to the small one on Gwyn's shoulder and his frown deepened. The beast was not in its usual position, but standing alert and quivering.

She turned toward the small creature and reassured it, "We will not speak of this longer than necessary, for I know it troubles you."

A curious noise came from the beast's mouth along with a disturbing keening sound. Gwyn reached up, gently touched the small dragon's head in commiseration and then turned her attention back to Dillan. The Master of the Guard had already divined what she was about to say.

"Powers, tell me this is just legend. Do not say such a thing exists!" The little dragon's intense reaction told him otherwise.

She nodded slowly. "A Stone exists and Phelan has it. He has bound a mother dragon to his will. She has laid a clutch of eight eggs and he knows of them. The men toiling at the Field of Stones work to uncover the cavern where the eggs reside. Once that happens, Phelan will order the mother to fire them, to ignite the life within them. When they hatch he will command nine dragons, not just one."

"Powers," the man murmured, comprehending the horror that would spread on the wings of the beasts.

"The newborn dragons will be at risk from us mortals for a considerable time, though they are quite capable of killing a man if provoked." The one on her shoulder began to relax, sensing the topic would shift away from the

Stone, a thing that all dragons feared.

"Then why were Morwyn and Belwyn called to the Ancient One if not to break his enchantment?" Dillan asked. He eyes moved to Pyrs and saw the boy was deep in thought.

"The dragon tested many a mortal, all men, and they all failed. He was seeking someone of strength and courage to wrest the Stone away from Phelan when the time came. When my mother was taken by Adwyth, against the rules of magic, it captured the Ancient One's attention. He watched the events play out at the riverbank that day as the crone spellbound my father instead of slaying him. My mother's courage impressed him when she saved my sire from hanging and so the ddraig called her north to test her. When my father joined her on that quest, the Ancient One knew they may be the mortals that could save his kin. He tested both of them in his own way. For his own reasons, he demanded that my mother lie with my father to break the enchantment."

Dillan was starting to see the direction of the story. "So that you two would be created."

"Yes, he did so knowing we would be born of that union. He marked us from the start. He sent a fledgling to carry us away from Braen and instructed us on how we may help rescue his mate, the mother of his children." Dillan's eyes widened, "We are now dragon kin, so no ddraig may harm us. They will slay themselves before harming another of their own kind, something we mortals have never aspired to. It is our task to keep the mother dragon from decimating Phelan's enemies, at least until we can free the beast from his thrall."

"Do your father and mother know all this?" he asked, his face full of amazement.

She shook her head. "They do not. They have no notion of the dragon's machinations to sire us nor to bring us to Phelan's fortress."

"Powers," Dillan murmured. He looked over at Aindreas and the man remained immobile and unaware. "Did you tell this tale to your grandsire?"

"Yes, we did," Pyrs finally spoke. He'd remained silent until now as he knew his sister would best explain this whole remarkable story.

"Then I must do as my master has agreed, though it pains me to leave you two alone and unguarded."

Gwyn knew his fears, at least for her. "I shall not become a wench in one of Kell's brothels, Dillan, have no fear. Between my magic and my guardian, I am safe from that. I will appear as an old and poor woman and will occasion no further interest." Her guardian was curled around her hair again, less tense, but still vigilant.

Pyrs added, "As for me, since I am young and healthy and not the least bit comely, I will no doubt become a slave, hopefully in the same location as father and Morgan. In that way I can bring them hope and keep them safe until you can rally your kinsmen.

"Then I must go to the remnants of the clans and gather them to fight."

"That is what is called for, Dillan. I think it would be best to free the captives at the Field of Stones first and then march on Kell," Pyrs remarked. That will give you the maximum number of men needed to besiege the city, if that need arises."

"How soon will Phelan unearth those eggs?" Dillan asked.

"Very soon," Gwyn answered.

"Then it is in the hands of the Powers," Dillan murmured.

"As it should be," Gwyn replied.

Dillan sighed and glanced back over at Aindreas. "Best to bring him back and we will talk of other things." Gwyn murmured something under her breath and the clansman returned to awareness without realizing that many minutes had passed. Pyrs requested another language lesson and after it was over Dillan appeared pleased with his progress.

"You do very well in our tongue," Aindreas commented politely.

"Thank you."

Dillan turned to his fellow clansman. "When we are closer to Kell we will leave Gwyn and Pyrs to their business and we will go to the clan to rouse them to war."

Aindreas smiled and nodded instantly. "Then the Gods will allow us our vengeance."

When the twins parted a day later it was extremely difficult for both of them. Pyrs only felt complete when his sister was beside him and now he was to be on his own.

"Be careful, Pyrs, Kell is a very dangerous place," Gwyn cautioned. Her eyes were full of worry and that unnerved him.

"I will. You be careful as well, for though you wield great magic, there is still danger for you." She sighed and nodded. Where she seemed invincible, she was not. There were chinks in her armor as well. She reached out and touched his chest and he felt a slight tingle. She'd put a protective spell on him.

He grinned. "You wouldn't have one for invisibility, would you?" She gave him a mock glare and shook her head.

I do, brother, but I reserve that for my use. They hugged one last time and he planted a gentle kiss on her forehead.

"Be well, dear sister, and we will meet soon." He turned and set off down the road toward the city one day's journey to the south.

After Dillan had cautioned her yet again, he and Aindreas set off to the east, into the forest. Five weeks had passed since Aindreas left his people and now he returned with a fellow clansman who would bring powerful allies to bear against their enemies. His steps were firm and his strength returning as they strode toward their destination.

Gwyn watched them for a time and then invoked a glamour spell of illusion transforming herself into an old woman, gnarled and crippled. The dragon was not visible now, cloaked as well. She would move slowly toward Kell, not at Pyrs' speed, speaking with those travelers who had just departed the city to learn of the latest news. Then she would set her sights toward the reason she was summoned south.

TWENTY

T he evening repast was subdued given the death of one of their own. Another one of the traders was missing, the one that no doubt worked for Phelan. The remaining trader from Kell said little, his business with the lord was concluded and so he slowly sank into his cups. After the meal the Southern girl was made to kneel on the floor in front of them. Her hands were not bound and the young trader found that rather curious.

Perhaps she is indeed the she-devil destined to build your wealth, Phelan.

He asked the obvious question, "Has she been searched?"

"By two women, so nothing has been hidden," Phelan replied and took a long sip of his wine.

"I am relieved, for I value both my life and my purse." He turned his eyes back on the girl, saw the black and blue marks on her face from her former master's attentions and the look of pure hate pouring out of those dark brown eyes.

His host gestured to one of the guards and commanded, "Bring in her brother."

The appearance of the iarel caused Fea to cry out and as soon as he fell to his knees next her she threw her arms around him. He wore ponderous chains and rags for clothes. Two nights previous Caewlin had found himself chained in the back of a wagon and spirited away to Kell, once again. It was obvious his guards did not know why the iarel was ordered before Phelan and he assumed it was for inevitable execution. It was only when he reached the city that he was told the news of his sister's capture. Now the threat of death seemed insignificant.

"Fea, dear sister," he murmured, embracing her tightly. His heart was anguished, for he had prayed this day would never come.

"Caewlin, you are hurt," she replied, seeing the drainage-soaked bandage on his leg. She kissed his check and smoothed back his hair from his dirty face.

"You are unhurt?" he asked, fearing so much.

"I am. Our Gods have kept me safe." He embraced her again, despite the chains.

Always the gracious host, Phelan made the introduction and relished it.

"This is Caewlin of the Southern tribes, the girl's brother. I had him fetched here from the Field of Stones so he could see what had befallen his sister. Pagan that he is, he does not speak our language, so I decided to let him know of his sister's ruin in a way he could understand. Unfortunately the sheets off of the other trader's bed this morning had far too much blood upon them to make them plausible."

"No doubt," was all the Northern trader could say, his mind reeling at the gross inhumanity of his host. He had thought Phelan had only meant to tell the girl's brother of her fate, not show him the very linens she'd been savaged upon. The man's cruelty knew no bounds.

"Hopefully tomorrow you will start your day in better condition than her previous owner and I can show her brother what I could not this morning."

"May the Powers allow that," was all the trader replied and he gestured the girl to come to him. She glared at him and refused to move.

"Bring her to me," the trader commanded. The closest guard wrenched her out of brother's arms and drug her to stand in front of him. The trader reached into his purse, counted out seven gold pieces, and handed them to his host.

"Your money, Lord Phelan."

"Your virgin, trader."

The transaction was not lost on her brother. Caewlin bellowed at the top of his lungs and attempted to rise. Forced back to the floor by two of the guards, he continued to shout until they silenced him. Despite the commotion, the trader continued to study his new purchase. Her face was set and he swore he could see his death in her eyes. He pulled out some of the rope he had purchased in the market and bound her hands together in front of her. The hatred in her eyes grew, mixed with fear. He pointed to the ground, indicating she should kneel. She did not move. He snapped his fingers in impatience and she still did not move. It was their first battle of wills and he dare not lose, especially in front of his host.

He had no choice – he cuffed her with his hand, sending her sprawling to the stone floor. Her brother erupted in fury, surging to his feet, and was driven to the ground by the guards, a dagger at his throat. The trader shot a quick glance toward the man and saw the raw look of hatred in his eyes.

Fea rose, slowly, feeling pain as it spread across her face. She wiped her mouth and was surprised it was not bleeding. Her fear grew, though burning hatred still ruled. She saw the trader point to the ground at his feet and she spat at him. She knew what would come next and it did, dropping her to the floor yet again. Their dance of wills was repeated three more times. Finally, after the fifth blow, she stood, wavered on her feet and then knelt as he commanded. All the while Phelan watched in fascination and her brother shouted his righteous fury.

The trader kept the look of triumph off his face. *This one is dangerous,* he thought. Though she appeared cowed by his violence, he knew that she only acknowledged his brute strength, but not his dominion over her. He and his host spoke pleasantly for a few minutes as the girl and her brother remained in submissive postures. Eventually the trader rose, bid his host good evening and gestured for his wench to rise. She did so without pause. He gripped her arm and began to stride out of the room.

His host's voice caught him. "By the way, trader, I have a question." He halted, his hand still firmly on the girl, and turned back toward Phelan.

"Yes?"

"There is a puzzle you can solve for me – it involves the knife this girl put in the other trader's throat last night. It seems that there were no serving dishes in his room so such a knife would not have normally been present for her to use."

"How interesting," was the reply.

"Would you know how she came by the knife?"

The trader smiled, broadly, and nodded. "Of course, I gave it to her. How else do you think she would have been mine tonight?"

Phelan began to laugh, loudly, slapping his thigh in complete merriment.

"I thought so! By the Powers, you are a cunning man! And you bought her for less than what you would have paid last evening."

"I did."

"You are a robber, there is no doubt of that."

"A robber with a wild girl to train, so if you don't mind …"

"I'll leave you to her, then. But one thing …" Phelan added,

"Yes?" The young man looked impatient to get on with his evening.

"I will place a servant outside your door, for I wish to be the first to learn if it is your blood on the bed linens or hers."

"And if my purse is yours as well," the trader shot back.

"Precisely."

Caewlin's dread for his sister overwhelmed him. He shouted in his own language and attempted to break free of his guards once again, but to no avail. On a gesture from Phelan they began to beat him unmercifully. Fea cried out and pulled back, trying to go to his side. As the guards battered the Southern iarel into unconsciousness, the trader dragged his latest acquisition out of the room.

As he had expected, it was a fight all the way. Though she had no weapon on her, her fury made up for that. She kicked him, hard, in the shins and then tried to bolt back to her brother's side. The trader tightened his grasp on her arm and tugged her along the hallway as startled servants scattered around them. She continued to shout, hiss and fight with him the entire way. He knew that by morning he would have bruises all over his body from this she-devil. To her credit, she was no longer screaming and that he appreciated. He regretted her brother's beating, but that was not his concern.

When he finally reached the door to his room he swung it open and then shoved her through it. She did exactly as he expected and immediately turned on him, attempting to break past him into the hallway. He grabbed onto her waist and this time she did scream, her curses filling the air, no doubt frightful oaths if he had understood any of it. He barely managed to shove her back into the room, for she had surprising strength for one so petite. Out of the corner of his eye he caught a glimpse of the servant Phelan had spoken of waiting further down the hallway. He would not have privacy with this girl and he regretted that. His host was too keen to torture her brother with the outcome of this evening's first lesson. The trader kicked the door closed behind him with a loud crash, strode over a few paces and then began to remove his clothes and weapons.

Fea's eyes darted around, desperately seeking a means of escape. Her assailant stood between her and door. She sized him up as he tugged off his boots and lay them aside and then removed his linen shirt, his sword belt and knife. Any feeling of gratitude was gone, by his own admission he had given her a means to fight the other trader solely so he could possess her tonight. He had no honor and intended the same violence as the other man, the one she had so righteously slain. Her eyes watched intently as he tucked his sheathed dagger behind him in the band of his breeches.

"Remove your clothes," he ordered. She shook her head violently. She was panting from exertion, her eyes wide in fear.

"As I thought, you do understand Northern speech." He paused and framed his words carefully, "Know that I own you and this evening can either go very pleasantly or go very poorly. I have no wish to harm you, but you are mine and you will do as I ask."

"I will kill you before you touch me."

"I doubt it, for no one has been so kind as to provide you with the means." Fear overpowered her good sense and she unwisely made a run for the door. He grabbed onto her as she darted past. She struck at him again, raining blows on his arms and chest and then she began to choke him. He carried her over and threw her on the bed to help break the chokehold.

"Remove your clothes or I will rip them off!" he commanded. She skittered away from him, going as far away on the bed as she could.

"I will not make it easy for you, you barbarian!"

"So be it, girl." He already regretted what he was about to do, but he had no choice, for Phelan had called his hand. It was not his usual style. He strode over, ripped the shift off her shoulders, dragging it down to her waist and then threw her back on the bed. He straddled her waist, pulling her bound hands over her head and then leaned over her. It was then she screamed, a high thin haunting scream reminiscent of an ensnared animal. It chilled him to the bone and he almost lost his nerve. He took a deep breath, knowing he had to go on with what he'd started given the sentinel in the hall. He clamped his right hand over her mouth, barely avoiding her snapping teeth. She attempted to scream again, but it did not come out as intended with his hand on her mouth. He leaned over and moved his hand from her mouth to her neck, pressing down with enough force to make her stop struggling.

He spoke to her in the most earnest voice he could muster, "I will not hurt you, but you have to stop struggling!"

She glared at him and growled back. "I will kill you!" He saw the raw anger in her eyes that had probably foreshadowed the other trader's death. She began to thrash again, despite the hand on her throat.

He whispered quietly so only she could hear him. "Girl, quit! Hold still and listen! There is a servant in the hallway, I have to do this, so stop struggling and help me!" In his haste to have her understand what he needed to do his ill chosen words only drove more terror in her heart. It confirmed his intention to take her, even if she ceased fighting. Her panic deepened and the need for flight ruled her mind.

His face turned grim, he would have to proceed and hope he did not hurt her too much in the process. He removed his hand from her throat and then tied her hands to the metal ring at the head of the bed with the tail end of the rope. It freed his hands for the work ahead. She struggled against the ring but without success. Another volley of curses came out of her mouth.

He reached behind him, pulled his dagger out of the back of his breeches and put it to her throat. She stopped struggling instantly at feeling of the cold steel at her neck.

"Now, hold still, please, I have no wish to harm you." He saw she was shaking now and he gritted his teeth at the sight.

"If you touch me, I will kill you!"

"Then you will have to kill me, for I intend to touch you, girl." Realizing the remaining tatters of the shift would have to go he took his dagger and cut it off at the side of her thigh and then pulled it away, leaving it under her. She was totally nude now and quaking in fright. She attempted to knock the blade out of his hands with her elbow, but failed, and he put it back at her throat. He gently touched her face, for she dare not move with the dagger in place.

"You are very brave, girl, and I promise this will be over soon." She closed her eyes, waiting for the inevitable. With her eyes closed she did not see him cut his left palm with the dagger's point, deep enough that blood flowed.

Leaving the dagger in place at her throat, he said quietly, "Forgive me this indecency." He turned and forced his hand between her clamped thighs. She started to struggle again and felt the blade push harder against her throat and she ceased her movements, sensing the end was near. She screamed again, that same horrific shriek and it had made his hair stand on end. He did not stop his actions, difficult though it was. She forced herself to lie still, praying, her eyes now focused on the dagger. Fea was determined to move forward and impale herself on it the moment her future ended. As she shivered uncontrollably she felt his hands on her, between her thighs and she waited for what had happened last night, the shift of the man's weight on top of her. It never came. She felt his hand on her, but no pain as she continued to shake in fear. He leaned forward once more and she caught the sight of his palm. It had blood on it. Without hesitating, she tried to force herself forward to skewer her throat on the dagger. He saw her intent and pulled the blade back where she could not reach it.

"By the Powers, stop that!" he commanded. It was then she began a strange keening noise and tears flooded her face. There had been no pain, but there was blood on his hand. Her life was gone, for the clan would never accept her back if she were not pure.

He shook his head and tried to explain in a whisper, "It is *my* blood, girl, not yours. You are still a maid and will remain so, Powers willing." Her keening continued unabated, a mournful sort of sound. He shivered for it struck every nerve in his body. She had her eyes closed as if waiting for him to finish what he'd started, for no doubt he would lie with her and take his pleasure. Sensing she was beyond comprehension, he took her face in his uninjured hand, forcing her to open her eyes and cease that unearthly noise she made. He held his bloody palm in front of her so she could see the deep cut he had made upon himself before touching her.

"The blood is mine," he said almost in a whisper.

He pulled himself off her and moved deliberately to the end of the bed. She sat up instantly, scooting as far away from him on the bed toward the wall as she could and then looked down. The bed linen and her ripped shift bore the stain of her honor as did her thighs, just as if he had been with her. She shook her head in confusion, understanding none of this. She watched him bind his wound with a piece of her ripped garment as he sat on the end of the bed. After binding his hand, he pulled the sheath out from his breeches, replaced the dagger within it and moved it near his sword. He strode over to the bed, his face resolute. She shrank back in fear as he pulled the bed linen out from under her and gathered up the tattered shift as well. He marched to the door, opened it and then summoned the furtive figure down the hall,

"You there, come here!" The servant scurried up and bowed. "Tell Lord Phelan that this is her blood, not mine, so he'll not have my purse in the morning. Bring fresh linens and some food, for I am hungry. Knock on the door and await my command to enter, do you understand?" The servant bobbed his head as the trader shoved the linens into his hands and then slammed the door behind him. The lackey set off in search of his lord.

After ascertaining the servant was off on his errand, the trader stoked the fire to warm the room. He feared the girl would go into shock and take ill after his rough treatment of her. He pulled the coverlet off the floor where it had fallen in the struggle and covered her with it, for her hands were still bound. He returned to the end of the bed and spoke, his voice softer.

"Phelan now has his proof that you are no longer a maid. It was the only way to keep you safe."

Her voice quavered. "I do not understand. You could have …" She continued to shiver, despite the coverlet. He poured her a cup of wine and then sat on the bed near her and offered it to her. She shrank away from him and shook her head. "If you mean to drug me to …" He sighed and drank out of the cup himself and then offered it to her again. Belatedly he realized that her hands were still bound. He thought a moment and then shook his head.

"I do not think it wise to untie you just yet, for you are still determined to kill me one way or another." He handed her the cup and then retreated to a nearby chair, putting some distance between them. "I must apologize for what I just did to you, it was most … indecent. I deeply regret it, but you were too frightened to help me and it was important that you appear fair and properly ravaged. I also apologize for striking you as I did, but I had to show my mastery of you. Lord Phelan doesn't entirely trust me." She watched his eyes carefully and saw only truth in them. He added, "Your actions, attempting to escape and those most dreadful screams, will add credence to what they believed happened here tonight."

"If this is some ruse to have me let down my guard," she began and he immediately frowned and shook his head.

"Girl, we both know that if I had wanted to violate you the deed would be done twice over and that would be your blood on the linens, not mine. There was nothing to stop me when I had my blade at your throat." His voice was forceful and growing irritated.

"Only my death," she said and he knew immediately what she meant. She would have found a way to kill herself at the first opportunity.

"I swear by my family's honor I will not harm you. I have yet to take an unwilling woman, virgin or no, and you will not be the first. I had hoped that if I gave you the knife last night you could kill that bastard and escape, but that did not happen. Did you know your brother was here and that is why you stayed behind?"

She shook her head and hugged the coverlet closer to her.

"No, I did not. The guards came too quickly after the trader's death. Apparently there was a servant on watch, as there was tonight."

"Well, if I am to return you as a maid to your brother, girl, we shall have to be very clever at this."

"You never intended to …" she asked in a shaky voice, still in shock.

"No, I never did." His voice was firm. "I have a sister of my own and I would hope that if I was not there to save her from such a fate, someone else would. I also believe you were a clever trap, though you were not aware of it. A slave trader would have no difficulty buying and ruining a girl and I think our host wishes to insure I am what I claim." His face was deeply lined, his eyes registering extreme weariness, as if this evening's work had been hard on his soul in some way.

"But you bought girls in the market," she protested.

"I did. They are now being taken to a safe location until Phelan no longer rules Kell."

"Were any of them clanswomen?"

He shook his head in the negative and offered nothing further as to his identity. She handed him the empty cup and then lay down in the bed, tugging the coverlet over her for warmth. Her bound hands made the task difficult so he assisted her. Her brown eyes remained wary.

"The servant will be returning soon with the fresh linens and the food I requested. It would be doubtful that a girl of your ... temperament ... would be so easily cowed and so I must leave you bound. When he returns, a few tears and curses would be in order. We need to keep this charade up as long as possible for both our sakes." She nodded and sunk further into the covers.

"Then if you are not a slaver, what are you?" she asked, but the question was lost as a knock came at the door. When the trader granted the servant leave to enter with the tray of food, he found Lord Phelan was right behind him. His host had a broad smile on his face and his hands on his hips. The trader's heart skipped a beat.

"Lord Phelan," he said as nonchalantly as possible. He only had his breeches on, nothing else, and that would look correct. His chest bore the marks of the girl's violence and would add credence to the servant's report that the Southern wench had indeed proved to be a she-devil. Fea immediately shrunk further under the covers and began to shake, violently. That strange keening noise came out her mouth again and he could not tell if it was forced or genuine.

"I thank you for your prompt delivery of the linens. I trust all is going well here?" his host asked jovially.

"Just the initial training session and then we begin to work on the basics."

"Which are?"

"Responding to my every command."

"I see." Phelan had his eyes on the girl and the trader knew what he wanted. He turned his head toward her, snapped his fingers and pointed to the floor at his feet.

"Here, girl, now!" Fea tried to do as he bid but the rope held her to the ring and she tugged on it in apparent fear that she would be punished. The important point was made, she had attempted to follow his orders although it was impossible.

He smiled, nodded, and then walked over to untie the bonds. He returned to his place by Phelan and then ordered her to him once again. She did as he bid, climbing out of the bed and falling to his feet, completely nude. She shivered on the floor, hugging her arms around her for warmth and modesty.

"Well done, I'm impressed and she's less bruised than I thought she'd be. Quite a beauty."

"It's all in the training," the trader replied modestly.

"Now that she is a maid no longer, would you consider sharing her with me for the night?" Phelan asked, his eyes lingering on the girl. Fea shivered violently at the thought.

"I'm afraid I must decline, Lord Phelan, and not because you've been an inhospitable host. The training is a precise thing and to have a girl with another man too soon will ruin her and reduce her value. This girl must be initiated very carefully because she is so willful."

"Perhaps in time?" Phelan's voice was laced with lust.

"Yes, that is possible once the training is complete. I would appreciate your estimation of how she turns out. Of course, it would be without charge," he replied magnanimously.

Phelan nodded and smiled again. His trust of the trader had risen significantly with the delivery of the linens and the marks he'd just seen on the girl. He'd clearly seen blood on her and that was the final proof in his mind.

"Then I leave you to your work. I will have the servant deliver the morning repast to you here in your room."

"That is very thoughtful, Lord Phelan, for I have no doubt I will be weary from the night's labors." He reached down at that and ran his hand under the girl's chin and she turned her head away in apparent revulsion.

"Into the bed, girl, for it appears you need another lesson in manners," the trader commanded and she rose, unsteadily, and crawled back into the bed, huddling against the far wall in apparent fright. She reached for the coverlet and his voice caught her, "No! You do not cover yourself unless I permit it!" Her hand fell away from the cover and she began to cry softly once more, wrapped into a tight ball.

Phelan snorted and slapped the trader on the back.

"By the Powers you are good at this!" He left the room at that juncture, the servant right behind him. The trader waited until they had disappeared down the corridor and then shut door firmly. When he turned, he found Fea was still curled up, tears in her eyes. He moved to the bed, sat on it and enveloped her in the warmth of the coverlet.

"You were perfect, girl. Just perfect."

She gave him a rueful smile. "He will not stop asking for me until he beds me."

"He will not touch you as long as you are with me. You must remain at my side at all times, for nothing prevents him from demanding you be with him if I am not present."

She sighed and nodded. "You are quite good at this, sir. How is it you know how a trader acts toward his girls?"

"I have been to slave markets and watched the cruel mastery of those considered property."

"It is a wicked thing," she replied.

"Yes, it is." He walked over to the tray and then returned with a small plate of cheese and beef and set it on the bed near her. She pulled herself up and began to eat. It was obvious she had not eaten such rich food for a long time for her ribs were plainly visible. He returned with a full cup of wine for her and they ate together for a few minutes, each deep within their own thoughts. The girl only broke the silence once the plate in front of her was empty.

"Sir, might I know the name of the man who has so creatively defended my honor?" He turned his blue-grey eyes on her and gave her a slight smile.

"I am Elrehan, son of Pyrs, a warrior in Lord Bardyn's service." Her eyes widened at this. "I am in Kell to seek the release of my liege lord's son and my brother-in-law."

"The Northern lords Phelan holds hostage?" she murmured, her eyes wide.

"Yes. Lord Morgan and Belwyn of the House of Aderyn. I was supposed to be in Kell when they met with Phelan, but my horse went lame and it took me three days to find another. I arrived too late to help them." His voice was guilt-ridden.

She observed him for a moment and replied quietly, "I am Fea, daughter of Brecc and shield-maiden of the Red Hawk Clan."

"Please pardon my ignorance, Fea, daughter of Brecc, but what is a *shield-maiden?*"

"I am permitted to fight in battle," she replied straightforwardly. He involuntarily shuddered at the thought.

"That I would not care to see, dear lady, for you would be more deadly than ten warriors. You have no fear of death, that is very clear."

"I fear it as much as any person, Elrehan."

"Yes, but you hide it well." He paused and then muttered, "I am weary, this has been a trying day." Involuntarily she yawned long and hard. "We must sleep in the same bed together for to bolt the door would invite suspicion." She eyed him and reluctantly agreed. He walked over to a nearby chair and selected one of the chemises he had purchased that afternoon.

When he handed it to her she asked, "I have your word of honor, sir, that you will not touch me unless I will it."

"You have it as long as I have your word you will not slay me in the middle of the night as I lay sleeping." He noted that she thought about that for a while as if weighing it as a definite possibility.

"You have it." She handed the chemise back to him. "It would not be right for me to be found wearing any garment in your bed, sir."

He nodded, reluctantly, and lay the chemise aside. He stoked the fire again and then sat on the edge of the bed, preparing to lie down.

"Your breeches must go," she said in a surprisingly mellow voice.

"What?" he asked, surprised.

"There is no guarantee that Phelan will not find a reason to interrupt us in the middle of the night. Everything looks as it should, except for your breeches."

He looked down and then unwilling nodded, "Unfortunately you are right." He turned his back on her, stripped off the breeches and climbed into the bed. He shifted his weight away from her and attempted to tuck the coverlet around him. She knew he was uncomfortable being in the same bed as her, no doubt concerned at offending a maiden.

"You are not the first man I've lain next to without clothes," she said quietly. His face turned towards hers but she noted he kept his body from touching hers.

"But I thought you are a maiden …"

"I am, but in our clan we share the furs of any young man we fancy, though we do not make joined love if we are pure."

"That is a curious custom and one that might be hard to enforce if all the maids look like you," he replied honestly.

She smiled slightly and added, "It is not hard to enforce when the maiden's mother and father share the same tent as the couple and her father's sword lays unsheathed lest it be needed."

"Yes, that would keep any man honest, would it not? But what is the point of sharing the furs, as you say, if you are not there to make love?"

"To learn if the man is skilled in ways that give a woman satisfaction, for we have other means to make love than joining."

"Oh," was all he could say, not wishing to go further into this unknown area. She saw his discomfort and inwardly smiled. Apparently Northerners were more constricted in their ways of passion. She felt some explanation was in order.

"The only women who are required to be virgin are the daughters of the iarel. The rest may invite any man to their furs whenever they wish, providing neither of them are wed. When they grow tired of them, they no longer permit them to share their furs and the man must depart without complaint."

"That is a truly an interesting custom. So if you were not the sister of an iarel ..."

"You and I would be free to love if I wished it."

"Ah, I see," he said as he turned back, his mind reeling at the thought.

Fea gave him a half smile and said, "Not to fear, Elrehan, son of Pyrs, your honor will be safe with me this night." She heard a low chuckle from the other side of the bed at that. She moved over next to him for warmth and as he fell asleep he felt her two small breasts pressed against his back. He began to regret that she was the sister of an iarel.

Lord Phelan made one more stop before he went to his bed – he visited the iarel where he sat chained to a damp stone wall deep within the fortress and presented him the evidence of Fea's ruin. Caewlin sobbed, openly, though he knew his mortal enemy was relishing every tear he shed.

Phelan gestured for a nearby guard to translate for him,

"One less virgin in your midst, Iarel. Her screams echoed throughout the fortress, but that did not save her. She killed the first man who tried to have her, but the second proved equal to the task." Phelan studied him for a few moments longer and then strode out of the cell, a cruel grin on his dark face.

The guards began to speak amongst themselves and Caewlin understood every word, every crude joke made at his sister's expense. He clutched the linens in his hands and then tore a strip of fabric from both the sheet and the shift. He tied one around each wrist. It was his intention to find his sister, learn how many times the pagan had lay with her against her will and then he would capture and torture the man for that length of days. When he finally was ready to kill him, he would plunge his sword into the bastard's throat, making him choke to death on his own blood. Then he would tie the linen scraps to the man's neck, grim evidence of the fate of one that would dare touch the sister of an iarel without her consent. He grew quiet as the grave and an hour later they shoved him in a wagon and sent him back to the Field of Stones. Tears burned his face as he wept in the cold night air, drenching the ripped rags on his wrists, for his sister was lost to him and his people.

TWENTY-ONE

The servant appeared early in the morning, sent by his master to determine if the trader still lived despite his subjugation of the Southern girl. A knock on the door awakened the sleeping couple and Elrehan immediately pulled Fea over to him and put his arms around her, heedless of the fact they both were nude.

"Enter!" he replied and the servant came through the door bearing a tray full of food.

"Your morning repast, sir."

Elrehan nodded. "Set it down for I have other things on my mind at present." He turned his eyes back to Fea and then began to kiss her. She struggled at that, as expected, and he growled at her and kissed her harder. She struggled more and he had to force her back down on the bed as a mock sob of despair escaped her lips. Her performance impressed him. In due time the servant left the room, closing the heavy door behind him.

Elrehan muttered, "I hope that did it."

"Phelan believes what we wish him to believe."

"Yes, but others will as well," he replied solemnly.

"You mean my brother?"

"Yes. Phelan will be sure to tell him of your fate and he will vow to kill me for what has befallen you. It was what I would do if it was my sister," he said softly and then quickly shifted his weight off her and lay on his side. The closeness of the woman had fired his ardor and he was somewhat embarrassed given that she was not an experienced woman. He quickly offered his apology, "It was not my intention to ..." he started, chagrined, but she cut him off.

"I am not offended, sir. One cannot expect a man to be made of stone when he is lying near a woman, even a maid."

"Thank you for your understanding," was all she heard him mutter. She leaned over him and gently put her hand on his chest.

"I owe you my future, Elrehan, son of Pyrs."

"Perhaps," he answered, uneasy. "The best way to show your appreciation is to keep your brother from killing me in some long and very painful fashion."

"That may prove difficult. There will be those in the clan who would believe you should die solely for having touched me, even though I am still untried." His head raised at this and he gave her a long look.

"Now that *is* reassuring news, Fea," he commented in a sarcastic tone. "I cannot partake of your charms because you are pure yet I can die horribly for having supposedly done just that. Or worse yet, for the minor sin of just lying next to you. That is hardly fair."

"No, it is not. Some would believe my life should be forfeit as well since I didn't kill myself after your supposed deeds. Or kill you, for that matter." Elrehan sighed long and hard and Fea could tell he wasn't pleased by that news, either.

"Just wonderful." The man rose at that point and donned his breeches, still with his back to her. She grinned at his modesty and then rose to dress. He made sure to keep his eyes averted and she found it amusing that this Northerner had such a strong streak of decency within him.

Their host called the trader to his chambers later in the morning and Elrehan took Fea with him, loath to have her out of his sight. Lord Phelan greeted him warmly and gestured for him to sit by the fire. Elrehan pointed at a place on the cold stone floor and Fea settled there. He disliked that, but had no choice. At least this time she was clothed in the garments he had purchased at the market, so she was much warmer.

"As you can see I am in possession of both my purse and my life," he joked.

"You are. You know, I had my doubts about you, but you have put those to rest."

"Doubts, on what account?" Elrehan asked nonchalantly as he poured himself some wine and sipped it slowly.

"I had my doubts that you were a flesh trader."

"Really? What put those doubts to rest?" he asked lightly.

"The girl," Phelan said and gestured at the figure on the floor. "A honorable man would not have had his way with her nor treat her in such a fashion. I see you are not such a man."

"There is little honor in being poor, Lord Phelan, and this girl, properly trained, will bring a bulging purse of gold coins in Ilspath. Southern women, especially one as pretty as her, are rare up there. Men will pay well to enjoy her charms."

"As I said, you are not honorable, which is why I like you." He paused and then added, "I had the linens from your bed delivered to the iarel last night in his cell right before I shipped him back to the Field of Stones."

"Why do you hate this man so much?" Elrehan asked.

"He refuses to die like the others. He is the only reason the clan survives, for he is their strength. Now he is mine and when I delight in torturing him no more, I will personally kill him." He gazed down at the girl on the floor and a smirk crawled across his face. "And now I have the satisfaction of knowing that his sister will serve any man's pleasure in Ilspath."

"Not any man, Lord Phelan, for they shall have to possess considerable coin to partake of her."

"As it should be. Come here, girl." She rose slowly and walked to him, reluctantly. He pulled her chin up, gazed into eyes and saw the marks on her face. "You are a beauty, even through the bruises." He gestured for her to go back to spot on the cold floor and he reminded his guest, "Hopefully her training is complete before you leave Kell. I will hold you to my one night with her." Fea's eyes widened at this and Phelan caught it. His face curved into a lecherous smile.

Elrehan replied evenly, "It can be arranged, providing she completes her training before I leave Kell. We are making progress, but at this stage they are pliable one moment and intractable the next. Once she learns how to properly service a man, you will have your one night, Lord Phelan."

"I look forward to that," Phelan came back and saw the girl shudder slightly. "Though, it appears she does not."

"She looks forward to nothing but a dagger in me right now, for she has found me a hard task master."

Phelan began to laugh and added with a ribald jest, "The *harder* you are, the better, for soon she will learn to like it that way." Elrehan let the jest pass, sickened by the man's uncouth nature, though he kept it off his face.

"Then I shall take this opportunity to retire to my room and my work. Girl …" he called and Fea hurried to his side. He reached over, put his hand on her neck, and caressed her. As if on cue, Fea trembled and pulled away.

He frowned and Phelan chided, "It appears more training is in order."

"It does appear so," Elrehan growled as he grabbed her arm and hauled her out of the room, never once dropping the guise of a displeased trader. He shoved her through the door to his room and slammed it behind him. He let her be after that, settling into the chair by the fire, quiet. She left him to his thoughts, stripped out of her clothes and crawled into the bed for warmth. It was expected she would be there.

Once he sensed she was under the coverlet he looked over at her.

"You did well, but I felt for you on that cold stone floor."

"It is not as cold as Lord Phelan's heart. I fear my brother will take ill at the news of my loss, though I suspect his desire for revenge will keep him alive at least until he settles the matter with you. Of course, he will not be the only one hunting you …"

He shot her a slightly exasperated look and remarked, "Oh, of course! Now I will have half of all the Southern Isle men seeking my demise."

"Some of the women, too, for as you well know, we are as dangerous as a man."

"That brings me no comfort, Fea." A resigned look crossed his face.

"That means that the only one I dare share my bed with for the time being is you, for you have vowed not to kill me."

"I have, for the time being." She shot him a half-smile and burrowed under the covers and soon fell asleep. Elrehan remained by the fire, thinking, turning their situation over in his mind. He finally gave in to the need to rest and lay down beside the girl, still fully clothed.

Caewlin returned to the worker's hut in a daze. It was obvious something of a grave nature had befallen him and the clan fell unnaturally silent, concerned for his health. With gentle questioning Dubhan learned of Fea's fate.

"By the Gods," the young clansman murmured in shock. At one time he'd considered asking for her hand, before Isen made it known that the girl was his and warned all others off.

There was silence for a time and then Caewlin murmured, "I will survive if for no other reason than to see his blood on my sword."

"May the Gods make it so."

The grim news spread through the clan and eventually reached Aithne. She heard the tale of the iarel's sister and the slaver from one of the guards, retold in a ribald fashion that made her nauseous. She kept the shock off her face and sent the guard in search of the iarel, insisting he needed treatment for his leg.

Caewlin appeared as the other workers shuffled their way to the boats the next morning. His eyes were haunted and his skin pale. She treated the wound and gave him a herbal mixture to boost his strength. She did not have a chance to speak with him as the latest guard had a strong stomach. She watched her beloved exit the hut, knowing the profound grief he carried within him. She waited until she was alone and then allowed the silent tears to track down her face.

Pyrs's time in Kell was brief, he had managed only two days in the city before being captured. He did not mind that at all. Once he had learned where Morgan and his father were he made sure to attract the attention of the guards and the rest was easy. He knew the odds were in his favor that they would send him to the Field of Stones. Gossip on the street said that every ablebodied man went there. He gave his captors only token resistance to avoid being beaten senseless and then he was tossed in the back of a wagon, arms and feet bound, on the way to join his father and Morgan. The journey was cold and unpleasant, but he had the resiliency of youth at his disposal and the smug satisfaction that all went as planned.

Once the journey ended, Pyrs worked his way out of the back of the wagon. A guard cut his bonds and then shoved him in the direction of another that led the newcomers to where soup and dry bread awaited them. While he waited, Pyrs stomped his feet to try to warm up. He took what was offered to him, though the meal really didn't look that appetizing. He was apportioned a thin blanket and then pointed toward the workers' quarters. Once he entered the building he stood for a moment to allow his eyes to adjust to the dimly lit interior. Now came the difficult part, for he knew his presence would infuriate his father. He took a big deep breath and began his hunt for the two men he knew were sheltered within.

Belwyn and Morgan were in their usual corner, talking quietly, as they tried to ease the aching cramps out of their backs and legs. Pyrs walked up, sat down near his father and remarked casually,

"Good evening, father … Morgan." He sounded just like he arrived a bit late for dinner at his grandsire's holdings. It was the first time he had ever addressed Belwyn as *father,* but his sire did not notice.

Belwyn's eyes shot to the source of the voice and he growled, "Pyrs?" He grabbed the boy by his shoulders, jostling the cup in his son's hand.

"Careful, father, you will spill this fine soup they have given me and I doubt they will allow me another cup." He kept his voice light and cheerful, hoping to keep his sire from exploding in fury. It did not work.

"What in the Powers' name are you doing here?" Belwyn's voice was instantly wroth and Pyrs knew he was in for it. He looked over at Morgan for support and then inwardly winced. His friend was glowering at him, equally upset to see him in this place.

"I am here to rescue my father and my liege lord's heir," he said in lighthearted fashion, but the jest fell flat.

"Why are you not at your grandsire's?" Belwyn demanded. His mind raced. "Is your grandfather ill or injured? Why are you here?" He could not imagine Owain the Elder allowing the boy to undertake such a dangerous journey on his own.

"Grandsire is well," Pyrs replied and sipped on the now cold soup. He suspected that even if it were hot the taste would not improve. There appeared to be something resembling a root vegetable in the thin broth, but just what that might be eluded him.

"I need to know why you're here, Pyrs!" Belwyn actually lowered his voice and his son realized the man was only growing more irate. His father's anger grew in direct opposite to the volume of his voice. In that, Belwyn was the antithesis of Owain the Elder.

"I was told to come here."

"By whom?"

Pyrs dropped his voice to a near whisper, "The dragon."

That stopped Belwyn cold. Pyrs looked over at Morgan, who still appeared extremely displeased at his presence.

His father sighed, "At least your sister is safe." When Pyrs did not reply Belwyn asked, "She is still at Aldyn's, isn't she?" That was the last place he knew her to be.

"No." *No reason to lie, he'll learn it anyway.*

"Then she is at the Circle or at Aderyn?" Belwyn pushed, increasingly nervous.

"No, she is not."

"Oh Powers, tell me she did not come with you!"

Pyrs said nothing, confirming his father's deepest fear.

"She is *here*?" Belwyn glanced around the room as if he expected to see Gwyn standing nearby. He shared a troubled look Morgan when their eyes met.

"Near here. She is safe, father." He paused and added, "She was told to come south, as well."

"Powers," Morgan muttered, running his hand through his long hair in exasperation.

Belwyn's voice was even quieter now, revealing his deep fury. The realization that the Ancient One had put his only son in danger was disturbing, but to hear that his daughter was equally at risk was more than he could handle.

"I do not care *who* demanded she come south, you are her brother, Pyrs, and I expected better of you. Where you may have felt compelled to follow *its* orders, your sister is another matter. Do you have any concept of what these fiends do to young girls?"

Despite his acknowledgment that his father had a right to be incensed at this news, Pyrs's eyes flared and he answered a bit more forcefully than he intended.

"I am not a child, father! I was forced to watch people be burnt to death in Kell. Their only crime was to attempt to hide their daughters from the guards. The girls were found, stripped and sold in the market as you'd sell a spring lamb. One went to a brothel in Kell, the other to a merchant from Ilspath. They were no more than Gwyn's age." He paused and his eyes betrayed his horror at what he'd witnessed. "Yes, father, I am *very* aware of what evils they commit." He paused again, took a deep breath and then continued, "You must remember that Gwyn will never allow a man near her unless she wills it, for the magic she wields can kill with a thought. If anything, I'm the one in danger, not her. So please, be quiet, and let me savor this bounteous meal."

Pyrs dropped his eyes back on the chunk of dried bread in his hand and began to chew on it vigorously. He slowly let his ire pass. He'd been overly harsh with his father, but perhaps that was what he needed. He was no longer a child, no matter what his sire thought. Belwyn glared and then exhaled deeply. His son had grown up faster than even he had thought possible.

"I am sorry, son. I worry so much about you and Gwyn."

"I know, father. I worry as well."

Belwyn frowned for a moment and then it hit him.

"You called me *father*."

Pyrs looked up and a half grin appeared on his face.

"So I did and more than once I believe."

Belwyn put his hand on his son's shoulder. "Thank you." Pyrs only nodded. "Did you run away from Aderyn or did Gwyn spellbind your grandsire?" Pyrs didn't answer right off as he sucked down the last of the soup and set the wooden cup on the ground near his feet. He was pleased the dismal stuff was gone.

"We explained why we needed to come to Kell and he allowed us to leave with Dillan and Aindreas."

"Powers." It must have been a powerful argument to convince his father to allow the twins to leave the safety of Aderyn. "Dillan goes to the clan?"

"Yes."

"Good, I grow weary of toting rocks to please Lord Phelan," Belwyn muttered.

Finally Morgan spoke, "Your mother is here, working with the healers."

"What!" Pyrs's reaction was instant. "Why is she here? It is too dangerous for her! Why did you allow her to come here?"

Belwyn actually started to laugh and Morgan joined him, enjoying the irony of the situation.

The frown on Pyrs's face deepened and he demanded, "Why do you think this is so funny? She is not safe here!"

"Just like you, your mother did not give us a choice. She appeared out of nowhere," Morgan explained.

"Oh …" Pyrs murmured. He looked a bit chagrined and turned his attention to the dry bread in his hand, more to keep from feeling the fool than the need to eat the tasteless lump.

"I suspect Morwyn will be quite upset to learn you are here," Morgan added.

"No, she'll understand, I think," Pyrs replied hopefully and continued to try to eat his stale bread.

"Have you heard more about your Uncle Owain?" Belwyn asked, his mind switching to his brother.

"He is walking again, though slowly, and heals more each day according to the reports we have from Lord Bardyn. Uncle promised to write grandsire as often as his health would permit."

"Powers be Praised," his father murmured.

"Has there been any movement against Aldyn's holdings?" Morgan inquired. Pyrs nodded and choked down the last of the bread, equally happy to see it gone.

He dusted off his hands and then replied, "Yes, but it was easily put down."

"Was it Fercos?" Belwyn asked.

"Yes. Though I believe he would have moved faster if he had actually planned the assassination. As it was, he waited four full days before making his attack. He was the sacrificial lamb, not the real evil behind the scheme," Pyrs remarked.

"You see so deeply for a lad your age," Morgan said. The boy only shrugged. Such insights came naturally to him and so they did not amaze him in the least.

"Lady Aldyn was the one who killed Fercos, she put a arrow in his heart."

Morgan actually laughed at that. "By the Powers, my cousin is remarkable. That should warn a few of those vultures to mind their manners."

Belwyn nodded and remarked quietly, "Well, if that is settled then our liege lord will soon be making a call upon Lord Phelan's hospitality."

"He was delayed for a time, but no doubt is on the march at this point. His wrath and that of Aderyn runs deep and is not likely to be quenched without a battle," Pyrs commented.

"So it will come down to the sword, once again," Morgan said.

Pyrs nodded and then curled up and fell asleep next to his father.

"The Powers will keep him safe, Belwyn," Morgan remarked as his friend tucked his blanket around the sleeping boy.

"That is my prayer."

Pyrs missed seeing his mother, for she refused to wake him when she returned later that evening. When he awoke in the morning she was already at her duties. He regretted that, for he missed her constant and uncomplicated love. Judged old enough to move stones, Pyrs made the first boat over to the island. All the while his heart pounded for he felt the power of the place. He glanced at his father and saw the man nod faintly, acknowledging he felt it as well. Pyrs held his tongue, it was not yet time to explain why he and Gwyn were here. It would weight down his sire too much and he sensed the work they performed was stressful enough on his father's health.

The work proved backbreaking and endless. It was cold and the wind would whistle around them as they worked in front of the cavern or further down the side of the mountain. Pyrs was exhausted but he put that aside and strove to reduce the amount of labor his father performed. It was evident the exertion was slowly killing him, just as it was Morgan.

I only need have them hold on for a few more days, Pyrs thought, as he struggled to move a stone that weighed three times his weight. *Only a few more days.*

He felt asleep in the boat as it made its way back to the shore that night, lying in his father's lap, covered by his cloak. He awoke when the boat beached, woodenly trudged through the soup and bread line and then leaned, exhausted, against the frost-covered outer wall of the worker's building as he ate his meal. He had barely finished when his mother appeared. They embraced eagerly and her smile made some of the pain disappear.

"I have missed you, son," she murmured and held him close. Where other boys his age often spurned the need for affection, he did not. He held his mother tightly and thanked the Powers she was alive. As she sat with her arms around her son, Morwyn caught her husband's frown and knew their vulnerability disturbed him.

"Let the Powers work as They will, Belwyn," she murmured.

"I will try," he answered and then fell silent as he consumed his tasteless soup.

"As I thought, the fools intend to challenge me!" There was a note of glee in Phelan's voice as he read Bardyn's terse and threatening reply. He tossed the response on the table in front of him and poured himself more wine from an ornate golden jug inlaid with jewels. Gorsedd stood at his side, uneasy. His recent success at ferreting out the Northern lord's wife had earned him a place even closer to his master. Though others envied him, it was not recognition he relished. He had no choice, he dare not refuse his elevation in status. He now stood as Master of the Guard, for the previous occupant of that position had died at Phelan's hands only the week before. No one seemed to know what offense the man had committed, only that Gorsedd now held his rank.

"I want to strike at his heart, let Bardyn know I am no mere upstart lord that will wet himself and run when he comes for me." He was talking more to himself at this point than to Gorsedd. He pondered for a bit longer, continuing to take sips of wine. "Yes, that will do nicely." He set the cup down forcefully on the table and commanded, "I will need to go to the Field of Stones immediately. Make the arrangements."

"Yes, milord."

Gorsedd vanished to make the preparations as Phelan sat and thought through his options. A smile flitted across his face. Today's report from the Field of Stones contained good news; the workers were nearing the end of the excavation and the cavern would be open within a few days. Even more interesting, a new arrival at the camp was apparently the son of Belwyn, the Eldest of Aderyn.

"Yes, that would make a very big impression." He rose and headed to his rooms to fetch what he needed for the journey to the Field of Stones.

His host's parting words were not comforting – Lord Phelan would be journeying to the Field of Stones and planned to return in two or three day's time. When he did, he expected to collect his one night with the Southern girl.

"I am usually as patient as you, but not in this case. I have waited too long to possess her. She has come far in the two days since you bought her. In three more, I will be willing to risk having my throat cut to lie with her."

Elrehan knew better than to argue. He nodded in agreement.

"I will assure she is as ready as she can be." The object of their conversation was kneeling at his heels. She swayed a bit. He put his hand on her head and patted it as if she was a well-trained hunting dog. "She will provide you good sport or I will insure the punishment she will receive will be excruciating ..." he paused and then added, "but leave no marks." He felt her shiver under his hand.

His host laughed and then as quickly his face grew serious.

"What do you know of Lord Bardyn?" Elrehan's eyes widened at that, as expected.

"He is a man of honor, well-regarded by his people, one of courage and strength. His rule over the Eastern March has brought a period of prosperity." He did not overstate the case for he suspected Phelan knew this already.

"And what of Aderyn?"

"Aderyn has been joined with Bardyn for a very long time. They are an old house with two promising young sons to carry it forward."

"I see. Are you aware that I hold Bardyn's son as hostage?"

"I had heard rumors on the street. I also heard you have the Eldest of Aderyn in your prison, as well."

"I do, as well as his wife and son," Phelan replied, casting his final test before the man.

Morwyn and Pyrs? Elrehan steadied himself, sensing the trap. Using all his verbal skill, he replied in a casual tone, "Then you hold Aderyn in the palm of your hand."

Phelan nodded. The trader's reaction was not untoward. "Does it not trouble you that war is coming because of it?"

Elrehan shook his head. "No, for if Bardyn wins I will still buy and sell flesh."

"And if I win?" Phelan hedged, his eyes curious.

"Then I will expect to see your lordship in Ilspath and I will be sure to recommend the best wenches to your bed."

Phelan snorted and shook his head. "You are a man for profit, aren't you?"

"Rich beats poor any day, my lord."

"Rich you shall be, for I will return one of your gold coins for one night with this one," he said, looking down at the immobile figure at the trader's feet.

"You are very generous, Lord Phelan," Elrehan replied in a genial tone.

"To those I favor," the man replied and then limped out of the room to make his journey. The next few days promised to be full of small triumphs, each carefully crafted to extract the most pain from his enemies. That is what he lived for.

Once the door closed Fea shot her eyes up at the man who supposedly owned her. "I will not be with him, I will kill myself first!" she hissed in a whisper.

He helped her up and shook his head. "You won't have to, we will leave tonight."

"Perhaps that's what he wants! How do you know he is not baiting you to see if you will run?" she asked, concerned.

"I don't."

"Is the woman he mentioned your sister?"

Elrehan nodded. "Yes, she is my twin." He waited for a moment and offered, "We will make our way toward my liege lord's column, for by now he should be marching south with an army."

"Then there will be war," she said quietly.

Elrehan planned for this moment since the day he arrived in the seaport. He had spent considerable time wandering around the city just to obtain a feel for the general layout of its streets. He knew that if Phelan would not negotiate, Bardyn would advance to Kell and a siege mounted. It was his duty to scout the city and, in the process, secure a means for his escape from Phelan's fortress if the situation arose. He only needed a bit more intelligence to complete his plan.

He took Fea to the market that afternoon to buy her heavier clothes. No less than four men tailed them. They made sure he saw them.

"What do you think of this color?" he asked as he held up a green silky gown to Fea's face. He was not addressing her but the vendor in front of them. Fea's eyes were wide, for the garment was made of rich cloth and quite sheer.

"No, this color, for it will look very nice with her hair," the vendor replied and held up a black gown.

Elrehan thought for a moment and then asked, "What color does Lord Phelan prefer for his wenches?"

The vendor's eyes enlarged and he smiled knowingly.

"This color, sir, he is fond of red, the color of fire."

"Good, then give me one in the red and one in the green," Elrehan ordered and paid for the gowns. They were wrapped in light fabric and tied with thick twine. Elrehan handed the parcel to Fea and the light tingle of her waist chain rattled as she clutched it to her. The chain ran around her waist and then extended another six feet or so to his wrist. It was delicate but strong chain, and it announced that the girl was a very valuable commodity.

As he walked away he remarked to her so others could hear, "You must look pretty for your night with Lord Phelan."

"Yes, master," she said quietly, keeping the smile off her face. She suspected that Kell's lord had nothing to do with it the trader's choice in gowns.

He stopped at various stalls and purchased heavy leggings for Fea, thick rope and then some scented oil. He made her carry all of it, except the rope. As he turned to walk back toward the fortress he collided with a young man, one dressed in a heavy cloak and fur boots. They traded apologies and parted. None of his watchers realized a message passed during the encounter – help would be waiting for them tonight outside the fortress.

Elrehan did nothing out of the ordinary for the rest of the evening. He ate his repast and later, after dark, he asked Fea to put on one of the gowns, just so he could see how it looked. She chose the green one, knowing it was the color he preferred. He turned his back to allow her some privacy as she removed her heavier clothes. Once she had the gown in place, she indicated she was dressed. As he turned back toward her, his mouth fell open in astonishment.

"Fea, you are … you are so beautiful!" She actually blushed, for the gown clung to her like a second skin and only flared outward at the multi-layered skirt. It was cut low in the front and though she still sported bruises on her chest from the first trader's hand, she was beautiful.

"It is so fine, Elrehan, I've never worn such a garment as this. We have ceremonial clothes that we don for special holy days, but none are like this." The clan tended toward the practical when it came to clothing.

"That is fortunate, or you'd have been married years ago and I'd not have the chance to meet you," he replied sincerely.

She shivered. "Only, it is cold." She reached for her cloak and donned it, reluctant to remove the wonderful fabric that enveloped her skin.

He thought for a moment and smile spread on his face. "You have given me an idea, Fea. I warn you, it will be difficult for you, but it will allow me the final opportunity I need to plan our escape."

"Do whatever you wish, for I trust you," she said back lightly, smoothing her hand over the skirt. Her tawny hair curled over her shoulders and fell below her waist.

She is the most gorgeous woman I've ever seen, he thought.

"I like the green gown better than the red," he said, masking his feelings.

"I thought so."

TWENTY-TWO

h e strode outside with Fea in tow to one of the higher terraces, in plain sight of the guards. As expected, he was instantly challenged. He explained he was there to discipline his girl.

"How so?" the guard asked, wary. All of the guards had orders that the Northern trader was not to leave with his prize. He may go alone, if he chose, but the girl must remain. They knew it would be their heads if anything happened to the iarel's sister.

"She has displeased me. I commanded that she serve me in bed in a particular way and she refused. I have struck her and it has proven to only increase her rebelliousness. Rather than bruise her beyond reason, I bring her out in the cold to teach her a lesson," Elrehan responded calmly. Fea was on the ground near him, head down, appearing miserable. He walked a bit further, the two guards behind them, and then stopped, nodding.

"Here is perfect." He gazed down at Fea as she began to sink to her feet and ordered, "Up!" She struggled up and stood next to him, head down. He jerked back the hood in a rather savage motion, gave her a sneer and then commanded, "Remove your cloak."

"Master?" she asked, her eyes enlarging at the suggestion. It was brutally cold outside and even more frigid up on the terrace in the light wind. She could freeze to death in a matter of minutes.

"Now!" She hesitated for only a minute and dropped her cloak onto the snowy stones at her feet.

"Place your cloak under you and kneel there until I tell you to rise."

"Master, please, no," she began in a serious voice, unsure of what he intended. He raised his hand she shrunk back. This time the fear in her eyes was real and it knifed into Elrehan's gut. He sensed how easy it was for someone to learn how to dominate another. The feeling of power was a narcotic and each action demanded another as the brutality increased. He was finding it easier to prey upon her and that frightened him deeply.

Sensing he would not back down, she made a small cushion of her cloak and knelt upon it in the open air. She was already shivering, huddling in an attempt to keep warm. The thin green gown was useless in the cold.

"Good." He turned his attention to the two guards. As he had hoped, the gown and the woman had done just what he wished. Their lust flared while their attention level dropped.

"Powers, she is a beauty, just as they say," one of the said, his eyes not straying from the shivering form as he elbowed his fellow guard in a knowing gesture.

"She will do," Elrehan remarked. He turned back toward Fea and threatened, "If you move from the cloak, you will be punished." She nodded and then the shivers became more intense. Knowing the two guards were riveted for the moment, he made his way over to the side of the terrace as if to enjoy the view. Over the next minute or so he methodically catalogued the street layout, rooftops and other avenues of escape from Phelan's fortress as Fea shivered in the cold. Once he finished with the view he would walk to her, tug her face up to him to ascertain how cold she was.

"No, not yet," he muttered and then strode to the second side of the terrace to study that venue as well. He repeated the gesture twice more and by the time he had completed his survey, Fea was near collapse. Her violent shivers were more than even he wished and though he wanted to rush to her side and comfort her, he dare not. He strode back, noting the guards were kneeling only a short distance from her now, eyeing her every move. Only their fear of their lord and the trader's sword kept them from taking their pleasure with her.

"Girl!" he snapped. Fea's head came up slowly, too slowly for his liking. He grew anxious, concerned he had miscalculated how long she could tolerate the cold. "What is your purpose in life?" he asked. A slight murmur came out of her lips. "Louder!" he pressed, a knot of worry in his stomach.

"To … serve you … master," was the final reply as it filtered through blue lips. He snorted in apparent satisfaction.

"You answered too slowly. Consider yourself lucky I did not allow these two to have you here on the stones. Now rise!" Fea attempted to comply but her knotted muscles failed her. She rose only half way and another vicious chill overtook her.

"That will do," he murmured. In short order he scooped her up in his arms, collected her cloak and bid the stunned guards farewell.

He'd not even taken the time to remove her gown before placing her in the bed. He tugged off her boots and ran to stoke the fire. Her lips were blue, her teeth chattering as her violent shaking continued. He cursed himself as he placed the coverlet and then both their cloaks over her. He climbed into bed, under the covers, pulling her as close to him as possible.

"What … were you … dddoing?" she stammered, her eyes finally beginning to focus.

"I am so sorry, Fea, I misjudged how long it would take and you grew too cold." Her shivers were lessening and so he released his grasp and held her hands in his to warm them. "I was determining the best way for us to leave tonight." He had found the route and been pleased to see it would not prove that difficult for either of them to traverse.

"Ttthat is why you aaaallowed me to ffffreeze to dddeath?" she asked, her brown eyes beginning to snap. Her mind was clearing rapidly.

"You are still alive," he observed, immensely guilty. No matter how he apologized, it would be insufficient. She frowned at him and swore in her own language. He did not argue and gathered her into his arms again, transmitting his bodily warmth to her. She relaxed and then actually dozed for a time. When she woke she found his blue-grey eyes still watching her intently.

"How soon do we leave?" she asked. The cold was steadily melting out of her bones, though she suspected it would be some time before she felt warm again.

"In a few hours. I want the household to settle down before we begin creeping through the halls."

On impulse she reached over and kissed him in a tender fashion. He responded without thinking and the kisses only grew more passionate, their hands roaming over each other's bodies. Her passion easily equaled his and for an instant he forgot she was forbidden to him. He found his hand inside her gown, caressing her breast and reality intruded. He pulled back suddenly.

"No, this will not do. Your brother will have a maid returned to him, not a compromised sister."

"I do not wish to be a maid any longer," she said firmly. "I want you to make love to me." He was stunned at her candor.

He swallowed and shook his head. "It is not a choice you will be given, Fea. I will not harm you, even if you wish it."

"I would not consider that harm, Elrehan,"

A jolt of desire hit him but he immediately forced it down. "No, I cannot. Powers, I wish you were any other woman, for I would warm you in a way we both would enjoy, but I cannot."

"If they allow me to return to the clan, I will have marry a man I do not love," she said in explanation.

"Then do not marry him," he replied, as if it were that simple.

"I will have no choice. Isen seeks rank for his family and marrying the iarel's sister will give him that."

"I see." He thought for a moment. "Does he love you?

"No, he seeks only rank, though I do not think he will mind sharing my furs."

"No man would." Her eyes acknowledged the compliment

"I may be outcast or forbidden to marry within the clan. It all depends on so many things, for our traditions are changing as quickly as our situation."

He frowned, upset at this perverse form of clan logic. "If they will not accept you, then you should come north with me," he said sternly.

"As your slave?" she asked, a slight crinkle of amusement at the corners of her mouth.

"As my wife," he replied evenly. The surprise was hers this time.

"You would marry me?"

"Yes, I would, here and now, if the clan did not stand in the way of it."

"But what of your people, what would they think of the Southern wench you brought home to them?"

"They would think she is intelligent, beautiful and full of courage, just as I do."

"I see," she replied and fell silent. When she spoke again she made sure to look deep in her rescuer's eyes. "The Gods will send us along the proper path, Elrehan, though it may not be the one we would choose." He sighed and tugged her closer to him, savoring the feel of her body next to his. It was his only solace for he sensed his time with her drawing short.

As Lord Phelan made his way toward the Field of Stones, his most vaunted prize escaped his net. Fea and Elrehan crept out of their room in the middle of the night, unseen. Using his incredible memory for detail, he sent them in the correct direction to where they could exit the fortress proper and then skitter across the courtyard. There were two or three near misses as guards tramped by, but after a tense half-hour of skulking, darting and hiding, the pair exited onto one of Kell's city streets.

They rendezvoused with Elrehan's contact near Kell's west wall and the rope he'd purchased in the market proved of value. Fea and her trader levered their way down the outer stone wall, one slippery footstep at time, until they both reached the ground outside the city. His accomplice hoisted the rope up and walked away as if nothing had happened.

They found two horses waiting for them in the forest beyond the city. Their saddlebags were full of food, blankets and other provisions, just as Elrehan had planned.

"Perfect," the warrior crowed, allowing himself a moment of supreme satisfaction as he gazed back at the city walls in the distance.

"I can't ride," Fea said more to herself than him.

"What?" He wheeled around, sure he hadn't heard her correctly.

"I have never ridden a horse before," she admitted, her voice tense.

"You can't ride a horse?" he asked, amazed.

"No!" She snapped in irritation. He began to chuckle, softly, and that angered her. She demanded, "Can you steer a ship across the open sea using only the stars for a guide?"

He allowed that he could not. "I will help you," he offered. She shook her head and he decided he had no choice. "Sorry, but we have do this." He scooped her up and deposited her on her horse. Fortunately, she did not fight him, only muttered oaths in a low voice while glowering at him. He loosely secured the reins around the saddle horn and then dug in his saddlebag and came up with a length of rope. He tied it to her horse's bridle then mounted his steed, the rope in hand.

He advised, "Just hold onto the saddle horn and you will be fine." She gave him a blank stare and he pointed to the corresponding part of the saddle. He started forward and she paled noticeably. He stopped, immediately, concerned she would fall off the mount and injure herself.

"Grip the animal with your thighs, Fea, and I will do the rest. We will go slow for a brief time until you feel better about the horse. Then we must pick up speed, for Phelan's men will hunt us without mercy." She swallowed and did as he instructed. As promised, he did not push the pace as they set off across the terrain, leaving Kell and its inhabitants behind. She sat rigid for the first hour of the ride and then the inevitable cramps in her back and thighs forced her to relax. Elrehan allowed a small smile to flit across his face, though he knew she could not see it. By the time he rendezvoused with his liege lord he was confident the iarel's sister would be handling her horse as if she was born to it.

Phelan's precipitous dawn arrival at the Field of Stones made everyone uneasy, from the Master of the Guard to the lowest camp wench. His unplanned visits usually spelled doom for some unfortunate. The Master of the Guard was especially nervous, his reports to Kell were more glowing than the actual truth of the matter. Summoned out of his bed, his master put the same question to him again.

"How soon will the cavern be open?"

The Master of the Guard had no precise answer, however this time his superior did not shout at him or threaten him as he had in the past.

"Soon, you think?" Phelan's voice was surprisingly amiable.

"Yes, milord. We are over ten feet inside the opening and can feel the cool air of the cavern coming around the stones."

"Good. Let me know as soon as you can see inside. I must be there before the last stone is removed. Do not allow anyone to enter into the cave, do you understand?"

"Yes, milord," the man muttered. "I shall keep an hourly watch on the progress and send you sufficient notice."

"Good. Now bring me Lord Morgan and the healer, the one that is the wife of the Northern lord."

"Yes, milord."

The man bowed and scurried off to do his master's bidding. Intercepted at the shore, Morgan was marched back toward the camp right before he could climb into one of the boats.

"What are they up to, father?" Pyrs asked as he hefted himself inside the nearest craft.

"I do not know, son." Belwyn answered, his voice full of concern.

Morwyn was collected from her duties in the middle of applying a dressing. She did not even have time to finish tying the bandage. She gave Aithne a nervous look and followed the guard through the camp to Phelan's rooms in the guards' quarters, her heart pounding. This time she had the opportunity to study the tyrant who had ruined so many lives, for previously she had been far too ill to take stock of the man. He was not tall, nor heavy, but his dark eyes seemed bottomless and his face was a cold mask. He suffered from some withering of his right leg, it appeared, and it made him hobble at an awkward gait.

Such evil for one so young, she thought. Her senses whirled for a moment and she struggled to understand what it was she felt. *What is this?* She identified the sensation and it brought her no comfort. Phelan glanced in her direction for only a moment, as if she was of no import. He said nothing to her, waiting. Morgan entered the room shortly thereafter, escorted by two guards. He gave Morwyn a worried look and moved to stand next to her. Phelan addressed the captive lord first and he made no attempt to hide the smug tone in his voice.

"Your father has declined the privilege of paying ransom for you, as has Aderyn."

"My father has too much honor to agree to such a ridiculous demand," Morgan retorted.

"Perhaps. On the other hand, maybe he does not quite understand with whom he toys. I think that Lord Bardyn needs a lesson in manners, so I intend to deliver it. While I was tempted to cut off some part of your person and send it to your sire, I will not do that, for you are too valuable. However, the strong connection between the House of Aderyn and your father will work to my benefit – a sacrifice from *their* House will hit as hard as if I had harmed you."

Morwyn's throat grew tight. It was obvious why she was here.

"It has been noted that there are feelings between you and this woman and that her son, the heir to Aderyn, is in this camp. That was a bit of a surprise, I must admit, but I am willing to accept what fate gives me. I hear you care as deeply for the boy as if he was your own. I wonder, perhaps is that the case? Is that why Bardyn is so fond of Aderyn?" He kept his eyes on the pair in front of him, watching for any subtle nuances that might betray them. He was testing, probing them to find their weaknesses.

Morgan thought for only a moment and lied with great skill, "Yes, Pyrs is my son," he stated firmly. His eyes flitted to Morwyn and she gave him a look of gratitude. If Pyrs were Bardyn's grandson Phelan would be less inclined to harm the boy. She would allow the lie to stand if it meant saving Pyrs.

"No, I don't think so. The Eldest of Aderyn would not hold you in such high regard if you had bedded his wife and sired a son upon her, one that claims Aderyn's lineage. Besides, from what I hear, the boy strongly resembles his father. I suspect you and this woman may once have been lovers, but you are not the boy's father." His informant had been most helpful, a quiet presence in the workers' hut that carefully cataloged every conversation he heard. The lack of privacy had been a boon.

"Whatever you wish to believe."

Phelan snorted, "What I believe isn't the issue."

"It will not avail you to harm any of the House of Aderyn," Morgan replied solemnly. "It will only hone my father's anger toward you.

"I doubt it will stop his doomed march to the sea, but it will prove my resolve in this matter. Respect is only learned at the sharp edge of a sword." He paused and then grew a wicked smile. "I am not totally heartless, though, for I will give you an opportunity to choose – tell me which of them I put to death, the mother or the boy?"

"By the Powers, you cannot do this!" Morgan snapped, but Phelan ignored him and shook his head. Morwyn went white at the mention of her son.

"I can and I will. You choose which one dies or I shall. Be assured, one will be executed on the morrow."

"I will not be part of this lunacy!" Morgan shouted back, furious.

"Then I shall choose." Phelan remarked casually and gestured to a nearby guard. "Give me a copper and silver coin." The young guard fished through his pouch and then handed them to his lord. Phelan picked up an empty goblet off the table in front of him and displayed the two coins in his slim hand. "The copper coin represents the woman, the silver coin is the boy. That is only fitting as silver is worth more than copper and an heir is worth more than his mother." He tossed the coins into the goblet and let them clatter around inside as he swirled his hand. He shoved the goblet in Morgan's direction. "Choose."

Morgan snarled and lunged at the man, but the guards immediately restrained him. He struggled and cursed, but to no avail.

Phelan gave him a disappointed look. "How undignified. Now I must choose myself." He reached in to select a coin and then paused, eyeing Morwyn. She was shaking in fright, knowing this madman would kill her son without hesitation.

"No, I shall have the mother choose. That is very fitting." He extended the cup in Morwyn's direction and she realized the Powers had given her an opportunity to save her beloved son.

She pushed her fears down and replied, "I will choose."

He moved the cup above her line of sight so she could not tell which coin she would select, for they were of equal size. She murmured under her breath what sounded like a prayer and pulled out a coin, holding it between her shaking fingers. It was the copper one.

"Well, woman, you have just chosen to die for your son." Morwyn uttered another prayer as she dropped the coin back inside. Phelan handed the cup off to the guard without pause.

"I will meet my death as you command, as long as you vow Pyrs will be safe."

Phelan appraised the woman in front of him and nodded with a slight measure of respect. "He will be, providing Bardyn does not anger me further." He paused again as a bloodthirsty smile filled his face. "I can promise you that the manner of your death *will* become legend." At that he left the couple, their guards still in place.

Morgan began to curse again, loudly, his fury building by the minute.

"It does not matter," Morwyn assured him as she walked over and opened her arms to embrace him. Her hands were still shaking. His guards released him and he returned the embrace, clutching her tightly. Taking a last look at the cup that held the coins, she turned to leave the room. As she reached the door the young guard tipped over the cup to retrieve his money. He blinked in surprise for both of the coins were copper.

"Powers, how can that be? I gave Lord Phelan a copper and silver. What is this?"

Morgan shot his eyes toward Morwyn as she turned toward him from the doorway. The expression on her face told him what had happened.

"It does not matter, Morgan. Pyrs is the future of Aderyn and the realm." She paused and then added, "It is for the best."

Morgan's voice betrayed his distress. "You should have …"

"No, Morgan, it is done!" He nodded his acquiescence. She smiled, as if somehow satisfied, and left the room as the guards continued to stare at the coins on the table, talking amongst themselves.

"This is strange magic!" the young one sputtered.

"Can a healer do such a thing?" another one asked.

"If the Powers allow a mother's love to become manifest," Morgan replied. He stared at the coins for a moment longer and then asked, "May I keep them?"

The young guard nodded, "If you wish. They are ill fated in my mind."

The residual tingle of magic sparked the lord's fingers as soon as he touched them. It was as he suspected, Pyrs's mother had changed the silver coin to copper so that her son might live. Apparently, Morwyn did not have enough power to change the coin back to silver once the choice was made.

His mind searched for a means to withhold this knowledge from Phelan. It was up to him to silence the guards.

As he examined the coins he said, "We have been witness to an amazing deed, for the Powers have worked this magic to keep the boy alive." The guards traded uneasy glances. Morgan continued, "I ask that you not tell Phelan of this and allow Them to act as They will. It is best not to anger Them when the Powers manifest Their will so plainly." He forced himself not hold his breath and maintain a calm and reverent expression on his face.

"That was no mere conjurer's trick," one of the guards observed.

"No, it was not," the younger replied, a frown on his face.

Another said, "I have no desire to anger Them. It is of no matter how the woman was chosen, it is done." The other guards mumbled their agreement, in part fearing Phelan's wrath if he learned he was duped. He would never accept a divine explanation and the blame could easily fall on one of them.

The younger guard announced, "We will leave it be."

Morgan murmured his thanks and then placed the discs in his empty pouch. No doubt the tale would eventually be told, for it was so remarkable, but hopefully not too soon. He felt his heart twist at that, for it seemed so cold-blooded.

It is what she wishes, he told himself, but his heart did not stop hurting.

He was escorted to a spot near the workers' quarters and made to wait there, still surrounded by guards. He found it odd that he was not heading toward the island and when he asked about that he received no reply. Eventually he saw Pyrs, Belwyn and two other workers trudging toward him in the ankle-deep snow. Fetched off their labors without explanation, they were all wary.

"Lord Phelan says you are to haul wood," an older heavy-set guard ordered and pointed into the nearby forest. Pyrs shot his father a raised eyebrow but only received a shrug in return. They marched into the woods with a small phalanx of sentries around them, each man deep in his own thoughts.

Morwyn was sequestered in a small hut and not allowed to return to her duties. The hut was rather stark, but more comfortable than the workers' hut. She sat on the lumpy cot for a considerable time, then finally lay down and fell asleep, weary from the intense stress. As she slept her mind replayed the choice of the coin and this time it came up silver. She awoke with a start and then calmed herself, realizing it had only been a dream. As her racing heart settled back to a normal pace she offered yet another prayer of thanks. Her rudimentary magic had actually worked and the silver coin had changed. When the coin proved to be copper she kept her astonishment to herself, sensing her prayers were answered. It was Their intention that Pyrs survive.

In that I am content, she thought. For some morbid reason her mind turned toward the manner of her execution. Kell's lord seemed fond of the use of fire, though some of his victims had been drawn and quartered and others impaled on spikes. All his methods created the greatest amount of pain and suffering. She closed her eyes and prayed for a quick end.

The task was simple, they were to haul freshly cut and limbed trees out of the forest to the center of the camp. Once there, the logs were sawn into smaller sections and stacked under a tall wooden pole standing some twenty feet in the air. The men hauled, stacked, and then returned for another load. All day the work continued, tree after tree, log after log. The work was tiring, through less strenuous than manhandling huge boulders. The moment they began to stack in the wood in such a manner Belwyn suspected its purpose. When he looked over at Pyrs, he saw the boy's face was haggard. They caught each other's eyes and knew their foreboding was identical. They could very easily be building their own funeral pyre. As the morning slowly passed into afternoon and evening the pile only grew higher, now some ten-feet off the ground.

Morwyn had heard the sound of the wood being cut and then heaped up and had tried to calm her mind. When she was allowed to walk outside of the small hut that served as her prison, she saw that they had employed her husband and her son to help build the pyre. She prayed they had not been told why. *Phelan's cruelty has no end, for he makes them build the instrument of my death.*

When evening arrived, the older guard assigned to watch the healer brought her food to eat. It was not the usual fare, but cooked beef and fresh cheese. It was unmistakably her last meal.

To ease the guard's extreme discomfort she joked, "So there *is* a way to obtain decent food in this camp. Unfortunately is not a way that can be repeated."

He looked at her and swallowed, hard. Her humor caught at his heart.

She saw his emotions and said, "Sir, your kindness has been noted by me, and more important, noted by the Powers. I go to my grave in peace for my son will live in my stead."

A slight smile flittered across the guard's face. "You are a very brave woman, healer."

"No, sir, only one at peace with herself. I am sure when the flames are licking at my feet I will be less … composed." He nodded grimly and left her to her meal.

Belwyn learned of his wife's death sentence that night after the evening repast. When Morwyn did not return to the hut after dark he grew concerned, but no one would speak with him about her. He sensed a definite change of

mood in the workers' quarters, for small knots of clan were sitting by themselves talking in whispers. It was not their usual behavior and he noted that
they often looked his direction with sorrowful gazes.

He wanted to question Morgan, but Pyrs was nearby and so he kept his
worry to himself. It was later that night when a guard came to fetch him long
after his son had fallen asleep. As Belwyn rose from his blanket he caught the
expression on Morgan's face – it was one of profound anguish. He knew then
that his suspicions were warranted.

As he and the guard tramped across the campground he asked, "Where
are you taking me?"

"To your wife."

"Why is she not with us tonight?"

"The pyre you built today is for her on the morrow."

Belwyn's heart froze.

He found her inside a small hut, a candle and a small cup of wine on
a rickety table. The old guard had scrounged what he could find for the prisoner. Other had helped him with the simple provisions, for the woman had
treated more than one of them during her brief stay at the camp. They were
no more pleased to learn of her fate than her fellow prisoners were.

"You can only have a few minutes. Phelan will skin me alive if he learns
you have been together," the old guard said and Morwyn nodded. He closed
the door behind the couple and waited outside, praying he'd done the right
thing.

"Morwyn," was all Belwyn could utter before they embraced and began
to kiss each other with a passion born of desperation. When they finally broke
from the kisses, he opened his mouth to speak. She shook her head to silence
him.

"Just kiss me and hold me, for we have little time." He complied and
they lingered over another kiss and then embraced tightly.

"I regret not having spent our wedding night together," she said in his ear
as he felt the warmth of her tears on his neck.

"At least we had one night," he answered, trying to find some way to
comfort the woman. His heart was breaking, for there was so much he wanted
to say to her.

"I want you to marry again. I do not want my children to grow up without
a mother."

He pulled himself out her grasp for a moment and studied her blue-grey
eyes. They were brimming with tears.

"I cannot promise I will do that." He would not lie to her at such a
moment, even if only to give her solace.

"You must, if nothing more than for twins' sake. You need a wife,
Belwyn, one that will love you, bear you children and care for you. I will not

rest easy if I know you are alone." Her voice was pleading, begging him to continue living though she would not be at his side.

"I do not know if I can love again," he replied sincerely.

"You will, the Powers will send you someone." She pulled her wedding ring out from under her clothes and passed it to him, her hand quaking. It felt warm as he clasped his fist around it. "When you find a woman to love, wed her with this ring so that my soul will be within your new union." His strong reserve fled at this and tears coursed down his dirty bearded cheeks.

"You will forever be in my heart," he murmured and kissed her tenderly.

"Then I will be at peace," she said. She heard the door open and knew their time had ended. After one last kiss and embrace, they parted.

He said nothing as he was marched back to the workers' quarters, tears still on his cheeks. The bitter night air began to freeze them in place and he reluctantly wiped them away, as if once gone Morwyn would be no more. He entered the hut and worked his way through the slumbering bodies back to the corner where his son lay asleep. The iarel was nearby, awake, his eyes troubled, for he knew what the morning held. Belwyn slumped to the ground near his sleeping son, his strength exhausted. He felt Morgan's strong hand on his shoulder.

"I could not save her, Belwyn. I would have gladly taken her place or that of Pyrs."

"As would I."

He felt another hand on him and it was Pyrs, for the boy was not sleeping, but lying there, quiet, his heart in turmoil.

"Son …" Belwyn's eyes were awash in tears and he had no means to conceal them.

"I know, father, I heard some of the clansmen speaking about it, though they thought I did not hear them."

Belwyn pulled his son into a tight clasp and they wept as one.

TWENTY-THREE

orwyn faced one final indignity before execution. She knew that often they shaved prisoner's heads or cut their hair before they were burnt, but there seemed to be no point. She found the guard absolutely unmoved by her request that her hair be left intact.

"Why?" she asked for the second time.

"My master wants some of your hair to send to the Northern lord so he knows that you are no more," the young guard replied, no sympathy in his voice or in his attitude. He was the same one who had supplied Phelan the coins that had earmarked her for death.

Morwyn sighed and turned her back as he pulled out his knife. She felt a firm tugging motion as he cut her braid off at about shoulder length. Once she knew he was done, she reached up and undid the leather tie that held her hair in place and offered it to him. He secured the top of the braid with it and then left, his task accomplished. As she slumped down on the cot she realized how heavy her hair had been, for it had always been long since she was a child.

I should have cut it years ago, she thought ruefully.

As sunlight poured through the trees Morwyn began her morning prayers. She sent her thoughts to Gwyn and to her brother, Elrehan. A smile of memory crossed her face at the thought of him and she reminisced about their simple life near the village of Argel. The image of her mother floated into her mind and her voice was as clear as if she stood next her, chastising her young daughter for shirking the work at their homestead in favor of watching the sunrise each day. *I will see one more sunrise, mother, and then I will be with you and father.*

It was not the older guard who came for her, but the younger one who had cut her hair. His lack of compassion was evident, though it felt forced in some way.

"Out, woman, your time has come," he ordered.

She nodded, rose from the bed and calmly exited the hut. The walk to the clearing was full of wonder, for the threat of death seemed to alter her senses. They were heightened, almost as keen as the sensations she once felt during the Ritual of the Third Path. She could almost taste the cold crispness of the morning air as her breath billowed around her like a white veil. She heard the delicate scampering of a squirrel in a tree nearby and the solid crunch of the snow beneath her soft boots as the intense cold permeated them, chilling her toes. Even the weight of her cloak made its presence known. It was that rare moment of intimate contact with the world around her, the ultimate acknowledgement that all things are transitory and should be experienced to the full.

'Your days are numbered and few,' she murmured, reciting an ancient prayer she'd learned as an adept. *'View each moment as precious, each day as a treasure worth hoarding, for soon they are no more. Blessed Be the Powers for the Gift of Life and the Mercy of Death.'*

Lord Phelan made sure to array himself as if he were a king, for this day would prove to be one of his crowning moments. He sat on a massive wooden chair with a long table at his side in middle of the camp. A golden pot of warmed mead sat steaming in the cold air at his elbow and he had a heavy embroidered robe lying over his lap. His face radiated supreme omnipotence. Today his enemies would learn that he, Lord Phelan, the baseborn son of a merchant, wielded a power beyond their comprehension. He had barely rested the previous night, anticipation driving sleep away. His eyes wandered down to his heavy leather jerkin. Lying under the leather was the cold orb that made him master of all. He smiled and laughed aloud, the lifeless sound startling those around him.

"Milord?" the Master of the Guard asked apprehensively as he stood poised at his lord's side.

He waved at the man in a dismissive gesture. "Just enjoying a private jest."

"Yes, milord," the man replied, confused.

Morwyn found her executioner no less arrogant than he was the day before. He was sitting in a noble pose, his subjects behind him. As she approached her senses began to tingle again, pulling forward vivid memories. Her mind was more focused at this point and she was able to determine the source emanated from the center of the man's chest. She glimpsed a thick gold chain that disappeared beneath his jerkin. She frowned, for the last time she had felt this type of power was when she stood in front of the Ancient One with Belwyn at her side.

Her captor mistakenly thought her attention was riveted on her braid in his lap. He held it up in amusement and remarked, "Lord Bardyn will find it hard to deny your death when he holds the only part of you that remains in this world."

"More of me remains in this world than you might believe," she replied as she raised her eyes to his.

"If you mean your son, that can be changed," Phelan threatened.

She shook her head immediately, "That was not what I meant. I have come to know that I have made my mark in ways I had never thought possible."

He frowned in displeasure, for he had expected a frightened and pleading captive. This was not the spectacle he desired. He snapped an order to his Master of the Guard. The crowd began to murmur as Morwyn's family and the iarel drug themselves forward in a clattering of chains. The sight of her son enmeshed in the heavy shackles was almost too much for Morwyn to bear.

Phelan fears them, even now.

Flinging the lap robe away as he rose from the chair, Phelan dropped the braid on the table and poured himself a cup of warmed mead. He savored every swallow as if to show his contempt for the freezing, half-clad bodies near him. He set the cup down and addressed the multitude that stood behind him, whispering amongst themselves. He had decreed that every worker, even those who were ill, were to be in the clearing this day. All were there and their fear was palpable.

"Yesterday I gave my enemy's son a choice – he was to choose whether the wife of the Eldest of Aderyn or her son would perish today. He refused, so I allowed the mother to make the determination by choosing either a copper or silver coin. She chose the copper coin rather than the silver one and sealed her fate." A collective gasp flew through the crowd and more whispering ensured. Morwyn's throat knotted for fear he had learned of her ploy and she turned to catch a glimpse of her husband's face. It was a mask of distress. At his side, Pyrs was barely holding back his tears. She sent him a soft smile, that from a mother to her child. He was too overwhelmed to return it. Morgan was near him, his hand on the boy's shoulder for comfort.

"Bid farewell to your family, woman," Phelan ordered. As she was pushed toward where her husband and son stood, the lord tugged the heavy chain from underneath his jerkin and let the orb fall free.

The moment he uncovered it a wave of sensations struck her and she faltered on her feet. *Dragon power,* she thought. Her courage began to wither. She found herself with Belwyn's arms around her, despite the encumbering chains and then Pyrs joined them as well. She used what little magic she had and placed a healing spell on her husband, though he did not appear to notice her efforts. He murmured his love in her ear and then they kissed. She broke her embrace and her son took his place. He was weeping, unable to speak, overcome with emotion. She kissed his forehead, ruffled his hair one last time and then found herself in Morgan's arms. Their farewell was touching, for it obvious that the man cared for her deeply.

As she turned away she heard the iarel say, "Ask for the mercy of the Gods and They will take you home." She turned toward him and their eyes met. His strength flooded into her.

"Bless you, Iarel, for you have given me the courage to do this. May the Powers free you and your people." He nodded in respect as she was yanked away to stand in front of her captor.

She brought her eyes up to those of her executioner and asked, "Do not make them watch this, I beg of you. My death should be enough, but to make my family watch me perish this way is inhuman."

Phelan only snorted and threw a sideways glance at Morgan as he retorted, "I have been told I am a barbarian, so I shall live up to that."

It was Belwyn who replied, his voice even and strong, his last gift to Morwyn. "I will remain here until it is over, for she is my wife."

Phelan ignored him, keeping his eyes on the condemned woman.

"I promised you a death that would become legend and so you shall have it." He gestured and she was led out into the snowy field and pointed toward the mound of logs, as if she had no idea what it was there for. She gifted the young guard accompanying her with a disgruntled look.

"You mean I have to climb this?" He frowned at her attitude and pointed upward again. "The least you could do is carry me," she jested, "for once I'm up there I have to do all the work." He frowned more, her odd humor was disquieting.

"Go!" he commanded.

"Oh, very well," she murmured and began the ascent to the top of the pile, scrambling over the logs as she worked her way up. Once there she watched the guard follow her up, thick ropes in his one hand. She pulled the hood of her cloak up just before he secured her hands behind the pole with the coarse rope.

"You have no need to make them so tight, I have nowhere to go." He scowled at her for a moment and then, quite suddenly, his mask of indifference evaporated. To Morwyn's astonishment, he loosened the bonds.

"Thank you."

"I have a wife about your age," he explained, his voice now filled with compassion.

"Is she here with you?"

He shook his head in the negative. "I have sent her north to her people so that she will not come to harm."

"The time comes when she may return to you," Morwyn murmured.

The young man's eyes widened. "Then it is true that the Northern lords will march against us?"

"As true as night follows day. Lord Bardyn will not allow such evil to thrive. It will be your choice as to where you stand when the battle begins." The man murmured something she could not hear and then slowly retraced his steps down the mountain of logs. He gave her one last look from the bottom of the pile before marching back across the snowy expanse to where his lord stood, waiting.

Morwyn closed her eyes and let her mind go as the smell of freshly cut wood enveloped her. For a moment she was small child back at her home in Argel, watching her father cut fuel for the winter. She envisioned her twin brother as a small boy playing near by, scampering amongst the dried autumn leaves and giggling in delighted tones. The memory was overwhelmingly pleasant and a feeling of deep loving warmth encircled her.

I am not alone in this world or the next.

A quiet unease fell over the field as they waited for the command to fire the wood. It did not come. She saw Phelan grasp onto the small orb on his chest and hold it up in the air as far as the chain would permit. Exclamations flew from all sides. A few suspected what he held in his hands and they prayed there were mistaken.

"By the Gods, it is a Stone of Summoning," Caewlin murmured in the Northern tongue without realizing it.

"You speak our language," his captor observed, a small expression of respect appearing on his face. He paused for only a moment and asked the one question that had been burning in his mind since the moment he had obtained the orb. "Why did the iarel of the clan that held this Stone not use its power against me?"

Caewlin's eyes betrayed his amazement at such a query. "It is not for a mortal to summon one of their kind!"

Phelan gave him a look as one would a slow child.

"What a foolish answer."

"You cannot …" Caewlin began, his eyes widening in horror.

"I have already." Delighting in the moment, he began to murmur under his breath, watching the iarel's face the entire time.

"No!" Caewlin shouted as his eyes swept upward instinctively. An enormous shadow passed over the field, sheltering them from the morning sun in a long sweeping arc. A thunderous bellow cascaded around them, dropping some to their knees in abject horror. Morwyn closed her eyes and prayed, her whole body quaking in fright. Terror billowed in her mind and only her strong will kept it from issuing forth from her mouth.

"I must not show fear in front of my son," she murmured. Her heart ached knowing what her husband and child would witness and she begged the Powers to give her the strength to die with dignity. She sucked in deep breaths, struggling to calm herself, to force herself to think through the situation. *He does not mean to have the dragon devour me or he would not have the pyre built.* She gazed downward and realized there was no kindling at the base of the woodpile. It was then she discerned Phelan's plan and though it chilled her heart, she saw the mercy of the Powers woven within it. He clearly intended that the beast roast her alive with its fiery breath and that was why she was bound in the midst of the wood, to make the execution even more horrific for the bystanders. As she died, the wood would ignite and the blaze would soar into the sky. He said her death would become legend and he had not lied. It would be a hideous death either way, but she would perish more quickly by the dragon fire than if she burned on the green wood pyre. In that way the horror would be lessened for those she loved.

"I bow to Your Will," she murmured as she kept her eyes firmly closed. "I ask forgiveness for all those I have harmed."

As the beast worked its way down to the earth in slow arcs, many in the crowd tried to bolt from the clearing. The guards held them in place on Phelan's orders, beating some severely in the process. As he watched the creature descend, Kell's master decided he would not bother to set the beast upon the remaining clansmen hiding in the forest a few days to the east of the camp. In his mind that was a waste of power. He did not plan to restrain himself, however, when the Northern lords inevitably came to rescue their sons. Then the dragon would serve him well. He allowed himself a bloodthirsty smile and glanced up as the monstrosity landed some twenty feet from him, kicking up a whirlwind of stinging snow. For a moment he was disconcerted, for it was one thing to summon the beast and see it in the sky far above you and quite another to see it so near to him. It stood at least fifteen-feet tall with deep-ridged scales rippling down its back and onto its long tail. Its brilliant blue wings contrasted against the white snow. The heavy choking smell of sulfur hung in the air and made his eyes sting.

Phelan swallowed and took charge. "I have summoned you." The beast only slightly inclined its huge head, its multi-hued eyes deeply unsettled. "Destroy her with your fire," he said and pointed toward the healer perched on the mountain of wood. The dragon shook its head in the negative. "I command you, destroy her with your fire!" he said pointing in Morwyn's direction again. The beast knew it had no choice. The one who wielded the Stone had command of her and all of her kind who came within reach of the orb.

The creature slowly turned those deep eyes toward Morwyn and she realized it must be a female. She was not as large as the Ancient One, yet was as beautiful to behold with that same regal bearing and the immense depth that resided in her eyes. Morwyn realized that it was only fitting she died this way, for the last time she had stood before a ddraig she had survived his breath only because he had not employed the dragon's fire. This time no vision would be planted in her mind, only the searing heat as the inferno engulfed her. She gazed into those unending eyes, seeing her death clearly, and invoked all her remaining courage.

"May the Powers see fit to set you free of this man's yoke, ddraig." The beast eyed her and Morwyn swore she could see regret.

Be at peace, Morwyn the Adept, the dragon's voice came clearly back into her mind. **Be at peace.**

Phelan uttered a few sharp words and the beast could tarry no longer. The power of the orb made no other choice possible. It rose on its powerful back legs, inhaled and sent a scorching blast of dragon fire toward the bound woman. Morwyn dropped her head forward so the hood of her cloak would obscure her face as she died. An overwhelming sense of peace flew through her and she murmured one last prayer right before the blast struck. The pain was instantaneous, intense beyond her comprehension. She felt her clothes ignite, the smell of her burning flesh in her nose, her limbs shortening as the heat encompassed her. Her binding ropes broke free but she could not save herself. She screamed in immeasurable agony and the sound rose in intensity as the heat engulfed her. Her death cry ended as a high pitched wail.

Pyrs's impassioned shout was almost as loud as his mother's final cry. He felt strong arms pin him down as he struggled to rush forward to be with her.

"NO!" he shouted and continued to flail as his father and Morgan threw all their weight on him to keep him immobile. "No! No!" The blast of flame ended as the dragon's front paws returned to the ground with a jarring thump. The sound of a concussion rocked the clearing as the woodpile literally exploded from within. As pieces of flaming logs and dirt shot in all directions, even Phelan and his guards threw themselves to the ground. The dragon shielded its face with a wing as debris rained down upon them. One of the few that remained standing was the iarel, for he sensed a presence beyond the power of the beast.

A flare of red dived through the air and as he shielded his eyes from the smoky ash, he saw it wing its way toward the pile. The hawk sailed directly into the middle of the conflagration and then out the other side, smoke twirling in eddies behind its powerful wings. The bird rose in the air, gave a coarse shriek and then sailed off toward the sea.

"It is Her!" the iarel cried. "The Red Hawk has come!" He fell on his knees in reverence, joining all the rest who had flung themselves to the ground in either panic or homage. "She has come for the healer and bears her home!"

When Pyrs finally rose to his knees, the weight of the chains seemed inconsequential to him. His mother's death scream reverberated in his ears. His face was dirt-covered, a mixture of tears and soot from the fire. He felt strong arms around him and realized they belonged to his father. His whole body shuddered as he allowed the grief to consume him. Slowly the other onlookers regained their feet. The clansmen murmured amongst themselves and if Phelan thought they were speaking of the dragon, he was wrong. They spoke of the Red Hawk and how She had taken the soul of the healer to the lands beyond. Only the most important of their people were granted such a blessing and they knew they had witnessed a miracle this day.

"Well done," Phelan remarked to the beast as if it was a well-trained hound. The dragon snorted indignantly, a small blast of fire spouting out of its broad muzzle. Its eyes were no longer mellow, but narrowed and irate. Ignoring the lord it turned those eyes toward the man and the boy who had just lost the center of their world. There the eyes softened while it dipped its head in sorrow. The eyes grew unsettled again as it turned back toward Phelan.

"You may go," he commanded. The beast deftly shifted its weight, ran a few steps across the snow and then beat its wings, sending a blizzard billowing around it as it lifted into the air. It rose, steadily, circled in the air above them and then with a mighty trumpet disappeared into the morning clouds.

Eerie sounds continued to emanate from the burning mass of wood. Melting snow hissed and sizzled while the green wood split apart with sharp cracks. Morwyn's footprints had vanished when the mass disintegrated, it was as if she had never been. Belwyn was on his knees now, weeping, holding his son as the boy sobbed inconsolably. Morgan stood behind both of them, his hands on their shoulders as he watched the flames swirl into the sky. Tears tracked down his face in a never-ending stream. *Farewell, my love, may you find peace.*

Deeming the spectacle quite satisfactory, Lord Phelan tucked the orb beneath his jerkin and announced, "I promised her a death unlike any other and I think I have succeeded."

Morgan called across the short expanse of field in answer, "And what message have you sent? Her death will not change the course of things." His voice was cold and dark.

"Perhaps not, but it was most satisfying," Phelan replied as he reached down and plucked Morwyn's braid off the table. He turned to the young guard, the one who had secured the healer to the pole.

"Take a swift horse and deliver this to Lord Bardyn. No doubt you'll find him on the march toward Kell, full of bravado and righteous indignation. Tell him that the wife of the Eldest of Aderyn is no more and how that came to pass."

"Yes, milord," the man murmured, grasped the braid and left the field. The only remnant of Morwyn the Healer felt cold in his bare hands and it mirrored the feelings in his heart.

Phelan departed, his face full of a smile as he gimped across the field to his quarters. He left behind a burning pyre and a devastated family.

Aithne had watched the execution from the edge of the crowd, her hood down to mask her tears. She had never met Belwyn or his son, though she knew of the House of Aderyn. Her grief was strong for the loss of a fellow healer was always grave. Though she had to admit it was more than that. A few days after she arrived, Morwyn had asked if they had ever met in Kell, for Aithne's face looked familiar to her in some way.

"No, I do not believe so."

"Pardon, then, for your face is one I have seen before," Morwyn remarked and then shook her head in confusion.

"Many say that," Aithne replied, offhand, then let the matter drop. Now with the woman gone Aithne regretted not telling her why her face was familiar, how it was Morwyn knew of her.

"It is too late," she murmured and turned her troubled thoughts inward.

Despite Morwyn's execution the day was no different from all the rest, the workers went to the island to continue their tasks. Belwyn, Pyrs and Morgan went as well, still chained. Phelan did not trust them, even in deepest grief. Pyrs leaned over the edge of the boat, staring into the dark watery depths that called to him. He surmised that the chains would weight him down and he would sink before they could pull him to safety. He would be with his mother and the pain would stop. Caewlin sensed the boy's suicidal despair and bent over to speak to him in a soft voice.

"The Red Hawk came for your mother, Pyrs. She was winged home by our Goddess, an honor reserved for few in this world." The boy looked up in surprise. Caewlin nodded reassuringly. "She was highly favored and that brings me solace at this sad time. Let it bring you solace as well."

"I am so lost without her," the boy admitted.

"Your mother is safe now, for Phelan can never harm her again. As for you, it is best that you hone your grief and then wait for the moment when you can send it like a flaming sword into the throat of Kell's vile master."

Pyrs's grief-swollen eyes widened and he nodded faintly.

"You are right. I must live so that I can tell of my mother's bravery." *And fulfill the dragon's task.*

"It is a tale well worth the telling," Caewlin allowed and then fell quiet. He saw Morgan watching him and sent him a subtle nod. They knew they must keep the father and son alive, for grief could destroy as well as give purpose to one's life.

The journey up to the mountain was nearly impossible with the heavy chains. For some inexplicable reason Caewlin's were removed, so he assisted Pyrs and some of the other workers helped Morgan and Belwyn as they inched their way upward. Belwyn's color was grey and he had not said a word since his wife had died. Morgan feared for him more than he did Pyrs, for the young man's anger would no doubt keep him alive. Belwyn could easily slip into the darkness that had claimed Morwyn.

The hawk landed on a thick pine branch sending it swaying at its sudden arrival. Its keen eyes studied the smoke from the pyre as it coursed high into the air in endless streams. It could see the boats upon the water heading toward the island where it now rested. Turning its eyes toward the far side of the mountain it searched out the opening to a small cavern. It would go there and seek shelter. It shifted its hold on a small object in its right talon, insuring it was firmly in its grasp. Satisfied, the bird of prey leapt off the branch, sailed on a thermal and then began its descent to the sanctuary below.

TWENTY-FOUR

The entrance to the cave was finally cleared of stones except for one massive boulder firmly positioned at the very end of the passageway. It appeared as if had been placed there deliberately and then the other smaller stones swept down to cover the opening. The Master of the Guard swore a vehement oath. They were so close to their goal that he could hear the sound of dripping water inside the cavern. He pushed against the stone in infinite frustration rather than with any hope he would be able to move the obstruction single-handedly. It was far too huge for any of his men to move, even working in concert.

"Perhaps if we can tunnel around it we can send men behind the boulder and shift it outward," one of the overseers suggested. The Master of the Guard pondered on the idea and then shook his head.

"It is too big. Even if we had all the men in the camp push against it, it would not budge."

"This is ill," the overseer replied.

"For me, especially," the Master of the Guard replied in consternation. His lord would not be pleased. He took one last look at the monstrous stone and then began his trek down the mountain to inform his master of the situation.

Phelan's displeasure was muted by the knowledge that only one more obstacle stood between him and his prize. He immediately set off for the mountain to determine the magnitude of the boulder, lest the Master of the Guard's estimation prove overblown. After the lengthy climb to the site he stared at it and realized his servant had not exaggerated in the least.

"I am sorry, milord, we have no means to move it," the Master of the Guard admitted with regret.

Phelan nodded in agreement. "No, you cannot, but then that's why it's there. I will deal with it."

"Milord?"

"Clear the men from the mountain and I will deal with it."

"Yes, milord." Despite his utter confusion, the Master of the Guard gave the order nonetheless. It took over three-quarters of an hour for all the workers to hike their way back down to the boats. They clustered near the waterline, edgy, unsure of what would come next.

Pyrs knew precisely what lie behind that boulder for that was why he was here, why he had sacrificed almost fourteen years of his life in only a few days. He rubbed his wrists to ease their discomfort. Their chains were removed right before their descent, more to speed their movement off the mountain rather than as a gesture of compassion. His father was sitting on a nearby rock, pallid and silent. In the distance, the still smoking pyre was visible in the late afternoon air and Pyrs shivered at the sight. He pulled off his ragged cloak and put it on his sire's shoulders. Belwyn did not even react.

"Father?"

It was an eternity before he answered. "Yes?"

"Mother would not wish you this way." There was no reply. "Father, please …" That brought a response as Belwyn raised his head, evidently hearing the loving tone his son had used. It was so completely at odds at the furious young man who had almost impaled him in his wrath. Pyrs knelt by him, took his father's cold hands in his own, and rubbed them for warmth. "We must survive, father. Grandsire will come for us and this nightmare will end."

"I do not know."

"I am sure of it." The boy's voice brooked no argument and that seemed to pull his father out of his darkness.

"I will lean on you, son, for you have strength for both of us, at present."

"We will survive," Pyrs replied, keeping his own uncertainty hidden.

High above them the booming sound of the dragon reverberated and it terrified those gathered at the base of the mountain. Men fell on their knees, invoking their Gods, sure the flying death would strike at them this time.

"Powers, he summons the brute again!" a guard cried. The hulking shape of the beast hovered in the air above them and then it slowly descended to the ground near the mouth of the cavern. Very shortly thereafter an object flew off the side of the mountain and careening down its rocky shoulder, smashing everything in its path until it plunged into sea and sank beneath the surface. Though the stone did not fall anywhere near where the workers were gathered, it did not matter. The vast majority of the men cowered and prayed.

"The final stone has been removed," Pyrs reported. He had suspected Phelan would do this.

"What is it he wants so badly?" Morgan demanded, infuriated at this endless quest for Phelan's secret treasure that had cost men their lives. "Why go to all that effort?" Pyrs thought for a moment and knew the time was right. He glanced around and noted that they were alone at present, some twenty paces away from any of the other workers or the guards. The time for secrecy was at an end.

"More dragons," Pyrs replied in a level voice.

"What?" His father's voice joined the discussion as he rose from his rocky seat.

"It is a female dragon that Phelan holds in thrall. She has a clutch of eggs in the cavern. He will demand she fire them and then ..."

Morgan demanded, "How many more of the beasts will there be?"

"Eight more."

Morgan's face paled. "Powers!" Belwyn clearly saw their future. When the dragons hatched Phelan would launch them against his father and his liege lord. None of them would survive, all burnt or crushed into their graves. The image of Malvern's rent body surged into his mind and he shuddered violently.

"We are lost," he said with finality and sank back down on the stone.

"The situation is no worse than before," Pyrs remarked in a calm tone.

His father stared at him. "You knew this was going to happen, didn't you?"

"Yes." Pyrs shot a quick look around them again. They were still by themselves, the other workers huddled in groups pointing upward and conversing in excited tones.

Small glimmers of insight filtered into Belwyn's brain.

"Is that why you are no longer a child?"

"Yes."

"Is that why your sister is somewhere nearby?"

Pyrs nodded and then murmured, "To say more would be unwise."

A faint smile crept on his father's weary face. He put his arm on the lad's shoulder and sighed. "I should have known you had a plan." Pyrs allowed himself a small grin at that compliment.

"I do not understand!" Morgan retorted. Belwyn attempted to explain, if nothing more than to keep his friend from losing his temper and attracting unneeded attention. At present the guards were riveted on the top of the mountain, too occupied to keep the prisoners from speaking freely amongst themselves. That would end.

"Do you remember the journey we undertook to bring the twins back home?" Morgan nodded. "Do you remember *who* rescued them from Braen and *why* they were older than when they were abducted?" his friend asked cryptically. Morgan's frown deepened for only a second and then it began to vanish. *Gwyn said their youth was in trade for the knowledge they received.*

"I think I see." He paused and added, "Powers!"

"Then let us say no more until such time as it is needed," Belwyn said quietly.

"So be it," Morgan replied, sealing the conversation.

A low sigh of relief came out of Pyrs's mouth. Now his father and Morgan knew as much as his grandsire, and by extension, Lord Bardyn, for Owain the Elder was tasked to tell their liege lord what they faced. There was more, but the lad did not speak of it, for that would be revealed during the battle that loomed just days ahead.

Dillan's task proved difficult for reasons he'd not fully anticipated. The omens had prepared his way to some extent and so he found the remaining clan members reasonably eager for a fight, tired of skulking around the forests. Nevertheless, the capture of the iarel and his sister were twin blows that cut deep within the marrow of the clan. Caewlin was their center, the rock they'd clung to over the last few horrific years. He was gone now and very likely would not survive captivity. Fea's loss was an equally unimaginable blow.

"You are sure the iarel is at the Field of Stones?" Dillan asked Nerian. A nod returned. "Good, then when I return to Lord Bardyn I will recommend we attack there first." Pyrs had made the same suggestion and it appeared that was the best option. If the iarel survived the clan would rally to him. Dillan knew that Bardyn and his men were traveling down the old road until they reached Mersey, one week's ride north of Kell. His lord intended to swing east at that point, into the forest, though it would slow their journey. Then he would resume the march south, for staying on the main road invited an ambush and made it too easy for Phelan to learn the number of men he brought to battle.

Wielding his right as eldest of the iarel's family, Dillan called the clan together and told his people about Lord Bardyn and Aderyn. His words were received with a mix of skepticism and hope. His chief difficulty lay in that not all of his kin were pleased to see him, no matter the message he delivered. For the most part, the older men he had known were dead, except for Nerian. The younger clansmen viewed his return with suspicion, for he was a powerful contender for the position of iarel should Caewlin not survive Phelan's imprisonment. Given his lineage, Dillan could rightfully become iarel and not all were pleased by that possibility. More than a few voiced their opposition to uniting with the Northerners, Isen included. Fortunately, Nerian and Galen stood by him and within three days time they had roused the strongest of the clansmen to battle. Once assured that Nerian could keep their kin under control, Dillan and Galen rode northwest in search of Bardyn and his men.

News of Morwyn's execution traveled swiftly to Kell. The young guard, Nyle, made his way there first before striking out on the great road that stretched north toward Ilspath. He spoke only with Phelan's Master of the Guard, for he had served under the man before going to the Field of Stones. Gorsedd was the young guard's father-in-law.

"I cannot believe it. I knew it was likely the woman would perish, the lack of food and the cold claims many in the camps, but not in such a horrific way," Gorsedd said in despair.

"The man is a butcher," Nyle said evenly, knowing such a thing could have him executed as a traitor. They eyed each other for a moment and then

Gorsedd nodded his agreement.

"Pick out a fresh mount and take what provisions you need so that you can deliver our lord's heinous message." He had offered to substitute another man in Nyle's place, but his son-in-law had refused. They both knew the danger he faced.

"I shall." Nyle paused and then reached out to clasp Gorsedd's hand. "Please, tell Ena how much I love her."

"I'll pray for your safety." He paused and then said, "I would not think unkindly of you if you do not return to Kell after you have fulfilled our lord's task, but go to be with my daughter. That is where you should be, for she carries your first child within her." The young man's mouth fell open as his face flooded with joy. He murmured a short prayer of gratitude and heartily embraced his wife's father. His euphoria quickly faded as reality returned.

"I expect my end will come at the point of a sword after I hand the Northern lord the evidence of Phelan's cruelty."

"Perhaps, but do not sell them short. All I have heard," Gorsedd paused there but did not mention the source of his knowledge, "tells me they are honorable men." Benen had been most forthcoming about the Northern men. Gorsedd's mind lurched at that, for he would have to deliver the grim news of the healer's death to her friend.

"Honor is one thing, Gorsedd, righteous anger, another."

Nyle's father-in-law met him at the city gates as he rode out later that day. He and Gorsedd embraced and after shifting his eyes around to insure no one was within hearing range, the older man said solemnly, "It is our hope that a strong north wind will soon come to Kell, one that will clear the city of the stench that lives within it."

"I will relay your hope."

"Good. We will sharpen our swords and await the shift in the winds, for he will not find all are displeased with the change in climate." Nyle nodded, pulled himself back on his horse and galloped out of Kell's gates. He was on the main road toward Ilspath in a very short time, passing caravans and other small groups of travelers with ease, for new snow had not fallen in the last two days. He set his fears aside and rode in search of the Lord of the Eastern March.

Fea finally begged Elrehan to stop. It was late in the afternoon and they had ridden steadily since their departure from Kell. She now held the reins to her mount and had managed to handle the beast tolerably well for someone new to the task. He dismounted and tied his horse to a nearby tree and then noted she did not join him. Something appeared wrong and so he strode up to her horse with concern. A thin sheen of tears appeared in her eyes and she muttered through clenched teeth, "I cannot get down, my legs are too cramped and …" He gave her a gentle look and very carefully eased her down from the horse. He felt her shaking in his grasp and knew the tremors were from the spasms in her legs. He wrapped her in as many blankets as their saddlebags carried, gave her wine, food, and then let her rest without intrusion. It was some time before she spoke.

"I feel like a new bride after her first night in the marital furs." It was not her usual type of humor and he began to chuckle at the bawdy nature of it.

"No doubt worse, for there is usually *some* pleasure involved in one's wedding night." At that he grew a slightly wicked glint in his eyes. "I do hope you can adjust to the riding before your clan sees you, for your current state will nullify any chance I have of claiming that I left you untouched." She returned a similarly wicked grin and then drank more of the wine. The ache in her thighs was lessening, but her bottom was completely numb, as if she'd been sitting in a mound of snow all day. He knew exactly what she was feeling.

"It will ease the longer you ride. The worse day will be tomorrow."

"What?" she sputtered. She could not imagine anything could be worse than today.

"You will hurt like fury at first, for at this stage everything is sore. As the day progresses, it will improve. You may be able to dismount on your own by tomorrow night. The key is learning how to remain on the horse without clenching your thighs."

"I can only imagine there are blisters …" she began and then stopped. Crimson crept over her face, for that had been a bit too personal.

Elrehan was honest. "There may be. I had some the first time I rode for any length of time. As a warrior I dared not complain, so I held my silence and gnawed the inside of my cheek until it bled." His candor made her smile.

"You did not own a horse before you became a warrior?"

"No, I was a poor village lad and we could not afford a horse."

She blinked, surprised. "I had thought, given your manners, you were of noble origins."

"No, my father was a warrior and my mother a village girl. He left his position with Lord Bardyn when they wed. I learned my court manners from him. It proved very helpful when I sought service with our liege lord."

"I see. And yet, your sister married into nobility," she mused.

"She and Belwyn fell in love despite impossible odds. He did not care that she was of common birth, for love meant more to him than wealth or a title."

She grew pensive. "I sometimes believe our clan's laws are too rigid."

"All things change, Fea."

"*Some* things change," she allowed. He waited a moment and changed the subject, for he knew both of them were uncomfortable with the topic. He switched back to riding, which seemed relatively safe.

"Do not worry, your blisters will heal and you may grow to like horses." A light laugh came back to him. "I prefer the open sea."

He shook his head immediately. "I do not like boats, they wobble too much." She gave him a curious look and then a wide smile graced her lips.

"You are afraid of the water, aren't you?"

"No, not the water, for I swim fairly well. I fear boats and no land in sight around me. You could easily be lost forever on the sea," he murmured and involuntarily shivered at the thought.

"Then we are poorly matched, trader," she chided. "I dislike horses and you dislike boats. Obviously the Gods did not intend us to be together, for if you stay in the south you would spend considerable time in my brother's longship."

He frowned and retorted, "Well, if you came north with me you would have to ride the entire time."

"Then it is not to be," she said, amusement in her voice.

"Apparently not." He gazed at her fondly and placed a light kiss on her cheek. "I love you, Fea, daughter of Brecc."

"And I love you, Elrehan, crafty trader and son of Pyrs."

He pulled her into his arms, her head resting on his shoulder, and they remained that way as the sun set.

Lord Phelan wandered around the inside of the enormous cavern with a flaming torch in his hand searching for the treasure. He noted the burbling waterfall in the far corner, the shaft of muted sunlight that drifted downward from a crack in the vaulted roof scores of feet above him. None of that mattered. Finally, he demanded the beast tell him where the eggs were secreted, they were that well hidden. Clearly not pleased, the mother dragon angled a wickedly sharp claw toward a half circle of stalagmites. Employing his cane he brushed back a mound of dried leaves and beneath them were eight faceted orbs lying in a bed of sand. They were different from the one he possessed, larger and with more texture to them. He leaned over and stroked one. It was lifeless to the touch.

He snapped upright and snarled, "These are like the other one, cold and hard. Do not think to trifle with me!"

The spout of dragon fire that issued from the creature's mouth drew him up short, for it came unsettlingly close to his body.

They are not fired, mortal.

"Then fire them!" he commanded, not sure of what that meant.

All must leave, the beast hissed as she moved herself toward the rear of the massive cavern. Her tail drug along one wall in a long irritating scrape.

"Fire them!" he commanded again and this time he was rewarded by a thunderous reply that echoed off the cavern walls and nearly deafened him.

All will leave!

He glared at her and realized he had no option. She would do as he said, but apparently this was something private to the creature. He scowled and nodded his acceptance of her demand.

"I will go, dragon. How soon will they hatch?"

Soon.

"How many days?" he pressured. He knew Bardyn's army would soon be arriving and though this one dragon would be means enough to destroy his foes, a sky full of the winged menaces would be far more impressive.

The answer was immediate and sharp. **We do not reckon in *days*, mortal.**

Only with great effort did he hold his temper in check.

"I would be here."

No answer came forth as the creature glowered at him.

"Fire them," he commanded. He shuffled his way outside the cave and then ordered his men and all the workers off the island so the dragon would do his bidding.

Once assured the mountain was deserted, a figure shimmered out of nothingness and took form near a towering stalagmite. She had waited in the shadows, invisible, as Lord Phelan and his minions had come and gone.

It is time, the dragon said, its voice surprisingly gentle.

Gwyn nodded solemnly. Her small guardian was not at his usual post on her shoulder, but clung to her forearm, his eyes entranced by the sight of the eggs within the circle. He made a small noise and his mother answered it as she hoisted herself up on the rocks just to the rear of the nest. Gazing down fondly at the eggs, just as a human mother would her baby within a cradle, the dragon began to trill contentedly and the sound echoed off the moist stone walls.

Gwyn rummaged in her pack and pulled forth a small sphere, roughly the same size as the one Phelan wore around his neck. Dropping the pack to the floor she encased the sphere within her hands and began to murmur to herself, weaving a spell around the object. The orb grew, becoming multi-faceted like the ones within the nest, though this one was larger and seemed to glow on its own accord.

She felt her guardian's talons digging into her forearm more than she would have wished. She knew he was anticipating this moment as much as she was. A high-pitched humming sound echoed around the cavern followed by a blast of dragon's fire, different in nature than what arced toward Braen in the forest. This was the dragon's inner essence, carefully directed so that it curved around the facets of the eight stones as they lay in the nest. The dried leaves flamed and disintegrated immediately, though the eggs did not change.

The mother continued her labors and the glow of the fire began to dance off Gwyn's gown, her blue-black hair and the towering sandstone walls around them. Inexorably the eggs began to change color. Grey reluctantly gave way to black, then brown and then finally a fiery orange-red. The high-pitched whistling sound ceased and the echoes faded. The eggs made no sound, but glowed red, small eddies of heat rising off each one of them into the cool air. Gwyn took a cautious step forward, fascinated. Inside each egg was a young dragonet, completely formed, only requiring the life-giving breath of its mother to set it free. She studied the orb in her hand for a time then placed it in the center of the eggs, pulling her hand back quickly for the heat was intense.

"Will it be enough?" she asked in concern, her eyes lifting to gaze into those fathomless blue eyes above her.

Perhaps.

Dawn was only a short time away and that saddened Owain the Younger. He looked forward to the nights Aldyn remained in his bed. It was not every night, for she was careful, but those evenings she tarried were beyond compare. Since that first night his health had improved dramatically and Owain knew the real reason behind his recovery was Aldyn's love, in all forms. Whether it be her kind words when he stumbled, which was less often now, or when she coupled with him – it was her strong love that sustained him and gave him a future.

Where he had originally determined to ask her to wed him as soon as he could fall to his knees, he knew now that he did not want to wait any longer. Life was too unsure. But for a misstep in the forest or Gwyn's powerful magic, he would be dead. He glanced over at her as she lay sleeping next to him, her gorgeous hair fanned around her face like an auburn halo.

Now, he thought. He kissed her tenderly and continued his attentions until she woke. She readily returned his passion and though she was keen to be with him, he restrained himself. He reluctantly pulled himself away from her increasing desire.

"My love?" she asked, catching the strange look in his eyes.

"I am not going to do this properly, but I don't care. I cannot wait another moment." He paused and cleared his throat. "I ask, Aldyn, that you marry me. I would have asked you on bent knee, but there I would remain unable to rise, so this must do." His mind cringed at his verbal clumsiness. He hoped she would forgive him for his lack of eloquence on this most important of occasions. Her eyes were instantly moist and her voice loaded with emotion.

"I will marry you, Owain, for you are the only one in my heart."

A triumphant smile erupted on his handsome face and he replied,

"Good, that's settled. Now, where were we? Ah, yes, you were about to continue my healing, I believe." The sudden surge of desire in her eyes told him it would be a vigorous session.

Lord Corryn sat in his study and pondered his next move with all the skill of a tactician. The majority of his fellow lords, greedy though they were, lacked imagination and sheer guts. They were too fearful of losing their holdings to wager it all against the most precious treasure this realm offered – the circlet of the High King. Corryn was willing to risk it all, his life included, for he knew that Lady Aldyn and her holdings were only the beginning of a long and tedious fight to place himself on the throne.

The latest intelligence from Aldyn's holdings told him that Owain the Younger was walking again, his health improving daily. That was regrettable and though he much preferred that the man had died as planned, he would adapt. There was no word that Lady Aldyn found any of her suitors of interest, the youngest of Aderyn included. Corryn suspected that might change. He had learned she'd spent much time nursing the man back to health and that might tip the balance in her patient's favor.

Corryn held his tongue and bided his time, devising his scheme with care. He wanted every possible avenue of escape closed for the auburn-haired wench. The recent events in Kell had especially piqued his interest, for rumors were circulating that Lord Bardyn had marched south in an effort to secure the release of his son and the Eldest of Aderyn. That was splendid news as far as the devious lord was concerned. Two of his rivals would have their minds and the bulk of their men elsewhere while he set his trap for the lady. He could not have crafted it more perfectly if he'd tried.

"Patience, that is all it requires," he murmured to himself and settled back in his chair with a knowing smile. "Timing is everything."

"Hold there!" a voice shouted from their right and Elrehan quickly reined in his mount. Fea stopped just behind him, instantly on guard.

"We hold," Elrehan shouted back and made sure not to make any untoward moves. He prayed it was one of Bardyn's sentries, not one of Phelan's roaming bands of mercenaries. Given that he was still alive and not cut down from his mount the moment he'd been spotted, he felt reasonably secure. Five men appeared out of the cover of the forest, as if by magic. Two were archers, the rest had their swords drawn. They all wore the hunter green livery of his liege lord.

"Thank the Powers," he murmured and shot Fea a reassuring glance before returning his attention to the men around them. One of them marched up to his horse and grabbed the bridle. Fea, he noted, sat absolutely still, her face unreadable.

"What is your business?" another voice demanded, for apparently they did not recognize him dressed as he was.

"I am Elrehan, warrior in Lord Bardyn's service. I return to him with information regarding his son."

"Elrehan!" a voice called. "It is you? What are these clothes you wear? Have you taken to selling apples in the market?" The chiding voice belonged to none other than to Ulwyn, the Bard.

"Ulwyn, is that you?" Elrehan strained his eyes and watched as the young man appeared out from behind a gnarled oak tree. "What are you doing out here? I thought a bard's only thought was for food, drink and a warm fire." He gestured around the snowy landscape. "Surely there are none of those out here!" Ulwyn strode up to stand next to his friend's horse, a warm smile on his face.

"No, there is little comfort, I've found. Nevertheless, often one must forsake the enjoyable things in life just to remember how truly pleasant they are." He shot a gaze over at Fea and then just stared. She sat straight on the horse, her long blonde hair flowing around her shoulders. "Powers, you keep handsome company!"

"Fea, daughter of Brecc, meet Ulwyn the Bard, singer of songs, a man of much jest and a true friend."

"I am pleased to meet you, Bard," she said, inclining her head as she answered in the Northern tongue.

"The pleasure is more mine, milady, that is true," Ulwyn replied as he bowed to her in a sweeping gesture.

"Fea is the iarel's sister and we are late of Kell where Lord Phelan treats his enemies and his citizens alike."

Ulwyn gave him a knowing glance and replied, "So I've heard. Come, I will escort you to our liege lord. He has been most keen to see you."

"And I, him," Elrehan replied. He offered his hand and pulled Ulwyn up behind him on the horse. They set off immediately, Fea trailing behind them as her mount picked its way through the underbrush.

"Dillan arrived last night and he said that Belwyn and Morgan are at a place called the Field of Stones," Ulwyn explained.

Elrehan nodded his agreement "The news gets worse – Pyrs and Morwyn are there as well."

"What?" Ulwyn sputtered.

"I know, that stopped my heart to hear of it."

"Apparently your plan went awry."

Elrehan nodded. "My horse went lame on the road and try as I might, I could not buy another until I reached Mersey."

"That is ill."

"By the time I reached Kell they were gone."

"Well, you seem to have done all right for yourself. Is she married?" Ulwyn's musical voice asked in his friend's ear, careful to insure the lady did not hear him.

"No, she is not. However, I do remember that you are wed and have two fine children to call your own."

Ulwyn shook his head. "No, silly, not for me. You!"

"Me?" Elrehan played the fool just to bait his friend.

"You! She's gorgeous, far prettier than Lady Aldyn and that's saying something."

Elrehan did a quick mental comparison and realized his friend was right. "She is, isn't she?"

"Yes, indeed."

"She's an iarel's sister, she can't marry outside the clan."

A snort of derision came into his ear at that. "Nonsense, there is always a way around these things."

"There is. All I have to do is compromise her and she's most likely mine. However, that might occasion my hideous death at the hands of her kinsmen."

Silence fell behind him, followed by a long sigh.

"There is always a catch."

"There is. Since I do not intend to do anything of the sort, it appears she will marry someone else." There was a definite hint of loss in his voice.

"You're smitten with her, aren't you?"

"Yes, I am, and the feeling is returned."

"Powers!"

"So, infinitely wise bard, what should I do?"

"Marry her. What have you to lose? The worst that can happen to you is that they'll kill you, though from what I hear from Dillan it might take some time given how they seem to delight in settling scores. Nevertheless, all the while they're torturing you to death you can think of your beautiful bride and the passionate lovemaking you enjoyed on your wedding night." Ulwyn's voice was rather lighthearted given the seriousness of the subject.

Elrehan half-turned and gave his friend a disgruntled look. "You are not that helpful on most occasions, Ulwyn."

"You did ask."

"The Powers will sort it all out," the warrior replied, swiveling back around. He tried to sound confident, though his heart knew better.

"Let us hope They sort it out in your favor, my friend."

When they made the center of Bardyn's camp, Fea made sure that she dismounted her horse as a noblewoman would, with confidence and not a hint of discomfort on her face. Elrehan had been right, she had hurt for the first two days and then the third day's riding proved tolerable. She now felt reasonably secure on a horse and that was a gift from the Gods in her mind.

"Lady?" a voice asked and one of the guards bowed instantly. Her regal bearing was evident, even when clothed in heavy winter garments. Elrehan allowed himself a hidden smile. He knew she worried that some would treat her as a wench, but he was certain it would not happen. Between her noble demeanor and his sword, no one would dare cross that line.

"Elrehan! Powers, it is good to see you are unharmed!" His liege lord's voice called across the compound. He felt a slight swell of pride at that for he was highly favored by his superior.

"My lord," he replied as he strode to stand in front of the man. He instantly fell on one knee and bowed. He felt a strong hand on his shoulder and knew it belonged to Owain the Elder.

"You may rise, Elrehan," Bardyn ordered. Elrehan rose and found Owain at his side. They embraced without reservation.

"It is good to see you, we feared your mission had ended badly."

"No, it did not, thank the Powers. Unfortunately, though, my horse went lame and I did not reach Kell in time to help Lord Morgan and Belwyn. However, I was able to assist in another way." Elrehan turned at that and gestured Fea forward. "My lord, I wish to present Fea, daughter of Brecc, shield-maiden and sister of Caewlin, the Iarel of the Red Hawk Clan."

Bardyn gave her a kindly smile and moved forward to take her hand. He noted she did not bow and that was to be expected given her lineage.

"Welcome, Fea, daughter of Brecc. You are a welcome sight for we had heard of your capture. We feared … much," he said letting his voice fall off.

"I am well, Lord Bardyn, because of your warrior. He risked his life to keep me from harm," she said sincerely.

"Dillan will be pleased to learn you are safe," Bardyn said. "He has been to your people and roused them. The decision has been made to attack the Field of Stones first, to free the captives, and then we will march to Kell and confront Phelan."

"Thank the Gods. I pray Caewlin still lives."

"I am sure the Powers watch over him. But come, join us. You are weary and need food and rest," he replied, gesturing toward a large green tent in the middle of the encampment. Elrehan gave her a reassuring smile and they set off behind his liege lord and Owain the Elder as they crossed the short distance to the marquee. The bard paused for a moment and then set off in search of Dillan to tell him of Fea's arrival.

TWENTY-FIVE

*a*s they dined Elrehan made a full report to his lord. Fea sat next to him, with Owain the Elder at his liege lord's side.

Bardyn asked, his face full of worry, "Then they were alive the last you heard of them?"

"Yes, milord."

Owain the Elder sighed. "Well, that is some news. I am not pleased to hear that Morwyn is in the middle of this. Pyrs set his sights to be with his father, so that does not surprise me. Apparently Gwyn remains free and that eases my mind somewhat."

"Gwyn is in the south as well?" Elrehan asked, shocked.

"Yes, she was with her brother."

"Powers …" Elrehan muttered.

"It will all fall out soon enough," Bardyn observed. "You both need rest, no doubt, so go and we'll talk more in the morning." Elrehan rose, bowed and escorted Fea out of the tent.

Dillan was waiting for them. Fea gazed at the time worn face and was enveloped in his arms instantly.

"Grand Uncle!" They embraced tightly. When they separated his eyes were twinkling.

"Fea, I don't remember you being so tall!"

"I was a little girl the last time you saw me, Nuncle," she chided using the pet term she'd called him as a child.

"You are a child no more," he said, marveling at the beautiful girl in his arms. His face grew serious and he said, "We must talk."

She gave Elrehan a quick glance and then nodded. "Yes, there is much to speak of." He watched them walk arm-in-arm across the camp and then headed off to find some place to sleep. He knew he would be lonely tonight as she would not lie in his arms.

Dillan talked to Fea for over an hour, though not alone, for Galen was present. It was a gentle interrogation for they needed to know what had befallen her after her capture, The subject was delicate and it was not easy for any of them.

"You swear you are untouched?" Dillan asked solemnly. Her story about her purchase by both the first and the second trader had stunned him.

"I am untouched. Elrehan fooled Phelan by cutting his own hand and placing his blood on the linens."

"Yet you have been alone with him?" Galen asked.

"Yes, we have slept in the same bed, unclothed, for to do otherwise would have jeopardized our ruse. At all times I had to appear as his slave." She didn't want to discuss this, but she knew they had a right to the truth.

"That will prove a problem," Dillan sighed. "I respect Elrehan as an honorable man and what he did to save you was ingenious, but your kin will not see it as such. They will not believe a Northern man could hold his lust and not be with you."

"Then they are wrong!" she snapped back. Dillan shot Galen a look. The Saga asked the obvious question.

"Fea, do you have feelings for this man?"

Her anger melted and she sighed. "Yes, I am in love with him."

"What are his feelings for you?" he asked.

"He has offered me marriage if the clan will not accept me as I am."

"What do you intend to do?" Dillan queried, for the girl had a right to her own future.

A somber look covered her face. "I really have no choice, I must marry within the clan, providing a man will accept me. It is my duty. There must be an iarel and if my brother has passed beyond ..."

"You love another man," Galen said.

"It is my duty," she repeated, more to convince herself than the two clansmen seated near her.

"A duty that involves no love," Dillan observed, his eyebrow arched.

"Yes." Her voice was softer now.

"Are you really willing to sacrifice that much for the clan?" he asked.

A glisten of tears appeared in her eyes. "I have no choice," she said.

"You say you love this Northern man. Why did you not lie with him?" Galen asked as gently he could.

Fea replied honestly, "I wished to, for I knew that I loved him and that he loved me. I was willing to share myself with him, but he would not allow it, though he offered to marry me. He vowed he would return me as a maid to my brother and he held to that vow."

Dillan and the Saga traded looks again. The elder clansman cleared his throat and announced, "I will think on the matter and make my decision by morning."

Fea was startled. "Surely you will wait and have my brother judge this matter."

Dillan shook his head. "As eldest of the iarel's family I am within my rights to make such a ruling when the iarel is not present. Though I pray it is not the case, your brother may not survive, and this issue must be sorted out as quickly as possible for it has serious ramifications for our people."

"Is it your wish to become iarel if Caewlin does not return?" she asked coolly.

"No, I do not. However, there are clansmen who seek his rank and will do almost anything to acquire it."

"Isen, you mean," she replied with a frown.

"Isen, for one. He is not the only young buck desiring your brother's title."

Galen cleared his throat and explained, "Since you and Caewlin were captured there has been much discussion about whether to continue our war with Phelan. Some believe we should return to the isles even if the Northern lords came to our aid, for they think that Phelan will no longer pursue them now that he has your brother in chains. In essence, they want to abandon our enslaved kin to their fate."

"By the Gods!" Fea spat. "That is profane!"

"That is why it is so important that we settle the issue of your honor, Fea, for you are the best means to secure the rank of iarel given the situation. Some will try to take advantage of your supposed ruin to further their own ends."

"Is Isen one of those that would sail south and let our people perish?" she demanded.

"He did not say such a thing to me, only that he still seeks your hand and that he'll acquire it anyway he can," Dillan said, hedging. Isen had been most derogatory toward the iarel, something that had incensed the older clansman, though he noted the man had enough cunning to keep his plans to himself.

"I had thought he would not want me if …"

Dillan interrupted, "On the contrary, he has said he will marry you no matter your state. He seeks the position of iarel as fervently as any."

"Then it is settled," she said in a bitter voice. "I will marry Isen and my honor will be retained. He will, no doubt, be surprised to discover I am a maid on our wedding night, but I suspect that will not prove much of an obstacle to his ambition. If he is indeed one of those who would dare think to order the clan to leave its people behind, he will find his new wife a formidable foe." Her eyes glinted in anger. "I will not allow anyone to abandon our people."

"I will think on the matter, for Isen is not the best choice," Dillan repeated, unwilling to approve such a match. "Go and rest."

She rose and left the tent in extreme weariness.

"It will go ill if she marries Isen or any of his ilk," Dillan observed.

"Most likely. Where he would not speak plainly with you, I have heard he is one of those urging the clan to flee southward. If he marries Fea he will claim the position of iarel, even if Caewlin still lives, and then order the boats to sail. Not all will comply with his order nor tolerate his leadership, for he is not well regarded. I can easily see Fea leading the rebellion against him or anyone who does not seek to rescue our kin."

Dillan swore softly under his breath. "I do not know what to do! I cannot allow her to be hurt nor, more importantly, the clan to be fragmented."

"We both know it will be more than a split, Dillan, it will lead to internecine war," Galen replied. "In our foolish pride we will finish what Phelan began and the blood on our swords will be our own."

Silence fell between them for a time.

Dillan murmured, "Fea reminds me of Vala. She has the same inner strength and clarity of purpose." He looked up at that and for a moment his eyes clouded in memory. "I have been where Elrehan stands and lost the only woman I ever loved. Vala's marriage to my brother was never a happy one but full of strive and bitterness. He married her only to spite me. To see such sadness again ..." He fell silent.

"There is an alternative, one that will keep the clan together until the iarel returns to us." The Saga paused and then added, "You must marry her."

Dillan's mouth fell open at the suggestion. "Me? But ..."

Before he could refuse Galen explained, "Clan law allows for such a close marriage, for you are her *grand* uncle, not her uncle. You have the weight of authority to guide us through this difficult time until Caewlin returns. You will insist the clan fight Phelan, as they should."

Dillan allowed the suggestion to work through his brain. Reluctantly, he had to admit it had merit, for as eldest male member of the iarel's bloodline he would stand as a shield against those who would usurp Caewlin's position.

"Many will believe I do this to become iarel."

"Some will."

"They may try to kill me for it," Dillan observed, acknowledging all the ramifications of the Saga's proposal.

"They may, especially if you sire a child on Fea."

Dillan shook his head instantly. "That will not happen."

"The Gods can be rather precocious when they choose," Galen said with a smile.

"No, I am too old for children."

"If the iarel does not survive, you will become our new leader and there must be a son to succeed you," Galen murmured, sensing his discomfort with the topic.

The older clansman groaned, "This will destroy Elrehan, for it would be one thing for Fea to marry a clansman he does not know, but to marry me will seem like betrayal."

"Do you wish me to talk to Fea of this?"

A nod returned immediately. "Yes, please, for this will be difficult enough without seeing her tears."

"I will speak with her in the morning, after she has rested."

Dillan clasped the man's arm and murmured, "Bless you, Saga. You have offered wise counsel to this old clansman."

"We have much in common, my friend, for I am a man who knows what it is like not to be with the woman he loves."

"I think I like this work better," Pyrs muttered quietly to his father as they gathered dry brush in the forest. Around them most of the workers were gathering either brush or logging. The number of guards had increased, as if they feared the men might band together and try to escape despite their ill health. Pyrs suspected that very thought had occurred to the iarel.

"I wonder at its purpose, son. We have not gathered such an amount of dry wood in the past."

"Our lord and master wishes to keep us busy," Pyrs replied in a sarcastic tone.

"Perhaps."

Nearby, one of the workers remarked to another that he was sure that the strange glow emanating from the cavern mouth was gold and that the amount was so great that it reflected even across the sea. Pyrs shot his father a look and winked.

Belwyn whispered back, "If it were only gold."

Fea was distant all day, riding quietly next to her warrior as Bardyn's men progressed south toward the Field of Stones. Conversation was minimal and the longer they rode Elrehan's unease grew. She appeared to be physically distancing herself from him, though in a gentle way.

"Is there something wrong?" he finally asked.

"No," she answered, but the answer felt forced.

"I worry about you when you are so quiet."

"I am well," she answered, as if that would soothe him. It did not, but he let the matter drop.

That night he was summoned to Owain the Elder's tent. He found Fea, Galen, Ulwyn and Dillan waiting for them. Owain joined them only a moment later. Fea was nervous and Dillan's face was unreadable. Only the two bards appeared at ease.

Dillan steeled himself and addressed Elrehan directly.

"I have summoned you and Fea so that I may tell you what has been decided about her future."

"Surely the iarel is the only one to make that decision," the warrior began in protest, unsettled by this unforeseen development. He had felt sure the clan would wait until Caewlin was in their midst to discuss Fea's future.

"I am the eldest of Fea's kin until Caewlin returns. A decision has been made and she is aware of why I do this." There was a pause as if the older clansman was reluctant to take the next step. Finally he pulled out his dagger and offered it to Fea. He struggled to keep his hands from shaking.

"I, Dillan, of the Red Hawk Clan, ask that you guard this dagger, protect yourself with it and keep it as long as you love me. If you accept this dagger, you accept my proposal, and so doing you agree that you will share my furs, bear my children and tend to me all my years, no matter what the Gods set before us. In return I vow to honor you, keep you safe and love you as the Gods have always loved us."

"What is this?" Elrehan demanded in a sharp voice.

"Is there no other way?" Fea asked, strangely calm at the offer put before her.

"No, there is not. I am willing to accept you as you are and will not hold your time with Elrehan against you. I will protect you and your brother from those who would seek to become iarel and destroy our clan from within."

Their eyes held each other for a time and then she nodded in resignation.

"Fea, what is this?" Elrehan demanded again. Ignoring the older clansman for the moment, she moved to the man who held her heart, kissing his cheek gently as her hands lightly caressed him.

"It is the only way, Elrehan."

"I love you Fea," he said.

"This is not about love, but duty." He pulled her close and heard her whisper to him, "I will always love you." He buried his face in her hair as tears burned in his eyes.

"I know. I will only love you for all my days." She pulled herself away from him and returned to her place by Dillan. She wiped the tears out of her eyes and intoned, "I, Fea, daughter of Brecc, do accept your dagger and your proposal. I acknowledge that is best for the clan." She took his blade and sealed the bond.

"We will wed immediately," Dillan replied. He could sense the weight of Elrehan's dark eyes on him, knew the man's world had just ended. He had once felt exactly the same way.

"I agree."

Elrehan felt the earth open under his feet. He remained oblivious to anything else around him until he felt Ulwyn's comforting hand on his arm.

"Come, let us get you some warmed mead, you look pale."

He sought his friend's eyes and murmured, "If only that were the cure."

The wedding between Dillan and Fea occurred only a short time later. It was conducted near Owain the Elder's tent with the Saga uniting the curiously paired couple. The ceremony was short and to the point. Dillan promised to wield his dagger in Fea's honor and keep her safe for all her days. She promised to bear his children and bind his wounds. They drank a cup of wine to their health and then Galen sealed the rites.

"You are bound together until such time as the Gods tell us otherwise," he recited solemnly. Dillan pulled his new wife into his arms and kissed her soundly on the lips. Congratulations were offered for several of Aderyn's men had gathered to witness the nuptials. He smiled, pulled Fea to him and kissed her again, this time on the cheek, obviously enjoying himself. He shook hands with Owain the Elder and his liege lord, continuing around the circle of men until he finally stopped in front of Elrehan. He knew whatever bond they had forged over the years, both in battle and in friendship, was destroyed. The young man's face was immobile, his eyes fixed.

"Elrehan, I had no choice," Dillan said remarked quietly.

The warrior's blue-grey eyes arced up and his voice was deathly quiet, "If you harm her …"

"I will cherish her as if she is my own daughter," Dillan replied.

Elrehan's face filled with scorn. "Do not hide your lust behind such honorable words. Be honest, you only sought to bed her so you can feel young again," the young man spat back, still so quiet only Dillan could hear him.

"I am her husband and I will share her furs for my own reasons." Dillan's voice was now cold, his pride hurt.

"I pray she finds you *equal* to the task," Elrehan replied bitterly. He turned on his heels and vanished across the encampment, his mind in turmoil.

In honor of their marriage Owain the Elder granted the couple the use of his tent for their first night together and that had proved most comfortable. They were supplied wine, meat and fresh bread to dine on and left alone. No further sound was heard from them, so all assumed that the couple found their new marital state satisfactory. Men would jest amongst each other about how fortunate Dillan was to have such a young woman in his bed, but they made sure not to say a word if Elrehan was anywhere near to them. The expression on his face spoke of sheer devastation.

There were a goodly number of eyes on the couple when they exited the tent the next morning. Both seemed in good spirits and Fea was smiling, though guardedly. Galen greeted the couple and spoke quietly with them for a time. He gestured toward the white piece of folded linen Dillan held in his hand, the *bride cloth,* as it was called. The elder clansman shook his head.

"We have spoken and decided that no one, besides myself, need know of my bride's purity. Both she and Elrehan spoke the truth. To display this cloth would only declare that I did not trust her word. That is not the way a husband should treat his wife," Dillan explained. Galen arched an eyebrow and then nodded his understanding.

"As you wish." The couple walked to the nearest campfire and together they threw it into the blaze. The ultimate proof of Fea's honor burst into flames and vanished. Dillan gave her a gentle smile, kissed her cheek and then set off to find his master. He sported the appearance of a man who just had spent the night in the arms of a young and beautiful woman.

The Watcher sat just outside the circle, gazing outward. Its blue-faceted eyes saw far in the distance, beyond the mountain, beyond the camp below, deep into the woods hundreds of leagues away. Time was of no importance for the forests were far older than the mortals who dwelt within them. The trees sang of their antiquity, the stones of their endless quest for warmth. The Watcher saw it all without any veil. It watched and waited, for it was Sentinel to the small lives that sat entombed in the shells at its clawed feet.

For two days the workers collected kindling and cut logs, as per their master's orders, without a clue as to why the task was deemed so important. During that time Phelan paced his rooms, eagerly awaiting the summons from the dragon. It did not come. Finally, in a fit of pique, he took a boat to the island and made the time consuming hike up to the cavern alone. He knew it was not a sound move, but he could wait no longer.

The fiery glow within the cave had diminished since the mother originally ignited the eggs, but still it nearly blinded him. Once his eyes had adjusted, he peered at the contents of the stalagmite semi-circle. All eight eggs were there, intact, glowing deeply within. Heat plumes billowed off them in the dense chilly air of the cavern. His fascination with the eggs kept him from seeing the menace that stood watch.

Why are you here? the voice hissed. Phelan started and glanced around, expecting to see the mother dragon glaring at him. She was not present, the massive space in the back of the cavern was empty.

"I came to see if the eggs had hatched," he replied, buying time. His eyes kept searching. Given the shape of the cavern it was difficult to determine from which direction the voice had originated. Frustrated, he turned back to gaze longingly at the eggs and there he found the source of the cold voice. Just outside the ring was a large beast, a dragon, pure white in color. It was about the size of a man and it seemed to shimmer in form. Its folded wings were nearly iridescent, tucked neatly near its body. The beast's fathomless blue eyes caught his and pinned him down. Around it swirled a haze of fire, floating around the beast as if it were composed of a myriad of tiny flames. He grasped onto the Stone of Summoning, intent on using it.

The Stone will not bind me.

He hesitated for a moment just in case the thing was lying.

The Watcher does not lie. The speed of which the beast could read his mind alarmed him.

"How soon will they hatch?" he asked, switching tactics as he carefully placed the Stone back down on his chest.

A strange hissing laugh echoed throughout the cavern.

You mortals, so tied to time, for you have so little of it.

"How soon?" Phelan demanded, his anger climbing. He disliked being taunted by something he could not control.

Sooner than you will wish.

He picked up the Stone again, feeling its weight against his palm. He decided it was worth the chance if he could actually bind the thing to his will. As he opened his mouth to issue the command the apparition in front of him began to increase in height, swirling upward, ten, fifteen, twenty or more feet. Its brilliant cold eyes bore down on him and a sense of unreasoned fear overwhelmed him, robbing him of his ability to speak. He turned and stumbling out of the cavern into the night. His terror did not diminish until he reached the shore where two of his guards waited for him by the boat.

"Milord?" one of them asked, sensing something was amiss. His master did not answer but climbed into the boat, his face a dark cloud that threatened violence.

Owain the Elder sat in stunned grief in his tent, his trembling hands tenderly cradling the coal black braid, the only part of his daughter-in-law that he would ever hold now. On one side of him was Lord Bardyn and on the other, his Master of the Guard.

"Tell us all of it," Dillan commanded to the young man on his knees in front of them.

"I shall, sir, for it is a grievous tale." Nyle had finally found Bardyn's column and after a considerable delay, he was permitted to speak with his master's enemy. He delivered the message as ordered and waited for the sword to fall. It had not. Bardyn was furious, but kept his wrath in check. He marched Nyle to another tent where he fell to his knees in front of an older, solidly built man. It was easy to see the man's resemblance to the captive Northern lord whose wife had perished only a few days earlier.

His father, no doubt, Nyle told himself. That made sense.

As commanded, he told the tale of Morwyn's execution leaving no part of the story hidden. He related how Phelan had made the mother choose between herself and her son. He spoke of how she came to die. As he talked he watched Owain the Elder's face the entire time. When he spoke of the dragon and Morwyn's fiery death, the man's jaw tightened in anger and tears coated in his eyes.

"Why?"

Nyle's eyes were tormented as he made the explanation. "He wished to send the message that your son, grandson, and your lord's heir are alive solely at his whim. I know him well, for I have served him for two years. Phelan will kill anyone if it suits his current fancy. He is a butcher who cannot be satiated." Nyle had cloaked his heart in the mantel of indifference, trying to shut out the horrors that had encompassed him almost daily. His sham of indifference perished on the fire with the healer. He could no longer stand and watch as so many died at his master's fancy. Ironically, he realized, his prick of conscience had come too late, for no doubt these men would have him slain. It was not honorable, but given what he had just told them, totally reasonable.

"Elrehan must know," Bardyn murmured. Owain's head came up at that and he nodded in slow motion.

"This will destroy him, especially after ..." He did not finish his sentence as Dillan was so near. "I will tell him." He rose from his seat as if two more decades of age now resided on his shoulders and left the tent, the braid still clutched in his trembling hand.

"There is one more message," Nyle began and then hesitated.

"Then deliver it," Bardyn's voice was somber.

"Not all the citizens of Kell are under Phelan's spell. They suffer at the hands of that monster as much as the clansmen. There are those who wish you to know that should you march on the city you will find allies within, for they are tired of watching their daughters sold like cattle in the market and their sons burnt to death in the city square."

Bardyn raised an eyebrow. "I see." He shot a glance over to Dillan and then back to the man on his knees. "How many men does Phelan have at the Field of Stones?"

"One hundred and ninety, the last time a count was taken," Nyle answered instantly.

"And in Kell?"

"Less than that, perhaps one hundred and fifty. His power derives from fear, not strength of arms."

"How many people reside in Kell?"

Nyle thought for a moment and tried to guess. "I would think about three thousand. The number changes daily given the ships in harbor and the market traffic."

Bardyn said nothing for a time, pondering on what he'd learned.

Finally, he commented, "It might be said that only a fool would attack a man who wields a dragon as a weapon."

"The Powers will stand with you, for They cannot support such evil as Phelan brings into this world," Nyle replied honestly. Bardyn shot Dillan another look and a faint nod came back from the clansman. All the while Nyle's eyes were level, staring forward.

"So, what shall we do with you?" Bardyn inquired.

"I am at your mercy, my Lord." His voice and expression spoke of resignation to his fate.

"I cannot allow you to leave, you have seen our camp and know our strength."

"No, that would not be prudent," the man replied.

"Who do we notify of your death, messenger?" Bardyn asked in a controlled voice. Only a slight intake of breath marked Nyle's reaction to the death sentence.

"My father-in-law, Gorsedd, is Phelan's Master of the Guard in Kell. You can tell him once you take the city, providing he survives."

Bardyn marveled at the man's composure. This was clearly a messenger who had not enjoyed his task, but had felt remorse, even guilt, at bringing the news of Morwyn's death to them. He was not merely some minion fulfilling his master's order. This man had a conscience and that had pricked Bardyn's interest. He gave Dillan another long look, moved to stand nearer to the clansman and then mouthed, *Test him.* He made sure Nyle was unaware of the nonverbal exchange.

"Deal with him," Bardyn ordered aloud and stood aside.

"Yes, milord," Dillan replied, a knowing smile on his face. "Make your peace, messenger, for your choice of whom you serve has cost you your life."

"Phelan's guilt is my guilt, for I was the one who cut off her braid and bound her to the log pyre," the man replied. "I did not think to survive this mission."

"I see." Bardyn gestured at Dillan and the man pulled his sword from the scabbard.

"Pity you are not Phelan," Dillan remarked dryly as he raised the sword above him.

The doomed man uttered a short prayer and remained on his knees waiting for the killing blow. He heard the sound of the sword cutting through the air. He steeled himself and refused to flinch, his last thoughts on his wife and their unborn child. The sword flashed by the end of his nose and still the pain did not come. He heard the sound of the blade sheathed and with a jolt, he realized he was still alive. He frowned and ran his eyes back and forth between the two men.

"Playing with me is cruel, something my master would do. Just slay me and be done with it!" His voice was angry but there was no fear in it. With a slight nod from his liege lord, Dillan offered the young man his hand so that he could rise from the floor. His thumb was bloody, the ritual offering to a naked blade.

"You didn't even wince when the sword went by you, that is impressive," Dillan remarked. Nyle's anger melted into pure confusion.

"I don't understand."

Bardyn explained, "You are obviously an honorable man for you showed deep remorse at the death of our kinswoman, nor did you deny your guilt in the matter. I need men such as you to aid us against Lord Phelan. I will treat you fairly, providing you do not betray me. If you prove false and all this has been some sham, Dillan's sword will have your life's blood on it the next time."

Nyle blinked in stunned surprise. It took him a moment to realize what had happened. He fell on one knee and offered his service to the Northern lord without hesitation.

"Rise, then, and go with Dillan. He will find you food and a place to sleep. Your sword will be returned to you."

"Thank you, my lord," Nyle replied, still in shock. He bowed yet again. As he followed the clansman out of the tent he murmured, "Powers!"

Dillan allowed the man a moment to compose himself. Nyle's courage had impressed him and he decided to take the young man in hand.

"I am Dillan, of the Red Hawk Clan, Master of the Guard to Owain the Elder." He stuck out his hand and Nyle took it readily.

"I am Nyle, son of Kern."

"You'll find things are different in our lord's camp, young man. We are quite capable of making war, but that is not our preferred way. Lord Bardyn is a decent and honorable man. He expects his men to be the same."

"So it shall be," Nyle replied.

Only Owain the Elder and Ulwyn were present when Elrehan learned of his sister's death. He sat in shock for the first minute, holding the braid in his hand as if it was an illusion. Finally he pulled it up to his face and anointed it with his unrelenting tears. Once before he had believed his dear sister dead at Belwyn's hands, a fallacy born of the warrior's enchantment. This time there was no mistake for the braid was proof she was gone. He grew grey, his eyes fixated on the object in his hand. Owain sent for the healer, concerned the man may collapse under the twin blows of his sister's death and the loss of Fea to another man. The healer prepared the grieving warrior a sleeping draught and made him drink it. He remained silent from the instant Owain told of Morwyn's fate until he fell into a deep slumber.

"I will stay with him," Ulwyn offered, his eyes wet with tears.

"Thank you," Owain replied and touched the bard's shoulder in comfort.

"I fear for him, for he has nothing to live for."

"Your fear is valid, Bard. The Powers have struck him in both his heart and in his soul. It will be up to us to help him find a reason to carry on." Ulwyn nodded and settled on the ground next to his sleeping friend. He tucked the blanket around Elrehan's shoulders, but did not remove the braid from his fingers. It was all the man had left in this world.

The Watcher sat immobile. It saw the face of a bereft young man as he clutched a braid of hair to his face in fathomless grief. A single tear tracked down its pure white face, luminescent in quality. It fell onto the ground near the eggs and existed for a second before vanishing in the withering heat.

A life as short as a mortal one, the beast thought as it sensed the death of the tear. *So short, so short.*

Bardyn's column was on the march at dawn the next day. Nyle found himself stationed near Dillan, no doubt so the clansman could keep an eye on him. He did not need anyone to tell him who the solemn, grim-faced young man riding at the side of Lord Bardyn was. His hair was the color of the braid he'd brought from the Field of Stones, his eyes the same as the woman he'd bound to the pyre.

Dillan noticed the focus of Nyle's attention and he said quietly, "It is her brother that rides near our liege lord."

"I thought so. His grief is so deep."

"She was his twin sister, his only living kin."

Nyle throat seized and he choked on the thick feeling of guilt. He had led her to her death, did nothing to try to save her from such an end.

"I …" he stopped, unable to voice the feeling of revulsion that spread through him. He tried again, "I was the one who led her to the pole and tied her there. She jested with me that I made the bonds too tight, as if she had some means of flight."

"And what did you do?" Dillan asked, curious.

"I loosened them, it was all I could do." His admission was one of deep remorse.

"Then you did something. Others would have taunted her or ignored her request. You tried, at least."

Nyle shook his head. "I did not do enough."

"That is for the Powers to judge, son, not you."

"I did not do enough," the young man repeated and fell silent.

Nerian was pleased to find the longships were in good condition, though more than one had a nest of woodland mice in them. The clansmen carefully scooped out the nests and placed them beneath some nearby bushes, superstitious about angering any of the Hawk's fellow creatures. They cleaned out the ships, checked them for soundness and the news was good.

"All of them are seaworthy, Nerian," one of the clansmen reported.

"Then let us go to sea and turn it red with the blood of our enemies," he commanded. A ragged cheer rose from the eighty or so men, women and young boys who had gathered near the shore. As each of the ships launched, he handed a feather to the first man on board so that it could be attached to the mast. Devona had blessed their mission and he knew it would end in victory. To think otherwise was not possible.

"We head for the Field of Stones. We must arrive at night and moor behind the island so that Phelan does not know of us. There we will wait until the Northern lords attack our enemy and then we will join the battle."

"His dragon will see us," one of the men warned. Nerian paused, knowing this objection would be raised. They had already learned about the beast and its role in the healer's execution, for they kept constant watch on the Field of Stones. The use of the dragon in such a way had stunned the clan and fomented even more dissent in their ranks.

"What of it, Nerian, what of that beast?" another man asked, one of those who had spoken in favor of sailing away from the danger.

"The Red Hawk will protect us," Nerian replied.

"She did not save the healer from death!" another protested.

"It is Her decision who lives and dies," Nerian replied. There was more murmuring and then a cool voice carried past all of the conversations.

"The Red Hawk protects those who follow Her," Devona intoned, her eyes dark and incensed. She knew the years of starvation had worn down the clan's taste for battle and she was keenly aware of the politics behind the murmuring. "It is for each of us to make our own choice – go to war or stay and cower in the woods like small children." She strode to the closest longship and was helped aboard. "Who will go with me and rescue our people from bondage?" Only a moment passed and then her challenge was accepted as shouts erupted around them. There was a surge toward the longships. As he took his place beside her, Nerian gave the Wise a look of deep appreciation and whispered, "Bless you, Wise."

"We will prevail, for we do Her will." He turned and watched the ships load.

Once they were ready, he shouted into the morning air,

"The Clan of the Red Hawk goes to war!"

TWENTY-SIX

Caewlin, Morgan and Belwyn kept a wary eye on the piles of dry branches as they grew over the two days of work in the forest. Each was thinking the same thing, though none put voice to it – the amount gathered would make a massive bonfire. It wasn't until late during the second afternoon that the piles of branches were transferred to big stacks near the workers' quarters.

"Powers," Belwyn murmured and he caught Morgan's eyes. The iarel stood nearby and his face was stern.

"He wouldn't …" Morgan began.

"Without a thought," Caewlin replied. He dusted his hands off on his filthy breeches and uttered a prayer he was wrong.

"Tonight?" Belwyn asked.

"No, I'd do it in the morning so that if any escaped the inferno they could be easily spotted and cut down by the guards." The men fell silent and continued to haul the dry limbs to the brush piles, knowing in their hearts they were stockpiling fuel for their own funeral pyre.

"You are sure of what you heard?" Caewlin pressed, talking so quietly the other clansman had to lean very close to hear him. Usually the clan kept a respectful distance from the iarel and so it unnerved the man to be seen in such close proximity to their leader. They stood awaiting their ration of food.

"I swear it. A guard said that the Northern lord should be here very soon, if not in the morning. Phelan has set his sentries to watch for them." Caewlin sighed and that made the clansman even more nervous. He had thought this was good news.

"Thank you, you've been a great help," the iarel said, touching the man's shoulder in appreciation. "You've given us hope when we needed it most." The man gave a slight bow and moved forward to collect his meager repast.

That night they gathered the most senior men and women of the clan and talked out the problem. The situation was grim. Phelan would no doubt order his men to pile the brush up against the building and fire it sometime over the next couple of days. It would be his final blow against the clan as Lord Bardyn arrived at the Field of Stones. Solutions were tossed around and most were not very practical. They had no weapons of any sort, only the clothes they wore. The old boards of the building were weak at some points, but they needed a way to batter their way through them so that a large number of their people had a chance to escape. Once outside they'd be caught in the conflagration and if they survived, they'd face the swords of their enemy.

"He will not allow me to die this way," Caewlin remarked as he stared off into nothingness.

"I doubt you are immune to this end, Iarel," Morgan replied politely.

"He will make me watch, for in that way he can torment me more." Morgan did not contradict him, for the iarel was probably correct.

"Our problem is that we have no notion of when our liege lord will arrive," Belwyn commented. "If we are to survive, it will have to be on our own merit."

"Why don't we uncap the well and see if there's water in there?" Pyrs offered. He'd been sitting and thinking through the situation while the adults talked.

"What well?" Morgan asked, confused. Caewlin understood the boy immediately.

"Of course, the one in the other hut. It's covered in stones at present, for the water is not healthy to drink."

"That's fine, but what will a bit of water do against the inferno Phelan will unleash?" Morgan asked, confused.

"If we use the stones to batter at the walls and wet the blankets as protection against the fire, we might have a chance," Pyrs ruminated.

"That's a bit farfetched," Morgan replied.

"Pardon me, *my lord*, but do you have a better idea?" Pyrs shot back in a sarcastic voice. He saw his father's eyebrow raise but no rebuke came from that direction. Morgan was frowning at his tone.

"*You* are bit too much like your grandsire on occasion, far too much cheek."

A wide smile lit up the lad's face. "Thank you, I shall take that as a compliment." Morgan groaned and gave in, knowing he'd never win the argument.

In the end, it was the best plan anyone could devise and though full of holes, they accepted Pyrs' scheme without delay. They spent over an hour toting rocks to uncover the well, lining the stones along the south wall of the building. After he had hefted a particularly large stone, Pyrs cracked,

"First I haul rocks for Phelan and now for the iarel. My life is in a rut." He caught Caewlin's eyes and a weary wink came his way.

"Remind yourself of that the next time you grumble about all the studying you're forced to do," Belwyn replied in a joking fashion. Pyrs sighed to himself. The warm and comfortable rooms of Aderyn, full of books and laughter, seemed so far away now.

The well cap took some prying and a lot of manpower, but it finally came off. Pyrs leaned over and peered into the depths, praying the well was not dry. It was full of brackish water, a decaying mat of debris floating on the top of it. The stench was nearly overwhelming.

"Perfect," he muttered and lifted his head back up out of the well and gulped down a lung full of reasonably fresh air. He gave the anxious adults around him a positive nod.

"Thank the Powers," Morgan muttered. He had feared there would be nothing there.

"Once the guards are settled for the night, I'll start telling my people what we face," Caewlin said. Before he began his rounds he took two of his most trusted men aside and gave them an order that if anyone attempted to leave the quarters before morning, they were to be subdued, or slain if necessary. There were spies in his midst, for Phelan knew too much of what went on in the quarters solely by chance.

"Our fate lies in your hands," he added and the two men soberly gestured their understanding.

He began his rounds, talking to his people in small clusters, explaining what the morning might bring. There was frank fear on their faces, but when he told them of their plan, they reined back their apprehension and stoically followed their leader's orders. There was no sleep that night, for the clan moved around quietly like mice, tugging the stones within the hut and lining them up along the south wall. It had been Pyrs suggestion that they consider attacking that wall instead of any one of the others. Bardyn would no doubt attack from the north and so it would be best to flee toward the sea and not between two armies. They inspected the wall carefully for loose boards, any means of egress that, when enlarged, would allow them to flee the building once it was fired. Women donated whatever extra skirts or petticoats they had and made a pile of them near the well. Near dawn all the blankets were collected, ready to be dipped in the water. Two lookouts kept watch through the wider cracks in the walls. The mood was somber, but at least they felt they were doing something that might increase their chance of survival.

Bardyn's forward scouts found the exact position of the Field of Stones right after sundown. He ordered his men on, fearing that if Phelan knew they were this close he might execute his hostages. His men trudged on through the snowy forest, the waxing moon providing some slim light. On their master's orders they covered their shields and cloaked themselves to hide any glint of steel that might give indicate their presence. The army moved as silently as the terrain would allow and there was no conversation. As luck would have it, two sets of Phelan's sentries were caught from behind by Bardyn's stealthy scouts and they fell dead in the snow without a sound. Slowly and with great care the army moved forward and though they were weary, no complaint was heard. Elrehan was still in the saddle, though Bardyn's healer had suggested that he lie down in one of the wagons to rest. He had refused and continued to ride, oblivious to everything but the need to stand in front of Lord Phelan and drive his sword into the man's heart. Then he would seek out where Morwyn had perished and grieve there, perhaps never to rise. He saw no future, only a past full of pain. Inside his shirt his sister's braid itched against his skin, a grim reminder of all he had lost.

"Well?" the impatient lord demanded. He had waited what he deemed an unacceptable length of time to learn his enemy's precise location. The sentry at his lord's feet was quaking. His physical state was not from the frantic ride to reach his master, it was because the Northern lords were closer than any of them believed.

"They are but a third of a league away," the man stammered. How their enemies had marched through the night and evaded their sentries, he did not know. He only knew he was the unfortunate one to bring this dire news to his lord. He continued to shake from fear.

"What?" Phelan hurled up from his chair near the fire. His morning repast was half-eaten and his mood labile.

"We lost a number of our sentries, milord. We only learned of the Northern lords' position an hour or so ago." He kept his head down, praying.

"How many of them are there?"

"A hundred or so, milord, as best as we could tell."

"Excellent!" his master crowed and pounded his fist on the table in exuberance rattling the serving dishes. "That is perfect!" He strode past the man and flung out a series of orders in rapid fire to the Master of the Guard. All the while the sentry remained on his knees, hoping his master would not burn him to death as he had others who had brought him ill news. Phelan marched by him again and sat back down to his meal, obviously pleased with the news. He stared down at the figure at his feet, surprised he was still there.

"Is there anything else?" he demanded.

"No, milord."

"Then go! I wish to eat my meal in peace."

"Yes, milord." The man rose from his feet, his knees knocking, and fled the room. Once he reached the safety of the guard's quarters he collapsed on his bunk and started crying in sheer relief.

Orders were barked out and the hut's inhabitants began to hear the sounds they dreaded; the dragging and scratching of branches being placed up against the outside walls. The iarel glanced over at one of the lookouts with an inquisitive look and the young man nodded grimly.

"Just once I wish I was wrong," Caewlin murmured and returned to the delicate task of keeping his people from mind-numbing panic. Once the preparations were nearly complete, the clansmen and the Northerners paused for a moment of prayer to their respective deities. Caewlin began with a plea to the Red Hawk for the safety of his people and for the Gods' assistance in defeating their enemies. His voice was strong and it carried throughout the building.

"As foretold in prophecy, the sixth clan has come to us and joined us in bondage. They have shared our tears of sadness and grief, stood by us as our enemy continues his futile attempt to destroy us. I ask the Red Hawk and the Gods to which we owe our lives, to give us courage, strength of arms and cunning so that when all is done, we will live to tell the tale of the Red Hawk Clan." He bowed his head for a time and then looked over at Belwyn.

The warrior cleared his throat and began, "Life is a precious thing, more precious than even we are aware. Only when strife and death encompass us do we stand still long enough to realize how precious our days truly are. Phelan, in his murderous ways, has taught us that lesson a thousand-fold. I ask the Powers to aid us in our battle and to grant us the right to once again have a life full of peace."

"May They make it so," Morgan murmured, sealing the supplication.

Silence claimed the hut as each worker offered their own individual prayers and then without a word, they returned to their tasks.

The summons came without warning and a noticeable ripple of tension flowed through the building – Caewlin, Morgan and Belwyn were to exit the workers' quarters immediately. Belwyn realized that Pyrs's name was not amongst those called.

When there was no immediate exodus the Master of the Guard growled, "Come on, move yourselves!" Belwyn tugged onto Pyrs, intent on insuring he came with them. A hefty guard immediately pushed the young boy back.

"No, not him, only you, your lord and this Southern rat," he said, pointing toward Caewlin. Belwyn paused, his heart in turmoil.

"Go, father, we will see each other soon," Pyrs said in a light voice. He did not overplay the moment, concerned the guards may take a closer look at the interior of the hut and the alterations they'd made. All the while the clansmen remained huddled in their small groups, the blankets quickly redistributed and hanging around their shoulders as if nothing was amiss.

"Stay well, son," Belwyn replied, placed a comforting hand on the lad's shoulder and then followed the other two men out of the door into the chill morning air. His eyes immediately sought the five-foot high pile of brush all along the side of the building. The point of a dagger pressed against his throat before he could speak.

"Keep it quiet, we don't want to startle the vermin, now do we?" his guard menaced. A glance out of the corner of his eye confirmed that Morgan and the iarel were in similar straits. Once their hands were bound and gags in place, they were marched away from the hut. Above the gag, Belwyn's eyes were rampant with worry.

Lord Phelan sat astride his horse and savored the moment. He had actually relished the usually difficult task of tugging himself up on his mount. This time it was different, for today he would prove that a gimp-legged illegitimate son of a merchant was a man who ruled without mercy. Today the clans would fall and the Northern lords, in their infinite arrogance, would watch their sons die at Phelan's command. If he was honest, he had to admire their courage and their rather ingenious plan. Where the bulk of the fighting would occur at the line between his men and the Northern lords, he had divined that the clansmen would have their own scheme. He had prudently placed two sentries on the island with strict orders to watch for longships. It was only logical to assume his enemies would attempt a two-pronged attack. His sentries had proven their worth. A shield reflecting off last night's setting sun passed the message that there were ships heading for the island, no doubt to lie in wait for the Northern lords' assault. Through a prearranged code Phelan even knew how many ships his enemy brought against him. This morning the island was shrouded in fog, something he found odd given the cold weather. Though it might prove a hindrance to his plans, in the end it would not matter for the dragon would fly no matter the weather. He'd heard no word from the beast and assumed the eggs were still incubating. That, too, was of no concern, for one adult monstrosity would be quite enough for his plans.

He glanced back at the workers' quarters and the large pile of brush surrounding the building and he allowed himself a slight smile. The fire would lure the Southern men out of their ships in a futile attempt to save their kin where they would be slaughtered to the man as their kinsmen writhed in their final death throes. If all went according to plan, it would prove to be the biggest pyre he would ever build.

From his position on the horse he did a quick sweep of the camp, pleased with the defensive fortifications now in place. He'd purposely left an open area between the forest and the center of the camp to funnel his enemies to him. In the very center of that space was an iron stake, the vantage point from which the last iarel would watch the final destruction of his people.

"Ah, what a day," Phelan sighed as he turned his face back toward the north, searching for some sign of his adversary. He heard the sound of shuffling feet behind him. He gazed down as if from some lofty summit on the dirty, ragged men at his feet. Magnanimously, Phelan gestured for the gags to be removed as the captives were too far away to warn the other workers.

"Your sires come to claim you," he said as he studied each captive's face in turn.

"Good," Morgan replied as soon as the dirty piece of cloth left his mouth. "Then we can return the gracious hospitality you have shown us." His voice was biting.

Phelan chuffed. "I've not been ungracious, I believe." He saw Belwyn's dark eyes on him and felt the man's unending hatred.

"Morwyn might say otherwise, if she were alive," Morgan replied.

"She has no right to complain. I did not make her suffer any longer than was needed. I could have easily have let her be used for sport amongst my guards before she died, but I did not."

"I'm sure the Powers will note your compassion and be sure to reward you appropriately," Morgan replied.

"Lord Phelan," Caewlin began, though he almost choked on the title, "I ask that you not harm those in the workers' hut. They are no threat to you." Phelan studied his most hated enemy for a time and then gave the iarel a knowing smile.

"*Lord*, is it? You never have used my proper title before, not even when I held your sister's life in my grasp." He paused and then could not resist the temptation to gloat. "But you have not heard! Your sister has taken to being a sporting wench as if she was born to it. She cowers at her master's feet like a dog and from what I hear, she denies him *nothing*. She has progressed so far in her training that I intend to enjoy her myself once I return to Kell. That will be a night she'll never forget." Caewlin clenched his teeth and kept the seething rage off his face. He forced himself to remain composed, knowing Fea was beyond his help at this point.

"If she still lives, I have no sister. It was her duty to slay herself the moment she was touched," he said in an icy voice. He sounded genuine, though his heart was hemorrhaging in torment. He struggled to retain control. "My concern is for my people. If you must have your revenge, then revenge yourself upon me. The workers still have value."

Phelan nodded. "They do have value, for they will make a jolly bonfire that will lure your kinsmen from where they lurk behind the island. Your clansmen will not resist the temptation to rescue their own and they will find my men waiting for them." Caewlin's eyes widened in stunned surprise. His enemy began to chortle as he reveled in the ultimate supremacy over another.

"I will enjoy killing you, but not yet. I want you to know what it feels like to have failed your people. I want you to beg for death and then, maybe, I will grant you your end."

Their eyes locked. "My people will survive, even if I do not." Phelan's mirth overtook him again and another lifeless laugh echoed around them.

"My lord, they come," his Master of the Guard said as he pointed into the forest. Phelan turned his eyes back and squinted. He could barely make out the banners and the glint of steel, for Bardyn was no longer concerned whether his enemy knew of his presence.

"A worthy rabble," Phelan observed. "Secure the iarel to the stake so he may enjoy every moment of this day." Caewlin murmured something under his breath, a prayer perhaps, and then hauled to the stake in the center of the camp. His eyes flitted over toward the hut and all he could do was pray that Pyrs's plan met with the Red Hawk's favor.

The appearance of the tawny owl on the prow of the longship occasioned considerable comment amongst the clansmen.

"Wise, is that is an omen?" Nerian asked, his eyes narrowed. The bird cleaned a wing and appeared to be waiting for something.

Devona studied the raptor, sensed the power in it and shook her head.

"No, this would be an ally." As if that was what the bird was waiting for it sailed down from the prow and onto the deck. Within seconds it transformed from an owl to young girl, one with black hair and blue-grey eyes. For a time she seemed to glow around the edges and then the illusion faded.

"By the Gods, it is her!" one of the man in the boat murmured. He was one of the sentries who had witnessed Morwyn's death on the pyre. "She is alive!" Nerian waved the man to silence and waited for the girl to speak.

"I am Gwyn, daughter of Morwyn, Dragon Kin and Wielder of the Old Magic."

Devona acknowledged her. "I am Devona, Wise of the Red Hawk Clan, Seer and Servant to our Goddess."

"It isn't her," the man mumbled, confused. "I would swear …"

"I am not her," Gwyn remarked. She turned her attention back to Devona. "I have come to stand at your side against your enemy." There was an audible gasp as the small dragon became visible on her shoulder. Only the Wise kept her composure, but her eyes widened.

"Your magic is needed, Gwyn, daughter of Morwyn," Devona replied. Gwyn gave a solemn nod as Nerian addressed this strange arrival.

"We are saddened by your loss," he said.

"All things must pass, clansman," the girl replied as the dragon eyed the man.

"Yes, but some pass too soon."

Lord Phelan waited patiently until Bardyn halted his march, arrayed his men and then rode forward approximately forty or so feet. Behind him, Phelan heard the sound of his own men assembling in battle formation. Only two hundred feet of snowy field sat between him and the Lord of the Eastern March.

"Ah, what a day," Phelan repeated in obvious pleasure as he shifted his weight on his mount.

Bardyn knew it was sheer futility to negotiate with the man on the other side of the field. He made a statement instead, one that left no confusion as to their purpose.

"We have come to claim our sons and to free our Southern brothers of your tyranny."

"So you have," Phelan called back. He gestured to the figures kneeling in the snow at his feet. "Tell me which son's head you would like me to send to you first – yours or Aderyn's?"

Bardyn strained his eyes and then realized who it was that knelt on the ground near Phelan, bound in thick ropes. His mind reeled, for it brought back memories of another battlefield almost four years earlier. He had nearly lost his only son that day and now his future lie in the hands of a maniac once again. *Powers, I gladly offer my life for his,* he murmured to himself. He shifted his eyes to Owain the Elder and saw barely contained anger flickering across the man's face. He, too, had determined who knelt on the ground near their foe. Belwyn was easily recognized. Search as he might, he did not see Pyrs. At this distance, he could read nothing in Belwyn's face to divine his grandson's fate.

Bardyn cleared his throat and shouted back across the divide, "We wish our sons returned in good health. To harm them will cost you your life." His words sounded weak in his own ears.

"I have long wondered what manner of man you are, Bardyn. I must say, I am not impressed. Apparently, Merioneth was not that clever, or he would have defeated you. Of course, he did not have the power to summon a dragon, as I do." The mention of the beast caused an instant ripple of unease to pass through Bardyn's host. All of the men knew what they faced, but to hear their enemy invoke the creature in such a casual fashion unsettled them.

"We will persevere, Phelan," Bardyn replied. He found himself at a loss of words. Where Merioneth had been a craven and vicious man, Phelan was a monster of a different cast. Bardyn did not know how to appeal to him.

Phelan shot a command to his Master of the Guard, "Take his bastard and tie him to the stake with the iarel."

"Milord?"

"Secure Bardyn's son to the stake and have one of your men escort the Eldest of Aderyn to his father."

"Milord?" the Master of the Guard asked again, confused.

"Send him back to his father!" Phelan repeated, his irritation rising.

"Yes, milord." The man gestured and Morgan lurched to his feet, drug upward by a hand on his collar. He was marched across the field to join the iarel before he could say a word to his friend. Belwyn rose to his feet and his bonds were cut, though not with care. He felt the dagger nick his palm and blood oozing forth. Drops of it fell into the pure snow at his feet and with some irony, he realized that the blood of Aderyn was the first drawn this day. *May it be all of Aderyn's blood that lies in the snow ere the day ends.* "Tell your liege lord what awaits his son and your whelp. Perhaps it will cool some of his arrogance." Prodded forward at sword point, Belwyn marched toward his liege lord's line.

As Morgan drew close to the iron stake he received the strangest thing from the iarel – a big smile.

"Good, I was getting lonely out here."

"It is not a good place to be, if you haven't noticed," Morgan remarked dryly as he was tied on the opposite side of the stake. "Arrows are rather indiscriminate weapons." He was facing toward the south where the clansmen would come from the sea.

As the guard marched off Caewlin commented, "No doubt, but we will be in the middle of the battle and that is not necessarily a bad location. The clan will be able to see me and draw strength from the fact that I live."

"Well, personally I'd rather be drawing strength from a sword and shield."

Caewlin chuckled at that. "Those will be ours soon enough, my friend." Morgan half-turned and looked into the iarel's intense brown eyes.

"You are indomitable, aren't you?" A curious look descended on the young clansman's face.

"I have no choice, Morgan." For an instant they shared the combined weight of their responsibilities.

"Then some day I may need to ask you how you do that," Morgan replied.

"I do what I must, that is all the advice I can give."

"I feared that," Morgan replied and then set to work on loosening his bonds.

Across the field, Owain studied the figure coming toward them.

"What is this?" he asked, more to himself than to his liege lord. "What devilry does he have in mind?"

"I do not know, my friend. I am open to suggestion on how to deal with this butcher." He had watched as his son was marched to the iron stake and secured there. Now Belwyn strode toward them. None of it made sense.

Owain shook his head. "I am sorry, I have none, our enemy is not rational." His eyes were riveted on the figure of his eldest son trudging across the field, a guard behind him with a drawn sword at his back. Once they reached the mid-point between the two armies the guard turned and left him to walk on alone. Once he realized the guard was no longer behind him, Belwyn's throat knotted. How far would Phelan allow him to go before the order came to cut him down? Would he be so cruel as to wait until he could see his father's eyes? He tramped on, pushing his fear down as far as he could, refusing to show cowardice and break into a run.

"Was this what you felt, Morwyn?" he murmured to himself. He remembered her solid steps as she walked toward her final moments on the pyre. She had shown extreme courage and he would do the same. If Phelan had him killed then he would join her in the next life. That thought instilled him with resolve. Perversely his mind began to count his steps; ten … eleven … twelve … as he listened for the characteristic sound of an arrow as it winged its way across the field and into his back. It did not come. Twenty … twenty-one … twenty-two … still no sound behind him, no order flung into the air that would end his life. Forty-three … forty-four … forty-five …

"Powers, let me live! I must save my son," he murmured, sweat now glistening on his forehead despite the chill morning air. As he drew close to the line he caught Dillan's eyes, for he was on horseback next to Belwyn's father. He drew strength from the clansman's stern face and continued to march until he stopped in front of his lord. He took a deep breath, ordered his legs to stop trembling and thanked the Powers for Their protection. Once in control of his emotions, he gazed up at the troubled face of his master.

Belwyn bowed. "My lord, father, Dillan …" he paused and sought the grim face of his dead wife's brother. Their eyes held for a moment, a world of grief exchanged without a word.

"Though I am pleased to have you with us, why has he released you?" Bardyn demanded.

"He wishes you to learn that he intends to fire the workers' quarters with the clan inside the building."

"Powers!" Bardyn's voice carried. His eyes shot up toward the figure in the distance. "He would do this?"

"Yes, the kindling is already in place. We suspected his intentions and have made some provisions so that a few may escape the blaze." He paused for a moment and then added in a strained voice, "Pyrs is in that building."

Owain the Elder closed his eyes and murmured a prayer.

Dillan asked, "Surely he would not fire a structure that stands in the line of his retreat. It makes no tactical sense!"

"He does not intend to retreat, Dillan. He sees only victory," Belwyn explained.

"His delusions make him unpredictable, far more dangerous than Merioneth ever was," Owain the Elder observed, his hands knotted around the reins.

"He knows that the clan has gathered near the island. He is intent on

using the blaze to force their hand and ours as well," Belwyn continued.
"What will it take to call this madman to heel?" Bardyn asked in desperation.

"I do not know, my lord. He is crazed with the power the dragon has given him," Belwyn replied, trying to keep the hopelessness out of his voice. "My lord, if I may make a suggestion," Dillan offered. Bardyn nodded at him. "Send ten of your men back into the forest so they may come in from the west, to the side of the building. In that way they may be able to help some of the clansmen escape and kill any guards that would harass them."

Belwyn interjected, "That would be of value, my lord. The workers intend to make their escape through the south wall as they hope there will be fewer guards in that direction." Bardyn nodded and the order issued. He turned his attention back to the figure across the field.

"What is it you wish, Phelan?" he shouted and his voice carried easily in the near silence of the morning.

"Victory," was the answer shouted back at him.

Bardyn sighed and did not answer his foe. He spoke so only the men around him could hear his words. "Let us hope we do not give it to him."

Phelan tugged the Stone outside of his leather jerkin and studied it in fondness. He seriously wished this moment would last forever, for he had never felt so alive. Almost reluctantly he summoned the dragon and it appeared in the air above them, for it had no choice.

"What of your brood?"

They are not born yet.

"Pity." Phelan waited and then gave the order, "Fire the hut!" He pointed toward the workers' quarters with a flourish. The dragon wheeled in the air with a deafening roar and the sound terrified both man and beast alike. Horses bolted, throwing their riders, both in Phelan's ranks and in Bardyn's company as well. Only the most seasoned or fortunate of riders remained in their saddles. Phelan was one of the lucky ones, for a guard held his horse's bridle and managed to keep the steed from bolting.

He commanded again, "Fire the building!" The beast dove through the air toward the structure and then spun sideways, executing a midair roll and shot off in the opposite direction. A massive bellow of pain came out of its mouth along with streaking arcs of golden red flame.

"Why do you hesitate?" Phelan shouted.

I cannot harm one of our kind.

Phelan shouted back, "There is no dragon in that hut! Fire it!"

One of our kind is there, I cannot harm him!

Phelan repeated the order at the top of his lungs, but the dragon writhed in the air and cried out as if in pain. The lord's face was crimson with fury at this unforeseen development.

He snarled at his Master of the Guard, "Fire the hut!" Men scurried off to perform the task and soon a dozen or so ignition points were burning in the bone-dry brush along the sides of the building

"Then I will burn them myself, dragon," Phelan growled and returned his attention toward Bardyn's line.

"Powers, save us," Bardyn murmured, incredulous at the size of the beast that now flew above them. Belwyn, who was donning his sword, glanced upward and then back down. He knew the beast's size and capacity for death as well as any. He felt a hand on his shoulder and gazed upward into his sire's eyes.

"We will prevail," Owain the Elder said. Belwyn only nodded. He noted that his father had given him one of Aderyn's older swords, but not the lineage sword, the pride of their family. *He has left it at Aderyn for my brother, should we all not return.*

Once he had the sword in place, he found Elrehan standing next to him, for by now all had abandoned their horses as the beasts were uncontrollable. His brother-in-law's eyes were devoid of emotion and that made him shiver.

"The Powers will aid us, we will prevail," Belwyn said, echoing his father's words. Elrehan did not speak, his eyes firmly set on the figure of the man who had taken his sister's life. Belwyn tried again, "I know that look, my friend, for I too have courted death when there seemed no reason to live. Do not seek to end your life before the Powers deem it time, for there are many who would miss you." Elrehan slowly turned his head and studied his fellow warrior for a moment.

"I know," he murmured and returned his eyes to the only thing that mattered in his life.

The dragon's booming call proved too much for the men and women imprisoned in the hut. Panic reined for a time until some of the older clansmen and Pyrs pleaded for calm. The fear was palpable, for all their well-laid plans would be for naught if the dragon fired the hut instead of Phelan's men. The building would explode in a fireball before any of them had a slightest chance to escape.

Finally, Pyrs made his voice heard over the tumult of voices, shouting in the Southern tongue, "It will not fire the hut, for I am here. Phelan's men will have to set fire to the building and that will save us!" The message made little sense to those who heard it.

"Why will it not burn us to death? Why are you so special?" a rough voice demanded.

Before Pyrs could shout an answer one of the sentries cried, "He's right, they come with torches!" He sighed in obvious relief, although their situation was not much improved. He saw several clansmen eyeing him closely but he did not bother to explain. Smoke began to filter through the cracks of the building. A battle cry rose in the hut and Pyrs added his strong voice to the din as a surge of bodies moved forward to attack the south wall, the one toward the sea and freedom.

TWENTY-SEVEN

The dragon's refusal to follow Phelan's orders disconcerted him and cost him precious time. No matter how rapidly his guards could fire the dry tinder, it was not the spectacle he desired. He turned his eyes back toward the north and saw a solid line of steel charging toward him, a cacophony of voices shouting for his blood. For a brief moment he quailed. The jeering voice of Taran, his heartless brother, echoed in his mind, calling him a cowardly dog, one only worthy of abuse and table scraps.

"No, the Master of the Hounds will not run," he murmured. "I am equal to *all* of them." He clutched the Stone in his hand again and commanded, "Kill those who dare to oppose me, kill them all!" This time the dragon did not hesitate, did not cry out in pain at the order, but turned and dove straight at Bardyn's line. Phelan watched his enemies' eyes widen in horror as the monstrosity dove out of the clouds like a lightening bolt. To their credit they held their line even as five of them vanished in a fiery cloud of flames, their death shrieks splintering the air.

"Impressive," he murmured to himself and tucked the Stone beneath his jerkin. He watched the dragon rise again, clipping the tops of the trees as it winged off to make another approach. "Very impressive."

Bardyn's line wavered and a command was issued for them to spread themselves further apart. They had lost the advantage of the horses and so had to slog across the snowy ground in full armor as Phelan's archers rained arrows on them. As the wave of bolts came pelting down the men crouched, placing their shields over them to shelter against the missiles. Once the arrows thinned they would rise and march a few more yards until the assault began anew. When the dragon struck there was near hysteria, but the line reformed and surged ahead, knowing to stay in one place was to invite the airborne killer to target them.

"We must find Pyrs!" Dillan shouted over to Belwyn. "He will keep the dragon at bay!" Belwyn gave his friend an astonished look and then suddenly more became clear to him.

"Is that why the beast did not fire the hut?"

"Yes!"

Belwyn pushed his march across the field. He could move faster than the others for he wore only a ringed mail jerkin, not full armor. The shield he carried now had four arrows embedded in it. Soon they would be too close for the archers to be of use and then it would come down to his agility with the sword.

"Powers, save them," he murmured as he saw a plume of smoke rising from the building in the distance. A phalanx of Phelan's troops stood between him and Pyrs. It would not have mattered if the dragon stood there, for he would find his only son or die in the process.

What had not been visible through the fog now became clear. Columns of smoke rose steadily upward and removed any doubt that it was the workers' quarters ablaze.

"By the Gods!" Nerian exclaimed in horror as the ships beached on their foe's shore.

"It is a trap," Gwyn said with remarkable serenity given that her twin was inside the burning building. She had already sensed Phelan's cunning maneuver and knew the danger it posed to both Bardyn's army and the clansmen. The plan had been for Pyrs to make his way to his liege lord and his grandsire to keep the dragon from targeting their men. That had been thwarted by Phelan's obsession with fire. *Could he know of our purpose?* she thought, her mind suddenly much less calm, nearly bordering on panic. She fought to regain control, sensing that Pyrs was still alive inside the growing inferno. She felt his raging fear as if it were her own. *No, Phelan does not know or he would have removed Pyrs from the hut before he ordered the dragon to fire it.* She took a deep breath to calm herself. Panic would not help her brother or the other members of her family.

"A trap you say? So be it," Nerian replied gravely. The clansmen poured out of the ships and sped toward the billowing fire and the mass of guards that eagerly awaited their arrival.

The flying death roared down again and this time seven men flamed into nothingness. Bardyn's line wavered and almost broke, for even battle hardened warriors found their resolve tested.

"Onward, it cannot strike too close to its master!" Bardyn shouted and strode forward. For a time only a handful followed him.

"Come on! You'll die if you stand still, move on!" Owain bellowed and the warriors hurried as fast as their heavy chain mail would allow. They were outnumbered and now the odds were even less favorable. A dozen had died in the dragon's fire, a handful by arrows. Phelan's men strode toward their foes, sensing their advantage as the battle began in earnest.

It seemed an eternity before the first holes in the south wall appeared. All the while they battered against the boards smoke and flames poured inside the building. The clansmen were clad in sodden blankets in knots of fifty or more near each potential escape route. In desperation they began to throw their shoulders against the timbers. A hole appeared and then another and another. Knowing Phelan's men would be waiting for them, the strongest men climbed out, threw the wet wool blankets on the blazing branches and then began to battle with Phelan's guards. Man after man followed, each gripping a stone, a piece of board, anything that could be used as a weapon. More holes appeared and as the soot began to choke the life out of those still inside, lines formed to crawl to safety. Surprisingly there was no stampede, for the light of freedom poured through the hissing flames and the dense acrid smoke. With a loud crash the main double doors smashed open and dozens poured into the fresh air shouting their gratitude to their Gods.

"Go on, go on!" Pyrs hollered as the roar of the flames rose behind him. He continued to shepherd the workers forward toward the wall. His mind screamed at him to flee, that he would burn to death if he stayed any longer. The intense heat bore down on him and he felt the sharp prickle of burns on his back as bits of flaming debris rained down on them. He steeled himself and refused to succumb to either the panic or the fire. He continued to wave more of the clan forward through the smoke, unaware that his unfailing courage hailed his passage into manhood.

Pyrs nervously stared upward at the flaming roof timbers and then returned his attention back to the south wall. The other three walls were ablaze from the floor to the roof, which began to groan from the shifting weight. He continued to guide people through the flames, lining them up for their escape into the fresh air. He knew it was vital he survive, but he would not leave until he knew that the majority of the clansmen were safe. Instinctively he glanced upward again and saw the north wall sway ominously as it tipped inward. A nearby clansman shouted a warning, but the wall fell before Pyrs had a chance to flee. Intense heat engulfed him and he was flattened to the ground. He smelt the stench of burning flesh, his own he supposed. He lay there for a moment and realized, to his stunned amazement, he was still alive. He heard frantic voices and felt hands digging him out from under something heavy. The comforting cold of a sodden blanket helped extinguish the burning spots on his ragged clothes. He shivered and then opened his eyes to see that a section of the hut had collapsed into a fiery heap.

"Powers!" He looked around and saw only a few of the others who had been standing near him. Two or three dozen of his fellow workers were gone, buried under the flaming wall. "No, no," he murmured, his eyes watering from the smoke and from the acute sense of failure.

"Come on, young man, it is time you left," a voice said near his ear. He felt himself pulled up and pushed bodily toward one of the openings, though he tried to protest. Once outside he found himself surrounded by clansmen, for they intended to keep this resourceful lad alive, no matter the cost.

Pyrs's eyes involuntarily lifted upward to see the massive form of the dragon sail over his head. He was jostled and then chastised himself for not paying attention. They were not out of danger, for Phelan's men were still pressing them. He noted that several of the clansmen now had swords, no doubt liberated from their slain enemies. He heard a battle cry and then had to duck to avoid being decapitated by a guard. He had no weapon so he snatched up a piece of wood employing it as a staff. The guard did not have a chance to kill the defiant lad as other clansmen piled on him using their rocks to beat him into the ground. The guard's sword went to Pyrs and now properly armed, he set off to try to determine where in this hellish melee he might find his liege lord and his grandsire.

The guards tasked with the job of slaughtering the clansmen as they came off the beach found the work hard going. There was a bitter battle as the clan fought with growing desperation to reach their trapped kin. The screams of their dying kinsmen inflamed them and they hacked their way through their enemies, struggling on the uneven sand until they reached solid ground. No quarter was given, if a guard fell to his knees grievously wounded, he was butchered. More than one corpse lacked its head as Phelan's troops began to surmise how merciless the clan could be. They were stunned to find women fighting against them, but their arrogant laughter withered away when they saw that the shield-women were even more brutal than their male kin. The carnage was horrific as guard after guard fell to the sand dead or mortally wounded. Mounds of corpses accumulated, staining the snow bright crimson as their lifeblood drained away. A cacophony of cries flooded the morning air, for so many were stricken.

Inexorably Phelan's men found themselves backed toward the inferno with no avenue of escape. They formed a tight knot and desperately attempted to contain the onslaught that seemed to come from all directions. Bardyn's small group of warriors waded in from one side as rocks and flaming timbers assailed them from behind. The liberated clansmen, newly fled from what was supposed to be their burning tomb, took their ferocious revenge. In the end there was only a handful of Phelan's men alive and they fled the field in mortal panic.

"I repeat, Iarel, this is *not* where we want to be!" Morgan shouted over the chaos of battle. They were helpless in the sea of arrows, flaming dragon fire and enraged enemies. No matter how hard he struggled, his bonds would not yield. He felt blood on his wrists from his efforts, but still he could not break free.

"The Gods will see to our freedom, have patience," Caewlin replied in complete confidence. Morgan began to swear in aggravation and fury, for the iarel's irrational bravado was starting to wear on him. Before he could complete his oath his eyes caught sight of a cloaked figure working its way across the field toward them. It appeared to be a clansman, but then he was not sure. One of Phelan's men challenged the individual and a battle ensued. As the figure delivered a wicked slice, the cloak hood fell back and he saw a torrent of red hair.

It was Caewlin's turn to swear.

"No!" he shouted. "No!" Morgan held his tongue and watched as the red-haired woman methodically parried the guard's thrusts and then felled him. He slid to the ground, her short sword deep in his throat. The woman pulled the blade free and continued her progress toward them.

"Fire-hair! Go back!" the iarel shouted, anxiety overwhelming him. Despite her desire to run to him, Aithne kept her head and worked her way over to them in a cautious fashion, keenly aware of the dangers around her.

"Iarel," she said with a smile, a smear of her foe's blood on her cheek. She glanced around once more and then cut his bonds. Morgan was freed a moment later.

"What are you doing here?" Caewlin demanded.

"Rescuing the father of my child, Iarel. Now go and save your people," she said with a smug grin and tried to hand him her sword. He shook his head vehemently, refusing to take her only means of defense. He pointed toward the woods.

"Go away from here! I cannot worry about you as well."

"You don't have to," she said, knowing now was not the place to discuss this. She gave him a kiss and then scurried off toward the woods. He wanted to follow her, keep her safe, but he could not. The workers' hut was in full flame and the sound of his clan's battle cry called him to war.

"Let us see if there are any of our enemy left to kill," he said and strode across the field in search of an unwary guard and his sword.

Morgan shot a quick glance toward the north and the skirmish line. He had little chance of joining his father so he sighed and followed the iarel on his quest for a weapon.

Nerian had detailed two clansmen to guard the Wise and Gwyn, but they were not the only force that kept the two women safe. Phelan's men quickly realized that horrific death flew off the shoulder of the mysterious black-haired girl. As a guard stormed toward Gwyn she uttered a spell of protection, reaching for her knife. It was not needed. Sensing danger her guardian rose, hissed ominously and shot toward the man's throat like an arrow. A spray of blood exploded around the warrior's head and he fell to the ground nearly decapitated. The dragon returned to hover over the top of its charge, its eyes whirling in fury.

"Powers," Gwyn murmured in awe. She gestured for him to come to her and he did. As he settled on her shoulder, she noted with a shiver that his claws were covered in gore.

The clansmen issued a mighty cheer when their iarel joined them in battle. He had acquired a sword, now stained with the blood of three of his foes. Morgan appeared only a few minutes later, a sword in his hand as well.

"Ah, there you are, I though perhaps you'd gotten lost," Caewlin chided.

"No, just collecting weapons," Morgan replied as he calmly thrust his sword upward into a foe's belly, laying him open like a ripe gourd. As soon as the disemboweled man fell to the ground in a dying groan, another guard took his place and the death dance continued.

Dillan and Elrehan flanked Fea as Phelan's men made their assault. Invoking her right as a shield-maiden, she had refused to stay out of the fray. She stood by her husband, a blooded sword in her hand and her long hair in distinctive battle braids. She moved quickly and with surety on the uneven ground as her opponents' weaknesses were ascertained and turned against them. Dillan fought equally well, though a bit slower because of his age. He kept a wary eye on his wife and knew that Elrehan was doing the same.

The broad slice of a sword glanced off Dillan's shield and caught him in the upper arm. He lurched back and Fea stepped forward instinctively and blocked his opponent, allowing her husband to regain his footing. He stepped forward again and engaged his foe. In time, the guard slumped to the ground, Dillan's sword in his chest.

"Fea!" Elrehan shouted and she whirled to find a man behind her. His blade caught her in the left side and despite her injury, she pressed forward and finally planted her sword firmly in the man's abdomen. He went down with an oath.

Dillan called to her, "How bad is it?" Fea winced and tried to move her left arm, feeling the blood under her leather jerkin.

"Not that bad, I can continue," she replied. She caught Elrehan's worried eyes and shook her head. Taking a deep breath, she rejoined the battle.

Pyrs had the unenviable task of working his way through Phelan's line in an attempt to reach his liege lord. He was at equal risk from both sides. He set his eyes on an opening between two lines of men and hurried forward, clutching his sword tightly in his hand. The path closed and he had to dodge around a different way. It was unnerving that death could come from any angle, either from one of his own or one of his foes. He felt the dragon's presence in the air above him and knew it would soon swoop down and kill more of Bardyn's warriors, perhaps even his father and his grandsire. That thought made his gut knot. He clenched his teeth so tightly his jaw ached and continued his push forward. He found his way blocked by a large warrior, one of Phelan's brutes, who studied the lad in front of him.

"You're Aderyn's brat, aren't you?" he snarled and strode forward to engage him, sure the boy would be easy to overwhelm.

"I am the youngest of Aderyn, if that's what you ask," Pyrs retorted.

The man snorted and jabbed at the lad with a vicious thrust. "A whoreson, no doubt. Your mother looked to be a wench, available for any man with a copper coin. Pity Phelan didn't let us enjoy her before he had her roasted."

Pyrs's temper flared into an inferno, infuriated at the man's vile comments about his beloved mother. He shouted his fury and instantly Dillan's voice echoed in his mind. *'Anger makes you weak. It is as much a weapon as the sword in your foe's hand.'* He scrutinized his assailant and knew that was his game. *No, this is my game.* He let his anger fade and kept his mind on his enemy's next move.

He quickly realized his adversary was a seasoned fighter and knew all the moves. Pyrs pulled forward Dillan's patient teachings, hearing the man's voice in his head as he battled his wily foe. He jammed his fear into his boots and fought with all the strength he could muster, knowing that if he died his father and his grandsire would as well. As he methodically worked the man's blade to determine a hidden weakness his arm began to shake from the exertion. His senses were keen, for he could hear the thick slash of the blade as it cut the air and smell the sweet stench of blood mixed with offal as it rose around him. A nick to his shoulder brought his mind to heel.

"One more inch and I would have had your throat!" the man crowed.

Pyrs finally determined the weakness he'd been so desperately seeking. It was not the man's lack skill with the blade, but his arrogance.

"Why haven't you killed me yet? Apparently this whoreson is better than you," Pyrs taunted as he ducked a wide swipe. It was a dangerous gambit. Anger could also give his foe the advantage.

"Not to worry, you'll be dead soon enough. I'll cut you open like a pig when I'm done," the man boasted back.

Pyrs had to jump to avoid another wicked stab toward his midsection. "No, you're not *that* good. Perhaps you spend too much time sporting with trollops rather than learning how to fight." He tried again, "Or perhaps you're more fond of lads my age." That insult was grave.

"You little bastard," the man growled and rushed forward intent on eviscerating the boy "I'll rip your lying tongue out before I kill you!"

A little closer, Pyrs thought. The mere seconds it took the man to reach him seemed to last forever. *Now!* He thrust his sword forward catching his foe in the lower abdomen and then ripped the blade upward with both hands.

A shriek erupted and then a spray of blood flew into the air splattering Pyrs's face. He felt the taste of blood in his mouth and it sickened him. He saw incomprehension and then mortal fear cross the man's face as he died at the hands of the youngest son of Aderyn. Pyrs stepped back, pulling his sword out of the body, his moment of triumph clouded by the overwhelming need to retch. He had killed a man, a despicable one it appeared, but a man nonetheless. He shivered as the adrenaline caught up with him and then jerked himself back to reality. An arrow sailed past him, impaling itself into one of Phelan's man and he fell to ground thrashing in agony. Pyrs shook off his queasiness and judged his position. He still lacked his liege lord's line by another fifty feet or so.

"If I were only invisible!" Pyrs complained aloud.

And so you are. It was his sister's voice and he jumped, for it sounded as if she was right next to him. He spun around but did not see her. When he looked down he saw the ground, but nothing else. He and his sword were invisible.

"Now that's *real* magic!" he announced and continued on, weaving his way over the blood-encrusted snow and around the countless wounded. He heard his sister instructing him how to make himself visible and invisible by using certain words. "I understand," he said, this time more sure of his steps as he continued his quest to join his liege lord.

He made the final fifty feet to stand near his liege lord without further difficulty, avoiding any combat to speed his movement. It would have been easy to slay those who could not see him, but he did not. He was intensely relieved to see his father and his grandsire were still alive. He murmured the word that made him visible and joined in the battle, much to the consternation of a guard in front of him. He fought to within a few feet of his father, keeping a wary eye on him and his grandsire as they fought back-to-back. A roar passed over their heads and all the men ducked, even Phelan's guards, for they feared the beast as well. The fire did not discriminate between friend or foe.

"It did not strike!" one man called out in surprise. Belwyn cast a quick look around and found the reason why. Some ten feet to his right he found his son engaged in a fierce sword fight with a man half again his size. Belwyn shifted his attention back to his assailant and after a few more thrusts he sent the man to the ground mortally wounded. He fought his way over to stand by his son, giving him an approving nod.

"Father," Pyrs said, ducking and then jabbing upward as Dillan had taught him. The old clansman was correct, his upward thrusts were weak and he made a note to work on that if he lived through this day.

"Son." Belwyn's voice was weary, but relieved. "I am pleased to see you live."

"No more than I am, father." Pyrs was mortally tired for there seemed to be no end to those who would square off against him. His youth made him a target. He heard another roar pass overhead and knew the dragon would not strike now that he stood amongst his fellow fighters.

At least this part of the plan is working, he thought wryly and kept his eye on his latest adversary's double-bladed axe as it sung through the air.

Phelan's voice erupted in fury as the dragon refused to slaughter his remaining enemies.

"Why?" he shouted in indignation as he kept a wary eye on Bardyn's men some one hundred feet in the distance.

One of our kin is in their midst. I cannot harm him.

Phelan opened his mouth to protest the absurdity of this claim when he stopped and thought it through.

"Which one is your kin?" His eyes strained through the battle attempting to search each figure individually. It was a difficult task due to the fluidity of the conflict. The dragon did not answer and Phelan felt its torment through the mental link.

"Who is he?" he demanded.

The descendant of a dragon slayer.

Phelan snarled back, "Young or old?"

Young, the youngest of his own kin. The dragon remained cryptic, hedging the truth as far as it dared. Phelan's mind was frantic as his eyes continued to scan the battlefield. He caught sight of a shorter figure and knew who it was in an instant.

He was in the hut and now ...

"Is it youngest son of Aderyn?" he demanded.

There was silence.

"Is it him?" Phelan shouted, incensed at the dragon's continued defiance. A cry of agony went up in the air as the dragon barrel-rolled in exquisite psychic torment.

Yes.

Phelan waved over his Master of the Guard. "Have an archer kill the youngest of Aderyn. It is he that keeps the dragon from fulfilling my commands." The Master of the Guard gave Phelan a puzzled look but issued the order. An archer began the tedious process of stalking the boy across the tumultuous field. All he needed was a clear shot and the lad would be dead before he hit the snowy ground.

A cry of anguish went up from the mountain as the Watcher observed it all, for the fog did not hinder its sight in any way. It felt the deaths of the mortals, the dwindling moments of life for those yet to perish this day. Tears fell again, hissing into the red-hot orbs at its feet. Its mourning turned to infinite fury when it found two men standing in the cave entrance. The sentries had completed their master's biding and decided to find out what actually lie in the cave.

"I told you it wasn't jewels, Phelan's not that way. It has to be something truly powerful, for that's all he seeks," one of the sentries said to the other.

"No, I'll not go in, it does not feel right. We should not be here!" the other man insisted and slowly backed away, his inner caution ruling him. He felt something he could not comprehend, something that frightened him to his very bones.

"Nonsense! The beast is not here and I want to see whatever it is for myself. Perhaps I can learn how to bind a monster to my will, as well." He strode forward, his sword drawn. "Powers, look! There are … eight of them!" He never finished his thoughts as his torn and bloody corpse flew out the mouth of the cavern in a wide arc. It tumbled down the side of the mountain and finally wedged up against a broad rock some sixty feet below, a grotesque parody of a discarded puppet. The other man fled in stark terror. A roar came out of the cavern and then silence. The Watcher settled back down on its haunches in loving protection of its kin and turned its bottomless blue eyes toward the battle once more.

Most great warriors sense when death stands ready to claim them and Lord Bardyn was no exception. He had fought in a many a battle, but he knew this one he would not survive. He felt a presence, one that he could not comprehend, but he remembered his father speaking of it as he lay dying on a battlefield decades before. It was the specter of death that beckoned to him, called him home to be with his beloved Morgane. The foe in front of him was masterful, his equal, and Bardyn was tired. He saw his end as clearly as one could and he uttered a heartfelt prayer.

My life for my son's, that is all I ask.

In the end it was not his lack of skill, but his foe's misstep and his own weariness that cost Bardyn his life. When the lord strove to take advantage of his foe's error, the guard recovered quicker than anticipated and drove his sword into the lord's upper chest before he could block the thrust with his shield. The wound was not mortal, but as he careened back the second blow was, striking just below the heart. Bardyn fell to his knees and then to the ground before his opponent could behead him. He heard a strange roaring in his ears and realized that it was his own men, howling their fury as they surged forward to surround him. He knew they were too late and felt strangely at peace.

Owain the Elder was at his old friend's side only moments after he fell. Heedless to his own safety he fell on his knees and pulled his lord's body off the ground into his arms. One look told him the deep chest wound was mortal as blood bubbled through the tight rings of chain mail and his friend's face grew ashen. Owain shoved his palm over the wound, pressing down, and felt an ominous sucking sensation. The blade had missed Bardyn's heart, but impaled his lung. The guard who had struck the killing blow had no time to rejoice as he was being hacked to death in righteous fury by two of Bardyn's men. It did not matter, for the great lord lay dying in his best friend's arms.

Bardyn's fall and the subsequent rush to his side cleared a path for the archer and he used it to his best advantage. The missile struck Pyrs in the upper left chest, clipping his collarbone and riding upward. He fell backward instantly as the pain overpowered him. He screamed and rolled to his right side to try to end the agony. His father moved to stand over him, to protect him from those who would finish what the archer started.

"Pyrs, you must rise!" he shouted down to the boy. Pyrs gradually worked his way up to his knees, his sword still in his hand. Finally with a massive groan he rose, wavering from the intensity of the pain and the loss of blood. He knew he could not fight, the wound was too grievous. He had only one option and he took it. When Belwyn glanced back his son was gone from sight.

"Pyrs?" he shouted. His opponent attacked with a rain of furious blows, knowing the man to be distracted.

"I am okay, father," Pyrs lied. "I am invisible now, that way they cannot find me. The dragon will stay away as long as I am alive."

"Where are you?" his father demanded as he finally wounded the guard that pressed him so tenaciously. The man fell back and hobbled away, sensing his advantage had evaporated.

"I am behind you, but I will move from time to time." Pyrs glanced over to where Bardyn lay on the ground, sensing the man's death was imminent. "Our liege lord dies, father," he said sadly. For a moment the grief was stronger than the throbbing pain in his chest. Belwyn turned and gazed toward where his father held Bardyn's body in his arms.

"May the Powers escort him home with all the honor he is due."

"They are, father, They are," Pyrs murmured and then sank to his knees. Despite his words to his sire he could move no further. With tremendous effort he reached up, grasped the bolt that protruded from his chest and broke it off. He fainted before he had a chance to scream from the pain. He lay on his side in the snowy field, invisible to everyone but the dragon and his sister.

TWENTY-EIGHT

P helan's Master of the Guard delivered ill news as the sounds of battle came closer from their rear. He glanced nervously in that direction, sensing their time was short.

"Milord, the Southern men have broken through. They are behind us and gathering strength." Phelan shouted an oath. He judged the remainder of Bardyn's army to be no less than sixty feet from where he sat on his horse. His dragon would not kill any more of them so he jerked the reins and rode toward the south, toward the clan. Clasping the Stone as he rode, he set his fiery weapon against his most hated enemy. The dragon's first pass over the clansmen made them drop to their knees and shield themselves as best they could. To their amazement no flames engulfed them. Again, the dragon cried out in torment and refused to follow its master's orders.

Phelan's control snapped. "Why are you not attacking as I ordered?" he bellowed, spooking his horse. A guard fought to keep it under control.

One of our kind ... the beast began and Phelan cut it off.

"Who?" This time the dragon did not hesitate, but told him what he wished to know. The power of the mental connection was wearing on its ability to withhold the truth.

The daughter of Morwyn is our kin.

"Which one is she?" he demanded, searching over the heads of the clansmen in the distance. They were in bunches as they worked their way toward the Northern line. There were far more of them than Phelan realized.

The dragon paused only a moment. **She is her mother.**

Phelan kept looking for the girl and finally spied her, knowing what the dragon meant by its answer. He opened his mouth to order her killed when he saw what sat on her shoulder. He studied it again as it rose in the air, threatening a guard who came too close. It settled back down on her shoulder in a vigilant posture. He smiled and grasped the Stone in his hand.

"Is that a dragon?" he asked. There was silence. "Is it?" he cried.

Phelan could feel the fear through the link. He surmised the answer without having the beast speak it. He howled in delight, knowing what fate had delivered him.

The impact of the missile into her twin's chest caused Gwyn to reel. She shouted his name in anguish and instinctively surged protective energy toward her brother, leaving her guardian unprotected against the Stone's power for only a moment.

Phelan's voice called in high triumph, "I summon you, you are bound to my will!" A huge cry echoed above him but he ignored it and continued to call the small beast into bondage. "I summon you, by the power of the Stone."

Caught between her devotion to her brother and the desperate need to protect the small dragon, Gwyn's magic faltered. Her guardian's claws dug into her shoulder causing her to wince in pain.

I cannot, I cannot! the little one screamed in her mind and she knew Phelan was hearing its thoughts as well. It cringed and then with a hoarse cry it rose from her shoulder and began its flight toward its new master.

"No!" Gwyn shouted, "no!" She tried a counter spell, but it failed. She shouted another, but it was of no use for the Stone had captured the little beast's mind. Terror ripped through her, for she feared for its life. Above them the mother dragon flew like a storm, circling and thundering in anger and concern.

The small dragon hovered only a few feet from Lord Phelan's face.

"You are more tractable than the other one," he observed.

I cannot serve you!

"You shall, for all of your kind are bound to the Stone." He paused, thought and then asked, "Why are you with the girl?" The little one did not answer immediately. "Why?"

It teetered in the air as if in distress and then replied reluctantly,

I am her guardian.

A strange grin appeared on Phelan's face and then a truly cold smile.

"I order you to kill her."

The tormented shriek that came out of the small dragon's mouth was heard throughout the battlefield. It started to twist in the air in front of its new master, as if trying to tear itself apart rather than follow his orders.

"Kill her, now!" he said clutching the Stone and shoving it forward toward the ddraig as far as its chain would allow. A barrage of bellows came from the sky above them and many of the warriors fell to their feet, sure the end was near.

"Go now!" The small dragon lifted into the air, whirling and tumbling like a leaf in a gale, shrieking and crying as it moved inexorably toward the girl it had sworn to protect with its own life. Gwyn stood absolutely still, in shock, terrified for the small creature. She muttered a protective spell, stumbling on the words. The spell might hold, she could not tell. Even if it worked, the little one would destroy itself. If the baby perished, the mother high in the air above them may well forsake its vow and slaughter all of them in righteous retribution.

The little dragon gazed upward toward the massive figure of its matriarch, gave a strange cry and then dove back to the ground. It arced over the top of Gwyn, coming so close that she felt its wings stir her hair and then it swept back toward Phelan at full speed. It traveled so fast he could not track it until he saw it bearing down upon him. He raised the Stone to deliver a command but the small beast struck before he could open his mouth. It caught the Stone straight on and there was brilliant explosion of light. It tore the orb from Phelan's grasp, breaking the gold chain. As it tried to fly away its wings beat irregularly, for it was badly injured. Instinctively it headed toward Gwyn, its cries of distress echoing in the air. It was drown out by the immense blast of sound coming from above them. The adult dragon turned and then plummeted toward the earth, its huge form generating a wide shadow as the mother dove straight toward the mortals who had harmed her baby.

"Powers, no!" Gwyn shouted, knowing the huge beast's intent. "No!" Heedless to her own safety she sprinted through the field as the darkness grew closer. Riveted as they were on the massive body hurtling toward them, no one challenged her. The mother rushed towards the ground, desperate to vent her rage against the mortals. This time hundreds would die, not just a few, for she had withheld the full measure of her fire when pitted against Phelan's adversaries. Gwyn flung her arm up, yelling at the top of her lungs and the small dragon came to her. It fell into her and almost to the ground. She cradled it, pulled the Stone out of its damaged claw and shouted to the mother as it approached at blinding speed.

"Come to me! Do not harm them, come to me!" she commanded. The dragon cried out but had no choice, for Gwyn held the Stone. She saw the hulk abort its dive at the last moment, the blast of its wings hurtling many to the ground. Gwyn dashed to an open space in the field and called again, "Come to me!" The beast turned in the air and came to land only a few feet from the terrified young girl. Its eyes were glittering and its chest heaved. Gwyn took a deep breath and murmured a prayer, shaking intensely. The small dragon lay in Gwyn's arms, keening in pain.

Now you command us, dragon daughter? The mother's voice hissed ominously.

"No. I did not want you to harm my kind."

If you hold the Stone, you hold us in thrall, the voice came, an explosive combination of fire and ice. Gwyn looked down at the small dragon and though she could not stop it, tears fell. She murmured a healing spell, but it appeared to have little effect.

She looked back up and asked, "How can I heal him?" The mother angled her head, attempting to gauge the emotions she was sensing in the girl. There was no desire to rule, only anguish at the little one in her arms, unending guilt for failing to protect him. She felt the girl's fear for her wounded brother and its tone softened.

Only we can heal him. Gwyn looked down at the small twisted body. Bones were obviously broken and the pain had to be unbearable. She reached down and kissed the little dragon on its head.

"Be well, dragon brother," she said. She took a deep breath and walked toward the huge beast, all the while keeping her eyes on it. She stopped within the range of the claws and the fire and held out the little body in her hands, trusting the mother would not seek revenge. Tears fell at the sight of her guardian's blood on her pale shaking hands.

"Take him, heal him, please. He has done what you asked, he has guarded me."

The beast studied her and then delicately accepted the small dragon from the girl, cradling it to her own chest. A strange humming sound erupted as the mother crooned to her child. The pensive face lifted back up and continued to study Gwyn, for she still held the Stone.

You hold the Stone, what is your command?

"How do I destroy it?" Gwyn asked, holding the orb up.

That is for us to do. The girl nodded and held out the fragile cord. The dragon shook its head. **I dare not touch it.**

"Carry me and I shall bear the Stone," the girl offered, her heart still pounding. She was aware of countless eyes nervously tracking every movement the dragon made. The beast thought for a time and then shook her head again.

Your skills are needed, for many of your kind perish here.

"But the Stone …" Gwyn sputtered, surprised.

Bring it when the hatching begins, for you must be there.

"By the Powers," Gwyn murmured in astonishment. She well understood the sacred trust that had blossomed between them in this desperate moment. "I will come with the Stone, I vow it."

The dragon's head nodded ever so slightly. It crooned one last time to the small one tucked up against its wide breast and then executed three of four hops into the air. A blast of snow swirled around the clearing as it launched itself off the ground. It turned once in midair and then flew toward the mountain. It did not cry out this time and the resulting silence was eerie.

Shorn of his power and thrown from his horse when the guardian attacked, Phelan found himself at the mercy of his foes. Only Nerian's presence kept him alive. Hauled to his feet and drug off toward the iarel, he was abused at every turn. His Master of the Guard was not so fortunate and his dying cries echoed across the field as the clansmen settled their score with practiced brutality.

Morgan knew something was wrong the moment he found two of his father's men at his side. Their expressions were telling.

"Milord, you must come with us, now!" one of them commanded, his face pale and drawn. They had fought their way around the burning building to find their liege lord's son, praying he still lived. They knew time was precious.

"What is it?" Morgan asked. As they were no longer being pressed, he had taken the opportunity to catch his breath.

"It is your father, milord." The man's eyes conveyed his grief.

"Powers, no!" Morgan set off across the field, the two men acting as escort. Caewlin gestured and four more clansmen joined them to assure that the young lord would reach his father safely. The iarel knew they would not summon him unless the matter was grave.

"May the Gods care for him," he murmured and turned his mind back to his own people.

A knot of people stood around the fallen man, for the battle was nearly at an end with Phelan's capture and the departure of his dragon. Without a word Morgan made his way to his father's side. The expressions of those around him told him his father's injuries were mortal.

"Father?" Morgan said gently, taking his sire's cold hand in his. The older man's eyes flittered open and slight smile creased his ashen face.

"My... son." His chest heaved with every breath.

"Father, we have summoned a healer ..."

"No ... it is not a time ... for healing ... it is a time for passing." Morgan pulled his eyes up to Owain the Elder. There were tears coursing down the older man's cheeks. Morgan's fragile hope fled.

"Yes, father." He moved over to where he could be close to the dying man, cradling him in his arms. Blood was pouring from his father's chest. Bardyn's face drew dusky and his voice progressively weaker.

"You are my only son ... and heir. I love you ... as much I have loved anyone ... even your mother." Morgan abandoned the futile attempt to hold back his grief and tears ran down his smoke-stained face.

"I love you, father. I will do my best ..."

"That is all that is ... required ... my son. Trust Owain ... he is ... best friend ..." The effort to speak was too much and for a time the great man fell silent. Then a smile of recognition passed over his face as his eyes gazed at some apparition none of the others could see. "Morgane? Do you ... call me? I hear you ... my love." He turned his head toward his son again and murmured as if in answer to a query, "Yes, he is ... a fine son."

He looked back toward the vision who waited for him beyond the Veil and said in a calm voice, "Yes ... I come ... I come." He took two shuddering breaths and then no more.

Morgan let his head fall onto his sire's blood-soaked chest and he wept. He felt Owain's strong arm on his shoulder, trying to transmit what strength and comfort he could. It was the only thing that connected him to this world.

"Your mother was waiting for him," Owain said in a grief-stricken voice.

Morgan raised his face and nodded numbly. "He is at peace, but now I am alone."

"No, you are never alone, Morgan, never," Owain's deep voice said. Morgan closed his eyes and let the loss envelop him. He did not know how long he knelt there, for time seemed to have no meaning. In the distance he heard the sound of weeping and of battle.

"Powers!" Owain exclaimed. Instantly on guard, Morgan's eyes flew open and followed the older man's line of sight. Staggering across the field was Pyrs, his shirt thick with blood, the remnants of an arrow in his chest. His father intercepted him immediately and urged him to lie down so they could find a healer to treat him.

"No, I must go to Morgan," the lad said and pulled out of his father's grasp, intent on his mission.

"Pyrs, you are too badly injured," Belwyn tried again, but to no avail.

"Help me, father, I must do this!" Belwyn knew to argue would be futile and perhaps cause the boy more harm, so he helped him across the field to where Morgan grieved for his sire.

"Pyrs ..." Morgan started and the boy shook his head. He slowly eased himself down on both knees and then swore under his breath. He did not have a sword, he'd lost his when he fainted. His eyes reached those of Owain the Elder.

"Grandsire, I need a sword."

Owain instantly knew what Pyrs intended. "Yes you do, my grandson. I am sorry, but the lineage sword is not with us or you would have it." He looked at Belwyn and said, "Give the lad a sword, my son." Belwyn thought for a moment and then finally understood. He handed Pyrs his weapon. The boy took the naked blade in both hands and with great effort extended it out towards Morgan in the timeless offering of a warrior to his liege lord.

He took a deep breath and forced down the blinding pain in his chest.

"I offer my fealty ... and my sword to you ... my lord. I wish to be the first to do so. I ask that you find me acceptable." It took everything for him to get the words out of his mouth as he fought to stay conscious.

Morgan's mouth fell open at the gesture. The moment of transition had come, he was no longer Lord Bardyn's heir, *he* was Lord of the Eastern March. This young man, barely sixteen years of age, sporting a wound that would felled men older than him, was on his knees offering his sword in service. It was a poignant symbol of the bond between Aderyn and his family.

He rose, crossed the short distance to where Pyrs knelt and stared in wonder at the young man. Pyrs's face was ashen, the end of the arrow plainly visible as it protruded through his blood-soaked shirt. The young lord raised his eyes to find a ring of men around him and he made sure his voice rang out.

"As Lord of the Eastern March I accept your blade and your oath of fealty. Let all know that I, Lord Morgan, do hold the House of Aderyn as kin and in particular, Pyrs, son of Belwyn, grandson of Owain the Elder, as dear to me as a brother." Morgan took the sword from the lad and then knelt in front of him. "Bless you, Pyrs, bless you." Pyrs gave him a weak smile and then fainted dead away at the feet of his new liege lord.

"Galen?" It was Ulwyn's voice as he stood over the wounded clansman. A wide swatch of blood extended down the Saga's right shoulder.

"Who calls me?"

"It is your fellow bard, one who would hate to have you die and leave me to sing all your clan's impossible songs at our victory feast."

"We won?"

"It appears so. The dragon has departed and the word is that Phelan is our prisoner. His men are fleeing for their lives as your people aren't very forgiving."

"What of the iarel?" the man asked, prying open his eyes to find Ulwyn kneeling near him. His companion had blood on his forehead from a cut, but his eyes were bright and his smile was genuine.

"I have not heard anything untoward, so I assume he has survived."

"And your liege lord?

A sad shake returned. "No, Lord Bardyn has passed beyond." Galen saw the glint of tears in the fellow's eyes. He took his hand and squeezed Ulwyn's arm. They had grown close on the march south, one bard to another.

"I will sing of his honor as they light his pyre."

"As I will sing of the bravery of your people." Ulwyn glanced around and spied where the healers had set up their temporary camp. He leaned down and helped Galen sit up. "Come, we must get you some care for that shoulder." He saw the man shoot a look of concern across the battlefield. "Is there something wrong?"

"I just wondered if she was safe." Ulwyn did not know who the man was referring to and so let the comment pass. He leveraged Galen up to his feet and set off to find a healer.

Phelan was on his knees in front of the iarel. Tempting though it was, Caewlin did not gloat. He steeled himself and made sure to keep his hand off the hilt of his sword where it now sat inside a plundered scabbard.

"I do not intend to beg. I spent far too many years crawling around, sleeping with the hounds to allow me to beg to one such as you," Phelan said defiantly.

"I didn't expect you to." Caewlin gestured to Nerian, "Keep him under tight guard, for there are more important things to worry about than him at present. Once we have treated our wounded and sent our dead to the Gods, then we will determine his fate."

"Yes, my iarel," Nerian replied, giving a short bow. He waved over four clansmen, gave the order and Phelan was trotted off sporting the chains that had once graced their leader.

"Nerian, I must know that Aithne is safe," Caewlin said. "I sent her into the forest and I've not seen her since." He was struggling to keep his worry at a manageable level.

"I am sure she is unharmed," Nerian remarked.

"Most likely, for I saw her kill one of Phelan's men with all the skill of a shield-woman."

Nerian knew what his leader wanted. "I will find her, Iarel."

"Thank you. Bring her to me, for I want her guarded as she bears the next iarel inside of her." Nerian's old eyes widened and then a smile erupted. Forgetting rank, he slapped Caewlin on the back, regardless of the iarel's wounds.

"By the Gods, we are favored!"

"Yes, we are. Find her for me, Nerian, for I must attend to our people."

"I will find her." Nerian ordered two men to accompany him and then vanished across the field on his quest. The further he walked the more he smiled. Their clan had survived and now a new iarel was being nurtured within the Red Hawk's Chosen.

"We are highly favored," he murmured to himself.

"Pardon, Iarel," Dubhan said and bowed.

"Dubhan?"

"I saw your sister this day, Iarel."

All the words came tumbling out of Caewlin's mouth at once. "What? Here? By the Gods! Where?"

"She was with the Northern lords, fighting, my iarel."

"Are you sure?" That made no sense.

"She had a clansman near to her. He looked to be of your kin."

"Dillan? It must be him! If she is with him then she is safe. By the Gods, that would be good news!"

"Do you wish me to find her, Iarel?" the man asked, pleased to be of service to his leader.

"Yes, Dubhan, find her! I hope you are right, for that would bring me such joy." Caewlin's face was full of excitement.

"I will find her and bring her to you, Iarel," the man replied and he set off across the field, unknowingly tracking in the same footsteps as Nerian.

Owain the Elder carried his grandson away from the carnage to a place near the woods where the healers had established a temporary camp for treating the wounded. He'd wrapped Pyrs into his own cloak to try to keep him from going further into shock. As soon as he placed the boy on the ground near another wounded man, a healer appeared at his side. It was an older woman, one of the clan.

"Where is he hurt?" she asked in the Northern tongue as she knelt by the boy, peeling back the cloak to check for wounds.

"He has an arrow wound in his chest and burns on his arms and shoulders," Owain replied, keeping his eyes on his grandson. He held the boy's right hand in comfort, though Pyrs was not aware of it. A slight intact of breath was all that told him that the healer found the chest wound grievous. She covered the boy and rose immediately.

"I will send over one of the more skilled healers, his wound is beyond my abilities." She scurried off, moving rather quickly for a woman her age. Owain returned his attention to his grandson. The boy's face was deathly pale and his breathing labored. Owain had watched men die from such a wound and his fear ran deep. Prayers tumbled out of his mouth, one after another. Another woman appeared, one in a heavy cloak with the hood up against the morning chill. She appeared to be younger than the other healer, given her gait and her ease of movement. She knelt by the lad, pulled open his cloak, examined the wound and then asked, "Does it penetrate through to his back?"

"No," Owain said quietly.

"Any other wounds?"

"A few burns, nothing compared to the chest wound."

"Good, then we have a chance."

Pyrs awoke to find a vision in front of his eyes. It was a woman, a very pretty one, her face framed by the hood of her dark cloak. He smiled at the sight. His chest ached in pounding waves, but the lady somehow made it better.

"You are very pretty," he said in a thick voice. Her eyes flickered over to him and she chuckled.

"You are too young to try to seduce me, son." Her hands were removing his blood-soaked shirt, carefully cutting it away to reveal the wound in its entirety.

"I am ... sixteen," he answered, hopefully. He'd worked that out in his head and it hadn't been that easy.

"And badly wounded, so I think your charms will have to wait."

"Oh," he said, somewhat deflated. Pyrs felt a squeeze on his right hand and moved his head ever so slightly. His grandsire's tired face came into view.

"Grandsire," he said and smiled more. All was well if his grandfather was with him. "Is it over?" he asked.

"Yes, it is. We have the day, but the cost has been beyond our bearing."

"Lord Bardyn ..." Pyrs murmured, remembering that the man was dead and that he'd knelt before his son, offering his sword in service. It seemed an impossible feat now.

"Our family is intact. Dillan was injured, but not badly."

"Thank the Powers," Pyrs murmured. "And the iarel?"

"He survived with only a few injuries."

"Then the Powers have been merciful to us all." He caught a curious look from the healer as she cleaned the wound.

"Almost a third of our men are dead or wounded and the iarel guesses that nearly one hundred of his people perished."

"Powers, what a cost." There was a pause and then, "I ... killed a man, grandsire." He paused again and then continued, "More than one, I think. It was a vile thing. It made me ill for I saw fear in their eyes as they died." His voice was no more than a whisper now.

"Killing is a vile thing, my grandson, but sometimes it is a needed thing."

"I do not like it and I pray this is the last battle I ever see."

Owain sighed. "You sound like me when I was young. I killed my first man when I was nineteen. I was newly married, my wife carried our child within her, and all I could think of was that I'd just ended someone's life, someone who would never experience the joys I would have in the years to come." As he spoke the healer continued cleaning the wound, though it was obvious she was listening to every word.

There was silence for a time and then she said, "I need to sit him up so I can clean his back." Owain helped her lift Pyrs up off the ground, letting the cloak fall back underneath him. As the boy leaned forward he brushed against her hood and it fell backward revealing a cascade of red hair. It caught his attention for a moment and then he closed his eyes, as the cleaning was very painful. Finally he was eased down on the cloak. He tried to shift to his side but the healer shook her head.

"I know it hurts lying this way, but it will make it easier to remove the arrow." He nodded his understanding and studied her for a minute or so more.

"You have the most beautiful hair," he said and another chuckle came out of the healer.

"Here, drink this and stop trying to court me," she said in a joking tone and made him take a long sip of herbed wine. It tasted good, for his mouth was dry, his throat thick from the stench of battle. She made him continue to drink for a few moments longer and then let him back down. The herbs in the wine made his head spin, dulling his pain and loosening his tongue even further.

"I think I am a very lucky young man, for I have my grandsire here to keep me company and a beautiful woman to care for me," Pyrs said, slurring his words. "What is your name pretty lady?"

"Aithne," she replied and then raised her eyes and caught those of the older man. He had an odd look on his face, one she could not quite fathom.

"Marry me, Aithne, of the gorgeous red hair. I am Pyrs, son of Belwyn, son of Owain the Elder, youngest son of the House of Aderyn. I am an honest lad, good with a sword and full of witty jest. I promise you would not have to scrubs pots or clean chimneys or ..."

"Pyrs!" Owain interjected, surprised at the lad's cheek.

Aithne explained, "It's the wine. It has herbs in it to decrease the pain so it will make it easier to remove the arrow. It also liberates the tongue."

"No, it's not the wine," Pyrs protested as he tried to ignore the fact the healer now had a knife in her hand, one no doubt destined to pry the bolt from his chest. "You are so pretty and I know our children would be very handsome! I think we should have at least five." He paused and noted the lady wasn't leaping at his offer. "Well, then if you won't marry me, then marry my father."

"Pyrs!" his grandsire sputtered.

"What, grandsire? Father is a very honorable man and I wouldn't mind this pretty lady as my mother. Far better than some he might marry."

Owain the Elder groaned.

"Drink more of this," the healer advised and Pyrs took a big gulp of the wine. His eyes began to flutter and he was chattering almost constantly. Some sentences made sense, most did not. His mind flitted to the matter at hand.

"I suppose this will hurt a bit ... when you take out the arrow," he observed as he studied the short-bladed knife in her slim hand.

"No, it will hurt a great deal, that's why I had you drink the wine."

"Oh. Can I keep the piece you take out?" the lad asked groggily.

"Yes. Now relax for me."

"Yes, pretty lady. Do you have any sisters that are as fair as you? If so, I could marry one of ..."

"Grandson, be quiet!" Owain ordered and to his surprise the boy actually complied. Aithne waved over another healer to assist them. Between the three of them, the arrow was deftly removed from the boy's chest. Though the pain was excruciating the lad did not scream, just clenched his teeth and bore it.

Sweat popped onto his forehead and at the very moment he thought he might faint, the agony relented.

"There, it is out," Aithne reported as she placed a clean linen on the wound and applied pressure. She thanked the other healer who rose and left them.

"Hurts ..." Pyrs murmured and then drifted off to sleep, the ordeal over. She lifted up the linen, examined the wound and nodded in approval. There was blood on the linen, but it did not flow copiously from the wound.

"Perfect," Aithne said and then looked over at the anxious grandfather. "He will sleep now. The arrow came out clean and he should heal given his youth and his feisty temperament."

"I apologize, he is usually fairly circumspect," Owain said rather contritely. Pyrs's comments had been amusing, but over the mark.

"I do not mind. At least I can still turn the head of a young lad." Her voice was strained, at odds with her casual words.

There was a very long pause and then Owain the Elder replied in a gentle voice, "Your mother turned my head, why should it be different for you?" Her eyes slowly rose to his, widening in apprehension. It confirmed Owain's suspicion that the healer knew who he was.

"I thought you might be *him*, but I was not sure until the boy said your name."

"I am he." He still held Pyrs's hand, but his full attention was on the healer. Her unique hair and elegant face had triggered a long buried memory, one of another young woman and the loving they had shared almost three decades before.

"When did you know?" she asked in an uneasy voice.

"The moment your hood fell back. Your hair is the exact color of hers and your eyes are ... well, I remember those eyes as if I were eighteen again." She fumbled with the linens and turned her mind back to her duties, disconcerted by the revelation.

"Help me bandage his wounds." They worked together and Pyrs's wounds were soon snugly bound. He slept through the whole process, snoring lightly. They carefully laid him down and she covered him with his grandfather's cloak.

"We are taking some of the more seriously wounded to the guards' barracks for it is out of the weather. I will see that he is moved there." She began to tidy her things, stuffing herbs and linens back into the pack she carried, anything to escape this awkward situation.

"Aithne ..." Owain started and then stopped. Her eyes crept up to his and for an instant there was only the two of them.

She swallowed and explained, "I do not know what to believe. I have heard things about you, about your family and ..." She stopped and then took one long breath and then exhaled to calm her racing heart. "I must tend to the wounded, for they have priority over this."

Owain nodded in agreement. "Know that I gave your mother a vow almost four years ago that I would find you. The Powers have allowed that to happen because of my boisterous grandson. I am content, Aithne, even if you never accept me for who I am, for I have fulfilled my vow to the woman I loved and lost."

She studied his worn face for any sign of falsehood and did not find it, only tenderness poured out of his eyes. She rose, gave Pyrs one last look and set off to help the other wounded warriors. A tempest raged within her heart, for she had met her sire and she feared he was not the monster she believed him to be.

Gwyn appeared only a few minutes after Aithne left them.

"Gwyn, Powers Be Praised, you are safe!" Owain the Elder cheered. She nodded, but he noted her face was pale and her usual level of self-assurance was absent.

"Has he been seen by a healer?" she asked.

"Yes, Aithne has removed the arrow and it came out clean."

"Thank the Powers," Gwyn muttered and then fell on her knees by her twin. She smoothed a small strand of his hair out of his face and then bent over and kissed his forehead in a loving gesture. Tears were in her eyes and for once Gwyn looked like a young girl, full of all the anxiety that life could bestow on her. She swallowed down her tears, placed her hands on her brother's chest and spoke a powerful spell of healing. Pyrs's color improved but he continued to sleep undisturbed. She leaned back, weariness and worry taking its toll.

Her grandsire sought to reassure her. "He will be fine. He is a very brave young man."

A slight smile appeared on her face. "He is, isn't he?" Owain noted the dragon was not on her shoulder and that boded ill.

"Your guardian?" he asked gently, fearing the beast had perished.

Her eyes caught his. "He is badly hurt. His mother has taken him. I did not … I could not protect him, grandsire." Her resolve fled and she cascaded into tears. Laying Pyrs's hand down Owain embraced his granddaughter and offered solace as she wept against his shoulder.

"You did what you could. You are not invincible, you know. That is something your mother had to learn as well." The sobs lessened and he felt her nod. Her visions during the Ritual of the Third Path had never revealed Pyrs's near fatal injury, only his time within the blazing building. She had not been prepared for what the Powers had placed before her.

"I know. When Pyrs was struck down I shifted my mind to him and that is when Phelan bound my guardian."

"All is well now, Gwyn. You have done such remarkable things for a girl who is only three-years old." She looked up at that and her tears began to fade.

"I am only three, aren't I?"

"And already a legend, like your cheeky brother. Did I tell you that he offered marriage to the healer who treated him?"

Gwyn actually laughed. "That I wouldn't doubt. He is a menace, grandsire!"

"She is very pretty," he said quietly.

His grand-daughter caught the odd tone to his voice. "Grandsire?" Her mind was too full of the events of the day to sense any deeper meaning.

"She is my daughter by Adwyth." The words hung in the air. "Her name is Aithne." He saw her in the distance, rising from the care of a wounded warrior and he pointed toward her. "She is there."

Gwyn turned toward where her grandfather pointed and sensed life coming full circle.

"So she is. Father will be very pleased." She looked back at her brother's inert form. "Does Pyrs know who she is?"

"No, he does not. We spoke after he fell asleep."

Gwyn started to laugh and to Owain it was the most beautiful sound he'd heard in ages. It was musical and full of life, like a young girl sharing an innocent jest with a dear friend.

"Please, let me tell him he was trying to court his own aunt. That will be precious! It will be so delightful to see Pyrs in full retreat!" She laughed again, reached over, kissed her grandsire, and then set off toward Aithne. She was determined to offer her magic to help the wounded and learn more about her newly discovered aunt in the process.

TWENTY-NINE

Dillan looked up into Isen's stern face from where he sat on a blanket awaiting Fea's return from the healers. The younger clansman had an expression of extreme displeasure on his face.

"By the Gods, you live," he cursed.

"Apparently They did not think it was my day to die," Dillan replied coolly.

"Pity, for I would not have mourned your passing, old man."

Dillan shrugged. His eyes went past the clansman and saw Fea drawing close. Next to her was Elrehan, as he'd been throughout the battle. In some strange way that had brought Dillan comfort, for he knew if he died the warrior would see to his wife.

"If you think marrying Fea has brought you the position of iarel, you are wrong," Isen muttered, unaware of the pair drawing closer to him.

"That was not why I did it."

"Old men such as you can die from many things – life is very precarious. I intend to bed your bride even as your funeral pyre burns, for nothing will keep me from her and the rank of iarel, in time." Dillan's eyes grew cold at the clansman's unusually candid remarks. As he opened his mouth to retort Isen suddenly shifted uncomfortably. He felt a sword at his back, pressing inward.

"If something untoward should happen to my husband, Isen, be aware that your throat will be cut before I even light his funeral pyre."

"You wouldn't dare!" Isen said, anger in his eyes. The sword shifted to the base of skull and pressed in to the point of pain.

"I vow it before the Gods." He shivered involuntarily, knowing the weight of such a covenant.

"I will keep my distance."

"Then all will prosper," Fea's stern voice replied.

The sword retreated and he turned to find the iarel's sister standing behind him, a dark expression on her face. The Northern man stood next to her and he glowered at him. Elrehan only regarded Isen with passing interest, his mind still numb from the events of the past few days. Isen stalked off, murmuring to himself in anger.

"Nicely done, wife," Dillan remarked and smiled broadly.

"I should put him to the sword just for practice," Fea said. She sheathed her weapon and took her place on the blanket next to him.

"How is your wound?"

"Feeling much better. You must go get yours treated now."

"It appears I owe you an apology," Elrehan muttered. The older clansman scrutinized the warrior as he rose from the blanket.

"No, you do not. I married the woman you love. I never forgave Geraint for that and so I suspect the Powers are allowing me to learn how it feels to be despised."

"No, my anger got the best of me. I …" he stopped and gazed fondly at Fea. "I will always love her but I know you will keep her safe from those like Isen."

"That is one of the reasons I married her."

"I wish you both happiness."

Fea gave Dillan a long look and then replied, "That is for the Gods to decide." Elrehan frowned at the odd remark.

"Indeed, that is for the Gods to decide," the elder clansman replied. As he walked away he could hear the warrior and his wife talking quietly.

May the Gods be merciful to us all, he thought.

Aithne found the young woman very disturbing. She was a near match to the healer who had perished on the pyre and that troubled her.

"Healer," Gwyn said lightly and then stooped down to ascertain if the wounded warrior at her feet was in need of magic or should be allowed to heal at his own pace.

"Girl," Aithne replied uneasily.

"I am Gwyn, daughter of Morwyn," the girl announced and then moved to another wounded man. His leg was in poor shape and she murmured a healing spell over it.

"I am Aithne," she replied, offering no lineage after her name. When Gwyn finished her work their eyes met.

"Greetings, aunt." Gwyn said nothing more and moved to the next patient and continued her healing. Aithne forced herself to remain focused on the wounded. Her island of denial was being breached, one compassionate family member at a time.

She was relieved when only a few minutes later Nerian found her, two clansmen in tow. She walked toward him, concerned, wiping her hands on her skirt.

"The iarel, is he unharmed?" she asked, wishing to verify what she had heard.

"He has wounds on him, but his enemies lay dead at his feet," Nerian replied, paraphrasing an old clansman's song. When he realized that hadn't mollified her, he added, "The wounds are not mortal, Aithne, do not fear."

"Thank the Powers," she intoned and sighed in obvious relief.

"He asked that I bring you to him." She shook her head immediately and gestured to the multitude of wounded behind her. Healers flitted from body to body like bees visiting tattered and wilted flowers.

"I cannot leave, there are too many in need of my care. Tell him I will find him later, once we have everyone settled." Nerian had wisely foreseen this moment and knew to argue would be futile, a healer would remain with her patients, no matter what his iarel ordered. He waved forward his men.

"Guard this woman with your life, for she is the Iarel's Chosen." The two clansmen bowed and from then on Aithne had an armed escort as she performed her tasks.

Belwyn remained at Morgan's side, confident that his father would see to Pyrs's treatment. He vividly remembered the fog he had lived in when his own mother had died and he knew Morgan needed a strong presence at his side.

"The casualty figures are grim. I had hoped we would lose less than we have. It will weaken us for a time," Morgan observed as he walked amongst his men. He stopped from time to time, speaking to individual warriors, offering his praise and his support. It was what a leader did after a battle, though he had lost his own father to the carnage.

"I would not doubt news of this battle will reach certain ears far sooner than we would wish."

Morgan nodded. "We can expect a challenge, for they have never held me in high regard." He was struggling to keep focused and wade through the duties of the day. His mind kept calling him back to his loss.

"That is their error. I would suggest we finish our campaign as soon as possible and head north." Belwyn knelt down at this and helped a warrior take a drink from a wineskin as his bandaged arm hindered him.

"That is the best course. It depends on Kell." He knelt and offered a few comforting words.

The wounded man answered, "Thank you, milord. We are all grieved at the loss of your father, but we know you are cut of his cloth." Morgan kept his emotions off his face and smiled gently.

"I will do my best." He rose at that and continued to make his way through the camp, seeing to his warriors' needs, instinctively assuming the role of his father.

Dubhan located Fea and Dillan and requested them to attend the iarel. When Elrehan rose, intent on accompanying them, Fea asked him to remain behind. He did so, though she could tell it was not to his liking.

"Caewlin must know my tale before he sees you or I fear he will kill you outright."

"I understand." His tone indicated that it did not matter.

As soon as he saw her, Caewlin immediately embraced and kissed his sister, overjoyed to find her alive.

"You are wounded?" he said, seeing the bandage on her side. He was keenly aware that a small knot of clan closely watched the encounter. To the man, they were curious how Caewlin would handle the matter of his sister.

"I am, but it is of no consequence."

"How did you come to be with the Northerners?"

"I was set free by one of Bardyn's warriors. He brought me to his liege lord and there I found Dillan."

"I worried so much about you after Phelan sold you." His eyes tracked down to the linens on his wrists. She studied them for a moment and realized what they were.

She shook her head. "No, it is not as it seems, for I was a maid when I reached Bardyn's camp." Caewlin's eyes widened. She shot a look over at her husband and continued. "I am now married … to Dillan."

"What?" Caewlin asked in surprise. "How is it that you were still a virgin and then wed so precipitously?"

"My honor was spared as Bardyn's warrior was the trader who bought me. His name is Elrehan and he made Phelan believe I was a maid no longer."

He demanded in a tight voice, "Explain." Fea saw the fire in his eyes and knew he was upset by this sudden revelation. She cleared her throat and began her tale. The small crowd around them grew as she progressed through to the end.

"You swear you were untouched?" Caewlin asked, incredulous. He lifted his wrists and displayed the torn pieces of fabric. "These say otherwise."

"I swear on the bones of our father and mother. The blood was the Northern man's, not mine." Murmurs swirled around them.

"Why did you agree to wed without my permission?" he asked, his mind reeling. Though Dillan, as eldest member of the iarel's family, did have the right to order her to marry during the iarel's absence, he was stunned.

"My iarel," Dillan interjected and bowed. "I wed your sister to remove any taint from her person. If I, her grand uncle, accepted her word that she was untouched and was willing to marry her, then it would be unreasonable for anyone else to judge her otherwise." Caewlin studied him for moment, his eyes narrowed. Dillan's face was unreadable and that told the iarel there was more behind this than Fea's honor.

"And the bride cloth?" he asked.

"We burned it, Iarel. To do otherwise would say I did not trust my wife's word." Caewlin's eyebrow inched upward.

"I see." He looked over a Fea and caressed her bruised cheek gently. "I must ask, did you wed willingly?"

Fea looked over at Dillan and then back to her brother. "I did, for I understood what being wed to Dillan would mean for our clan's future." Caewlin thought it through and realized he had few choices.

"Iarel," a voice said, "I challenge this marriage."

As I knew you would. "On what grounds, Isen?"

"It was known that she was to be mine."

"Did you offer her your dagger?"

A sullen glower appeared on the clansman's face. "No, she made sure not to allow me the opportunity."

"Fea?" Caewlin asked as he turned toward her.

"I did not wish to wed Isen, for he would not treat me with respect. He only sought to have me so he could improve his status within the clan. His ambition would make him an unsuitable husband and a poor lover." Her brutally frank comment occasioned an scathing oath from Isen.

"Hold your tongue," Dillan warned, his hand on the hilt of his sword.

Caewlin examined the two men. His grand uncle had always made the clan his first priority, as had Fea. Isen put himself first, above the clan.

There is more here than I see, Caewlin thought, *or Dillan would not have done this without my permission.*

He took a deep breath and announced, "I accept the bond between my sister and my grand uncle, Dillan, brother to our grandsire, for it benefits the clan. May the union be fruitful and our people grow stronger because of it." A murmur of approval wove its way through the now sizeable crowd. Isen swore again and stormed off in fury.

"Thank you, brother," Fea said and gave him a light kiss. He leaned over and whispered in her ear. "We will speak further in private." She nodded and then moved to stand near her husband. Dillan slipped his hand around her waist and gave her a kiss on the forehead. To Fea's brother it was a paternal kiss, not one of a husband to his bride.

Elrehan found the point of a sword hovering only a few inches from his throat as he sat on a rock close to the shoreline, nearly oblivious to everything around him. He knew to whom the sword belonged and when two pieces of bloodstained cloth fell at his feet, he muttered, "Iarel."

The Southern leader sported an intense look and the sword point did not waver. "Trader."

"I trust you have found your sister," Elrehan replied. He did not attempt to pull his weapon, it would be pointless.

"Yes, I have found her."

"She is an incredibly brave woman."

"She told me her tale. Apparently she was not ruined by you."

"No, I would not do such a thing. If you intend to kill me, please do so now. Gloating does not become you and I am weary and am ready for rest." There was an immense sadness in his voice.

Caewlin frowned and shook his head. "I think not," he replied and sheathed his weapon. The expression that appeared on the Northern warrior's face almost bordered on regret.

"I suppose you know that Fea is married," Elrehan said in an uneven voice.

"Yes, I do. Do you know why Dillan asked for her?"

Elrehan nodded, "I have come to see some of the reasons. I once believed it was because Dillan wished to reclaim his youth through the body of a young woman. Now I know it was more than that."

Caewlin glanced around to insure there were no clansmen nearby.

"I spoke at length with both my sister and my grand uncle. Dillan married my sister for a number of reasons, the most important of which was to keep the clan from fragmenting. There are those who keenly wish to be iarel and will only achieve that rank if they are wed to my sister. Since it was unsure if I would survive, Dillan married Fea to protect her. He is the eldest of my family and felt a duty to keep her safe." There was even more to it than that, but he felt this explanation would suffice.

"I will accede to that, though it makes the loss no less hard to bear." At that, Elrehan rose from the rock, dusting off his breeches. "All I pray is that she finds happiness," he said quietly. The tone of his voice spoke reams to her brother.

"I am sure she will," the iarel replied, watching the man like a hawk. Elrehan turned and walked across the sand leaving Caewlin to his thoughts.

"By the Gods, he *is* in love with her." He scooped up the two pieces of bloodstained cloth and set off to find a campfire in which to burn them. In that way he would break his vow to destroy the man who had supposedly harmed his sister. Ironically, the Gods had already inflicted a punishment far more painful than any torture he could invent.

Aithne knew it would only be a matter of time before her betrothed found her and so it was no surprise when she heard him shout, "Fire-hair!" He rushed across the field, heedless as to how that might look to any of his people and then assaulted her with a barrage of kisses within a very tight embrace. "By the Gods you are safe!" She finally pulled out of his ardent clinch and realized his wounds were neither clean nor bound.

"Your wounds are not treated!"

"Not yet." His voice told her he could care less.

"Come and I will treat them or they will infect. I can't have the father of my child die because I didn't care for him."

"I'd rather make love to you here in front of all the Gods and my people," he replied in a playful voice, trying to pull her into his arms again. She restrained him.

"Stop that, there are people watching us."

"Then let them see how much I want you," he murmured back as he tried to slip his arms around her waist. She pushed him away and pointed for him to sit on a nearby blanket. He gazed at her sensuously and she ignored it.

"Sit down!" He complied rather reluctantly. As she checked the numerous wounds, all of which appeared relatively minor, she realized that one of them smelled. It was not her.

"You need a bath, Iarel."

He gave her a surprised look and then chortled. "You are right, I do stink."

"No, you're worse than that," she replied, wrinkling her nose. "Even I will not be with you until you bathe." She was pleased to find that wounds did not need much care, at least not until he was clean, and then she could apply ointments and bandages as needed. "Bathe so I can bind your wounds. To do so now will only allow the dirt to settle within them." She removed her hands and stepped back out of reach, knowing where his mind resided at present.

He rose, bowed, and said rather graciously, "Well then, my love, I am off to find water to bathe and perhaps even some clean clothes. Then I'll be back so you can tend *all* my hurts." She shook her head at him and watched him wander off on his quest. She knew it might be some time before she saw him again.

The afternoon progressed as the wounded were treated, the dead prepared for burial and the living tried to accept their miraculous survival. Though Pyrs did not know it, he had a steady stream of visitors who stood near his bed in the guards' barracks and offered prayers for his recovery. His father, grandsire and sister stayed the longest, but little groups of clansmen and women would filter in as well. They prayed for his healing and gave thanks to their Gods that the fearless son of the Northern lord lived. His daring plan had saved countless lives in the fire and he was already renowned for his bravery and his intelligence. Fortunately, he was unaware of the awe he was generating and slept soundly through the visitations.

The iarel's desire for cleanliness proved to be a common theme for all the workers. Once the more important work was completed, as a whole the clan turned its mind to food and bathing. The camp's stores were raided and food distributed. Cooking pots were set up and soon the smell of rich stews and roasting meats began to waft through the night air. The food was readily shared with their Northern counterparts so it was not uncommon to see a knot of clan sitting with a few of Bardyn's men, all eating and trying to understand each other.

Phelan's men were fed as well and Caewlin was surprised to see that the clan had not given them only bread and water. Cups of stew were in their hands along with bread. He found more than one clanswoman hand feeding an injured guard and he suspected those particular men had not been brutal in their treatment of his people. He had realized quite early in the conflict that the more heinous guards were swiftly dispatched, but those who had shown some mercy were treated with a measure of kindness.

"As the Gods would wish it," he murmured to himself. "Perhaps we will not become like Fyren or Phelan." That gave him hope.

"Iarel?" Nerian appeared at his leader's side.

"Ah, Nerian. How are things progressing?"

"Very well, Iarel. The wounded are cared for, the dead are being prepared for the rites tomorrow and sentries are in the woods in case there is an attack from Kell."

"There won't be, not with Phelan here. He will be left to perish for his men feared him as much as we did." Nerian's eyebrow went up at that and Caewlin caught it. "Yes, I feared Phelan and I will admit it. I could see the end of us, Nerian, as clear as I could my own hand."

"It was not to be, Iarel," his second-in-command replied.

"No, we were favored and have lived to tell the tale." He glanced around and the sight of two tents caught his eye. "Are those what I think they are?"

Nerian nodded. "Yes, we have set up two tents for bathing. Our people are tired of being filthy. The Wise blessed them so they are a means to cleanse the stench of our servitude and the filth from our bodies."

Caewlin grinned. "That is perfect! Do you need anything else of me at present?" His voice begged that the answer be negative.

"No, Iarel, all is settled. Phelan is under heavy guard, those captured have been treated and fed and the Northerners are mourning their lord."

"Then I am off to bathe and then warm the furs of my beloved fire-hair," Caewlin announced.

Nerian smiled and replied, "We have secured a room for you in the guards' barracks. We felt it safer than having you sleep in a tent in the middle of an open field while enemies are still about."

Caewlin nodded his agreement and clasped the man's arm. "You are my strength, Nerian."

"As you are mine, Iarel." He watched as the young man strode across the field toward the tents with a determined look in his eyes. "May you find much happiness tonight, my iarel."

For once, Caewlin took advantage of rank and jumped ahead of those waiting in line. No one said a word, but motioned him forward eagerly for he had certainly earned his right to the hot water. He had no way to immerse himself, but pouring water over his body and using the soap they'd found made all the difference. He emerged clean, in borrowed clothes, his hair shining. He felt like a new man, despite the discomfort of his wounds. After one last check to insure all was secure he set off for the guard's barracks. It was easy to guess which room held his fire-hair for there were two clansmen stationed at the door. They bowed the moment they saw him. Caewlin noted neither of them had bathed yet.

"She is inside?" he asked, though he knew the answer if they were on guard.

"Yes, Iarel."

"Good. Then go find food and bathe, for there is nothing like being clean after such a long time. I will guard her tonight." The men bowed again and departed. As soon as they were out of sight Caewlin smiled and sighed in virile anticipation. He did not knock on the door, he was iarel after all and she should expect him. She was not the least bit startled, in fact she was in the narrow bed, now lined with warm furs. Her clothes lay on a nearby chair and there was a cozy fire in the hearth. Everything told him the night would be full of passion.

"Fire-hair, I am clean." He shut the door, noted the heavy bolt at the top of it and pulled it shut with a strong tug.

"Then you are presentable to share my furs." The look on her face beckoned him to join her.

"Not yet, for there is a matter we must resolve." Her face grew puzzled. His grew a stern expression. "I have heard a rumor that you shared your bed with another man in Kell, one with brown hair. I heard that you found much pleasure in his loving. Is that true?" Her eyes widened and she recognized the game he played. It was unlike him. So much weight had fallen off his shoulders that he could now jest like this.

"Yes, I did sport with another man, Iarel, and I enjoyed his time with me very much. He was very vigorous and gave me many nights of pleasure."

"And where is he now?" he demanded as he started to remove his clothes, never taking his eyes off the beautiful form in the bed.

"Alas, he has left me. Once he got me with child he has abandoned me to my fate."

"With child, you say?"

"Yes, I am nearly three months gone."

"Well, this bodes ill. He has taken advantage of you and that will not do." He crawled into the furs with her, watching her intently. "I must remove his nights of lovemaking from your memory."

"That will take much," she replied, an erotic glow in her eyes.

"I have the power to do it," he confidently.

"I am willing to bet you cannot." She felt his hand on her hip and she jumped involuntarily. It was ice cold. "Powers, your hand is freezing."

He pulled her over on top of him and commanded, "Then warm me up."

It took some time, but eventually the iarel admitted he felt warm enough and Aithne agreed that some of her memory of that *other* man had faded to some degree. They lay together, savoring the love they had made. Her mood shifted and he sensed it immediately.

"What is it, my love?" He kissed her gently on the cheek and waited for her answer. She spun the tale of her mother and herself, how the House of Aderyn had sought their deaths and of the improbable meeting with her sire on the battlefield.

"What do you intend to do?"

"I wish to know if I should acknowledge or spurn him."

"I can only speak of what I have seen, my love. Both his son and grandson have great honor and genuine compassion for those who suffer. Men do not usually obtain those qualities unless their sire teaches them. I cannot speak of Owain the Elder, but Dillan can. Speak with him, for he has served him for more years than I have been alive. That may help make your decision easier."

"I will."

He pulled the heavy coverlet over them and then murmured in her ear, "I love you fire-hair."

"I love you, Iarel."

"We will wed in five nights," he announced, "for I want you at my side for the rest of my life."

"Then I am favored by the Gods," she replied.

Once Elrehan had taken his place at Morgan's side, Belwyn succumbed to the need to be clean. It took little persuasion. He found himself in the men's tent with three other clansmen who were singing and jesting as they scrubbed themselves. His itchy beard was the first thing to go and then he applied the soap and water with vigor. It was a merry time as the men traded jokes and tales, the weight of the battle gone and the thrill of being alive making the moment memorable. Belwyn's recounting of some of Morgan's more bawdy jokes earned him hearty laughter. Finally, almost reluctantly, he rose, donned the clean clothes his father had brought for him from Aderyn, and left his jolly companions behind.

Lord Bardyn's body was at rest in his tent, two of his men standing outside in tribute. They inclined their heads as Morgan entered to pay his respects to his sire. His father was in his battle garments, his face tranquil as if he found death a pleasant respite from the cares of this world. Morgan understood that now, for his title bore down as heavily as the massive stone that once stood in the cavern's mouth. He was not surprised to find Owain the Elder sitting vigil in the candlelight.

"Owain," he said in a quiet voice. The man sat on a bench near his friend's feet.

"My lord."

"Please, call me Morgan."

Owain inclined his head. "I shall call you Morgan in private, then." He paused and then asked, "How do you fare?" The young man settled onto a bench near his sire's head.

"I am overwhelmed. I knew this day would come and still I am not ready."

"One is never ready for such a task. I was not. I know Belwyn and in time, Pyrs, will feel the exact same way. To feel otherwise means you are not fit for the task."

"I hoped he would live forever."

"He would not have wanted it that way. From the very second he learned who you were, he was at peace, for he knew you were the best son he could possibly have."

"I must look to siring an heir," Morgan said. He sounded like it was a penance.

"Yes, you must, but choose your wife wisely, for she can either stand as your rock in difficult times, or weigh you down like a millstone." His voice was edged in sadness.

"I will try to find one such as you describe, but I knew only one woman who …" He stopped. It was inappropriate to speak of Owain's deceased daughter-in-law in such a way.

"You have kept your heart in armor since she refused you and no doubt have missed more than one opportunity to wed."

Morgan nodded his agreement. "You are right, for I have met more than one good woman since Morwyn."

"Put her memory aside and you will find a woman comparable to her."

"I have tried to but …"

"My lord!" A voice called from outside and both men stood up instantly, for the voice was urgent.

"What is the matter?"

One of his guards entered, bowed and then stammered, "Our enemy has escaped!"

"What? How?" Morgan demanded.

"His guards' food was tainted and they fell asleep."

"Who fed the guards?" Owain quizzed.

"One of the clansmen, sir."

"Then wake the iarel!"

The incessant pounding on his door and the grim news that Phelan was gone interrupted the iarel's blissful evening with his fire-hair. He dressed and flew out of the chamber after commanding Aithne to bolt the door behind her. She did as he asked and then weary from the day and the evening, she fell back asleep immediately.

As they feared, Phelan's escape was made possible by commandeering one of the small boats in the harbor. It was obvious he had set off for Kell to rouse his troops and seal the city against the invaders.

"Powers, how could this have happened?" Morgan stormed as they stood at the water's edge where their foe had so brazenly sailed away.

"I will learn who has betrayed us and they will meet with clan justice," Caewlin replied in a low tone. He was deeply disturbed, for he sensed the treachery lie within his own people rather than with the Northern men.

Morgan was incensed. "Fine and good," he growled sarcastically, "but now I must lay on a siege for which I have neither time nor the provisions. Is there nothing else we can do?"

The iarel shook his head. "The guards have been asleep for at least two hours by their reckoning. Phelan chose a small boat and that makes him hard to track. He will be in Kell before we find him." He was angry as well, but kept that from his face.

"This is impossible!" Morgan growled. Gwyn was standing nearby, listening. She moved her eyes toward the mountain in the distance and sent a request. It was answered immediately.

That is possible, dragon daughter. A small trumpet of sound issued from the island as a blaze of white glided through the night, back lit by the moon as it set off across the sea.

"Powers, what was that?" Morgan asked.

"That was the sound of a dragon hunting for our errant enemy," Gwyn murmured. The Watcher had much better prospects at finding Lord Phelan than did any of the mortals.

Morgan called Elrehan, Owain the Elder and Belwyn to his tent for counsel, though he was exhausted and needed sleep. He pointedly informed the iarel his presence was not needed, for the discussion would focus on Kell and the clansman had already indicated his people would not take part in a siege of the great city. Caewlin, sensing Morgan's volatile attitude, wisely refrained from comment and returned to his betrothed.

Morgan's usual tact was gone, worn down by the events of the past few days. "Whether that flying menace finds Phelan or not, I intend to march to

Kell tomorrow. I am astounded the clan let Phelan escape! Now he will have ample opportunity to raise his men before we arrive."

"I do not think Phelan will find as hospitable a reception as he believes," Owain explained. He related Nyle's comments in detail.

"Did this man survive the battle?" Morgan demanded.

"Yes, he did. Do you wish to speak with him?" The lord nodded and a warrior was dispatched to find him. While they waited, Morgan talked at length with Elrehan about the layout of the city.

"It was built to withstand a siege," the warrior explained. "It boasts ten wells and plenty of fresh water. Since we don't have sea capability, it will be nearly impossible to starve them out." Morgan nodded in agreement, he suspected as much. Shortly thereafter Nyle appeared and was questioned closely about the internal politics of the city. Morgan listened intently though his attitude was brusque.

"I do not want to lay siege to such a strongly fortified city. I need to return home as soon as possible, for we have our own set of villainous nobles to deal with," the lord explained.

"If my father has his way, you will have no war."

"Then let us pray that is the case."

ThiRTY

As the Lord of the Eastern March stood in the morning light he gazed in unbridled awe at the funeral pyre the clan had built in honor of his sire. It was meticulous in every detail. Rather than randomly heaping up wood and laying the corpse on the top, they had painstakingly built layer after layer, each piece precisely alternating with the other underneath it. It stood some ten feet off the ground and his father's body lay at the very top, magnificent in every form.

Those of his men who had perished with him were layered down the sides of the pyre as if his father still commanded an army in death. It was a work indicative of deep respect and Morgan found it very difficult to hold back his tears at the sight of it. The pyre for the clan's fallen was equally intricate, but Phelan's men warranted no such care. Situated away from the two main pyres so as to not taint the honorable dead, it was indeed a heap of logs with bodies strewn on it. He knew the clan would have preferred to bury those corpses rather than give them the rite of a pyre, but the frozen ground did not permit it.

Morgan would come to know this day as the hardest of his life. Holding his father as he took his last breath was devastating, but igniting the pyre and watching his body consumed into ash was far more agonizing. It was truly the end. Standing at his side was Owain the Elder and on the other, the iarel. Arrayed behind them was every member of the clan who could was capable of walking. Morgan's men were present as well, mixed within their Southern brethren.

The funeral rites were performed with utmost dignity. Devona offered prayers to the Gods and both Galen and the Ulwyn sang of the honor and bravery of those that fought and died on this field. Owain the Elder invoked the Powers, calling Them to witness the ascension of so many worthy men and women.

Morgan stepped forward and ignited his father's pyre, watching it blaze into life. Caewlin did the same to the clan's pyre. The tinder caught instantly and then worked its way through the carefully selected dry wood. The pleasant smell of pine filled the air as the flames shot upward. A strange unearthly keening noise assaulted Morgan's ears, filling the void around him. It came from the clan, their way of showing their grief at such a time. The sound faded away and they fell silent in tribute to those who were no more.

Morgan pulled his sword, dropped to one knee and held the blade out to the growing inferno that engulfed his father's corpse, returning him to the elements of the earth.

"I shall carry forward your sword and your life's work as long as the Powers deem me worthy. I love you, father."

Behind him, all grieved, tears flowing from every face. Morgan finally permitted his grief to show and tears rained down his face. He did not know it, but the iarel wept as well, no longer concerned that his people would think him weak. Strength came from the ability to grieve, to acknowledge the loss and to value life even more. Morgan remained in place for the time it took for his father to vanish completely in the roaring flames. He rose, sheathed his sword and then turned to find hundreds of faces behind him, all sharing his loss.

At his side, Owain the Elder murmured, "Remember, you are never alone." Morgan searched the face of his father's dearest companion and found loss heavy on him. In his eyes, he saw compassion.

"Powers, guide us and help us find peace," Morgan intoned and then marched off the field to prepare his men for the journey to Kell.

Lord Phelan enjoyed the joke once he was far enough away at sea to laugh aloud. "The irony of it," he chortled. It was not one of his men that had allowed him to escape, but one of the iarel's own. "How delicious!" he chortled again and kept his craft near the shoreline as he worked his way toward the fortified city. Once there he would raise his troops and when the new Lord of the Eastern March came to call, as no doubt he would, the war would tilt in his favor. He had readily granted the rogue clansman everything he'd asked for, but that was not a bargain he would keep. All of the clan would perish, his misguided rescuer as well, and then the Lord of the Hounds would reign supreme.

He continued to watch the sea behind him as night turned to dawn, vigilant for the pursuing longships, but he saw none. What he did not realize was that his greatest peril would come from the sky, not the sea. A bolt of white dove out of the air and catapulted his boat across the water. Phelan sank and then frantically pulled himself to the surface, his heavy cloak weighting him down. As he thrashed he saw the white demon skimming across the azure water as a hawk would in search of a fish. He ducked, but it did not save him as a claw deftly plucked him out of the water. The dragon soared into the air with a cry of triumph, its prey in hand.

The morning did not go as Belwyn had planned, for he learned he was not to accompany his liege lord to Kell. When he asked his father the reason, he was told it was because of Gwyn. He sought her out and rather ungraciously demanded to know why he was not to be at his liege lord's side.

"You and I are to go to the mountain, father, for the hatching," she replied and gave him a demure smile. The smile usually worked on her grandsire, but it failed with her father.

"I have no need to be there. I must be at Morgan's side," he replied in a flat tone, irritated.

"No, you must be at the hatching, father, for there is a purpose for your presence."

"I don't care," he snapped. "I have had quite enough dragons for one life."

She chuckled, took him by the arm and starting leading him toward the seashore. "Neither of us have a choice, father. We *must* be there." The disgruntled frown on his face did not disappear, even as they boarded one of the small boats and made their way to the island.

It was a moment to savor and the Watcher did just that. A slight chuff of smoke issued from the white dragon's mouth as the mortals scattered in panic front of it. It found that endlessly amusing. It had landed some distance from the still smoldering pyres, kicking up a blaze of snow that obscured it for a moment. When the cloud dissipated, it bided its time waiting for one of the leaders of the mortals, Caewlin he was called, to come forward. The dragon observed the blonde-haired young man march forward to within only a few feet or so. He was clearly within the range of its fire and its claws, yet he showed no fear. The beast was impressed and addressed its thoughts directly to him.

Gwyn, dragon daughter, asked that I return our enemy to you. The dragon's right claw opened and spewed forward a cloaked form onto the ground in front of it. Lord Phelan rolled some distance as the garment unwound from around him. He sat up and started hurtling oaths at the beast behind him. An immense hiss erupted and he fell into silence as the dragon's eyes bore into him.

You lack manners, mortal. The dragon gazed back at Caewlin and announced, *His fate is yours. See that he troubles us no more.*

"We shall, dragon. Peace be to your kind." The beast paused for a moment and then inclined its head at the gracious remark. It took to the air only a few moments later, covering those nearby in a thin layer of powdery snow.

"Bind him in chains in the middle of the compound where all can see him," the iarel's stern voice decreed. He shot a look at Dillan and then returned to his morning repast. Phelan was drug across the field without ceremony. He held his silence and set his mind on escape.

"Did they learn who helped him?" Dubhan asked Dillan as they followed their leader back to their meal. A shake of the older clansman's head was the answer.

"The clansman who fed the guards is dead, his throat cut. He is not under suspicion, for he hated Phelan – his wife is in one of Kell's brothels. We believe another tainted the food and then committed murder to cover his identity."

"By the Gods, that is ill. We have a traitor in our midst and no knowledge of who it is."

Dillan held his silence. He and his iarel suspected who had altered the food, but there was no proof and so the matter would pass without resolution. *A traitor in our midst,* he thought, *one that would be pleased to see both Caewlin and I dead.*

As Belwyn hiked up the side of the mountain he tried to work out in his mind how many times he'd made this same journey. He couldn't determine the exact number, but the weariness in his body and the ache in his bones told him the few weeks he had worked as Phelan's slave had taken its toll. He felt at least a decade older and wondered if the intense exhaustion would ever pass. Gwyn climbed ahead of him in the sunshine, the exercise not tiring her like it was her father. He paused and leaned against a rock to rest, weary beyond measure. The invigorating sensation of magic coursed through him and he realized Gwyn had returned to his side.

"You are more tired than you should be, father. Your health is weak," she said in concern.

"I know, it is from all the rock toting and the loss of your mother."

"You will grow strong again, have no doubt." She removed her hand and he found his strength returning. He rose and continued the hike up the side of the mountain with his daughter leading the way.

He stepped into the cave with his heart in his throat. Her insistence that he leave his sword outside the cavern did not play well with him, but he did as she asked. His eyes immediately went to the brightest area and the glow of the eggs blinded him for a moment. He shielded his eyes as they began to water from the characteristic smell of sulfur. He heard a low rumble emanating from the back of the cave.

"Come, father," she said and guided him forward, shielding her face. Once their eyes had adjusted they studied the contents of the nest.

"Powers!" he said, for the eggs immediately caught his attention. In the center of them was the little guardian dragon, curled up like a contented cat basking in the warm sunlight.

Gwyn, dragon daughter, you have come.

Belwyn recognized the voice instantly and he strained to see further into the murky interior of the immense cavern. The rumbling sound increased and he found two sets of brilliant dragon eyes peering back at him. Without hesitation he bowed, deeply.

"Ancient One." Not quite knowing how to address the mother dragon he bowed again and said, "Mother of Dragons." He hoped it would suffice.

Welcome, Belwyn, Eldest of Aderyn. The Ancient One's voice sounded amiable and not the least bit threatening.

Belwyn looked down at the clutch of eggs and remarked in a congenial tone, "You have a fine brood here. I am pleased to see them unharmed."

As are we. It was the mother dragon this time. Her voice was more lyrical than that of the oldest of their kind.

"Am I to guess these are your children, Ancient One?" Belwyn asked.

Yes, they are mine. She is my mate. A number of things tumbled into Belwyn's mind at that point, more pieces of the puzzle. He now had a reasonably clear picture of why the dragon decried that Morwyn be with him to break the enchantment, why the children existed. Try as he might to summon righteous anger at being so keenly used, he could not. The Ancient One was a father protecting his own.

"You have lead us on a merry dance, dragon."

A chuckle rumbled throughout the cave.

We have. You have done very well, better than even we hoped.

"I regret Morwyn is not here to see this day," the warrior said with deep sadness.

There was no reply.

Gwyn said, "I have brought the Stone. What do you wish me to do with it?"

Place it in with the eggs, for that is where it belongs, for then it will be consumed, the Ancient One ordered. **Do not try to touch any of them.**

Gwyn nodded and pulled the cord out from under her dress, dangled the cold orb for a moment and then gave it a toss into the center of the ring. It flared for only an instant as it sailed through the golden haze that surrounded the eggs and then landed in the sand. The gold chain instantly melted into nothingness, leaving only the orb behind.

"What is this Stone?" Belwyn asked his daughter, curious as to the nature of such a powerful amulet that could make dragons fear it.

"It is an egg that did not hatch. Though its life has not come to fruition, it is linked to those who created it and its fellow hatchlings," Gwyn explained. "That is how it can be used to bind a ddraig, for all their kin are related." She motioned to a nearby outcropping of rock that rose from the cave floor. "Come, father, sit and wait, for the hatching time will be soon."

He settled down on the cold stone, put his one arm around his daughter's waist and watched. Time passed and as it did the glow in the middle of the ring appeared to increase. The small dragon woke and sent out a plaintive little noise, instantly answered by its mother. When it spied Gwyn its head tilted as if in greeting.

"Little one, you are much better!" she said in obvious joy, a mist of tears in her eyes. A faint little nod returned as it burrowed its way further down into the warm sand. Only its head and the tips of its wings were now visible. It seemed to revel in the heat the eggs radiated. "But how?" she asked, not comprehending. She rose, reached to touch him and then pulled her hand back in obvious discomfort as soon as her hand encountered the haze. "Oh, my!"

"What is it?" Belwyn asked, concerned.

"It is some sort of dragon essence, I think. It must be coming from the eggs. I believe that's why the guardian is healing." An affirmative snort came from one of the parents. Gwyn sat back down and Belwyn put his arm around her again. When he gazed back up into the eyes of the Ancient One, he saw parental concern and surprisingly enough, nervousness.

Just like any new father, he thought in amusement.

The first eggshell burst open sending shards into the air. Belwyn immediately pulled Gwyn toward him, covering her with his cloak, for they were no doubt sharp. The sounds of the eggs breaking outward and upward continued like miniature explosions, echoing around the cavern. Fragments rained against his cloak and struck the floor around them. Once the sounds ended Belwyn and his daughter cautiously peered back into the nest. The reddish gold glow was gone and in its place were small bits of shell and eight newly hatched dragonets. Caught on the remaining portion of its shell, one them frantically gnawed on the edges with its needle sharp teeth. Gwyn knelt by the circle and began to extricate the small beast. It nipped at her and she scolded it.

"Stop that, I'm helping. You shouldn't try to bite your kin." The dragonet angled its head in thought and then nodded as if in understanding. Belwyn knelt on the other side of the nest and beheld the small ones in wonder. He heard a contented purring sound from the back of the cavern and he knew the new parents were pleased as well.

"Your children are marvelous, dragons," Belwyn said, his eyes amazed by the little creatures as they began to try to walk around. They were awkward and stilted in their movements, but he knew that in time they would take to the sky in a graceful dance that no mortal could hope to achieve.

Very fine. The Ancient One responded in a voice full of fatherly pride. His mate crooned to them in a low voice. Gwyn reached down and delicately removed the guardian from the middle of his cousins. They were bumbling around a bit too much and kept knocking into him.

Sister, the small one said in her mind.

"Dragon brother. Are you well?" A nod came back and it began to arch and exercise its wings as it sat on Gwyn's lap. "Powers be Praised!" she said in delight and then reached down and kissed his small head. He trilled back in contentment. She gazed downward again and realized the Stone was now ash, being scattered under the feet of the new dragons. "The Stone is no more," she said and heard an affirmative noise from one of the parents.

Belwyn's face furrowed. "I don't understand. If it didn't hatch the first time around, wouldn't the other eggs burn it into nothingness?" There was an uneasy shift in the back of the cavern and then the mother's voice explained, **Another of our kind was not vigilant. She did not remain to watch over the eggs. One became separated and then lost to us.**

"The one that became the Stone?"

Yes, the mother said.

She is not longer favored as a mate, the old dragon replied. Deep displeasure tinged every word.

"I see," Belwyn murmured, sensing the delicate nature of the situation. He decided to change topics. "It must be amazing to be a dragon and be able to fly through the sky at will," he marveled. The Ancient One gave him an inquisitive look.

You wish you could fly?

"What mortal doesn't?" Belwyn answered. He watched a particular dragonet make its way over toward him. "May I be permitted to touch this one?" he asked.

The Ancient One thought for a moment and gave his approval and then a curious rumble. The little one answered in a smaller version of his father's noise. As he reached down to touch the baby dragon, Belwyn was rewarded with a set of wicked teeth clamped firmly onto his thumb. He clenched his jaw in pain but did not pull back nor attempt to dislodge the baby. He knew it was just exploring.

"Your children have a taste for us mortals," he joked while holding his hand very still to avoid injury to the dragonet or to himself. It studied him with those deep eyes, seemingly enjoying the encounter.

The eldest of dragons snorted back, **We all do.** With a start, Belwyn remembered the bleached bones that were scattered around the dragon's lair. He wisely did not reply. The dragonet eventually grew tired, unclamped his teeth, and went to explore a sibling's tail, using the same method of investigation. That set off a minor row that ended as quickly as it started.

"They are a handful," Belwyn murmured. He looked up at the two adult dragons whose heads were not more than ten feet above him. For some reason the smell of sulfur in the cave was less now and he appreciated that. His eyes were no longer burning, though his thumb was.

"Pyrs would love to see these little fellows" Gwyn said, a genuine smile on her face. She was acting her age, for once, now that the battle was over and the dragons born.

"Your mother would enjoy this as well," Belwyn said, "despite her end."

He studied the wee dragons closely and puzzled, "Which ones are males and which ones are females?"

We do not know until they are older, was the answer from their mother.

"How old?" Belwyn asked in return.

Two hundred of your mortal years.

He guffawed at that. "I shall be long dead before you know if this one," he carefully pointed to one of the hatchlings while keeping his finger at a respectful distance, "is a he or a she. It does put our lives in perspective."

You are the rare mortal who understands that, the Ancient One replied solemnly.

"I suppose we are rather engaging to watch as we go about our frenzied activities that really mean nothing in the end. Only in death do we find peace."

Not even then, a voice replied, one that sounded different from the other dragons. He turned to see a white figure at the entrance to the cave. It was just a head taller than his height and its deep blue eyes pulled at him immediately.

Daughter, the old ddraig intoned as his mate dipped her head in greeting.

Greetings, Ancient and Favored Ones.

Is the troublesome lord now with his foes?

I delivered him to them as you asked, though he did not like riding inside my claw. Fortunately, the wind drowned out most of his shouting.

Then it is up to his own kind to determine his punishment.

Belwyn shifted uncomfortably and with a look towards Gwyn he indicated it was time for them to leave. She nodded in agreement and rose from her position by the nest. He bowed again and cleared his throat. All dragon eyes moved to him immediately.

"By your leave, Ancient One, we should return to our own. It has been deeply moving to watch the birth of your children."

We are pleased you have survived to see this day.

The warrior paused and then offered the thanks he felt he owed the ddraig. "It appears I must thank you for allowing my children to be created." He looked over at Gwyn, "They are my solace." A pleasant rumble issued forth for obviously the beast harbored deep affection for the twins.

You are free to depart, Eldest of Aderyn. All has come to pass as we hoped. Go now and treasure what days you are granted, as we will treasure our freedom.

Belwyn bowed again. "May the Powers make it so."

The mother dragon spoke, **Gwyn daughter, allow our child to stay with us. You are safe amongst your own kin now.**

Gwyn stroked the little dragon's head once more and then walked him to his mother where he curled up on her massive tail in a contented heap.

"I will miss you in my hair," she said with a twinge of sadness.

As I will miss you, dragon sister, even though you never listened me.

"I didn't, did I?"

Not once. Gwyn chuckled and followed her father out into the twilight where he collected his sword and began the trip back down to the shore.

"You were right to insist I come for hatching. It was wonderful."

"I knew you would enjoy it," she said and followed him down the mountain, one cautious step at a time.

The Ancient One's eyes fell upon the white dragon once more. His tone shifted to one of inquisition.

You felt no inclination to allow the lord to plummet to his death? The question was direct and caught the smaller dragon off guard.

I ... I admit I did think of it, given his crimes, the white beast reluctantly admitted.

Why did you not do it? None would regret his passing. You could have dropped him and he would have shattered to pieces in the sea.

It was not for me to choose whether he lives or dies.

Even though he tried to kill you and your kin?

Even so.

You have learned much, daughter.

Not all of it do I like, was the candid reply.

We rarely like what the Powers wish us to learn. He shifted his iridescent eyes toward the cavern's entrance, knowing that Belwyn and his daughter were descending the mountain now. **Tonight the warrior will learn what it is like to be a dragon, as he wished.**

I do not understand, the white dragon replied, unsure.

The bite my hatchling gave him will cause him to journey with our kin this night. If you wish to be with him ...

There was silence as the smaller dragon thought it through.

I will take him flying and show him how beautiful the moon really is.

Come morning he returns to his kind, the ancient dragon cautioned.

I understand. One night is enough. At that the pale beast pulled itself out of the cave and winged high into the air to await the soul that would fly with it this night.

You are clever, my only one, for you know they will bond, the female dragon observed.

A curious chuckle issued from the Ancient One's mouth.

I am doing it again, aren't I?

You are, though I do not see children of this night's union.

No, that is not the reason I send them together.

The mother leaned down, nuzzled one of her little hatchlings, and was rewarded with a chirping sound of recognition. Her melodic crooning filled the cavern and hummed off the towering stone walls.

I am at peace, the Ancient One thought and allowed himself to drift to sleep to the soothing sounds of the new mother and their children.

By the time Belwyn reached the encampment, he was ill. His thumb had swollen and his head burned like fury. Gwyn had to guide him back to his room in the guards' barracks for he could barely walk. He fell on the bed with a deep moan.

"I cannot believe such a little thing could harm me so badly. What is it about dragons?"

Gwyn examined the thumb, did a healing spell and then realized it had no effect whatsoever. She tried again and the spell failed. She cleansed the wound, stripped off her father's boots and sword and set off to find Aithne.

Belwyn's fever rose and peaked somewhere near midnight. He was clearly hallucinating for he talked of the wind, the stars, and the silvery moon over his shoulder. He spoke of ancient kings and of realms no one had ever heard of. Aithne used all her skill to bring down his fever, but it was to no avail.

"I am at a loss, Gwyn. I have administered herbs to decrease his fever and they do nothing. The thumb is not infected, it is as if some venom was in the bite." She found the whole story of the newborn dragons quite riveting, but her concern for Belwyn was uppermost in her mind.

"I do not believe the Ancient One means to kill him," she said solemnly. Her eyes were full of worry.

"Then it will have to run its course."

"Go to bed, I will watch him." Aithne nodded, for she could not stay away much longer or the iarel would come hunting for her, concerned that she was not getting her rest. He was, if anything, overly protective of her and their child.

"Call me if his condition worsens."

"I shall."

ThiRTy-OnE

In dragon form, Belwyn winged through the misty clouds, feeling the damp coolness on his thick black skin. The moon shown to his side and the earth below was dark with only tiny spots of light. He rolled through the air, reveling in the freedom that flight gave him. It was magical and he loved it. He dove toward the ground and then back up again, now knowing that the little bits of light were the campfires of the mortals below.

Mortals? It was odd to call them that when he was one. *No! I am not mortal, I am one of the eldest, a ddraig, those the mortals call dragon!*

A strange feeling of exhilaration thrummed through his veins and he felt invincible. He barrel rolled in oblivious glee, unfettered for the first time in his life.

Greetings, a voice called to him and as he banked he found a luminous white dragon, a female, off his left wing tip.

Greetings, fair one.

How do you like being a dragon?

I find it wonderful! He rolled again and then returned to glide near her.

I, too, have found it to my liking.

He tumbled around her, unknowing beginning a courtship ritual older than time. They raced through the sky, playfully ducking through the clouds and emerged with mist glittering on the edges of their wing tips. Their courtship dance continued and without a word, they made their final roll together and then joined in mid-flight. Trumpeting bellows issued from both of them as they found the ecstasy that dragons savor and that mortals can never attain.

As the moon set they lie together on a rock, curled around each other in a tight embrace to share their warmth. She carefully kissed a spot on his shoulder where her claw had cut him during their mating. She bore small wounds as well, for their desire was so intense they felt nothing else.

I have missed you, my love, he said, for in dragon form he had recognized the soul that inhabited the female's body the moment they met in the air.

As I have missed you.

How is that …?

Do not ask, only be here with me, for our time passes too quickly.

He settled his neck around hers and allowed himself to accept that she lived, though not in the form he once knew as Morwyn.

When dawn broke Belwyn was awake and curiously well. His head was full of images of flying and of the white dragon, but he was not sure if it was real or a dream. When he sat up in bed his shoulder throbbed intensely. Under his linen shirt he found an ugly gash deep into the flesh.

He smiled and laughed aloud. "It did happen! By the Powers, it did!"

"Father, what is this? This was not here last night!" Gwyn asked, incredulous. She had listened to his ranting and wondered if her father rode the winds with the dragons. The wound added credence to her suspicions. Belwyn told Gwyn of his dream and of her mother. The girl did not act surprised.

"You knew she was alive, didn't you?" he asked, unable to grow angry with her.

"Yes. I kept her from serious injury by the wood fire, but I could not prevent the dragon fire from touching her. It permeated her, merging with her soul. She is in dragon form now as it is the easiest way for her to cope with the changes within her."

"Well, she is far more amorous as a dragon than as adept," he observed with a libidinous grin. He did not ask the question she expected and so she answered for him.

"She is neither dragon nor mortal at this point, father. She is *between.* If she accepts the dragon form she will be like them, but never really *one* of them. She will die earlier than a dragon would and there will be no hatchlings for her even if she takes a mate."

"And if she returns to mortal form?" he asked, his heart beginning to beat harder.

"She will bear the scars of the dragon fire and be plagued with visions that will be very hard for her to bear. Dragons see things we mortals cannot fathom. I fear they would drive her mad if she did not learn to control them."

His good humor evaporated at that. "It is her choice. I was with her one night as a mortal and one night as a ddraig. That is more than I deserve."

"The Ancient One will make her choose, whether she wishes to or not."

"I wish him luck," Belwyn murmured and then lay back down on his bed to rest.

Morgan was overly tired and that made him inclined to be less than patient. He found himself biting his tongue repeatedly as they made the journey to Kell. Sensing his labile mood, Owain the Elder demanded he partake of a sleeping draught once they'd made camp. Although Morgan fought him, Owain would not desist.

"It does not matter how quickly we get to Kell, the situation will not change. You need sleep!" the older man advised.

Morgan gave him a foul look in reply.

"Sleep, Morgan! And have no doubt, I've given the same order to your father more than once." The young lord glowered and then acquiesced, downing the draught. He was asleep in minutes. He slept heavily for over ten hours and when he woke in the morning he felt well rested and more in control of his temper.

"My lord," Owain said as Morgan sat down near the campfire and helped himself to a plate full of bread and cheese. He could have dined in his tent, alone, but too many years serving as Merioneth's Master of the Guard had taught him it was best to eat with his men.

"Owain."

"You look rested," the older man observed. Morgan gave him a sideways look and nodded.

"I took the advice of a friend and got some sleep. It proved to be sound advice."

"That is good news. Perhaps your friend will not find it so hard to have you listen the next time." Morgan shot him a stronger look but Owain ignored it. The young lord began to see why his father had enjoyed this man's company over the years. Rank did not intimidate him, though he could be deferential when needed. *A true friend,* his father had said, and in that he did not exaggerate.

"What do the scouts report?" Morgan asked as he reached for a wineskin lying nearby.

"Kell's gates are open."

Morgan frowned. "That doesn't make sense. Is it possible that Phelan did not return there?"

Owain shrugged. "We won't know until we're there."

Morgan sighed, rose and dusted off his hands. "Well, let's go see what that fair city has to offer for entertainment. The last time I was in Phelan's fortress I passed on the most gorgeous sporting wench I've ever seen. Perhaps she's still willing and then I won't have trouble sleeping at night."

Owain laughed heartily and the order was given to march.

Gorsedd did a quick count of the men arrayed in columns in front of the main city gates. There were fewer of them than he had anticipated and they were not in battle formation. That surprised him. Once they had been spotted he'd sealed the city, praying that a battle might be avoided. The news that the Northern lord had perished at the Field of Stones had chilled Gorsedd's heart. He feared retribution, but the men waiting patiently at Kell's gates did not appear to be so inclined. A polite request was made to speak to whoever currently ruled the city and there they waited for an answer.

"Well, Benen, it appears that I must go greet our Northern neighbors. If this should go ill ..."

The innkeeper shook his head vigorously. "It will not. They do not want war, Gorsedd. Tell them the truth and we may yet avoid conflict." He gave his friend a comforting smile and watched as the Master of the Guard worked his way down the ladder from the wallwalk.

Gorsedd exited the city through one of the small side gates, not willing to open the main gates with such a force at their doorstep. As he rode, he spied his son-in-law in the first rank of warriors. Nyle gave him a slight nod in acknowledgement. Gorsedd sighed in obvious relief, his prayers answered. He halted his mount in front of the young blonde-haired lord and waited for the man to speak, for he had superior rank.

"I am Morgan, Lord of the Eastern March. I come to find Lord Phelan and finish this business he has started." The young lord's face was grim and his eyes unyielding.

"I am Gorsedd, one-half of the ruling council that now serves Kell. Lord Phelan is not here, for he did not return to us from the Field of Stones."

"Then where is he?" Morgan asked, disconcerted.

Gorsedd shrugged in reply.

"Hopefully in the belly of his dragon," he said in a sarcastic tone and then added, "Then again, best not, for a ddraig with indigestion could no doubt be a frightful thing."

Morgan blinked in surprise, puzzled at the man's attitude. He did not appear the least bit apprehensive. In fact, he was jesting at such a time. Sensing no threat, the young lord went for the lighter touch.

"In that you are right. Well, sir, must we war or can we end the bloodshed here and now?"

"Kell has no taste for war. It depends on you, my lord." The peace hung between them.

"I have no taste for it either, for it has cost me dearly as of late."

Morgan stuck out his hand and Gorsedd rode forward and shook it. A series of jubilant shouts erupted from both inside the city and within the lord's contingent.

"What can we do to help you?" he asked. Gorsedd sensed the offer was genuine. Benen had been right.

"We need help ferreting out the remainder of Phelan's men. Many have gone into hiding and we fear what insurrection they may launch against us. We need help setting up a strong and just council to manage the city. And most of all, we need an ally that we can count on if another Phelan should rise in the future."

Morgan weighed the requests and found them entirely reasonable.

"You have all of that and more, Gorsedd."

"Then welcome to Kell, my lord," the old guard replied with a huge smile on his face as gestured toward the city with a decided flourish.

The new Lord of the Eastern March rode through the gates of Kell to a hero's welcome, though in his mind it was not deserved. Cheering citizens lined the streets and celebrations erupted spontaneously. Morgan caught Owain's eye and a wink came back to him.

"Enjoy it, it never lasts," was the older man's sage observation.

"Powers!" It was the fourth time Pyrs had uttered the word and it didn't appear he would stop saying it in the near future. The news that his mother was alive had stunned him.

"She is well," Belwyn said in a cheerful voice. He had straightforwardly related the events of his evening to Pyrs, knowing his son was a man now and needed to hear the truth.

"Well, at least you had the pleasure of her company," the boy said and then beamed. It was as bawdy as he dare get given the subject was his mother.

Belwyn saw no reason to lie. "I did and I enjoyed it immensely."

"I knew Gwyn wouldn't let her die! Of course, my all knowing sister didn't say a word! Confound her!" the lad went on. He thought for a moment and then asked, "Have you told Uncle Elrehan?"

Belwyn shook his head. "I must think on that. I do not know if it will help him to learn that his sister is now a fiery creature with claws who preys upon deer or humans for food. Perhaps it is best if he believes she is at rest with the Powers." He and Gwyn had spoken at length on that very topic and a decision proved difficult.

"I see your point," Pyrs murmured.

"Pyrs?" a soft voice called. A young girl near his age appeared at the end of his bed. She was obviously one of the clan for her tawny hair hung in two lengthy braids. In her hand she held a plate full of food, mounded high.

"Oh, hello." He didn't blush, but his father knew it was a near thing.

"Well, it appears you have a fine meal and good company," Belwyn said and surreptitiously slipped his son a wink. A manly smile crept across Pyrs' face.

"Yes, father, I shall be quite well tended." Belwyn rose, gave the girl a smile and set off for his room. *Soon I'll be a grandfather.* He shuddered at the thought, given his young age. *Not too soon, I hope.*

Dillan and Aithne talked for over two hours. Aithne learned how her father had been imprisoned and kept from her mother, exactly how her mother had died and what horrors she had visited upon Belwyn with her enchantment. Aithne took everything Dillan told her and weighed it in her heart. Once her decision was made she would wait for the proper time to speak to Owain the Elder.

I did not see you dancing near the moon tonight, daughter, the eldest of dragons noted.

The white beast shook its head. *It is not the same now.*

The Ancient One felt his mate shift her weight ever so slightly, a subtle way of acknowledging that he was right once again.

Why is it not the same? he asked, though he knew the answer better than the soul in front of him.

He is not there.

And that matters to you?

Yes, it does. It is easy to become enraptured with this form, for there is much power within the life of a ddraig. But it is not enough …

You always sought to be special. Now that you are, that is not enough?

No, it is not. I have nothing, for without him, without my children and without my mortality, I am not Morwyn. I am a mortal pretending to be a dragon, nothing more.

But who is Morwyn? Is she not that wistful girl who would sit and watch the sunrise praying that she would be special, worthy of a life beyond what fate had decreed for her?

Yes, but I have remained that little girl my entire life. I have been consumed by my search for the elusive thing that would make me special.

But what of your magic, does that not make you special? Do you now say that your magic is not worth the love of your husband and that of your children?

Magic is magic, Ancient One. It exists. Gwyn once said that I must learn to rule the magic rather than allowing it to rule me. It has reigned over me since the moment I became an adept. I have sacrificed my life to it and still, it is not enough.

Then you are not special? the dragon pushed, knowing the moment of decision loomed.

Eldest, I was special long before the magic, I was special the moment I was conceived, for I am Morwyn and there are no others like me. I was born in a caul, did you know that? I was extraordinary and did not realize it. My life has been a constant quest for a treasure I already possessed.

What is your decision, daughter?

There was profound silence as the white dragon with the soul of a woman made her choice.

I am Morwyn, I am mortal and I seek to live among my own kind.

Your life will be short.

I know. I will value each day and treasure the nights I share with the man who owns my heart.

And what of your magic?

It is magic, nothing more.

A long sigh erupted out of the Ancient One and for a moment it confused the young dragon that waited in front of it.

Finally, Morwyn the Adept, *finally* you have learned what the Powers decreed. Go and take up your life where it stopped the night you broke the enchantment.

The white dragon's eyes flared at that, incredulous.

Do you mean that if I had chosen to be with him from that night on then all of this ... she paused and let the question carry her down a different path. The Ancient One did not reply and that was answer enough. *So much time lost. No more, I swear it!*

The white ddraig shrunk in height and shimmered into the form of a young woman, clad in all white like her dragon counterpart. Morwyn gazed down and smiled. The claws were gone, replaced by the thin hands she remembered.

The visions will haunt you, for you cannot stop them as you have our essence within you. You must learn to welcome them or they will destroy your mind.

"I will try," she said and then walked directly up to the Ancient One and bowed. "Thank you for your lessons and patience, Eldest." His huge claw delicately touched her head in genuine fondness. She hesitated and then asked, "If Belwyn and I should be granted more children, will you vow that they will be allowed to grow at their own pace, not aged overnight and sent on some dragon quest?"

He gave her a measured look. **Your future children will be your own.**

It was not a complete answer and Morwyn suspected she'd not get one.

"So be it." After she bowed to both of the beasts, she left the cave and strode into the moonlight. Her eyes could pick out the faint dots of light in the distance, the multitude of campfires in the clearing. She heard laughter and music filtering across the water.

"I come, my husband. I pray you find me as enticing as a woman as you did when I danced with you in the sky." She began the tedious journey down the side of the mountain, picking her way over the uneven stones, trying to stay on the rudimentary path built by the workers.

"I should have flown to the clearing and *then* changed," she grumbled to herself.

She swore she could hear the eldest dragon's voice in her mind.

Rule your magic!

On impulse she muttered a spell for light and held out her right hand. Nothing happened. She frowned, thought about it, and repeated the spell, adding the one word she had forgotten the first time. A glow of light appeared in her palm and she stared at it in amazement. The lighting spell was one she could perform before she had broken Belwyn's enchantment, but not after. Gwyn's words came back to her in full force, *'Not everything requires a sacrifice.'*

The magic had not fled her that night she lie with Belwyn. Accepting the adept's creed, she had believed it would diminish and so it appeared, for one's mind often rules one's reality. She muttered another spell and a shower of light erupted around her in a fountain of magical power. She threw back her head and roared in laughter. It felt marvelous. Morwyn the Adept ruled the magic and in all things, she was special.

Gwyn was laughing as well, aware of the events on the mountain and endlessly amused by her brother's startled realization that Aithne was a blood relative, his aunt.

"Oh, Powers, tell me I didn't proposition my own ... Oh, Powers!" He fell silent and refused to say anything further. Gwyn couldn't resist and added the last bit of the story that put him in full retreat, just as she'd hoped.

"She's the iarel's betrothed, brother. No doubt Caewlin will want your head for daring to court his lover and the mother of his unborn child." She howled in absolute mirth as Pyrs's face disappeared under the covers and steadfastly refused to reappear.

Devona finally summoned the courage to speak with Galen. She had sat near his side as he slept after the battle, worried about his wound and their future. As soon as he had started to rouse she'd left, unsure. Now she was back and needed to speak to him about all the things that fluttered in her heart.

"I am pleased to see you are better, Saga," she said.

"I am healing. I heard that you sat near my side for a time. I thank you for that."

"I ... did."

His eyes pinioned hers. "Did you sit near to me for some formal reason or for a personal one?" he asked abruptly. He saw her blanch and wondered if he had been too blunt.

"I sat at your side for both reasons. As Wise it is important for me to offer prayers for the Saga of our clan."

"And as a woman?" he pressed, his bard gift urging him to push forward.

"I also sat next to you as a woman, for I care if you live or die." A sigh came out of his mouth accompanied by a warm glow in his eyes.

"Then I am favored by the Gods." A shy smile appeared on her face at that.

"When you are well, I would wish you to share my furs." Her heart beat loudly in her chest, worried he might now refuse her for some unknown reason.

"For the Gathering Night?" he asked, wishing to be certain of what she sought.

"No, far more often than that." They gazed at each other for a time and then she reached over and delivered a light kiss on his cheek.

"Then I am truly favored by the Gods," he said and pulled her into a loving embrace.

Elrehan sat on a rock near the sea stewing in his gloom. Even Ulwyn had not been able to cheer him up. The knowledge that Dillan had married Fea for reasons other than lust had helped, but not much. His beloved sister's death had only added to the misery. The Powers had been unwilling to allow him to die in battle and so he was in oblivion, unable to discern where his future lie.

He had found little comfort confronting Lord Phelan as he sat in his chains. No matter how he tried, the thought of killing the man brought him no peace. He had received some satisfaction in presenting Fea and telling their former host the whole tale of how he'd been duped. That had sent Phelan into a round of raging oaths. Still, Elrehan's heart was empty. His sister was gone and Fea now belonged to another. In retrospect, Phelan was the victor.

His keen eyes picked out movement on the water and he watched as a small boat drifted up onto the shore. A cloaked figure alighted from the craft, deftly jumping to avoid getting its cape hem wet. In the person's hand was some sort of glowing object that lit the way as they headed toward the encampment. The pure white cloak seemed to reflect the bluish tint of the moon. As the figure approached he caught a glimpse of black hair under the cloak hood.

"Gwyn? Is that you?" The figure stopped and then headed toward him. "You should not be out alone, it is not safe," he said as he rose. The figure strode up to him and he was astounded to find the glow came from a small ball of light resting in a woman's hand. As the hood fell back the intense blue-grey eyes of his sister greeted him.

"Not safe, you say? And who would dare challenge someone freshly returned from the grave?" Her voice was full of amusement. It was only fitting that the first person she encountered was her twin.

"Mor … wyn?" His face went pale and he cautiously reached out to touch her hand, as if she was an apparition. The flesh was solid and his mouth flew open in surprise. "You're alive!"

"I am. Now stop staring and hug me, for I have missed you greatly, my brother." He launched into her and in so doing nearly knocked her to the ground. She extinguished the light in her palm and returned the clinch.

"Morwyn, Powers, you are alive!" He hugged her fiercely and though her skin was still sensitive from the dragon fire, she did not tell him.

"I am quite alive and quite happy to be back amongst the mortals … my people." She had used the dragon's term unconsciously.

"Does Belwyn know?"

Given his reaction, Morwyn sensed her husband had not imparted the events of the previous evening to her brother. She spun the truth, "He does not know I am here, neither does Pyrs."

Elrehan noted the absence of a name. "Gwyn knew you were alive?"

"Yes, she knew I lived but could not tell you of it."

"But where have you been?" She pulled out of his arms and pointed toward the island and the mountain resting upon it.

"I have lived with the ddraig, brother. They are interesting hosts," she said lightheartedly. She swore she could hear a dragon chuckle in her mind at that point. He started to sputter and then hugged her again, not knowing what else to do. When he released her, he said, "Come, we must find Belwyn and tell Pyrs and …"

"Elrehan, please calm down. I will tell Pyrs and then find my husband."

He studied her for a moment. "Is it your intention to stay with Belwyn?"

"It is my intention, if he accepts me," she said back, uncertainty in her voice.

"He will, even if you grew claws and looked like one of them," he said pointing back up at the mountain. Morwyn barely kept from breaking out in laughter.

Little do you know, brother.

He embraced her again and finally her tolerance for hugs ended. She pulled completely out of his grasp.

"Stay here and watch the moon, it's quite lovely tonight."

Elrehan looked up and murmured, "It is, isn't it? I hadn't noticed before."

"Have patience, brother, the Powers haven't finished spinning their magic yet." He frowned at that but she would say no more. Morwyn left him sitting on the rock, gazing at the moon, his heart partially healed.

τhirτγ-τwo

Morwyn visited Pyrs next and found him alone. His father, he said, had told him the tale of his flight with an amorous white dragon. She gave him a wide smile in response.

"You are different," he said, eyeing her. She was more at ease, he thought, and appeared her age now, less haggard and worn.

"I am and yet I am the same."

"You talk like a dragon now," he observed with a shrewd frown.

"I do, don't I?" She laughed at that.

"It sounds good to hear you laugh!" Pyrs replied, allowing the frown to evaporate into a wide grin. She hugged him again, careful not to touch his healing wound.

"The little dragonets are quite fun, if your sister hasn't told you."

"I want to see them!" he begged.

"You have to heal first and then I'm sure Gwyn will take you to them. Have no fear, they will stay small for a very long time."

"I hope so. I want to see my kin." He glanced up at that and they shared a smile. He added, "I hoped Gwyn had a plan to save you."

"She foresaw my death when she undertook the Ritual of the Third Path and then rather rashly decided to change what she saw. It almost failed. Gwyn's magic is not foolproof around the power of a dragon. I am a bit singed, but I will not complain."

Pyrs nodded contentedly. "Then go find father, for he misses you so very much."

"I shall. Rest now and I'll see you in the morning." She leaned over, put her hand on his chest and murmured a spell of sleep and then one of healing. "I love you son," she whispered as his eyes fluttered. Soon he was lightly snoring, his face radiating supreme happiness.

After one or two inquiries, she found Belwyn's room. It was empty. After stoking the fire she settled into the chair near the blaze and warmed herself, waiting in a unique mixture of anticipation and nerves. As Morwyn gazed into the fire the flames seemed to dance upward and then whirl in a strange pattern. The vision that struck her was blinding in its intensity. If she'd been standing it would have driven her to her knees. She clenched her fists and let the revelations wash over her. None of it made sense, for though she carried the essence of a dragon within her, she was experiencing the vision as a mortal, limiting her ability to comprehend what she saw in her mind. She winced as a blinding headache blasted her and then it just as quickly it disappeared. Exhausted, wet with sweat and her mind in complete tumult, she lay her head against the cool wood of the chair and drifted to sleep.

Belwyn found himself staring up at the moon in fond remembrance. He knew he would never gaze at it again in quite the same way. He watched the orb rise for a time, hoping to catch a glimpse of a certain flying form, but it was not to be.

"Live well, Morwyn, for I will always love you," he said quietly and then crunched across the newly fallen snow to his room as the sounds of merrymaking continued. The clan would celebrate most of the night, a prelude to the iarel's wedding. Usually they would revel for one full week, but Caewlin had ordered the time reduced given their situation.

Belwyn nodded in the direction of a couple of his father's men as they passed in the barracks hallway and then entered his room. He did not immediately notice the figure by the fire, for she had fallen asleep in intense weariness after the vision. He doffed his cloak and his sword and when he moved to the chair to remove his boots he found it occupied.

"Powers," he said softly and reached up to caress her cheek as if she was a mere figment of his heart's imagination.

The touch caused her to open her eyes and she found her husband kneeling at her side, his dark eyes full of love. Her head no longer hurt and she felt strangely refreshed, as if the vision gave her strength in compensation for the pain it inflicted.

"You were celebrating rather late," she observed.

"Why is it you are not dancing with the moon on those beautiful wings of yours?" he asked as she slowly straightened up in the chair, dropping her cloak hood back onto her shoulders.

"The dance is lonely without you, my love," she answered honestly.

A soft smile crossed his face. "Are you here for only one night?"

"I am here for as long as you wish it."

His eyes sparked and he asked, "Why have you come back when you could be everything you've always wanted?" Having taken their form he understood how special the ddraig were. As he waited for her answer, his heart pounded.

"In the end, it was nothing, for you were not there." Her hand reached out and pulled him toward her and they kissed deeply. When he drew back, he found her eyes mirrored his own desire.

"Are you here as a companion or as a wife?" He had felt her passion behind the kiss, but dare not assume.

"I would be your lover and your wife, if you wish it."

"I wish it more than anything in this world," he said. "But what of your magic?"

She grew an odd expression on her face. "It is magic, nothing more. It is there because I command it. It will not diminish because of loving you."

"But how?" he asked, stunned, not understanding how this could have changed. She rose and took him in her arms.

"I will explain it later, my love." She kissed him more earnestly now and then abruptly drew back. "I am not like I was, for I bear scars from the dragon fire."

"I do not care."

"You may, once you see them." He saw the concern in her eyes, that he might reject her.

"Then show me," he said, sensing the direct approach was the best. She made her way over to the bed, removed her boots and her cloak and then slowly unlaced her gown. It fell to her shoulders and then to just above her breasts where she held it in place.

He gazed upon what part of her he could see. Her skin was different now, it reminded him of the luminescent quality of the white dragon's hide. He gingerly reached out to touch her chest near her breastbone and felt a faint spark flicker through the tips of his fingers.

"It is so …" Her soft blue-grey eyes sought his and he saw trepidation in them. He chose his words carefully for he knew how fragile the moment was. "It is so exquisite, soft, like wind rippling across the snow in the moonlight. It seems to shift like that. I had thought it would be more like a scar, but it is not."

"The dragon fire is different, for it burns into your soul."

"Does it hurt for me to touch you?" he asked in a concerned voice.

"I am more sensitive than I once was, but your touch is very welcome."

A slow smile came to his face. "Then I shall touch you, wife, for you are even more beautiful now than you were before. Besides, I believe we have not yet consummated our marriage." She opened her mouth to protest and he shook his head. "We were not in human form when we joined the last time." Morwyn nodded. "Let me see you as you truly are, for I love you."

A demure smile appeared on her face and she allowed the gown to drop to her waist. Her hands covered her breasts for a time and then she removed them, shyly, as if it was the first time he had seen her naked. There were random cuts in her skin, testimonial to their fiery lovemaking in the sky the night before.

He gazed at her in utter adoration. "Powers, you are beautiful, even when kissed by dragon fire."

He rose, strode to the door and threw the bolt, shrugged off his clothes and crawled into the bed next to her. Her gown was now gone and she held her arms out to embrace him. He hesitated for only a moment and then pulled off the rawhide cord that held her ring. A few moments passed as he fumbled with the knot and then dropped the cord to the floor.

"Your ring, my wife." He placed it on her hand and then pulled her to him. "May it stay there from now on."

"It will," she said. He kissed her in a needy way, as if he could not believe she was really in his bed, had consented to be his lover.

Suddenly he pulled back and stated rather sternly, "If you are planning to leave me in the morning tell me now and I will secure you to this bed once I've made love to you. I have twice had you in my bed and twice you have run off."

Her eyebrow arched and she gave him a slightly lecherous smile, in complete contrast to her modest behavior earlier.

"Perhaps you'd best tie me to the bed once you've satisfied your lust, my lord, for you never know what I will do next." Her look and the sultry promise behind it completely overwhelmed him. He abandoned all decorum and claimed her as his own with a fervent prayer that she would still be with him at dawn.

Gwyn sat meditating in the moonlight, allowing the events of the past few days to settle in her mind. She could easily see the little dragons sleeping in their nest, their mother and father watching over them. Pyrs was asleep as well and she sensed her mother's hand at that. A smile of contentment played on her face – she knew her parents had found love once more and this time her mother would stay.

"Powers, you are merciful," she murmured and then her mind strayed, no longer anchored by pressing concerns. The bard she had met at Lady Aldyn's came into her thoughts and she pondered on him for a time.

Come home soon, dear Gwyn. I miss you.

She jumped up and shot her eyes around in agitation. It had been Dru, the bard, his voice as clear as if he was standing next to her. She found no one close to her, only a couple kissing near a small tent in the distance.

"Powers, how does he do that?" she muttered, a frown on her face. When no answer was forthcoming she finally went to her own bed, unsettled at the strength of the connection between her and the mysterious bard.

"Lord Morgan?" a voice called out pleasantly. Morgan turned to find Owain standing in the doorway of the large room he had chosen for his stay in Kell. By Owain's side was a face he remembered.

"Powers," he muttered under his breath. It was the sporting wench he had so graciously declined during his last visit to Phelan's fortress. "Owain?" he said in a more firm voice.

"I believe you indicated a need for a good night's rest, my lord," Owain said with a sparkle in his eye.

"I did. Welcome, girl, we meet again." The girl bowed and smiled.

"This young girl has offered to help you find that good night's rest, my lord," Owain explained.

"You are willing to be with me tonight?" Morgan asked.

"Most certainly, milord, it would be a pleasure," the girl replied. "I regretted not being of service the last time you were here."

"I was not sure of your former lord's motives." She nodded in complete understanding.

Morgan seized the moment.

"Owain, if you please, assure we are not interrupted tonight. I am quite tired and will need a full night's rest." His face spoke of anything but weariness.

Owain bowed at that. "As you wish, my lord." His smile was almost as wide as the room. As the door closed, Morgan gestured, "Bolt it – I'm sure neither of us want to be disturbed." The girl's smile rivaled Owain's as she pushed the bolt home and headed for Morgan's open arms.

May the Powers bless you, my friend, he thought and drew the girl to him in a rustle of silk.

As Belwyn sat by the fire slowly tugging on his clothes, his mind was full of memory. Last night had been beyond his ken, full of passionate love-making. There had been nothing held in reserve, for both of them knew they had waited far too long to share themselves. It was a fresh start and they embraced it fully. There had been laughter, tears of joy and fiery passion as the night progressed. He was determined she would not leave him, not ever again. As he heard Morwyn shift in the bed his face grew a mischievous grin. He turned to watch her reaction to his handiwork.

"Belwyn, what is this?" she sputtered. Her left hand was secured with a long piece of cord and then tied to the frame of the bed. He had padded under the cord near her wrist so it would not harm her, but she was bound nonetheless. Only her deep sleep prevented her from knowing his actions.

"Securing my wayward wife to prevent her from running off as she is so inclined to do. Perhaps I can talk to Elrehan and purchase one of those light slave chains I saw in Kell. That would work nicely." He had a wicked glint in his eye.

"Powers, you are a beast!" she grumbled though her voice sounded amused.

"No, just a man determined to keep his wife for more than one night." She tugged on the rope and then tried to work the knot.

"Quit that!" he ordered.

"Belwyn, undo me!" The point made, he walked over and began to untie the knot and then thought better of it. He began to kiss her and then pulled down the coverlet a bit further exposing her lithe body underneath. She responded in kind and his dressing proved for naught as his clothes landed in a heap on the stone floor.

After the loving he murmured, "I must rise from this bed."

"So you must." Her voice said otherwise.

"I must," Belwyn said and rose. She protested and he shook his head. "I will dress completely this time and then untie you." She did not reply. "Perhaps I should have let you run off. I fear a good night's sleep is something in the past."

Morwyn smiled lecherously and he chose to ignore it for it only would delay him even more. In time he was dressed, his bride was unfettered and her clothes in place.

"Be sure to rest this afternoon, for we have more consummation to consider this evening," he advised.

"More?" she asked, a twinkle in her eye. "We've consummated at least four or five marriages already!"

He winked and took his leave at that moment, knowing if he stayed any longer he would have to dress yet again.

There was one reunion that Morwyn did not relish, but it had to be. Ever since Belwyn had told her how her son had inadvertently discovered his missing aunt, Morwyn knew she must make peace with the woman, if possible. She questioned her husband closely and learned as much about his sibling as possible. He could not tell her of Aithne's feelings toward the House of Aderyn, for the fire-haired healer had kept her distance since encountering her father on the battlefield four days earlier. After speaking at length with Dillan, Morwyn set her mind to the task and sought out Aithne. When the iarel's betrothed appeared outside the healer's tent and spied Morwyn, her eyes grew wide and then unreadable.

"So you *are* alive," she said in a noncommittal voice. The news of the healer's miraculous return had flown through the clan.

"The Powers were merciful." Morwyn replied and then composed herself as best she could. "We must speak, for there is much between us."

Aithne nodded and then gestured for them to walk. As they strolled into the forest, her ever-present escort some distance behind, neither said a word. In time they stopped by a fallen tree. Aithne settled on the log and tucked her cloak around her for warmth. The sun was out but there was a chill in the air and in her heart. What she did not realize is that Morwyn was in similar emotional turmoil.

"You have my attention," Aithne announced.

Morwyn cleared her throat, apprehensive. "I have spoken with Dillan and he tells me that you are aware of what fell out between your father and your mother, how Aderyn kept him from the woman he loved." Aithne nodded. "I felt we should speak about what led to the battle that caused your mother's death."

A frown formed on Aithne's face. "You make it sound as if the battle killed her."

Chagrined, Morwyn apologized. "I am sorry, that is not what I meant. I am responsible for her death, that I cannot deny." She paused and added, "She forgave your father as she passed over."

"I know she forgave my sire, but I did not hear that she forgave you." The voice was cool and unyielding.

Morwyn swallowed and continued, "Your mother placed an enchantment on Belwyn in retaliation for Aderyn's foul treatment. It was her choice to wield the magic for ill purposes and there are consequences for those who do so."

"Are you saying she was evil?" Aithne demanded. She desperately needed to know more about Adwyth, the woman who had given birth and then relinquished her baby to save the infant's life.

"No, not as such. Your mother did seek out her darker nature and allow it to rule her, but she was not evil."

"The tales I have heard have made her the cruel villain."

Morwyn's voice grew in strength. "To some she would seem a villain, for the enchantment she placed on Belwyn was truly horrific. He would have killed himself to end the visions that haunted him day and night if the Powers had not intervened. As it was, the gallows almost claimed him for my supposed violation and death. Yes, to many, your mother was the villain."

The image of her half-brother dangling at the end of a hangman's rope caused a shiver to course through Aithne's body.

"Tell me how she came to die."

"We confronted each other at the battle between Merioneth and Lord Bardyn. She had sided with Merioneth to bring about Aderyn's destruction. We engaged in magical combat and I prevailed."

"Have you no guilt in this?" Aithne demanded. The two guards sensed the increased hostility and their vigilance grew.

"I carry much guilt. I took a life, one that was not full, but a life nonetheless."

"It was not a full life because of Aderyn," Aithne replied sharply.

"In part, perhaps. Aderyn wielded its might against her unjustly. Your grandfather's actions were unconscionable, for he had no right to intervene between your parents. Trahern was a domineering man who believed he could mold his sons as he chose."

"Yet, you still blame my mother?"

"Instead of confronting her loss and living her life to the full, she sought the darker path."

"Is that wrong, given what she suffered?"

Morwyn sensed there was more here than reconciling Adwyth's actions.

"Yes, it is. We all have darkness within us, Aithne. Your mother chose to cultivate it. She lost so many years to the anger and bitterness. At the end, she realized that and made her peace."

"How do you know that I do not harbor that same bitterness, that same desire for revenge?"

"I do not sense it within you. You appear to have chosen to acknowledge the hurt and carry on as best you can. Your mother did not, she honed her anger until she could wreck her revenge on Aderyn, very nearly killing your father and your brother as a result."

Aithne was silent for a time, as if in deep thought.

"I did not know I was a fosterling until my mother … my foster mother died. Ide told me the tale of Aderyn on her deathbed. I was not raised in anger, but knew only a loving family. I had no idea I was not their child, though I did find it odd that I was the only one with red hair." A slight smile appeared and then vanished almost as quickly. "I found myself alone, for first my foster father, Loman, died and then my foster mother." Her eyes were full of memory and glistened with tears.

Morwyn looked down at her boots. "You grew strong and wise without feeling a need to hate."

"What is it you want of me?" The question fell between them and caught Morwyn off guard. To allow her time to think, she turned and studied the two clansmen. They were still watching the pair intently.

"I ask that you not allow what happened between your mother and myself to affect how you deal with Aderyn. Your sire has not known a moment's peace since he learned of you. Belwyn and his brother have searched for you in vain, trying to fulfill the vow Owain the Elder gave your mother. *They* are your family, Aithne, no matter what has happened in the past and no matter my part in the loss of your mother."

"I do not know if I can ever forgive you for killing her."

Morwyn closed her eyes, the guilt driving deep. "I do not expect absolution. I took another's life, lost though it was. I took your mother away from you and that is a burden I will bear until I die."

The red-haired woman shifted her eyes into the forest, breaking the difficult connection between her and the healer. They still glinted with tears.

"After my foster mother died, I went north in search of mother and found her buried in a cairn of stones near Bardyn's Keep. I journeyed to Ilspath and heard the tale of Morwyn the Adept and the great battle with the evil crone. I heard how the eldest son of Aderyn had been enchanted. I admit I found that righteous, regardless that he was my half-brother. My bitterness grew and I sought to repay Owain the Elder in kind."

"Why did you not go to your father and talk with him?" Morwyn interjected.

"I planned on worse than that, for I sought to plant a dagger in his heart. I spent my time in Ilspath planning his assassination. It gave me purpose."

Morwyn shuddered at the thought. "Why did you not follow through?"

"I was in the common room of a pub and heard the innkeeper speaking about the master of Aderyn. I listened intently, for I wished to learn anything I could about the man. He'd been staying at the inn the week previous and found out that the innkeeper's young daughter was having a birthday. Apparently he grew very melancholy at the news and said, 'A daughter is a precious thing. I have one myself, but I do not know where she is, for I have foolishly lost her. Guard yours, innkeeper, for children are a treasure beyond gold.' He'd bought a small present for the little girl and then returned to Aderyn only a few days before I arrived in Ilspath."

A soft smile settled on Morwyn's face. "That is Owain at his best. I have to be honest, Aithne, I love him as much I did my own father."

"After that I could not continue with my plan to kill him, so I left Ilspath and returned south."

"Why did you not go to Aderyn?"

Aithne shook her head. "I could not. I would have slain him if the Powers had not intervened. How could I then go to his home, eat his bread and claim to be his daughter when only a short time before I was planning his murder?"

"He would have understood."

"Perhaps, but I could not do that. I returned to Kell and built my own life."

Morwyn dropped her gaze to Aithne's midsection and said gently, "Your son will need a grandfather."

The healer blinked in surprise. She quickly regained her composure and replied, "Caewlin says it's a boy."

"It is, a strong red-haired one." As the Watcher, Morwyn had seen the lad clearly. His future was remarkable, but she did not speak of it to his mother.

"My son needs a grandfather," Aithne repeated, "and he shall have one, for I have decided not to hold the events of the past like a dagger to my sire's heart. I have sent a message to Owain informing him of my decision."

A deep sigh came out of Morwyn's mouth. "Then I am content, Aithne."

"As am I, Morwyn the Adept," Aithne replied and then made her way back to the camp, her guards in tow.

Owain the Elder was shouting at the top of his lungs and for a moment Morgan feared that something ill had befallen them.

"Morgan!" He heard the sound of the man stomping across the cobblestones in the courtyard and turned toward him, his hand on his sword by instinct. Owain's face was full of astonishment and outright joy. "It is good news!" Throwing decorum to the wind Morgan sprinted the remaining distance and found himself engulfed in one of Owain's massive bear hugs.

"What is it?" The embrace ended and a piece of parchment was waved in front of his nose. Owain was too busy rejoicing to speak of whatever the message contained. Slightly irritated, Morgan deftly plucked the parchment out of the man's hand and read the note himself. Belwyn's message set him to rejoicing as well.

"Powers!" he shouted and then joined Owain in an impromptu jig in front of their men and a goodly number of the bewildered citizens of Kell.

Nearby Gorsedd gave his son-in-law a quizzical glance and remarked, "Perhaps they've found Phelan."

"That would be good news indeed."

"Gorsedd!" Morgan's voice sang across the courtyard and when they all had gathered around the young lord the contents of the parchment were revealed.

"Lord Phelan has been captured," Morgan started and then looked directly at Nyle, "and Morwyn the Healer is alive!"

All Nyle could do was stammer. "Bbbuttt …"

"Gwyn used magic to save her. She is alive!" Morgan said and then realized the man had no idea who Gwyn was. "Gwyn is her daughter and she wields the Old Magic," he said in explanation, hoping that would suffice.

"Thank the Powers!" Nyle shouted and his father-in-law clapped him on his back surmising the guilt that had just cascaded off the young man's shoulders.

"Come, news like this must be shared!" Gorsedd ordered. "Benen will want to hear this!" The pair strode off leaving Morgan and Owain behind. The older man pulled out another parchment and gently unrolled it.

"I have another message, Morgan, one from … my daughter." Morgan widened his eyes a bit, but didn't reply. He'd already heard of the incredible battlefield encounter and had prayed all would turn out for his father's dearest friend and his newfound daughter. "She has accepted me and asks that I be present at her wedding as her sire should be. If you have no objections that I …"

Morgan was already waving his hand in approval. "Objections? You are to be there! From what little I saw of her, she is a marvel. Go, Owain, and rejoice, for your daughter has found it in her heart to forgive you."

"Thank you, my lord," Owain said and bowed to the younger man.

"Come to me before you leave for I will wish to send something appropriate to the wedding of the only daughter of Aderyn and the Iarel of the Red Hawk Clan."

"I shall." Owain turned on his heel to make preparations as Morgan savored this pleasant moment.

"Enjoy yourself, Owain, for you so richly deserve all you have," he said quietly and then set off across the courtyard to speak with the bard about a wedding gift.

Since his capture, Lord Phelan had graced the same iron stake that Caewlin and Morgan had once occupied and he was considerably worse for wear. Though no one dare kill him, blows and kicks were acceptable and so he sported a number of ugly cuts and bruises. He'd been given only meager food and a pitifully thin cloak against the cold. Despite his situation, he remained arrogant. That arrogance vanished the moment Morwyn appeared not three feet from him.

"How …?" he stammered in complete disbelief.

"The Powers were merciful."

Phelan began to swear vehemently, his anger directed at the dragons for having failed him.

"They are the spawn of evil!" he bellowed. "I curse them all!"

Morwyn shouted, "Silence!" A ball of flame flew toward him and then evaporated before it could do any harm. "If you continue, I will roast you where you stand!"

The flames did stop his ranting. "You are a witch!"

"I am an adept and I wield the Old Magic."

"A witch and a sorceress in league with the forces of …" Morwyn had enough.

"You lack manners, mortal." She murmured a spell under her breath and his vile curses ended as his mouth slammed shut. He could not open it, no matter what he did. His nostrils flared as he breathed hard, but he could not speak. Her final words finally caught up with him and Phelan's eyes grew large in remembrance at when he'd last heard that phrase. The image of the white dragon flew through his mind and his eyes only grew larger.

"Perhaps I should have dropped you in the sea after all," she muttered.

Phelan's trial lasted for over an hour. It was not a trial centered on the matter of guilt, but rather a debate on how to execute this most brutal of men. The suggestions had varied from the more common methods of execution, including hanging and beheading, to more exotic ones such as giving him to the dragons as a meal for their new brood. Morwyn had strongly favored that one, but held her tongue.

Caewlin suggested, "To be fair, our Northern neighbors have suffered as well. I ask Pyrs his thoughts, for at one time he believed his mother dead at this butcher's hands and was forced to watch her gruesome end." The young lad was sitting nearby on a thick fur, leaning against a rock snuggled in even more warm furs. He had insisted on the right to be present during the trial. He was there under the watchful eyes of both his aunt and his mother.

He shot a quick look over at his father and then answered in a strong voice, "I would suggest that you secure him to the center mast of a vessel, tow him out to sea and set the ship alight so he will perish. In that way, his remains will not taint this ground and his soul will never find respite. He will be no more."

A shiver actually passed over Morwyn.

Caewlin caught her reaction and asked, "What is it?"

"It is the Will of the Powers, Iarel," she said instantly. "I feel Their hands in this."

Devona agreed, "I sense it as well, Iarel, the Gods wish it this way."

Caewlin rose and announced solemnly, "So it shall be. Collect the wood and select a suitable boat. We will execute him tonight at sundown so the Gods will take notice and carry him to his eternal torment." The once high lord could say nothing, the spell upon his mouth. Morwyn sought out his eyes and saw defiance blazing within.

She had to give the man grudging respect, he did not beg. Morwyn removed the spell of silence the moment they tied him to the mast of the small boat. They heaped tinder and dry wood in the vessel and still he did not beg or plead in any way. Once the preparations appeared complete, he studied them and then addressed Caewlin in the arrogant tone that was his hallmark.

"I go to my grave undefeated." Phelan's heart pounded but he would not appear weak, even as he died. He would see his brother soon enough and that would be his solace.

"You have only made us stronger for the blood letting. Your defeat will be at the hands of the Gods, not us," the iarel replied, a flaming torch in his steady hand.

"In the end, it does not matter. I have proved to be more than the Master of the Hounds, as my kin once called me. My dearest brother, Carr, will be in awe of me. He awaits and I go to my grave in triumph," the man's voice crowed. As soon as Phelan mentioned his brother's name Morwyn head spun. She felt Belwyn's arm on her arm, steadying her.

"Are you unwell?" he asked concerned. She was ashen and did not answer him.

"Gwyn?" she asked and felt her daughter's hand in hers. "Do you sense it?"

"I do, mother, though much less than you." Gwyn had an equally distant look on her face.

"It is nothing like I have ever felt." Morwyn closed her eyes. She did not need to see the scene in front of her as the small boat blazed, set alight by the myriad of torches hurled into it. She did not need to watch it be towed out a few hundred yards into the sea as it flamed brilliantly in the twilight.

"By the Gods!" Dillan invoked and drew Fea closer to him in protection. The Wise wavered on her feet and Galen took hold of her. She had a detached look on her face, one that made him shiver.

"What is it?" he asked and then began to sense the presence of something not of this world.

"They come," Devona said in awe and dread.

"All of them?" he asked incredulously, for he now understood her meaning.

"Yes, to the smallest child."

To the assemblage it appeared as if shadows floated across the placid water. There were murmurs within the crowd, for some of the shadows they recognized. The dead walked upon the water in small groups of twos and threes. Some were families carrying babes in arms, others were alone, toting only their weapons. They were clothed as they were when they died, their gaunt faces hauntingly sad. Spectral in form with the sea visible behind them, they journeyed toward the burning ship, as if it were a beacon in the night that called them from their graves. The *fades* gathered around the boat, for almost all of them had passed beyond because of this one man's deeds. As the blistering heat reached Phelan, he clenched his fists, defiant to the end.

"I will not be weak!" he shouted to himself. He saw the shadows clearly and felt a presence, one that brought back what scant loving memories he possessed. "Carr? Is that you?"

"Brother, what have you done?" a young voice called back and the once mighty lord of Kell searched through the flames to see his beloved sibling standing on the water near him, his face bewildered. Behind him were the legions of the dead, thousands strong, their eyes accusing as they pointed at the bound lord, murmuring against him.

"Carr?" he called in hopeful voice. "I come to be with you!" *He is here, he waits for me!*

"What have you done? They call your name, blame you for their deaths. This is not the brother I know." Carr's voice wavered as if in emotional pain.

"I am strong, Carr, not weak as father said. They are of no import!" Phelan called as the flames began to lick closer to him. He kept his eyes on his brother, ignoring the pain as his clothes began to ignite.

"I see plainly what horrors you have committed! How could you? There are so many! Why have you done this evil?" the agonized voice called out.

"No one will call me a cripple again. All will remember Lord Phelan for his strength!" he cried as the flames began to engulf him.

The specter shook its head in horror. "No! No! For the Love of the Powers, I renounce you, for you are not the brother I love!" Carr's voice cried and then he stepped back to allow the multitudes to press closer. He disappeared into the sea of faces, his own heart broken at the knowledge of what his beloved brother had become.

"NO! Carr! NO!" A firestorm erupted in the center of the ship, engulfing the Lord of Kell as he died in a spasm of torment, for the loss of his brother's love was what destroyed him, not the burning pyre. The *fades* watched silently as he perished and then as the ship began to break up, each one picked up a small piece of burning debris. Cradling the small light next to their faces they began their journey back across the sea. In time no piece of the ship remained, only a myriad of small lights shimmering in the distance like the stars in the dark canopy above them. The illuminations faded on the water as the dead returned to their world. There was complete darkness, for even the moon hid behind a veil of clouds as if it mourned the loss of so much light in the world.

"His evil is gone, carried away by those he harmed," Morwyn said. She turned and walked away from the shore, her mind overwhelmed by the visions she had seen. Each *fade* had a story and she had not been able to hear all of them. *So many lives lost to the inner torment of one man.*

"May the Gods grant them peace," Caewlin murmured and then led Aithne back to the camp in silence. The celebrations that night were subdued in memory of all the lights that had disappeared into eternity.

Thirty-Three

The surviving members of the Southern Isle clans reunited over the few days leading up to the iarel's wedding. Families filtered in from the forest and joined into one large encampment at the Field of Stones. It was a bittersweet time as they embraced their loved ones and rejoiced at their survival. Others found only grief when they learned that a family member had perished during the battle or during their enslavement. There were marriages, births and solemn mourning, all part of the fabric of clan life.

Though remnants of the five clans now lived together, often with different religious rituals and customs, their fervent desire to rebuild their lives was the uniting factor. An iarel's wedding was always cause for jubilation and so the clan threw themselves into the preparations. As the rumor regarding Aithne's pregnancy spread, so did the sense that all would be right. Their iarel prospered and so would they.

Large quantities of deer and rabbit were felled, more campfires built and food preparation begun in earnest. Owain the Elder and Ulwyn returned before the ceremony with a caravan of ten wagons full of food and goods, courtesy of the citizens of Kell. The ruling Council of Kell, Gorsedd and Benen, felt it wise to make amends with their Southern neighbors, hoping to forge a pact of peace with them. While the food was appreciated, the clan was even more thrilled to find boots, blankets, clothes and personal items in the wagons. All of it was carefully distributed according to need and there was much merriment as the clothes were handed around until they found someone they would fit.

In particular, Pyrs was very pleased to see an influx of young girls his age. They had hidden in the forest with the older men and women and now that all was safe they came to the Field of Stones to be with their families. He quickly found himself the center of attention as the tale of his exploits made the rounds of the campfires. He would have been embarrassed to learn that the anecdotes recounted how he had killed ten men at once and that he had held the walls of workers' hut up with his bare hands so others could escape. The clan knew the stories were embellished, but they retold them anyway, along with tales about their iarel, Dillan, Fea and her mysterious trader. All along Pyrs reaped the benefit of attention and basked in it. Despite his youth, he knew it would all end and life would soon return to normal. He looked forward to sitting in Aderyn's library, delving through his family history.

Owain the Elder searched around the campsite until he found his daughter. He'd been bursting at the seams all the way from Kell and even Ulwyn had found the man's exuberance rather tiring.

"For your wedding, daughter," he announced gleefully as he held out two large parcels. Startled, Aithne took them from him and then removed the fabric wrappings. One held an elegant gown constructed of finest linen with delicate embroidered flowers on the bodice. The other was a beautiful black wool cape with rich fur trim.

"Owain, these are …" she stopped, stunned.

"These are for my daughter," he said simply. "The gown is from me and the cloak is from Lord Morgan in honor of your wedding." She hugged him hard and then held the dress up to her body. It looked to be an exact fit.

"How did you guess my size?" she asked in amusement and saw Owain redden a bit.

"I searched through Kell until I found a girl of your build and then took her shopping with me." He'd actually gone to one of the brothels and sought out a young woman. The girl had been quite surprised when the man only wanted to purchase clothes. He'd paid her handsomely for her time and after assuring himself she did indeed wish to remain in service at the pleasure house, he'd departed.

"I see. Did she get a dress as well?" she teased, in awe at the generosity of the gifts.

"Yes, she did."

Aithne gave him a gentle look. "Thank you, Owain."

"Thank you for forgiving me, Aithne." He planted a kiss on her cheek and left her to prepare for the wedding.

Some five-hundred members of the clan gathered around their iarel and his betrothed as the sun set. The ceremony was as old as the clans themselves and followed a prescribed ritual. Galen recounted tales of Caewlin's father, grandfather and great-grandfather, all sung in his melodic baritone. Ulwyn sang of Aderyn, of their strong and honorable sons and of their courageous and beautiful daughters. All the while Aithne stood next to Caewlin, her hair plaited in the ritual braids of a new bride, her face full of love. He couldn't pull his eyes off her, entranced by her beauty. The deep love they shared was richly evident.

The vows were simple and recited with great care.

"I, Caewlin, Iarel of the Red Hawk Clan, son of Brecc, grandson of Geraint, do claim Aithne, Chosen of the Red Hawk, as my mate. I vow to guard her, love her and care for her until the end of our days. As an iarel cares for his clan, so shall I care for Aithne, for she is my beloved and mother to my children." He took a sip of a wine and then passed the goblet to Aithne.

"I, Aithne …" she paused and turned her eyes toward Owain the Elder and then began again, "I, Aithne, daughter of Owain the Elder and Adwyth the Adept, foster-daughter of Ide and Loman, do claim Caewlin, Iarel of the Red Hawk Clan, as my beloved mate. I acknowledge that the child within my womb is of his loins. I vow to guard Caewlin, love him, bear his children and bind his wounds. I promise to care for only him until the end of our days." She drank from the wine, handed the goblet back to Devona and then the couple clasped their hands together.

Devona intoned, "The Gods have blessed this union from the moment you first met. Go forth, Caewlin and Aithne, for you are bound together!" An immense cheer rose from around them and the clan erupted in unconfined joy. Toasts were made and dancing circles sprung up around many of the camp-fires.

"I love you fire-hair," Caewlin murmured, his brown eyes reflecting an inner contentment he never thought he'd possess.

"As I love you, you wild-eyed iarel." He looked around at his clan now engaged in full revelry and then murmured in her ear, "How soon can we retire to our marital furs?" As was custom, they had remained separated for the last few nights and that had clearly whetted his desire.

"You have duties to perform, remember? Patience, Iarel."

"I cannot be patient! I can only think of …" Owain the Elder unknowingly cut him off as he strode up to his daughter in obvious pride.

"Aithne, you are gorgeous! May I claim a kiss?" Owain asked as he reached out to embrace her. She melted into his strong arms and then allowed him a kiss.

"Sister, welcome to our family," Belwyn said and claimed his embrace and kiss. Pyrs was next and though he still looked a trifle pale, he was not about to miss this moment. The instant Aithne saw him she gave him a knowing smile and he knew what was coming.

Caewlin eyed him and asked, "Wife?"

"Yes, Iarel?"

"Is this the young man who was courting you so earnestly, offering you a fine home and numerous children?" Pyrs groaned. Belwyn shot his father a look and they traded winks.

Aithne nodded. "It is, my husband. He was most persistent."

The iarel put his hand on his sword hilt and growled in mock displeasure, "What have you to say, Pyrs?"

Pyrs decided to bluff it out and assumed his most gracious voice.

"I readily admit I proposed to this pretty lady. Who wouldn't? However, at the time I was unaware you had already asked for her hand. Alas, your hold on her heart was stronger than my offer, which is fortunate as she has proven to be a close blood relative and apparently already bearing your child.

I accept defeat, Iarel, for she has chosen very wisely." He bowed at that, though it made him wince.

Caewlin began to chuckle.

"A very gracious retreat, Pyrs, and one I will accept."

"Thank you, Iarel." Pyrs straightened up at that, glad that was over. "I am pleased to welcome all of Aderyn into the Red Hawk Clan, for you are now family."

"We are all honored, Iarel. To be part of the Red Hawk Clan is a tribute we will hold dear," Pyrs replied sincerely. He moved forward, collected his kiss and then returned to where two young girls waited for him by a nearby campfire. They fell to conversation immediately as one of the lasses tucked furs around the young man. Another girl appeared with a plate of food and then one with wine. It was apparent Pyrs was not lacking in attention.

As was custom the iarel began the rounds of the clan, talking to as many as he could possibly greet in one evening. He performed the duty in a jovial mood, but Aithne knew where he'd rather be.

"Dubhan!" the iarel called and the man rose to greet him. He had a bandage on his head, a wound sustained in battle, but his eyes were bright.

"My iarel," was the reply along with a bow. Mada rose from the furs near the campfire, her two children at her feet.

"Iarel," Mada said. Her son tried to perform a little bow as well. Caewlin cheerfully acknowledged it and the boy beamed.

"We are all blessed, are we not?" their leader asked, particularly pleased to see that the family had prospered despite Fyren's execution.

"More than we deserve," Dubhan replied. He hugged Mada closer.

"Your wisdom has given my children and I much happiness, Iarel," Mada said, her voice almost cracking.

"We all deserve happiness, Mada, for we have passed the tests the Gods have sent us and now we can live in peace."

"May They make it so," Dubhan intoned. He watched as the iarel and his new bride moved to the next campfire.

"You didn't tell him our news," Mada murmured.

"I will, in time. I suspect our child will only be one of many born before Gathering Night." Mada nodded and sat back down on the furs and pulled her children into her arms.

Morwyn sat with Belwyn near a campfire and together they watched Pyrs and his bevy of girls. Dillan wandered over and knelt beside them for a time.

"He is in complete glory, isn't he?" the older clansman remarked in some humor. Fea was only a few steps away, speaking with Orva and laughing lightly at some jest.

"Pyrs is full of himself tonight," Belwyn agreed. "I do not mind, though, he is a sensible lad and won't let it go to his head." He looked over at Dillan and changed the subject. "Did you tell father of your decision?"

Dillan nodded. "I did." He caught Morwyn's puzzled look and explained, "I am staying with the clan, with my new wife, for Caewlin will need help to keep the wolves in our midst in check." Morwyn nodded in understanding even as he spoke.

"There will be challenges, Dillan, but nothing you and the iarel cannot handle. The arrival of the iarel's son will settle some of that."

"I hope so. Aithne has asked if you would return for the birth of the child. She wishes that one of her own kin be present at the birthing." Morwyn's eyebrows raised in surprise, for the request was completely unexpected.

"I will be here, Dillan, and I am honored by the request."

"Good, I will tell her." He rose and rejoined his wife, slipping his arm around her waist. She gave him a gentle smile and then her eyes flitted over to Elrehan where he sat by himself near the fire. Their eyes met and then she shifted her attention back to Orva and her husband. Elrehan rose and walked away into the night, his heart heavy.

A round of laughter came from the knot of girls around Pyrs in response to a joke he'd related. He was plainly at ease, reveling in the attention.

"I cannot remember having that many girls dancing attendance on me when I was that age," Belwyn remarked.

Morwyn chuckled. "You didn't hold a burning building up with your bare hands."

"No, I didn't." Belwyn paused and looked around. "Where's Gwyn?"

"On the mountain, with the dragons. She left right after the ceremony."

"She is a unique, even more than her mother." Morwyn crooked an eyebrow but didn't reply. Belwyn moved his gaze back to Pyrs. "Do you think I should rescue our son from his ardent admirers?" he asked in considerable amusement.

"No, let him be. He's earned this night." She snuggled into her husband's arms and watched the jubilant clansmen dance in honor of their iarel and his bride.

Aithne and Caewlin finally left the celebration some three hours later, though both of them had wanted to escape much sooner. A large marital tent sat in the center of the campground, in their honor, and within they found food, a blazing fire, wine and thick furs. Outside, discretely placed at a distance, were his guards, for even tonight they would not drop their vigilance.

The iarel pulled down the tent flap behind them and immediately took Aithne in his arms. His voice was thick with both heartfelt emotion and desire.

"I never imagined I would be granted such a bounty as you, fire-hair."

"Nor did I think to find such happiness, Caewlin."

"Come, my love, let us start our new life together as the Gods would wish." They undressed, settled into the furs and then he poured her a drink of wine. After they shared the drink he placed the cup down on the ground and began to undo her hair from the ritual braids. He kissed each section of glowing red hair as it came loose. When all her hair was free, it flowed around her shoulders and down onto her chest in gentle waves. The scent of herbs wafted around him and he could wait no longer.

"I have much need of you, my love," he said.

"I am yours," she said. He pulled her into his arms to begin their new life together.

The next morning Pyrs got his wish and had the opportunity to visit the little dragonets. How he got to the top of the mountain did not please him in the least – being changed into a dormouse and hauled in the claws of one's sister, now an owl, was not a pleasant experience. He shrieked in a little mousy voice most of the way, furious as she had not warned him how she intended to convey him to the island. Nevertheless, once he knelt at the nest restored to his own body, he knew it was worth it.

You are healing? It was the voice of the mother dragon as she peered down at him in concern.

"I am, Favored One," he replied politely. One of the small dragonets moved over to the edge of the nest and studied him intently. "Greetings, cousin." The little one kept studying him and then hopped in the air, flapping its wings a few beats before settling back down into the sand in apparent dismay. It tried again and gained a bit more altitude before plopping back to earth scattering sand around its claws.

"They will fly soon," Gwyn observed. "I will warn the clansmen so they are not startled to see wee dragons buzzing around their heads." Her guardian was on her shoulder now, pleased to have his tail wrapped around her hair once more. He was trilling contentedly in her ear.

As soon as they can fly I will take them to another place, the mother replied and a rumble of approval came from the Ancient One lying near her.

"Very wise. Mortals and dragons aren't good neighbors," Pyrs remarked.

Another rumble and the Ancient One spoke.

There is a mortal you must watch.

"Braen?" Pyrs asked, suspecting he knew of whom the dragon spoke. The fiend had been on his mind for some time.

An incline of the dragon's massive head was confirmation.

According to his grandsire, Braen had vanished since the incident in the clearing, for Aderyn still hunted him. When he'd queried his sister, Gwyn reported that the brute was somewhere in the forests near Ilspath. She'd murmured that his evil had grown since they'd last encountered him. That had unnerved Pyrs and he'd asked nothing further.

The touch of our fire has changed him.

"Will he have visions like mother?" Gwyn asked, her eyes troubled.

In his own way.

"I will hunt him, Ancient One," Pyrs offered.

Caution, for he is not as you remember him. He will find …

The oldest of dragons uncharacteristically did not finish the sentence. An uneasy silence fell in the cave.

"I will be cautious, Ancient One," Pyrs replied and then turned his attention back to the little dragons in front of him. He only wished to enjoy the company of his kin, not think of yet another quest.

The clan appeared to be settling in for the duration. Food was readily available and the location near the sea seemed to please them. Certain elements, such as Isen, were under scrutiny as the iarel began the difficult task of rebuilding their lives. Caewlin decided they would remain at the Field of Stones until after the Gathering Night in the fall. If the food stocks were plentiful and the drought lifted further south, then those that wished to return to the Red Hawk's isle would do so. Though he did not speak of it openly, it was his intention that Dillan would become the iarel for the new clan. In that way, both clans would be united by blood and future conflict avoided.

Caewlin was determined to remain on the Northern shore, for he felt it was a good location for their new life. They began to construct huts and shrines, gradually transforming the Field of Stones into their home. The Red Hawk had led them here, so here they would remain.

Two days after the iarel's wedding, the remaining Northerners departed. It was a difficult time for many. Fea and Elrehan's farewell was conducted in private, away from curious eyes. Dillan excused himself and left them alone in the tent. It spoke reams to Elrehan and he knew he would not violate Dillan's trust. He took Fea in his arms and kissed her on the forehead, only, though he wished to do so much more.

"I will miss you, Fea, daughter of Brecc."

"I will always love you, Elrehan," she said.

"As I will love you," he replied and then kissed her again. She reached out, took his hand and placed three ribbons within his palm. There were the ribbons he'd purchased for her in Kell.

"Keep these in memory of what we might have had." He closed his eyes, fighting the tears, and clasped them in his hand.

"May your Gods give you a life full of joy and peace."

"May it be so," she said. They broke the embrace and he left her to her tears. A few minutes later Dillan returned to the tent and she felt his arms encircle her waist in a gesture of comfort. A light kiss fell on her forehead.

"I am truly sorry there was no other way, Fea," he said gently.

"I know," she said.

Aithne and her father parted reluctantly.

"Once you have your fine son, come to Aderyn and see your ancestral home. If you cannot travel, then I will come here to you. I want to hold my newest grandson while he's still a baby," Owain said with a flourish. He'd been overjoyed to learn Aithne was with child.

"You are always welcome, Owain. I will try to make my way to Aderyn, though I suspect my iarel desires a number of children in a short period of time."

"Tell him to allow you some time between them! Powers, what is it with us men? You'd think we did all the work," he jested. "Besides, you're a healer, you can work that out!" he said and winked. She hugged again and then handed him a fur pouch adorned with seashells. He found it contained a braided lock of her red hair. He kissed her, hugged her hard and then climbed up on his horse. Belwyn was next, then Gwyn and Elrehan, for he was now her kin by marriage.

Morwyn hung back, unsure how to proceed. She murmured a spell of protection for child in the healer's womb and felt the young life respond accordingly. Aithne clutched her stomach, for her son had delivered a strong kick. She shot a glance over at Morwyn.

"You did that, didn't you?" Her fellow healer grinned in response.

"A spell of protection never hurts. He appeared to like it."

"Please, no more, he kicks enough as it is."

"Eager to be out and seeing the world," Caewlin replied as he appeared at her side.

"Far too eager, like his father," she replied and warm laughter was the response.

Pyrs was on a horse, though he suspected a full day's ride was not in his future. He admitted it was vain, but he wanted to ride out of the clan's camp rather than sit in one of the wagons with the other wounded warriors. His father helped him up on the steed and he stayed there though he was light-headed and his shoulder ached like fury. He shot a glance over at his mother and she glowered in return. She had cautioned against such a thing, but he was stubborn and had his own way. She made sure to reserve a space for him in one of the wagons, knowing that in about two hours he would be lying down, fast asleep from one of her healing spells. He offered his farewells to a gaggle of young girls and received small presents in return. He was clearly enjoying himself.

As they rode out of the encampment into the forest, Morwyn turned back for one last look at the mountain and sent her farewell to the dragons.

Be at peace, dragons.

Be well, Morwyn, for you are special.

I know.

"You are sure?" Corryn pushed, his eyes wide and his mind spinning.

"I am sure, my lord. A message was sent to his Master of the Guard and I heard it in Ilspath."

"Powers!" Corryn muttered. "Bardyn is dead! How perfect!" He thought for a moment and asked, "How soon will our new liege lord return to his holdings?"

"It will take almost a fortnight, my lord. The only reason we know of Bardyn's death so soon is that they sent the message by winged courier."

Uncharacteristically, Corryn allowed his exuberance to show and he pounded the table in front of him. His wine glass sloshed but he did not notice. He glanced up and waved the messenger away.

"It could not be more perfect."

They found Kell a city in flux. The new council was trying to come to terms with the human cost of Phelan's rule. Slavers worked openly in the city, many of the city's guards continued in their lecherous ways and the brothels were still crowded with those forced into that profession. Reform was needed and it would take time and perseverance.

Morgan realized he didn't have that time, despite his offer to assist the council in any way they needed. He was desperate to return to his holdings, concerned at what devilry the likes of Corryn or Vaddon were planning. Belwyn, inadvertently, gave him the means to solve his problem.

Belwyn's dilemma was Morwyn, for he knew she would not want to leave Kell until a new House of Healing was established. She'd not said a word, but he saw it coming, no doubt at the last possible moment. He had prepared endless speeches in his head to convince her to return with him to Aderyn, but he knew it was not to be. He shoved his disappointment down and waited for her to bring up the subject. To ease his conscience and insure she was safe, he brought his problem to his new liege lord.

"You are right, she will not leave," Morgan replied when presented with the situation. Owain the Elder sat nearby and he readily agreed.

"I would like to ask your permission to leave Pyrs here to keep an eye on her," Belwyn requested. He'd thought it through and felt it was the most sensible thing. Morgan pondered for a time and then smiled, broadly.

"I agree. And in that way, Pyrs can solve my problem as well." Belwyn's quizzical look prompted the answer. "I need to leave someone of authority here in Kell to help them over the next few months. Pyrs, though young, has a presence that inspires confidence. His bravery in battle and his ability to see into the heart of matters will serve him well. I'd like to ask him to stand as my representative to the Council of Kell. He would act on my behalf."

Belwyn's eyebrow rose, considerably, and his father was equally surprised. "I agree Pyrs is quite capable, but his is only sixteen."

"Sixteen going on forty, as we've all joked," Morgan replied. "That will free an experienced warrior for whatever greets us upon our return home."

"There is that, " Belwyn allowed. He looked over at his father. "What do you think?"

Owain the Elder nodded in affirmation. "I believe he'll do very well, though he will be disappointed not to return with us."

Morgan sighed in relief. "Well, then, that's that. Have him come to me and I'll tell him what I want. Oh, and Owain, arrange for us to leave on the morrow. We need to return home as quickly as possible."

"I will set it in motion, my lord."

Morwyn's heart demanded she go with her husband, but she was a healer and duty demanded she be here for as long as it took to train healers and raise a new House of Healing. The news that Pyrs would be staying on as Morgan's representative had endlessly pleased her, though her son had reacted in stunned amazement at the incredible responsibility that now lay on his shoulders. Morwyn suspected Belwyn's fine hand behind some of that, for she knew he'd not leave her to her own devices. No doubt he had worked out her plans, but he obviously did not intend to make it easy for her. She waited until that evening as they lay in each other's arms after the loving.

"Morgan returns north tomorrow?" she hedged.

"Yes, we are to be ready after the morning repast. He has concerns about the safety of his holdings and of Aldyn's, given that Bardyn is dead."

"Until they learn he is his father's son and worthy of respect, he will be mightily tested," she observed. That much she had gleaned from the intense visions which continued to strike her down without warning.

"News of Bardyn's death has already traveled north, of that you can be sure," Belwyn replied solemnly.

She could put it off no longer. "Belwyn, I wish to remain in Kell until the new House of Healing is established."

He crooked up an eyebrow and asked, "You do not wish to be with your husband?" He would not make this difficult, for he acknowledged the need, but he wanted her to understand how it affected him.

"I do, but just as you have a duty to our liege lord, I have a duty to those who need healing." She watched his face intently. He could deny her the right to do this, but it would generate a wide rift between them, one not easily set aside in the years to come.

"I will not be pleased to ride north without you by my side, but I understand the need. How long must you stay?" His heart ached at the thought of it.

"I would say eight to twelve weeks."

"Plus two more weeks travel time makes it almost four months," he said quietly.

"I will push to have my part of this completed as soon as possible, Belwyn, for I have lost too many years with you."

"And now we lose a third of yet another year."

"It will go quickly, for Morgan's homecoming is fraught with peril. You will be busy."

"Then it is fortunate that Pyrs was asked to remain in Kell for he can keep you out of trouble."

"As if you had nothing to do with that."

"I only asked that he remain in Kell, not be given the duties Morgan laid upon him."

"I see. You knew I'd want to stay."

"Yes, though I prayed it wasn't so." He sighed and lightly touched her hair. Kissing her cheek he murmured, "Then if I am to be away from you for so long, let us spend the night in loving so that we have memories enough to sustain us."

"Memories are not as passionate as you are, my love," she replied honestly.

A smile appeared on his face, "Remember that, wife! If you do not appear in four months time I am riding south to fetch you home even if I must kidnap you from your fellow healers and tie you to my saddle."

Her eyebrow raised and he saw that look he loved in her eyes, the one that promised him untold pleasure.

"Oh, my ..." she started and then said no more.

The next morning's farewells were difficult.

Belwyn and Morwyn embraced, kissed and then he chided, "Perhaps it would have been easier if I'd slipped out the door before dawn, like someone I know usually does." Morwyn gave him a frown and then another long embrace.

"Hurry home, mother," Gwyn said, her eyes misty. They kissed and hugged.

"I will, dear. Watch over your father for me, for the next few months will be trying."

"I sense that, mother." She kissed Morwyn again and then climbed up on her horse and took her place next to her grandsire.

Elrehan collected his farewell and murmured, "Be safe, sister." He ruffled Pyrs's hair and then mounted his horse. It was plain his heart was troubled and Morwyn knew of no way to comfort him.

"I hope everything goes well," Pyrs muttered.

"It will be difficult for Morgan, but it will resolve," Morwyn said, though she did not see the future that clearly. "Gwyn is with them and that will be a boon."

Pyrs nodded. He'd already said his farewell to his sister earlier in the morning and it hadn't been any easier than the day they'd parted on the road to Kell.

"Farewell, wife, remember my warning," Belwyn called over with a certain look on his face.

"I am duly warned, husband," Morwyn replied with a twinkle in her eyes. He wheeled his horse and followed Morgan out of the main gates, Owain the Elder and Gwyn right behind. Ulwyn and Elrehan followed them, the bard choosing to ride near his morose friend with the intent to cheer him up.

As the remainder of the column exited the city, Morwyn ascended to the wallwalk. She watched as her family moved along the road that ran from the old seaport to Ilspath. Once the last figure disappeared into the distance, she murmured a prayer for their safety and turned her mind back to her work.

It was near midday on the fourth day's ride north when the winged creature overtook them. A bellow in the air startled the horses and all eyes shot upward in reflex. The dragon, though hundreds of feet in the air, still looked huge. Their mounts skittered a bit and then settled back down as the beast flew ahead of them and disappeared into a bank of clouds.

"The Ancient One?" Belwyn asked, guessing by the creature's size.

Gwyn nodded. "No doubt returning home to his lair now that his children can fly."

"How appropriate," Belwyn murmured. "The males go north while their mates stay south." Elrehan's eyes met those of his brother-in-law and they traded melancholy nods.

"So it appears," he murmured.

epilogue

The partially unrolled parchment on her lap was not the letter of condolence she had expected. The Council of Nobles had seized the opportunity to strike when Lady Aldyn was weakened by grief. Demonstrating unusual swiftness, they commanded her to stand before them and answer a number of charges, including her part in the death of her husband, the late Lord Merioneth.

Her fear and fury were equal.

"You would never have dared do this if my uncle were alive!" Her hands knotted in anxiety as tears fell onto her mourning gown. She was dressed in solid black once more, her hair caught up in a silver net. Her eyes were red and her face lined as she sat near the hearth in her chamber, her heavy cloak around her shoulders against a chill she could not break.

A knock came at her door and she hastily dried her eyes, knowing who it was. It was important that she appeared strong, for he would need her strength to face their future together.

"Enter."

The grim face of her councilor appeared. Owain the Younger shut the heavy door behind him and worked his way over to her with the aid of a cane.

"Aldyn," was all he could say. He had just learned of the contents of the message and had hurried to her side. As he made his way through the corridors he'd witnessed the shock and consternation on the faces of her servants, the ill news had traveled swiftly throughout the castle. He did not know the best way to comfort his mistress and lover, for the loss of her uncle was a bitter blow compounded by the Council of Nobles' despicable actions. He stood at the side of her chair and took hold of her pale hand. It was disturbingly cold to the touch. She pulled her hand out of his grasp, as if not wanting the contact and picked up the parchment, offering it to him.

His reaction mirrored hers.

"The bastards! How can they ask you to account for something that happened almost four years ago?"

"They have the right, Owain."

"They only do this because …" he stopped. There was no point in stating the obvious.

"I see Corryn's hand in this," she said, her eyes hardening. Her initial flight of tears had withered. "He has learned of my uncle's death and pushed this through the Council." Owain nodded and tossed the parchment on a nearby table.

"*Shoved* is a more accurate term, for they are usually slow in their decisions. Corryn no doubt bought some of them off." He paused and then added, "I will stand as your councilor, if you wish."

She nodded. "That brings me much comfort." She waited and then asked, "How long before Morgan returns?"

"At least a week and a half, at the shortest. No doubt he left Kell as soon as the situation permitted." Aldyn thought for a time and then nodded in acceptance.

"Then it is our battle, my love." She grew quiet and stared into the fire. It seemed no matter how close to it she sat, she could not break the frost in her bones. It took all of her will to hold her composure until her councilor left the room.

Once Owain closed the door, he leaned his forehead against it in despair. All their recent happiness had been washed away by the death of her uncle and the machinations of the Council of Nobles. As he turned to leave, his ears caught the sound of weeping from within.

GLOSSARY

Glossary

Note: pronunciation does not necessarily follow the rules of the parent language. Liberties have been taken.

Aderyn (add-er-in)
One of the oldest houses with a distinguished history of service to the High King. Heraldry features a falcon.

Adwyth (ad-with)
Former adept of the Circle of the Swan (deceased).

Aindreas (ahn-dree-ahs)
Red Hawk clansman.

Aithne (ath-nyuh)
A healer.

Alarch (al-arch) The Swan
The eldest adept of the Circle of the Swan.

Aldyn (all-din)
Only child of Lord Bardyn's sister, Ebrill, and Lord Morgan's cousin.

Ancient One
The oldest male of dragon kind, a ddraig. Wielder of the Old Magic.

Argel (ar-gel)
Small village located near the main road from Ilspath to Kell.

Awstin (aw-stin)
Brother of the High King who was assassinated by Lord Wann. Presented Rhyd of Aderyn with the lineage sword in recognition of his loyalty.

Bard (bard)
Singing poets who carry forth the oral tradition of their people. Blessed with the *gift*.

Bardyn, Lord (bar-dyn)
Most senior nobleman in the realm, noted for his fair and just rule. Heraldry features a dragon.

Belwyn (bel-win)
Eldest son and heir to the House of Aderyn. Brother to Owain the Younger.

Benen (ben-in)
Innkeeper of *The Old Port* in Kell.

Braen (bray-en)
Villager from Argel.

Brecc (brek)
Caewlin and Fea's father.

Brenna (bren-na)
One of Ilspath's healers.

Bride Cloth
A white square of linen used to verify a bride's purity.

Cadmon (kad-mon)
Lady Aldyn's Master of the Guard.

Caewlin (kah-lin)
Iarel of the Red Hawk Clan and Fea's brother.

Cara (care-a)
A seamstress who is Ifor's lover.

Carr (car)
Lord Phelan's eldest half-brother.

Ceffyl (keff-il)
Belwyn's bay horse.

Circle of the Swan
A Circle of adepts trained in healing.

Corryn, Lord (core-en)
Northern noble.

Ddraig (threyeg)
The word in the old language for dragon.

Devona (de-vona)
Wise of the Red Hawk Clan.

Dillan (dillan)
Owain the Elder's Master of the Guard.

Dru (drew)
A bard in service to Lady Aldyn.

Dubhan (duh-van)
Red Hawk clansman.

Duncan (duncan)
Lord Bardyn's Master of the Guard.

Elrehan (el-re-han)
Twin brother of Morwyn and son of Pyrs (The Elder) and Enit of the village of Argel.

Erc (er-ik)
Iarel of the Badger Clan.

Fade (fayd)
Shadow form of a deceased person.

Fea (fey-ah)
Sister of Caewlin, the Iarel of the Red Hawk Clan.

Fyren (fie-ren)
Red Hawk clansman.

Ferco, Lord (fehr-kos)
Northern noble.

Galan (gahl-en)
The Saga (bard) of the Red Hawk Clan.

Geraint (ger-**aint)**
Caewlin and Fea's grandfather.

Gorsedd (gore-seth)
One of Lord Phelan's senior guards, father-in-law to Nyle.

Gunn (gun)
An orphaned boy of the Red Hawk Clan.

House of Healing
A collection of healers located within a city.

Iarel (earl)
Title of the leader of a Southern Isle Clan. Equivalent title to Lord.

Ifor (yah-for)
An archer.

Ilspath (ils-path)
A large fortified trading city in the North.

Iola (yoh-lah)
House of Aderyn's healer.

Isen (eye-sen)
Red Hawk clansman.

Jestin (jes-tin)
Owain the Younger's page.

Keely (keel-ee)
One of the serving girls at *The Old Port* in Kell.

Kell (kell)
Major seaport on the southern shore.

Lowri (low-ree)
One of the serving girls at *The Old Port* in Kell.

Mada (meh-duh)
Fyren's wife.

Mair (mir)
Lady Aldyn's maid.

Meara (meer-ah)
One of the serving girls at *The Old Port* in Kell.

Merioneth (merion-eth)
Lady Aldyn's husband (deceased.)

Moina (moin-a)
Owain the Elder's wife, Belwyn and Owain's mother.

Monksbane (munks-bane)
A plant used for its poisonous properties.

Morgan (morgan)
Bastard son and heir of Lord Barydn, Lord of the Eastern March. Lady Aldyn's cousin.

Morgane (mor-gain)
Lord Morgan's mother (deceased).

Morwyn (mor-win)
Twin sister to Elrehan, daughter of Enit and Pyrs (The Elder).

Nerian (nair-ian)
Iarel Caewlin's second-in-command.

Nona (noh-nah)
Youngest adept of the Circle of the Swan.

Nyle (nile)
Guard in the service of Lord Phelan and Gorsedd's son-in-law.

Owain the Elder (oh-wain)
Eldest of the House of Aderyn, Belwyn and Owain the Younger's father.
Second son of Trahern.

Owain the Younger (oh-wain)
Second son of Owain the Elder, Belwyn's brother, and councilor to Lady
Aldyn.

Peter (pee-ter)
Riona's son.

Phelan, Lord (fey-lan)
Baseborn son of a wine merchant who rules the seaport of Kell.

Pyrs (the Elder) (piers)
Father of Morwyn and Elrehan, grandfather of Gwyn and Pyrs (The
Younger).

Pyrs (the Younger) (piers)
Son of Belwyn and Morwyn, Gwyn's twin brother.

Rhyd (reed)
Belwyn's great-great grandsire who fought to place Awstin on the High
Throne.

Rhosyn (hrose-in)
Healer in the service of Lord Bardyn.

Riona (ree-nah)
Apprentice healer who lives with Morwyn at the mirrored lake. Peter's
mother.

Ring of the Fey
A fairy ring wherein the Elders reside.

Saga, The (sa-gah)
A Southern Isle bard.

Siarl (sharl)
Lead healer in the House of Healing in Kell.

Southern Isle Clans
A collection of five distinct tribes who dwell in the Southern islands. They are named for the deity they worship: Badger Clan, Black Stag Clan, Grey Wolf Clan, Red Hawk Clan and the White Owl Clan.

Taran (tear-in)
Lord Phelan's half-brother.

Ta'wel (ta-**wel)**
The second youngest in the Circle of the Swan.

Trahern (tra-**hern)**
Owain the Elder's tyrannical father.

Ulywn (ull-win)
A bard in service to Lord Bardyn.

Vala (val-lah)
Geraint's wife and grandmother to Caewlin and Fea.

Vaddon (vah-don)
Northern noble.

Veil, The
The nebulous boundary between this world and the next.

Wann, Lord (wann)
Lord of the Eastern March during Rhyd's time. Slew the High King (Awstin's brother) in a bid for the High Throne.

Wise, The (wise)
The priestess of a Southern Isle Clan devoted to acting as an intermediary between the Gods and the people.

Zinna (zin-ah)
Carr's wife and Lord Phelan's sister-in-law.

Jana Oliver is the author of the **DragonFire Fantasy Series** which includes **The Circle of the Swan** and **The Summoning Stone.** She has also penned a hot and spicy supernatural romance, **The Lover's Knot,** based upon the classic Alfred Noyes' poem *The Highwayman*. Her next project, a Victorian murder mystery set in late 1880's London, is in the research stage. A native Iowan, Jana now lives in Atlanta with her husband and Midnight, the cat.

MAGESPELL PRESS
Book Order Form
www.magespell.com
Paranormal Romance
____ **The Lover's Knot** 0-9704490-0-3 $12.95US/$19.95CAN

DRAGONFIRE FANTASY SERIES
_____ **The Circle of the Swan** 0-9704490-1-1 $12.95US/$19.95CAN
_____ **The Summoning Stone** 0-9704490-2-X $15.95US/$23.95CAN
_____ **Summoning Stone Color Poster** 24"x36" $15.00US/$23.00CAN

Order online at www.magespell.com or use this form to order by mail. We accept personal checks, money orders or MC/Visa/Amex.

Name_____

Address_____

City_____ State_____

Zip Code_____ E-Mail_____

Please send me the book(s)/poster(s) I have indicated above.

Total for book(s)/poster(s) $_____

Sales Tax (in Georgia - 6%) $_____

Postage & handling (see below) $_____

Total Amount $_____

Postage Options:
Media: Add $3.00 for first book/poster and $.50 for each add'l book.
Priority Mail: Add $5.00 for first book/poster and $1.00 for each add'l book.

Credit Card Information (MC/Visa/Amex)
Name on card_____ _____
Card Number_____
Expiration Date_____
Signature_____

MageSpell Press
P.O. Box 1126 Norcross, GA USA 30091-1126
Phone: 678.438.4010 Fax: 770.216.1571